KU-707-873

Cynthia Harrod-Eagles won the Young Writers' Award with her first novel, *The Waiting Game*, and in 1992 won the Romantic Novel of the Year Award. She has written over sixty books, including thirty-one volumes of the Morland Dynasty – a series she will be taking up to the present day. She is also creator of the acclaimed mystery series featuring Inspector Bill Slider.

She and her husband live in London and have three children. Apart from writing her passions are music, wine, horses, architecture and the English countryside.

Visit the author's website at
www.cynthiaharrodeagles.com

Also in the *Dynasty* series:

The Abyss

DYNASTY

18

Cynthia Harrod-Eagles

sphere

SPHERE

First published in Great Britain in 1995
by Little, Brown and Company
This edition published by Warner Books in 1996
Reprinted 1996, 1997, 1998, 2000
Reprinted by Time Warner Books 2006
Reprinted by Sphere in 2009

A CIP catalogue record for this book
is available from the British Library.

ISBN 978-0-7515-1745-3

Typeset by Palimpsest Book Production Limited, Polmont, Stirlingshire
Printed and bound in Great Britain by Clays Ltd, St Ives plc

Papers used by Sphere are natural, renewable and recyclable
products sourced from well-managed forests and certified
in accordance with the rules of the Forest Stewardship Council.

Mixed Sources
Product group from well-managed
forests and other controlled sources
www.fsc.org Cert no. SGS-COC-004081
© 1996 Forest Stewardship Council

Sphere
An imprint of
Little, Brown Book Group
100 Victoria Embankment
London EC4Y 0DY

An Hachette UK Company
www.hachette.co.uk

www.littlebrown.co.uk

DYNASTY 18

The Abyss

THE ANSTEY FAMILY OF YORK

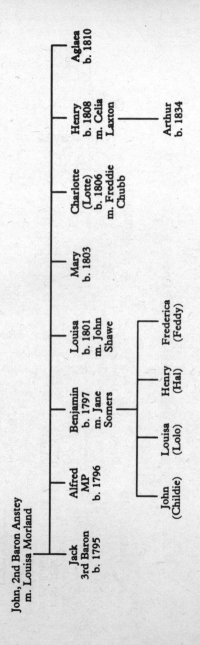

John, 2nd Baron Anstey
m. Louisa Morland

Jack
3rd Baron
b. 1795

Alfred
MP
b. 1796

Benjamin
b. 1797
m. Jane
Somers

Louisa
b. 1801
m. John
Shawe

Mary
b. 1803

Charlotte
(Lotte)
b. 1806
m. Freddie
Chubb

Henry
b. 1808
m. Celia
Laxton

Aglaea
b. 1810

John
(Childie)

Louisa
(Lolo)

Henry
(Hal)

Frederica
(Feddy)

Arthur
b. 1834

THE MORLANDS OF MORLAND PLACE

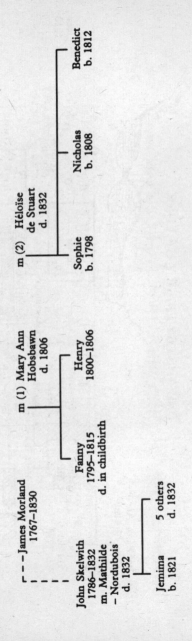

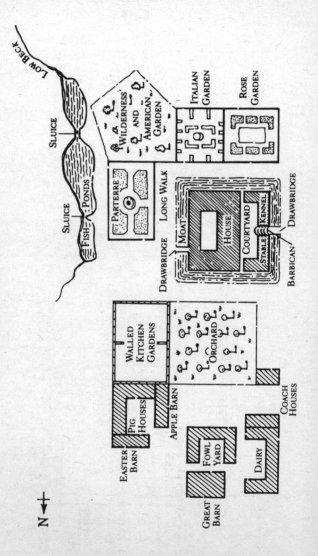

MORLAND PLACE AND GROUNDS

N

LOW BECK

SLUICE

SLUICE

FISH PONDS

WILDERNESS AND AMERICAN GARDEN

PARTERRE

ITALIAN GARDEN

ROSE GARDEN

LONG WALK

DRAWBRIDGE

MOAT

HOUSE

COURTYARD

STABLE

KENNEL

BARBICAN

DRAWBRIDGE

WALLED KITCHEN GARDENS

ORCHARD

EASTER BARN

PIG HOUSES

APPLE BARN

COACH HOUSES

GREAT BARN

FOWL YARD

DAIRY

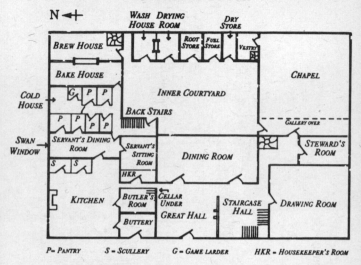

MORLAND PLACE IN 1830
GROUND FLOOR

N

WASH HOUSE · DRYING ROOM · DRY STORE

BREW HOUSE · ROOT STORE · FULL STORE · VESTRY

BAKE HOUSE · CHAPEL

COLD HOUSE · G · P · P

INNER COURTYARD

P · P · P · P

BACK STAIRS · GALLERY OVER

SWAN WINDOW · SERVANT'S DINING ROOM · SERVANT'S SITTING ROOM · DINING ROOM · STEWARD'S ROOM

S · S · HKR

KITCHEN · BUTLER'S ROOM · CELLAR UNDER GREAT HALL · STAIRCASE HALL · DRAWING ROOM

BUTTERY

P = PANTRY   S = SCULLERY   G = GAME LARDER   HKR = HOUSEKEEPER'S ROOM

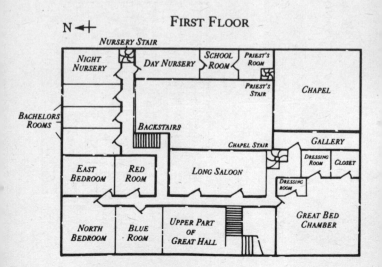

FIRST FLOOR

N

NURSERY STAIR

NIGHT NURSERY · DAY NURSERY · SCHOOL ROOM · PRIEST'S ROOM

PRIEST'S STAIR · CHAPEL

BACHELORS ROOMS · BACKSTAIRS · CHAPEL STAIR · GALLERY

DRESSING ROOM · CLOSET

EAST BEDROOM · RED ROOM · LONG SALOON

DRESSING ROOM

NORTH BEDROOM · BLUE ROOM · UPPER PART OF GREAT HALL · GREAT BED CHAMBER

AUTHOR'S NOTE

For those who would like an overview of the way early railways were built, I recommend *The Railway Builders* by Anthony Burton. For more about the life of the navvies, the excellent book *The Railway Navvies* by Terry Coleman is both detailed and immensely readable. For the lives of the Stephensons, I recommend *George and Robert Stephenson, The Railway Revolution* by L. T. C. Rolt. And finally, for the life of George Hudson, *The Railway King* by Richard S. Lambert is the most detailed and accessible study.

BOOK ONE

The Imagining

Hurrah for the mighty engine
As he bounds along his track;
Hurrah for the life that's in him,
And his breath so thick and black!
And hurrah for our fellows, who in their need
Could fashion a thing like him –
With a heart of fire, and a soul of steel,
And a Sampson in every limb!

Alexander Anderson: *Songs of the Rail*

CHAPTER ONE

May, 1833

The private parlour at Markby's Hotel in York was up a
steep and narrow flight of stairs, and Martha Moon had
not been designed by Providence for climbing. When
she reached the top she was completely out of breath.
Alarming red and black spots danced before her eyes and
she had to stop and bend forward and rest her hands on
her thighs until they went away.

'Stop a bit,' she gasped as Mrs Markby, a decade
younger and half a hundredweight lighter, wanted to
show her into the parlour. 'Wait till I catch my breath.'
Mrs Markby waited, eyeing her coldly. She disliked any
call on her time that was not directly linked to profit.
Showing gentlemen up to their rooms was one thing;
hopping attendance on such a creature as this quite
another.

Bit by bit Mrs Moon straightened up and her face resumed its normal colour. 'Eh, what a climb! I'm sweatin'
rivers. And all a goose chase, I wouldn't wonder. Like as
not you've got it wrong, Liza Markby.' She glared at Mrs
Markby with the resentment that could only be felt by a
fourteen stone woman who has just raised herself by her
own efforts nearly thirty feet above ground level.

'Got it wrong? T'isn't likely, is it, with Mr Ferrars
hisself asking me to fetch you here? The steward of
Morland Place might know a bit about what goes on

3

there, I should think,' Mrs Markby concluded with exquisite irony.

And you might know a bit about Mr Ferrars, you skinny cat, Mrs Moon retorted, but only inwardly. It was not wise to get on the wrong side of anyone when a position like Housekeeper at Morland Place might be at stake. It was a position to make one's mouth water, and she was still sure there was a mistake somewhere; but if there were any chance at all – 'Well, well,' she said with a placatory smile. 'I'm ready now, Mrs Markby, thank you.'

Mrs Markby opened the parlour door, announced Mrs Moon with an air of taking no responsibility for her, and removed herself with a toss of the head. Ferrars, seated at the table by the window, did not get up, but gestured Mrs Moon towards a chair opposite him, which she took gratefully.

'Thank you for coming to see me,' he said. 'Your husband is here too?'

'I left him below, Mr Ferrars,' Mrs Moon said. 'Moon likes me to take care o' business. To be open with you, he hasn't much to say for himself, hasn't Moon. I speak for both, Mr Ferrars, rest assured.'

'Very well.' There was a silence, while they eyed each other speculatively. Ferrars, Mrs Moon thought, was a nasty sight on a fine morning – an undersized and ugly man, with thinning, scurfy ginger hair, bad teeth, and a pasty face in which freckles, blackheads and blemishes jostled for space: if it was true about Mrs Markby and him, she must do it with her eyes tight shut. More importantly, Mrs Moon thought, he looked as though his character was as maculate as his complexion, and this raised her hopes of the job. Ill-luck likes company, as the saying went, and if a man like him could get to be Steward of a fine old gentleman's seat like Morland Place, he wouldn't be likely to want a paragon of beauty and virtue in a subordinate position to himself.

'So, Mrs Moon,' Ferrars began, 'you are looking for a position.'

'I do find myself in that unfortnit case, Mr Ferrars, so I won't deceive you,' Mrs Moon said with a large air. 'Me and Moon, we had our own little place – the Black Bull out at Osbaldwick – but things didn't work out just as we planned.'

Ferrars nodded. He had heard of the Black Bull's misfortunes from Captain Roger Mattock, a boon companion of his master's who liked to frequent low alehouses; and further enquiries had told him all he needed to know about the Black Bull's landlord and lady.

'It'd be a step down for me to go into service, I don't deny,' Mrs Moon went on, 'but such an establishment as Morland Place – one of our oldest families – everything most respectable – well now . . .'

'It might be a step down you'd be prepared to take,' Ferrars finished for her.

'It might hardly seem like service at all,' she suggested hopefully.

'It's my turn to be open with you,' Ferrars said, leaning forward confidentially. Mrs Moon watched the eyes, which were as confidential as a viper's. 'The service at Morland Place has declined from what it once was. In the last few years of Lady Morland's life, she did not concern herself much with the household, and the servants got lazy and careless.'

'As servants will, Mr Ferrars, if they are not kept up to the mark, the bold-faced, idle hussies. You don't need to tell *me*!'

'Quite so. Well, my poor mistress died last year, as you may know, during the cholera outbreak—'

'Aye, God rest her soul, poor Christian lady – for all I heard she was next-door to a Roman. But very kind and charitable all the same, so they say.'

'– and now, after a period of respect for her memory,' Ferrars went on as though she had not spoken, 'I am

5

reorganising the household, removing all the servants I don't find satisfactory and replacing them with others of my own choice.'

Mrs Moon's attention sharpened. Now they were coming to it. 'Has your master nothing to say in the matter, Mr Ferrars?'

'Mr Nicholas Morland is a gentleman of affairs. He inherited the entire Morland estate from his mother, as well as the trusteeship of the Skelwith estate. He is both immensely rich and immensely busy. Such a man has no time for trivial domestic matters.'

'Which gentlemen don't hardly understand such things anyway, Mr Ferrars, in my experience,' Mrs Moon agreed comfortably.

'My master leaves everything to me. As long as he is well served – and his needs are simple – he makes no enquiry into the running of the household.'

Mrs Moon sat back a little, her stays creaking as though sharing her satisfaction. She'd got Ferrars' measure all right. 'A gentleman – nor a lady neither – shouldn't be troubled with poking into cupboards and looking at account books and so forth.'

'Just so.' Ferrars came abruptly to the point. 'I am looking for a new housekeeper, Mrs Moon, and a butler. The present housekeeper and butler have arrived at too comfortable an understanding with each other. For that reason I would prefer to take on a couple, so that I know where I stand from the start. Divided loyalties make for an unhappy house.' Mrs Moon nodded. 'The new housekeeper would be in authority over the rest of the female servants.'

He paused with an enquiring look, and Mrs Moon took the cue. 'As to that, Mr Ferrars, there's not much I don't know about keeping girls in check.' Before her marriage she had been a wardress on the Women Felons' Side at the County Gaol: the flightiest maid would be no match for her.

6

'Discipline is a great thing in the servants' hall. And I'm sure we could manage with fewer girls if they were kept up to the mark. The saving in wages could be considerable.' He gave Mrs Moon a steady look. 'The master, I'm happy to say, never enquires into the household budget. A sum of money is allocated to me, and I dispose of it exactly as I see fit.'

Mrs Moon almost licked her lips. 'That's as it should be, Mr Ferrars. A gentleman should be above wondering what becomes of every ha'penny piece he parts with.'

'I would also wish the new housekeeper to oversee the kitchen. Her late ladyship's cook was a profligate and wasteful man – French, you understand. He left when her ladyship died, but some of his ways linger on. I should like the new cook to be under the authority of the housekeeper, and for the kitchen to be run as economically as possible.'

'There are many ways of saving money in the kitchen, for them as knows 'em,' said Mrs Moon. One of a wardress's duties was to feed the prisoners on the fixed amount per head granted her daily by the governor, and a wardress usually reckoned on making a profit to repay her for her trouble. 'Provision of food of all marks I understand very well, Mr Ferrars. There are ways to make a little look a lot.'

'There is the reputation of the house and the family name to be upheld,' Ferrars warned. 'We do not entertain very often, my master being a bachelor, but when we do—'

'I understand you, Mr Ferrars, never fear! Economy in the kitchen – style upon the table. Everything just so and nothing wasted. There is just the one gentleman in residence, I take it?'

'Mr Nicholas Morland, the master, and his ward, Miss Skelwith, a child of twelve. Her entire family died of the cholera and she was left to Lady Morland's care.

7

Unfortunately her ladyship lived only long enough to pass the trusteeship to Mr Morland.'

Mrs Moon nodded. 'Quite a bachelor household, then – and just such a one as the lower servants take advantage of, in my experience. Oh, I don't doubt there are plenty of economies to be made.'

'Now as to the butler – since we have few visitors and entertain little, his duties will be light,' Ferrars went on. He placed his hands on the table. 'Your husband, I hope, will be equal to it? The failure of your last undertaking—'

Mrs Moon interrupted hastily and firmly. 'Don't you worry about that, Mr Ferrars. Moon has his weakness, I can't deny it, but I can keep him in check. He's a good man at heart, and as honest as the day, except for his little weakness, but, bless you, that's only a matter of keeping him out of temptation's way. An alehouse was too many opportunities, you see, and I couldn't always be on hand in the taproom – for, not to mince matters, it's ale as he hankers for; wine nor brandy he will not touch, and so I warrant you. But a better man with the silver and such there isn't, and knowledgeable about the cellar like you wouldn't believe. Don't you worry, I have him under my thumb. Moon will do whatever I say.'

Ferrars nodded coolly. 'That's as I should want it. I have a great many things to do about the place, Mrs Moon – indoors and out – and my master to care for. What I want is one person who is absolutely loyal to me, who will be my second-in-command in all matters to do with the household. Such a person, giving satisfaction, would find me generous. And, let me assure you, with the way things are arranged, I have it in my power to be very generous indeed.'

She met his eyes. 'I understand you, Mr Ferrars. I'm sure I am the person for you. Me and Moon, we're the ones. You won't regret giving us a chance, I warrant you.'

8

Ferrars was sure she did understand him; and he understood her very well. She was unprepossessing of appearance, but then what did that matter? A useful tool didn't need to be nice-looking. He was pretty sure that he would be able to spot the ways in which she would inevitably try to cheat him; and they would be small ways – it would merely be to salve her pride that she would feel obliged to rook him of a few pence here and there. He had felt sure she would suit when Mrs Markby had told him about her. An ex-wardress and alehouse keeper; and a brothel-keeper at one time – and in her very young days, probably a prostitute too. She had all the experience of mankind she needed, and there'd be nothing she didn't know about keeping order in a closed community like Morland Place. Only a prioress from a convent would know as much, and he wasn't likely to be offered one of those, he concluded with a smirk.

Mrs Moon saw the smile and didn't like it. He was a snake, that one, she thought; but if life had taught her one thing it was that you didn't have to like someone to make money out of them. Better, in fact, if you didn't: Moon was her one weakness, and he had caused her more trouble because of her puzzling and foolish fondness for him than all the other men she had known rolled together. No, she'd be better off disliking Ferrars. She'd make more money that way. Morland Place – the thought of it! The Morlands had been one of York's first families for hundreds of years, wealthy, respected, almost revered; and Morland Place itself was an ancient, moated manor-house built, as they said locally, 'any time after t'Flood'. It was regarded almost as a palace, the very apogee of service, every servant's golden dream. It must have fallen on hard times, she thought, for someone like Ferrars to be in charge. In the old mistress's day, the likes of her and Moon wouldn't have got past the gate, leave alone be made housekeeper and butler. For a moment she felt almost uneasy at the idea of taking advantage of such a noble old place, but then she shook away stupid sentiment. Sheep were for fleecing, that was all; a house had no feelings one way or t'other, and the dead were dead. If Nicholas Morland was daft enough to let his patrimony run through his fingers, she had as good a right to cup her hands under the flow as Mr Snake-eye Ferrars any day o' the year! Those as had must hold, and those as hadn't must take; and if Morland Place turned out as good a billet as she suspected, she and Moon could salt away enough to spend their old age in comfort.

'Very well, Mrs Moon,' Ferrars said, 'I will offer you the position. When can you start?'

'Whenever is conformable to you, Mr Ferrars,' Mrs Moon said grandly; the lofty position she was about to assume required a certain amount of style. 'Moon and me is entirely at your command.'

Nicholas Morland checked his horse at the top of the rise and sat looking down at his home. He had been born there and would no doubt die there, and now, after trials and vicissitudes he preferred to shut out of his memory, he owned it. He was the Master of Morland Place. The house looked beautiful in the afternoon sunshine: mellow rose brick and softly yellowed stone, surrounded by its gardens, orchards, barns and stables; the light glinting from its moat and fish-ponds; its paddocks and fields rolling away on all sides dotted with ancient trees and grazed by Morland cattle. All was harmonious, solid, long-established. And it was all his.

The Morlands were sheep-farmers and clothiers from ancient times: villagers spun and wove the wool from his sheep, and rolls of Morland Fancy were still sold throughout the Kingdom and born by ship to far corners of the earth. In more recent times, the Morlands had become breeders of horses: racehorses, delicate and strong like silk; saddle-horses, gentle and clever with mouths soft as kid gloves; and, the backbone of the business, the special breed of carriage horses called Morland Yorks which were so much in demand up and down the turnpike there was always a waiting-list. Post-houses knew they could not get better, for strength and speed combined with beauty and good manners. And whenever there was a wedding of the well-to-do in the York area, and the bridal couple took delivery of their nice shiny new carriage, their highest ambition was to see it drawn up to their front door by a pair (or, if Papa came down handsome enough, a team) of finely matched Morland bays or chestnuts.

All this had made the Morlands rich. They were also respected: Justices of the Peace; holding commissions in peace and war; from raising militia to conserving woods and highways, they were the dispensers of local law, arbiters of the fate of tenants, servants, pensioners and villagers. And now he, Nicholas, was master; the house, the park, the farms, the stock, the property in York, the interest in the factories in Manchester and the rows of houses the factory workers lived in – all were his. It was what he had always wanted; why, then, did he so often feel restless and unhappy?

The good times were when he was able to forget himself – like this morning, when he had been so busy schooling a pair of fine carriage horses that he had not noticed the time pass. There was oblivion to be had in drink, too, and opium, and in those pleasures of the flesh his friend Mattock had so successfully introduced him to. When he was carousing with a group of his cronies, drinking, gambling, laughing, making a lot of noise, he felt cheerful enough; but when the whirlwind of gaiety died down, and he was left alone with himself, then he felt, as he felt now, that there was something missing from his life, without which the golden prospect lying at his feet, the ownership of everything any man could desire, was dry and tasteless, mere Dead Sea fruit.

Checkmate sighed and shifted his weight and then tried to get his head down to graze, and Nicholas checked him

11

automatically, frowning through his thoughts. Perhaps the trouble was that he was lonely? Every man needed someone to love, someone to love him. He was singularly lacking in that commodity, he thought with rising self-pity. His mother, his adored, his sainted mother, who had always loved him best in the world, had died of cholera exactly a year ago, in May 1832. He could feel the tears rising at the very thought of that dreadful time. The loss to him – the agony: the wonder of it was that he was still alive! As if it wasn't enough for fate to have taken his noble, respected father three years ago, in a riding accident (shocking irony for a man who had been known as the best rider in the Ridings!).

His mother's death was typical of her unselfishness: her ward, Mathilde (with whom Nicholas had been brought up as if she were an older sister) had caught the cholera, and she, her husband John Skelwith and five of their six children had all died. Nicholas's mother, nursing them faithfully, took the sickness home with her and died in a matter of hours, leaving poor Nicky an orphan. Poor, poor Nicky, all alone in the world! Papa and Mother dead; Mathilde dead, who had been like a sister to him; his sister Sophie married and gone away to Manchester, which might as well be at the other end of the earth for all he ever saw her or heard from her. All alone! It was cruel!

It was more than cruel – now his self-pity spilled over into anger – it was wicked! If his mother had had any consideration she would not have gone off to nurse Mathilde, risking infection like that. It was quite unnecessary – there had been plenty of servants to do it. It was thoughtless, too – exposing Nicky to such anxiety on her behalf, endangering his life by bringing the infection home, especially when he had always been so delicate, which his mother of all people ought to have remembered. And then to die in that selfish way! But it was always the same, he had always been surrounded by heartless people who thought of nothing but their own concerns. It was a miracle he had survived to his present age, twenty-five, in such a callous world. He had always known, he thought pathetically, that he would not make old bones.

Here he had to pull out his handkerchief to blow his nose and dab his eyes, so affected was he by the contemplation of his own misery. Perhaps he ought to marry, he thought suddenly. He needed someone to care for him, and Morland Place ought to have an heir. All his acquaintances were married. His erstwhile closest friend, Harry Anstey, with whom he had shared a tutor, had got married last October to the love of his life, Celia Laxton – and apart from a 'come and visit us any time at all, our door is always open', Harry had completely abandoned Nicholas to his loneliness. Everyone but him had someone. Even Harry's older sister Charlotte, whom everyone had expected to remain upon the shelf for ever, had married two years ago and become châtelaine of Bootham Park; and a very good match it was for her, for though she was handsome enough, the Ansteys were too numerous a family for her to have much of a portion. Well, if Lotte could marry, Nicholas Morland of Morland Place ought to be able to.

The difficulty was, to whom? Heiresses were not so plentiful one could browse amongst them and take one's pick. Of course, Nicky had one of the most substantial of them under his own roof – Jemima Skelwith, sole surviving child of Mathilde and John, was heiress to John's not inconsiderable property as well as his building business. At the moment the business was being run by agents, and Nicky himself was trustee of the estate. Yes, Jemima was a very substantial heiress indeed, and it was a good thing that she was only twelve years old, for it would pain Nicky mightily when the time came to hand over control of her wealth to whoever she eventually married.

Checkmate sighed again, felt his bit, and edged a step

or two towards home: it was very hard to be held back when his stable was almost in sight. Nicholas patted his neck and gave him the office to walk on. In the distance, coming along the track which led from the South Road, he saw a horseman whom he had no difficulty in recognising as his former groom, now steward of Morland Place – Ferrars. Nicholas smiled to himself with agreeable malice. You could tell Ferrars a mile off from his seat on a horse, which must be the worst in the Ridings! The poor man must have no idea how dreadful he looked, or he would go into the city in a gig. If I looked such a muffin in the saddle, Nicholas thought, I'd never cross another horse all the rest of my life!

Ferrars reached the junction of the two tracks first, and reined his horse to wait for his master.

'Good day, sir.'

'Well, well,' Nicholas said, turning Checkmate's head as he tried to take a bite out of Ferrars' gelding in passing, 'and what have you been up to?'

'Looking after your interests, sir, as I always do. Indeed, it is my pleasure as well as my duty,' Ferrars said, falling in beside his master. 'Have you passed an agreeable day?'

'I've been schooling the blacks up at Twelvetrees,' Nicholas said, 'and now all I have in contemplation is dinner alone in my big empty dining-room, and an evening alone in my big empty drawing-room with nothing to do.'

Ferrars glanced sideways at him. Now what start was this? he thought impatiently. 'I'm sure, sir, if it would amuse you, I should be willing—'

'To play chess with me? or tables? or piquet?' Nicholas interrupted with a sarcastic sneer. 'And no doubt you think that is all the solace a personable man of fortune is entitled to expect when he has finished his day's labours?'

Ferrars was feeling his way in the dark. Solace? What was this? Was he seeking encouragement to go into York

14

to the Willow Tree, Mrs Jeffreys' discreet establishment in Straker's Passage, or the new and wildly expensive Golden Cage whose little birds did a lot more than sing? 'Pleasures of all sorts are available to the gentleman of sophistication, sir,' he said carefully, 'who knows where to look for them.'

But Nicholas was not in the mood to be reminded of the things he did that he would not have liked his mother to know about. He blushed with a mixture of embarrassment and fury. 'I'm not talking about pleasures, you block! Not – not *that* sort of thing! I'm talking about marriage.'

'Marriage?' Ferrars said incredulously. This was as bad as could be. Better nip it in the bud.

'Yes, marriage, what else? Why are you looking so stupid?' Nicholas turned on him in exasperation. 'What could be more natural than that a man in my position should be thinking about marriage?'

'Many things, I should think,' Ferrars said boldly. 'Most men in your position would be only too pleased to have their freedom to enjoy themselves and spend their own fortune, instead of having a wife and a baggage of brats to spend it for them.'

'You know nothing about men in my position,' Nicholas said scornfully. 'How could you? Son of a servant, born to service – never owned anything but what your master puts on your back – how should you understand the feelings of a gentleman and a landowner? Morland Place is the most important estate in the Riding, and the Morlands have lived here since – since – well, they've always lived here. My position demands that I marry and get an heir. It is my duty as much as the King of England's.' Nicky liked that analogy, and paused to hear it again in memory.

Ferrars shrugged. 'Oh, well, sir, if it is your duty – but there's no hurry about it. Plenty of years yet to enjoy yourself, before you need worry about the getting of an heir. Getting heirs is a sport for old men, when their hunting days are over.'

Nicky wasn't impressed. 'Don't talk nonsense! It's not just that the estate needs an heir. Morland Place needs a mistress, and I need a wife. How can I entertain and take my place in society without a hostess? And –' he forestalled the next interruption from Ferrars, 'I want a companion. It is pitiful that the man who owns all this—' he waved his hand to signify the house, the land, and all the invisible assets of the estate, 'should have no company or affection by his own hearth.'

Ferrars was contemplating the ruin of his dreams, but he knew better than to go on opposing Nicholas directly. Instead he tried a sideways approach, pretending to consider the matter seriously.

'Of course, sir, I understand. But you know, it occurs to me – forgive me if I speak out of turn – that if you were to marry now it would put out of reach for ever your wonderful opportunity with Miss Skelwith. Even if—'

Nicky stared. 'What are you suggesting? Jemima is a child – twelve years old.'

'Only two years, sir, from marriageable age,' Ferrars reminded him.

'You don't understand these things,' Nicky said. 'It would be scandalous for a man to marry his own ward before she came of age. I don't even know if it's legal. But even if it is, it would be shocking bad form to take advantage of a girl in a position where she would find it difficult to refuse.'

Ferrars looked away. 'Well, sir, you might wait until she comes of age. There could be no objection then. If you marry now, you may come to regret it later when Miss Skelwith is able to choose for herself.'

Nicholas had thought of that – of the pain of losing Jemima's money – but there was another consideration which he could not voice to Ferrars. Jemima's mother, Mathilde, had been brought up almost as a sister to Nicky; but more importantly than that, there was a persistent rumour, which Nicky had long been aware

16

of, that Jemima's father, John Skelwith, was in fact a by-blow of Nicky's own father, which would make him Nicky's half-brother and Jemima, therefore, Nicky's niece. Uncle-and-niece marriages were not unknown, but they were not considered the thing, not at all the thing. Nicholas didn't want a marriage that was in any way to be frowned upon; he wanted people to shake their heads in wonder at his acumen and good fortune, not in pity for his shame.

'Even when she's twenty-one, it would still have a very off appearance for me to be marrying my ward. No, what I want is a woman of large fortune and great beauty; a docile, good-tempered, affectionate, virtuous girl, who will admire me and look up to me. If such a woman should come in my way, why, I would marry her tomorrow and make her mistress of Morland Place – and that's as good a bargain as any female could want, considering who and what I am.'

'Yes sir,' said Ferrars with such profound gloom that Nicky's momentary golden vision faded. He sighed. The trouble was that it seemed about as likely that such a woman would appear tomorrow as that it would rain seven-shilling pieces.

Mr and Mrs Henry Anstey had a small house in Gillygate – not a fashionable street, and the house was old and inconvenient for the servants; but it had all been newly painted, and Henry, who was a great contriver, had by having a door rehung here and a chimney improved there made it snug and comfortable. All his friends said it was the completest thing and wondered afterwards what it was about the house that struck them so homelike. Few of them realised that it was the quiet attentiveness of the hostess that made the difference, and went home babbling of patent-fires and muffin-warmers. But Celia Laxton had long done the honours of her father's house before she married Henry – her mother being semi-invalid and wholly idle – and since her father's friends were solid, prosperous, elderly men of business, she had early learned what constituted real comfort without show.

She had had something to do to persuade her father to let her marry Henry, who was only a youngest son and dependent on what he earned by his endeavours at the offices of Greaves and Russell, attorneys, of High Ousegate. Sir Percy Laxton did not despise men who lived by their wits, and he knew Henry Anstey well enough to acquit him of being a fortune-hunter; but after all, Celia was his only daughter, beautiful, treasured and – he believed – delicate. He wanted her to be comfortable and secure; and besides, all fathers want their daughters to make great matches. But Celia was single-minded for all her air of fragility. One evening she had sat upon Papa's lap and wound her soft arms round his neck and told him that if she could not have Harry she would never marry at all. Sir Percy had sighed and yielded, resolving privately to tie up little Cely's fortune good and tight, just in case he had been mistaken about the Anstey boy.

He need not have worried: in a pre-nuptial interview the happy couple informed him that they wanted to live simply on what Harry earned, and suggested that Celia's dowry be put in trust for their future children. Sir Percy bristled at the idea of his beloved child making economies and having no money of her own to spend, and at last agreement was reached that Celia's pin-money should match shilling for shilling Harry's salary, to be spent as she saw fit without enquiry from anyone, husband or father. It still did not really satisfy Sir Percy, who salved his pride by deciding to come down pretty handsome at the time of the wedding. Lord Anstey – Harry's brother who was now head of the family – gave the lease of the little house as his wedding-gift, and a beautiful set of china; Celia had all her grandmother's plate, and her aunts provided her with linen; so Sir Percy had nothing to do but insist on furnishing and decorating the house

18

from top to bottom, and buying them a smart new chaise. For their first wedding-anniversary he had already put in an order for a pair of Morland blacks to draw it – Morland horses were so much in demand, an order six months ahead was not too soon.

The result was that everything in the little house was bran-new and modern, and Celia and Harry started married life in want of absolutely nothing – except perhaps the fun of make-do and manage. But they were an intelligent pair, very much in love, and with an evenness of temper which made them equal to facing even the awful prospect of being completely happy. The house in Gillygate had proved an irresistible draw to their friends, and it was rarely that they sat down to dinner alone.

Nicholas knew all this, of course. He had been at their wedding – he had even agreed to school the pair of blacks himself, when Sir Percy made it plain he expected him to offer to do so – but he had never been to their new house. His lifelong intimacy with Harry had cooled of recent years, though Harry at least had no idea why. Nicky thought Harry disapproved of the set he went around with – though the fact was that Harry's life was so crowded with his own concerns he hardly knew who they were, and he missed Nicky only when the sight of him passing down the street reminded him how rarely they met these days. But had he known the direction Nicky's interests had taken he *would* have disapproved, and that was enough to make Nicholas hate him.

However, Nicholas's thoughts about marriage, and a disinclination for his own undiluted company, made him at last decide to go and view Harry's marital bliss for himself, and to take up the invitation to 'take his pot-luck any evening' which Harry had pressed upon him with the parting clasp of his hand at the wedding-breakfast seven months ago. Nicholas left his horse at the York Tavern and walked through to Gillygate. As he drew nearer, his steps slowed of their own accord. He began to grow nervous. Suppose they were dining out? Suppose they had company? Suppose he was simply told 'not at home' – how would he ever rid himself of the conviction they had refused to receive him? He was suddenly aware that they had never issued any formal invitation to him, though newly-married couples generally could be depended on to be sending out cards at least twice a week.

Then he drew himself together: this was all nonsense. Who was Harry Anstey? No-one! Should Nicholas Morland of Morland Place feel anxious and humble about visiting him? Never! It would be an honour, and more than they deserved, for the Henry Ansteys to receive him, especially without invitation, which was treating them with all the distinguishing privilege of long friendship. He ought really to have called on them before, just so that they could have his card on display for everyone to see. It was remiss of him not to have conferred his public approval on the match by calling on them. Two of our best families, he told himself magisterially; very good sort of people indeed; an unexceptionable match. And they would be grateful for the attention. Buoyed by this view of the situation, he found the house and rapped authoritatively on the front door.

His anxieties returned in full force as he trod up the stairs behind the servant, and he was in such a state of nerves when he was shown into the parlour that he was able to take in nothing except that Harry and Celia were not alone. But Harry's greeting was everything he could have hoped for.

'Nicky! How good of you to call! I've been hoping so much you would. Cely, my love—' He drew her forward, and she greeted Nicky with matronly calm and said she was pleased to welcome him to their new home.

Nicky immediately became acutely conscious that he had sent them no wedding-gift – something which must have been remarked by everyone. True, he had still been in mourning for his mother at the time of the wedding, which could be held to excuse a certain absence of mind, but he might have made the omission good at any time since.

'You will stay for supper now you're here?' Harry was saying, and Celia added, 'Oh please do. It's only what we were having ourselves, but we should be very glad if you'd stay.'

'We mean to have a formal dinner party soon, but I wanted to wait until you were fully out of mourning,' Harry added. 'I know how seriously you Morlands take the formalities – and your mother's death was such a shocking blow to us all, we could only guess what it meant to you. But you will stay now you're here?'

Clouds of various sorts seemed to clear from Nicholas's eyes. 'But I'm afraid you aren't alone. I don't wish to intrude—'

'Lord, it's only family – Aggie and Ceddie, and George Cave, who's as good as family,' Henry said, waving a dismissive hand towards the three who were waiting in the background.

Well, so they were, Nicholas discovered, able at last to turn and look at them: Harry's younger sister Aglaea; Ceddie Laxton, Celia's vacuous elder brother; and George Cave, son of the rector of Middlethorpe, who had been at school with them. They came forward now and shook hands, and Nicky began to feel more comfortable. Ceddie's languid 'How d'e do?' was the same one he gave to all creatures as he ambled through life, amiable and uncritical: Nicky could never feel threatened by Ceddie. George Cave was just the sort of person he could and did ignore: a quiet, rather scholarly young man in orders, whose father had a small estate which he would inherit along with the living. And Aglaea he had known literally all her life, from the time he had first peered critically into her cot when he was two years old.

She was the youngest of the Ansteys and Harry's particular pet: because they came together at the tail end of a large family, she and Harry had always been especially close. Nicholas was not unaware that Harry had once cherished the idea that Nicholas might marry her one day. It had not seemed out of the question then. The Morlands and Ansteys were close – Harry's mother had been a Morland of a collateral branch – and fourteen-year-olds don't understand the full implications of marriage, rank and interest. But the Ansteys were not landed, and Aglaea would only have three thousand pounds, and in reality such an alliance was far out of her reach.

Nicky had not seen her since Harry's wedding, and as she placed her hand in his he realised that he had not really looked at her in years. She was not 'Harry's little sister' any more. She had not grown up handsome or tall, but she had a pleasant face, a womanly figure, and soft brown hair. She smiled at Nicholas, but her expression was otherwise rather grave: she had always been the quiet one, shy and reserved. It was a pity, he thought, that she had not more of something – more beauty, more sparkle, above all more dowry – for if he had to marry, it would be pleasant, he thought, to marry someone he knew very well and could be confident of controlling. Aglaea would never argue or criticise or want her own way; she would not be dashing about the country paying visits, talking about him behind his back. She'd have made a comfortable, economical, stay-at-home sort of wife.

But it was out of the question – Nicholas Morland of Morland Place to marry a plain girl with three thousand pounds? Not to be thought of! How would that arouse the envy, the wonder, the respect of the world? He would be laughed at, pitied even – they would think he had asked her because he despaired of anything better. No, poor Aglaea must take her chance; and with her limited assets she would likely end up an old maid, and be grateful to live with Harry and Celia as unofficial governess to their children.

As the evening passed, Nicholas noticed several things: that Harry and Celia were very much in love and very happy; that everyone but him felt very much at home in this snug, well-furnished house, which they had obviously visited on many occasions; and that George Cave was more than a little interested in Aglaea. These two had several quiet conversations together, and though there was nothing either pointed or improper in his attentions, it became clear to Nicky from the way Cave looked at her that he was on the way to being in love. As to her feelings for him, Nicky could not be so sure. She was uniformly quiet and modest, but there was at least something comfortable in the way she spoke with him that suggested this was not the first evening they had spent together by the same fire.

Nicholas was intrigued; later the intrigue turned to annoyance when he caught sight of Henry's face as he watched George talking to Aglaea. Harry's expression was fond and complacent, as one who has successfully made a match. So, Harry was planning a wedding for Aggie, was he? He had lowered his sights somewhat in the last ten years, Nicholas thought peevishly. Now a priggish parson with a mouldy Elizabethan manor, hardly better than a farmhouse, was good enough for the sister Harry had once wanted to see installed as mistress of Morland Place! Nicky found that insulting. He wasn't sure whether it was an insult to have George Cave preferred to him, or whether the insult lay in having planned to wed Aglaea to him in the first place; but that Harry was insulting him he had no doubt.

When they sat down to supper, Aglaea had been placed at Nicky's side (to George's obvious disappointment) and he took the trouble to talk to her, meaning to draw her out and discover what lay beneath the quiet exterior. He was only partly successful: conversation certainly flourished between them, but he soon found it was he who was talking about himself. He liked the subject, however, and she seemed really interested in what he had to say, and deeply sympathetic to all the ill-luck and lack of understanding that had bedevilled his life. He found he was enjoying himself much more than he had expected to, and the occasional glances that George Cave cast at them across the table enhanced his pleasure.

Not that conversation flagged elsewhere – the other four had plenty to say, and obviously found each other amusing company. Much of what they said was exactly of that trivial and esoteric kind that marks really close friends who meet each other often, which Nicholas found most annoying in other people, because it made him feel shut out. That, of course, was the purpose of it, he knew quite well. They were going to some lengths to make it plain that they hadn't missed his company at all. They wanted him to know that they could get on very well without him – that George Cave, in fact, was a perfectly acceptable substitute for Nicholas Morland of Morland Place.

His habitual resentment was fed by the sound of their laughter, the warmth and comfort of the room, and the good claret which flowed unstintingly into his glass, all of which, oddly, made him feel more and more left out, cold, miserable, unloved. Only Aglaea's kindly interest in him saved the evening – and it was that which gave him the idea for his revenge. He saw it all, with the perfect clarity and logic that comes at a certain stage of drunkenness: he would make it his business to cut George Cave out. He would court Aglaea, make her in love with him, and show Harry, who was so stupidly content with the grubbing little Cave fortune, exactly what he had missed. And then, when everyone was expecting him to make a formal proposal, then – then he would drop her. That would teach them all a lesson! That would show Harry Anstey! He was not entirely sure *what* it would show Harry Anstey, but he had no doubt that Harry deserved a lesson, and that Nicholas Morland was the man to give it to him.

* * *

24

Harry walked downstairs with Nicholas when it was time for him to go, shook his hand with the utmost cordiality, begged him to come again soon.

Nicky decided it was time to pave the way. 'I'm sorry I can't ask you and Celia to dine, but of course I have no hostess. We sad bachelors—' he sighed and let the sentence hang.

Harry seemed not to be listening. 'Nicky,' he said hesitantly, 'there was something I wanted to mention to you in private – about your brother.'

Nicholas's face went stony. 'I have no brother.'

Harry persisted. 'About Benedict – someone I know said they saw him in Selby, that he's living there, or nearby, and working on the railway. Is it possible?'

'I know nothing about it,' Nicholas said harshly. 'I've told you, I have no brother. He who was my brother is dead to me. You will not mention him to me again, if you please.'

Harry bit his lip. 'Nicky, old fellow, you know I would not do anything to offend you, but I must say I really think you were mistaken about Bendy. You see, last year I heard something – I came upon some evidence – well, it convinced me that he was innocent of the things you—'

Nicholas gripped him by the upper arms, looking levelly into his face, and said gravely and sincerely, 'Harry, old friend, I'm not offended, but you must allow me to know my own brother better than you. The worst thing about him was the way he managed to conceal his depravity from everyone but me. I assure you it is you who are mistaken, not me. Good God! Do you think I would banish my own flesh and blood without the clearest, most incontrovertible proof of his guilt?'

'Why – no, of course not – but—'

Nicky gave him a little, friendly shake. 'Dear old Harry, always so generous, always so reluctant to think ill of anyone! That's why we all love you so.' Harry was touched – it was long since Nicky had shown him so much affection. 'You're a good man,' Nicky went on. 'But don't be deceived about Bendy. Believe me, I know a great deal more than I can ever tell you. Trust me – and never mention his name to me again. He is dead to me now – let him be dead to you, for our friendship's sake.'

Harry was not proof against such an appeal. 'Very well, old fellow, if you say so.'

Nicky released him, and smiled. 'Thank you again for a most pleasant evening. You are a lucky man in your domestic happiness.'

Harry watched him walk away down the street, still a little puzzled; and then shrugged and dismissed the matter from his mind. He was a practical creature, and a Nicky in the hand was more important to him than a possible Bendy in the bush.

CHAPTER TWO

The coach rocked and bounced, shooting a loose stone away from under its wheel rim with a crack like a rifle-shot; the roof passengers lifted an inch or so off their seats and dropped again on their rumps with a hard smack. Benedict clutched at his hat and grinned with exhilaration. When you were twenty-one and full of the juice of life, it was a wonderful thing to ride on the top of one of the great flying coaches, bounding along at more than twelve miles an hour with the wind whipping past your cheeks. Ah, this was the great age of road travel! Everything got out of the way of the *Ebor*: at the sound of her horn the pikes opened like magic before her, humbler vehicles drew hastily aside from the crown of the road. Unchallenged they swept through the countryside, whipping past trees, farms, villages in an instant, leaving astonished cows and wondering children gawping in their dust.

The bright May air was warm and filled with the scents of the land. Coming through the Midlands they had passed through open champion, unfenced fields of young wheat and beans rolling away on either side like the sea, the scent of beanflower as powerful and elusive as a waking dream. Now there were deep hedgerows to either side, heavy with perfumed hawthorn, the grass verges were frothed with lacy kex, the glossy trees were fat with leaf and gently waving in the breeze. This was Yorkshire, the old enclosures – his home country. Now there were neat fields, tidy cottages and prosperous yeoman-farms, small brown brooks and slowly turning windmills, mild-eyed cows grazing under the broad shady skirts of chestnut trees. And everywhere sheep and lambs, dotted like daisies across the pastures, were busy about their old Yorkshire alchemy, turning grass into wool and sweet mutton – turning green into gold.

Benedict was a Morland, and the land and the sheep were in his blood. He could not see these well-kept, productive acres without pleasure; but now other interests fired his mind. All the way up he had been thinking of man's inborn delight in speed, and of the means of rapid travel which had been developing in the last ten years. Telford and Macadam between them had provided the science to build roads smoother and harder than the world had ever known. From London they reached out to the most distant parts of the Kingdom, and fine English horses and the flying coaches bore men and women along them at speeds never before dreamed of. It was no idle boast that the *Shrewsbury Wonder* and the *Hirondelle* competed for the title of fastest coach in the world: nothing in any other country could come near them. It was said that the *Shrewsbury Wonder* covered one of her eight-mile stages in thirty minutes, and could complete a change of horses in thirty seconds. Of course, the *Ebor* was not quite in that class, but she was still a marvel: London to York in twenty-three hours! And yet Benedict carried in his heart the secret knowledge that there were things afoot which would soon make the *Ebor* and her sister-flyers seem as archaic as pack-horses. And there was a part of him that would regret it. There was nothing, *nothing* like this!

They were coming into Selby now. The horses' speed fell off a little as houses sprang up on either side, separated at first, and then joined together in one neat, prosperous terrace, seeming to narrow the road, as though funnelling life into the town. Suddenly there were people, and dogs, and carts, and traffic. Now other noises intruded through the diminished thunder of the *Ebor* – voices human and canine, the banging and rattling and thumping of workmen, and far, far overhead the screaming of swifts remote in their insect-filled heaven. There was a smell of coal-dust in the air and an atmosphere of purpose. Bendy looked about him eagerly: this was the new England – young, bustling, thrustful. Selby was a busy town. From its impressive wharves, steamers went down the river to Hull, and from Hull to London and the Baltic ports, so it was an important staging-post for trade of all kinds, both import and export; but especially for the coal from the South Yorkshire mines. And it was the coal, of course, which ultimately accounted for his being there—

The guard's horn interrupted his thoughts. They were rattling into the cobbled Market Square, under the elegant, pale bulk of the Abbey, whose lacy pinnacles were etched against the sky like a rehearsal for York Minster. The White Lion was just ahead, the last change before York, before the final destination of the Pack Horse Inn in Micklegate. The horn sounded again and again to clear the way, but the guard found time between toots to remove it from his lips and tap Benedict briskly on the shoulder. 'Now then, young gentleman, look alive! Selby is not a bait, y' knaw, and the old *Ebor* waits for no man.'

'I won't hold you up,' Benedict said cheerfully. 'I've just the one bag – that one there.' He nodded to it, and slipped his fingers into his waistcoat pocket for the shilling he had put there in readiness. The guard's eye, bright and quick, observed the movement as a blackbird spots the flicker of a worm in a wet lawn. His leathery hand reached out and spirited the coin away.

'Ah'll th'ow it down to thee, maister,' he said, and his descent into the vernacular was a friendliness. 'Haud tight, now.'

The warning was timely, for the coach swayed violently

as it swung off the road and into the inn-yard, and there was a muted chorus of shrieks from the inside passengers as they were flung against each other. The whip called 'Hoa, hoa, sta-a-and', the guard applied the brake, and the horses halted with a scrape and a clatter. They stood blowing and shaking their heads, dripping foam onto the cobbles, and in the enclosed space of the yard the smell of their hot sweat rose up suddenly like cooking-steam from a pot.

'Now then, maister, wick now!' the guard prompted tersely. Benedict stood, turned, swung himself over the side, found one metal rung with his left foot and then dropped the rest of the way. Even as his feet touched ground his bag came flying at him, and he had to catch it high to save his hat from being knocked off. The coach looked massive from down here, and the ground under his feet seemed to jolt and twitch; the thick smells assailing him after the freshness of the drive were making him want to sneeze. But there was no time for leisurely observation. The yard was seething like a kicked ants' nest and if he didn't move out of the way he would be knocked over.

A stagecoach change was always a great thing to watch, and the windows of the inn were thronged with onlookers, idlers hung about the yard, and several gentlemen had appeared at the coffee-room door, glasses in hand, to watch the fun. The fresh horses had been ready and waiting, held by the ostlers precisely positioned to either side. The instant the coach stopped the boys had dashed in and unhitched the spent team, and were now running them forward and away as the fresh horses were led into place, the wheelers poled-up, and the leaders' traces attached. The guard meanwhile was throwing down parcels to a waiting porter, and receiving a box labelled for York in return, while a well-dressed schoolboy of about fourteen was furtively negotiating with the whip for Bendy's empty place on the top. It was against the law to carry anyone not on the waybill, but there was always a chance that a driver might be venial.

Bendy found himself standing beside a prosperously portly man in an old-fashioned mulberry coat and striped waistcoat, who had emerged from the inn door and was holding in his open palm a huge gold hunter.

'I always like to time her,' he remarked as he caught Benedict's eye. 'One minute exact, never more, never less. Runs like a machine, the old *Ebor*. Set your watch by her.'

It was done, it was all done already. The ostlers were stepping out of the way, the whip shouted 'Stand clear!', the guard sounded the horn. The leaders pranced a little as they felt the bit and then flung themselves into their collars, and the coach gave a great lurch and started forward, the roof passengers (the schoolboy now among them) jerking first backwards and then forwards as if they were all-of-a-piece. The boys ran ahead of her like spilled peas to make sure the road outside was clear; the horn sounded again and the *Ebor* rushed through the arch, swayed violently to the right and was gone.

'One minute to change, just as I said,' the gentleman remarked with as much satisfaction as if he had been personally responsible. 'Marvellous, marvellous!' He snapped his watch closed and returned it, with some difficulty, to his tightly stretched fob-pocket. 'What do they want railways for, answer me that, when they've coaches like the *Ebor*? Railways, bah! Stuff and nonsense! Give me the open road and a flying coach any day.' He eyed Benedict a little belligerently. 'What do you say, sir? You ain't one of these railway-loving folk, are you?'

'I just came in on the *Ebor*, sir,' Benedict said, neatly avoiding the question. 'She's a wonderful vehicle.' The crowds were dispersing now as the wet rumps of the weary team disappeared into the stables; the windows had cleared of heads and forearms, and the normal life of the yard was resuming. Two post-boys with dust-jackets over their livery came out to sit on the bench, sparrows flew down to peck between the cobbles, and a cat who had fled at the first sound of the horn came slinking back to her sunny doorstep to watch the sparrows. Somebody's delayed departure was evidently imminent, too, for a nice-looking team of chestnuts was being led out, while two men dragged up a chaise which had been pushed back into the corner of the yard.

'She's more than that,' the portly man was saying, 'she's an institution. And if I meet any of these railway people I'll have something to tell 'em. Tearing up the countryside – they should be horsewhipped! It'll be the ruin of hunting, you mark my words. Stephenson, pish! Probably never crossed a horse in his life.'

But Bendy was hardly listening, for over the portly man's shoulder he had seen the form of a young woman appear in the doorway. She was divinely fair, dressed in a wide-caped, nip-waisted mantle of deep green velvet and a huge, preposterous hat decorated with ribbons and feathers and flowers, under which clusters of golden curls framed her face. She carried a muff of banded black fur and a lacy parasol, and a beaded ridicule hung from her arm: everything about her was the pinnacle of fashion. She allowed her glance to rest just an instant on Bendy's face before lowering it as she picked her way down the two steps to the yard as though it were a task that needed all her concentration. The glance had not been long enough to tell, but Bendy was sure her eyes must be as blue as her delicate cheeks were pink.

She was followed by a stony-faced maid, and an inn-servant carrying a dressing-case and a basket. Bendy, stepping politely back out of the way, looking in vain for whatever gentleman she might be travelling with – for it was unthinkable that such a goddess should stir out of doors without a protector. The portly gentleman – the railway-hater – turned to see what Bendy was looking at, and his expression softened.

'Bless my soul, there you are, my dear! Are you feeling better now?'

'Yes, Papa, thank you.'

Her voice was sweet and tuneful – but, oh horrors, this man her father? Could that delicate Meissen shepherdess really be related to this crude Staffordshire toby? Bendy could only stare and doubt.

'Good, good!' the toby continued. 'And I see they are bringing up our chaise now.'

'Yes, Papa. I ordered it when I put on my hat.'

'That's a good girl. Well thought of, yes, yes. We can get on our way, then.'

'Yes, Papa,' she said demurely; but she peeped again at Bendy – blue, he thought, quite, quite blue. The portly gentleman appeared suddenly to realise that his proximity to Bendy must be giving a false impression of being acquainted with him. He cleared his throat sternly and frowned, and moved to place his body deliberately between Bendy and the vision of loveliness as he offered her his arm. There were to be no more glances, then – though the maid, as she passed, gave Bendy a full-bodied glare of comprehensive disapproval. The ostlers were still putting the horses to in a leisurely manner (they would not hurry for a mere private chaise) but the portly man assisted his daughter into the carriage anyway, plainly thinking she'd be safer there. Bendy thought with an inward grin that it was lucky the gentleman didn't know the kind of ne'er-do-well he was really dealing with.

It would not be the thing to stay and stare now he'd been warned off, so he picked up his bag and set off out of the yard and along the main street. He had a longish walk home ahead of him, and he debated briefly whether to take the shorter route across the fields, or to stick to the road in the hope of a lift from a friendly carter. It was growing dusk, and there were big, dark-edged clouds coming up from the south-west, which decided him. The fields looked pretty wet, and in the gloaming he would not be able to see the puddles: he had doubts about his boots. He hitched his bag more comfortably and set out on the road towards Monk Fryston. Soon he had left the houses behind. The empty road seemed at once darker, and a cold, evening smell rose up from the earth. He set himself a swinging, regular pace along the crown of the road, and for occupation let his mind linger on the pleasure a tiny foot in a well-turned boot could give. She had been the essence of femininity: absurd hat, bobbing curls, shy blush and air of fragility. He wondered who she was, and concluded that it hardly mattered, for he would never see her again. If they were travellers, they must live far from here.

With one part of his mind he was listening for the sound of wheels behind him, but when it came at last, it sounded like a gentleman's carriage, not a farm-cart. He had little hope that a gentleman would offer him a seat. He moved to the side of the road and looked round – yes, a smart black britsky and a pair of Morland bays – and stood to let it pass; but to his surprise it began to slow, and pulled up just a little beyond him. The nearside window was let down and a man's head in a tall hat poked out.

'Doost want a ride? It's like to rain any minute.'

'Why – yes, thank you, sir. I should be much obliged.'

'Jump in then. Look lively!'

Bendy obeyed, and a moment later was seated in one corner of the carriage amongst the agreeable smell of new upholstery, while his benefactor lolled in the other corner and examined him lazily from beneath his eyelids. He was a strange-looking man, tall and heavily-built, with an air of physical strength lately turned to fat, like a hard man come upon soft living. He seemed about forty years old, but it was hard to tell exactly – he might have been older or younger. His face was broad at the eye and his cheeks were like slabs, but his mouth was small and full like a girl's and his chin a little round button. His nose was an indeterminate splodge, which looked as though it might have been broken at some time, and his skin was rough and coarse-pored. Altogether they seemed not the features of a gentleman, and his speech had been broad; but his carriage and his clothes were expensive, and his air was one of ease and authority – not an easy man to classify.

His eyes, behind those thick, heavy lids which drooped so strangely at the outer corners, were as flat as bootsoles; but something told Bendy this was not a stupid man, nor a slow one. Not a man to cross, either – there was temper in that small, petulant-looking mouth. Bendy wished he could have got a look at the hands, which might have revealed something, but they were covered by expensive gloves of soft York tan with jet buttons, which looked new.

'Well,' the man said suddenly, 'tha'll know me again, that's for damn' sure. Tha's looked me over careful enough.'

It was said good-humouredly, so Bendy said, 'And you have me.'

'Aye.' No more than that was vouchsafed. 'Where s'l I take thee, then?'

'To the crossroads at Monk Fryston, if you are going so far,' Bendy said. It was only about a mile from there to his house.

'I'm bahn to Ledsham,' the other said neutrally. 'And where might you be heading, young man?' Bendy hesitated, and the man cocked an amused and knowing eye at him. 'To th' workings, is it? Nay, tha's nowt to fear from me, I'll not break thee head for it. I've a great interest in railways.'

'How did you guess?' Bendy asked, intrigued by his companion.

'Here's a young gentleman, good walker, surveyor's eye and an all-weather face. Even hunting four days a week doesn't complect a man like that. My face was hardened on a farm, as you may guess from my talk – born in Howsham, son of a farmer, that's me – but if you weren't born a gentleman my name isn't George Hudson.'

'Many things can give a man a brown face,' Bendy said.

'Eh, well, tha's not a jolly jack tar!' the man chuckled. 'Nay, with a bunch o' seals on thy weskit and that nip-waisted coat and that hat, th'art a railway man if ever I saw one. Engineer, is it?'

'Yes sir,' Bendy gave in with good grace. 'Benedict Morland's my name. I'm overseeing the cutting near South Milford, and I have a house there. That's where I'm heading.'

Hudson's interest seemed to kindle. 'Morland, eh? Not related t'the Morlands of York? Morland o' Morland Place?'

'I am – connected,' Bendy said warily. 'Are you from York, sir?'

'I thought any York man might have heard of me,' Hudson said, though he didn't seem offended. 'Mine is a very big name in the drapery business. Nicolson and Hudson's, on College Street, that's my place. Started as a prentice at fourteen and now I own it, lock, stock and barrel! Married the boss's daughter, and now I have a business that turns over thirty thousand pound a year, at five and twenty per cent profit. Now then!' There was something almost endearing, Benedict thought with faint amusement, about his boastful pride in his achievement; but still there was more to this man than bombast. Something warned Bendy to be careful.

'That's very praiseworthy, sir,' he said.

'Aye, tha's not been picked oop by Johnny Nobody,' Hudson declared. 'A man o' substance, that's what I am.' And then he added casually, 'But tha must have been in my shop a time or two. Most gentlemen are in and out of ma shop like lambs' tails.'

Bendy was glad that the gathering dusk inside the carriage was masking his face a little, for the subject of drapery was embarrassing to him, and he would have given half a guinea to know how much this man knew and how much was mere coincidence.

'I – I don't recollect,' Bendy said vaguely. 'Perhaps I may. I haven't lived in York for some years.' It was necessary to change the subject. 'If you are interested in railways, sir, you will be interested in the news from London today.'

'What news is that, then?' Hudson asked, humouring him.

'The two Railways Acts have gone through – for the Grand Junction and the London and Birmingham. Both gone through the same day.'

'Have they, by God?' Now he was genuinely interested.

'In a few years' time it will be possible to travel by railway all the way from Liverpool to London, with only a few trifling baits.'

'And what would they be for, sir?' He seemed almost annoyed by the idea of stopping for anything.

'Oh, for changing lines, and buying tickets. There would be three different companies involved, of course, for the first part would be on the Liverpool and Manchester's lines.' Hudson nodded thoughtfully. 'But even so,' Bendy went on, 'the whole journey will likely take no more than ten or twelve hours – can you imagine it!'

'That I can,' said Hudson with some vigour. 'I tell thee, young man, I've been reading everything I can lay my hands on about the railways. It fires my mind like nothing else!'

'It will be a tremendous undertaking,' Bendy said, glad of an interested listener. 'Especially the London and Birmingham – that cuts through some of the most difficult terrain in the country. Why, the first incline out of London is so steep they will probably have to use a stationary engine for it. And then there's the Chiltern Hills – the workings will be prodigious, cuttings and tunnels longer and deeper than anything yet seen!'

'Aye, well, George Stephenson will put it through, I have no doubt. He'll know what to do right enough,' Hudson said with enthusiasm. 'He's the man for it, by God!'

'Well, sir, in fact it is Mr Robert Stephenson who will be in charge of the London and Birmingham,' Bendy corrected. 'And I must say, though I owe his father everything, to my mind Robert is the better engineer. Old George has the vision, but Robert gets things done.'

Hudson's flat eyes seemed to examine Bendy in new detail. 'Do you know them, then?'

'Mr George prenticed me and taught me my trade, and I had the honour to work with both of them on the Leicester and Swannington. It's only a little coal line, but it presented us with some interesting problems.'

'Well, by God, did you now?' The words were said in a voice devoid of emphasis, and the eyes that were fixed on Bendy's face were not seeing him. Bendy's curiosity was stirred. What was going on in this man's mind? He certainly was a strange one. But while the silence still endured, Bendy saw that they were coming into Monk Fryston – there was the Blue Bell, and the Crown, and the yew-shaded gates and grey stone boundary of the Hall.

'I wonder if you'd be good enough to stop your carriage here,' he prompted, and Hudson came back to himself with a jerk.

'Eh? Oh, aye, that's right.' He elevated his stick and rapped hard on the roof with its silver top, and the carriage slowed and stopped.

'Thank you very much, sir,' Benedict said, preparing to dismount. 'You have been most kind.'

'Tha's welcome to it,' Hudson said absently. 'Good night to thee, Benedict Morland.'

A moment later Bendy was standing by the roadside and the carriage was rattling away from him in the dusk. It was lighter outside than it had been inside, but the dew had fallen, and the air struck cold after the protected stuffiness of the coach. In the west there were long streaks of damson cloud still edged with faded pink, but above them the sky was deep luminous turquoise with approaching night, and the evening star shone still and steady against it, like a diamond set in translucent shell. It was the time of day when men's thoughts turn to home, the yellow light of lamps and the warmth of company. Bendy turned up the Milford lane and set off homewards, and Hudson dropped cleanly out of his mind.

The clouds came up before the moon, and Bendy did the last part of his journey in darkness. There were no houses on this part of the high-hedged road until his own, which was one of a group of three which stood just around a bend, so no distant light showed from them. He picked his way gingerly in near blindness, with no company but the occasional whispering of unseen leaves as they moved in the light breeze, and the sounds of nature – a furtive rustling in the hedgerow, the distant bark of a vixen. The dew had penetrated his boots – he had been right to be doubtful of them – and his feet were numb, but the cold air on his face was refreshing and had that wonderful mossy, well-water smell that only comes on damp May and June evenings.

A piece of the dark suddenly took substance and flung itself at him, making his heart contract painfully as the atavistic part of his mind cried *wolf*! He could not see his attacker, but as he thrust out his hands defensively, expecting the rending of teeth, instead a cold, wet nose was jabbed into his palm and he felt the familiar battering against his legs of a long, close-haired tail. He laughed in vast, shamefaced relief. No wild wolf, this, but his dog, Fand, come to greet him. Hounds of her breed did not bark, and this silent onrush had disconcerted many a visitor. She must have been waiting on the doorstep for him, which meant home was not far away.

'Get down, you fool,' Bendy said, thrusting her off his

chest as she frisked like a puppy in her gladness to have him back. Another few steps and they rounded the bend of the road, and there was the glimmer of lamplight, yellow as butter in the blue-blackness, where the shutters had not been pushed quite to. Fand rushed to the door and lifted the knocker with her nose, and ran back to Bendy again, her white teeth and yellow eyes catching the light, the rest of her a moving shadow.

The door opened, and there was Liza holding a lamp up. 'Be careful of the puddle by the door,' she said in her flat-vowelled, unemotional, Midlander's voice. 'The gutter over the porch is cracked, and we've had such rain these last two days.'

Benedict flung his bag past her into the tiny hallway and grabbed her round the waist. 'Is that all the greeting I get after my long absence? I am Odysseus home from my ten-year wanderings!'

'I don't know about that,' she said stoically, but her free hand crept round his waist and held him hard. Like Fand she was silent in her joy.

'You didn't have the bolt on,' he observed sternly. 'Don't you know these are dangerous times?'

'I knew you were coming home tonight.' He raised an eyebrow. 'Fand said so. She wouldn't come in when it got dark, not even to eat.'

'I can't keep any secrets from her,' Bendy said, and stooped to run his hands over his dog. 'She's very thin. Have you been starving her?'

'She's been starving herself, the great gowk. Made up her mind to die if you didn't come back.'

Bendy caught Liza's chin and planted a kiss on her lips. 'What faithful females I have.'

'You'd better come by the fire. Your feet are sopping wet,' she replied; but she looked pleased with the kiss. He followed her in, shutting the door behind him. The hall was tiny, no more than a passage running from front door to back, with a floor of uneven herringbone bricks and a smell of damp earth even on the hottest summer day. To the left was the parlour, a dark little room lined with wainscot, which was used only occasionally, when Bendy's friends came for the evening and wanted to smoke. To the right was the main room, the kitchen-cum-sitting-room where all their living was done – Liza from her childhood's dialect called it 'the house'. From this room a staircase, concealed by a door beside the fireplace, wound round the chimney to the bedroom above. There was a second, smaller bedroom leading off the main one, and a scullery behind the kitchen, and that was all. To Bendy, who had been born at Morland Place, it was almost a joke, a little doll's house; but he knew it was everything to Liza – her home, and the best she'd ever had.

The fire was bright, but there was a clothes-horse in front of it, on which a variety of baby-linen was drying. Liza put down the lamp on the table and went quickly to whisk it away into the scullery, but it had already left its smell in the room, an unpleasant fustiness after the freshness of the air outside. Babies seemed to create an inordinate amount of washing. Bendy pulled up his armchair and sat down with a sigh, pushing Fand's head out of his lap so that he could reach down to take off his boots. Liza, coming back in, almost ran to kneel before him. 'Let me do that.'

'No, no, let it be,' Bendy said quickly. He sometimes felt smothered by her attentions. It was true what the cynical sage had said: when you save someone's life, you belong to them for ever. Liza desisted, sitting back on her heels in case help was required. Bendy examined her covertly as he took off his own boots. In the firelight, illumining her from the side, she did not look her best. Girls of her class bloomed early, and faded quickly. Since the baby she was looking more than her age, and what prettiness she had ever had, had been the effect of youth. She had lost a couple of teeth, too, which made her cheeks look sunken. She was, as always, as neat as a pin, but everything was plain about her: her hair drawn back into a chignon without curls or side-ringlets; her dress rather old-fashioned in cut, worn over the lightest of stays, high-waisted and with not even a hint of bustle, so that she looked the same thickness all through, without curves. Of course, since she was bending and reaching all day about her house work she could not lace herself tight as ladies did, and long side-curls would be always in the way; but a man did not want a woman always to be sensible. The image of the goddess at the White Lion came for an instant into his mind, and he smiled at the memory. He'd like to bet those little gloved hands had never done anything more practical around the house than arranging flowers.

'What is it?' Liza said, seeing the smile.

'Nothing,' Bendy said quickly. 'I'm glad to be home, that's all.'

She looked pleased. 'Give me those boots. I'll stuff them with straw and set them in the fender, or they'll not be dry by morning.'

'They're all but worn out,' he said ruefully. 'An engineer's life is hard on boots.' He stretched his feet towards the fire, and steam began to rise from his stockings. 'How has everything been here? Any news while I was away?'

'Part of the new embankment came down after all the rain and two of the men were hurt.' She knew it was railway news he wanted, not domestic.

'Who were they?' Bendy asked quickly.

'Two of Spider's gang. Tunnel Jack was one – I don't know the other.'

'A digger? Probably Blueskin, then – they always worked together.'

'They're not bad off,' she reassured him. 'Cuts and bruises, so they say. A man was killed on the line Saturday, but not one of yours – a miner from The Warren. He was walking home from Newthorpe dead drunk and fell into a pit in the dark.'

'The usual thing, I suppose – staggered out of the inn and thought the permanent way looked a nice straight, flat road home,' Bendy said with a shake of the head. These accidents to outsiders were the deuce, giving ammunition to the anti-railway party. 'How are people taking it?'

'Most are saying it was the man's own fault. Seemingly he wasn't much liked, foul-mouthed and too ready with his fists. There's to be a Crowner's inquest, but everyone knew he was always drunk of a Saturday night.'

'That's just as well. We don't want any more trouble. We're unpopular enough as it is in certain circles.' He thought of the portly man at the White Lion. 'Well now, the news from London is that both Acts have gone through. The railway from Liverpool to London will be built.'

'There,' Liza said, pleased because he was pleased. 'And who'd've thought it, after all the fuss the great folk made about their land?'

'Once they get used to it, they'll find it isn't as bad as they think. There was so much scare-mongering, terrible stories being circulated about the Liverpool and Manchester – all lies, you know, about accidents and fires and sheep losing their lambs and two-headed calves and so on. The reality will be so much better than their fears they'll feel grateful.'

Liza stood up, boots in hand. 'Are you hungry? Would you like a bite o' supper? I've bread and cheese and beer and a bit o' cold bacon.'

'That'll do.'

Liza crossed to the big cupboard and took out a tankard, and turned towards the scullery where the beer was kept; but before she reached the door the penetrating wail of a baby started from upstairs, and Liza halted doubtfully, tilting her head sideways to listen for the quality of the cries. Perhaps they would stop. They didn't. Her eyes slid round to Benedict.

43

'I'll get your beer first,' she said, weighing the expression on his face.

'No, go and see to him,' Bendy said. 'I can see you can't bear to leave it.'

She put down the tankard and disappeared up the stairs, leaving the door open so that a cold draught slithered down into the room from above. The crying intensified for a moment, and then stopped with a hiccough or two, and a moment later Liza came carefully down the steep twist with the baby on her hip.

'He's wet, I'll need to change him,' she said apologetically. Young Thomas, six months old, rested drunkenly against his mother's neck, red-faced and preposterous-looking between his white knitted cap and the bundle of clothing that covered the rest of him. He snuffled a little, having managed to squeeze out a real tear or two, but he looked around him with the air of one who does not intend to waste the golden hours of opportunity in slothful sleep. Bendy wouldn't have put it past him to wet himself on purpose to be brought down, as soon as he heard voices below.

Bendy could smell him now, and wrinkled his nose. 'Can't you do that upstairs?'

'It's so cold up there,' Liza said. 'I don't like to bare him to it. He's not been quite well this last week.'

'Oh very well,' Bendy said. He knew babies were supposed to be kept in hot rooms, and suspected that if she hadn't believed he'd be coming home that evening, she'd have had the baby down here with her – as it probably had been all the time Bendy was away.

'I'll get your beer first,' she offered.

'No, I'll get it,' Bendy said. 'You get on with what you have to do.' This, of course, was the other side of the equation, the negative side. Liza kept house for him, cooked and cleaned and washed and ironed, and warmed his bed. She had provided him with the comforts of home, which he would not have enjoyed in bachelor lodgings;

44

but she had also become pregnant. When it first happened she'd plainly expected him to turn her out, but he could not be such a brute as that. He was fond of her, and he knew that, little as she spoke of it, she loved him fiercely and wanted nothing more than to be allowed to stay with him. Well, now there were two of them for him to belong to, the life he had saved and the life he had created.

But all this was a far cry from where he had started, Benedict Morland of Morland Place, scion of one of the leading families of York – a city that was not short of the eminent and the wealthy. For nine tenths of the time he took his situation for granted, but just now and then something occurred to make him compare the promise of his childhood with the present reality, and the contrast was startling, almost ludicrous. If his mother could see him now – ah, but he didn't want to think about his mother. That was too, too painful.

Liza, busy on the other side of the room, with her back to Benedict and her body tactfully interposed between him and the awful sight of what she was doing, seemed to hear his thought. She turned her head a little and said diffidently, 'Have you had any news of your brother?'

'No,' he said shortly. 'How should I?'

'Oh, I thought in London you might have met up with someone. Though, if you remember, you said it was to keep an eye on Morland Place that you took this job with the Leeds and Selby. It's not much use if you never go near the place.'

'I'm not welcome there. And you know perfectly well that I can't go into York.'

'Oh, that old thing,' she said dismissively. 'I warrant nobody thinks of it now. It'll be long forgotten.'

'Yes, well, you can warrant what you like when it isn't your neck that's at stake. But if I get clapped into gaol, who'll look after you?'

She saw she had annoyed him and said nothing more. He sat staring broodingly into the fire, and when she had finished her task, she lifted up the baby and brought him over, and said, 'Would you like to hold him a bit?'

Bendy lifted his head to say no, but at that moment Thomas, held towards him, reached out his hands and beamed his toothless smile. There can be few things as flattering as such evidence of preference from a baby. 'Just for a minute, then,' Bendy said.

The baby smelled not quite so sour now, and Bendy set him on his knee and pulled out his watch to be played with. Thomas was fascinated by anything to do with his father, and clutched at the shiny thing inefficiently, listening to Bendy's voice and burbling in reply as if he could understand what was said. When he reached up and grabbed at Bendy's nose, Bendy pretended hurt and yipped like a puppy, making Thomas laugh. Fand came over and put her muzzle up, and the baby grabbed that too, and Bendy yipped again. Thomas spilled over with chuckles as though his fat bolster of a body had been full to the top with them, and repeated the delicious joke until Fand, patient though she was, had had enough and backed away, shaking her head and sneezing. Thomas, deprived of his sport, stared open-mouthed for a moment and then burst into wails of protest. Liza hurried over and plucked him from his father's lap, and at the same moment there was a rap at the front door, which gave her the excuse to carry the howling out of the room before Benedict could offer to go. A moment later she returned, followed by George Findlay, one of Benedict's fellow engineers on the Leeds and Selby, and a particular friend.

'What ho, old fellow!' Findlay said over the top of Thomas's noise. 'Am I interrupting?'

'Not at all, it's good to see you,' Bendy said, jumping up and shaking his hand.

'I wasn't sure if you'd be back, but I'd thought I'd take a chance. I wondered if you might like to take a turn down to the Black Bull and have a spot of supper with me – my treat. I happen to know Mrs H made a beefsteak and oyster pie today – there may be some left. Or have you eaten already?' He looked vaguely round the room as though for evidence of feasting, and then glanced doubtfully at Bendy's stockinged feet.

Benedict knew that Liza was looking at him, and avoided looking in her direction. There was cold bacon and cheese and ale in the scullery, and the obvious thing to do was to invite George to join them there, at home. He hesitated; but the baby was howling, and he felt stifled. He had had wider horizons about him, and all the stimulation of London for days past, and he could not bear the closeness of the walls and the encroaching smell of baby.

'Excellent idea, George. A stretch of the legs is just what I need, and I want to talk to you about the embankment.'

'Oh, you heard about that, did you?'

'I haven't heard the details yet. But it shouldn't have come down, even with all the rain we've been having. I wonder if the angle was too steep?'

'Oh, I can tell you all about it,' George said cheerfully. 'I was there. It isn't as bad as it sounds, although—'

'Hold up, old fellow, until I find a pair of boots, and we can talk about it on the way to the Bull.'

A few minutes later he opened the front door and Fand slipped out ahead of them into the mild damp night. George followed, and Bendy turned at the last moment to say goodbye to Liza, but the baby was still crying, and she had turned away to take it back to the fire and nurse it. Bendy shrugged inwardly and closed the door behind him. The clouds had parted and there was enough moonlight to see the puddles, which was just as well, for he hadn't another pair of boots for tomorrow if he soaked these.

CHAPTER THREE

Mrs Moon stood impatiently in the kitchen passage outside the door of the housekeeper's room. At last her husband appeared; with his slow, old-man's gait and his hunched shoulders he looked like a shabby heron testing an unpromising backwater.

'Well,' she said impatiently, 'is he up?'

'No,' said Moon. 'Not likely to be neither, after last night. Six o' claret and four o' brandy between four of 'em, besides the port, and a decanter o' whisky which that Captain Mattock saw off by 'isself – and him the only one walking straight afterwards.' He shook his head, torn between wonder and disapproval.

Mrs Moon tutted, and walked briskly to the end of the passage, pushed her head round the kitchen door and said, 'Nursery breakfast only, Mrs Codling.'

The cook, a cowed, bony, wispy creature, as pale of face as she was red of knuckle, looked up from the kidneys she was coring. 'These won't keep until tomorrow, Mrs Moon.'

Martha considered. 'The chickens will, though. Make a beefsteak and kidney pie for dinner, and Master can have the chickens tomorrow. I'll send word to the poultry-maid not to kill the ducks after all,' she concluded with satisfaction. The ducks were already killed – had come up just this morning – but only she had seen them; and she had a good use for them.

Mrs Codling wiped her nose on the sleeve of her upper

arm. There was usually a drop at the end of her nose and her eyes were always watery. There seemed altogether an excess of moisture about her, perhaps because her previous service as a cook had always taken place in basement kitchens: Morland Place was a step up for her in more than one sense. 'Master ordered Davenport fowl,' she objected damply. 'He enjoys my Davenport fowl.'

'Then he'll enjoy it all the more tomorrow, for the wait,' Mrs Moon said impatiently, turning away. 'For all he's likely to notice today you could feed him out o' the hen bucket,' she muttered to herself. Moon was still standing where she had left him, and she brushed past him into her room. 'Haven't you got anything to do?'

'I've got plenty,' Moon defended himself. 'I were just thinking.'

'That'd be the day,' Martha said, sifting amongst the bills on her table for the grocer's account she had been doctoring. Moon drooped against the doorframe watching her.

'It's that little lass,' he said. 'I were watching her play a bit since out by the orchard, and thinking what a lonely life it is for her. It doesn't seem right to me. I wonder Master doesn't send her away to school.'

'Oh you do, do you?' she replied. 'A fine thing that'd be, tearing her away from her home and all she knows, sending her off amongst a lot o' strangers. Thinking, you call it? *I* wonder you don't save your head for keeping your hat on, for it's not much use for anything else.'

She didn't look at him and was only half listening: her scorn was automatic. Moon saved his breath and chose instead a dignified retreat across the passage into the butler's room, to seek the solace of cleaning silver. He found it satisfying, covering the dim metal with the brown paste, as though hiding it in a muddy ditch, and then rubbing the mud away to reveal the bright, moony silver underneath. It was his own little act of creation, to make beauty out of dullness, to make perfect what was spotted: it made him think how good the world would be if the spots on men's souls could be cleaned away so easily, and all the sin and naughtiness got rid of by the exercise of a little elbow-grease. Entering his room with a gentle sigh of relief, he closed the door quietly behind him, not wanting to provoke his life's companion. Fretty this morning, she were. Probably something to do with Master's jollifications last night. Moon smiled softly and permitted himself a little joke. Wouldn't want *his* head this morning, any road!

Mrs Moon seemed hardly to have got started on her bills when the little French clock on her chimneypiece ('borrowed' from the unused Red Room) chimed ten. She gave it a startled look – she hadn't realised it was so late. She got up and cautiously opened her door, noted with satisfaction that her husband's door was closed, and came quietly out. She looked into the kitchen – Codling was bent over with her back to the door, poking the fire, and the kitchen-maid was out of sight, though perfectly audible, washing crockery in one of the sculleries. Good! Mrs Moon could move softly when she wanted, for all her bulk. She was across the kitchen like a shadow, across the servants' hall, and out into the cold stone passage that led to the backstairs, the courtyard door, and a warren of pantries and store rooms. It was empty at this time of day, as she had expected. In the cold-house, in the shadows under the slatted bench, was the basket she had filled early this morning. She took it into the game larder and added the ducks, covered it with a cloth, slipped it over her arm and went quickly to the courtyard door, pausing a moment in the shadow of the backstairs to listen for movement. But all was quiet.

Across the courtyard, down the brewhouse passage, past the nursery stair, and out through the back door she tripped like a vast red-riding-hood; across the drawbridge, breathing heavily with concentration, for it was hardly more than a couple of broad planks fixed together, and she went in terror of going over the side or through the middle and into the moat. Those black and haunted waters frightened her more than anything in this ancient house; she had the horrid feeling that if she looked at them for long enough she would be driven to throw herself in, as people are said to be fascinated into throwing themselves off cliffs.

Safe on the other side she hurried along the path which ran beside the orchard. There was a clump of elder growing up against the orchard wall, and in the shadow of it a man was waiting. He was well camouflaged, for his clothes were no-coloured, like earth and stone, and his skin was weathered with a natural dirt which had not been disturbed in years. I suppose if I was a dog, I could smell him, Mrs Moon thought with fastidious disdain, but quite wrongly: in fact since he lived out of doors, sleeping most nights like a hedgehog, curled up in the woods under a covering of leaves, he was as near to scentless as any living thing could be. It was important, in his line of business, to be able to get close up to animals before they noticed him.

He flattened himself against the wall to make room for her as she stepped into the shadow of the elder.

'Here it is, then,' she said. 'Got your sack?'

He nodded and held it forward, open. His hands and the soiled hessian were hardly distinguishable. She transferred the goods from her basket carefully, telling them off so there could be no mistake. 'A nice pair o' ducks, just killed. Brace o' Cornish hens, dressed.' They were from last night – she had reckoned the gentlemen wouldn't know the difference between Cornish hen and pheasant by the time they got to the table, and she had a brace of pheasant spare, which Ferrars had confiscated from a poacher and left for the kennelman, because they were too mutilated for the table. She had simply diverted them to a dark corner of the game larder, reasoning that what the kennelman had never had, he'd never miss, and got Mrs Codling to decorate them on the platter with watercress and such, to hide the ragged bits. 'A smoked hindquarter of ham – tell him I can get more if he wants.' The pigman, who also took care of the smoke house, was not only stupid, but because of his smell was a social outcast. Even if he noticed a ham was missing, who could he tell? And who would believe him? 'Two pound o' butter. A dozen eggs – be careful o' those. Don't swing the sack about like you usually do or it'll be you that pays. This is a pineapple – don't put it on top of the eggs, now! And watch out for this, too,' she said with the last cloth-wrapped bundle. 'Dessert grapes, two bunches. Black Hamburg – the best.' Who but she was to know how much fruit the gentlemen had eaten last night? Certainly not the gentlemen, who had been incapable of counting their own heads by the time they left.

'That all?' the brown man said at last.

'All? Aye, and plenty! I want a good price for these, mind. Tell him I don't forget those pigeons. Three shillings indeed! And me risking my life for the likes of him.'

The brown man carefully closed the sack and lifted his eyes to hers for an instant. It was not a thing he often did, and she didn't like it. His eyes were dark brown, shiny and still, and seemed to have no whites. They were like an animal's eyes – an animal that watches from cover and has no thoughts but of life and death. She felt her bones crunch and her blood spill when she looked in those eyes.

'He said he'd take liquor,' he said. 'Brandy or port-wine.'

She clucked with a mixture of annoyance and alarm. 'Aye, I don't doubt he would! And where does he think I'd get liquor from?'

The brown man inclined his head briefly towards the house. 'He says your man could do it.'

Mrs Moon put her hands menacingly on her hips.

'Never! You tell him, never! Moon's an honest man. I won't have him brought into it. Besides, a bit o' food left over or gone missing, that's one thing, and neether here n' there. But bottles o' liquor's different. That'd be stealing. I don't doubt he'd like to see me hanged at Tyburn, but I wouldn't dangle alone, I warrant you, and so you may tell him!'

The man nodded indifferently, and seemed even before her eyes to be fading into the background, dislimning in the disconcerting way he had.

'Bring the money Tuesday,' she said sharply. 'Usual arrangements. You know.'

He nodded again. He knew. Then he stopped fading and his face seemed to sharpen and point like a gun-dog's muzzle. 'Someone watching,' he murmured, without moving his lips. Mrs Moon turned in alarm, but she could not see anyone. 'Where— ?' She turned back, but he had gone. She shivered and folded her arms round her. There was something unchancy about him, and she disliked having to deal with him; but he was the perfect go-between, invisible except when he wanted to be seen, and standing so far outside civilisation most people would hardly class him as a human being. He brought her the money in a sealed envelope which listed the goods and the price paid, so that, since he could not read or write, there was no possibility he could cheat her or her customer. She paid him out of the contents of the envelope, and he never questioned the amount. What he did with the money she could not imagine and did not ask. It wouldn't have surprised her if he simply played with the coins for a while and then abandoned them, like a monkey with a shiny bauble.

She started back to the house, the empty basket over her arm and held close to her body. She hadn't gone more than a few steps, however, when a rustling and a slipping sound of stones stopped her short beside the broken bit of the wall. A tree had fallen on it last year, and no-one had got round to repairing it, partly, no doubt, because a scramble over the pile of rubble, earth and weeds made a convenient short-cut to the barns and outbuildings, and cut off a corner of the walk to Twelvetrees.

'Who's there?' she said sharply. 'Come on out, I know you're there. Show yourself, or I'll know you're up to no good. D'you want me to call the dogs out?'

A face slowly appeared above the wall, and Mrs Moon sighed with annoyance. 'Miss Jemima! What are you doing skulking there?' Too late she remembered Moon's words. If she had been listening to him properly, she might have kept a better look-out. 'Come over here at once,' she commanded sharply.

Jemima stared at her for a moment as though contemplating defiance, and then slowly, by inches, eased herself over the broken wall and down onto the path, where she stood just out of hand's reach. Mrs Moon examined her with disapproval. A nice, plump, pretty child, with rosy cheeks, golden curls and blue eyes she might have found a tolerable addition to the household, but not this pale, stick-limbed creature with her straight, ruddy hair and watchful brown eyes. There was something unpleasant about a child that looked so critical at grown-ups. You never knew what she was thinking – and what cause had a child to think anyway? She was an incubus, that was what!

'What were you doing over there?' she asked sharply.

'Playing,' Jemima said, the minimum of answer.

'Who with? Who else is there?'

'Childie, but he's gone now.'

Mrs Moon stiffened. Childie was the pet-name of John Anstey, eldest son of Ben who was brother to Lord Anstey, and, like so many of that clan, resident under his lordship's roof in the family mansion. He was a few months younger than Jemima, said to be a very clever boy, but the worst thing about him as far as Mrs Moon was concerned was that his uncle was a Justice of the

Peace and his aunt was being courted by Master, who was running tame about Anstey House these days.

'Very nice behaviour for a young lady,' Mrs Moon snapped, 'skulking about in the shadows like that with a boy!'

'We weren't doing anything wrong.'

'Don't you be pert with me, miss! There must have been bad in it, for you to be so underhand, creeping about in hiding, spying on people—'

'Spying?' Jemima said indignantly.

Martha scowled horribly. 'What did you see? Come on, out with it!'

'I saw you talking to the gypsy,' she said.

'Oh you did, did you?'

A wiser child might have noted the menace. 'And I saw you give him things out of that basket. Stolen things, I expect.' She ducked back in surprise as Mrs Moon moved with unexpected swiftness; but Martha held back her hand at the last moment, and let it fall slowly to her side. For a moment they stared at each other like two cats weighing the odds. It was not Mrs Moon's place to strike the ward of her employer; but a complaint from Jemima would take a long time to trickle through to authority, and might easily run out into the sands along the way.

'My business with what you call the gypsy is my own affair,' Mrs Moon said coldly, 'and you'd be wise not to repeat slanders like that about honest folk. Why were you out here without your maid?'

Jemima looked slightly puzzled. 'I was playing,' she said.

'Where's Matty?'

'In the nursery, I expect. Matty doesn't play out with me.'

We'll see, Martha thought. We'll see about that. 'You'd better come in,' she said shortly, 'and brush your hair and wash your hands. You look like a ragamuffin.'

She turned away, and Jemima fell in behind her, not particularly apprehensive. Just as there was no-one for her to protest to about ill-treatment, equally there was no-one to punish her for wrong-doing. The nursery maid Matty looked after her, but Matty was a bit simple and had no influence over her; and she never saw her guardian except accidentally, in passing, for which she was quite grateful. In the one interview she had had with him since Grandmama's death, he had instructed her to call him Uncle Nicholas and promised to take care of her, but there was something about him she didn't like. It was unfair, as she acknowledged to herself, for he had given her a home, and fed and clothed her, and had never said or done anything unkind; but he had a sort of sick look about him, a sort of bruised look about the eyes, and he was always pale, and sometimes he smelled strange. Whenever she saw him she wanted to run away and hide. Her greatest fear was that he might one day touch her: an instinctive and illogical repulsion made her fear his touch would be cold and slimy, and that he would stick to her skin like a slug.

But their relationship was distant, and he never seemed to concern himself about what she did or where she went, which was good in a way, for it meant she did no lessons and wandered about the estate with a freedom a schoolchild would have envied. But sometimes she felt so bored and lonely she would have welcomed lessons as something to stem the pain. When she was alone with nothing to do she thought about Mama and Papa and her sisters and Little Josh, all dead from the cholera, and most of all about Grandmama, with whom she had been staying when the epidemic broke out. If she had been at home, she would have died too; and sometimes she wished she had. Uncle Nicholas had given her a home, but there was no-one left in the world to love her. And when you were quite, quite alone and something as dreadful had happened to you as losing both your parents and all

56

your siblings at one go, you couldn't really feel much fear of being scolded by the housekeeper.

In the brewhouse passage Mrs Moon turned and waited for Jemima, told her to go and find Matty, and watched her up nursery stair, her expression thoughtful. Then she retraced her steps, put the basket back, and went to find her husband.

'But I don't like to, Martha. It isn't my place,' Moon protested feebly. 'Why can't you do it?'

'Me speak to Master? You great gaby, if it isn't your place, how can it be mine?'

'But, Martha—'

'You do it casual,' she rode down his objections, 'just bring it up in conversation, when you're serving him or taking orders. Just mention it, exactly as I said – put the idea in his mind, like. I'll do the rest. Now don't look at me like that! You told me yourself you were worried about the child, didn't you? It was your idea to begin with.'

'But I don't like to presume—' He was almost tearful at the idea.

She took him by the arm, her fingers biting to give him courage. 'You do this right, Moon, and I'll let you go to the Have Another one evening. You can spend a whole evening there and get as drunk as you like. I'll give you the brass, and I'll fix it up so's no-one asks after you.'

He looked at her rather sadly. 'Thank you, Martha, but I don't want to. I'm surprised you think of it. When we came here you said the best thing was I'd be out of temptation's way. I'm enjoying feeling respectable again. I don't want to spoil that.'

She let her hand drop and watched him walk away with a painful mixture of emotions. The damned old fool, she thought; and then, damn *me* for a fool! Why should I be so fond of the silly old codfish? It was a weakness, and she knew it.

*   *   *

Anstey House was a vast rambling mansion on the Lendal, smelling of and sometimes invaded by the river, and always seething with generations of Anstey brothers, sisters, cousins and aunts. They were a home-loving clan, left the ancestral roof with the greatest reluctance, and made any excuse to return there.

Mary Anstey, sister to Harry, was thirty and the plain one of the generation. Since their mother had died she had mothered (and grandmothered) the family and accepted the position of daughter-at-home as a permanency; she had taken to wearing matronly caps and developed a brisk and, some might say, bossy air. Being free, as she thought, from the lunacies of love, marriage and procreation, she naturally saw more clearly and knew better than her polyphiloprogenitive siblings, and if her advice wasn't sought she delivered it unasked. When she found her sister Aglaea 'mooning' in the garden after a visit from Nicholas Morland, she knew exactly what it was all about.

'Now then, Aggie, you'd better come indoors and find something useful to do. There's plenty in the poor basket, if you haven't any work of your own.'

Aglaea, startled out of her reverie, turned away from the view of the river she had been contemplating and began obediently to move towards the house. Obedience was in her nature – youngest of nine, she had always had plenty of people telling her what to do – but a sigh escaped her almost without her knowing. It had always been a place that attracted her, this corner of the garden from which you could see the boats going up and down the river, and a glimpse of the wharf on the far side where broad-shouldered men laboured to load and unload them. The boats waited, sails furled, their wooden waists jostling the quayside like a comfortable animal rubbing away an itch; nowadays there were steamers too, leaner and noisier, churning the river to grey-brown soup as their paddles manoeuvred them in and out of mooring. Where they went to, she did not know. To the sea, of course – she had never seen the sea, and simply could not imagine a stretch of water so wide you could not see the other side of it – but beyond that she had no idea. The Ansteys, unlike the Morlands, had no tradition of educating their females; Aglaea could play the piano, but could not have found England on the globe. Yet watching the boats had always given her a keen pleasure, and of late years had eased an ache in her that she was hardly aware of. Sometimes she dreamed that she was standing on the deck of one of them, sailing away down the river, away and away, with York getting smaller and smaller in the distance behind – yet remaining minutely clear, so that when she looked back she could see every house in perfect detail. She could even see into the garden of Anstey House, and it would be filled with people, packed from side to side with Ansteys, and she would name them as she sailed away – Jack and Alfie and Ben and Jane, Childie and Lolo and Hal and Feddy – seeing each face as she named it in a soothing litany of farewell . . .

'I want to speak to you, Aggie, about Mr Morland,' Mary said, drawing Aglaea's hand through her arm the better to command her attention – and also to show her that it was not to be a scolding sort of talk, for Aglaea was timid and easily downcast.

'About Nicky?'

'Yes, and there, you see, is one of the points I want to make. Because you and Harry saw so much of Mr Morland when you were all children doesn't mean you ought to call him Nicky now. You're grown up, and it isn't fitting.'

'I don't, much,' Aglaea reflected. 'When you are talking to someone, you don't often use their name, do you?'

'That's all well and good, but I would recommend a certain degree of formality, love, until he actually makes his declaration. Has he hinted anything to you yet, about it?'

Aglaea frowned. 'Declaration?'

'I imagine he'll speak to Jack first, as head of the family, to ask his permission. With his upbringing – Lady Morland was so strict – he'll want to do everything properly, which is just as it should be, of course. If nothing else he'd want to make sure there can be nothing for the tabbies to fasten on. The Mistress of Morland Place must be above reproach, you know, like a queen. But as a gentleman he ought to give you a hint when he is going to do it, so that you aren't taken by surprise, which would be undignified.'

'Do you mean you think he wants to marry me?' Aglaea managed to get a word in at last.

'Now, child, don't play the innocent with me. Of course he wants to. Why else do you think he's been haunting the house ever since he met you at Harry's? His dangling after you has been noticed, I promise you. Mrs Bolter said something to me only the other day in Blake's – though being Mrs Bolter it was something catty, but that's only jealousy on her part. No doubt she wishes she'd done as well herself, but for all her airs when she came out, she was wearing last year's hat with a new ribbon, so Bolter can't be doing too well for himself. But Mr Morland's attentions to you have been too marked to be mistaken, and God knows it's time and past for him to choose a wife. I quite understand that he wouldn't wish even to be thinking of it while he was in mourning, but life has to go on, and he's been after you long enough now for him to come to the point. So tell me, dear, has he said anything to you?'

'No,' Aglaea said. She thought of his visit that morning. He had come looking, he said, for Harry, but that must have been a fiction, for there was no reason for Harry to have been there and not at his place of business. And then he had brought out of his pocket the book of poetry he had been talking to Celia about at dinner the night before at Anstey House. Aglaea, being seated on the other side of him, had listened to the conversation and, when driven to it by Nicky's persistent questioning, had professed a liking for Gray, though in reality she had only ever read the *Elegy* and would only have recognised the first two stanzas of that. But he had produced a nicely bound volume and had sat down and talked to her about it, reading bits aloud to her, and when he had left had begged to be allowed to lend her the book. 'He just talked about poetry,' she said at last.

Mary laughed. 'That was such an excuse, even you can't have been taken in by it! And saying that that book belonged to his mother, when anyone could see it was bran-new from the bookshop, with half the pages still uncut! Of course he dearly wanted to make a present of it to you, but he's too much of a gentleman to do that until you are betrothed. I think, love, that he will speak soon. The poetry-book suggests impatience to me.'

'If he asks for me, must I have him?' Aglaea asked timidly.

Mary looked astonished, and stood still to emphasise it. 'You can't be thinking of refusing him? My dear child, whatever for? He's the catch of the county – Morland Place and all the rest of the property, an income almost beyond counting! You'd be mistress of Morland Place – which is far beyond anything we could have hoped for you,' she added seriously, 'things being as they are, but I suppose he's been in love with you since the schoolroom without knowing it, for it's my certain knowledge that he's never offered for anyone else, nor even shown any interest in another woman. The luck of it, to have Nicholas Morland in love with you! You'll have everything you could possibly want – *and*,' she added cunningly, 'which is an added benefit in your particular case, you'll only be a mile or so from home – near close enough to walk! Not that you'd have to walk, for the Mistress of Morland Place will have the finest carriage and horses in the Riding, I promise you.'

'But I don't—' Aglaea began, and then stopped.

'You don't what?' Mary asked sharply.

Aglaea thought it was too bold a thing to say; but then her feelings rushed up in her, a stifled feeling, as though she was in a cage and the bars were moving in on her. She would be crushed, snuffed out like a candle. All her life she had been surrounded by people, and being the last and least had done their bidding, and thought it her lot. There was no rebellion in her: she accepted the way life was; but even a mouse might make one squeak of protest between the cat's jaws.

'I don't love him,' she said at last, but on a dying fall, her courage running out even as she spoke.

Mary looked at her in silence for a moment, and felt an unexpected and unwelcome access of sympathy. She had sometimes been pitied, she knew, for being 'upon the shelf', but the position of a maiden lady, if she had a secure home and a sufficient allowance, was far preferable in her opinion to that of a woman married to a man she disliked. But after all, Aglaea had known Nicholas all her life, so she could hardly *dis*like him, and certainly not fear him. To marry him would be preferable, surely, to marrying a comparative stranger? As to love – Mary shrugged inwardly. A good establishment was much more important.

There remained one question. 'You aren't in love with anyone else, are you, dear?' she asked with unwonted gentleness.

Aglaea looked away. She had thought she was in love with George Cave, and he with her, but since Nicky had begun to pay her attention, he had simply absented himself; and when they did meet, by accident as it were, he was cool and polite to her as if they were the merest acquaintances. Surely that could not be love, to put up no struggle for her? If she had been a man, and free, she would not have stood by idly and allowed Nicky to have his way. So she must have been mistaken after all.

'No,' she said. 'I'm not in love with anyone.'

Mary felt an enormous relief. There had been something about Aggie lately – not that she wasn't always quiet, but she had seemed almost *depressed*. 'Well then, you goose, there's nothing to stand in your way. Your duty is to marry as well as possible, and as long as the match is respectable and your settlements are generous, enough of love will follow, I assure you. It always does.'

'You think I ought to accept, then, if he offers?'

'I think you *must*,' Mary said. 'You would disappoint your family dreadfully if you were to refuse such a good match for no reason. And besides,' she went on gravely, 'Mr Morland has paid you such marked attentions that it would be quite a scandal if you were to refuse him now. Everyone would think you a jilt. You would be ruined, and we would be shamed. Think of poor Charlotte, and Celia, how unpleasant it would make everything for them.'

It was an odd kind of world, Aglaea reflected, where you had to marry a man because he had singled you out, even if you hadn't wanted to be singled out and couldn't have done anything to stop him. But perhaps Mary was mistaken after all, and he wouldn't ask for her. That thought, however, did not bring with it the full and free sense of relief that it ought to have. Morland Place, she thought, was gloriously empty compared with Anstey House. Perhaps she should look upon it as being a little further down the river of her dream, which never went *to* anywhere, only *away* from what she knew. Perhaps as the wife of a wealthy and important man, she might even get to see the sea, and find out what place it was she had always wanted to get to.

Ferrars sought out Mrs Moon, and found her in the linen room upstairs, examining sheets for wear. He closed the door behind him and set his back against it to forestall any interruption, and Mrs Moon looked at him nervously and measured the distance between herself and her large cutting-out scissors on the work-table. It was well known that little, ferrety men usually preferred ample women, so it was quite possible that Ferrars had been overcome with lust for her, given his unmarried state and the degree of her amplitude.

But no, it seemed that anger and not desire was inflaming his pustules. 'What are you about, you meddling old besom?' he snarled. 'What's this you've been telling the master?'

Mrs Moon bridled. 'I don't know what you're talking about. I haven't been next or night the master in two days, not since he ordered his dinner yesterday morning.'

'You know exactly what I mean, so don't bandy words with me. It was your fool of a husband spoke the words, but it came from you all the same, as I know very well. The master has just been asking me what I think about sending Miss Jemima to school, because she "seems rather lonely and wants companions". And when I dig further I find Moon has been maundering about the poor little orphan having no-one to play with. So I repeat, what the devil are you about?'

Mrs Moon's mind was working quickly. Ferrars wanted the child kept home, did he? But why? Asking him would do no good, and she couldn't tell him the real reason she wanted that creeping, spying, unnatural child out of the way. She must have a plausible excuse.

'Why, Mr Ferrars, I don't know what all the fuss is about,' she said slowly, marking time. 'I swear to you it was Moon's own thought that the child was lonely. He came in and said to me this morning that he'd seen her playing all alone and—'

'You told him to tell the master. Why?'

'Well, it did just occur to me, as Moon was saying that, that here was a good opportunity –' Ah, she had it! '– to save some money. School would be a deal cheaper than the child's food and clothes, and I know what an economist you are, Mr Ferrars. If she was sent to a nice, cheap school, you could close the nursery altogether and save coal and candles and servants wages—'

'And have her meeting God knows who and coming under the influence of God knows what?' Ferrars snarled. 'I have my own plans for Miss Jemima, and they do not include letting her leave Morland Place.'

'And what would those plans be, Mr Ferrars?' Mrs Moon asked, on the basis that it could do no harm. But to her surprise he answered.

'I mean the Master to marry her when she comes of age, that's what. I would be failing in my duty to him if I allowed an heiress like her to slip through his fingers.'

Mrs Moon looked at him with some surprise. As a plan it fitted perfectly with Ferrars' character: the Master has control of Miss's fortune, and Ferrars has control of Master – she had been in the household long enough to know how the land lay, how the steward encouraged Mr Morland in every vice that was likely to weaken his hold upon affairs. But Ferrars must know, because everyone knew, that Master had been paying his court to the youngest Miss Anstey and was expected to pop the question any day. So what was Ferrars up to? A horrid suspicion crossed her mind, that the fate he had in mind for Miss Jemima was to be a lot sooner and more final than matrimony at age twenty-one. She wouldn't put a spot of homicide past Mr Snake-eye, provided he had worked out a way to get his share of the dividend. It would be easy enough in this big, half-empty, shadowy, gothic old place to arrange for a foot to slip or a battle-axe to fall off a wall; or perhaps a slow and mysterious wasting illness might find its way to her via the nursery porrage. Well, she shrugged inwardly, it was none of her business. Nobody wanted the child. She'd be better off put out of her misery.

'Well, Mr Ferrars, I'm sure it would be a comfortable thing for Master to marry someone familiar, instead of a stranger with who-knows-what dreadful secret in the cupboard. But I will say that if I was Master, I shouldn't want my future bride to be running about the country unchaperoned as Miss does. She may only be twelve, but it's old enough to get in trouble, and when I see her morrissing about with rough boys and talking to gypsies as she was this morning—'

'What?'

Yes, that startled you, Mrs Moon thought. Kidnapped by gypsies – that'd put a stop to your plan, wouldn't it? 'As I live and breathe, Mr Ferrars, the dirtiest scoundrel you ever saw, and she was chatting to him like her own brother. The child has low tastes, I'm sorry to say – and with no supervision, for Matty is as much use as a wet week at harvest. She needs watching close, does Miss Jemima, every minute of the day.'

Ferrars gave her one piercing look, which she withstood firmly, having said no less than she believed in the last sentence, at least. And then he was gone. Hotfoot to Master, Mrs Moon thought indifferently. We'll see whose plan succeeds, Mr Spotted Toad-face. You can't out-manoeuvre me, so don't think it.

'I've been thinking, sir, about what you said earlier,' Ferrars said. He was standing behind his master holding his neckcloth, while Nicholas stared in the mirror, struggling with the top button of his shirt.

'Eh?' he said shortly

'About sending Miss Jemima to school.'

'Oh,' said Nicholas. The points of his shirt were too high and the neck too tight for him comfortably to turn his head. Instead he reached a hand straight up for his neck cloth, and met Ferrars' eye briefly in the glass. The truth was he had not really been serious about it. He had just floated the idea idly, with the vague notion that it might annoy Ferrars. He didn't seem annoyed, however, but gravely thoughtful. 'Well, what about it?'

'I don't think it would do, sir.'

'What the devil are you talking about?'

'At school she would come under the influence of people over whom we – you, I should say, have no control. You would have no knowledge of what they might be teaching her. And she would make friends amongst the other girls and want to go and visit them at their homes. She would meet a whole circle of people – men included – unknown to you, sir. And sooner or later she would fall in love and want to marry. Or some plausible rogue might compromise her to force you to let her go. She would be lost to you—' He let the rest of the sentence suggest itself – *and her fortune would be lost to you as well*.

'The deuce!' Nicky exclaimed, between alarm and annoyance. He didn't like Ferrars poking into his private affairs, but there was sense in what he said. 'What do you suggest, then?'

'A governess,' Ferrars said. 'She should be watched close the whole time.'

Nicholas tied his neckcloth carefully, his senses alert. Ferrars never said exactly what he meant; what was there behind this new suggestion? He was still hankering after his old scheme, wasn't he, for Nicky to marry the girl himself. That was why he didn't want her sent away to school. And he hadn't been in the least convinced by Nicky's courting of Aglaea, damn him. Well, there was no reason why Ferrars should know everything that went on in his master's head. And he didn't care one way or the other whether Jemima went to school or stayed home. Even at home, with a governess to 'watch her close' she would still meet people, eventually. Sooner or later someone would propose to her. Ferrars hadn't thought out his case very well, and the realisation put Nicholas in a good mood. He liked to be one up on Ferrars.

'I'll think about it,' he said loftily.

'Very well, sir,' Ferrars said. 'But it is a matter of some urgency. The present arrangement—'

'It's not something to be rushed into,' Nicholas said. 'I said I'd think about it. That's all.'

Ferrars bowed and retreated, and Nicholas's sense of triumph lasted until the man was out of the room, and then began to evaporate. It wasn't like the man to accept defeat so meekly. What *was* he up to?

Matty stood before Mrs Moon, her face swollen with weeping, her hands nervously twisting her apron strings.

'I'd never let Master Nicholas down,' she vowed passionately, 'never! Him what I fed at my own breast? I've knowed him since the very day he were born, Mrs Moon. No mother could love a son more.'

'Well you have let him down, and perhaps if you'd thought a little more respectfully about your master, and a little less about yourself, you might have done better.'

'But what have I done?' The tears were flowing freely again.

'You know right well what you've done – letting Miss Jemima gallivant about like an urchin with no-one to watch her. While you sat at your ease and smoked a pipe by the nursery fire, I've no doubt.'

'No, I never! I swear it! But what was I to do? Miss Jemima wouldn't've wanted me to play with her, not a great girl like her.'

'You fool! What did you suppose you were there for? Your job was to chaperone her, not just help her on with her stockings in the morning.' Matty was silent, trying to understand. She had been brought into the family as a wet-nurse, and had stayed on as a nursery-maid under the direction of a nurse and a governess. They had been dismissed and she had been kept on, for reasons she had no way of understanding, but no-one had ever told her what her duties were, so she had gone on doing what she did when she was the lowest of four or five.

Mrs Moon stared at the half-daft, blank face and took a step down towards her level. 'Suppose Miss Jemima, wandering about all alone like that, had been attacked? Or carried off? Or *ruined*?'

Matty understood that breathless horror all right, and turned pale. 'Eh, no! Oh my Lord! She's never!'

'No thanks to you if she wasn't. Well, you understand now why you must go – and thank Providence and your generous master that you are not to be clapped up in gaol for your wicked negligence.'

Matty hung her head, still weeping, but submissive now. She had nowhere to go – no family – no money saved – she might well starve to death 'out there' where she had not set foot in twenty-five years. But she was not capable of looking that far ahead. She thought only of the baby she had nursed at her breast so long ago – the one incandescently wonderful thing that had ever happened to her.

'Can I see Master Nicholas – just to say goodbye, like?'

'See Master, after you've let him down so bad? T'isn't likely! No, nor Miss Jemima neither. You're to go at once, without speaking to anyone – and never come back here, do you understand?'

A knock at the door heralded the kitchen-maid, lowest form of creation, lower even than Matty and too timid even to speak as she curtseyed, put down the bundle of Matty's belongings, and curtseyed again for good measure. Mrs Moon dismissed her with a nod, handed the bundle unceremoniously to Matty, and said, 'I'll see you off the premises.'

It was hardly necessary – the girl was too cowed and heartbroken to have disobeyed – but there was no sense in taking chances. When Matty was out of sight, Mrs Moon went and found her husband and told him to ask the Master for a private interview with her – urgent.

*   *   *

'Gone, you say? I don't understand. Gone where?' Nicholas snapped, wondering why he was being bothered with domestic matters.

'Left your service, sir, the ungrateful hussy. I'm sorry to say, sir, that she's been giving unsatisfactory service for some time now. She got ideas above her station and nothing was good enough for her. Complaining about the food and her quarters and I don't know what besides. Now she's upped and gone, without a thought for your convenience, because she'd heard of a better place – up Thirsk way, so I understand.'

'Matty?' Nicholas shook his head disbelievingly. If any servant had been loyal, he'd have expected it to be Matty – but they were none of them to be trusted. 'Well, what's to be done?'

'Well, sir, if it will help you, I can look after Miss Jemima for a day or two – keep her with me – while you look about for someone else.'

'Someone else?' he said vaguely.

'I beg your pardon, sir, but she did ought to have a governess – someone to keep an eye on her all the time. She's a growing girl, sir. And Matty gave her all too much freedom.'

'Yes, quite,' Nicholas said hastily.

'Unless you might be thinking of sending her away to school, sir?'

Nicholas shook his head. 'Where the deuce am I to find a governess,' he muttered. 'It's the devil of a nuisance.'

Triumph sang in Mrs Moon's heart. 'Well, sir,' she said meekly, her eyes lowered, 'if it would of any help to you, I do happen to know of a young lady who's looking for a position. In fact, not to mince matters, she's a cousin of mine once removed. A most genteel person, and excellent references. She was looking after a baronight's two girls – and a proper handful they was, until Miss Smith took 'em over and got 'em into order. Now they are a credit to society, sir

70

– you couldn't find two more quiet, good, obedient girls.'

'Yes, yes, you needn't trouble to give her a character, I'll interview her myself. Just get her here as soon as possible, will you?'

'Very good, sir.'

She left the room, quietly closing the door behind her. All well, she thought. Just as I planned – and as long as May Smith remembers she's my cousin, and that the bridewell she's been wardress in was a baronight's schoolroom, we shall have no trouble. As she crossed the staircase hall, she had the feeling of being watched, and lifted her head sharply. Jemima was standing at the turn of the stair, looking down; her face was paler even than usual, and her eyes were red. Mrs Moon couldn't help a little smile of triumph curling her lips, upon which Jemima turned away with a stifled sob and ran back upstairs. She rushed blindly along the passage towards the nursery, where now no Matty would be waiting, comfortable and comforting, to give her bread and milk and listen, uncomprehendingly, to anything she had to say. As she ran past the backstairs she brushed past Ferrars without even noticing him. Ferrars drew back and let her go, following her with his eyes as she disappeared round the corner. All well, he thought with satisfaction. His real plan was different from anything either Nicholas or Mrs Moon supposed. He meant to have everything in the end, and that included Jemima's fortune – but not by the chancy expedient of Nicholas's marrying her. Good God no! Ferrars would deal with Miss Jemima much more thoroughly than that.

CHAPTER FOUR

Harry Anstey knew quite a bit about George Hudson, who was becoming something a public figure around York. A few years back he had inherited a fortune from a great-uncle, which had enabled him to leave his drapery business in the background and go into politics. He had got himself made treasurer of the York Tory party, and during the first General Election of the Reformed Parliament in the autumn of 'thirty-two he had organised the Tories' campaign supporting John Henry Lowther. Though it had been unsuccessful – the Whigs had won, and Harry's brother Alfred now had the seat the Tories had earmarked for Lowther – Hudson had gained much credit for the enthusiasm of his effort. Another new interest of Hudson's was finance: he had recently opened the York Union Banking Company, a new joint-stock bank, in company with a number of co-investors including Sir John Lowther, father of John Henry.

The summons – for it was hardly less – to Mr Hudson's house in Monkgate took Harry by surprise, for Greaves and Russell did not normally handle his business, and Harry was not personally acquainted with the draper. It was, moreover, a summons out of business hours, which he would have been within his rights to refuse; but simple curiosity was enough to make him turn right instead of left at High Petergate on his way home, skirt the Cathedral Close, and walk out to the new paving and bright gaslighting of Monkgate.

Ten minutes later he was sitting in the comfort of a deep crimson velvet upholstered armchair before a large fire in Hudson's business-room, a glass of sherry in his hand, and his bemused eyes fixed on the large figure of his host as it walked about the room. For such a bulk of man, Hudson's feet were remarkably small, and his constant little steps hither and thither in sudden spurts of movement seemed like the operation of a safety-valve for a head of steam building up inside him.

'I am a cooming man,' Hudson was saying in his broad accent and broader way. 'That's what they say of me, Mr Anstey, aye, and they're not wrong! Coom I mean to, and coom I shall – and I 'ave the method all ready up 'ere—' He tapped the side of his head. 'I mean to get ahead, and get ahead fast, but one thing I do know is that you must prepare the ground first, or you'll "coom a cropper", as you hunting folk say.'

'Indeed sir,' Harry said, since a response seemed required.

Hudson turned and looked at him keenly from under those heavy, pale lids. 'You married that pretty little Miss Laxton, daughter of Sir Percy Laxton of Heslington Grange,' he said abruptly.

Surprised, Harry took refuge in facetiousness. 'I admit the soft impeachment.'

Hudson ignored the interruption completely and resumed his restless teetering. 'Sir Percy is a friend of Sir John Lowther, who is a friend of mine in the business way. I hear things about thee, things to thy credit, young Mr Anstey. Sir Percy – who was doubtful tha was good enough for Miss, as any father'd naturally feel about a 'prentice attorney wi' no expectations from his family— nay, let me finish! Sir Percy, I say, thinks a bit about thee, now. Sound, he calls thee. He means to set thee up in practice, now then!' A sidelong glance at Harry, who was utterly bemused by all this. 'Aye, it's true what I tell thee. Tha's a cooming man thyself, seemingly.'

Harry made an effort. 'I really don't know what your source of information might be, sir—'

'Nay, don't frost up with me, lad, I mean no harm. My source is good, you may rely on it. You will be a big man in the legal way; and your brother-in-law will be a rich 'un one day, and completely under your thumb, as well I know.'

'Ceddie Laxton?' Harry said, growing more confused by the minute. 'What has he to do with it?'

'He will inherit his father's fortune, and knawnt what to do wi' it. Where else should he turn for advice but to you? And you will serve him well, I know. You are a man of integrity – all your friends say so, and a man's friends are the mark of him. I think I shall be in the way to put a lot of business your way, Mr Anstey, and a chance to investment in summat new and exciting which you will relish, I promise you. You are going to be useful to me, and I am going to be useful to you. Why, you might even find yourself one day naming one of your younger sons after me!'

This, Harry saw, was a joke, but he managed no more than a feeble smile and a, 'Mr Hudson, I really don't—'

Hudson held up his hand. 'I know, but you will. Be patient. Let me fill your glass.' This done, Hudson filled his own glass and abruptly sat down in the chair facing Harry's, leaning forward confidentially. 'Your friend, Benedict Morland – I've seen him, spoken to him. He's working on the railway undertaking near Selby. Did you know that?'

'I'd heard – a rumour,' Harry said cautiously. 'Someone – a common friend of ours – said they had seen him, though not to talk to, so I thought it might have been a mistake.'

'No mistake – it's him all right. It seems he left York in some kind of disgrace. I've been making enquiries about him, but I can't get to the bottom of it. The stories are that confused, all I know is you and your brother were in

74

it somehow. That's why I've come to you. I want to have the truth.' Harry stared at him doubtfully, and Hudson, straightening, added, 'I bear your family no grudge for winning the seat. All's fair in war and love, they say – and talking of love, young Mr Benedict was having a bit of a do with the widow Makepeace, warn't he? Was that why he left home?'

'Good God, how did you— ?' Harry began to exclaim, but Hudson chuckled and shook his head.

'Eh, tha's got a streak of the innocent about thee, Anstey! It's right refreshing! I am a draper by trade – Makepeace was a draper. Did tha think I wouldn't know everything there is to know about my chief rival? Of course I knew young Benedict Morland was servicing the widow – and good luck to it, for my part! I hope it gave 'em both pleasure, for I'm sure it harmed no-one. That's why I'm puzzled if he left home because of her.'

'He didn't,' Harry said quickly. 'At least, not directly, although – look here, Mr Hudson,' he began again, searching the face opposite him for guile, 'I want to know why Bendy is any of your business. Why are you asking me all these questions?'

Hudson seemed to consider. 'I cannot tell you everything yet, because my plans are not complete, but I can tell you that I want to offer Mr Morland – Bendy, you call him – a position. More than a position, an opportunity. If he takes it, he will never regret throwing his lot in with me. But I must know what sort of man he is. You were his friend, and you knew all about it. Now tell me, what did he do to be sent away, and if he was innocent, why has his name not been cleared – by his friends, if not by him?'

Harry flushed. 'I was not at liberty to – I had no idea where he was until recently, and there was no need—'

'Nay, tha needn't make excuses to *me* – I'm not thy conscience. Just tell me what happened.'

Harry considered. 'Well, I don't see how it can do any

harm to tell you. I would like to clear Bendy's way to come home again – if he wants to. If that's your purpose too, well and good. But I must tell you it's a confusing tale.' He sipped his sherry, composed his thoughts, and began. 'Years ago Bendy had a youthful adventure with a farm-girl, who disappeared quite suddenly, and years later reappeared in York. She was then living in a room above a workshop, and the artisan said that he saw a gentleman coming and going regularly, as if the girl was in keeping.'

Hudson nodded, and reached over to refill his glass.

Harry resumed. 'He didn't recognise the gentleman, who was always muffled up and took good care not to be seen. Then one day the girl hanged herself. The artisan found her; but he knew that her keeper had been there before him, and simply left her hanging and did not report it to anyone. That was bad enough, but on the same day, in the same area, a pauper was attacked without provocation, beaten about the head by a gentleman with a stick, who then ran off and left the pauper to die.'

Hudson pursed his lips and frowned. 'And why do you think it was Benedict Morland as did those things?'

'I don't,' Harry said quickly. 'I'm quite sure he is innocent. But there was a time when, albeit reluctantly, I thought – you see, he was seen in the area; in fact, seen coming out of the very street where the pauper was attacked.'

'By you?'

'By his brother. Nicholas Morland.'

'Ah!'

Harry waited to see if the *ah* would be explained, but it wasn't so he went on, 'I saw his brother shortly afterwards and he told me about it. And later a pair of gloves was found near the girl's lodging, which proved to belong to Bendy. Nicky told me that he had known for a long time that Bendy was – was going to the bad – though

I think he only meant that he drank and gambled and philandered—'

'As gentlemen commonly do,' Hudson said neutrally.

Harry shrugged. 'Lady Morland – their mother – wouldn't have thought so. And as she was so frail, it was decided to save her the shock of knowing about Bendy's crimes by sending him away. Jack – my brother – and I agreed to keep the secret provided Bendy went away and did not come back.'

Hudson nodded. 'So then, what has changed your mind? Why do you now think he's innocent?'

'Firstly because I've known Bendy all his life, and I can't believe he's that kind of person. As a boy he was the soul of generosity, and tender towards all creatures weaker than himself. He would never have harmed any living thing. And secondly because I've spoken to Mrs Makepeace, and she tells me that Bendy was with her the whole day when those awful things took place.'

'And you believe her?'

'Yes,' Harry said. He thought of adding something, but the word stood better alone.

'So why have you done nothing to clear his name?'

'His name was never publicly blackened. Nicky gave out that Bendy had run away to seek his fortune. I don't know what rumours have grown up since, but there was nothing to be done about them, except simply to deny them. All that needs to be done to reinstate Bendy is for the record to be put straight with Jack and Nicky.' Harry bit his lip. 'The difficulty is that Nicky really believes in Bendy's guilt, and when I try to speak to him about it, he refuses to listen.'

At the conclusion of this speech, Hudson got up and began walking about again, his little steps seeming to express disapproval. 'It seems to me you've all behaved like a lot of green girls with the vapours. You'd nothing to say that Benedict Morland did anything, bar a pair of gloves, which he could have lost anywhere, and his brother saying he was nearby when someone knocked down a beggar. By God, I wouldn't hang a cat on such stuff as that! Why you didn't – but haud back a minute!' He stopped himself suddenly, narrowing his eyes. 'If Benedict was all innocent, why did he let them send him away?'

'To save his mother, and to protect Mrs Makepeace. He didn't want to tell anyone he had been with her, for fear of hurting her reputation. And knowledge of that affair would have been very shocking to Lady Morland.'

Hudson's eyes widened a moment, and he muttered something under his breath which had the words 'young' and 'fool' in it. 'Aye, well,' he said aloud, 'maybe he was happy enough to get out, any road. He's done well enough for himself – engineer on the Leeds and Selby Railway, did you know that? – but the time has come to bring him back to York. Can you get his brother to receive him?'

Harry looked troubled. 'I can try. But Nicky is – passionate on the subject.'

'You must go and see him and tell him how he was mistaken. He's courting your sister – aye, I know! – so you must want that matter cleared up before the wedding. It would be awkward to have such a cloud hanging over your brother-in-law, wouldn't it?'

'I hadn't thought of that. But you still haven't told me what it is you want Bendy for.'

'You and him both can do me a power of good. I'll tell you when the time is right. First you must clear the way. When you've spoken to your brother and Mr Nicholas Morland, let me know, and I will go and see young Benedict. And then all will be revealed. But you must get on with it, Mr Anstey. Time is precious.'

It was a long time since Harry had been to Morland Place, and when he rode in under the barbican that fine autumn day, he had a feeling like the Sleeper in the old story, who returns home to find a hundred years have passed, and all he knew dead and gone. The yard was empty except for a few hens scratching at the broken cobbles. There had never been broken cobbles in the old days; the paint was peeling on the main stable door, too, where the sun had silvered and blistered it. The yard would never have been empty, either: there were always servants about, horses in the stables, the great door standing open to a multitude of comings and goings. The silence was disconcerting.

Morland Place had been Harry's second home. He had come here every day to do his lessons, carried pillion behind a servant; brought in the carriage on wet days, bouncing and slithering on the buttoned leather cushions, his legs too short to reach the ground, clutching at the silken cord with the turk's head knot to stop himself falling off into the straw on the floor; later riding proudly on his very own pony, his bundle of schoolbooks bumping the small of his back. A thousand memories peopled his mind: of Father Sparrow, the stout French émigré who taught him and Nicky – and later Bendy too – who beat them rarely, told them stories of French giants and witches and talking animals (so much fiercer and more unpredictable than the home-grown sort) and kept a store of fragrant liquorice-bark in a secret pocket inside his robe.

Memories of Lady Morland: so little and dark and quick, with a voice like music, and hands that seemed to heal where they touched. When he'd been bad, she would brush the hair out of his eyes and speak to him in French, smiling down into his face, and the sweetness of her seemed to slide right into his soul, like honey soothing a sore throat. Her kingdom, this: no-one ever said the words to him, but he knew it all the same, that this world revolved around her, and her rapid steps and flashing glance were the momentum that kept it spinning in its place.

The house itself: always welcoming, full of the smells of home, of beeswax polish and woodsmoke downstairs, the starched smell of sheets and the fibrous smell of drugget upstairs; hints of coal and soap drifting up the backstairs; the suggestion of dinner and pies and cinnamon buns wafting from the kitchen passage. It was always full of the sounds of life, too, servants moving about their tasks, a footman whistling as he polished, a housemaid tutting at fingermarks, the clicking of a dog's nails across a polished floor. There had seemed so many servants, one for this and one for that, a sewing maid, a boot boy, a footman for messages, an old man whose sole occupation seemed to be filling coal scuttles and log boxes. They crowded his memory as they had seemed to crowd the house, all the same and all different: a stream of new young housemaids with downy bare arms and wispy hair and shiny faces; parlour-maids with shoes that creaked as they crossed the stone floor of the hall and starched aprons that crackled like minor lightning as they bent; kitchen-maids with cheeks hot from tending the fire and hands hard as floorboards from scrubbing pots, hair that smelled of bread and fingers that smelled of onions. He remembered daily mass in the chapel when all the household assembled, and the maids in serried rows were suddenly all grown beautiful, dewy-eyed with piety, while the men-servants were shy and knobbly, hands between their knees twisting for comfort, eyes cast down lest anyone embarrass them with a question.

And Nicky, of course: his first and closest companion, sharing with him all the minute and wondering, carefree and noxious concerns of small boys. With Nicky he had explored the country, muddied himself in streams, stung himself in nettly ditches, caught sticklebacks, fallen out of trees, learned to drive a plough-horse, been bitten by an angry sow; with Nicky he had travelled the trackless wastes of Latin grammar and Greek prose, and penetrated the steamy jungle of adolescence. You did not lightly stop loving the companion of your growing up. And Bendy had always been there too, a plump, dark, good-natured baby tottering after them, smiling through every bump and disappointment; later a stocky boy wandering off alone to watch birds and gaze at frogs and learn the secrets of spiders. The three of them; then the two of them, and then, by degrees and never somehow noticed until it was too late, one alone. What had happened? Where was the Nicky he had shared every thought with?

And what had happened to Morland Place since he was last here? Shadow, dense in the bright sunshine, lay cold as water across one side of the yard, and he could smell the blank, dank odour of the moat which seemed, in this moment of emotional confusion, like a sound as well as a smell, the sound of emptiness, the sigh of nothingness that comes up out of an unlit cellar. Sitting his horse, he looked up at the face of the house, and for a moment the windows were the blank and empty eyes of a corpse. When Lady Morland had died, had its spirit died with her? Darkness, dankness, silence – then his horse sneezed, and the familiar, living sound broke the spell. The shutters had been closed in the bedrooms, that was all – against the sun, or because the rooms had been shut up, perhaps, to save work. (Yet that alone was unlike Morland Place.) He dismounted, tied his horse to the ring by the steps, and walked up to the great door. In the old days, he would have been just as likely to go in by the buttery door to see if old Monsieur Barnard, the cook, had anything delicious lying about the kitchen to be sampled. But this was not the old days, and he was not sure whether he would be welcomed, or have the dogs set on him.

But all was not as deserted as it seemed: the great door was opened before he reached it, and a butler stood before him, butler-faced – neither welcoming nor forbidding. The master, Harry was to learn, was walking in the Wilderness. Yes, Harry thought, bending his steps thither, that seemed an appropriate analysis of the situation.

The formal gardens lay mostly to the south of the house, and Harry could see that they were neglected – not fatally so, but simply enough to notice: a raggedness about the hedges, dead heads upon the roses, a strand of bindweed waving triumphant and defiant out of the box edging, weeds growing confidently in the gravel of the paths. It had not gone to rack, but it was no longer loved, he thought. The Wilderness, at least, would show no difference, as was its nature, and he thought sadly that it was typical of his present relationship with Nicky that he should have to seek him out in its gloomy shades, which he had always disliked. Harry liked everything open, broad and fair, with plenty of sky above and a good view all round; the convoluted paths and dense growth of the Wilderness had never invited him, even for the achievement of finding the Roman spring in the centre, with its greenish satyr-mask dripping, dripping into a mossy alabaster bowl all grown around with ferns. Sometimes a single beam of sunshine penetrated there, but it seemed little compensation.

In the Wilderness you could be feet away from a person and not see them at all, but to his surprise and relief Harry came upon Nicky almost at once, sitting in an arbour of laurel, on a moss-stained stone seat, with his mournful whippet, Minna, lying between his feet. She rolled an eye whitely at the sight of Harry, but did not get up. Nicky looked up too, and without showing any surprise or offering any greeting said, 'Do you remember the time we thought Aglaea was lost in here? We searched and searched, tearing our hands, scratching our faces, weeping because we thought we'd never find her. And all the time she'd gone off with Sophie to see some puppies.'

Harry remembered. 'I got a whipping when I got home, for not looking after her.'

'Did you? I didn't know that. But it wasn't your fault. Sophie shouldn't have taken her away.'

'If you remember, Aggie wandered out onto the Long Walk, and Sophie found her there all alone. She might have fallen into the moat and drowned. That's what the whipping was for.'

'I don't believe babies fall into moats anywhere near as often as servants expect them to. Look how many generations have been brought up here. As far as I know only one person has ever drowned in my moat, and that was deliberate.'

It struck Harry as odd, he didn't know why, that Nicky should have said 'my moat'. 'You mean the White Lady? I thought that was supposed to have been an accident?'

'She was mad, poor lady, and a prisoner. Who can say how much she meant when she went walking beside the moat in the middle of the night?'

Harry shivered. 'I say, Nicky, do you think we could go out into the sunshine to talk. It's cold in here.'

'No,' said Nicky, quite unemphatically. 'What do you want to talk about? If you choose the subject, I choose the place.'

This seemed odd talking. 'You're not bosky, are you?' Harry asked with a sudden suspicion.

Nicky laughed – a whispery sort of laugh. 'The place is bosky, I am not. Do you remember your Horace – "the horrid wood"? Choose your words with caution, Harry, you never know when they might come back to haunt you.'

This was not promising, but Harry determined to plough on, planted his feet firmly and clasped his hands behind his back, the better to withstand the wind of passing ghosts. 'I want to talk to you about Bendy.'

'Ah, a discussion about the dead, is it? How appropriate in this place.'

'Nicky, do stop talking nonsense,' Harry said robustly. 'You know perfectly well Bendy isn't dead. Well, you might not have known that for certain, I suppose, but I've come to tell you that I know where he is, and that I know he is innocent of the things you suspected about him. I know that for certain sure, and I want to be able to bring him back to York.' He had not expected to get so far without being interrupted, and now he stopped, disconcerted. Nicky was smiling benignly, but not at him, and there was no knowing if he had even been listening. Harry felt a cold finger of unease around his collar. Was Nicky just being annoying as usual, or was he really beginning to lose his wits? 'Nicky, do you hear what I say?'

'Be careful what you wish, for you might just get it,' he said, faintly, as though from a long way away.

'Nicky – about Bendy—'

'I hear you,' still absently. 'What do you want from me?'

'I want you to receive him here, at Morland P—'

'Never!' It was spoken sharply, though not loudly. Minna, her muzzle on her outstretched leg, rolled an eye again to see if she was called. Nicky stared ahead at nothing. 'It's mine,' he said, as though to himself. 'Mine. All I wished for. The little fingers fastened tight around my neck, the little voice whispering, whispering in my ear.'

'Nicky, please listen,' Harry said desperately. 'I tell you I know Bendy didn't attack that pauper, as you thought he did. He wasn't even there. I know you thought you saw him, but you must have got confused about the day. On the day that pauper was knocked down, Bendy was with a lady, all day. I know her, and I have her signed affidavit. You can be quite sure it's true. And he had nothing to do with that poor girl, either. It was all a mistake.'

'All?' Nicky said. 'You don't know the all, nor the half. You don't know the depth and breadth of his crimes.' He spoke rapidly and low, almost panting for breath, his eyes squeezed tight with the force of emotion held back. 'He was evil, evil all through, I tell you! The things he did to that poor wretch – vile, degrading things – I cannot bring myself to speak of them. And not only her – others, sluts in brothels – dozens of them – young girls defiled – a virgin, once, who couldn't have been more than ten years old, though they said she was thirteen. Oh, it's unspeakable!'

Harry stared, shocked. 'No, Nicky, no, not Bendy. You're wrong. It's a mistake.'

'There's worse,' the relentless, dreary voice went on. 'Much worse. More deaths – not just the pauper, not just the girl – but others.'

'You mustn't say these things. You're upset, I can see – your Mother, poor lady – all the things that have happened to you lately. Sitting in this gloomy place makes you imagine things. None of that's true – Bendy isn't like that, and you know it in your heart.'

'In my heart? The heart of darkness – all dark, everywhere.'

'It's dark in here under the trees, that's all. Come on, old fellow, come out of here into the sunshine, and you'll see things differently.'

Almost reluctantly, he laid his hand on Nicholas's shoulder, and was shocked to feel how thin and how taut it was. Surely such tension must snap his bones? But when he coaxed, Nicky came, and allowed himself to be led towards the light. Minna trotted behind, tail clamped down, anxious eyes glancing from one to the other. Oh, the sunshine, the air, the space outside was wonderful! Harry gulped it down like water, leading Nicky like an invalid to a bench in the middle of the Long Walk, where there was no shadow. Though it was not hot out here, there was a dew of sweat on Nicky's upper lip, and his white face looked clammy. But after a few minutes' sitting, he began to look more normal.

Harry said tentatively, 'Are you all right now, old fellow? In there – well, you said some odd things. You didn't sound quite yourself.'

Nicky turned his head and looked at his old friend. The sun was in Harry's eyes, and he couldn't see Nicky's, but his voice sounded normal as he said, 'It's the curse of a sensitive nature, to be affected by one's surroundings. There are those to whom ghosts manifest themselves, you know, and then there's the rest of humanity, plodding, practical, blind to everything but the here and now. You Ansteys never had any imagination, did you? The salt of the earth, of course: the world could not do without you.'

If Harry had been an imaginative man, he'd have thought that sounded contemptuous. 'There's always been enough in the real world to keep me busy,' he replied mildly.

Nicky sighed. 'Yes, I know it! I always knew you could never really understand. No-one ever really understood me except my mother, and she—' A deeper sigh.

Harry was touched. 'It must be lonely for you here without her. But all the more reason, surely, to welcome Bendy back.'

'No,' Nicholas said at once, his frown reappearing.

'Nicky, I promise you, you were mistaken about him. I give you my word. Surely you don't doubt my word?'

'You may bring him back if you choose. That's your affair. But I won't receive him here.'

'But you must, or it will be no good,' Harry said urgently. 'Think what a scandal there would be. And you know,' he hesitated, but ploughed on, 'you know the scandal will harm you as much as him. People being what they are, they'll find a vicious amusement in brothers quarrelling, and they'll laugh at both impartially.'

Silence. But Nicholas was looking thoughtful. The idea of being laughed at . . . 'Very well,' he said at last, 'I will receive him – once! – for form's sake. But there is no question of any friendship between us.'

'But Nicky, *why*?'

'I have my reasons,' was all he would say.

They sat in silence for a while. Harry, looking about, saw that the grass of the Long Walk needed cutting, there were weeds growing up under the bench on which they sat, and the hedge that divided them from the parterre was needing its October trim without having received its April one. The shutters were closed in the rooms along this side of the house as well, except at the far end – the night nursery; and there was a piece of guttering hanging loose on the chapel roof.

Another delicate subject, to be broached with care. 'Nicky, I couldn't help noticing that – well – the grounds are looking rather neglected. And there was no groom to take my horse when I came into the yard, and a lot of the windows are shuttered. Have you – are you – have you dismissed a lot of the staff? I don't mean to be impertinent, but—'

Nicky looked at him with a sort of grim humour. 'But you are going to be all the same,' he finished for him.

Harry shifted uncomfortably. 'As your oldest friend, I'm naturally concerned—'

'Oh, don't worry, I'm not under the hatches yet!' Nicky said harshly. 'I can quite see you wouldn't want to be seen in the company of a pauper—'

'It isn't that at all!' Harry said indignantly. But it was true he had had a thought about Aglaea and her position, if Nicky were in financial trouble. But surely the vast Morland estate could not have fallen low so quickly, and without anyone's knowing?

'The truth is,' Nicky went on as if he hadn't spoken, 'my revered mother was not such a good steward. Far too unworldly; and her method of keeping accounts— !' He shook his head and chuckled, but it was not a warm sound. 'However, not to worry! A little retrenchment will soon have all in order again. And as I am a bachelor, and do not need to keep any state, the easiest way to retrench is to cut down my establishment.' He flicked his head round as though to catch Harry's expression unawares. 'Does that answer your questions?'

'I was only worried for you,' Harry said. 'I'm glad there was no need.'

'Naturally you were. And naturally you are,' Nicky said; but he smiled and laid a hand briefly on Harry's

87

arm. 'My good friend. Always my good friend, aren't you, Harry Anstey?'

'Of course,' Harry said. The smile seemed a quite normal one, and he relaxed at last, and smiled back. 'More than that, really. I've always looked on you as a brother. We were almost born on the same day, after all.'

'Yes, we should have been twins,' Nicky said, 'but you were in such a hurry to get here first—'

'Never mind, you've led the way ever since,' Harry said.

'Yes, I have, haven't I?' And Nicholas seemed pleased with that idea. 'But then I was always an eldest son: it makes a difference, you know.'

Benedict probably wouldn't have gone to the dance at Selby, had not a ticket been sent to him. It wasn't that he didn't like dancing, but tickets cost money, and money was in short supply at the moment. Somehow or other his expenses had increased considerably during the year, added to which the baby hadn't been quite well, and though Liza wouldn't hear of his sending for a doctor, even apothecaries had to be paid. But when a ticket arrived with a scrawled message across the back, 'Compliments of Sir Carlton Miniott', he felt he would be obliged to use it, and was glad to be obliged. All work and no play made Jack both dull and restless; a young man not yet twenty-two has need of a regular intake of jollity, noise and glitter if he is not to be bent out of his nature.

'I ought to go,' he said to Liza, fingering the heavy card with its handsome, elaborate inscription. 'Miniott is one of the directors of the railway, you know – Miniott of Ledston Park – a very important man of these parts. It would be almost an insult if I were to ignore his invitation. It's dashed good of him to think of me.'

Liza studied his flushed cheeks under her eyelashes. 'Of

course you should go,' she said unemphatically. 'Whoever said you shouldn't?'

'It's just that – well, my things, you know. I shall certainly have to have a new shirt and neckcloth at least if I'm not to disgrace myself. I just hope my evening clothes are not too shabby. My black pantaloons – I've had them two years and I've put on an inch or so round the waist since then. You feed me too well.'

'We'll get everything out and look it over,' Liza said placidly. 'If you need new, you must buy new.'

'Oh yes, and with what?' Bendy laughed. 'The tailor would never let my bill run past the month, and even if he did, how should I pay him off?'

She went across to him and laid her hands on his chest, looking up into his face. 'You would pay him out of your salary, and give me less. I can always make do somehow. You know I've done it before.'

He smiled at her. 'Oh yes – gleaning in the fields and hedgerows, snaring rabbits, collecting windfalls. A fine way for me to be treating you, putting you to that labour!'

'Bendy, don't joke me. I know as well as you do why your salary isn't enough. We cost you plenty, me and the baby and my brother.'

'There's no need to—'

'It must be said! You've been too good to us, and there's no need. To be paying for Diccon to have schooling as well as everything else—'

'Dear Liza, that is my pleasure, indeed it is. He's such a bright boy, and he's going to be a credit to you. I couldn't leave him to waste his talents as a horse-boy on the railway at tuppence a day.'

'No, you couldn't leave him, like you couldn't leave me. You must needs rescue us from the gutter, and we hold you back. If we'd any gratitude we'd take ourselves off out of your road—'

'Now don't talk like that,' Bendy said uncomfortably. 'I'll tell you when I want you to go.'

She removed her hands from his chest and took a step back. 'No you won't,' she said simply, and turned away. 'Let's have a look at your things and see what's amiss of 'em. You want to make a good impression – there might be people there who can help you get on.'

'It's only the Autumn Assembly,' he laughed. 'It won't be that kind of ball.'

'Then why did this Miniott person send you a card?' she said astutely, and he was bound to admit he had no answer to that.

Oh, but it was a great pleasure to be away from the little house and away from the workings, and heading for a little civilised pleasure in brightly lit surroundings. Selby was a prosperous town, and the Crown had new and handsome assembly rooms where there were regular balls and concerts throughout the season. There were plenty of wealthy people living in and around the town to justify them. Old wealth from wool and coal was joining new wealth from manufactures; Leeds was only eighteen miles away, and a more relentlessly pleasure-seeking society than that of Leeds was hard to imagine. The organisers of the ball had chosen a moonlight night, of course, and fortunately the weather held so that the clouds were well broken and there was no rain. Bendy was glad of that, for he had chosen to ride to Selby and had no desire to arrive splashed to his elbows. He had new pantaloons after all – the tightness of his old ones would have made dancing anything less stately than a minuet impossible, and Liza did not have much to do to persuade him to visit the tailor, though he still wondered how he was to pay the man next month. He had had to have new pumps, too, which were tucked into the saddle-bag, carefully wrapped in a cloth to keep them from scratching – in fact, his coat was the only part of the ensemble he had not renewed and his main worry now was whether it would proclaim its age too loudly. It would pass in a crowd, Liza assured him, and he hoped that the ball would prove such a 'sad crush' that no-one would be able to stand far enough back from him to see the worn seams.

He had arranged to leave his horse at the Grey Horse and take his dinner there with George Findlay, the only one of his friends who was going to the ball but had not been invited anywhere to dine beforehand. That was another expense, of course, but it could not be helped. It would have been paltry to refuse when George asked him particularly, and unfortunately he'd already told George he wasn't dining anywhere else, so he couldn't use that for an excuse. George had a handsome allowance from his family as well as his salary, so it was natural for him to suggest the Grey Horse, instead of some minor establishment where one could have dined cheaply at the common board, but Bendy, having gone so far, had decided to throw parsimony to the winds just this one evening, to enjoy himself and worry about the bills later.

So the two young men were feeling warm and mellow when they strolled towards the brightly lit windows and welcoming carpet of the Crown. They had been watching carriages draw up and disgorge their contents this half hour, and had judged that the proceedings would have 'warmed up' to just the right degree by now.

'Going to be a fine one,' George remarked with satisfaction as they stood aside to allow a party to mount the steps ahead of them: a party of four, Papa, Mama, and two nubile daughters. 'Right proportion of females. That's everything at these affairs,' he added wisely.

Bendy had some idea of finding his benefactor and thanking him for the ticket, but there was such a crowd in the vestibule, and particularly near the fire, where George assured him an old gentleman like Sir Carlton would be bound to be holding court, that he allowed himself to be persuaded to go straight into the ballroom, and leave the courtesies until later. As he stepped in through the double doors, he drew a breath of complete satisfaction. Nothing could have been handsomer than the room, with its high ceiling, fine plasterwork, and tall windows with heavy crimson drapes, the whole lit by a multitude of candles – nothing in the least paltry about it. The music was playing, and already people were dancing: in his state of euphoria they all seemed to Bendy to be young, handsome, and dressed in the first style.

George was not proof against the magic either. 'Dashed if I ever saw a greater number of pretty women in one room,' he murmured. 'And, by Jove, I see someone I know! What luck, Bendy, here are two partners for us!'

'Who, where?'

'Sitting over there, with the aged female in the purple sack. It's Miss Phillips and Miss Georgiana – the old girl's their mother, of course. I've known 'em for ever. Went to school with their brother Ned – ran tame about the nursery for years, pulled Georgy's pigtails and so forth. Splendid girls, not a bit affected. Come on, hurry up before some dashed bounder cuts us out.'

He grabbed Bendy's hand and towed him through the crowd, and in a moment they had arrived before the party amid cries of welcome, and breathless introductions were being made, enquiries after the brother, who was discovered to be with his regiment in Hounslow, and tentative enquiries about the next dance. Miss Georgy was evidently delighted to put her old friend's name on her card, but Miss Phillips was already engaged – though the kindness of her smile and the glumness of her assurance that she had been engaged 'these two weeks' suggested she wished she wasn't.

Mrs Phillips, vast, kindly and simple, intervened. 'Never mind, my precious, never mind, it can't be helped. But there are so few young men arrived yet we can't waste you, Mr Morland. We must see you dancing, or it will be quite shocking. Let me present you to a friend of Lizzie's, who is staying with us for the ball, and who is pining to be up and doing. Rosie, my dear! Rosie, let me present Mr Morland to you – a friend of Ned's – or at least – well, well, it is Mr Morland, at any rate! Mr Morland, Miss Fleetham.'

The young woman had been standing back from the group, half-hidden behind Mrs Phillips, her back to them, talking to a friend. Now she turned and was drawn forward into full view. Bendy found his mouth was dry, and closed it hastily so as not to look completely the idiot. Exquisite in white gauze over sky-blue satin, with many-ruffled sleeves, and feathers and flowers in her hair, was the golden beauty of the White Lion Inn yard.

CHAPTER FIVE

Harry put his head round the sitting-room door and saw Aglaea sitting at the table by the window with her sketching-book before her and a paintbrush in her hand. The small sitting-room at Anstey House was on the first floor overlooking the river, but even so the light at this time of day was very poor.

'You'll ruin your eyes,' he announced himself.

She looked round, and smiled a welcome. 'I'm more afraid I'll ruin my work.' He walked across and looked over her shoulder. It was a picture of their brother Ben's youngest daughter Frederica, always known as Feddy, since that was the closest she could come to her own name when she first learned to talk. She was four years old now. Aglaea had drawn her standing in the garden with the house behind her and a basket of flowers in her hand. 'I want to get it done for Jane's birthday tomorrow,' Aglaea said.

'It's very good,' Harry said. 'You do this sort of thing uncommonly well, Ag. I'd have known in an instant who it was.' Aglaea gave a small smile at this sincere if untutored praise. 'Perhaps you could do Celia some time, if you didn't dislike it. There would be a pretty subject for your pencil!'

'Very pretty indeed,' Aglaea agreed.

He stepped to the window, looked out into the dusk for a moment at a barge moving downriver, ghostly in the afterlight, her sprits'l hauled out almost at right-angles to

94

catch the light airs; and then turned back to look at his sister. She was bent over her painting again.

'You like that sort of thing, don't you?' he said diffidently. 'I suppose you are the artistic one of the family. We're practical people as a rule, we Ansteys – wouldn't you agree? Here-and-now sort of people.'

She only said, 'Mm.'

He looked at her bent head, at the pale parting in her brown hair, dividing her scalp exactly in two, the hair drawn neatly into four plaits, two at the sides and two at the back, which were pinned up into a knot at the crown. What could be more neat and sensible? She had always been neat and sensible, but he realised that he had very little idea what went on inside that familiar head. She had always seemed quietly happy with her lot, and his was not the nature to look for things to be different from what they seemed. Besides, all girls had been undifferentiated in his eyes until he had fallen in love with Celia. Aggie sewed a great deal and played the pianoforte quite nicely, as did every young female he had ever met, was as docile and pretty-mannered as they, and as pleasantly, flatteringly ignorant of everything except domestic matters.

Lots of girls sketched and painted, of course – Cely had once done quite a good thing of her father's collie, asleep with its head on its paws, which hung, framed, on the wall of Sir Percy's business-room. But with Aggie it was more than a ladylike pastime. And, now he came to think of it, some of her pictures were rather odd for a female. Likenesses and landscapes was what they mostly did, and vases of flowers and bowls of fruit. But none of the other girls drew boats – books and books of them, Aggie had, sketched as she sat at the window or in the garden, watching them go by on the river. And sometimes she drew boats that she had never even seen, going along rivers that weren't anywhere. 'Where's this?' he had asked her once or twice, and she had replied, 'Nowhere. It's just a fancy.' She made up boats out of her head – now that was odd, wasn't it? His brother Jack, having been a sailor before he came into the title, laughed at them, though not unkindly, saying they were drawn all wrong and would never have stayed afloat. Harry didn't know about that, but to him they always looked as if they were really *going* somewhere. You could almost feel the wind and hear the water.

So now he said, 'You're different, though. You have imagination, haven't you?' She paused in her work, lifting her brush carefully from the paper. 'Does it make you unhappy?' he asked her awkwardly. 'I've never asked you – I've always just assumed – but I wonder—'

'Wonder what?' she prompted.

'All those boats – why do you draw 'em?'

'I don't know,' she said. Her face was as calm and inexpressive as always, but she seemed really to be considering the question. The room around them seemed almost to be holding its breath, as though they were on the brink of some important discovery. 'They aren't unhappy pictures,' she said at last, as though offering a consolation.

He felt relief. No, they weren't, of course, not *unhappy*. There was a quality about them that was – he struggled with unaccustomed ideas, seeking a word for something as intangible as a mood – *wistful* perhaps? 'What I really wanted to ask you,' he said hurriedly, before the flow of communication dried up, 'was about Nicky Morland. Do you mean to marry him?'

'He hasn't asked me,' she said calmly. 'I keep telling everyone—'

'Oh, but he's bound to, it's only a matter of time. I just wanted to know – how he seems to you.'

She looked up now, meeting his eyes. 'I've known him all my life. You have, too. Why do you ask?'

Harry hesitated. He didn't want to put any doubts in Aglaea's mind. 'Does he seem different to you recently?'

'Of course he does,' she said. 'We're all grown up

now. He is Master of Morland Place – that must make a difference.'

'But how is he – towards you?'

'He is very pleasant. He admires my drawings and talks to me about a lot of different things.'

Well, thought Harry, giving it up, perhaps they would suit each other, both having imagination. Aglaea would be able to understand him when he said strange things – or perhaps, with the love of Aglaea to support him, he wouldn't say them any more. Marriage was a great thing for a man. Every man ought to marry, if he could find the right girl. 'When he asks you, Aggie dear, will you say yes?' Harry put to her now, very gently, wanting to be sure.

A rowing boat was going up the river, just visible by the lantern hanging from a pole in the stern, which jerked back and forth with the pull of the oars. Aglaea watched it, the last boat she would see tonight; after this it would be too dark. She would need a candle to finish her painting – unless she got up very early to do it by the dawn light. But someone was waiting for an answer from her – oh yes, it was Harry. What had the question been? No, not a question, a request. Well, if he wanted it too, what was there to say?

'Yes, Harry,' she said obediently. 'I will say yes.'

Bendy posted rhythmically to his horse's steady trot, his hat brim pulled down against the fine mizzle, his mind a litany of Miss Fleetham's perfections. Her tiny waist, so small he could almost have spanned it with his two hands – oh to be permitted to try! Her gown, the colour perfect for her, the huge sleeves, all layers of ruffles, from which her white shoulders and slender neck rose so pure and fragile. Her little hand, resting in his light as feather in its long glove, so that he had been afraid of crushing the tiny fingers by holding them too firmly. Her smile – perfection! Her voice – a nightingale was coarse by comparison! Her eyes – oh, she was altogether lovely. She was as exotic and delicate as an orchid – and she had danced with him – with *him*!

Miss Fleetham. Rosalind Fleetham. Miss Fleetham of Fleetham Manor, dancing with him – if indeed it was dancing, and not simply floating an inch or so above the floor. He had been almost too happy to speak, certainly too much astonished to say what was uppermost in his mind. It was she who broke through the absurd commonplaces he was spouting about the floor and the company, saying, with a very pretty mixture of humour and reproach, 'I'm afraid you don't remember me, Mr Morland. Though we had not been introduced, we *have* met before.'

'Remember you! I hardly dared think you remembered me! But indeed, I have thought about you very often, and wondered – wondered—'

'It was at the White Lion Inn, on the twenty-eighth of May,' she said, tacking the occasion down with a firm stitch. 'I wrote it in my journal.'

'Miss Fleetham!'

'Oh yes, I always keep a journal when I travel. One sees so many places and meets so many people. It is hard to remember them all,' she added, with a haughty look from under her eyelashes.

Benedict tore his mind from wondering that a girl so divinely fair could have such very dark eyelashes, and said, 'But I never thought I would see you again! I made sure you must live a long way away, or why should you bait at Selby?'

'Fleetham Manor is near Micklefield, about ten miles from here,' she said. 'We only stopped at the White Lion because I had a fainting-fit.'

'You are of a delicate disposition,' Bendy said.

'I assure you I am very well in general. Carriages always make me ill. The stuffiness and the jolting – there is no bearing them.'

'No indeed. I am not fond of carriages myself. I much prefer – prefer to ride,' he changed tack quickly, remembering her father's prejudice. 'Do you ride, Miss Fleetham?'

'Oh yes, I am never happier than on a horse. It is the only thing that never tires me. Why, in the hunting season I am out all day, and it is only the horse that comes back weary.' She lowered her eyelashes again. 'You are fond of horses, Mr Morland?'

It was wonderful, he thought, that she did not instantly associate the name Morland with horses. Evidently she had no idea he was connected to Morland Place, and as things were, that was just as well.

'Yes, very,' he said, and changed the subject quickly. 'May I ask how you come to know the Phillipses?'

'Oh, I've known them for ever. My mother and Mrs Phillips were childhood friends, and so naturally I was taken to play with Lizzie and Georgy as soon as I could walk. My mother is dead, you know – that's why I come here with Mrs Phillips. It's very kind of her to chaperone me, otherwise I shouldn't go anywhere, for I have no aunts.'

'How very sad,' Benedict exclaimed.

'Yes, isn't it?' she said with a sigh, and then dimpled irrepressibly at him. 'But Mrs Phillips is better than a mother because she is not so strict. I'm sure Mama would not have let me dance with you on so slight an acquaintance.'

He saw that she was teasing, and it made him feel powerful and sophisticated. 'I assure you I am very respectable,' he said with a smile. 'Mr Findlay can vouch for me – and if you have known the Phillipses from childhood, you must know him, because he says he used to run tame about their nursery.'

'Oh, Mr Findlay is a very nice young man, I'm sure, but one cannot place any confidence in people who have pulled one's apron strings undone and put frogs in one's workbox, even if it was all a very long time ago.'

'No, did he? The villain!'

'You must call him out for it,' she suggested with a sparkling look.

'I would I had the right to,' he said gallantly. It was the sort of conversation he had never expected to hear himself having. And she danced like an angel, and when their two ended she very properly said she could only stand up with him once more and offered him the last two before supper. 'Then, if you like, you might take me in to supper.' Benedict accepted with joy. 'I might perhaps manage to sit out with you some time after supper,' she murmured as he walked her back to Mrs Phillips, 'but I must dance with some other people – I *must*,' she added, as though it was not entirely what she wanted. 'I could never bear to do anything at all particular.'

'Whatever you did, ma'am,' he said with a gallantry that surprised him for its readiness, 'I'm sure you would grace it.'

It struck him afterwards that this was a speech capable of misinterpretation and he was glad that she took it as a compliment. Indeed, he went afterwards over and over every word spoken by either of them, trying them out for meanings, nuances, hidden hints until he hardly knew what he thought of the evening – except that Miss Fleetham was the most beautiful girl who had ever lived. He had almost come to blows with Findlay when he met him later between partners, for saying that 'Georgy was heaps prettier – he preferred dark girls – fair girls were insipid – and anyway, everyone knew Miss Fleetham was a shocking flirt.' Bendy obliged him to take back the latter statement, though he held firm by Miss Georgiana's superiority of looks.

But there was more incident yet at that remarkable ball, as Benedict reflected, hacking along the now hallowed road towards Selby. He had begun to feel guilty about not paying his respects to Sir Carlton, especially since he was the ultimate source of all Bendy's present happiness; and as they walked back to Mrs Phillips after their second pair Miss Fleetham gave him more cause of unease by saying, 'I really ought to take you to Papa before we go to supper. He is very particular about such things, and really, one can hardly call your meeting with him at Selby a proper introduction.' Benedict was afraid that it would all too soon come to light that he was a railway engineer – indeed, it would probably be Mr Fleetham's first question – and then he would be barred from ever speaking to the divine Miss Fleetham again. If it had to come, he would as soon put it off, and he was thinking of what excuse he could possibly make, when his partner cried, 'Oh, but here is Papa coming now. He means to know who I have just been dancing with!' She gave a pretty laugh. 'He is such a strict, proper old Pa, and growls around me like a dear old bear! I swear there are people who think him quite an ogre on that account.'

Bendy looked round and saw the ogre bearing down on them, his face much the colour that his coat had been at Selby, though it may well have been the effect of the heat and a tight stock. He was not alone, however, and it was his companion who in fact addressed Bendy first: a tall, handsome man of mature years, whose face looked younger than his thick grey hair, and whose dark, keen eyes presented a further intriguing contrast.

'Mr Morland? I have not had the pleasure yet of meeting you, but I know you very well by report. My name is Miniott.'

'Sir Carlton,' Benedict stammered, taking the hand that was offered. 'I am very glad, sir – I was meaning to present myself – I am most obliged to you for sending me the card.'

Miniott's smile was friendly. 'The pleasure, I assure you, was mine. It must have puzzled you a little, but I was acting on behalf of a friend, of whom I would like to speak to you later. I see you have had the rare pleasure of dancing with Miss Fleetham.' He took her hand and carried it to his lips, smiling at her over it. 'Rosalind, my dear, I claim the privilege of an old family friend! And now, Mr Morland, I must beg to be allowed to present you to the fair Rosalind's father, who is dying of curiosity to know who it is that has been tripping so featly with his only chick! Fleetham, pray let me introduce to you Benedict Morland, one of our coming young men.'

'Morland, d'ye say?' Fleetham shot a piercing stare at Bendy, whom he obviously recognised but could not place. 'Yours, Miniott? How is he yours?'

Benedict cast an anguished glance at Sir Carlton, and to his astonishment received the ghost of a wink in return. Could it be that Sir Carlton understood the situation?

'Oh, indirectly, you know,' he answered Mr Fleetham airily. 'We are connected in a business way through Mr Hudson. Do you know Hudson, Fleetham? No? But you must let me introduce him. He has made me a great deal of money in the past, and will do so again, and he might do the same for you, you know. The York Union Bank, Fleetham! Put your money in the York Union! Morland, come and speak to me later. Do you dance after supper?'

'Oh – er – no, Sir Carlton.'

'Good. Come and find me, and we'll talk.' And he walked Fleetham determinedly away, leaving Benedict feeling profoundly grateful for his escape.

Rosalind watched the retreating pair thoughtfully. 'Well, that was a piece of luck,' she said at last. 'Now we may go in to supper with light hearts. Sir Carlton is our neighbour, and Pa thinks the world of him, so you could not have had a better introduction. Sir Carlton is such a droll. Is he your patron, Mr Morland?'

Bendy hardly knew how to answer. 'Indirectly,' he said at last. 'As he said himself, indirectly.'

When Miss Fleetham's first partner after supper had

taken her away, Benedict went to seek out Sir Carlton. His pleasure in the evening was finished now, as he supposed, for he could not dance with Miss Fleetham again, and there was no-one else he wanted to stand up with. Sir Carlton was standing by the fire in the vestibule, talking to two serious-looking men whom Bendy took to be manufacturers or something of the sort. He turned away with an excuse when he saw Bendy, took him confidentially by the elbow and led him off a pace or two.

'Well, sir?' he said with an amused look. 'So Miss Fleetham's arrows have found another victim?'

'I am most grateful to you, sir,' Bendy said, 'for not telling Mr Fleetham – I mean, I suppose you know—'

'That he hates all things to do with the Devil's Horse? Yes, of course! He harangues me about it every week. We are neighbours, you know, and we have both lost land to the railway, but Fleetham minds it twice as much as I do, though he has given up far less. But he will come around. They always do! It is the fear of the unknown, you know, which makes them bark so loud. However, to business: Mr Hudson of York wishes to see you on a matter of business. You know of whom I speak, I take it?'

Benedict was astonished. 'I – I have met him once, to my knowledge, sir. He was good enough to take me up in his carriage. But I cannot think—'

'Then don't, there's a good fellow. All will become clear to you in time. Hudson will be here, at the Crown, tomorrow. Will you wait on him at noon? He charges me to beg that you will find it convenient.'

'I fear it will be out of my power. I must be at the workings tomorrow.'

'Ah, yes, but that is why I have been charged with the agreeable duty of playing Mercury,' Miniott smiled. 'As a director of the railway, I am able to smooth your way. I shall make it all right, never fear: messages will be sent to everyone who needs to know. Hudson and I would not have you suffer by this.'

So Benedict had nothing to do but agree, gracefully, to the arrangement, and Miniott dismissed him with a friendly nod and went back to his conversation.

Bendy wandered away to try to find a vantage point from which he could watch Miss Fleetham dancing, but the Master of Ceremonies had other ideas, and having ascertained that he had no partner, insisted on presenting him to a young lady who was sitting down. He led her into the second set which was just forming, and forced himself to smile and be pleasant, for the young lady was looking chagrined, as though she knew he had sooner not be dancing. His diligence was rewarded, for halfway through the first dance he and his partner came alongside Miss Fleetham and hers, who were dancing in the first set. She raised her fan and spoke a few words to him behind it as they worked their way up.

'I have spoken to Papa – he does not remember where he saw you before. He thinks it was at Ledston Park – Sir Carlton's place, you know. I did not disillusion him.'

'You don't mean to tell him?'

'Goodness, no! It is much better this way. He has convinced himself he thinks very highly of you. It is the greatest joke!'

Bendy's partner was looking at him curiously, and he felt it was very impolite to be talking to someone else in this way, but there was one question he had to put before he lost Miss Fleetham's attention for good. 'Is it possible that I shall see you again?'

'Goodness, yes! That is, I have no idea! But I stay with the Phillipses until the end of the week, and George Findlay, you know, is always in and out. I think he half wants to marry Georgy, only Georgy has vowed not to marry before Lizzie, for she says it would be shocking.'

At that moment a gap opened above her in the set and she and her partner moved up, leaving Bendy behind.

104

He turned back to his partner, who said wistfully, 'Miss Fleetham is very pretty, isn't she? And they say she will have thirty thousand pounds. Do you know her well?'

'No, hardly at all,' Bendy said, and applied himself to being pleasant.

The rain grew heavier as the first outlying houses of Selby appeared, and by the time Bendy reached the Crown his knees were soaked and various trickles had found their way down the inside of his collar and into his boots. He rode into the yard and an ostler came running out from the shelter of the stable, his collar turned up and a reproachful look on his face as he grabbed the reins from Bendy and ran the horse away almost without waiting for instructions. Benedict squelched in through the back door, and was accosted by a pot-boy.

'Is you the party a-visiting Mr 'Udson, sir? Come this way, sir, if you please.' Bendy followed, suppressing the desire to shake himself like a dog as the rain dripping off his curly forelock fell onto his nose. He was taken up the stairs to one of the big first-floor parlours, where the boy announced him succinctly as ''Ere he is, sir.' Benedict saw straight before him a gloriously large and vigorous fire, before which the tall, bulky man he remembered was standing toasting his tail. Hatless, he proved to have curly hair, bushy over his ears and on the top of his head, but with deep erosions above the temples, as though a tide of skin were coming in.

'Ah, there you are!' Hudson said, surveying him quickly head to foot. 'Wet as an eel! Well, I have some hot porter coming up any minute, that'll warm you up. Meanwhile, come by the fire. Boy, tell Mrs Partridge to fetch up a towel, will you. Now, my other guest I think you already know.'

Benedict was only halfway towards that welcoming blaze when the last sentence and a wave of the hand drew his attention to the other man, seated well back in a winged armchair. Bendy stopped dead; the man rose and came forward; they stared at each other a moment in silence.

'Harry Anstey,' Bendy said at last.

Harry grinned and held wide his arms. 'Bendy! How good it is to see you again!'

Bendy glanced at Hudson, who was smiling to himself with satisfaction. 'Aye, it's all right. We're all friends here,' he said.

Ten minutes later, Benedict was sitting before the fire, his boots gently steaming, his hair awry from a rough towelling, and a mug of hot porter in his hand. Harry's chair was drawn up to one side of him; Hudson had drawn up another, but continuously got out of it to teeter about in that restless way of his, which Bendy, like Harry, was to find habitual in him.

'Now then, you'll be wanting to know what this is all about,' Hudson began. 'When I met you on the Selby road, Mr Morland, I told you I'd long been interested in the railways, and meeting you set up a train of thought in my mind, which brought things to a head. Since then I've been thinking and planning, and the upshot is this: I mean to bring the railways to York!'

Benedict's eyes opened wide. 'To York?'

'Aye, that's right. You are York born yourself – why should you stare?'

Bendy struggled to express it. 'But York is – is such an ancient, quiet place: the Cathedral close, the old city walls, the fine shops, the houses of the rich—'

'The sleepy folk, the mediaeval traditions,' Hudson nodded, 'not to mention the fat and lazy Corporation, more interested in putting on fancy dress and having civic dinners than getting anything done.'

Harry grinned. 'There is that to it, of course.'

'Aye well, all you say is true,' Hudson said, 'but that's no reason I shouldn't shake 'em up a bit. Why should we not have a railway, same as other folk? Every scratty bit of a place is putting up its railway plan nowadays. Why should Manchester have it, and not us? Manchester was nowt but a dirty village when York had been great a thousand year. Capital o' the North, that's what York was – and will be again when I have given it the railway! You don't need great dirty factories to be an important town in this modern England of ours.'

'Where would your railway go to?'

'To Leeds,' Hudson said promptly.

Bendy frowned. 'But what need is there of a railway to Leeds? The Leeds and Selby links up with the steamer trade, to take the coal and manufactures out – but Leeds to York?'

Hudson shook his head. 'And you a railway man! Don't you know better than to ask that? Look at the Liverpool and Manchester – planned and built for freight, but it's passengers as bring in the revenue! And you'll find it'll be the same thing with the Leeds and Selby, or I'll eat my hat. People want to be moving, the further and faster the better, and never mind where to! Don't you worry about need – once the railway is there, folk'll find reasons for using it. York folk want to travel, don't they, just the same as anyone else? Off to Leeds for the day, to the market, to see the sights and gawp at the people. And Leeds folk off to York for the day, to look at the fine shops and wonder at the fine women, to say nothing of the races, and the horse fairs. Back and forth they'll scurry like mice, and pay a fare every time, to warm the hearts and line the pockets o' the shareholders of the York and Leeds Railway Company!'

Bendy caught Harry's eye, and they both smiled at the eloquence. But Bendy said, 'Is this your vision as well?'

'Why not?' Harry said. 'Do you remember when my papa took us to Northumberland to look at the coal-mine tramways? Papa even said to your mother that it would be a good idea to have a tramway from his mines into York. He would be all for this scheme.'

'It would benefit Leeds coal mines, not yours,' Bendy pointed out.

'Once the railway from Leeds is built, others will follow.'

'You always were railway-nutty,' Bendy remarked.

'And so were you. Look at you now!'

Bendy turned to Hudson. 'I think you will meet with a lot of resistance,' he said. 'People are hard to persuade to anything new.'

'Not if you appeal to their pockets,' Hudson said. 'Think of the extra trade it will make. If I get enough of the leading traders and manufacturers on my side, the rest will follow.'

'But the landowners, sir?'

'If you were a landowner, wouldn't you want to take your fat sheep to Leeds market on a nice fast railway waggon, instead of walking them there and selling them thin?'

'I might take some persuading that that was a great enough benefit,' Bendy said, 'especially if I was one of the old families.'

'I know what you're thinking,' Hudson nodded. 'They say I'm a counter-jumper. It's true – no need to look embarrassed! I know what I am. That's why I need you two young men – to persuade the old families. You are of their kind. They'll listen to you.'

'Jack is all for it,' Harry assured Benedict, 'and I flatter myself the Anstey influence counts for something in York. I shall do my part.'

'We shall have need of a legal brain,' Hudson said, nodding at him. 'I'll be sure to put the Railway Company's business through your hands. One hand washes the other, you see. I mean everyone to profit from this scheme of mine. No-one shall be a loser if I can help it.'

'And what is my part to be?' Bendy asked, though he was beginning to suspect it.

'To persuade the landowners, of course,' Harry said.

'They'll worry about the hunting and whether their stock will be frightened to death. You of all people can reassure them. You have the experience—'

'And the Morland name,' Hudson said, watching him from under his eyelids. 'It carries weight. Aye, and not only with the landowners. When I call the first meeting, it'll weigh heavy in my favour if I can advertise an Anstey and a Morland already on my side.'

'But not the right Morland,' Bendy said. 'I think I smoke your plan, Mr Hudson. The logical line for a railway from York to Leeds would be across Morland land. You hope I will bring my brother in on your side, but I'm afraid you miss the mark, for two reasons: firstly, my brother hates the railways; and secondly, he hates me. I wonder Harry has not told you that. You have wasted your time with me – I can do you no good.'

Hudson lifted a hand. 'Hold hard, Morland – don't be so hasty.'

'You don't know all that's happened,' Harry said eagerly.

'I know that I can never set foot in York again,' Bendy said, 'so I would be little use to you in swaying the great families. Or do you expect me to hold court in Selby, and have them travel to me?'

'I said, hold hard,' Hudson commanded, as one who is used to being obeyed. Bendy looked at him coldly. 'Doost think I'm a noddy? I know all about thee.'

'Not quite all, I think.'

'Hoity-toity!' Hudson exclaimed, amused. 'I know why you left York, and I know the truth of it. The widow Makepeace spoke out on your behalf – aye, that surprises you! Thought to protect her, didn't you? But maybe she didn't want protecting, maybe she didn't like being kept in the dark. She sent for Anstey here, and between them they teased it out.'

'I've spoken to Jack about it,' Harry broke in eagerly. 'He now knows you are quite innocent, and he has spoken to Sir Percy. They were the only two who knew anything, apart from me – nothing was ever said in public, you know. As far as anyone else knows, you went off to seek your fortune, like any young man. You are free to come back to York any time you want.'

Bendy looked at them in bewilderment, his emotions in turmoil. It had all happened too suddenly for him to be able to take it in. But he caught up the one flaw he could immediately see in their argument. 'Nicky – you have not mentioned Nicky. He was quite convinced of my guilt.'

A shadow crossed Harry's face and was gone. 'I have spoken to Nicky – told him about Mrs Makepeace. He knows you are innocent.' Under Bendy's stare his own wavered. 'Did you know he is courting Aglaea?'

'No, of course I didn't.' He made an effort. 'That's wonderful! Isn't it?'

'It will be a great match for her. And it will bind our families closer. You will be my brother indeed! So you see, Nicky will not want anything to cloud our relationship.'

Bendy stared hard. 'You don't sound sure of that.'

Harry looked uncomfortable. 'He has agreed that you can come back to York, that he will receive you, that there is no question of public blame attaching to you.'

Bendy looked thoughtfully at the fire, saying nothing. After a moment, Hudson said, 'What your brother has against you I don't know nor want to. Family squabbles are always the bitterest, but they needn't concern anyone else. It's enough for me that your public name is clear. For the rest – why should you let it rule your life?' He watched Bendy for a moment, and then said, 'I have not told you what I plan for you, Mr Morland. I know nowt about railways, from the practical side. I'll need someone that knows to put me straight, so's I can sound right when I put my case before the good folk of York. And then, when we have formed our company and secured our investors, we'll need an engineer to run the show.

110

That's what I'll offer you. Engineer in chief to the York and Leeds Railway. What doost think to that?'

Benedict looked up. 'Chief engineer?'

'I've spoken to Sir Carlton, and I've corresponded with Mr Robert Stephenson about you. He thinks a bit about you, does Mr Stephenson – says you're the man for us all right. And think where this might lead you. Why, when I've done, you'll be famous! You'll be able to go anywhere in the world.' The heavy eyelids lowered over the shrewd eyes. 'And rich, too. I mean to make some brass out of this, I don't mind telling you, and those that come along with me will not be the poorer. You'll be able to buy Morland Place ten times over, if that's what you want.'

'It's a dazzling prospect,' Bendy said with a faint smile. 'A man would be a fool not to consider it.' He looked at Harry's eager face, and then back to Hudson. 'But you cannot be placing all your reliance on my persuading my brother to agree to the railway.'

Hudson said blandly, 'I reckon you'll find the way, if there's enough at stake.'

'And if I don't?'

'We'll cross that bridge when we come to it. But the Morland name is good for business, whatever kirsted name it's attached to. Now then, are you with me?'

Bendy shrugged. 'What have I to lose? Yes, I'm with you. Let's bring the railway to York.'

Hudson shook his hand heartily, and Harry was on his feet, pounding Bendy's back with glee. 'Good fellow! I said you were a right 'un! What a difference it will make to sleepy old York! And won't you like coming back? I can hardly believe you've been as close as Selby all this while and never set foot in the city. Not even a note to me – you're a sad friend! But you must come and dine at my house, and meet Celia. You knew she and I had tied the knot, I suppose?'

'Celia? Not Celia Laxton? However did you persuade her pa to let you have her?'

'I can't think. He must have been bosky! But of course Ceddie Laxton is my brother now – that's the handicap! And when Aglaea marries Nicky, he'll be yours too, in a roundabout way.'

'I think I can weather Ceddie Laxton,' Bendy said. 'I have weathered so many other storms.'

Harry looked serious. 'I know – poor fellow! Not to be at home when your mother died – well, it was a sad business indeed. She never thought of herself. She was a great lady.'

Bendy nodded; and then with an effort said, 'She would have approved of having Aglaea take her place. When is the happy day to be?'

'Oh, he hasn't put the question yet,' Harry said cheerfully, 'but it must happen soon. All of York talks about it.'

Hudson, who had been listening impatiently, said, 'York may talk of what it chooses, but we have more important things to discuss now. Can we get down to business, gentlemen? You may chatter about weddings when you're alone together.'

Having seen his horse bedded down at the Black Bull at Milford as usual, Benedict walked home through the dusk, his mind a whirl with the events of the day. A long talk with Harry had brought him up to date on the news from York, and he had an invitation to take supper with Harry and Celia the following week, Harry promising that there would be a number of old friends there, to welcome the wanderer home. Before then Benedict would have to present himself at Morland Place and see how the land really lay between himself and Nicky. Harry had been evasive about Nicky's state of mind concerning him, but in any case there could be no substitute for finding out for himself at first hand. And there was a number of things he wanted to ask Nicky about their mother's last hours. A talk

112

of that nature would be bound to have a softening effect.

That hurdle over, a bright future seemed to be promising over the horizon. The thought of Hudson's scheme put him in a glow of excitement: to be the engineer of a new line! The challenge, the responsibility, the glory! Could it be done? Sir Carlton, Bendy had learned, was quite sure it could, and had promised to bring in a number of investors. Harry's father-in-law and Sir John Lowther, both founder investors in the York Union bank, had also promised support, and through their connections with Glynn's bank in London expected to be able to raise working capital. If they could win enough support in York for the idea, and persuade the landowners over whose land the line would run, then there was nothing to prevent the success of the scheme – and the profits that would follow.

The dusk was sweet with the poignant smell of woodsmoke, and the light had that slate-blue glow to it that only comes in the autumn. His thoughts took a more tender direction. He had not thought of Miss Fleetham for hours, but he thought now, and wondered if being the chief engineer of the York and Leeds Railway would make him more or less acceptable to Mr Fleetham than being an assistant engineer on the Leeds and Selby. Then he chided himself for his folly. Even if they could get the support they needed right away, it would be years before work could start on the railway, and the delectable Miss Fleetham would no doubt be married to someone else long before he was in the position to support a wife. And anyway, what made him think she had the slightest interest in him? She had danced with him twice, and had seemed to like him, that was all. Probably he would never see her again. Her image sprang before his mind again, so tiny-waisted and fragile in the full-skirted, huge-sleeved gown that it seemed to be wearing her rather than vice versa. What might not a man achieve with such a wife on his arm? Ah well, dreams cost nothing, and hurt no-one!

As he neared his house he saw Fand sniffing about in the ditch, probably after a rat. He whistled her and her head shot up, and then she caught sight of him and came racing down the road, her whip-tail making circles of delight. A boy who had been helping her search also turned and then came running towards him. 'Bendy!'

'Hello, Dick. What are you doing here?'

'Waiting to see you. I've just come from my lessons. We were reading about the Siege of Troy. I say, who was your favourite? I like Hector best. Don't you think Achilles was a bit of a sulk-pot?'

'Definitely a sulk-pot,' Bendy said, amused. 'Have you said hello to your sister?'

'Oh yes. She sent me out to wait for you. Fand broke a plate with her tail, so she wanted to get her out of the house.' He fell in beside Benedict, and the three of them walked towards the house side by side. 'I've had an idea what I want to do when I grow up. Promise you won't laugh?'

'I promise nothing. Is it something very silly?'

'Not silly at all. It's to do with the railways.'

Benedict smiled. The railway was all Dick had ever known, since he ran away from a brutal home to be the lowliest of navvies of the Leicester and Swannington. 'A locomotive driver?' he hazarded.

'No, better than that. I want to be a contractor, like Mr Cook.' He looked anxiously to see whether Bendy would laugh.

'Why not?' Bendy said. 'You'll know all about it from the bottom upwards, after all. By the time you're grown up, you'll have been a navvy for ten years or more.'

'Yes,' he said eagerly, 'and I've seen how things go wrong, and I've a lot of ideas about that. And I know how the men think, and what makes 'em work hard.'

'But you'd need quite a lot of money to start,' Benedict

said gently. 'You'd have a lot of things to pay for at the beginning, before you earned any money at it.'

'I know,' Dick said quickly, 'and I have thought of that. As soon as I have a proper wage, and when I've paid you back for my lessons, I mean to start saving every penny I can.'

'You don't have to pay me back for the lessons.'

'Oh, but I must. It wouldn't be right.'

'Not at all,' Benedict said firmly. 'You save your money and become a contractor. You never know, by then I may be in a position to give you work. I may be engineer in charge of some great project.'

Dick whooped with approval of the idea, and turned a cartwheel in the road, which went wrong and almost put him in the ditch. Fand pranced round him and her tail caught him a fierce blow across the back of the head before she rushed off towards the cottage, where Liza had just appeared in the doorway with Thomas on her hip.

'Hello. What's all the noise about?' she enquired.

'It's just your brother, planning to be Prime Minister of England before he's done,' Bendy said. 'How's the boy?'

'He's been as good as gold all day,' Liza said. The boy struggled to get down, so she set him on his feet and he ran straight to Benedict, showing off his newly acquired mobility and smiling to reveal the little seed-pearls of his teeth.

'As good as gold? That doesn't sound like my Tommy,' Benedict said, scooping the boy up. 'As heavy as gold, though. What have you been feeding him on, Liza?'

'How was your meeting?' she countered.

'It was very well,' he said. He met her eyes reluctantly. He knew she was afraid of his old life, fearing it would claim him back from her one day; he had always denied the possibility, but now it looked as though she had been right all along. He thought of Serena Makepeace, who had been his mistress, and whom he had never written to since he left York, and hardly thought of. He had wanted to marry her once; how right she had been to refuse. 'One day you will marry,' she had said, 'and when you do, I hope she will be handsome, accomplished, young, and very rich.' She might almost have been describing Miss Fleetham. 'And by then you will be far away and I will be a distant – and I hope pleasant – memory.' At the time she had said that he had thought himself desperately in love with her. How young he had been, only eighteen! It seemed a world away. Now he was nearly twenty-two, he realised what a child he had been then. And now Liza—

He realised that Liza was looking at him curiously, waiting for a fuller answer. 'Hudson has a scheme,' he went on hastily. 'He thinks I might be useful to him. There might be some benefit to me eventually – a new and better position.' She was scanning his face, trying to extract the rest of the information from it – how it would affect her and the child. But before she could ask him anything, Dick interrupted boisterously.

'Liza, Bendy thinks I really might become a contractor! At least, he didn't laugh at me, so there!'

'Oh hush, Diccon. Who would give work to someone with a dirty face like yours? Go and wash yourself, for heaven's sake!'

He made the face that all boys make at their older sisters, and disappeared round the back of the cottage, saying as he passed them, 'Don't forget to give Bendy the message.'

'What message?'

Liza drew out a folded sheet from her apron. 'One of the boys from the Bull brought it down,' she said. He unfolded it, aware of her eyes on his face as he scanned it: she could not read or write.

'It's from George Findlay,' he said at last. 'An invitation to dine with him tomorrow.'

'At his lodgings?'

'No. As a guest, with him, at the house of some friends

of his, the Phillipses.' He spoke the words casually, for her sake. 'I met them at the ball. They are old friends of his family.'

'That's right civil of them,' she said, still examining him. 'Is it just old folk, then? Won't it be a bit dull for you?'

'Oh no, there will be young people there as well. George played with all the young Phillipses in the nursery.'

'I see.' She lowered her eyes and turned away, gathering up Thomas as she did and detaching his fist from the clod of earth he had been playing with just in time to stop it going into his mouth. He set up a wail at being deprived of his toy.

Bendy read the message again, trying to make it tell him more than it could. *Mrs Phillips is having a dinner party tomorrow and particularly asks me to bring you along, so do not fail me, or my credit is nil with her. In her eyes I am a dull dog with fascinating friends! Phillips has a good cook but a bad cellar, so we had better take one or two on board before we go. I will call for you in a chaise at half past six.* 'I think I should go,' he said casually.

'Of course,' Liza said. 'You'll want your new evening shirt again, then. It was a good job you bought it after all.'

'Yes,' Bendy said, following her in.

CHAPTER SIX

It began to snow at dusk on December the 30th, the very fine, powdery snow like confectioner's sugar which comes with the bitterest cold, and by dark the roofs and cobbles of Petergate were glittering white with it. The back parlour of Mrs Tomlinson's hotel had no fireplace, and the only source of heat in the room was a rather smelly oil-lamp with a green shade which hung from the centre of the ceiling. The air was so cold in the room, that the breath of the men gathered there was visible ('Steamin' like cattle!' said Mr Peckitt, the tanner and shoemaker) and the fingernails and cheeks of the more elderly amongst them had turned blue. The room contained a large round table, much scarred from years of service, and half a dozen plain wooden chairs, which were snatched up by the first-comers. Everyone else had to stand on the bare floorboards ('Not even a bit of drugget,' sniffed Catchpole, the carpet merchant) while Meek, the coal-merchant, whom Hudson had asked to chair the meeting, perched uncomfortably on the windowsill with the latch of the shutters digging into the middle of his back. Why Hudson had chosen this particular venue was canvassed in discontented undertones throughout the proceedings, and remained a mystery to all who did not know about his long-term friendship with Mrs Tomlinson. Indeed, if Mrs Markby's parlour had been larger, it might have been she who was favoured that evening.

Benedict, leaning against the wall out of the way,

looked around the assembled company as Meek opened the proceedings, and noted the substance and style of those invited. Mr Enderby, who owned the large draper's shop in Stonegate, was sitting next to Peckitt, and on his other side was Mr Pobgee the lawyer – always known as Young Mr Pobgee, to distinguish him from his late father, but himself now over sixty, and as ascetic as Enderby was corpulent. The other three seats were taken by Mr Cutts, who appropriately enough owned the largest glassworks in York, John Obadiah, the coach and carriage manufacturer, and the monobrachiate Mr Willans, owner of the vast livery and post stables, who was reputed to have had his arm bitten clean off by a mad horse. Such was his ferocity towards his post boys that it was widely believed he had got his revenge by killing and eating the offending horse.

Shopkeepers, proprietors of small businesses, leading citizens. The medical profession – and there were more physicians per capita in York than anywhere else in the Kingdom – was represented by Dr Havergill, whose father had been one of the founders of the Dispensary for the Poor. Thomas Bayliss was there, representing his father, the newspaper proprietor, and Billy Pemberton represented his mother, the confectioner, whose teashop in Blake Street, conveniently next to the subscription library, was a favoured resort for ladies at leisure.

Mr Meek explained the purpose of the meeting – to consider 'whether York should have the railway' (Bendy thought he made it sound like an infectious disease) – and outlined the case for a line to Leeds, via Garforth. He touched on the success of the Liverpool and Manchester, elaborated rather more on the Leeds and Selby – 'passing us by, gentlemen, passing us by altogether' – and waxed enthusiastic on the prospect of cheap coal which the railway would open.

'You are all businessmen, and you all know that the cost of transporting goods has to be added on to the cost of manufacture. Now for small, light goods, the roads serve well enough, but for large and heavy goods like coal, it's the canals we must use, and the canals let us down badly. It's a slow business, transporting anything by navigation. Unreliable too: in the summer when the water's down, the boats have to go half-loaded, and in the winter they can be frozen up for days at a time. Besides that, with no competition, the Aire and Calder can charge what they like – and they do, don't they, gentlemen? They charge like – like—'

'Bulls,' said Mr Peckitt helpfully, and there was a burst of laughter.

Meek reddened a little, but went on doggedly. 'Now if we had the railway, we could give the Aire and Calder a run for its money. The railway can carry heavy goods as easily as light, and at a speed you wouldn't believe if you hadn't had it proved to you. Twenty miles an hour, I'm told, fully laden! Coal brought up to the surface of a South Yorkshire mine on Monday morning could be in the coal-scuttles of York by Monday night. Now then!'

There was a muttering amongst the assembled, and Bendy thought Meek had rather overreached himself with his example. They seemed uneasy with such a fairy-tale picture of events: such rapidity was hardly natural, and what was not natural was inevitably cursed. Enderby spoke up in his fruity, bottled voice to express the general suspicion of haste.

'That's all very well, Mr Meek; you young men are all push and thrust and hustle and go-on. It's in your natures, I suppose.' Meek was in his thirties, but he was still only half Enderby's age and therefore, in Enderby's eyes, only half as worthy of being right. 'But what possible benefit could it be to us to have—' he looked round to gather his audience for the gem he was about to utter – 'to have *fresh-dug* coal upon our fires? Eh? Eh? Coal is not a delicate fruit, which must be caught at the exact moment of ripeness! Coal is not a new-laid egg, or a pitcher of milk,

120

to lose its attraction as time passes! This notion of rapidity may be exciting to young, less *weighty* minds, but we men of experience cannot be hoodwinked – yes, *hoodwinked*, sir! – with a promise of fresh-dug coal in every grate.'

This speech seemed to have done Meek more good than harm, Bendy noted, for Enderby was not much liked, and his laboured witticism was appreciated only by a few. Meek waited patiently for him to finish and then replied with contrasting succinctness.

'The speed, Mr Enderby, is what guarantees the cheapness. It is cheap coal I am advocating for York.'

Tom Bayliss spoke up mildly. 'Your plan would not be popular with the shareholders of the Aire and Calder – and there are quite a few of them in York, some of them powerful men.'

Meek turned to him. 'I don't mean to put them out of business, Mr Bayliss, only to give them competition. And I think I'm right in saying that the Liverpool and Manchester Railway has not destroyed the canals in Lancashire. They thrive even better, now they have been forced to attend properly to their business.'

Mr Cutts spoke up. 'I like the sound of it, Mr Meek – cheap coal would serve me very well. It's my biggest expense. I could increase my production no end if I could get cheap coal.'

'I don't know what all this talk about coal is for,' said Billy Pemberton. 'We don't want any railways here in York. We are a Godfearing, Christian town, which is why they gave us the Minster, and the Archbishop to look after. Railways are the Devil's work, everyone knows that, and they bring a curse with 'em. On the very opening day of the Liverpool and Manchester, a man was chased down and killed by one o' them engines of Hades, torn limb from limb so his own mother wouldn't have known him – and that's the truth I'm telling you! You ask anyone. He was a gentleman too, and a Member of Parleyment. Hunted down like a rabbit and killed.'

'Don't talk so far back, Billy Pemberton! The poor gentleman fell on the line, that's all,' said Mr Peckitt; but others felt unease about the strange new machinery, and were glad to hear it expressed, though they would not themselves have brought in mention of the Dark Gentleman.

'We don't want railways here!' 'Dirty, noisy things!' 'It would ruin our town for ever!' 'We've got on all right without railways for a thousand years.' 'It would be money wasted.'

Dr Havergill spoke up at this point. 'On the subject of money, I must agree with the objectors. I have read it somewhere that a railway costs seven thousand pounds a mile—'

'Ten thousand!' someone called out from the back of the room.

Havergill shrugged. 'Seven was what I saw. But seven or ten, it is a vast, vast sum of money. Even if we were capable of raising such a sum in the city, should it not be spent *in* this city, rather than outside it, on excavations and embankments and iron rails? There are twenty-five thousand people living within the walls, thousands of them crowded into tenements in the filthy courts and lanes without the vestige of sanitary provision, without drainage, without even clean water to drink. You all remember the cholera last year: four hundred and fifty cases, of which a hundred and eighty-five died! A thousand people draw their drinking water directly from the Ouse, into which their waste matter is directly disposed. The graveyards inside the city are so full that it is impossible to bury one person without turning up another. The filth and miasma—'

'I didn't come here to listen to this sort of thing,' said Mr Enderby, his ruby cheeks touched with green. 'If you've got a point, Havergill, for God's sake make it, and leave out this talk of graveyards and such!'

'My point is that if we have money, we should spend

it on civic improvements, not railways. Drainage, water-works, sewerage, and new housing for the poor.'

'Oh aye, I'm like to fork out my brass to give new houses to Irish vagabonds!' Mr Catchpole said stridently. 'Let them buy *me* a new house first.'

There was some laughter, but Mr Cutts broke through it. 'If I had cheap coal, I could expand my business, and that would make new jobs. Jobs would do the poor more good than giving them drains and water-pipes.'

'Wouldn't do your pocket any harm, either, would it, Cutts?' said the one-armed Willans, and there was laughter.

Hudson caught Harry's eye, and he stood forward and said, 'If I may speak, gentlemen?' All heads turned towards him. 'You all know me, and I speak for my whole family when I say we are all for this idea. We have mines at Garforth, as you no doubt know, and we would dearly like a railway to bring our coals to York more cheaply and quickly. If we could cut our transportation costs, we could sell more coal to more people, and that would improve our profits, I don't deny. But it would improve life for everyone in York. Think of the honest labourer, who can't afford to heat his home in winter. Because his home is cold and damp, he gets ill, which means he cannot work – so he and his family come on the parish.' There was a growl at that – the poor-rate was forever climbing, affecting every tax-paying citizen's pocket. 'Then there are the goods he can't afford to buy, because coal costs the manufacturer so dear he has to keep up the price. The man suffers – yes, but so does the manufacturer, with the sales he loses! I tell you, all sorts of trade would benefit from the railway, and what benefits trade benefits everyone.' A murmur of agreement round the room. 'My brother Lord Anstey is a Justice of the Peace, my brother Alfred a Member of Parliament; by marriage we are connected with the Chubbs, the Laxtons, the Shawes, the Somerses, the Morlands, and I don't know how many other leading families. We Ansteys have as big a stake in this city as anyone, and what affects it affects us. We would not be for the railway unless we believed it would be good for York – and we are for it, gentlemen, with all our hearts.'

'It's all very well for you to talk in such high-flown language,' said Mr Catchpole, 'but where's the money to come from? You haven't called us here tonight to hear our opinions,' he went on, glaring at Mr Meek, 'but to wheedle the brass out of our pockets to pay for this damn-fool scheme. I can see as the coal-merchants of this world would profit mightily if a bunch of noddies was to fork out the money to build them a nice railway line, but I don't see the rest of us coming out of it with a profit. "What benefits trade benefits York" – pah! Sugar words! If it's a choice 'tween being kind to coal-merchants and keeping a tight hold on my brass, I know which one I'm going to favour, thank you very much.'

This view found some favour. 'And what about the likes of me?' Willans cried over the outbreak of comment. 'You'd take the bread out of honest folk's mouths with your railways! What about the horse interest, eh? Livery stables and post houses, coach-makers, harness-makers, tanners, horse-breeders and fodder-merchants – there's a powerful few of us about, and you attack us at your peril!' He nodded at Mr Obadiah, and then swivelled his head round towards Bendy. 'Now then, Benedict Morland, your pa provided me with a good few horses in his time. What have you to say on the subject? Your brother has sent you here to speak out against it, I warrant.'

Bendy pushed himself upright, the better to be seen, and there was a general shifting and a murmur of comment as many caught sight of him for the first time – he was not a tall man. 'I have come to speak for the railway,' he said. There was a restless murmur of comment. 'I was born here in York, and I come from a family of horsemen, as you all know; but I have been working on the railways for the last three years, and I have seen the future.' He paused to let another ripple of comment die down. 'Others can tell you about the benefits to cost of moving goods by railway, but what I have seen is the benefit to people of being able to travel quickly and easily. In the first year of the Liverpool and Manchester, four hundred and sixty thousand passengers were carried between the one town and the other – that's four times as many as ever made the same journey by coach! People want to travel – they yearn to see new places and meet new people – and now that the railways exist, they *will* have them. Those towns that refuse to be connected will wither and die. York can have a railway, and become part of the wonderful new world which is being born, or it can ignore the future and sink into the stagnant waters of its past. The new world will not care one way or the other – but *I* care. I love this city, and I want it to live and grow and flourish. The railways are the future! We must seize our chance.'

There was a brief silence when he stopped speaking, and he heard the after-echo of his words and knew he had spoken well. He had stirred them. There was a visionary look on many of the faces.

And then Mr Catchpole said, 'Humbug! Where's the profit? I don't part with my brass for no profit.'

It was then that Hudson spoke. In physique he was a strong contrast to Bendy, and his words were as down-to-earth as Bendy's had been inspirational. 'Profit? You want profit? By God, Catchpole, you can't see the nose in front of your face! Ten per cent, that's what the Liverpool and Manchester paid its shareholders this year, and that's only the beginning! The railways are going to be the biggest thing this country has ever seen – bigger than wool, bigger than coal, bigger than cotton – bigger than you can imagine, you with your short arms and rusty elbows! Never could get your hand into your pocket, eh, Catchpole?' There was laughter – Catchpole was famed for never standing his round. Hudson resumed. 'Now there are plenty of business men in Leeds and Sheffield who are going to jump in and make their brass out of this, and it's up to us to jump in first and get our share. Why should we be left out? I tell you all, the railways are going to be a gold mine, and we'd be fools to let it all go to the smart folk in other towns. They won't be slow to catch on to this in London, I can tell you, and if a soft southerner can see where the brass is, I'd be sorry to think any northerner couldn't outsmart him!' There was a matter of approval at this. 'You all know me! I'm a warm man, and I've made a shrewd few bargains in my time. I've never been bettered in a business deal, and that is my boast. I tell you every penny of my fortune is going into this scheme, and I'll come out of it as rich as Croesus! So you can come in with me, or go home and take up knitting, it's up to you.'

Well, thought Bendy, that about covers it. The emotional appeal from Harry, the intellectual from me, and then Hudson hits them smack in the pocket with good, plain greed! How can they resist? We'll get our resolution through all right. That man Hudson is a good deal more cunning than he looks. I should hate to cross him – a simple engineer like me.

And he looked across and caught Harry's eye, and they both grinned.

The meeting finished very late, and as they walked out into the freezing night, Hudson said, 'Well, I suppose they had to have their havering and wavering, but we'd have got on a good bit faster if they hadn't set up that hare about taking the line to Selby.'

'You got your way in the end, though,' Harry said. 'A good majority for the Leeds route; the Railway Committee now officially exists, the Railway Company is to be set up, and you got yourself made Treasurer into the bargain. Not a bad evening's work, Mr Hudson.'

Hudson shook his head. 'I had to take up most of the

shares myself, though. It's all talk wi' them. They've none of them the bottom to send their brass in after their words.'

'You could have mine, if I had any,' Harry said, amused. 'You convinced me with your talk of ten per cent.'

Hudson gave him a narrow look. 'Are you making fun of me, Henry Anstey?'

'Not at all. But you must give people time to come round to an idea. You can't rush them at the fences, or they'll baulk.'

'They'll baulk whatever speed you take them: they are poor-spirited creatures. However, it's a start. Now we must get the report put in before they frighten theirselves right out of it. We must get the line surveyed, to start with.'

'Have you someone in mind?' Bendy asked.

'I've better than that – I've already engaged him. Mr Rennie only waits on my word to start.'

Bendy grinned. 'You were confident about the result of this meeting, weren't you?'

'I always get what I want,' Hudson said. 'My way lies this road. I bid you good evening, gentlemen. You'll be hearing from me soon.'

Harry turned to Benedict. 'It's late. Why don't you come home with me? You don't want to be riding all the way to Milford at this time of night, and in this freezing weather.'

Bendy smiled. 'I'd sooner do it now than before dawn. I have to be at the workings tomorrow. Thanks all the same, old fellow, but I'll collect my horse and be on my way home.'

'This home of yours must have some rare attraction,' Harry grinned. 'I wonder what it is?'

'You'll never know,' Bendy said. 'Fortunately, being a bachelor, I can't invite you and Celia, and I shall make good sure never to ask you on your own.'

'I shall come and call on you one day, without notice, and find out your dark secret.'

'You had far better stick to your own hearth and your pretty wife. When I am engineer to the York and Leeds Railway, and have a wife of my own, then I'll entertain you.'

Harry laid a farewell hand on his arm. 'Oh but you entertain me now, old fellow, more than you imagine! Good night!'

The snow had stopped and the sky was as clear as well-water, the black punctured by a million blue-white points of stars. It was freezing hard. The moon had risen, small and hard and bright like a white-hot sixpence, sailing clear of the chimneys to shine down serenely over the still and sugar-frosted world. It was so cold that it seemed to have passed beyond cold, and as he put his horse into a trot, Bendy felt tiredness drop away from him, and he was filled with a godlike feeling of lofty detachment, as if he were looking down on creation from the heights of Olympus. The roofs of the houses glittered black as obsidian through the rime of frozen powder; the shadows of the chimneys were short, as at some other-worldly midday. There was no-one about, and most houses showed no chinks of light at their closed shutters. Only somewhere – near, far, who could tell on such a night? – a vixen barked shrill and short, and nearer to hand a dog woofed a half-hearted reply, muffled from within whatever shelter he had sought.

An impulse made him turn his horse from the road and across Hob Moor towards Morland land: he wanted to see his home – his former home – by the light of this moon. One day, he thought, the railway will come along here; he tried to imagine moonlit rails, a locomotive, black as a running fox, its head clouded with luminous steam, the glow of its fire fantastically red-gold in the colourlessness of night. It would happen one day – but how to persuade

Nicky? He knew Hudson was relying on him, but he had not yet even managed to gain access to Morland Place. He made the attempt to call formally on his brother a few days after the meeting with Harry in Garforth, but he had found the barbican gates locked, and a stranger on guard there – a tough-looking individual who did not know him and was not to be swayed by his entreaties. Master was not at home, he said, and his orders were not to admit anyone, without direct instructions from Master or Mr Ferrars. Where was Mr Ferrars, then? He was out with Master, of course. They had gone to Tadcaster. He didn't know when they would be back. He couldn't undertake to say who else was at home. Ottershaw? No, there was no-one of that name at the house. Moon was the name of the butler. No, he could not call him – he was not allowed to leave his post. The gentleman had much better call some other time when Master was at home.

Bendy had retreated, baffled. Things were difficult, of course, and there was much unemployment, and in some parts of the country armed gangs had been known to break in to remote houses and sack them; but not in Yorkshire. Yorkshire had never suffered troubles like that. It was a prosperous county, and the rural poverty that affected the Midlands and the south was almost unknown. Surely Nicky's precautions were excessive?

He had met Nicky at last at Harry Anstey's, where they and several other old friends were invited to supper. It was an awkward meeting. Bendy had been frankly shocked at the change in his brother: Nicky looked ten years older than when he had last seen him and far from well. He looked, Bendy thought, as he had looked in childhood sometimes, during one of his attacks of asthma – hollow-cheeked and deathly pale. His hair was thinning fast, too, and the lines in his face seemed unnaturally deep.

When Harry led Bendy up to him, Nicholas had faced him with a profound lack of response, offering neither hand nor smile, merely staring at him as he might at a closed door.

'Hello, Nicky. I'm glad to see you again,' Bendy had offered. 'Are you well?'

'So, you're back,' was all that Nicky had vouchsafed.

'I hope you can welcome me,' Bendy said. There was no-one else within earshot, so he added, 'It was all a misunderstanding, you know. Harry says he has explained it to you. He says—'

'I know what Harry says,' Nicky interrupted. His eyes were flat and clouded like those of a long-dead fish, giving away nothing of his thoughts. Bendy felt they were not even seeing him. 'It seems I must share the world with you. I can't pretend I do it with enthusiasm, but you could not expect that. If you keep out of my way we should do well enough. Don't try me, or you will be the loser.'

'Try you? Nicky, I am your brother: can't we—' But he had walked away. Bendy watched him, baffled and hurt; but this was not the place to try to have it out. And since then they had met only in company, which precluded any frank talk. He wished he knew what Nicky had against him. He supposed when the time came to talk to him about the railway, it must all come out.

He knew this path so well that he asked Tonnant to canter, and the horse pricked his ears and put his feet down gaily, striking the tops off the frozen waves of the ruts in little dark spurts, and even finding the energy to shy playfully at his own moon-shadow. Bendy's mood matched Tonnant's: he was on Morland land now, and any Morland coming home felt a lift of the heart. On an impulse he turned right at the crosstracks and followed the Low Beck, putting Tonnant over it where Little Beck joined it and riding along the north bank so as to approach Morland Place from the other side, by the fish ponds. He would come upon it suddenly this way, surprising himself with the pleasure as he had sometimes done as a boy, creeping up on his home as one might on a beloved mistress dozing in a meadow. Ah, there it was, the moonlight shining calmly on it, turning the windows and the moat to beaten silver! His heart rose up into his throat, and he checked Tonnant by the second sluice, surprised by the strength of his feelings. Here he had been born, like generations of Morlands before him, five hundred years of them; and though in his restless years he had longed to try his wings in the wider world, it had been with the assumption that it would always be there to go back to. But now Papa was dead, and Maman, and Mathilde; Sophie was gone away, Father Sparrow and even old Barnard the cook – all the familiar servants, gone; and he was an exile.

He turned Tonnant's head and rode back the way he came. Now the earlier deific light-headedness had left him, and he was aware of being tired and horribly, creepingly cold. He thought of the feather beds of Morland Place, the fine linen sheets made almost too hot to bear by the application of a warming-pan: his frozen feet and chilled, aching bones longed for the comforts of wealth. He had to rise early tomorrow to go to the workings, and his day would be long and hard – an engineer's life was a strenuous one. He loved the work, the challenge and excitement, the satisfaction of achievements which were so very marked; but just at this moment he would have preferred to be Master of Morland Place, and to let it be Nicky facing the ride back to the damp cottage in Milford.

On New Year's Eve Nicholas had a party of his boon companions to dinner. These were not the worthies of York, not the Harry Ansteys of the world, as he thought of them sneeringly, but a jolly crew with whom he was accustomed to enjoying the manly pleasures, drinking and gambling, cocking and ratting and dog-fighting, and generally carousing and making a great deal of noise and nuisance. Tonight he was feeling particularly cheery, for

Ferrars had asked for and been given several days leave of absence, and there was something oppressive about Ferrars. Nicholas never felt he could quite do as he liked in his own home when Ferrars was about.

He had nine guests this evening; nine of the very best, he thought, looking rather crookedly round the table, with whom he meant to see the new year well and truly in. They had all sworn an oath early in the evening, over bumpers of champagne, not to go to bed before the sun rose on 1834, and so far no-one looked like reneging. Four were officers from Fulford – Roger Mattock, good old Roger, his guide and mentor through the world of sophisticated pleasures; an Irishman, Michael O'Rourke, a thin and sinister-looking man with a patch over one eye, whom Nicky cherished because he was so ugly he made Nicky look quite nice by comparison; and Kit Mullen and Jocelyn Tovey. Then there were Jack Cox and John Edmundes, the black sheep of their respective respectable families. The other three were all younger than Nicky – the infantry, as Mattock called them with a mixture of affection and contempt. They were all from good families, and the despair of their guv'nors, apprentices in debauchery who were in danger of overtaking their elders and betters: Felix Thirlby, Boy Jessop, and Digby Husthwaite – younger brother of Carlton, who had recently defected to the ranks of the respectably married.

Finding himself observed, Husthwaite goggled soddenly at Nicky and then raised his glass.

'Excellent dinner, Nicky old man,' he said. 'Excellent food, excellent drink, excellent company. Excellent evening altogether.'

'Excellent drink,' Boy Jessop amended seriously. 'You forgot to mention the most – the best—'

'I *said* that,' said Husthwaite indignantly. 'Excellent drink. Nicky is the most generous host in the Riding.'

'In Yorkshire,' Jessop amended.

'In the land,' Mattock concluded from the other end of the table. 'Let's have a toast – to our host!'

'Wait, wait, my glass is empty,' Husthwaite said in a panic, staring around him for something to put in it. They had been drinking port-and-brandy for some time now (except for O'Rourke, who preferred what he called Flesh and Blood – port and gin mixed).

'Fill him up, before we all die of thirst,' O'Rourke called down the table, and Jessop grabbed the nearest bottle and obeyed.

'Now,' said Mattock, who was either much less drunk than the others, or better at concealing it, 'the toast proposed is Our Generous Host, who has regaled us successively with champagne, claret, port and brandy, and never once flinched at the thought of the morrow.' He lifted his tankard. 'Nicky – in bumpers!'

They all roared 'Nicky!' – except for Jessop who, a little confused, shouted 'Bumpers!' – and a near-silence followed as the vessels were up-ended.

Afterwards talk and movement broke out as the glasses were refilled, and one or two got up to relieve themselves or to fetch something to eat from the side-board. Mattock, having carved himself a plate of cold beef with a remarkably steady hand, came up to Nicky's end of the table and sat down in the place Jessop had just vacated.

'What's this I hear about a brother of yours appearing suddenly in York?' he asked, folding a slice of meat into his mouth. 'Is he as good a fellow as you? Why have you kept him secret all these years?'

Nicky scowled. 'He's nothing like me. I have nothing to do with him.'

'Why ever not?' Mattock was amused. The reason he stayed comparatively sober was to torment others, his favourite occupation. 'What's he like?'

'He is the most thoroughgoing villain,' Nicky snapped. 'The most wicked, debased, Godless creature on earth.'

'My dear, why do you sound so disapproving?' Mattock

133

said. 'He sounds just our sort. Why don't you bring him along to one of our little *soirées*?'

'Never! I won't have him in the house!'

'Oh, come! He might liven things up. God knows these children haven't the least notion of sin – sticking out their tongue at their tutor still strikes them as wonderfully daring. Your brother must be a sophisticate if *you* disapprove of him. Perhaps he could show us a new vice, something we haven't tried?'

Nicholas was angry and confused. 'He's not a sophisticate!' he snapped. 'He's an engineer!'

Mattock roared with laughter. 'Oh, then he's beyond redemption! I see your trouble, and I sympathise entirely. Let us never say we have entertained an engineer in our midst! Even Edmundes over there would not sink so low, and he is almost the lowest form of life there is.'

'I say, Mattock,' Edmundes said, overhearing this, 'steady the helm. I'm not as low as your friend O'Rourke. I've heard he bites the heads off pigeons for a bet.'

Mattock gave his most contemptuous smile. 'Ah, but he does it with consummate style, something I fear is sadly lacking in the present company.'

'Roger's getting bored,' Jack Cox called a warning down the table. 'We'd better think of something new to do, or he'll be off.'

'You should have provided some women,' Husthwaite said to Nicky. 'A troupe of dancing-girls to entertain us.'

The idea struck Nicholas. 'I shall do that next time. When Ferrars is away.'

'Oh, be damned to Ferrars,' Cox said. 'Why do you have that fellow around you, Nicky? He's damned ugly. Puts me off my grub.'

Mattock put in smoothly, 'Yes, Jack, I've often wondered about that fellow Ferrars. It's my belief that he's blackmailing Nicky. Would you like us to kill him for you, Nicky? That's the only thing to do with blackmailers, otherwise they go on and on for ever.'

'Just say the word,' O'Rourke said with soft menace, 'and we'll slit his t'roat.'

Nicholas found his hands were sweating. 'No, no,' he said, trying for a light smile, 'you must leave the poor fellow alone. I assure you, he may look unpleasant but he's damned useful to me. I couldn't do without him.' He sought for something to distract them. 'What say we smoke a pipe? I have some very good stuff put by – you know, Roger, from that fellow you put me on to. What say we adjourn?'

The younger set, however, wanted women, and in the end were drunkenly prepared to break their oath to get them. They departed, along with Kit Mullen, who had to be on duty the next morning; and the rest of the company went to the drawing-room, where they disposed themselves in comfort while Nicholas prepared the pipe.

It had gone round only once when the door opened, and everyone fell silent with astonishment at the sight of Jemima standing in the doorway looking at them with a mixture of defiance and fear. She was fully dressed except for her shoes, but her hair was in its night plait. For a long time nobody spoke, and then Nicholas managed to croak, 'What in God's name are you doing here?'

She swallowed, and said, 'I could hear you laughing. I wanted to join the fun.'

O'Rourke whistled, and Edmundes leered at her. 'The boys didn't need to leave after all.'

'For God's sake,' Mattock said, looking at him in disgust.

'I like my chicken tender,' said Edmundes, smacking his lips.

Nicky was trying to clear his head. 'How did you come to hear us? Why aren't you in the nursery with Miss Smith?'

'You gave her leave of absence,' Jemima said. 'Sickness in the family. Don't you remember? Mrs Moon watches me in the daytime, but I'm alone after bedtime. I don't like Miss Smith,' she added boldly. 'She looks like a corpse.'

Nicholas began to laugh. He didn't mean to – he meant to be stern and send Jemima away – but it was true. Though superbly efficient at keeping Jemima under strict control, Miss Smith did look like a corpse. She had a hollow, pale face, and red-rimmmed eyes; her nose was truncated, so that the nostrils seemed unusually large and black, and her teeth were slightly prominent. The whole effect was of a death's head. Seeing him laugh, Jemima was emboldened to say, 'She's a horrible person, too, and she doesn't like me. Couldn't you send her away, Uncle Nicholas?'

He shook his head. 'Who would look after you then?'

'I don't need looking after,' she said. 'I can look after myself. I'm grown up now.'

'Are you indeed!' Edmundes said gloatingly. 'Come here, then, little miss impudence, and try a puff of this.' He had the pipe and held out the mouthpiece to her.

'No, don't,' Nicky protested, though Jemima was plainly only too willing.

Mattock intervened. 'Ladies never smoke pipes. Come and try a little wine instead.' He looked across at Nicky. 'Sound wine never hurt anyone.' He poured her a glass from the decanter on the table beside him, and she went and took it, drank, and coughed a little; but then to the immense amusement of all she pronounced loudly that she liked it.

'Drink it all up, then,' O'Rourke commanded. ''Twill make you feel good.'

Jemima, sensing approval, of which she had had very little in the past fourteen months, not to say companionship, drank again, and managed to get a good deal down without choking. 'It's quite nice,' she said, 'only a bit too peppery.'

Nicky tried to assert authority, feeling vaguely guilty, with a memory he didn't want to investigate too closely.

'Jemima, you must go back to bed. You shouldn't be here.'

The drink was already going to her head. 'I don't want to go to bed. I want to stay here. I never have company. It's not fair.'

'Hear, hear!' O'Rourke said. 'It's too bad of you, Nicky. Let her stay.'

'As long as she sings for her supper,' Edmundes grinned. 'Do you know "The Merry Troubadour"?'

This was a particularly obscene song that they sometimes sang after dinner. Mattock looked a little uncomfortable and said, 'Nicky, you should stop this and send her away.'

Nicky had been thinking the same thing, but O'Rourke, his one glittering eye fixed on Jemima, said, 'Ah, don't be such a spoil-sport, Roger. Sure there's no harm in it! Look how she's enjoying herself.'

'She's only a child,' Mattock said mildly.

O'Rourke turned his head to fix him with a meaningful stare. 'They have to learn some time, don't they? Ye've been quite a one yourself for teaching the young entry how to shoot, have ye not? At Mrs Jeffreys little establishment, for instance – I've not seen you worry there about their age. Nor you neither, Nicholas Morland, as ever is.'

'That's different,' Nicky muttered. 'They're – girls of a different class.'

'Ah, well,' O'Rourke said, the contempt audible in his voice, 'I don't see the distinction meself. My own mother was a girl of a different class, as you so delicately put it. She was wed in the end, but I don't see that made any difference – not to her, anyway.' He looked at Nicholas. 'Do you always do what others tell you? Or do you have a mind of your own?'

Nicky had been listening, half bemused, through bursts of laughter from the other end of the room, where Cox and Edmundes were amusing themselves by suggesting inappropriate songs, which Jemima was gravely regretting she did not know. O'Rourke was right, he thought: Roger was a hypocrite. Besides, there was no real harm in it. Jemima was clearly enjoying herself.

'She can stay,' he said. No-one heard him: there was too much noise as Tovey taught Jemima a version of 'Over the Hills' which, while not obscene, was full of *double-entendres*. Naturally she did not understand what they were laughing at, but she laughed all the same, to be companionable, and that in itself was exquisitely funny. After a bit even Mattock began to smile.

CHAPTER SEVEN

Morning service on the first Sunday after Epiphany was always well attended at the Minster. It was an occasion to meet one's friends, exchange news, make new plans for future entertainment, free of the tyranny of family obligations – and to show off one's new Christmas gown or hat to anyone who had not seen it yet. It was the time when you were pretty much assured of seeing everyone you knew in the one place, even those who usually attended more local services.

For this reason Benedict took horse and rode in, rather than attending the service at St Mary's in Milford as he usually did. He had received a curt note from Hudson early in the new year asking when he meant to clear the way with Nicholas over the railway plans. The surveyor was ready to start, and naturally preferred to do the job in order, starting at the York end, where he would strike Morland land almost immediately. Bendy thought the morning service would be a good opportunity to accost Nicky: he could hardly be unChristian towards his own brother in the very shadow of the Minster.

He sat himself at the side near the back, so that he could get out early and be sure of not missing Nicky. The disadvantage was that he could hear and see nothing from that position, so the service seemed endless and tedious. He thought of the homely service in the little church at Milford, where the vicar knew his congregation's endurance to a minute and never overtaxed it. Liza would be there now, with her brother Dandy Dick (he must stop calling him that if he was going to become a respectable businessman instead of a navvy-boy!) and little Thomas on her knee. They always went to the service together and sat in the decani aisle, at the back, behind the local domestic servants. Bendy arrived a little later and sat on the cantoris side, just behind the family pews, and did not look at her as he passed. The world accepted domestic arrangements such as his without so much as a raised eyebrow, provided its attention was not drawn to the irregularity.

The Minster service over at last, he hurried out into the sunshine. The world was still in the grip of the great freeze, but all the snow there was had fallen by now and been blown away, with the result that the ground was quite dry underfoot, and a sky of deep delphinium blue arched above them, framing the soaring towers and delicate pinnacles. There was no heat in the sun, but the sight of it was cheering, though the air was so cold it ached inside one's chest. Bendy stuffed his hands into his pockets while he scanned the crowd issuing from the door; but a moment later he dragged them out again and lost all interest in his brother, for coming towards him, actually making for him, he saw the figures of Mr and Miss Fleetham. She was wearing a lavender silk bonnet with very gay ribbons of dark lilac and white stripe and a white ostrich plume, and a mantle of lilac velvet lined and edged with white fur. Her little hands were stuffed in a vast white fur muff, and her face, framed by the poke of the bonnet and the thick fur of her collar, seemed the more exquisite for being so much smaller than its decorations.

She was smiling at him – quite definitely at him! 'Why, Mr Morland! Why, Papa, here's Mr Morland – you remember, Sir Carlton's protégé. How do you do, Mr Morland. What a surprise to see you here.'

'The surprise for me is surpassed by the pleasure, Miss Fleetham,' Benedict said, which he thought was

140

particularly sophisticated and ready of him, considering the unruly behaviour of his heart and stomach at the sight of her. 'How do you do, Mr Fleetham? I trust I see you well, sir?' he added respectfully.

Fleetham looked him over, and then offered his hand, which Bendy took with some relief. 'Do you come to morning service here every Sunday?' he asked.

'No, sir, it's rather far for me. But I do like to come sometimes. The Minster seems like an old friend,' Bendy said.

'Oh, it's a beautiful building!' Miss Fleetham exclaimed. 'I rave over it – don't I, Pa?'

'Are you interested in architecture, Miss Fleetham?'

'Excessively,' she said. 'Didn't I tell you this morning, Papa, that the Minster was the most beautiful building in the world?'

'Did you? I don't recollect,' Mr Fleetham said drily. 'Are you with friends, Mr Morland? You seemed to be looking for someone when we approached.'

'I was hoping to catch my brother,' Bendy said. 'I wanted to speak with him.'

'That's Mr Nicholas Morland of Morland Place, isn't it?' Miss Fleetham said emphatically, flicking a glance at her father.

Mr Fleetham accepted the look patiently, but he said with rather more interest, 'Is your brother here with his wife this morning?'

'My brother isn't married, sir,' Bendy said, suppressing a smile.

'No? Confirmed bachelor, is he? Leaving it all to you, eh? That's very well when there are two of you. I was an only child myself, so I had no choice in the matter. And I have but the one chick.' He smiled tenderly at his daughter. 'Fortunately Fleetham Manor is not entailed. Ah, Colonel Chubb! I must say hello to the good Colonel and his wife – he will expect it. Will you excuse me one moment, my dear, Mr Morland.' He turned his back to them to intercept Colonel Chubb as he strolled by with Mrs Chubb on his arm, and soon was engaged in conversation with him. Bendy and Miss Fleetham were therefore left alone together in the middle of a crowd, a delightful situation, ensuring both privacy and respectability.

'Well, Mr Morland, and what have you to say for yourself? What excuse have you to make?' Miss Fleetham began at once with mock severity.

'Excuse, ma'am? What do you accuse me of?'

'Why, of not having come near me these two months. Very shabby I call it, when I thought we were such friends.'

'Miss Fleetham— !'

'After that delightful dinner at Mrs Phillips's, when you and I sang a duet, and I thought our voices blended so well together. And then to see and hear nothing of you. It was too cruel.'

Bendy felt dizzy. 'I should have counted it my greatest privilege to have been able to see you, but I don't know how it could have been managed. I could not call on you without invitation.'

'No, I see that, but you might have contrived it all the same. You might have gone to places you knew I would be. I have been to I don't know how many balls since then, and you were not there. And I never see you in any of the shops or public places.'

'It's true I hardly ever go out—' Bendy began, but she cut him off in her enthusiasm to speak.

'So I persuaded Pa to come to service here this morning, for I knew you must be here. Lizzie Phillips told me everyone in York comes to this service. And here you are! But quick, tell me, for Papa will be finished with the Colonel in a moment, do you go to the concert?'

'The concert? In Selby?'

'No, silly, here in York. I shall think it very shabby if

142

you say no, for we are coming in a large party, and I depend on seeing you there.'

Bendy was bemused – he had never been flirted with so hard in his life – indeed, he had had so little experience of young women at all that he hardly knew it was flirting. She must have fallen in love with him at first sight, as he had with her, he thought dazedly. What a miracle!

'Which day is the concert?' he managed to ask.

'On Tuesday, of course, how could you not know that? Now do say you are coming, for I mean to sit in the first row, and you must get there early so that you can get a seat beside me and fill up the row. Caroline Cox has vowed she will sit in the first row, and I could not bear to be bested by her. Tush! Papa has finished. It's all settled then.'

Over her one shoulder Bendy could see that Mr Fleetham was indeed exchanging farewells with the Colonel, but over her other shoulder he could see Nicky approaching, and even dazzled by love as he was, he did not want to miss the very thing he had come for.

'Oh, there's my brother. Hullo, Nicky! Miss Fleetham, will you allow me to present my brother to you?' It was as well she was there, indeed, for Nicky was walking fast and might well have ignored Bendy, but could not in full public gaze brush past Miss Fleetham.

Mr Fleetham rejoined them in time to be introduced as well, and having shaken hands and looked Nicholas over keenly, he said, 'We have never happened to meet, sir, though I knew your father slightly. But everyone knows the Morlands of Morland Hall.'

'Place, Papa, Morland Place,' Miss Fleetham corrected urgently, and then flashed a smile at Nicholas. 'Your brother is but lately known to us, Mr Morland, but already we count him a very good friend.'

'Indeed, ma'am,' said Nicholas, with a daunting lack of interest. He was not best pleased to have been stopped, and was eyeing Benedict with suspicion, wondering what trick he was up to this time.

'Oh yes,' Miss Fleetham laughed gaily. 'We have so many friends in common we almost think of him as one of the family.'

Mr Fleetham, pursuing a train of thought of his own, addressed Nicholas in the sort of hearty voice an older man uses to a younger when he is bordering on the impertinent. 'You are unwed, Mr Morland: I almost envy you. The trials of matrimony are many, indeed.' Nicky gave him a look of astonishment, but he continued. 'Mark you, not every man is lucky enough to have a choice in the business, as you do. I dare say it is a matter of the greatest satisfaction to you to know that your brother, our good friend here, is behind you, ready to take up the reins when the time comes?'

'When the time comes?' Nicky said. 'What can you mean, sir?'

Bendy coughed furiously, but Mr Fleetham was not to be diverted. 'Marriage is a strain on the constitution which a wise man avoids if he can. *You* may leave the hazardous business to the young entry, while you continue to enjoy a life of single blessedness.'

Nicky turned a look of pure murder on Benedict, and then raised his chin and stared at Mr Fleetham with a shrivelling coldness. The proper thing in the circumstances would have been to ignore the impertinent curiosity and not dignify it with a reply. Benedict expected Nicky to excuse himself icily and walk away; but he had not reckoned on the strength of Nicky's desire to cut him down to size. If Benedict had been boasting to the Fleethams about his expectations, he should be shamed in front of them. 'You are quite mistaken, sir,' he said to Fleetham. 'I am no hermit. Indeed, the whole of York knows I am to marry Miss Aglaea Anstey, sister of Lord Anstey.'

'Lord Anstey, eh?' Fleetham said thoughtfully. 'I just know him. Well, sir, I give you joy. When is the happy day to be?'

'There is no date set at present,' Nicky said, looking annoyed at being forced to the admission; but it seemed to cheer Fleetham up, and he gave his daughter a little nod which said *there's many a slip twixt cup and lip.*

Nicholas made nothing of the look. Deciding he had successfully crushed Bendy's pretensions he began to make his excuses; and at that moment Fate played him a cruel trick. The four of them were standing in the main flow of people leaving the Minster, and now the current washed up against them Jack Anstey, with his two unmarried sisters on his arms. Naturally, seeing the Morland brothers, they stopped, and Benedict was obliged to make presentations all round.

'We have met, my lord,' Fleetham said to Jack. 'Perhaps you may remember – at the meeting at the Red House before the last General Election?'

Jack bowed slightly, too polite to say he did not remember, too honest to say he did. Miss Fleetham, having dismissed Mary at a glance as past her prayers, was examining Aglaea's brown felt mantle, simple bonnet and lack of side-curls with complacency. The cold air which made Miss Fleetham's cheeks rosy made Aglaea looked pinched and plain, and calculating her age on the generous side, she enquired sweetly, 'Do you dance, Miss Aglaea Anstey? I am sure I saw you at the Assembly the week before last.' Aglaea replied that she must have been mistaken – 'I have not been to any balls this year past' – and Miss Fleetham smiled with satisfaction and gave her father a little nod which said *too old to dance.*

Mr Fleetham, taking heart from the apparent elderliness of the unwed sisters, said, 'I understand felicitations are required, Lord Anstey. Mr Morland has been boasting of his happiness.'

'Sir?' Jack said, politely puzzled.

Fleetham bowed in the direction of Aglaea. 'Miss Aglaea Anstey and Mr Nicholas Morland – it will be the wedding of the season, I make no doubt.'

There was a brief and rather horrible silence, and Bendy looked from one face to another with acute sympathy. Mary had blushed with angry embarrassment, but both Nicky's and Aglaea's cheeks were the colour of clay. Jack made another slight bow to Mr Fleetham, and looked at Nicky with an eyebrow raised in eloquent enquiry. There was nothing Nicky could do but force a sickly smile onto his lips and murmur to Jack, 'I would like to have a word with you in private, if I may, later this morning. I – er – I was hoping to catch you. I came to morning service for that purpose.'

'Indeed,' Jack said gravely. 'I shall be happy to see you at any time. We are going directly home now. Pray follow at your leisure. Miss Fleetham, Mr Fleetham, I will bid you good day. It is too cold to keep my sisters standing.' And he gave a nod and a smile to Bendy, and walked away. Nicky watched them go with inner fury. This was not how it was meant to happen! When he had originally, idly, plotted to teach Harry Anstey a lesson, he had meant to bring down the Anstey pride by having them boast of catching Nicky and then proving to be uncaught. The Ansteys would then be the object of ridicule, Nicky himself of admiration and sympathy. But if he was known to have spoken publicly of being to marry Aglaea, and then did not, he would be shunned by polite society, and regarded as a dishonourable brute. He was trapped. His fury looked around for someone to blame, and did not have far to look. It was Bendy's fault! He had done this deliberately! It was yet another crime to be laid at his door. Oh, but you will suffer for it, Nicky vowed. I will have my revenge on you, if I have to wait until the last hour of my life!

When he presented himself at Anstey House, Nicholas was conducted straight to the library. Unusually, he did not encounter any other member of that numerous household on the way, and concluded that he had been

146

deliberately isolated, like a patient with a rash, until more was known about his condition.

In the library a good fire was burning, and the dark, comfortable room, full of old panelling, books, and accommodating chairs, seemed to radiate outwards from its glowing heart, reflecting cheerful glints from warm, shadowy corners. Jack was standing before the hearth, and looked at Nicholas rather quizzically as he came in. But he spoke cordially enough: 'Ah, Nicholas! Come and get warm. Will you take a glass of something?'

'Thank you.' Nicky received a glass of madeira and sipped it, wondering if there was still a way to get out of it. Perhaps Jack would refuse his permission; but that might be worse still. For a Morland to be refused by an Anstey – unthinkable!

Jack broke the silence at last, contemplating the amber glow in his glass and asking neutrally, 'You wanted to see me?'

Nothing to do, then, but put a bold face on it. 'I have come to ask your permission to address Aglaea.'

'I see,' Jack said. It sounded like the encouragement to a man only halfway through what he had to say, and it wrong-footed Nicky, who had expected an immediate answer. But Jack continued to wait, looking at him with mild enquiry, as though some further explanation was required.

'I assume,' Nicky said at last, since someone had to speak if they were ever to get any further, 'that as she is of age, she will be allowed to decide for herself.'

Jack did not answer the point, but asked instead, 'Have you spoken to her?'

Nicky hesitated. 'You are the head of the family. In all propriety I felt I should ask your permission first.'

'Propriety, yes,' Jack said thoughtfully.

Nicky frowned. Was he being toyed with? 'You have no objection, I imagine?'

Jack seemed to come to a decision. He drew himself

up a little. 'I am very fond of Aglaea, you know. She is a good girl. But she has little experience of the world outside these walls – this family. Exchanging one home for another will be a great step for her.'

Nicholas raised an eyebrow. 'Morland Place, I think, is an establishment to please any woman.'

'Quite so. Harry always used to say it was a second home to him. And you and Harry were like brothers, were you not? Of course, I was away at sea when you were all young, but they tell me that you and Harry and Aggie were always together.' Nicky assented with a slight nod, not sure where this was leading. 'I want to ask you something, Nicky. I hope you won't take offence.'

Nicky felt a chill. What was coming? What had he heard, or found out? Could it be— ? No, never! Not that. But what, then? He had thought his peccadilloes too discreet to be discovered. Whatever it was, he must brazen it out. Jack could know nothing for certain; it could only be rumour or innuendo. He managed a ghastly smile and said, 'You may ask me anything, of course.'

Jack nodded and asked in his blunt, sailor's way, 'Do you love her?'

The question threw Nicky aback. 'Love her?' It was the last thing he had expected, and he had no answer ready. He might have expected questions about his financial standing, his behaviour, the state of his soul – but *love her*? What the deuce had that to do with it? Here he was offering the establishment of any woman's dreams, offering the hand of Nicholas Morland, the most eligible bachelor in Yorkshire, to a woman who had neither beauty, rank nor fortune – who was not even in her first flush of youth – and her brother was talking about love as if he were a character in a three-volume novel!

And then suddenly Nicky thought he understood: it was not doubt he saw in Jack's eyes, but wonder at his astonishing good fortune. The offer for Aglaea was far beyond anything he could have expected; indeed he must have thought at times that he would never get her off his hands. Now it seemed she was landing the catch of the year, and Jack couldn't believe his luck. Of course, he was simply trying to account for it to himself: Nicky could not be fortune-hunting, therefore he must surely be in love!

Suddenly genial, Nicky smiled. The irony of the situation tickled him. 'Love her? Of course I do. I thought I had made it obvious enough to everyone. She is the only woman I have ever contemplated marrying.' That at least was the sober truth! 'You may set your mind at rest, Jack.'

'Thank you. I only want her to be happy.' Jack hesitated, and then asked, with a faintly puzzled air, 'Do you know the Fleethams well?'

'Hardly at all,' Nicky said quickly. 'They are Bendy's friends, not mine.' Jack was silent, plainly wondering how it came about that Nicky had told these casual acquaintances about his happiness even before securing it; but Nicky was growing impatient with the quizzing. Enough was enough. It was not for him to explain himself to an Anstey. He put on a lofty look and a formal air. 'Well, Lord Anstey, do I have your permission to address your sister or not?'

Jack seemed to rouse himself from his thoughts. 'Oh, you have my permission, of course. As you rightly supposed, I would wish Aggie to choose for herself in such a matter. Whatever she says, I will abide by it.' That did not seem very gracious to Nicky, considering all he was sacrificing for this family; but then Jack smiled and offered his hand, shook Nicky's heartily and said, 'You may go to her at once, if you wish. She is in the small sitting-room, alone. I imagine I have no need of wishing you well, so I wish you happy. I shall be glad to have a further connection with the Morland family.'

I have no doubt of that, Nicky thought, bowing and taking his leave. He knew the way to the small sitting-room, of course: he had run tame about this house all his life. It was not the room favoured by the ladies of the house in winter, when the red room was warmer and more convenient, but he knew Aglaea preferred it – and in any case, there would obviously be no privacy in the red room. Nicholas trod up the stairs, still in his mysterious isolation, which gave him the feeling of being watched covertly from dark corners. He knocked at the door and opened it in the same movement, and there was Aglaea sitting before the big window, looking out, her hands folded in her lap for once, no drawing or painting in progress. The short winter day was declining, and the westering sun was shining in rosy-gold, already touching the sheers on the roof of the warehouse opposite, so that they stood out blackly like gallows against the pale sky. The room was chilly – it was too big for its fireplace at this time of year – and there was something comfortless about dying day. Nicholas wanted to get it over with and go home.

Aglaea turned her head towards him as he came in, but made no other movement, and he suddenly realised that 'getting it over with' was the last thing he could do, for proposing marriage to her would put in train events that would change everything in both their lives. He had thought about a mythical wife, handsome, accomplished and wealthy, as an addition to his possessions and his standing; his next few sentences would put that out of possibility for ever. What he would get instead, in his home and at his dining-table, was Aglaea: familiar, plain, brown – worst of all, disconcertingly real.

He had to say something. 'May I sit down?'

She made a gesture towards the other chair which had been drawn up as though in preparation for this interview. Well, perhaps it had. How long had she been waiting here, alone? The room was chilly, but she looked cosy in her brown wool dress with the long sleeves and high neck – like a warm little brown bird. He studied her for a moment, her neatly braided hair, her wide, smooth forehead, her downcast eyes, her soft mouth. The lower lip trembled a little, and was pulled in with a little catch of breath. She was nervous, he thought, and the idea cheered him.

'I suppose you know why I am here,' he said at last. She made no reply, her eyes downcast. 'I have spoken to your brother, and he gives his consent.' Still no response. He supposed he would actually have to say the words. Women set store by such forms, of course. 'Aglaea, I am here to ask you to marry me. Will you be my wife?'

'Yes,' she said. That was all, and it was almost a whisper. But after she had said it, he saw her draw a deep breath, summoning determination, and she looked up at him flinchingly, as though she expected it to hurt. She scanned his face for a moment, and then something relaxed in her. What had she expected to see? he wondered. Perhaps she had thought he might laugh at her. 'You must have been very lonely since your mother died,' she said.

The simple words, the supposition, unlocked a door in him from which memories and feelings, shut away, rushed out like a black cold flood. He felt the ground under his feet tilt, and the mouth of chaos open to swallow him as he fell. His mother! She was before him instantly: grave face, accusing eyes. *Have you forgotten me, Nicky? Never forget me! Never forget!* His mother was dead; the centre of his world, the whole purpose of it, was gone, and he was alone in a howling wilderness. He gasped with the suddenness of the pain, and without realising he had done it, reached out his hands to Aglaea. Her hands were warm and dry to his cold and clammy touch; he tightened his grasp, her fingers closed round his, and he felt as though she were reattaching him to the world.

'You will be kind to me?' he heard himself say.

'Yes, Nicky.' There were tears in her eyes. 'Always. I will do whatever you wish.'

Miraculously, the blackness was sucked back in and the

151

door slammed shut. He was safe again. He sighed, and felt his assurance come back to him. Her warm, dry, small hands were still in his and she looked at him, he thought, humbly and gratefully. Perhaps marrying her would serve after all. A wealthy beauty might think too highly of her own worth, be inclined to expect things of him, and be disagreeable when he did not conform to them. Aglaea would never make a fuss. She would be uncritical – grateful to have been taken off the shelf. There might be worse things, he thought, than a grateful wife. He smiled, suddenly genial in his awareness of his own superiority, and wanted to give her something.

'It's usual for a man to give his bride a wedding-gift,' he said. 'Is there something in particular you would like? A riding horse of your own, perhaps, or a bird in a cage, or a new work-box?' She was a modest girl, and would not expect jewels or anything of the sort, which he might have to dig deep for. 'Anything at all,' he prompted.

She looked up, scanning his face anxiously, hopefully. 'There is one thing,' she said hesitantly.

'Yes, my dear. You have only to name it,' he said. Some foolish trifle, he thought, which in her humility she doubted she might ask for.

'I should like to see the sea.'

He was so surprised that for a moment he could not make sense of her request: see the see – what could that mean? And when he understood it, it was such an odd thing to ask for that he could think of no reason to deny her. 'Well, if you wish it,' he said at last, 'we could go to Scarborough for the wedding-trip.'

She smiled so radiantly that for a moment she looked almost beautiful. 'Thank you,' she said, quietly, but with great emphasis. He blinked in the sunshine of her gratitude, which made him feel strong and masterful. For almost the first time he knew the power of giving pleasure, and was glad he had followed his impulse.

*   *   *

The cold which had been exhilarating under a blue sky grew grim at dusk, and Nicholas was glad to get home at last. For the last half mile he had been pursued by an almost superstitious dread of being caught out after dark: that cold could kill, as the dead birds, found stiff on their backs in the morning where they had fallen from trees during the night, bore mute witness. As Checkmate trotted briskly homewards on the familiar path, Nicky looked forward to a neat supper and a bottle of claret and a quiet hour or two by the fire looking at some of his 'curious' books. That was the way to spend a cold winter evening! He was not best pleased, therefore, to arrive home and find Bendy there; not only there but admitted to the house – 'I didn't like to leave the gentleman waiting outside, sir, not in this cold,' said Moon apologetically. And not only was Bendy in the house, but he had made friends with Minna, who was wagging her whole hind-quarters while pressing her muzzle between Bendy's hands, as he squatted by the fire in the great hall. At least Moon hadn't installed him in the drawing-room with a glass of sherry, or invited him to dinner, Nicky thought with sour sarcasm.

'Well, what do you want?' Nicky demanded inhospitably as he stood pulling off his gloves. Minna came fawning round his knees, but he ignored her to punish her for infidelity.

Bendy stood up, brushing himself down with a nervous gesture. It upset him to be so little tolerated in his childhood home. 'I have been wanting a word with you on an important matter for some time now,' he said. 'I hoped to catch you after the service this morning, but other matters intervened, so I took a chance on coming here to wait for you.'

'You've had a long wait, then,' Nicky said, and the knowledge pleased him. 'I have been at Anstey House. I suppose you can guess what for.'

Bendy looked at him cautiously. 'I shouldn't care to. Your private business is your own.'

Nicky grinned unpleasantly. 'It also happens to be yours in this case. I am happy to tell you that I am going to marry Aglaea Anstey. I asked for her hand this afternoon and naturally she accepted me, so there's an end to your pretensions!'

'Mine?' Bendy said. 'What can you mean?'

'You thought you might outlive me and take Morland Place in the end. But once I'm married and have a child, your last hope dies. So there's for you, Benedict Morland.'

Bendy shook his head. 'You're wrong, Nicky. I've never thought that. I've known all my life that Morland Place would be yours and I've never minded it.'

'Ha!'

'It's true. You are the eldest and it's right and just that you should inherit. I don't covet what is yours – I never did. I wish you would believe me.' Nicky made a derisive sound, and Bendy shook his head in a puzzled way. 'I am very glad to hear your news. I wish you joy. I'm sure Aglaea is just the person to make you happy.'

'Good breeding stock,' Nicky said triumphantly. 'All the Ansteys are fertile. I shall have a string of sons in no time.'

'I hope you do,' Bendy said patiently.

'Well, what did you want to speak to me about?' Nicky asked, suddenly tiring of it. 'Say your piece and be done with it.'

Bendy quickly assembled his thoughts. 'You may not yet have heard that on December the thirtieth a group of leading citizens decided it would greatly benefit everyone to have a railway from York to Leeds. They have set up a company and retained a surveyor to investigate the possibility. I am here on their behalf to canvass your support for the idea.'

Nicky stared at him incredulously. 'For a railway? Are you mad?'

'The most obvious route for a railway to Leeds would be across Morland land, so naturally your agreement is very important.'

'And they think *you* can persuade me? It's they who are mad after all,' said Nicky contemptuously.

Bendy flushed. 'They know nothing of your – your hostility towards me. Naturally they think that as your brother—'

'You are wasting your time. And mine.' He turned away.

'I don't wish to persuade you,' Bendy said quickly, 'but to explain to you the benefits it would bring both to—'

'Fustian!'

'Both to you and to York. Indeed, the interest of one is bound up in the other.'

'Do you think *you* can tell *me* anything about railways?'

'I am a railway engineer,' Bendy said.

'Then you are hardly an unprejudiced source, are you? Why should I let my land be torn apart, and have those monstrous engines roar across it, terrifying my stock, destroying my crops, setting fire to my trees? They are an abomination – hideous, black, filthy, destructive – cursing everything they touch!'

'Nicky, it isn't like that. Won't you let me tell you what it really means?'

'Our mother,' Nicky said with narrowed eyes, forgetting for a moment that he had cast Bendy out of the family, 'did not approve of railways. She would never have allowed any part of Morland land to be sullied by one.'

'She would have listened before she condemned,' Bendy said. 'She was always just.'

'She knew she was the guardian of the estate. The duty now falls to me, to keep it intact, to see it prospers.'

'But it would. The railway would not need much

of your land, and you would be paid generous compensation. And the ultimate benefit to you would be the same as to all York businessmen: quicker, cheaper transportation of goods, and an increase in trade. York would be connected to the world instead of a stagnant backwater.'

'And all those people who now travel by road would travel by railway, I suppose?' Nicky sneered. 'Very good business for Nicholas Morland, when the turnpike revenues disappear, and no-one buys horses any more!'

'People will always buy horses,' Bendy said quickly.

'Oh, very good! And the post houses, I suppose, who buy Morland horses, will continue to buy them out of sentiment when there is no more traffic on the post road?'

'Yes, I know that's the way it looks,' Bendy said uncomfortably, 'but even if that trade disappears, other trade will arise, new trade, to take its place.'

'How many people have you heard say that the railways will spell the end of the horse? It's the greatest boast of people like you.'

'I know people say it, but I don't believe they are right,' Bendy began, but Nicky interrupted him.

'Thank you, but I don't care to wager my patrimony on your beliefs. You can go now, and tell your grubby friends you have failed. The railway will not cross Morland land.'

Benedict did not move, looking steadily at his brother for a moment. 'Nicky, you remember the story of King Canute?' he said. 'The railway will come, and if you refuse to allow it to cross your land, it will simply go another route. You cannot stop it. Why not be part of it, and get the benefit?'

He had not expected his words to have any effect, but Nicky stared at him, evidently running rapidly through a series of calculations. At last he said abruptly, 'What is it that you want of me?'

'To begin with, just to allow the surveyor to come and survey the land, to see if it's suitable. That's all. Nothing more can be done or decided until he has made his report.'

Nicky nodded slowly. 'Very well,' he said.

'You mean – you agree?'

'To see the surveyor, that's all. But he must come to me in person, and I will conduct him wherever he wants to go. And he must come alone.'

'He will need to bring an assistant,' Bendy said anxiously. 'Maybe two. Surveying can't be done single-handed.'

'He may bring his assistants, but I won't have any of you undertakers hanging on his sleeve. No-one from your railway company whispering in his ear. I want his report to be unbiased.'

'I'm sure I can promise you that,' Benedict said, surprised and relieved. 'Thank you, Nicky. You won't regret it.'

Nicholas saw him out, wondering privately at the conceit and folly of the railway-interest which really thought it could persuade the horse-interest to cut its own throat. Half his income came from providing riding horses, carriage horses and post horses, and what would become of that if everyone travelled by railway? Even hunters would be less in demand if all the hunting country was destroyed by having railways tearing across it. But Bendy's words had rung true in one respect. If he refused outright to have anything to do with the railway, he would find himself on the outside, with no means of influencing the decisions. Let the surveyor come to him, and come alone. 'Nothing can be done or decided until he has made his report.' There was no man on earth who did not have his price. He had only to find out what it was, and the report would be Nicky's report.

CHAPTER EIGHT

Hudson was fuming, actually prancing with rage on his little shiny-booted toes. Benedict noted with interest rather than alarm his suffused face, his eyes disappearing into slits, the speck of spittle on his lips. He had been working on a cutting and had not been to bed for two days, and he was too tired to be afraid of anyone who was not likely actually to hit him.

'Oh, your brother has done us up finely!' Hudson raved. 'He has trussed us up like Christmas geese all right! But if he thinks to have heard the last of us, he has another think coming! No-one gets the better of George Hudson! I will see him off! I will last him out and see him off, you see if I don't!'

'But what has he done?' Benedict asked patiently. His head was aching with weariness and he wanted his bed, and he just wished he could get to the denouement of the play without having to sit through the Burletta, Parody and Grotesque Dance.

'He has done us up, I tell you! He has made fools of us all! Oh, now I understand why he wanted to see the surveyor all alone. Now I know why he invited him to dinner in that ingratiating way. So very polite of the gentleman, wasn't it? I remember you were surprised at the time he should come off so civil – well, now we know! I wonder what else he gave him, besides a grand dinner and fine wine and soft words?'

'What are you saying, sir?' Benedict asked with scant patience.

Hudson bowed himself and thrust his purpling face close to Bendy's. 'He has bought our surveyor, that's what I'm saying!' he bellowed.

Bendy stared. 'Impossible. I don't believe it.'

Hudson straightened up, danced away to his desk, snatched up a document and thrust it at Bendy, smacking it with his other hand. 'If you don't believe me, read this! Here is our surveyor's report – bought and paid for by Mr Nicholas Morland of Morland Place! This here is the report I am to put before the Railway Committee; and do you know what it says?'

'I have no idea,' Benedict said wearily.

Hudson slapped it again with his hard hand. 'Horse-working! Aye, that's what our precious *independent* surveyor recommends! "I can see no occasion for the Committee to consider locomotive engines, which in my view would be unjustified on grounds of economy." Horse-working, that's the beginning and end of it! What he wants us to build is nothing more than a bloody horse-powered tramway!'

Despite himself, Benedict began to smile. He had underestimated Nicky; and the thing had a sublime quality of farce about it.

Hudson saw the smile, and flew into a greater rage. 'I see nothing to laugh about, young man! It's all your fault, is this! You were the one who was supposed to fix your brother, and he ends up by fixing you!'

'Oh, but he's done it so nicely,' Benedict said, giving way to a chuckle. 'And remember, I did warn you that I have no influence over him.' Hudson stamped away and let loose a flood of filthy oaths, pounding one palm with the other fist as if it were Nicholas Morland's face. 'Come,' Bendy said at last, taking a hold on himself, 'it isn't so bad, surely? At least he doesn't condemn the railway out of hand. And the other thing can be got over, can't it?'

Hudson whirled on him. 'A horse tramway is worse

than nothing! It would make us the laughing stock of the north!' His lardy cheeks trembled with emotion. 'I love this town, and I won't have it laughed at. York is the best town in England, and it shall be the marvel of the whole country before I'm done! I swear it by this head!'

'Well, then, why let this report cast you down? The Committee doesn't have to accept the proposition, does it?'

'What in Hades do you think we commissioned it for? Oh, this report is jam for the railway haters! It is ammunition. This gives all the excuse they need to the little men, the waverers – mealy, lily-livered, pussy-footing old women that they are!' His voice shot up into a grotesque falsetto. '"No need to decide on a railway – let's just have a nice, safe tramway and let someone else take the risk" – aye, and the glory, and the profit! What do they care – serving their time and sitting on their fat arses in their dusty little shops!' He turned away, stamping in rage, and whirled back again. 'But it's worse than that – oh, you don't know the half of it! It's not just this report: your precious brother has gone round the whole horse interest in York, and got them on his side. Obadiah, Willans and Peckitt – all on the Committee – they've already been to see me, bleating about a tramway, and we haven't even presented the report yet! Your brother's been round them all – the coach- and harness-makers, the turnpike shareholders, post houses, livery stables, horse-breeders, farriers, blacksmiths – even that bloody ket-feller from Heslington! Everyone whose livelihood depends on horses will be on his side. A solid wall of opposition. We'll never shift 'em. That plus the waverers will take the day all right. *And*,' he whirled again, 'we've lost the Anstey vote into the bargain.'

'Oh, surely not?' Benedict was surprised. 'Harry Anstey is as railway-nutty as I am.'

'Oh aye, Harry Anstey is as sound as you, for what use that is! But *Lord* Anstey now remembers that his father only ever wanted a coal line to bring his coals to York, and horse-drawn'd be good enough for that. And *Mr* Anstey, Member of Parliament, remembers that now we have a Reformed House of Commons he must do what his voters want and not what he wants. Mr *Benjamin* will follow whatever lead his lordship gives him, seeing he lives under his roof. And the former *Miss* Ansteys will take their husbands with them, if their husbands ain't already gone over, considering they are gentlemen with an interest in hunting. And besides all that, Lord Anstey has just agreed to wed his youngest sister to Nicholas Morland, and doesn't reckon to beggar her by killing the horse trade, nor make an enemy of her future husband.'

'Yes,' said Bendy, 'I do see all that.'

'Oh you do, do you? Well, where the Ansteys and Morlands go, many will follow. So now you tell me, Mr Engineer Morland, what the deuce are we to do next?'

'I don't know,' Benedict said. 'I really don't know.' He sought for some grain of comfort. 'The fight was always bound to be hard, you know. People take time to persuade. The argument for the London and Birmingham was not won in a day – in fact, I know Mr Robert Stephenson thought many times that the Bill would never go through, the landowners and the turnpike interest fought so hard against it. But they got it through in the end.'

'Aye, aye, and so will we,' Hudson said. 'I'm not finished yet. No-one puts one over on me and gets away with it, and Mr Nicholas bloody Morland will smile on the other side of his face before I'm finished. I will have my railway. I *will* have it!' He pounded his palm again, but more softly this time, and with a deadly determination rather than rage. Benedict found this mood more impressive than the other.

'If people can be swung one way, they can be swung the other,' Benedict said. 'You just have to find the right argument.'

161

'Aye,' said Hudson. He looked mournful. 'It's a set-back, though, I can't deny it, and I'm a man as hates a put-off. I like to be getting on, I do. I was hoping to be able to put a proposal to Parliament this year, but that's off now. We won't be starting anything for a long while yet.'

Benedict looked thoughtful. 'It's a blow to me, too. The Leeds and Selby is due to be finished this autumn. With no York and Leeds in the offing, I shall have to look for work elsewhere.' Nicky had done for him, too. He had hoped to be able to stay near York until he had improved his position enough to be able to support a wife. An engineer's life was never a settled one – he went where the railways led him – and if he was forced to go away from the district in the autumn he would probably never see Miss Fleetham again. Or at least, when he saw her again, she would be married to someone else, which would be worse.

The Easter Ball at Moreby Manor was one of the prominent events on York's social calendar. The present Viscount Howick was a lively man in his thirties who had not long succeeded to the title, and was in the process of modernising the estate and sweeping away all his father's old-fashioned ways. The Easter Ball, which had been a staid and private affair for family and a few friends, had under new management become a semi-public celebration of great flamboyance, to which it was only necessary to be gently-born and want an invitation to receive one.

Benedict had never been to Moreby Manor, so he was pleased to have the chance to go this year, in 1834. His invitation came from Sir Carlton Miniott, who was making up a party at the request of Lord Howick. Miniott also asked Benedict to dine for it, at Ledston Park, which meant he would be transported in comfort to the ball, instead of having to hack and arrive mudsplashed and windswept. Benedict was grateful, and said so, with a hint of surprise at such continuing attentions from the baronet, which he could not see why he deserved.

'Not kind of me at all,' Miniott said, giving his dark, sidelong smile which made Mammas with susceptible daughters wish that, whatever his age, he was safely married. 'I happen to know that Miss Fleetham will be there, and the only way I can get her to look at me at all is to stand directly beside you. You must forgive me if I make use of my proximity to you to steal a dance with her this evening.'

Benedict felt himself blushing idiotically at the mere mention of her name, but he said sadly, 'You have nothing to fear from me, Sir Carlton.'

'That's poor-spirited talk for a coming young railway engineer.'

'That's just the trouble, sir. Mr Fleetham don't approve of the railways. I've heard him say all railway men should be horsewhipped.'

Miniott grinned. 'I'm a railway man myself. I should like to see him try.'

'It's a little different with you, sir,' Benedict said ruefully. 'You *own* the railway, I only work on it.'

'Ah yes,' said Miniott thoughtfully, 'I do see your difficulty.'

The party was all male, and dinner was very merry, and it was past ten when they climbed into their carriages to drive out to Moreby Manor, about five miles to the south of York. Benedict was in a fret of excitement at the thought of seeing Miss Fleetham again, but almost the first person he encountered inside the anteroom was his brother. To his astonishment, Nicky greeted him openly and with a grin, which if not affectionate, was at least cheerful.

'Well, well, you here? How did you get in?' Nicky said.

'I came with Sir Carlton Miniott's party,' Benedict said cautiously.

'Miniott of Ledston Park? Oh yes, he's one of these railway backers, isn't he?'

'He's a shareholder in the Leeds and Selby.'

'I've heard he's in a good deal of trouble – too many fingers in too many pies. However, that's all gossip.' He waved a hand. Benedict could see he was already fairly bosky, though not yet quite at sea. 'You see me here *en garcon*,' he went on loudly, 'and perhaps for the last time. I suppose you have heard that I am to be married in June?'

'Yes indeed. I wish you joy,' Bendy said, fascinated by this expansive mood.

'You shall come if you please. You see I have nothing more to fear from you! Soon I shall have a string of little assurances in the nursery. Yes, come and see me turned off.'

'I'll come and gladly. Thank you. Where is Aglaea tonight?'

'My betrothed is confined to bed with some trifling indisposition, but I felt I owed it to Howick to attend,' Nicky said indifferently. His mind was evidently on other matters. 'I have scotched your railway plan, you see,' he went on happily. 'You aren't clever enough for me! You thought you could ruin me, but I have turned the tables on you. Yes, I'm very pleased with the way things have gone. Who is that young woman staring at you?'

The abrupt change of subject took Bendy by surprise. He turned his head and saw Miss Fleetham a short distance away looking at him with great urgency, calling him over with her eyes.

Nicholas snorted. 'Good God, yes, it's that bold female you were talking to outside the Minster. I did not recognise her in those feathers. What was the name, again? I wonder she still wants to talk to you, now she knows you have no fortune.'

Bendy could not resist the call any longer. 'Nicky, please excuse me, I must see what she wants.'

164

He made his escape, and doing his best to appear casual about it, soon fetched up beside Miss Fleetham, who was hanging back from a group of older women, amongst whom Bendy recognised Mrs Phillips. As soon as he reached her, Miss Fleetham put up her fan, and behind it laid her hand over Bendy's wrist, pulled him near and whispered, 'Sir Carlton told me he had brought you. I had to promise him the two first after supper for it, but you may have the two second. How late you are! I suppose you sat late over dinner, and now it is nearly supper time. Well, so much the better, I hate dancing, one can never have a proper conversation while dancing. Oh, it is an age since I saw you! I suppose you have been flirting madly with everyone in the Riding? Well, indeed, I have had plenty myself, what with the Mansion House Ball – how did you come not to go, by the by? – and the Barkers' evening party, and the Creed wedding. Mrs Phillips gave a dinner for that and I hoped she would ask you, because she asked George Findlay, but we were only twenty to sit down, and there were so many relatives there was not room. Molly Creed is a cousin, you know, of sorts. Well, Harry Coulsden, who she is marrying, was an old beau of mine, and I must say he looked *so* at me at the wedding I was quite ashamed! Jane Barker said she was sure he had sooner marry me than Molly, for she is not at all pretty, you know, only a very sweet girl, and my particular friend. I'm sure he is madly in love with her, and so I told Jane Barker. He used to moon over me so it quite put me out of patience, and I was glad when he fell in love with Molly, for it took him off my conscience at last. Well, and so Sir Carlton is taken Papa off to sing your praises to him, so he told me. He says he will make Pa invite you to our house, which would be tremendous, would it not? He is such a good friend, Sir Carlton! I have known him since I was a little girl, you know. He is such a flirt, it is quite shocking! All my friends have been in love with him for ever, though he's old enough to be my father. Lizzie Phillips can't look at him without blushing, for I told him once that she thought him the handsomest man in the world – which she did, for she told me so, only she didn't know I would tell him. But I always tell him everything, it is quite ridiculous! He is such an old friend.'

Benedict was almost drunk with delight at being near her. Her perfume made him feel dizzy, her sparkling eyes and white teeth dazzled him, her beauty made it difficult for him to concentrate on what she was saying. But he managed to say, 'I'm afraid Sir Carlton will not prevail over your father, for I know he hates anything to do with railways.'

Miss Fleetham laughed. 'Oh, there is nothing in that. Sir Carlton sold Papa some shares in the railway months ago, and he is all for it now. He used to be amazingly against it, because they made him sell some of his land for it, and he does not like to be *made* to do things, but then Sir Carlton said that if he owned shares in it he would only have sold the land to himself, and Pa was quite happy with that. He changes his mind ten times a day, you know. It used to make the other landowners mad because they never knew which way he would vote when there was a General Election, and Pa was worth ten votes before the Reform.'

Bendy now felt as light as a feather, his last worry gone. 'Oh, Miss Fleetham,' he murmured rapturously, 'I am so very happy to see you again! Would you – dare I hope – will you allow me to take you down to supper?'

'I'm afraid I have already promised Percy Barker,' she said, lowering the fans of her eyelashes in the way which enchanted him, because it was so utterly, frivolously feminine; and then, lifting them just enough to look at him from under them, she added, 'but I'm sure I can put him off. After all, he's just another friend of Ned Phillips's and I only said yes out of kindness.'

Benedict's happiness was complete. So far he had not

166

dared to dream of more than being able to dance with her and talk with her occasionally at public assemblies like this. But if Sir Carlton were really 'singing his praises' to Mr Fleetham, perhaps he might attain to the dream of being received at Fleetham Manor one day. That would be a step indeed! Perhaps he might even advance his case sufficiently by the time his present contract ended – suppose he were to be able to find another post right away, with a large enough salary – if Miss Fleetham really did favour him, as Sir Carlton thought—

His mind wandered off in a haze of delicious suppositions and imaginings; and across the anteroom, Nicky watched him with a malicious grin.

Mrs Moon and Miss Smith sat facing each other across the table in the housekeeper's room, a bottle of gin, a jug of hot water, a bowl of sugar, and two tumblers between them. Despite these comforts, their expressions were of matching gloom.

Miss Smith roused herself a little. 'It might be all right,' she said hopefully. 'Ferrars says she's as meek as a sheep.'

Mrs Moon made a noise of contempt. 'What does Ferrars know? And what unmarried girl isn't meek as a sheep? That's how they catch a husband. But as soon as he's hooked and landed, it's a different matter. She'll come marching in here spoiling to have her own way, you mark my words.'

'I dare say you're right,' Miss Smith sighed. 'And just when we'd got ourselves nicely settled.'

'I've been putting away a fair bit,' Mrs Moon admitted. 'In a year or two Moon and me could've set ourselves up comfortable somewhere. Now she'll come through like a whirlwind, poking her nose into everything and spoiling all my arrangements. And Moon isn't getting any younger. His constitution has never been strong. All I wanted was for him to be comfortable,' she added almost indignantly. 'I don't want anything for myself. I'm not a greedy woman, you know,'

'I know, dear,' Miss Smith said absently. She had one or two nice little schemes in operation herself, which she would be sorry to have to wind up. The pickings in this house were quite as good as in the bridewell, and the work was much less dangerous. And besides—

The burst of revelry interrupted their silent thoughts – a violent surge in the muted background sound of the bachelor feast which was going on in the great hall. The last report they'd had, the gentlemen were playing a game taught them by Major Tovey, which he'd learned in India – a sort of horseback hockey, using walking-sticks. Half the gentlemen were being horses, carrying the others pick-a-back. It was only a matter of time before something got broken, or someone got hurt.

'He'll have a thick head to take to church tomorrow,' Miss Smith commented, with a jerk of her head in that direction.

'Serves him right. What did he want to go a-marrying for?' Mrs Moon reached for the gin bottle. 'Will you have another?'

'I don't mind if I do,' said Miss Smith nicely.

Mrs Moon laid her hand against the jug's tepid cheek. 'Would you like me to hot the water up a bit?'

'Oh, don't bother. I don't mind it.' She watched Mrs Moon drop a piece of sugar into the bottom of each tumbler, add the gin, and top it up with water. 'Well, maybe we can work her round to our ways. It's two against one, after all.'

As if reminded by this comment, Mrs Moon said, 'Where's Miss, by the way?'

Miss Smith grimaced. 'In there with *them*, the baggage, and enjoying every minute, I make no doubt. Not that I care – she's no relative of mine, and I've no wish to stand guard over her every night, I give you *my* word. But I wonder what Master is about? She will be corrupted for

168

sure, and her an heiress and all. Who'll want to marry her, if it gets out how she goes on, drinking and cursing and singing those songs – not that she understands what she's saying, but she knows it's wicked talk all the same.'

'I don't suppose Master cares one way or the other about her morals,' said Mrs Moon. 'When he's got a few in, he hardly knows his head from his ha'penny anyway. Likely he thinks it's funny, no more than that. But that Ferrars— !' She shook her head with a dark look. 'We all know who's really master in this house.'

'Why should Ferrars care what she does, if Master don't?' Miss Smith said.

Mrs Moon leaned closer. 'It's my belief Ferrars *wants* her to be corrupted.' She sat back again, with a 'now then!' air.

'Whatever for?' Miss Smith asked, impressed despite herself. 'She'll never get a husband, the way she's carrying on.'

'He don't want her to get a husband,' Mrs Moon said with penetration, 'for where Miss goes, her money goes, and it's not her pretty face he's interested in.' She shook her head and sighed. 'Moon don't like it a bit, the great soft gowk, and one of these days he's going to say something to one of 'em, and then the fat'll be in the fire. I try to hold him off, but he had a little girl of his own once, and it makes him tender.'

'Where is she now?' Miss Smith asked with interest.

'Dead,' said Mrs Moon succinctly. 'She fell in the fire one time when Moon was s'pose to be watching her, only he was drunk and fell asleep. Her mother – his first wife – was in childbed, you see. Moon never got over it. He never touched spirits again after that – but, bless you, a man can get just as drunk on ale, if he puts his mind to it. O' course, she an' the baby died as well, which drove the lesson home, so to speak, though it was none of his fault – the fever took 'em both.'

Miss Smith sucked her teeth in sympathy. 'A chancy business, childbirth.'

'Thank the Lord I never fell myself,' said Mrs Moon briskly, 'though Moon'd've liked it. But now, you know,' she changed tack suddenly, 'a thought occurs to me, May, about this business – Master marrying and all. I wonder if Miss wouldn't be our best ally.'

'How's that?'

'Well, the new mistress will be expecting to be a mother to her, and she can't hardly have an idea of what's really going on. If Miss behaves as badly as she can, she might take up all the new mistress's attention, and keep it off us. Either she'll want to roll up her sleeves and bring the child to hand, in which case I doubt she'll have no time for housekeeping; or else Miss will make her life such a misery she'll want to keep out of the way entirely. If she spends her days carriage-visiting, I shall have no objection, I promise you.'

'Yes, but what about me?' Miss Smith said. 'Ten to one but I'll be blamed for Miss's behaviour, and she'll turn me off without a character.'

'She won't do that. Ferrars will speak for you. He won't let any harm come to you.'

Miss Smith looked incredulous. 'Why should he take up for me?'

Mrs Moon smiled and sipped her gin. 'Because if he don't, we'll tell what we know about him. I'm not blind nor deaf, May, and I dare say you've seen a thing or two as well. It's as long as it's broad: we've got the stuff on Mr Ferrars all right, and he knows it.' She stretched her feet under the table, a gesture of well-being. 'Oh, I think we might manage to hang on here a bit longer, you know. Could you fancy a spot o' toasted cheese to go with that? Feeb is still in the kitchen, and she does a nice Welsh rabbit – with a bit of onion to it. Just be so kind as to reach out and tug the bell, would you?'

*　　*　　*

Aglaea woke before dawn on her wedding morning, and lay quietly looking up at the tester, thinking. Since she had become a betrothed woman she had had a room of her own, but before that she had shared a bed with Mary for so long that she was unused to the idea that she could move or turn or even get up if she wanted without disturbing anyone. The months of her betrothal had gone by quickly, and in a whirl of activity. There were her wedding clothes, for one thing: her sisters and sisters-in-law seemed to be driven almost to a frenzy by the news of her engagement, and had determined between them that she should be dressed at the pinnacle of fashion if they died for it. Such porings over patterns and samples, such trampings around warehouses, such quizzing of other young ladies at balls and promenades, and such stern examination of mantua-makers went on that Aglaea thought a coronation could hardly have been more trouble. Besides the wedding gown itself, there was a going-away outfit, first and second day dresses, evening gowns, carriage dresses, nightgowns, mantles, bonnets, and quantities of underwear all had to be chosen, made, fitted, altered and trimmed; and that was not all, because there were boots, slippers, gloves, handkerchiefs, fans, muffs, caps, pelerines and parasols to buy as well. Sister Lotte, now Mrs Freddie Chubb, declared that not one thing Aglaea owned was fit to be taken with her, and Mary energetically agreed; and sister-in-law Celia was called upon to impose the restraint of her good taste upon the Anstey multitude to make sure that nothing had anything the slightest bit *demi-toilette* or awkward about it.

The wedding itself caused almost as much fuss, for there was the place to be chosen, the guest list to be drawn up, the invitations to be sent and checked off, the seating plan to be devised, and the wedding-breakfast to be organised, and the presents to be unpacked, acknowledged and displayed. In all this flurry Aglaea was dragged back and forth like a useless limb, appealed to for her approval and never heeded when she spoke, turned this way and that, pinned up, measured against, and constantly outvoted in any decision. She saw little of Nicholas, and never spoke to him alone; indeed she could have been forgiven for thinking that having proposed to her he had nothing more to do with the wedding, which seemed, like an over-starched petticoat, quite capable of standing up on its own without anyone in it.

But now all the preparations were over, and the day had come. Today she was to leave her maiden home for ever and become Mrs Nicholas Morland. The words even more than the thought frightened her. It sounded so strange that it seemed unchancy to pronounce them even in thought. That person, who would come into existence today, seemed as remote and fantastic as Nicholas himself had become since he had ceased to be Nicky-Harry's-friend and become her fiancé. What did she know about him? What would her life be like? What would be required of her? She knew nothing about marriage except that she knew nothing. The life of her mother and father as a married couple had been so remote and hidden that it might never have existed – except that there were eight Ansteys of Aglaea's generation to prove it. Life at Morland Place would be different from theirs, she supposed – but who was there to tell her what to do? She felt horribly unprepared, as though she were going to be examined in public on a subject she had never studied.

She heard the first questioning note of a blackbird outside – the beginning of the dawn chorus. Soon they would all join in, all the birds of the air singing to bring the sun up, so her mother had told her long ago when she was a little child. Remembering at last that she was free to move, she got out of bed and drew the curtains. It was still dark, but she could see the shape of the trees against the sky, black against less black, proof that the light was coming; after a while she could see where the garden ended at the river-bank, and all was mute and grey; then as the pearliness of dawn seeped into the sky she could see the wraiths of mist lying over the lawn and the river. She hoped the day would be fine. It would seem like a warning if it were not.

She knelt at the window to say her prayers, but after the first few automatic words she found she could not think of anything to say. It was as if her mind were asleep: she could not imagine what was to happen, nor even what she hoped might happen. She rested her chin on her folded hands and stared out at the broadening day, and thought of nothing. She was still in the same position when Mary came in, bringing her chocolate on a tray.

'What, are you up already? Kneeling on the floor in that nightgown, and bare feet too, you'll catch your death! Come, come back to bed, hop in and drink your chocolate. Goodness, your hands are like ice. There's no need to be nervous, you know. Everything's arranged down to the last dot. Louisa's gone down to the church already to make sure no-one's disturbed the flowers. Everything will be all right.'

'I know,' Aglaea said. Mary was nervous, she could tell. She was worried because the wedding was not to be in the chapel at Morland Place, like every important Morland wedding before. The fact was, since there was no mistress in the house, it could not play host to the wedding. Aglaea was to be married from Anstey House, and the ceremony was to be held in the Minster, which was very fine and grand, but for anyone who knew the history of the Morland family it was not quite right. Mary was close to feeling that despite all their care Aglaea would not be properly married to Nicholas.

'Louisa's coming to help me help you dress in half an hour,' Mary said briskly. 'And Celia's sending her Betty over to do your hair – you know what a light hand she has. So drink your chocolate like a good girl. Your hot water will be here any moment.'

Aglaea sipped obediently, eyeing her sister as she walked about the room, touching this and that, evidently working herself up to say something. Finally she came over and sat down on the bed, playing with the fringe of the counterpane and not meeting Aglaea's eyes.

'I want to speak to you, Aggie, about marriage,' she said. 'I know if our mother were alive, she would have spoken to you before this, and perhaps I ought to have asked Louisa or Lotte to do it, but you're such a shy thing, I was afraid they might upset you. So I feel it's up to me.'

Aglaea wondered at her embarrassment, and tried to comfort her. 'It's all right, Mary,' she murmured. 'You know you can say anything to me.'

Mary peeped under her eyelashes and looked down again, colouring a little. 'Yes, you may well say that, because you are as innocent as a baby, and don't know any more than a child of two! Well, dear, I don't mean to spoil your innocence, because I think the less you know the better. Certainly I would feel that way if it was me that was marrying. Marriage isn't all fine clothes and new carriages, you know.'

'I didn't think it was,' Aglaea said gently.

'All I want to say to you, Aggie dear,' Mary went on undeterred, 'is that when you are married, your duty will be to obey your husband in everything.'

'I should not think of anything else,' Aglaea said, a little puzzled.

'I know, dear, but men are different from women, and they have different ways. Your husband may—' she coughed, colouring deeper – 'he certainly *will* ask you to do things that you will not understand – things you may find strange or even distasteful. But you must do whatever he wants. Remember he is your husband and your master, and he knows best. It is your duty – your *sacred* duty – to obey him. Remember that God has ordained it so.'

'Yes, Mary. But what— ?'

Mary ploughed on, determined. 'You must try not to show any surprise or reluctance – they don't like that. Just do what he asks without making any fuss. Do you understand?'

Now she looked up. Aglaea met her eyes with complete incomprehension. 'What could he ask me to do that I might find distasteful? Surely a gentleman would not behave improperly towards his wife?'

Mary shook her head impatiently. 'It isn't improper between man and wife, you goose.'

'What isn't?'

'Anything.' She made an exasperated gesture with her hand. 'I can't explain it to you. You'll understand better one day. Just remember, as long as you obey his wishes, everything will be all right. You can remember that much, can't you?'

'That I must do as he wishes – yes, of course. You did not need to tell me that,' Aglaea said. It was the way of things. A woman was always under the command of a man: father, older brother, master, husband. It made no difference which.

Mary smiled, more at ease now the embarrassing duty was done. 'Yes, you always were a good girl. And we are proud of you, Aggie. Mother and Papa would have been proud of you too – especially Mother. She'd have been so happy today, to see you become Mistress of Morland Place.'

Aglaea smiled reflectively. 'That's one of the things I'm happiest about, that I'm going to live for the rest of my life in the house where she grew up.'

'And you'll be able to be a mother to that poor Skelwith child. Do you know, since Childie stopped going to play with her, I don't think she's had a person near her, poor mite. Nothing but servants.' Mary patted her hand and stood up. 'Here's Susan with your water now. I'll leave you to wash, and come back in a little while.'

To do whatever he wanted, Aglaea thought dreamily

as she watched the maid pour the hot water from the can into her basin. The youngest of the family, she had always been at the bottom of the family chain of command. Well, now she would have only one person to obey instead of dozens. The thought of it made her feel warm and languorous, though she hardly knew why: to do whatever Nicky wanted, however strange it seemed – that was her duty and her destiny. Mary had told her so, and Mary must know; unwed as she was, Mary was mother to them all now, and Mary knew everything.

It seemed to Nicholas little less than a miracle that he was at the church on time and standing, or rather swaying, in his place, shaved, brushed and correctly dressed. The carouse in honour of his 'turning off' had gone on until after dawn, and it was fortunate, he thought, that the wedding was not taking place at Morland Place, for they would never have got the bodies and bottles out and the damage made good in time to lay up the feast. As it was, he was to leave direct from Anstey House for the wedding-trip to Scarborough, so the servants could clean up at their leisure. Ferrars was to pack his box and bring it and the chaise round to the Lendal at three o'clock. With four horses they should be in Scarborough in time for dinner. Nicholas was glad that Ferrars was not accompanying him on his wedding-trip, although it had been threatened: the new valet he had been promised could not start for another week. Ferrars had expressed a desire to see Scarborough, and Nicholas had learned not to deny Ferrars his wishes. But at the last minute Ferrars had decided to stay at home. Moon could not be trusted to take care of things in his absence, he had said, and a footman was told off to go in his place.

Nicholas only hoped he would be able to eliminate all the scars of the bachelor feast before their return: apart from the horse-hockey (polo, Tovey called it), Jack Cox and Micky O'Rourke had been practising sabre-thrusts on the curtains, and he feared some of the wilder strokes might have nicked the woodwork. Moon had given him a deeply reproachful look this morning when he brought up his hot water, but that was probably more because of Jemima. Moon didn't think Jemima ought to be allowed anywhere near Nicky's friends on these occasions, and had come perilously close to telling his master so. Didn't he realise, Nicky thought peevishly, that he took care nothing too bad was said in her presence? And as for giving her wine, well, it was more the case that she took it. Besides, a little sound wine never hurt anyone. Why, his own beloved mother was as fond of wine as anyone, and had let him taste it, watered, when he was much younger than Jemima, saying that the younger he learned to drink it moderately, the less likely he was to become a slave to it in adulthood. And indeed, he was *not* a slave to it. He could take it or leave it alone if he wished; it was just that he much preferred to take it. Moon didn't realise how entertaining Jemima was on these occasions, how funny it was to hear the things she said, spoken in that childish voice, and to see her hopping about like an ape when she had had a glass or two.

The organ, which had been pootling quietly in the background of his thoughts, struck up with a violent tune which seemed through his pounding headache vaguely familiar. There was a creaking and rustling and scuffing sound as the congregation stood up, and a flock of vestmented clerics suddenly appeared from nowhere and stood in front of him with an expression of anticipation, like geese waiting to be fed. Nicholas turned and looked back towards the church door, and the sight he saw struck him cold to the stomach with a mixture of fright and awe and belated realisation of the irrevocability of what he was doing. Lord Anstey – Jack – was advancing along the aisle at something like a military slow march, the grimness of his expression probably due to a determination not to cry; and on his arm was Aglaea – an Aglaea transformed not only by the dressmaker's art, but by the glow of the occasion. The gown was beautiful – pink and white striped taffeta, small-waisted, full-skirted, with a deep frill at the hem, and puffed sleeves over which vast gauze *imbécile* sleeves ballooned to the wrist. The softly pleated lace tucker was held at the throat by a pink rose; the pink and white silk bonnet was set far back on her head to show the pink roses fastened like a halo round her head, from which her hair fell in bunches of glossy long curls beside her face. But most different of all was the face: Nicholas stared in sheer astonishment. Could this – this *beautiful* creature be the Aglaea he had known all his life? Where had the glowing cheeks, the softly red lips, the shining eyes been hidden before? He wondered briefly if one of her sisters had employed the arts of *maquillage* upon her, but even as he thought it he knew it was not so. He had had enough of painted women to know the difference, and not the most subtle painting could produce so natural a look. Something else was happening here, and the thought that it could have to do with the occasion and therefore with him both elated and frightened him. He wanted to run; he wanted to tell *her* to run; but it was not possible, of course. What was to come had been inevitable from the first time he had singled her out for attention at her brother's supper-party. He should have known then how it would end. He had seen enough singed moths flapping helplessly at the foot of the lamp.

Aglaea reached his side and looked into his face, meeting his eyes with a directness which was so unlike her it was almost exciting. It occurred to him that he did not really know her at all: she was a composite of all the modest young women he had ever had to do with in the drawing-rooms of polite society. The only thing he had ever heard her say of herself was that she wanted to see the sea, and that was odd enough in all conscience. The elation and fright which filled him took on a tinge of pleasurableness. Perhaps it might be an enjoyable thing after all, this marriage business, if it meant getting to know someone who was interesting as well as good, and who was dedicated to one's welfare. On the crest of the thought he smiled at her, and she smiled back. The smiles were seen with sentimental pleasure by a great many, who afterwards murmured that it was obviously a love-match after all. There were no witnesses who knew Aglaea well enough to be aware that her smile was three-quarters relief.

CHAPTER NINE

It was one of those perfect June days, when the sunlight falls with extraordinary transparency from a perfect lapis bowl of a sky. Small sounds – the sigh of waves, the high keening of a gull, a child's voice raised importantly in play – came to the ear so clearly they seemed to echo as though the world were hollow; and the heat was so clean and crisp Nicholas almost expected to see snow on the ground instead of sand. He was strolling along the promenade at Scarborough, the sea to his left hand beyond the broad sands, and his wife on his arm. That last was an astonishing thought, and one which he had difficulty in keeping in his mind. Her hand was so light on his sleeve that he could hardly feel it, and she only spoke when spoken to, so that when he looked the other way towards the sea, which naturally he often did, he found himself forgetting for minutes at a time that she was there. He was very tired and had drunk a great deal in the last couple of days, so his mind was, in any case, lacking in 'grip', tending to float aimlessly on the verge of blankness.

Yet he was happy. It was an odd thing that the simple presence of this quiet creature made it possible for him to do nothing and think nothing for long periods of time. Alone he could not have walked up and down the promenade in this aimless way, nor sat looking for hours at the sea; alone he could not have sat over a pot of tea in the tea-rooms watching the smartly dressed promenaders walking past the big bow windows. Yet with her beside him, even if he was not talking to her or even looking at her, he could do those things. A restlessness in him was stilled by her presence; a wound in his soul, which bled him constantly of ease, was staunched; the shrill, nagging voice inside which meant he had constantly to do something, anything, so as not to have to listen to it, quietened to a muted grumble.

My wife. What an odd thought! Mrs Nicholas Morland. He half expected some official to expose him for a fraud, some grown-up to tell him to stop play-acting and go back to his lessons. And yet everyone seemed to accept the situation as normal, natural, and even agreeable. Approving glances followed them as they passed in and out of the hotel. He had even seen, as they walked through the streets and along the sea-front, men glancing at her with admiration, and women surveying her dress with critical appreciation.

She had certainly turned out better than he expected, he thought: her various outfits were smart and very modish without being over-trimmed, and her new, softer way of dressing her hair made her look younger and almost pretty. She was a good companion, too. At dinner she had listened with real interest to him, and asked him just the right questions to keep him talking; and she fell in readily with anything he suggested by way of occupation. It was pleasant to have command of someone sweet-tempered, pliant, and so obviously approved by everyone else. Yes, she was his to command: whatever he said became the rule; he was the master. My wife. I have a wife. And he could walk openly into the hotel with her without shocking anyone, even go into the same bedroom with her, and no-one so much as raised an eyebrow. It was an extraordinary sensation.

Ah, yes, that was the one fly in the ointment, the one hair in the custard. His mind writhed away from the memory; but the fact of it was that when he had finally climbed into bed beside her on their wedding night, he simply couldn't – well, couldn't. Of course, he had been pretty castaway – the wedding feast had been liberal, and then he had had a flask in the carriage (in case of accidents) which it seemed a shame not to use, and then there had been dinner at the hotel, with champagne before and port afterwards, and he had taken a drop or two of brandy while she was putting herself to bed, in order to bolster his confidence. One way and another, it was not too much of a surprise that nothing happened that first night. But then last night, though he had had plenty to drink throughout the day, he had not been more than gently illuminated – certainly not bosky – and yet he still couldn't. He'd tried, he'd done his best, but somehow, with Aglaea, whom he had known all his life, quiet and sweet and smelling cleanly of soap, lying there willing and obedient beside him, he simply could not raise the recruits. It was an extraordinary thing, and it had never happened to him before, even with twice that amount of drink in him. He couldn't understand it; but he supposed it would sort itself out sooner or later. In this summer sunshine, with his mind idling, he found it hard to worry too much.

He looked at Aglaea, and she smiled at him, rather in the way Minna smiled when he looked at her. In a sudden burst of affection, he wanted to please her. 'What would you like to do this afternoon?' he asked.

'Whatever you like,' she said.

'No, you choose.'

'I had much sooner you chose,' she replied.

'But I want you to be happy. I want you to do whatever would make you happy,' he insisted.

'I like doing what you like doing. As long as you are happy, I am happy,' she said.

A frown appeared between his brows. 'Choose,' he commanded shortly.

She hesitated. 'I'm afraid it might be boring for you.'

'For God's sake—! What is it you want to do?'

Aglaea looked at him nervously. 'I would like to draw – make some sketches of the sea and the cliffs and the sand and so on. To remember it by afterwards.'

'Very well,' he said curtly. 'That is what we will do. Do you have your sketching things with you?'

'At the hotel,' she said. 'Mary said I should not pack them, but I put them in at the last minute. I – I feel lost without them near me.'

The foolishness of the admission calmed him, and he smiled again. 'You are a strange one, Mrs Morland.'

Aglaea blushed and lowered her eyes. Her new title sounded as strange to her as it did to him, but she was equally pleased, so far, with married life. It had not proved as different or as frightening as she expected, and indeed, being near the sea was such an intense joy to her that things would have to have been pretty bad otherwise to cancel that out. Nicholas had been an unexacting companion. She seemed able to please him, taking note of his different moods of loquacity and withdrawal, engaging him in conversation during the one and effacing herself during the other. In two days he had not lost his temper with her once, and had even smiled on her with all the appearance of affection. She thought she could be happy, and would have looked forward to going back to Morland Place if it had not been for the sea. She didn't want to leave the sea. She was aware of a painfully irrational feeling taking root in her that she never, ever wanted to leave the sea again.

But of course she would have to. And at Morland Place she would be able to be useful and not merely decorative. She had surprised herself by how decorative she had turned out to be – and she could tell from the way other people looked at her that it was the case – but her upbringing had schooled her for service. Lectured long and hard on the vices of vanity and idleness, she

183

was rather wary of human beauty, having been taught that it was often a tool of the devil. She was glad, really, that Nicholas was not handsome, so that when she grew to love him, as she knew was her duty, she would have no doubt that it was for his inner qualities and not for his outer shell. What those inner qualities might be she had yet to discover. He talked very little except at dinner, when he had taken wine, and then it was mostly of horses, and of great runs he had had at hunting and so on. He did, she had noticed, seem to drink an awful lot, more than her brothers at any rate; but she told herself that her brothers need not be the absolute, and that weddings were always vinous occasions.

So far she had seen nothing of the strange and shameful things Mary had threatened her with. It had been strange to share a bed with him, it was true, for though she had hardly ever slept alone, she had naturally always shared with women before; and she had felt very embarrassed when she had had to take off her robe and climb into bed in his presence in nothing but her nightgown. But when he put out the lamp and climbed in beside her, it was not so very different after all, except that he smelled so strongly of wine. Last night she had been afraid that the 'things' might be going to start happening, for he had kissed her on the mouth in the darkness, and then laid his hand on her body. It had felt very hot and heavy through the linen of her nightgown, resting on her shoulder; and then – then – he had moved it down to her breast and let it lie there for a bit. She had held her breath, for it had given her a strange and palpitating feeling, which had increased when he moved it to her belly. He had been doing something with his other hand – not to her, but somewhere in the bed – she could feel the movement through the mattress – but she did not know what it was. After a while he stopped kissing her, lifted his hand from her belly, turned over on his side, sighed, and went to sleep. If that was what Mary had been warning her about, she thought her sister had been frightening her for nothing. She could certainly bear *that*.

Aglaea did have a faint doubt that these activities could be all that there was to it, for there remained the question of where babies came from, and she couldn't see that anything Nicholas had done had altered her fundamentally enough for a baby to come of it. But she was willing in her humility and ignorance to suppose that Nicholas knew best, and that whatever happened, he would not do anything to harm or shame her. She was quite willing to put the apprehension aside, and tell herself that whatever was to come, it was worth having got married just to have seen the sea. Not, of course, that she had had the choice: she would have had to marry Nicholas anyway once he asked, sea or no sea, as Mary had explained to her; so she was right to be deeply grateful to him for having made the experience easy for her so far.

Whitby smelled of fish; no, more accurately, it smelled of the seaside, a particular mix of salt, tar, weed and dead crabs which was so powerfully evocative that it almost made Benedict cry to smell it. Would little Tommy remember it when – if – he came to the sea again, or was he just too young? Benedict watched him as he sat on the shingle, sometimes staring in wonder at the sparkling water, sometimes at a pebble he had picked up; then, as though his head were on a string, following a seagull which screamed aimlessly as it wheeled past. Now as Benedict watched, Liza took the boy's hand, and they walked together the few steps down to the sea's edge. The tide was out and there was a narrow strip of dark sand below the shingle, where the quiet waves lapped and expired, leaving a thin lace of bubbles. Fand was running back and forth along the water's edge, biting foolishly at the waves, and Thomas pulled his hand free and ran to stamp his fat feet in the water, then looked back at his mother, laughing. Liza stepped forward again to catch

185

his hand before he could overbalance and soak himself, and they stood together, mother and child, holding hands, outlined against the dazzle, an eternal shape, an eternal occupation.

Benedict's heart was painfully tugged in him. He could not regret the impulse of pity and chivalry which had prompted him to rescue Liza, but there was no doubt that they were a drag on him, his unofficial family. Without them his present salary would have been enough for him to live comfortably in fashionable lodgings, and he would not have felt the responsibility and guilt which took the edge off his bachelor enjoyments. The trouble he had originally rescued her from had been none of his doing, which sometimes made him feel resentful. It was as if he had been trapped; but of course it was his own fault that he had not got clear of her long since. His original motives were pure and disinterested, and if he had only resisted the urge to sleep with her, he could have packed her off with a clear conscience as soon as she was well again. It was a perfectly natural urge, of course. A young man had to sleep with somebody, and he had never cared for the idea of consorting with prostitutes, as some of his contemporaries did. Liza had been there, available, and more than willing, and he had given in to impulse; but the consequence had been Tommy, his little hostage to fortune. He loved the child, and it would be painful now to part with him.

They had not yet seen him watching, and for a moment he observed them with an outsider's eye. What would people think of them? Liza, neat and plainly dressed as always, was hard to place. She might have been a servant girl on her day out, except that a servant girl's holiday clothes would surely have been cheaper and more gaudy; she might have been a small shopkeeper's wife, except that she hadn't the overtly self-confident air of a respectably married woman. There was a diffidence about her, even in the way she stood and moved. He supposed the situation was hard for her, too – always to be kept in the background, to toil and labour for him without ever achieving respectability. That was why he had decided to bring her and the baby with him when he made this trip to Whitby: it would be a treat for her, and he was not likely to meet anyone he knew here. Staying in the cheapest of lodgings he could just afford it.

She turned with the baby away from the sea, and saw him. She was quite still for a moment, and then in a gesture he knew very well she put her fingers up to her temple, as if to brush away a strand of hair. From this distance she looked younger and better born than she did close up: she might have been the child's governess, were it not that a baby of that age would have been in the care of a nursery maid. Now she stooped to point him out to Thomas, who was too small to recognise him at that distance, and wanted to go back to the much more fascinating waves. She scooped him up, set him on her hip, and began to walk up the shingle, managing it with far more grace than he could have done, walking slowly with her head up, so that he was reminded of a deer stepping warily through a wood. There was a quiet fineness about her which always puzzled Bendy, which made it seem that she had come from better stock than he knew she had. Her dignity made it harder than ever for him to admit to himself that he wished her far away, for he knew she would go, if sent, without fuss. He was fond of her, but he had long since ceased to desire her, and he found the responsibility of her irksome. Oh, but there was little Tommy, and what could he do about that?

Fand saw him now, and galloped towards him, spraying shingle, leaped up the steps in one bound and circled him in mad delight. Liza, however, was waiting to see if he meant to acknowledge them, or if she must pass him like a stranger. Bendy felt ashamed, and smiled at her, and held out his arms for his child. Her pinched face bloomed with pleasure as she passed him up.

'Did you see him?' she asked.

'Yes, I saw him.'

'And what did he say?'

'All is well. Come, walk with me, and I'll tell you all about it.'

She came up the steps from the shingle to the road, and he offered her his free arm, which she took with a mixture of pleasure and hesitancy. 'You look very fetching in that straw bonnet,' he said. 'I like the way you've trimmed it.'

She looked down, too pleased to smile, and said, 'What did Mr Stephenson say?'

It was to see George Stephenson that Benedict had been drawn to this small and rather remote fishing port. The fact that the great man was here at all was typical of him. The good folk of Whitby wanted a railway to link them with the market town of Pickering, twenty miles inland across the North York Moors, so that they could sell their fish and buy their other provisions fresher. They were not overweeningly ambitious: it was only a horse tramway they proposed – they did not aspire to locomotive status. But one of their committee had written to the great man himself, asking his advice, and the great man had astonished them by coming in person to inspect the plans for their tuppence-ha'penny scheme and give them the benefit of his experience. Benedict had heard the story with affectionate amusement. There was no 'side' about the Father of Railways: his interest in any scheme, however small, was as fresh and uncluttered with self-conceit as a child's.

Bendy wanted to consult on his own behalf. He now knew that the Leeds and Selby was to open to passengers in September; his work would then be finished, and he needed new employment. The company of George Stephenson and Son was to build both the new railways which had received Royal Assent that year, the Grand Junction and the London and Birmingham, and Benedict urgently wanted to work on one of them. He would prefer to work with Mr Robert, but propriety, together with gratitude for all the old man had done for him, required him to apply first and foremost to Stephenson *père*.

Bendy found him quite unchanged, with his silky white hair, his mahogany face, and his lilting Northumberland accent which, when he got into a rage, made him quite – and probably fortunately – incomprehensible. He evinced a flattering pleasure at seeing Benedict again, praised him for what he had heard about his work on the Leeds and Selby, and, most opportunely, asked him what he meant to do next.

'I hoped, sir, that you might be able to find a use for me,' Bendy said. 'I know you are to build the whole of the new railway between Liverpool and London, and I thought on such a giant scheme there might be room for a hardworking assistant engineer.'

Stephenson chuckled. 'It's a giant undertaking, all reet! Just getting it past the landowners was hard enough: down south a railway's a complete novelty, y'knoa. But our Robert's a canny fighter. Three days he was on his feet before the Select Committee, and they never once threw him. By Gaw, that boy's got a mind like a machine!'

'The London and Birmingham in particular is going to need some tremendous works,' Bendy said. 'It's hilly country all the way. You'll need a man who's good with tunnels.'

'Y'wouldn't be referring to yoursen, by any chance?'

'Well, sir, modesty prevents—'

'Never be modest, laddie. Them as are modest usually have reason to be.' He rubbed his nose with his forefinger, and his eyes grew thoughtful, almost sad. 'You're wrong on one count, though. It woan't be me that builds the London and Birmingham. That's all Robert's own – and I wish him luck with it.'

It sounded a little bitter, and Bendy looked at him with concern. 'Oh, sir, don't say you've quarrelled?'

'Na, na, never fret. Me and Robert are grown men. We can settle wor differences without that. And he's reet, after all. He's not my boy any longer, and he's got his own way of doing things. Him and me could never agree for longer than five minutes. He drives me wild with his fussing over details, and I drive him wild with what he calls my carelessness, so it's time for us to part ways. I should have let him have his freedom long since, but when you've brought up a child, it's hard to remember they're twenty-nine and not nine years old any more.'

'So Mr Robert is building the London and Birmingham alone?'

'That's reet, lad. And I don't know a better man for the job,' he added in a burst of generosity. 'With difficult country like that you've got to pay attention to the detail if you're to come in under cost, and he handles the contractors better than me, that's a fact. Still, it tugs a bit, I don't say it doesn't, when your lad cuts away from you.' Again he rubbed his nose, and sniffed a bit, clearly struggling with emotion.

'But you are building the Grand Junction, sir?' Bendy asked.

The old man straightened up. 'Aye, that's reet, me and Jo Locke together. They've divided it between us – Jo gets the top half and I get the bottom, and we shall see who makes a cannier job of it. They've given him the easy bit, y'knoa, which is just as well, because between you and me Jo Locke has no vision. He's a clerk by nature, inky fingers and a cramped mind. If it had been left to him, we never would have had any railways at all. It took a man like me to see the possibilities. D'ye think Jo Locke would have got the railway across Chat Moss, with ivvry jack in Lancashire telling him it wor impossible? But I did!'

'It was a remarkable achievement, sir,' Bendy said warmly.

Stephenson looked at him sharply, his clear gaze seeming to cut to the centre of Benedict's mind. 'Y'should go and see Robert for a job, laddie. Na, don't look so blue, I'm not turning you away! But you're young, and you should be with him; and you'll never have better experience than you'll get on that contract. Range after range of hills, cuttings, tunnels, embankments, a quicksand to be crossed – by the time it's done, y'll know all there is to know about bad terrain. Go to Robert, with my blessing. I'll give ye a note to take to him, if you like, but y'll not need it. He'll be glad to have you.'

It was everything Benedict had hoped for; though he was sad at the hints of a quarrel between father and son, and he hated to think of the old man being superseded and left behind, for the country owed everything to him. But a moment later Stephenson was talking about the little Whitby tramway, and his vigour and enthusiasm even for such a small undertaking proved to Bendy that he didn't need to feel sorry for the great George Stephenson, who had the energy and self-confidence of a twenty-year-old.

He told Liza all this as they walked slowly up the town. It was built on such a steep slope that the narrow, cobbled streets tacked back and forth, interspersed by shallow-stepped alleys and flights of steep stone stairs by way of short cuts. They were just crossing one of the more fashionable streets when a large, flamboyant figure stepped out of the Angel, paused on the pavement to draw on a fat cigar, and then cried out, 'Well, well, well, if it isn't Benedict Morland! And what might you be doing here, ma lad?'

'Oh lord,' Bendy breathed. He had hoped not to meet anyone he knew; but it could have been worse. 'Good afternoon, Mr Hudson.'

Hudson's little eyes took in the woman and the baby, and he grinned. 'I'd say you were doing someone a good turn, except that that little lad is the image of his Daddy! Oh, never mind it, I won't tell. But what are you doing here?'

'I came to see Mr Stephenson,' Bendy said economically. He was aware of Liza's hand trying to escape from his arm; out of the corner of his eye he could see that her head was down, as though she were trying to hide under her bonnet. But however she effaced herself, there was still Thomas, who, beginning to be sleepy from all the fresh air, was resting his head against Bendy's neck and holding on to his collar in a most familiar manner.

Hudson was evidently more interested in Stephenson than in Bendy's family. 'Oh aye, you know him, don't you?'

'He prenticed me,' Bendy said shortly. 'I owe him everything.'

'Came to ask him for a job, did you?' Hudson said, eyeing him keenly.

Benedict saw no reason to be submit to questioning by this man without retaliation. 'And you, what are you doing here?'

'I came on business, about a property my great-uncle left me,' Hudson said, not seeming at all to resent the impertinence. His mind was clearly elsewhere. 'George Stephenson – now there's a man as could sway our waverers, if he would! Everyone's heard of him. What is it they call him? Father of Railways? If we could get him interested in our scheme, we'd have a lot more credibility with the investors, too.'

Bendy shrugged. 'I dare say he would be interested, if we had a scheme to tell him about. He's interested in everything. That's why he's here – to look at the plans for the Whitby tramway.'

'Is he, by God?' Hudson said, staring intently at Bendy. 'Now then, this might turn out to be just the piece of luck I've been waiting for! Here I am, and here he is, both in the same town at the same time – don't tell me that isn't Providence. And you nicely on hand to bring us together!'

Bendy hesitated. 'I hardly think—'

'Eh, now, don't give me that hoity-toity look. No gentleman's scruples from you, if you please, when you've just done telling me he's interested in every scheme. You shall take me to him and introduce us – aye, and stay and help me tell him about our plans, for you have the right words for railway things, which I haven't. He likes you, doesn't he?'

'I suppose so,' Bendy said, taken by surprise by the question.

'Aye, o' course he does, or he wouldn't have offered you a job. So now then, you can get him on our side, if he's got any doubts. Where's he staying?'

'At the Admiral Rodney – but—'

'That's only just along the street. You can go there now and find out when he will meet us. No, wait, tell him I want to buy him his dinner. They do a right handsome table at the Angel, here – famous for it! See if he'll come tonight, or if not, when. Now then, Morland, hop to it, lad! It's thy future too, tha knows! If we never build this railway, tha'll never get to be chief engineer of it.'

Benedict found himself trotting off like an errand boy, almost without volition. There was no resisting Hudson when he had his mind set on something; Mr Stephenson might find he had met his equal for determination.

It was late when Bendy got back to his lodgings, his hair reeking of cigar smoke, his head whirling with wine and images. He felt he had just witnessed an elemental reaction of the fundamental sort that changed civilisations, like the coming together of fire and water to make steam. George Stephenson and George Hudson, confined in the crucible of a small private inn-parlour: it might have been an explosion, but instead it was a fusion. They had taken to each other at once, the two Georges, though their backgrounds and characters were so different. When Hudson had talked about his beloved

York, Stephenson had listened with a glittering eye and a rapid nod of understanding.

'I want York to be great again. It was the capital of the north once – the seat of government and the heart of the Church for the whole north of England. There was a Roman city there, and a Danish. The trade routes north to south and east to west meet there, and it was the great market place, for things and for ideas. Time has passed us by in the last couple of centuries, but that doesn't mean we're finished, and when I see things starting up over in Lancashire, and everyone talking about Manchester and Liverpool and upstart places like that, it makes me mad. For what sort of places are they? What have they got? Nothing! York has everything – fine houses, educated people, the Minster, schools, shops, markets, libraries – the best doctors and lawyers in the north – more rich folks' estates round about than you could shake a stick at! We've got gas-lighting – I own part of the gas-works. We've got banks – I started one up myself. It's a crying shame we should be so far out of the way and neglected. Now if we had the railway, we'd be joined up to the world again. Folk would come to us – make no doubt about it. York would be the name on everyone's lips.'

It was the sort of large and visionary talk Stephenson liked. He spoke of his beloved Northumberland, and his similar desires to see it at the heart and not on the edge of things. Between them Benedict and Hudson told him the story of the York railway plans so far, and he came down at once on the side of locomotive power.

'Things have moved on since the old Stockton and Darlington days. We were just feeling our way then. We knew we could make a locomotive engine that'd work, but we had no evidence to prove it, and naturally undertakers were sceptical. An exploding tea-kettle on wheels: that's what one of the directors called the first engine in service there – the good old *Locomotion*! I drove her myself on opening-day – the first time we'd used coupling-rods on the wheels. She didn't explode, o' course, but she was unreliable. And even back at Rainhill we were still experimenting – you should have seen some of the queer things that went by the name of locomotive! – but in four years we've learned so much, the new engines make the *Rocket* look like a child's toy. There's nothing airy-fairy about it any more, Mr Hudson, nothing experimental. I can produce facts and figures, solid proof of performance, that'd knock your committee's eye out. No-one can afford to be thinking of horse-power, if they're really wanting to compete in the modern world. A horse can pull a load of ten tons along a permanent way, at a speed of five miles an hour. It can work for two hours before you need to rest it, and it can work for about eight hours a day all told, with one day in seven off if you don't want to knock it up entirely. Now a locomotive engine can draw a load of fifty tons at thirty-five miles an hour, twenty-four hours a day, seven days a week if you like, stopping only to take on water and fuel. It doesn't have to be tied up when it stops, it doesn't catch a chill if you leave it standing, it doesn't go lame or get harness galls or colic, it doesn't shy at sudden noises, or get sulky and refuse to go because the rain's blowing in its face. There's no comparison, Mr Hudson, none at all. A locomotive railway is a progressive, modern, commercial mode of transport. A horse tramway is a piece of blinkered nostalgia.'

'By God, sir, by God,' Hudson cried, his eyes gleaming under their thick lids, his fist softly pounding his palm with excitement, 'I wish my committee could hear you! You would convince a dead man! I wish you could address a public meeting on our behalf. Our waverers have been got at by the horse interest – you know the sort of thing—'

'Indeed I do,' said Stephenson feelingly.

'– but you would have them round in an instant. I don't doubt but you'd have the horse interest over as well!'

They had talked on while the level in the decanter

sank and the smoke from the cigars lay in blue strata to the ceiling. Discussing the intransigence of the horse interest, Stephenson had touched on something which had set Benedict's mind in motion.

'I don't believe the railway will spell the end of horse-power altogether,' he had said. 'Oh, it'll make a difference at first, I grant you, with the post houses closing and the stages and mails going out of business. The landowners that grow the fodder and breed the horses may feel a loss in the short run – though I'm not even convinced of that. But the railways will only run from town to town, not from village to village, and how will folk get from their village to the railway station? By horse. And how will the goods brought to the town get from the railway station to the shops and houses? By horse. It seems to me that every railway journey will involve a bit of a horse journey at one end or the other, more likely both; and it's just simple mathematics that if you multiply the number of journeys being made by a hundred or a thousand – and it could be more – you'll end up needing more horses, not fewer.'

The logic of the argument made absolute sense to Benedict, though he could see it was not something that could easily be put across to the average person, used to thinking only in concrete terms and about what was familiar. The harness-maker who made and mended the harness for a local post house would not be able to see beyond the closing of that establishment because of the coming of the railway. Experience alone could convince him that his work would increase: you would never get him to vote for an abstract idea. But Bendy could see vividly that a train arriving in York from London carrying, say, a hundred people, would require perhaps fifty horses to get them from the station to wherever they were ultimately going. He could envisage a line of cabriolets waiting outside the station to convey people who, without the railway, would not be there at all, would have stayed at home, creating no business, spending no money – needing no Yorkshire horses. That line of cabs meant work for coach-makers, upholsterers, harness-makers, wheelwrights, for blacksmiths, horse-dealers and breakers, corn-merchants, farriers, for drivers and ostlers, for whip-makers and hatters – an almost endless list, right down to the dung-collector and the ironmonger who made his shovel and bucket. And the increased and more widespread transit of goods would create a similar pyramid of horse-consuming occupation. But he knew it would be next to impossible to paint that picture so that Willans or Peckitt or Obadiah could see it. As some people were tone-deaf, and could hear dogs barking but not the music of Mozart, so the average small proprietor was deaf to all but the common sounds of the business he was accustomed to.

The meeting between the two Georges had ended with an undertaking on Stephenson's part to interest himself in Hudson's railway scheme at least to the extent of coming and addressing a meeting some time, thus adding the weight of his name and his reputation to the scales of persuasion. 'When you've got a proper proposal to put – with locomotive power – then I'll come and speak for you.'

Nothing was going to happen for some time, however – that much was obvious. The railway might be a burning interest with Hudson, but it was not his only one. There was to be a General Election in the autumn, and Hudson meant to renew his efforts on behalf of the Tory party – 'Lowther or bust!' – which would take up so much of his time and energy, he would not even be able to think about railways until next year; and without his driving force, the Committee would trickle ineffectually like a meandering stream, and decide nothing. So it seemed inevitable that Benedict would have to leave the environs of York to seek work with Robert Stephenson. He was only half sorry – the thought of working on such an undertaking

197

as the London and Birmingham was thrilling indeed –
but when the sorry half came uppermost in his mind, he
was very sorry indeed. To part with Miss Fleetham! The
idea made him frantic.

From across the room, Liza's voice interrupted his
thoughts. She spoke quietly, for the baby was asleep in
a crib at the foot of the bed, and she spoke uncannily to
the point, as if she had heard what he was thinking.

'This woman – are you going to marry her?'

He looked at her, startled. She was sitting on the edge
of the bed in her nightgown, and she was not looking at
him, but at her hands, clasped between her knees. He
knew perfectly well what she was talking about, and yet
he was so at a loss for an answer he could only repeat
stupidly, 'Woman?'

'I suppose I should have said "lady". I'm sorry.' Now
she looked up, but her eyes did not quite contact his. He
knew her well enough to know she was in the grip of a
strong emotion, but what emotion he could not guess.
'Are you going to marry that lady?'

'How do you— ?' he began, but then realised he
probably didn't want to know how she knew. 'I don't
know,' was all he could honestly answer.

'But you want to – you mean to?'

'I – yes, I mean to ask her. I don't know what she'll
say.' She looked down at her hands again, as if that was
all there was to know. 'I will take care of you,' he said.

'I know,' she said. 'You always have, and much more
than we deserve.' A little pause, and then she said, very
low, as if it had escaped her against her will, 'What will
become of us, me and the child?'

'What would you like to happen?' She didn't answer,
and he tried again. 'Would you like to go back to your
own people?'

'I have no people,' she said – quite simply, a statement
of fact.

'Your own country, I mean. Leicestershire.'

She shook her head. 'I would like—' she began, and stopped, as though she had dared too much, and then dared again. 'I would like to see you sometimes. I don't want never to see you again.'

'Of course,' he said awkwardly, 'of course I would come when I could.'

'To see Tommy,' she said quickly, looking up at him eagerly as if it were a clinching argument.

'And to see you,' he felt constrained to add. But it was not true, not any more.

She shook her head again. 'I always knew you would marry one day,' she said, as though explaining it to him. 'I knew that from the beginning. But Tommy – you'll want to see him now and then.'

'I'll provide for you both,' he said, desperate for something positive to say to her. In the bending candlelight her face looked fantastic, one half young and rounded, the other half, the shadowed half, like a death's head of cold hollows.

Her lips parted as if she would say something else, but then she got up and went round to the other side of the bed and climbed in, as if nothing of any moment had been said, and he had no idea whether it was a superb piece of play-acting, or if he had really fulfilled all she had hoped and expected of him. It was foolish to expect her to feel the same way about things as he thought he would in her position, he told himself as he climbed into bed too and blew out the candle. She was from a different world, had no education, was unaccustomed to analytical thinking or self-examination. Probably he refined too much on the situation. Even had she married, the best a girl of her background could ever have hoped for was a roof over her head, food for her and her child, and a man who did not beat her – and he had already given her so much more than that.

But tenderness for her claimed him even so, and when he reached for her in the dark she responded to him willingly, so that physical passion was aroused as well. When he had done, he felt satisfied and pleasantly sleepy, and grateful to her on both counts. He drew her into his arms and held her, as he knew – though she had never said so – that she liked him to do, and stroked her hair. Through his sleepiness he felt her wakeful: the lines of her body were still taut. She was thinking, and he could only guess what about. But after a while she sighed, not unhappily, and relaxed against him. Then he asked, feeling safe at last to do so.

'How did you know?'

Her answer came promptly. 'Sometimes you smell of her. She must put perfume on her hand, so it comes off when you shake it.'

He contemplated the idea, fascinated. What wile would women think of next? He adored Miss Fleetham's perfume, but thought it was his imagination that he smelled it when she was not present. Thinking of her, he almost drifted off into sleep; and on the edge of sleep another small sentence came quietly out of the dark from the woman lying with him.

'I'd have known anyway.'

CHAPTER TEN

Coming out of the steward's room, Nicholas saw that the chapel door was ajar. He stopped and looked at it with a faint shiver of horror as dark shapes stirred in the back of his mind; but then he thrust them down and made himself walk forward to investigate. No supernatural forces were at work: someone was in there, that was all. Minna pushed past him as he hesitated on the threshhold, and so he knew who it was. Minna had taken very kindly to Aglaea, to the extent that Nicholas felt jealous that his dog should fawn over someone else in that way.

As he stepped down into the chapel, the familiar sense of dread took hold of him. It was like cold nausea. He hated the chapel, with its smell of stale incense and dankness, but it frightened him too. That was why he had not shut it up, though the priest had departed when his mother died. He had a senseless fear of what might breed in the darkness behind locked doors, so the doors were left unlocked and the sanctuary lamp was kept burning by his orders. But as far as he knew, no-one went in there, except for the servant who refilled the lamp. All the old servants were gone now, and the new ones that Ferrars had recruited were not devout.

What was Aglaea doing in here? Exploring? She had done some of that since they came back from Scarborough: he had found her one day inspecting the family portraits in the Long Saloon, examining them one by one with grave attention as though she meant to catalogue them for a guide book. He had quite enjoyed telling her the background to them, old family stories about his ancestors which he had heard from his mother. It was pleasant so to be reminded that the Morlands had been important people when the Ansteys were still peasants. Aglaea had been suitably impressed with her good fortune in marrying into such a clan.

He stepped forward and looked around, and a fresh shiver touched his spine. She was in the Lady chapel. The candles were alight on the Lady altar, and there were flowers there, too: green stuff – myrtle, perhaps – and some late rosebuds which would never open, not at this time of year. Aglaea was just sitting there, staring ahead of her. His mother had used to sit like that, too, except that she had been conducting long inward conversations with the Lady. Aglaea could not be praying, surely? The Ansteys were sturdy, no-nonsense Protestants, with the Protestant dislike of anything that smacked of idolatry or Enthusiasm. They would sooner be hanged than caught praying outside hours. Nicholas began walking forward, angry, but reluctant. He didn't like to see Aglaea there – he wanted to make her leave – but there was something about the Lady chapel that made him walk on tiptoe. The wooden statue of the Virgin which stood on the altar was so old, so old; it made him shiver. There was a legend that when some disaster threatened the house, it wept real tears. There were many places in the house where he felt that there were eyes on him, the shades of his ancestors, perhaps, watching him critically, but he felt it here most of all. What had his mother told the Lady about him, in those long, long conversations of theirs? And the Lady – she must know plenty that his mother had never discovered. If she wanted her revenge, she had not far to reach. He must get Aglaea away from there.

Minna had reached her, touched Aglaea's hand with her cold nose and made her jump. She turned to look, saw Nicky, smiled; and then the smile faded as she saw his expression.

'What are you doing?' he asked – it came out in a whisper, though he had meant to sound stern.

'Just – just sitting,' she said nervously. 'I like it here.'

'Did you light the candles?'

'It seemed so dark without them. Was it wrong? I wanted to look at the fan tracery. It's such a beautiful ceiling.'

His scalp hairs settled down a little. If she were only admiring the architecture . . . 'It's fine work. But I don't like it in here. The smell makes me queasy. It always did, even when I was a child.'

'I'm sorry,' she said, getting up, always obedient to his wishes. He hurried out, trying not to run, and she followed him, and watched as he dragged the heavy door shut behind them, with a hollow slam like the slab dropping back onto a tomb. She could see that he was really upset: he was breathing fast, and there was a sheen of moisture on his face, though it was cold in the corridor here.

'What's the matter?' she asked, and then, 'I'm sorry if I did something wrong.'

'I don't want you going in there any more,' Nicky said; and then, hearing his own voice, he tried to speak more naturally, 'You shouldn't sit in there like that – it isn't healthy. You'll take cold. The – the air is very bad in these old chapels.'

She knew his health was delicate, and his concern seemed reasonable to her. 'Is that why you don't have a chaplain any more? It seems a pity to lose the old traditions, though. Your mother—'

'My mother was a papist,' he snapped. 'There was much too much of that sort of thing in the house in her time. Your family goes to church on Sunday, and that's that.'

'Yes,' she assented meekly. 'Though when Mama was alive we used to have daily prayers too.'

'That was different. That was in the drawing-room, and one of the family spoke them, not a priest.' But his control was returning, and he spoke more reasonably. Now he was out of the place with the door shut, he felt safer; normality was intruding into the nightmare. 'Well,' he said politely, 'and what do you do today, Mrs Morland?'

She hesitated. She could hear from his voice that the question was the precurser to dismissal. He might be busy – but moments alone with him were hard to come by, and she was loath the waste this one. 'There is something I would like to talk to you about, if you would spare me a moment.'

He looked at her askance, as one might eye a plum that probably had a wasp inside it. 'Come into the steward's room, then,' he said at last, his terseness concealing apprehension. So far, since they had come back from their wedding-trip, everything had been remarkably easy. He had hardly known he had a wife, except that when he dined at home, she sat at the other end of the table from him. Otherwise, he hardly saw her. He breakfasted before she was up and was out most of the day about his own tasks; he went in to York on business and to his club as before, and dined there when he felt like company. The only difference had been that he had not had any of his carousing evenings at home, and he had not visited any of those other places – places like The Willow Tree. He felt an awkwardness about that, now that he was a married man.

Still, even contemplating his virtue had a satisfaction about it. He had liked knowing that she was there when he wanted someone to talk to, and he had enjoyed her company in the evenings after dinner. Once or twice she had played the pianoforte for him, and they had even had a game of cribbage once – though that evening had not ended well, he remembered, because he had tried to teach her piquet, but she was too stupid to learn it.

But he had a nervous notion it was about the sleeping

arrangements that she might be about to beard him. At the very beginning he had tried sharing the Great Bedchamber with her. His parents had always slept there together; but he had found that in the ancient, traditional embrace of the Butts Bed, where he and generations of Morlands before him had been conceived and born, he was even less able to contemplate the carnal act than he had been at Scarborough. Perhaps it was a mistake to have gone along with the tradition. The Great Bedchamber was so much his mother's place, the bed his mother's bed, the furniture hers – there seemed even a lingering odour of her lavender sachet about the room – that it felt like a violation even to be contemplating fleshly activities there.

And Aglaea – she was too like his mother. Oh, not in looks, of course not, but in the *spirit* of her. She was pure and good, and he had never done it with a pure and good woman before. All his sexual experience had been with women and girls of the lower orders, prostitutes either paid or unpaid, defiled women whom it was no sin to defile further. But to do such things with a decent woman of his own class – it was unthinkable, and his manhood shrivelled before the enormity of it. It would have been like doing it to his mother. It was simply not – not possible.

Even sleeping in the same bed with Aglaea had begun to make him uncomfortable, and seeing her in her *déshabille* made him feel as though he had peeped through a keyhole to watch his mother undressing. It was all wrong. And so after an uneasy fortnight, he had moved back into his own bedroom, the North Bedroom, where he had slept before his marriage, leaving the Great Bedchamber to Aglaea. He had offered her no explanation, and she had asked for none – the most comfortable thing about her was the way she simply accepted things without comment – but he was horribly afraid it was all about to catch up with him.

In the steward's room, with the door closed behind them, he faced her sternly, with an intimidating frown which he hoped might even yet stave off the worst of disasters, by nipping any unwelcome curiosity in the bud.

'Well?' he snapped. 'What is it?'

Aglaea folded her hands together before her to keep them still. Almost she wished she hadn't begun this. 'It's about – about my place here,' she began with difficulty.

'Your place?'

She nodded. 'I don't know, you see, what I am supposed to do. When I was at home – I mean, before I was married – I had my own tasks about the household. I was brought up to be useful. Mama taught me housekeeping, so that when I was married, I would be able to run my husband's household efficiently.'

Nicholas began to relax. It looked as though the feared storm was not coming his way after all. 'Your mama did not expect you to marry as high as you did,' he said benignly. 'As a merchant's wife, perhaps you would have had to run the household. Here at Morland Place we have servants to do it.'

Aglaea persevered anxiously. 'I do see that, but am I not even to direct the servants? I feel I should do something, but if I try to speak to Mrs Moon she refers me to Ferrars, and Ferrars—' She stopped. She was afraid of Ferrars, that was the beginning and end of it.

'Ferrars is steward here, and directs everything, both in the household and on the estate. There is nothing for you to do. In fact,' he grew bold, seeing how uncertain she was, 'it would greatly offend the servants if you were to try to interfere.'

She flinched at the harsh word. 'Am I then to live a life of no purpose? I hoped to make your home comfortable for you, but others do that.' She was about to add a word about having hoped to be a mother to Nicholas's ward, but seeing his frown, held it back. The one time she had visited the schoolroom, she had been comprehensively rebuffed by Miss Smith, and Ferrars had come to her afterwards to request that she did not interrupt Miss Skelwith's regime unless requested to do so by the Master. She had assumed the rebuke had come from Nicholas, and did not care to provoke another.

He said coldly, 'Let me tell you, there's many a woman who would envy you your freedom from care. Perhaps I should have married one of them instead.'

Her hands fluttered anxiously. 'Oh, please, don't think – I am truly grateful to you, and I would not dream of going against your wishes in anything. Indeed I would not. But it seems to me that you would have been just as well off without me. I'm afraid I don't seem to make any difference to your life.'

'Nonsense,' he said, trying for a smile. 'Why you – you cut and arrange all the flowers. And you keep me company in the evenings and grace my dinner table—'

'But I do not order the meals,' she said nervously. 'Even when we gave our dinner party, I was not consulted about the menu.'

Any minute now, she would be complaining that he did not dine often enough at home! He wished he had not stopped to listen to her. He wanted to escape as soon as possible. 'You seem to have a mighty list of complaints, madam,' he snapped petulantly. 'But if you had a better understanding of your new rank, you would not be keeping me from my work only to complain that you are ill-treated!'

'Oh no – pray—!' She was stricken with remorse. 'I do not complain, I assure you! It is only my foolish ignorance. I do not properly understand what I am to do with myself day by day.'

'Anything you want to, of course,' he said. 'You have your drawing and painting and – and sewing and so forth. You have the gardens to walk in and the estate to ride over. What more can you want?'

She hung her head, ashamed of having annoyed him. The sight of her humility excited him in a strange way. It

207

made him want to subdue her more, to strike again where he had so obviously caused her pain. He breathed more quickly, and his hands clenched and unclenched down at his sides as he reined in his passion, to guide it better.

'Now, if you have no more complaints, I'm afraid I must terminate this delightful interview,' he said, and heard his voice trembling with the force of his control. 'I have a great deal of important business to attend to. Pray don't trouble me in this way again, Mrs Morland. If you cannot amuse yourself with all the resources of this house at your disposal, I fear *I* cannot help you.'

With the last cutting words he walked triumphantly past her and out of the steward's room, leaving her – he hoped – in tears. It was when he got to the Great Hall and discovered that Minna had not followed him that the reaction set in. He had behaved badly; Aglaea was a good, gentle woman – and a gentlewoman – and he had hurt her. His triumph seeped away, he felt the beginning of shame, and as always when shame attacked him he fought back, whipping up resentment as a defence against what he could not bear – self-criticism. What had he done to deserve this? he asked himself. He had thought he had a docile and loving wife, a helpmeet, but she was turning out to be troublesome after all. Wasn't it enough that he was plagued with work and worries all day long – and his health never of the best – without having to bear the added burden of a nagging wife? He didn't ask much out of life, he thought pathetically – just a little sympathy, and to have his wants – simple and few as they were – regarded. He worked his fingers to the bone to provide her with every luxury, and instead of being grateful she complained that – that – he paused a moment to try to remember what it was she had complained of, but it had passed from his mind, leaving only a general resentment against her.

Well, by God, he was not going to take it lying down! He would show her! He would show them all. They were

208

all against him, but he was not going to be anyone's dupe, anyone's puppet. He was Master of Morland Place, and he could do anything he liked. He cracked his knuckles and strode towards the door. He would just ride out of here and go into York and – and—

At the top of the steps he paused, seeing Ferrars walking across the yard from his quarters – the apartment in the gatehouse, over the barbican – towards the house. Ha, there was another conspirator! Nicky thought. He hated Ferrars. He hated being under his eye, hated that sly, knowing look that reminded him that Ferrars knew his secrets. Most of all he hated the feeling of helplessness, of knowing that he could not get rid of him. Well, he could get away from him for a time, if nothing else. A pleasant image was in the back of his mind, of the sound of pliant canes cracking against taut, springy flesh, of a rosy blush overspreading the nacreous curve of young buttocks. He had been celibate for a long time, and it wasn't natural in a young man, he thought. He had his needs, just as everyone had.

'Oh, Ferrars,' he said as loftily as he could, to forestall argument, 'I am going into York. I – I have one or two things to do. I shall probably not be back tonight. In fact, I certainly shall not. I will stay at my club, so you may close the gate at sunset.'

Ferrars bowed obediently in reply, but as he watched his master walk away, his face relaxed into an unpleasant smile. So it was starting already, he thought. The honeymoon was over. He knew that expression on Nicholas's face, that tone in his voice. He was not coming back tonight: he was going to Straker's Passage, or perhaps to the place in Dixon's Yard, which was lower and dirtier, and sometimes suited the Master's mood better. Well and good! The last thing Ferrars wanted was a dutiful husband in the control of a virtuous wife; but it looked as though this wife had very little influence over her husband. All in all, a satisfactory outcome, the best that could be hoped for, if the Master had to marry at all – and if he hadn't married, there would always have been women on the catch for him, whereas now they would leave him alone.

And if he could detach Mrs Morland from her inquisitive relatives, it would be even better. Ferrars pursed his lips soundlessly as he walked towards the house. It was one of the minor irritations of his life that he could not – had never been able to – whistle. Mrs Moon said it was the mark of the Devil, for a man not to be able to whistle.

It had not been possible for Benedict to secure an interview with Miss Fleetham, and now time was running out. He had been kept horribly busy ever since his return from Whitby, even working every Sunday, and frequently having to bed down on a paliasse in the back of a waggon instead of going home at night. Everything was moving so fast that he felt his life had run out of control. He cursed the restrictions of polite society which meant he could not write to Miss Fleetham, nor arrange a meeting with her, even for the very proper purpose of asking her to marry him. He could have approached her father in the old-fashioned way, but for one thing, he felt that a modern young woman like Miss Fleetham would resent not being asked for her views first; and for another, he wanted to get some idea of how her father regarded him, before he risked his neck.

The chance came at last, as chances often do, when he was not prepared for it, at the August race meeting. It was his first knock-off day in weeks, and Sir Carlton Miniott had invited him to share his box at the racecourse. Sir Carlton said with a charmingly self-deprecating smile that he wanted the advantage of Benedict's Morland eye for horses, to pick the winners for him. Benedict accepted the invitation gladly, though afterwards, thoroughly exhausted by work, he did think that it might have been wiser to spend his knock-off day in bed asleep. Liza's brother Dick had promised to take her to the fair at Milford, and their nextdoor neighbour, an elderly ditcher's widow, had promised to take care of the baby, so the house would be quiet. But the races were in his blood, after all, and chances to catch up with sleep would present themselves sooner or later, whereas the great race meeting happened only once a year – and who knew where he would be next year? So he went.

Being in Sir Carlton's box was a good way of meeting people, for a great many came up to pay their respects – Lord Howick, Lord Lambert, the Coweys and the Chubbs – Henry Bayliss the newspaper proprietor – 'Young' Mr Pobgee and his son – George Hudson, florid in the heat and talking loudly about the coming elections.

'We'll do it this time, don't you worry. Don't waste your time voting for Anstey, young Morland! Brother-in-law he may be, but the Whigs have won their last election in this town, I give you my word!'

'I don't have the vote, Mr Hudson,' Benedict reminded him gravely.

'Eh? Oh, no more you do. Well then, Miniott, what about you? Eh, I tell you what, young Morland – you might have a bit on my man, do yourself a bit of good! Mortimer at the Maccabbees is running a book, and he was offering fives this morning on Lowther. I should get a bit of that if I was you – the odds are bound to shorten.' He winked solemnly, showing his bad teeth in a rare grin. 'Mortimer's been got at, I fancy, by the Anstey interest. But I can assure you my man will win.'

'You mean you'll see he does,' Miniott said with a shake of the head. 'One day you'll come a cropper, Hudson, I warn you.'

'Nay, I'm light on ma feet, I always dance away,' Hudson said airily. 'By the by, Morland, there's an old friend of yours here today. I saw her over yonder, by the refreshment tent.' He jerked his head. Benedict heard the pronoun with a fluttering heart. Miss Fleetham here? Well, there was no reason why not. Perhaps he might get the chance to speak to her at last. Hudson was eyeing him closely, as if reading his thoughts without effort. 'Mrs Makepeace, I mean, o'course,' he said with a sly smile. 'You should go and have a word wi'er. She's looking as handsome as ever, I warrant ye.'

Benedict blushed hotly and could think of nothing to say. Sir Carlton, watching his face with interest and some sympathy, turned the conversation gracefully to allow him time to recover, and then asked him politely if he would be so kind as to go and place a bet for him on the next race. Bendy took the proffered money and gratefully made his escape. He felt a little embarrassed about Mrs Makepeace. Their affair had been torrid, and the last time he had seen her – the day before Nicky drove him from his home – he had been pressing her to marry him. Of course, he had been young and foolish – incredibly foolish, it seemed to him from his present eminence of maturity – and she had known it, and laughed off his proposals of marriage with a kindly grace. But he had never seen her since, and he thought she must know he was back in the district, and perhaps be hurt that he did not so much as pay his respects. He had little idea of the etiquette of the situation – what courtesies did one owe to an ex-mistress? – but in sheer kindness he felt he ought at least to have sent her a note. She had been good to him, and he felt he had not acknowledged it.

Still, it would be too embarrassing to approach her now, after all this time. Whether she were resentful or indifferent, it would put him out of countenance, and he was glad of the excuse to head in the opposite direction from the refreshment tent to place Sir Carlton's bet. He had only just finished that thought when he rounded the corner of the stand and almost walked straight into her.

She was standing with another young woman whom Bendy did not recognise: under the shade of Mrs

Makepeace's parasol they had their heads together over the race-card. He could not even creep away, for his sudden eruption made them look up. The younger woman eyed him with mild interest as a well-looking male stranger, but the widow seemed to grow very still, and her eyes widened, as though she were facing some unknown danger.

There was nothing for it. Bendy swept off his hat, bowed, smiled. 'How do you do, ma'am? What a surprise to see you here – a pleasant surprise, I hasten to add.'

The words seemed to hang on the air, and Benedict would have caught them back if he could. He sounded like a cad. But what else could he say? The presence of the other woman was inhibiting. As if she realised this, Mrs Makepeace turned to her companion and murmured something, and with a look and something like a shrug the girl turned her back and walked off a few paces. Now at least he had privacy to make an ass of himself, Bendy thought. He had been right about the embarrassment, though. Face to face with his ex-mistress he found himself comparing her with Miss Fleetham, and noticing her age and fullness of figure with disfavour. There were lines in her face and around her eyes, and her waist looked twice as thick as Miss Fleetham's – she looked almost stout. Her hair was as burningly red-gold as before, but he did not care for the way she had dressed it, and he couldn't help feeling there was something rather vulgar about the colour, especially compared with the pure guinea-gold of Miss Fleetham's. But she couldn't have changed so very much in four years, he told himself, and therefore it must be he who had changed. He despised himself for it, hated the fickleness of his own heart, but he could not help wondering what he had ever seen in her.

'Mr Morland,' she said now, since one of them must speak. 'I had heard that you were back.'

He felt himself blushing. 'I – yes – for some months now. I ought to have written – or come to see you—'

She raised a hand slightly to stop him. 'I didn't expect it.' She smiled, intending to reassure him, though to him it looked a troubled smile. 'You need not be afraid of me. I was glad when I heard you had come back, for it suggested all was well with you, and I worried very much when you went away. But our lives have moved on; I did not expect to see you again on the same terms.'

'You are very good,' he mumbled, ashamed. 'You always were. I ought to have thought – I should have written.'

She laid her hand on his arm: shielded from view by their two bodies, it was a discreet gesture. 'Oh, Bendy, I always told you you would grow out of me, and you have. It's natural. Don't reproach yourself, my dear. You gave me great happiness, and I have nothing but fond memories of our time together. I don't expect you to have me on your conscience for the rest of your life!'

He raised his eyes to hers, his face burning with a shame she had only made worse by her generosity. Now he remembered why he had loved her. 'I've treated you badly,' he said.

'Nonsense,' she said robustly. 'Don't talk of it any more, but tell me, how are things between you and your brother?'

Bendy shrugged. 'He hates me – I don't know why. It's hard to believe he still thinks I was guilty of those things I was accused of, but I can't think of any other reason. He seems to believe I'm a hardened villain.'

She looked grave. 'My dear, you allowed yourself to be accused rather than name me. If I had known, I would not have let it happen. As soon as I did know, I did what I could to put the record straight. I saw your mother—'

He started. 'What?'

'I met her by chance in the street, and asked her for the favour of an interview. I told her everything I knew about the business – including the fact that you were with me

214

at the time of the supposed crime, and therefore must be innocent. She believed me.'

'But how could you do such a thing?' he cried in distress. 'It was to save her from the shock of knowing that I went away.'

She shook her head at him. 'You think women are made of paper! We are rational beings, usually a great deal stronger in our minds than you men. Your mother wasn't endangered by the shock, as you call it. She knew what men were. Good God, she was married to your father long enough!' She stopped herself abruptly.

'What about my father?' he said suspiciously.

'Nothing at all,' she said hastily. It was common knowledge to her generation what kind of man James Morland had been, but probably Bendy did not know. 'I only meant that as a married woman she understood the nature of men. The important thing, Bendy, is that she believed your innocence. I think she meant to clear the whole matter up, but she was taken ill the very next day, and died before anything could be done. But I am sure – perfectly sure – that she meant to bring you back home and reinstate you. That is what I wanted you to know, my dear – that your mother knew everything. She died believing your innocence.'

He felt absurdly like crying, and swallowed once or twice before he could speak. 'Thank you,' he said. 'It does help to know that. Thank you for telling me. I only wish my brother knew it too.'

She opened her mouth to speak and then changed her mind. She withdrew her hand from his arm, preparing to depart. 'We should not stand talking like this any longer. You have your reputation to consider.'

He smiled a little uncomfortably. 'I don't think of that,' he said gallantly.

'Then you should. Goodbye, my dear. Think kindly of me now and then. But if we meet again in public, remember I am only the proprietor of a drapery shop which you sometimes patronise, nothing more. Give me just such a nod as you give shopkeepers, and pass on.'

He almost let her go. 'Serena!' She half turned, but he could not say what he had been going to say. Instead he blurted clumsily, 'I am going away soon. I may not come back.'

She looked at him for a long moment consideringly, and then said, 'Be careful of your brother. I think – I think he is not a good man.' And then she really did go, gathered up her friend and walked off with her arm in arm, disappearing into the crowd.

Bendy turned the other way, towards the book-makers, and threaded his way through the crowds, puzzling a little over her last comment. Nicky's animosity towards him was strange and hurtful, but he hardly needed to be ware of him; there was nothing Nicky could do to hurt him, beyond treating him coldly in public, and Bendy was resigned to that. Indeed, working on the railway amongst rough, sometimes violent and always uncultured navvies, he had learned to ignore the foulest abuse and sometimes even to dodge blows. The worst Nicky could say to him could hardly match that.

He was so deep in thought that he almost walked into the Phillips party without seeing it, though it was making enough noise. At the centre of it was a uniformed Ned Phillips, on furlough from his regiment, his every word being hung upon by two adoring sisters, his every glance directed in hopeless admiration towards Miss Fleetham. Several other young men and women were attached to the group, over which Mrs Phillips exercised her usual vague chaperonage, when she could spare the attention from the conversation of her bosom friend, Mrs Sedley Walker.

Brooding thoughts of Serena were vanquished as Bendy was absorbed into the group, greeted with noisy enthusiasm, and solicited for his opinion about the result of the forthcoming race. He was reminded that he still had to place Sir Carlton's bet for him, and began to excuse himself, but when Miss Fleetham wondered aloud how the placing of a bet was done, he discovered an unexpected quickness of wit in himself and invited her to go with him and see.

Miss Fleetham appealed to Mrs Phillips. 'Papa is off talking to his friends and won't be back for hours, so you must be the arbiter, dear ma'am. May I go? Do say yes – I should dearly love to know how to place a bet. Think how useful I shall be to all of you for the rest of the day!'

Mrs Phillips, her attention dragged from the thrilling story of Mrs Sedley Walker's daughter's confinement, looked around her and then up at the sky as though seeking Divine direction, and since none was forthcoming was forced to rely on her own wits. 'I'm sure there is no harm in it, my dear, in such a crowd,' she said. It could hardly count as being alone with Mr Morland, she told herself, when there were several hundred people pressing all about them. 'But come straight back – don't go wandering off.'

'I'll bring her back safe and sound, ma'am, don't worry,' said Benedict, offering Miss Fleetham his arm. She took it, gave her parasol a jaunty twirl, glanced back to observe the effect on the rest of the group, and walked off with him.

Benedict could hardly wait to get out of earshot. Her perfume was making his head swim. She was so beautiful, so elegant, dressed today in a dark navy-blue silk taffeta mantle and a matching bonnet with a ruched silk lining of pale sky blue, which set off the glorious gold of her hair and the fairness of her complexion. The narrow hanging ends of the mantle were tucked into the buckled belt of her muslin gown, as was the fashion that year, and he marvelled at the smallness of the waist within that narrow span. Her exquisite features, her daintiness, her tiny feet and slender hands, the pure unsullied gold of her hair – she was like a creature from another sphere, and he felt himself the object of every man's envy for having her on his arm. He wanted more than anything in the world to possess her, and knowing how few his chances of being alone with her, decided that this one must do. She had come with him with such complicit eagerness that he was filled with a rather shaky hope.

'Oh, I am glad to get away from them for a moment,' she was saying cheerfully. 'I do love the Phillipses, they are the dearest people, but sometimes one can have enough of them. I believe I am naturally more thoughtful than other people, and to be always in noisy company oppresses me. Some people cannot bear to be alone,' she added with a light laugh, 'but I must confess I relish it. I have such resources within me that I never notice the time pass when I am alone.'

'I'm sure you need never be alone unless you wish to,' Bendy said. 'Everyone must want to be with you.'

'Ned Phillips was just saying the very same thing. He is such a rattle, it is vastly amusing, but underneath I believe he has grown more thoughtful since he went away. His sisters don't notice it, but I am more sensitive than some people. There were times when he stood quite silent for minutes at a time, staring directly at me, his thoughts, I am sure, a thousand miles away. I confess I was quite embarrassed to have him stare at me so pointedly, but I believe his mind was quite on other things and he had not a notion how he was putting me out of countenance.'

Bendy shook his head. 'No-one who had the privilege of looking at you could have their thoughts elsewhere,' he said gravely. 'That would be impossible. Poor Ned, I'm afraid, must have been bemused, like a moth before a flame.'

She looked sidelong at him from under her eyelashes. 'Why, Mr Morland, I did not take you for a courtier! I had always hoped to hear nothing but the plain truth from you. Men are such idle flatterers! Pray do not go the same way. I depend on you not to bamboozle me.'

'I assure you I do not flatter. What I say is the plain truth. Miss Fleetham,' he gathered his courage and the correct vocabulary, and plunged on, 'I beg you to allow me to tell you how violently I love you!'

'Really, Mr Morland, I don't know that I should,' she said with a smile. But it was not a scornful smile – indeed, it seemed almost inviting – so he went on.

'I know this is not the best of places to make such a declaration, but it's so difficult to find the opportunity that I must take my chance. I have loved you since I first laid eyes on you. I think you must have noticed by now what my feelings are towards you – I haven't tried to disguise them, and you are, as you rightly say, a person of great sensibility.'

'I thought perhaps you preferred me a little,' she said modestly.

'I love you,' he said urgently, 'with all my heart and soul! Miss Fleetham, I beg you only to let me know whether I may speak to you further – whether it will be agreeable to you. I know that your father must be consulted, but I would not – will not – speak another word unless I know you do not dislike it.'

She lowered the dark fans of her eyelashes modestly to her blooming cheek and said, 'Pray go on, Mr Morland. I will hear you with the greatest pleasure.'

He heard her words with a leap of excitement which took away his breath for a moment, and he had to wait and assemble his words before he could begin. Then he told her, in what he felt was a logical order, about the Leeds and Selby contract finishing, and how he had written to Mr Robert Stephenson, and how Mr Stepehenson had offered him a position as an assistant district engineer on one of the sections of the London and Birmingham railway. After the first few words Miss Fleetham's eyes opened with a look of surprise, to which was shortly added the beginning of a frown. She did not seem to be hearing him with great rapture, and afraid she had not fully understood the position he had been offered, he hastened to elaborate.

'He's dividing the work into four sections, you see, each under an engineer, and the sections will be further divided into districts of about six miles of line each, together with separate contracts where there is a particularly difficult piece of work – like the Kilsby Tunnel, for instance. The engineers will have complete control over their own section, and the assistants, under them, over their own district. So you see it will be an important job, and it will mean I am fixed in one place, rather than travelling from one section to another all the time.'

'Well, and do you mean to accept this – this *job*?' she asked fretfully as he paused for breath.

He was surprised. 'It is a great advance in my career. I am to be assigned to the Tring cutting – an enormous undertaking, and a very great responsibility. It is an honour to be asked.' He saw this did not mean anything to her, which was understandable enough. He went on more specifically. 'The salary will be correspondingly generous, and I shall be able to take a house, and therefore – well, I shall be in a position to provide a home for – for a wife.'

There was a pause while he waited for Miss Fleetham's reply, and when he saw that she was not looking delighted with what he had said so far, he was plunged into reaction. Had he expressed himself clumsily, and offended her?

After a moment she said, 'Well, Mr Morland, and what is all this to me? This – this engineering talk might as well be a foreign language as far as I am concerned.'

He felt hot with chagrin. Had he misread the situation, mistaken her feelings? 'I beg your pardon,' he said. 'I should not have – I didn't – I thought you understood that I meant to ask you to marry me. I wouldn't have spoken if I had realised you did not care for me in that way. I have made a most embarrassing mistake. Please forgive me.'

The hand which rested on his arm tightened, and she smiled at him reassuringly. 'Pray do not be embarrassed. You were not mistaken. I do like you, Mr Morland, very much. But I do not fully understand what you propose. Pray speak plainly. I assure you I am very well disposed towards you.'

He gritted his teeth. 'In plain language, then, I love you with all my heart and wish you to be my wife. Will you marry me, Miss Fleetham?'

'When?' she asked. It was not a response he had expected, and it threw him off balance, for the question evidently did not spring from wild impatience to be his. It was a puzzled question.

'Why – as soon as you wish,' he said, puzzled in his turn. 'As soon as it is convenient to you.'

'You mean,' she said, striving for clarification, 'you want me to marry you *before* you go away to this job? Marry you and go with you?'

'Why – yes. That was my intention.'

She shook her head. 'Oh no, I don't think I would care for that. I would much sooner wait until you came back. I don't think I would care to live at this cutting place. It doesn't sound at all nice.'

He saw she had not understood. 'But I may not come back at all,' he said. 'An engineer's life is necessarily nomadic. We must go where the work is. When this contract ends – in three or four years' time – I must apply for another. Fortunately I believe I can say with assurance that I will not lack for preferment. With the Stephensons as my patrons, I hope to be able to support myself and my wife in increasing comfort.'

'But you can't mean to be an engineer for ever,' she said impatiently. 'You will come back to Morland Place.'

'Morland Place belongs to my brother.'

'But he is not strong. Everyone says he will not make old bones, and that he and his wife cannot have a child. So then *you* will inherit.'

221

He almost laughed, but stopped himself in time. 'I beg your pardon, but you have quite mistaken the situation! I am not playing at being an engineer just until I inherit my fortune. I am an engineer by profession, for my life.' He saw her brows draw together in a frown. 'Dear Miss Fleetham, I don't know how you have got the idea that I am the heir to Morland Place. Even if my brother does not have a child, even if he dies tomorrow, it will make no difference. The estate has never been entailed. That means Nicky can leave it to anyone he wants, and I assure you he will not leave it to me. He – he dislikes me, for reasons I will not trouble you with. Suffice to say I am the last person he would leave his fortune to.'

She was watching his face as he spoke with a mixture of feelings – puzzlement, disappointment, doubt, he read there – but at the end of it she looked away from him, her face became calm and inscrutable, and she said, 'I am sorry if I misunderstood the situation. I'm afraid it alters everything.'

His disappointment was so sharp that he felt almost sick. 'You mean – you mean you won't marry me?'

She twirled her parasol and gave him a faint smile. 'I mean that it is not in my power. My father would never permit it.'

'Because I am only an engineer and not the master of Morland Place?' he said, and then tried to compose himself. He would not endear himself to her by abusing her father. 'It is natural, I suppose, for him to want you to make a great match.'

'It's true, he does; but that is not all,' she said kindly. 'I am my father's only child, his only comfort now my mother is dead. I could not marry a man who would take me so far away from him. I have a duty to him – however much I might wish it otherwise.'

He stopped dead at that, and turned to face her, careless of the crowds. 'Do you mean that? Dear Miss Fleetham, *do* you care for me?'

She lowered her eyelashes. 'Yes, I do,' she said.

'You don't know how much that means to me. Even if my love for you is hopeless—'

'*Is* it?' she said quickly.

He shrugged. 'Unless I can make my fortune and come back to claim you as a gentleman of means, I must be an engineer. It's all I know how to do.'

'If you *do* make your fortune,' she said, 'you will come back, then?'

'Like a bird to its nest,' he said fervently. Then he sighed. 'But unless a miracle happened and I became very rich in a very short time, I'm afraid I would come back to find you married to someone else.'

'Well,' she said, looking down again modestly, 'that is a possibility, of course.'

'I couldn't expect you to wait,' he said.

'It would be my duty to marry,' she agreed. 'My father would need the support of my husband in his old age.'

'It hurts me to think of you married to someone else,' he said in a low, painful voice.

'Then you must make your fortune quickly,' she said. He dared to take her hand, folding it in both of his. She looked up then, their eyes met, and he saw something change in the depths of hers. Some particular and different contact between them had been made for the first time. She looked almost surprised, and her cheeks coloured unexpectedly; a violent thrill ran through him, which left him feeling hollow and weak.

'Do it quickly,' she said, and the words seemed bare, hard and undefended, like stripped bones. They came from a different place from all the other words she had spoken to him. 'Do it quickly and come back for me.'

He nodded and pressed her hand, feeling almost sick with longing for her. But how could he promise what was not in his power? He could not even say, 'I'll try', and so he said nothing.

*   *   *

When he got home, Liza and her brother were already back, and had collected Thomas on their way. Walking up the road towards the house, Bendy could see them sitting on stools outside the door, enjoying the westering sunshine. Little Tommy, sleepy at the end of a long day, was sitting in the dust at their feet watching Fand as she rolled, switching herself over to one side and then the other, rubbing the top of her head against the ground, her paws waving ridiculously in the air. She was so enjoying the process that she did not hear Bendy coming, and jumped up at the last minute to bow and yawn apologetically to him, one foolish ear turned inside out, and bits of twig and dried leaf in her coat.

Bendy stooped to sweep up his son in a welcoming embrace, and then turned to Liza and Dick, who seemed in high spirits, their faces animated, their eyes bright. 'You look as though you've had an exciting day. Was the fair very good?'

'Yes, yes it was good,' Liza said eagerly, 'but that's not it. Diccon has news! Tell him, Dicky.'

'The most wonderful thing has happened,' Dick cried. 'We met Mr Collins at the fair, and he said that he'd been talking about me to Mr Turner – do you know him?'

'No,' said Bendy. Collins was the vicar who had been teaching Dick. He had not heard of Turner.

'Well, Mr Turner's the land agent for Lord Howick at Moresby Manor. He and Mr Collins are special friends because he married Mr Collins's sister. I met him once or twice at Mr Collins's house. Anyway, Mr Turner told Mr Collins that he was looking to take on a new assistant, and that he specially wanted a young man that he could train to his ways. And what do you think? Mr Collins recommended me, and Mr Turner says he's willing to take me on for a trial.'

'Why, that's splendid news,' Bendy said, considerably surprised. Dick must have made a favourable impression on his teacher for him to have recommended a navvy boy to a position like that. 'But is it what you want to do? I thought you wanted to be a railway contractor.'

'That's my dream,' Dick said, a little embarrassed. 'But this is something real and solid. And – and the other thing needn't be lost for ever. A contractor needs money to start up, I know that. I'll earn more this way than as I am, and maybe I'll be able to save enough to be a contractor one day. But if I don't – well, I like Mr Turner, and if I work for him I'll be respectable and have a trade.'

'Well, then, I'm very pleased for you. You deserve it – you've worked really hard at your lessons.'

Dick's thin cheeks coloured. 'It's all your doing. Without you I'd be just a common ignorant horse-boy. Without you I'd probably be dead. I can never, never thank you enough.'

'All you need to do to thank me is to grow up a fine, hard-working man, as I know you will.'

Liza had been looking at him closely all this time, and as he turned to her enquiringly, she said, 'That's not all, though. There's more to it – tell him, Diccon.'

Dick cast a glance at her, and then addressed Bendy gravely. 'Well, sir, Mr Turner says there's a little cottage goes with the job – on the estate, you know. The agent has to be on hand.' Bendy nodded. 'It's a bit smaller than this one – only one room downstairs and two up – but it's sound, and it has a bit of garden at the back for beans and cabbages, and a pigsty, and room for a hen-run.'

Liza broke in and took the narrative from him. 'We thought, you see, Dicky and me, that I could go and live with him, and keep house. With his wages, and the garden, and a pig and some hens we could be comfortable—'

'And Mr Turner says there's always stuff from the estate, too – fruit and game and things – Lord Howick being a generous master.'

Dick stared at him appealingly, as though their lives and happiness were in his hands. Benedict was aware

225

that Tommy was growing heavier as he relaxed into sleep against his shoulder.

'You want to stay here when I go to Tring?' he said slowly, looking at Liza. 'You want to go and live with Dick rather than come with me?'

She looked at him piercingly for an instant, as though searching for something in his face; and then her expression became veiled. 'That's what I want.'

'You and little Tommy?'

'I'd take care of him,' Dick said eagerly. 'I'd never let him want.'

'It would be a new start for me,' Liza said, looking away into the dusk. 'Mr Turner don't know anything about me. Diccon means to tell him I'm a widow – no-one'll know any different. I'd be respectable, and bring up the boy respectable too, instead of having people look sour at me, and shake their heads.'

'I see,' said Bendy, feeling rather dazed. 'Well, if it's what you want, I am content. I'll still send you money for the boy, of course—'

'There's no need,' Liza said, with a sideways glance at Dick. This was something they had discussed, then. 'Diccon thinks we can manage all right.'

'I'll send you something,' Bendy said firmly, and after a moment she nodded.

'If you want, then.' A pause. 'You aren't angry?'

'Good God, no, I'm not angry.' He pulled himself together. 'I'm very happy for you both.' He had dreamed of being free of his responsibilities, and now they were leaving of their own accord. He could resume his bachelor life, carefree and footloose, do as he pleased, go where he liked. It was what he had wanted – so why did it make him feel sad? No Liza to hold him back – no Liza to welcome him home at the end of the day. No Tom to weight him with responsibility – no Tom to beam in blissful delight at the mere sight of him. He was afraid he was going to feel lonely without his burdens, although he could be nothing but glad at the way things had turned out. Dick was talking again, chattering happily about the little cottage and the garden and Mr Turner and the job. Bendy would rather have liked to go indoors and rest and have his supper, but he could not for the moment break into his delight. And besides, the weight of his drowsy child in his arms was a sweet weight, and he didn't want to put it down.

BOOK TWO

The Undertaking

To the tune of 'Believe me, if all those endearing young charms':

Believe me, if all those extravagant lines
They talk of so wildly today,
Were each made in the way its projector defines,
They're none of them likely to pay.

Punch, March the 8th, 1845

CHAPTER ELEVEN

One of Nicholas's young horses won the big race at the autumn meeting of 1835, and since he had had the foresight to bet on it himself, he found himself better off by more than just the prize-money. Moreover, there was a buyer already interested in purchasing the colt – a quiet, plainly dressed, well-spoken man who, Nicholas suspected, was acting on behalf of a Very Important Person Indeed. Hastings, the head man up at Twelvetrees, and Cooper, the rough rider, were both anxious that Brighteyes should be kept, for the old stallion was coming to the end of his good years. Nicholas replied that if the King wanted this particular horse, he would be prepared to dig deep for it. In vain did Hastings point out that over a lifetime at stud the colt would earn in fees ten times his purchase price, to say nothing of further possible wins at races: Nicholas insisted that a price in the hand was worth any number of fees in the bush, and that the colt might break its leg or die of colic before it had served a single mare.

The upshot was that Nicholas had a welcome roll of banknotes tucked into his pocket and the prospect of further riches to come when the sale was concluded. There were plenty of bills that needed paying, but Nicholas knew just what to do with the windfall. He had been working very hard lately, and felt ready for some merry-making, and he had not had a carouse of the old sort since the bachelor night before his wedding, well over a year ago.

So he gave his orders, issued his invitations to his old companions, and told Aglaea to go early to bed.

It was no different from his other bachelor parties – the food was indifferent and the wine plentiful – except that there were more toasts. Bumpers were raised over and over again to Brighteyes, in gratitude for restoring Nicholas to the fold, for his companions had missed him – or at least, had missed his hospitality. The room grew warm and the company noisy, but suddenly, towards the end of the meal, a silence fell. Nicholas turned to see what everyone was looking at, and saw Jemima at the open door, looking in hesitantly, to see if she would be sent away or not.

'Well now, and we was just drinking to Brighteyes,' Micky O'Rourke said with a slow smile. 'It must ha' been an incantation after all, for here's the Honorary Member herself, in person. Come in, me darlin', and join the fun!'

Jemima needed no second asking. Here was the only convivial company she had seen in sixteen months; here was the first break in the tedium of her life for she didn't know how long. Miss Smith was snoring gently in her bed in a juniper-scented cloud of oblivion. Lonely, longing for approval, and filled with the tomboyish energy of four-teen, she fell in with the group's ethos and fulfilled every request with innocent eagerness. Soon she was laughing and chattering, breaking into snatches of song and dance, grabbing food from the table and drinking wine as fast as she could. Nicholas glanced at her uneasily from time to time, thinking that anyone seeing her for the first time would be forgiven for thinking that she was quite wild. He half thought when she arrived that he ought to send her away, but he could not summon up the energy; now, some bottles later, he told himself she was amusing his guests, and it was a host's duty to provide amusement.

Roger Mattock, at the foot of the table, felt a lassitude which had come over him more and more often in recent months. Usually he put it down to his liver or the east wind; but tonight he felt oddly detached from the proceedings, and observed them with the jaundiced eye of surfeit. It was time to move on, he thought: but where could one move on to? He had tried all the vices he could think of, and all of them palled after a time. Would he be reduced to trying virtue? It was a terrifying thought.

Nicholas, looking up at that moment, caught his eye down the length of the table. He was very drunk, and it took a moment or two for it to impinge upon him that all was apparently not well down there. 'Whass marrer, Roger?' he asked tenderly. 'You look damn' miserable. Like a cow with colic.'

'I was just thinking,' Mattock said with insulting clarity, 'what dull company this is. Sin is so boring.'

Jack Cox planted his elbows on the table and leered at him. '*I* don't find it boring. I could never get bored with it. It's working for my damned living for my damned old drybones of a guv'nor that's boring.'

'I don't know how you can say that,' O'Rourke put in. 'You've never worked long enough to find out.'

Mattock shook his head kindly. 'It would be hard for you to be bored by anything, my Jack, since boredom requires some modicum of intelligence, and you haven't so much matter in your head as would clog the foot of a flea. But my mind is a powerful and sensitive instrument, and one cannot abuse it. One does not use a surgeon's scalpel to hew firewood. I am bored, my friends. I require new stimulation.'

'Something different – something a little out of the ordinary,' said Tovey, pretending to muse. 'Something fresh, let's say! Now, why does an image of bright eyes come to mind?' He stared thoughtfully along the table at Jemima, who was engaged in seeing how far across the polished surface she could flick a grape with a fingernail.

'What are you talking about, you damned dog?' Mattock asked pleasantly. 'Corrupting the innocent? You are behind-hand. I've tried that game years ago.'

'What, with Boy Jessop?' Tovey said with a curl of the lip. 'You can't count that. Boy was born corrupt: it left you with nothing to do. Now Miss Jemima is as innocent as a daisy. Isn't that so, Miss Jemima?' he raised his voice to her. 'Are you not as innocent and good as a newborn lamb?'

Jemima looked indignant. 'I am fourteen years old and nearly a half, so you can't call me a newborn lamb. And as for innocent and good – why I've been beat three times in the last week, so I can't be so very virtuous, can I?'

There was general laughter at that, though Nicholas frowned.

'Who beats you?' Cox asked with interest.

'Miss Smith, of course. But she don't beat hard,' she confessed reluctantly. 'Not like the Major when he was at school,' she added with a nod at Tovey. 'He told me when he was at Eton he got eighteen strokes once for stealing a ham.'

'No, no, it was six for the ham, six for denying it, and six for cheeking the Old Man,' Tovey corrected, amused.

'By God, Keate could whop a bit, though,' Cox said. He, Mattock and Tovey had been there at the same time, but two years apart. 'I got twelve once: a dozen strokes but only ten scars. There's accuracy for you! I showed 'em to the new boys for a ha'penny a time for three days, until they started to close up – my chamber of horrors, don't you know!' He grinned amiably at Jemima. 'Don't you wish you might go to school?'

'Not now. But I wish I might have when I was younger. I've never done anything really wicked,' she said wistfully. 'One can't, at home.'

'Now then, Roger, me buck, here's a lady after your own heart,' O'Rourke said. 'She's bored. It's our duty to try to amuse her. What do you say, Miss Jemima, to trying a new game?'

'What are you up to, you scoundrel?' Mattock asked with mild amusement.

'Oh, nothing very out of the way,' O'Rourke said. He looked round the table and saw the gleam of response in Tovey's eye. 'I believe we all have a tender interest in our fellow, if honorary, member.' He gave an ironic bow in Jemima's direction. 'We also know that our noble host is short of the readies, as always. Now don't look like that, Nicky me boy. Why else would you be selling that fine colt after its first good win instead of keeping it to add lustre to your stables? And if he's willing to sell one Brighteyes, lads, why not another? All I propose is a little auction.'

'Auction? What auction?' Nicky said, frowning. He was trying hard to concentrate, though since his eyes had lost focus he wasn't sure which O'Rourke he should be looking at.

Mattock said, 'I think he has quite a different fate in mind for the filly. Isn't that right, Morland? He means to run her in a maiden's race.'

'He'll never get her to the gate,' O'Rourke said seriously. He met Mattock's eyes. 'You know that, and I know it — and he'll know it when he's sober. So what do you say, Morland? A bird in the hand, so to speak, being worth two in the bush, what do you say to an auction now, pocket the funds, and the Devil take the hindmost. You could be dead tomorrow, after all.' He grinned suddenly. 'You don't look to me the type to make old bones. Come to that, nor does she. It's a fool's game to bet your all on a prospect as distant as the marriage of Brighteyes!'

'I don't know what you're talking about,' Nicky said, managing to rest his chin on his hand and his elbow on the table edge at the second attempt. 'What do you want to auction?'

'Miss Jemima.'

235

'Oh yes! What fun!' Jemima cried, jumping up. 'I'd like to be auctioned! Shall I parade round the ring? What do I have to do?'

Jack Cox looked from O'Rourke to Morland to Mattock. 'Wait now, you don't mean it? Morland, you ain't serious?'

'If the girl's willing,' Tovey said indifferently, his lowered eyelids hiding his expression.

'What would I have to do?' Jemima asked again, looking from face to face, all eager innocence.

'Just agree to dance with the winner,' O'Rourke said smoothly.

'Oh yes, I like to dance,' Jemima said.

'Any sort of dance the winner chooses,' O'Rourke added.

'Any sort! Any sort at all!' Jemima chirruped. She was flushed and over-excited with wine, and began to prance about the room, swinging her skirts like a Spanish dancer.

'That's right, my girl. A young lady should be biddable,' O'Rourke said.

'You are an unscrupulous rogue,' said Mattock, with a faint smile at O'Rourke's plausibility, though debauching gentry-girls was not to his taste.

'I'll start the bidding,' said Cox, laughing. 'Five guineas!'

'Paltry,' said O'Rourke, snapping his fingers. 'That wouldn't buy you a glimpse of a fetlock. Major Tovey here won't allow a lady to be insulted. Give me a proper bid, Tovey, you evil varmint, and put him to shame, for I see you slavering there at the very thought.'

'You ain't serious?' Cox said, slowly coming to grips with the realisation that this was not a joke. 'You really mean I get the girl if I bid most?'

'Only the girl, not her fortune,' O'Rourke corrected solemnly. ''Tis not marriage we're talking of today.'

Mattock looked down the table. 'Morland, you had

better put a stop to this,' he said lazily. So far no harm had been done, but he knew his companions, and he knew there came a point in any company where it went beyond controlling.

'Had I indeed?' Nicky said, straightening up. 'Are you telling me what to do in my own house?'

'Somebody had better. Send that child to bed, where it belongs, and let's have a pipe, and play at hazard.'

But Nicholas had reached the irritable stage of drunkenness, and was not to be coaxed. 'You are not master in this house,' he said, a little slurred. 'I decide what we do for entertainment and I decide – I decide—' He shook his head to try to clear it. 'What were we talking about?'

'The makin' of a little profit, is what we're talking about,' O'Rourke urged. 'It's business, Nicky, good business! Sell the same goods twice, and at the end, why, you still have the fortune. She's under lock and key in your own house, and no other relatives to object. What else is a woman for? They're all the same under the petticoat, me boy – as you know as well as any man.'

Mattock stood up, leaning his weight upon his hands. 'Nicky, you keep damn' bad company these days, and you are growing more sodden by the minute. Still, I will further mortgage my evening by offering to take you to the Golden Cage – my treat – if you break this party up now and send that child to bed.' Tovey caught hold of Jemima as she danced past and offered her his glass, talking to her in a low voice as she drank. To judge by Jemima's expression, she didn't understand much of what he was saying, which, knowing Tovey as Mattock did, was probably just as well.

Nicholas eyed the pair as well, and gave a contemptuous grin. 'Is *that* what you want to protect? By God, O'Rourke is right, they're all the same.' His head was swimming unpleasantly, which made him feel bad-tempered. Roger Mattock was getting above himself these days, he thought. He ought to remember the difference in their station, and be grateful that Nicholas Morland condescended to invite him to his house.

'You're only peeved,' he sneered at Mattock, 'because *you* didn't think of it first. You always want to be the one to decide what we do, don't you? Well this is *my* house, and *I* say what we do here. So you can pipe that in your smoke.' Jack Cox sniggered, and Nicholas, unsure what he had said that was funny but happy to accept the accolade to his wit, smirked as well, and drained his glass in a toast to himself.

Mattock looked at him for a long moment. 'What a bore you are, Nicky,' he said at last, softly. 'I should never have taken you up.' He pushed his chair back and left the table, clamping a hard hand down on Jemima's shoulder as he passed her, detaching her forcibly from Tovey's soft clutches and propelling her towards the door. A chorus of protest and complaint rose behind him, but he ignored it, opened the door, and thrust her through into the hall. 'Get to bed,' he said shortly, in the sort of voice that brooks no refusal.

Jemima, extremely pale and swaying a little, tried to look up at him, but had hastily to restore her head to the level as her stomach protested at the change. 'I don't feel very—' And she was gone, with remarkable rapidity.

Mattock turned back to address the room. 'Gentlemen – though that term is rather an exaggeration – I feel the need to exercise my wits in a game of chance. The night is still young. What say we adjourn to the Maccabbees, and try our luck at the wheel? And then perhaps back to the barracks for breakfast in the mess. Who is with me?'

Debate broke out noisily, but when Mattock left about fifteen minutes later he succeeded in taking with him O'Rourke, Cox, and Tovey. Nicholas had already forgotten Jemima and the cause of Mattock's departure, but he was angry at the early break-up of his party, and sat smouldering with resentment at the insolent way he had been treated, emptying glass after glass of brandy until he slid gratefully into the joined embraces of Bacchus and Morpheus.

Ferrars stood at the end of the bed looking impassively at the small figure as it writhed and muttered. He was thinking rapidly. 'How bad is she?' he asked.

'Pretty bad,' Miss Smith said. 'She's feverish, as you can see. I don't know what in God's name they gave her, but she was sick as a dog, and then lying on the cold floor all night, until I found her. I don't like the looks of her, I can tell you.'

He heard the alarm in her voice, and sought to reassure her. 'You did quite right coming to me. We've got to keep this quiet. Does anyone else know?'

'Only Martha – but she's a safe hand.'

'As long as she doesn't tell that sot of a husband of hers,' Ferrars muttered. 'I must have a word with her right away. No-one must know, no-one at all.'

'But she needs a doctor,' Miss Smith protested.

'No doctor!' He turned to her, exasperated. 'Do you want an outsider coming in here, poking his nose into your affairs?'

'*My* affairs?' she said indignantly.

'She was in your charge,' he said silkily. 'If she comes to harm, it's your responsibility. Do you want it all to come out?'

'What about the Master?'

'I'll talk to him. He won't be sensible for a long time yet, but I'll catch him when he wakes. If no-one knows she's ill, there'll be no harm done, will there?'

'But what's to be done about *her*?' Miss Smith made a nervous gesture towards the bed. 'She's sick.'

'You nurse her.'

'I'm no expert, Mr Ferrars. I know nothing about sick-nursing.'

'All women have the instinct in them. I'm sure you'll manage,' he said graciously.

239

'But what if she dies?'

He shrugged. 'Children do get sick and die. No-one will be surprised.'

Miss Smith was silent, unconvinced. If Jemima died, who would be blamed except her? She didn't trust Ferrars further than she could spit him, and if it came to saving his own hide or hers – but what else could she do? He had her in a cleft stick, and he knew it.

'I'll need help,' she said at last, sulkily. 'I can't watch her day and night.'

'Mrs Moon can help you. I'll speak to her. No-one else must know, no-one at all, d'you hear? Anything you want, ask me, and I'll get it. Lock yourself and the child in here, and don't open to anyone but me and Mrs Moon. We'll come out of this all right,' he added, bringing his face nearer to emphasise the point, 'if we keep our heads.'

Miss Smith would have been happier if he'd kept his out of her face, but she nodded agreement, and waited in silence for him to go away.

'Madam, could I speak to you?' said Moon tentatively.

Aglaea looked up in surprise. She was sitting at one of the windows of the Long Saloon with her watercolours, and had been so completely engrossed that she had not heard the butler come in. But her surprise stemmed more from being addressed at all. She sat here most mornings, after the housemaids had finished, and was never disturbed: life of the house went on, as it had from the beginning, without her.

'Yes, very well,' she said, putting down her brush. The picture she had been colouring was part of a new task she had set herself. In one of the drawers of the large armoire in her room she had found a series of leather-bound manuscripts, closely written in a strange and spiky handwriting. On the first page of the first book was the superscription *History of the Revolution*; and from scraps of remembered conversation she had realised it was the memoirs written by Nicholas's mother, the late Lady Morland, who had grown up in France and lived through the revolution of 1789. Aglaea had found the manuscript so fascinating that it had set her imagination alight, and for months now as she read she had been selecting episodes to illustrate. She had never been to Paris, of course, or anywhere else for that matter, but she drew from fancy, and the ongoing nature of the enterprise gave a sense of purpose to her days. Today she was illustrating a sea-voyage, and had been so much enjoying painting her favourite subject that she sighed at the interruption.

But here was Moon, drooping from the shoulders like a shabby parrot, a little moist of eye, and with a quiver to his jowls which suggested extreme nervousness; but he stood his ground resolutely, as though having screwed up his courage to the sticking-point he meant to speak or die.

'I don't mean to presume,' he began, 'but – oh, madam, I'm so worried about that little girl.' He clasped his hands together in front of him – large, chalky-knuckled, purplish old hands, clasped as though he were praying. The thumbs, crossed on top, were in her line of sight, and she noticed that the thumb-nails were long and discoloured under the rim, from a lifetime of slitting the seals on bottles. A butler's thumbs, she thought absently, and then dragged her mind back to what he was saying.

'What little girl?' she said. 'Do you mean Miss Jemima?'

He nodded. 'Oh, madam, I beg you not to tell I said anything – they'd have the hide off me if they knew – but I can't stand by and do nothing, not namore. I had a little girl myself once, madam, and I know I wouldn't bear it if she was mine. Which, I know gentry ways is different, but this – it isn't right, madam, whichever way you look at it.'

'*What* isn't right?' Aglaea asked patiently.

'Locking her up in that room, like as if she was a prisoner. She hasn't been out of it for weeks, madam, to my certain knowledge, and nobody isn't let to go in – not even the housemaid to make up the fire. Miss Smith does that, which is not normal, her being what she is. It's my belief there's something queer a-going on, and I don't like it, madam, 'deed I don't.' His face was trembling now with more than fear – it was outrage.

Aglaea frowned, completely at sea. She wondered if Moon had been drinking, early as it was; though he didn't seem bosky. 'Are you telling me that Miss Jemima is being kept prisoner in the nursery?'

'That's what it comes down to,' Moon agreed. 'No-one's let to come next or night her, and no-one's seen her except Miss Smith and Mr Ferrars.'

'Miss Smith is her governess,' Aglaea pointed out, perplexed.

Moon flicked a glance over his shoulder as if he expected to be crept up on, and bent a little more, as if the least encouragement would have him put his mouth to her ear. She drew back a little in compensation. 'I don't like to say it, madam, but May Smith is not a proper governess for a young lady.'

'I thought she was your wife's cousin?'

'Mrs Moon says so, but they are no more than friends. And she's a deal too thick with Mr Ferrars, is Miss Smith.'

Aglaea stood up abruptly. 'I don't know what you're suggesting, Moon, but I've heard quite enough. Please never speak to me like this again.'

Moon's jaw dropped. 'Nay, mistress, nay, divn't frost me so,' he pleaded, slipping in his agitation into a more native tongue. 'Ah'm not mad, nor drunk neether. That 'ittle lass is not treated right, Ah swear Bible-oath on it! Ah wouldn't durse speak to you if it weren't for her.'

Aglaea stared at him helplessly. His passion seemed genuine, but she didn't understand what he was afraid of. 'I don't understand you,' she said.

'Just think, madam, when did *you* last see Miss Jemima?'

Aglaea thought; but her days passed so quietly and in such solitude that she could hardly tell one from another; and besides, she didn't often see Jemima anyway, except to pass her occasionally when she was being taken for a walk or ride.

Moon watched her face earnestly, and seeing encouragement in her bewilderment, added, 'If there is no mischief in it, why are the nursery doors kept locked day and night?'

'Are they?' she said in surprise, and then pulled herself together. She mustn't encourage him. The poor old man was wandering in his wits, that was the kindest thing to think. 'You mustn't worry, Moon,' she said gently. 'Miss Jemima is the Master's ward, and he will not let any harm come to her. He takes the very best care of her, you may be sure.'

'I don't believe Master knows about it,' Moon said urgently. 'It's Mr Ferrars's doing, that's my belief.'

'Nonsense!' Aglaea said, though she shivered a little at the mention of the name. She had nothing of which to accuse Ferrars – he was always polite to her – but she held him in instinctive aversion. 'Mr Ferrars only carries out the Master's orders.'

Moon looked at her for a long moment, and then lowered his gaze and shook his head slowly from side to side like a goaded stirk. His bony hands were at his sides now, clenching and unclenching as if they had a life of their own. 'It's like leaving t'lamb to be guarded by t'wolf,' he muttered.

'What's that?' Aglaea asked sharply.

'I cannat say,' he said at last. 'I beg your pardon, madam. Please forget I spoke.'

He turned away slowly to make his exit, looking more than ever decrepit, as though the interview had taken a great deal of the life force out of him. Aglaea watched

243

him go, a poor old man whose wits had been addled by a lifetime of drink; but he plainly believed quite genuinely that something was amiss.

'Moon,' she said. He stopped where he was, halfway to the door, and turned on the spot, looking at her with an enquiring, apprehensive eye. 'Everyone has Miss Jemima's welfare at heart. Try not to worry.'

Moon nodded slowly, thinking now, where before he had not thought. He had come to her on impulse, driven by anguish which had got the better of his discretion and his loyalty to his wife, simply in the desire to help Miss Jemima. But now he had to think about it, how could the Mistress have helped even if he had convinced her of the truth? He knew, probably much better than she did, how little power she had in the house. He had been a fool indeed.

He hesitated a moment longer. 'Madam, you won't say as I said— ?'

'I won't tell anyone you have spoken to me. Now leave me.'

'Mr Morland,' Aglaea said at dinner, 'I was thinking I had not seen Jemima for some time.'

Nicholas looked up sharply from his plate, an access of guilty thoughts rushing like blood to his head. 'I was not aware,' he said at last, 'that you took an interest in her whereabouts.'

She smiled nervously, wondering how to phrase it so that he would not be made angry. Moon's words, 'I don't believe Master knows about it,' were all that drove her on. If it were possible that there was any truth in the notion of a conspiracy between Ferrars and Miss Smith, it would be remiss of her not to follow it up.

'I went along to the nursery wing this morning, and all the doors were locked,' she said, 'so I wondered if she had gone away somewhere?'

Nicholas found he was holding his breath, and made

himself breathe normally. 'Why did you do that? What business had you there?' he countered her question with one of his own.

She was ready for that – indeed, before she had dared go along the corridor to the nursery rooms, she had provided herself with an excuse. 'I came across a book in the Long Saloon which – which I used to love as a girl, so I thought – I thought – Jemima might like to see it.' She hadn't expected it to sound so weak, and her voice wavered.

Nicholas was staring at her unsmilingly, and she waited for the storm to break over her head; but after a moment he sighed and said, 'I suppose I must tell you the truth. But I must ask you for your absolute discretion. What I say must go no further – your promise.'

She nodded, startled; and Nicholas paused a moment longer to choose his words. He remembered all too well the interview with Ferrars, on the day after his last carouse. He did not know how Ferrars had learned about the auction which had almost taken place, but he did know, and he was furious: he had not even known before that Jemima came downstairs to his parties. Only Nicholas's sense of guilt, and his frightful hangover made him sit still under the tirade. But given the circumstances, he agreed with Ferrars that her illness should be kept quiet; his own hatred and suspicion of doctors made him glad to agree none should be called for the child.

It had been an anxious time, however: Jemima was very ill indeed, and more than once her life had been despaired of. And when she finally recovered enough to be expected to live, she seemed much altered: her previous liveliness had gone; she was listless and quiet, and her nerves were affected, too, so that she started at any little thing, and was easily reduced to tears. It was Ferrars who suggested that the situation might be turned to good. They had had a narrow escape that night, and it brought home to them how important it was to keep Jemima under close guard. Her altered spirits suggested the means.

So now Nicholas arranged his features in lines of stern sadness, and said, 'I'm afraid Jemima is not like other girls.' Aglaea looked startled, and he nodded gravely and went on, 'It was a weakness in her we – I suspected long ago. That was why I found a special governess for her. Miss Smith may look unprepossessing, but she has a great deal of experience in dealing with these special cases.'

'You mean – Jemima is— ?' Aglaea didn't want to say the word. 'Not – *mad*?'

Nicholas sighed. 'I'm afraid so. When she was younger, it was not so apparent, but these things often reveal themselves at a certain time of life, when other changes occur – you understand me. For her own protection, she must be kept under lock and key; and for the sake of the family, we must make sure as few people as possible know about it. Only Ferrars and Miss Smith – and now you, my dear – have any idea. You must promise to keep it that way.'

'Of course,' Aglaea said at once. 'But—'

'In time,' he went on quickly, 'and with careful nursing, we hope she may recover enough to take her place in society. In that case, the fewer people who know the better.'

'I understand,' Aglaea said. 'Poor little creature. But after what she suffered, I suppose it is not to be wondered at. To lose all her family in that way—'

Nicholas applied his handkerchief to his eyes. 'It breaks my heart,' he said, muffled by the linen. 'I do all I can to keep her safe and make her comfortable, but it grieves me bitterly that I cannot do more. I feel so guilty.'

'It is not your fault.' Aglaea's eyes were damp in sympathy. How kind he was, how truly kind and generous. 'How can you feel guilty? God sees,' she said. 'God knows what is in every man's heart.'

Under the handkerchief, Nicholas winced at her choice of words.

*　　*　　*

Harry Anstey was at his desk in his office when to his great surprise George Cave came in. 'I haven't seen you in an age!' he greeted him. 'Have this chair, old fellow, it's the most comfortable. A glass of sherry?'

'Thank you – no,' Cave said. He seemed ill at ease. 'I'm afraid you may not want to offer me sherry when you hear what I have to say. But I must—' He lapsed into a brooding silence.

Harry eyed him quizzically. 'Why, George, what's the matter? Are you in trouble? You've come to the right place if you are. You know I'm yours to command, old chap.'

Cave looked up. 'That's just like you, Harry. That's what makes it so difficult. It ain't a business matter, you see; it's personal.'

'Well, cough it up, then,' Harry said encouragingly. 'An attorney gets to hear most things, one way and another. I doubt if you can shock me. Is it money? A woman?'

'Oh, Harry, you dear old thing, just cork it for a moment, will you?' Cave said, smiling in spite of himself. 'I've got to say something that I don't at all want to say. And I shall have to broach matters which are none of my business, and perhaps set your back up and make an enemy of you; and how can I do all that if you keep burbling on and making me realise every minute what a good friend you are?'

'*What's* none of your business?'

'Aglaea – your sister – Mrs Morland. She's none of my business any more, more's the pity. Look here, you know how I felt about her?'

Harry frowned. 'Well, I thought I did, until you beetled off and left her flat.'

'Hardly that,' Cave said. 'She was being courted by Nicholas Morland.'

'Well, I call that spiritless! Why didn't you put up a fight for her?'

'I couldn't compete with Morland. How could I set myself up against all he has? The idea was ludicrous.

247

And Aglaea – your sister was so tender-hearted, it might have pained her to have to snub me. So I removed myself from the lists and saved her the trouble.'

'How do you know she would have snubbed you?' Harry demanded.

George gave a queer, twisted smile. 'Events have proved it. She is Mrs Nicholas Morland, mistress of Morland Place.'

'George, old fellow, you didn't give her much of a choice, did you?'

George looked carefully at Harry for a long moment. 'You can't mean that you would sooner she had married me? Have you some reservation about Morland?'

Harry hesitated; but his doubts about Nicky were so indefinable that it would have been hard to put them into words. Besides, he had no real reason to think all was not well. He saw Aglaea very infrequently, but when he saw her she was her old self, no different from the way she had been any time these ten years.

'It was her choice,' he said instead. 'I had nothing to do with it.'

Cave chewed his lip thoughtfully. It seemed to him a less than whole-hearted endorsement of Nicholas Morland, and any doubts Harry had would make his part easier. He decided to plunge on. 'Look here, Harry, I'm making a bit of a muff of this, but the point I was trying to make is that I have your sister's welfare at heart, or I wouldn't dream of saying anything.'

'You haven't *said* anything yet,' Harry pointed out.

'What I mean is, I'm not just making trouble. You do believe that, don't you?'

'You are the best-hearted man in the world, George, everyone knows it. Now do get on with it, there's a good chap.'

Cave took a deep breath and fixed Harry with his bravest and steadiest look. 'I don't know if you are aware of it, but there is an establishment in this city in Carr's Lane – you know, just off Skeldergate—'

'A choice part of town,' Harry commented.

'An establishment called the Golden Cage.'

'I don't know it. What is it? A tavern?'

Cave paused, wondering whether Harry's innocence made his job easier or harder. 'Not quite,' he said drily, 'though liquor's to be had there – and other stuff – but they are incidental to the services the customers pay for. I'd call them pleasures, but you and I wouldn't find them pleasurable.'

Harry was puzzled. 'What are you talking about? You mean it's a brothel? You needn't be so delicate, George, I ain't a spinster.'

'It's a particular kind of brothel. Well, not to mince matters, it is a house of flagellation.'

Harry's cheeks coloured a little. 'I know such places exist, of course,' he said, 'but I didn't think we had any in York. I thought one had to go to London for that.'

'It's very expensive, which is how it manages to keep itself exclusive. I only know about it because my friend Macadam, the physician, had to attend one of his patients who'd been there and had rather a lively session of it. He told me all about it – not mentioning names, of course – rather as a joke, but I could see even he was rather shocked at what goes on in there. There was a girl killed there once, apparently, though they managed to hush it up. There are floggers and floggees, you see—'

'Quite,' Harry cut him off. 'But why are you telling me this?'

'Because I was taking a short cut through Carr's Lane the other night, on my way home, and I saw Nicholas Morland coming out of the Golden Cage.'

'How did you know it was the Golden Cage?' Harry asked. His voice came out rather high. 'Presumably it does not advertise itself?'

Cave sighed. 'It was the Golden Cage all right. I'm

sorry, Harry. I thought long and hard before saying anything, but the thought of—'

'Yes,' Harry said sharply, cutting him off. 'I appreciate why you told me. It – it was brave of you. I might have knocked you down.'

'You still might,' George said ruefully. 'Maybe it's nothing. Maybe there's a good reason. I don't know. But I loved Aglaea. I couldn't bear to think – I thought perhaps you might be able to do something.' He shrugged. 'I don't know what.'

'I half wish you hadn't told me,' Harry said slowly. 'It's a hell of a thing to know what to do with.'

'I know, but – you are her closest brother. You were Morland's closest friend. I didn't know what else to do.'

Harry nodded, and then sighed, feeling ten years older than he had felt ten minutes ago. 'Leave it to me, George. I don't need to tell you to say nothing to anyone—'

'Of course not. But – if you need my help— ?'

'Thanks,' said Harry, but he shook his head. His mind was already far away, following a trail he had no desire to follow, and he hardly noticed Cave take his leave. He thought of Nicky's pallor and bruised, sickly look; his odd moods, his unreasonable dislikes. A man with strange vices and the money to indulge them might well have impaired the functioning of his mind. But surely, surely Aglaea could not know about it? *Surely* he would keep it secret from her? As long as he took his strange habits out of the house and was discreet about it, it was his business, and no-one else's. There was no justification for anyone to intervene.

He didn't do it with Aglaea. He couldn't. He couldn't.

Harry couldn't bear the thought. He knew he had to find out, or he would never sleep quietly again. But how to ask? Aggie was so gentle and innocent. Besides, it wasn't a subject he could raise with her. No, he must enlist the

250

help of a woman, an older woman. He must ask Mary. Mary would know what to do.

Aglaea was walking about the parterre as the heat went out of the day, enjoying the scents which the earth gave up at this time of the afternoon. The parterre was dreadfully neglected: the yew hedges around the perimeter were shaggy and overgrown and the gravel was worn from the centre of the paths; the box hedges which marked out the geometric beds were bald in places; weeds were rampant in some sections, unsuitable plants had taken over others. The four huge urns in the middle of the four sides had not been planted this year; and the fountain in the centre was full of last year's dead leaves.

Even so, she liked it here. The symmetry pleased her, the linked shapes which led from one to another gave her a sense of progression – and the pattern never ended, for like a circle it came round again. She had a half-daydreaming plan to revive it, replant it as a knot garden, as she had seen them in old books. If the right moment presented itself, she might even ask Nicholas if she could do it. She imagined the smell of lavender and rosemary and thyme, the sound of bees hungry for the sweet herbs, the sound of water splashing in the bowl.

Minna, who was running ahead of her, keeping to the narrow edging of grass to avoid the gravel, suddenly stopped and turned, one paw raised, her nose lifted, her anxious brown eyes wide. Aglaea turned, hearing at the same moment the sound of footsteps on gravel, and saw Nicholas striding towards her. He had been into York on horseback, which was why he had left Minna behind. She had not expected him back that evening, and was pleased to see him; but as he came closer, she saw thunderclouds in his face, and her pleasure seeped away. He was plainly in a foul temper.

'Well, madam!' He stopped before her, scowling. He had been striding so hard in his anger that he was almost breathless. 'And what have you to say for yourself?'

That was a hard question to answer. 'You are back early, Mr Morland,' she tried.

'I wonder I came back at all! I have been so *mortified* – put to the blush, madam, and by your relatives! What the deuce have you been at, talking to them about our private affairs? Have you no discretion at all? Have you no *shame*?'

Aglaea's lips moved soundlessly as she tried for a safe sentence. She shook her head minutely. 'I – I don't understand, sir. What have I done?'

'Done? Why, only exposed our intimate life to public view, that's all!' He walked a few furious steps away and back. Minna had crept behind a low box hedge at the first outburst and was quivering there, her tail clamped so far between her legs it looked unlikely ever to come out again. 'You went in to York to see your family yesterday, didn't you?'

'I went to see Mary, only Mary,' she said nervously. 'I wanted to ask how Celia is – she's with child again, you know.'

'Oh yes, with child,' Nicholas raged. 'There was plenty of talk about children, I don't doubt!'

Aglaea racked her brains to find the source of her fault. Talk about children? Well, yes, now she thought about it: 'Mary did ask—' She swallowed with apprehension. 'She only said that as we had been married more than a year, she would have expected me to be increasing by now.'

Nicholas put his hands on his hips in triumph. 'Oh yes! *Only* that! And instead of rebuking her impudence you gave her full licence!'

'She is my sister, Mr Morland,' Aglaea protested gently. 'Sisters do talk to each other. She's interested in my welfare.'

'And what else did she ask you?' he sneered. 'What was the next innocent question?'

Aglaea cast her mind back, and her cheeks began to redden. The questions had seemed innocent and straightforward to her at the time, but seeing Nicholas's rage, she began to misdoubt. 'I – I can't remember,' she faltered.

'How convenient! But perhaps you remember your answers, Mrs Morland? Perhaps you remember telling her that we sleep in separate rooms?'

'You – you said that was quite usual for people of our rank,' she said.

'It's not usual to discuss it with outsiders – and in such detail!'

Aglaea was remembering how Mary had accepted the separate rooms with no more than a raised eyebrow, but had then gone on to ask how often Nicholas visited her. Aglaea had not understood the question. 'How often does he visit you in your bed, dear?' Mary had pressed her. 'Oh, I do not see him at night,' Aglaea had answered. 'His room is at the other end of the house.' 'He *never* comes to your bed?' The question had seemed such an odd one she had neither confirmed nor denied. She did not know what it was Mary was after, and she was sure her sister would not ask anything improper – but she could see that Nicholas was really angry.

'How – how did you— ?' she began falteringly.

'How did I know what you have been saying?' he anticipated. 'Because, madam, your sister relayed it all to your brother Harry, and he was so obliging as to accost me this afternoon at the Maccabbees club and subject me to a most impertinent examination!'

'Oh, no!' a gasping little denial.

'Oh yes, Mrs Morland! I was obliged to speak quite cuttingly to him. I don't know what I may have said. There will be bad blood between us now, and it's all your fault.'

'I'm so sorry!' She put her hands to her hot cheeks. 'I never meant to do anything wrong. I would not upset you for the world.'

'Aye, well you have,' Nicholas said, a little mollified by

her distress. 'He seemed to think I had treated you badly. I don't know what impression you managed to give your sister—'

'Oh no, sir, I swear! She couldn't have thought that! You have always been so good to me. I will go and see her tomorrow, and put things straight!'

'No, by God!' Nicholas cried hastily. 'I'll have no more meddling and gossiping from you! It's plain that you can't be trusted any more than a poll-parrot to keep a still tongue in your head!' He observed the tears spilling down her cheeks, and modified his tone. 'Come, come, I don't altogether blame you. I expect you were too innocent to know what was being wheedled out of you.' She nodded, and took with touching gratitude the handkerchief he offered her. 'But, that being the case, you still cannot be trusted to go alone amongst devious, underhand, sophisticated people like your family. From now on, you will not visit anyone, nor have anyone to visit you here, unless I am with you. Do you understand?'

'Not – not see my family?' It was the mildest of protests, but she couldn't help making it.

'No, nor receive them. I won't have you paying carriage calls, either – all your friends are as bad as each other. You will confine yourself to the house and grounds in future, unless I am with you.'

'Not – not even go to the library? Or the shops?'

'Not anywhere. You will be taken advantage of for sure, if you meet with anyone alone. A servant can change your library books and do whatever shopping you want. I may invite some of your family here sometimes, for propriety's sake, as long as I am on hand to guard you – and guard your tongue.' He eyed her mournful face. 'Come, there should be everything here at Morland Place to make you happy,' he said. 'I wish *I* need never go away, even for an hour: I am never happy anywhere else. But a man has so many cares and responsibilities that a woman knows nothing about. We labour and suffer out in the world, so that you may stay at home in safety and repose. You are lucky to have me to keep and protect you.'

'Yes,' she said, struck with the image. 'You are right, of course. And I am grateful. I made a foolish mistake, and I am very sorry for it. I will not give you cause to be angry again.'

He laid his hand on hers. Despite the warmth of the day, his was as cold as stone. 'I know you won't. You are a good wife – Aglaea.'

She was touched by his tenderness, his use of her name, and could only smile back at him in wordless gratitude.

CHAPTER TWELVE

On October the 13th, 1835, Sir John Simpson, the Lord Mayor of York, presided over a meeting in the Guildhall, called by the York Railway Committee. The purpose of the meeting was to decide on a railway for York, and it was attended by every prominent citizen of York and its surroundings. The weather had been warm, and emotions were warmer: Harry Anstey was glad in the end that he had dissuaded Celia from attending, for the meeting grew heated in both senses.

She had miscarried of their second child, and needed something to occupy her mind and keep her from fretting. In desperation Harry had tried to interest her in the railway question. The debate had widened during the summer, for the committee had been considering proposals for railways not just to Leeds, but all the way to London. This idea had raised Celia a little from her depression. 'If one is to go to the trouble of building a railway at all,' she said to Harry, 'one might as well think on a grand scale. Imagine being able to ride all the way to London in a railway coach! One could have the new fashions almost as soon as they had them in Bond Street. And—' she sought for a masculine enticement – 'and London newspapers the same day. Think of that, Harry!'

'Think of the expense, too. It's all very well, Cely, but we can't get our local worthies to put their hands in their pockets for a line to Leeds. We'd never get them to sponsor something that passes through Lincolnshire and Northamptonshire and every other southern shire they've never visited and never want to. And there's the turnpike interest to take into account. They wouldn't lose much by the Leeds scheme, but the Great South Road is meat and drink to them.'

One proposal had come in from the good citizens of Doncaster for a line from York to London, passing through Doncaster and jointly funded by the two towns. When Celia heard that the Doncaster deputation was to attend the York meeting, to say nothing of the elder Mr Stephenson, she was determined to go and see the fun, but Harry in the end persuaded her that the meeting would be long and tiring and, since it would be largely a masculine affair, the hall would be full of smoke. As it turned out, it was well she stayed at home: Nicholas Morland was present, and Harry wouldn't have wished her to see how far apart they had grown.

He deeply regretted having tackled Nicholas on the delicate subject; it was an unwarrantable liberty, and Nicholas had every right to be furious. Yet with another part of his mind, he wondered what else he could have done. How could he have ignored George Cave's revelation? He had hardly seen Aglaea since her marriage: she and Nicky entertained very little, and rarely accepted invitations. Once George had raised doubts in his mind, he had known he would be uneasy until he had consulted Mary; and Mary had been decisive.

'You can leave it to me,' she had said firmly. 'I'll talk to Aggie. I've been wondering myself if all was well: they've been married over a year, and not a sign of a baby. I'll get it out of her, don't worry.'

Mary was the best creature who ever lived, but Harry was a little alarmed at what he'd started. 'Don't frighten her, Pol. You know how innocent she is.'

Mary snapped her fingers. 'I know how to deal with Aggie. Just leave it to me.'

Two days later he had called in at Anstey House in response to a terse note from Mary, and she had told him in shocked tones what she had gleaned from Aglaea's innocent responses.

'You'll have to speak to him,' Mary had said. 'It isn't right.'

Harry felt uneasy. 'I don't know, Polly. After all, it isn't as if he's harming her in any way—'

'Not harming her? He's not doing her duty by her, and someone's got to talk to him.'

Harry thought of the brothel, and Nicky's pale, marked face and his strangeness, and his mind shied away from the speculations those things prompted. 'But it isn't really any of my business,' he said unhappily.

Mary was rock-firm. 'Aggie's our sister, and it's up to us to look out for her. Obviously *I* can't talk to Nicholas, so it's got to be you. You were always the closest to him.' And when Harry had still demurred, 'If you won't talk to him it'll have to be Jack.'

And so Harry had bowed his head and walked away to his doom. Alienating Nicky had been all to no purpose, of course – had probably made things worse. Since then he had seen Nicky here and there about town, and had come face to face with him outside the Maccabees once, on which occasion Nicky cut him dead. But he had not seen Aglaea at all, and according to Mary, she had not visited Anstey House either, and no-one seemed to have seen her in York. In a state of contrition he had ridden out to Morland Place, but had been told 'not at home' at the door, and had had to go away again. Apparently, then, Aglaea was taking Nicky's part: he had lost a sister as well as a brother-in-law. It was all very sad and unnecessary, and he cursed George inwardly for having told him in the first place, and himself for having plunged in where a wise man would have feared to tread.

The meeting at the Guildhall brought surprises. In accordance with an agenda decided by the Committee

– which meant decided by Hudson – Harry spoke first in favour of the original York to Leeds scheme, repeating the arguments for it, and mentioning the names of local luminaries who supported it. Then in turn came speeches by the proponents of three separate York to London schemes, ending with a most eloquent appeal by Doncaster's wealthiest resident, who made the substantial and telling point that the scheme he favoured would be supported by his private fortune.

'Aye, that's the point,' somebody in the audience said. 'You don't get owt for nowt in this world. Who's to pay for all these fancy undertakings?'

'Why, they mean us to pay. That's why we're here,' said Meek the coal-merchant loudly, looking round at his fellow citizens. 'We're the milch-cows, don't you see?' There was uneasy laughter. A buzz of conversation started, and Hudson cast a meaningful look and a prompting cough at the chairman; but before Sir John could initiate the next part of the agenda, Nicholas Morland stood up and said, 'I will tell you, gentlemen, who will *not* pay for these schemes.' The talk died down and all eyes turned to him. Sir John glanced at Hudson and shrugged slightly. It would not look well for him to silence such a leading citizen. 'I have been consulting amongst the landowners of York,' Nicholas went on. 'We, who own most of the wealth of the country, have the best right to determine what happens to the land; indeed, the only right to decide what happens on our own estates. I can assure you there is not a man of us who would put a penny into any of these harebrained schemes!'

Now there was complete silence. He turned his head one way and then the other, gathering attention. 'These schemes are not merely foolish, they are wicked,' he went on. 'All of you remember my late, revered mother, Lady Morland. You remember her nobility, her virtue, her great generosity, her uncounted good works. She was the very epitome of what it has always meant to be a Morland:

a great lady, working tirelessly for the good of others, for the preservation of the land, for the advancement of the worthy and the succour of the poor. Her very death speaks of the life she lived: fearless in the face of hideous disease, where others fled to save their selfish lives, she nursed the sick with her own tender hands, day after day, until she took the sickness herself.' His voice wavered and he paused and put his hand over his eyes, bending his head for a moment, and there was not a sound in the hall. Then he removed his hand, lifted his head, and spoke more strongly. 'My beloved mother believed that the railways were the work of the Devil, and could never bring any good to the people of York. The lure of travelling further and faster is one of the Dark Gentleman's idlest and most subtle wiles, and it will destroy our society. What use will all this travel be, except to take men from their proper work and their responsibilities? To breed envy and make everyone dissatisfied with their lot? To make women frivolous and vain, young people restless, idle, disrespectful? Yes, these are the evils – not the benefits – of rapid travel. Compare them with my mother's tireless dedication to duty, her industry and piety, and tell me, any man who dares, that I should go against her express wishes and allow this infernal undertaking to cross my land!'

There was a murmur at that, and out of it Willans, the livery stable owner, spoke up. 'Well said, Master Morland, well said indeed! You have all of us in the horse trade behind you, sir, that you do!'

'Thank you, my friend,' Nicky said, turning a rather horrid glance on him. 'I know that I have the good will of every man of sense. The fact of the matter is that this railway scheme is the fancy of one or two in the coal-mining interest – I mention no names, but you all know who I mean, for they are headed by a prominent family of this city, with whom I am closely connected. These people wish to use their position of influence to dupe the honest citizens of York. With lying promises of benefit, they would trick us into allowing our fair countryside to be torn asunder by workings, and our lives to be defiled and made hideous by these infernal machines. And why? So that the coal from their mines can be carried more rapidly to our hearths, and our cash to their pockets. Who benefits?' he added, raising his voice over a buzz of comment. 'Ask yourselves that, gentlemen. And to add insult to injury, they mean to dupe us into *paying* for this railway too – and pay we will, in more ways than one! We will be paying for the rest of our lives!'

Harry listened with a sense of shock, and saw from the expressions on faces in the audience that there were others who were shocked and puzzled at this obvious reference to the Anstey family. Everyone knew Nicholas Morland had married the youngest Anstey girl – or woman, rather, for she was no spring chicken, which was why everyone had assumed it must be a love-match. But it made his words the more impressive to them, Harry saw; those who reasoned at all were reasoning that he must be truly and sincerely against the railway, so to attack his own wife's family. Others were merely glad to have their instinctive prejudices given voice and justification.

Harry had known for a long time – since they were boys together – that Nicholas followed his mother's opinion of disliking the railways; but the venom with which Nicky had just spoken puzzled him. Was it possible he felt so very strongly about the railways? Or was this reprisal for Harry's having questioned him about his married life? At all events, there was no doubt he had had an effect. One after another the honest citizens of York were standing up to voice their doubts. There were many in the horse interest who spoke, and it seemed to Harry that in some cases their words were not unrehearsed. It looked as though someone had been talking to them, coaching them even, and glancing every now and then at Nicky's face, he began to suspect that it was Nicky himself

261

who had gone around from wheelwright to liveryman to corn-chandler, orchestrating their opposition.

Up on the platform, Hudson listened impassively, his heavy eyelids lowered inscrutably, his meaty face expressionless; his hands rested on the table top in utter immobility, as though nothing that went on below him could move him. Beside him Mr Stephenson listened with obvious interest, moving restlessly now and then, his quick eyes darting back and forth, occasionally shaking his head or grimacing at one opinion or another. It was not until the tide of talk slackened and ran out in a trickle that Hudson gave the nod to Sir John to call on him, and he stood up and commanded the attention of the meeting.

'Friends,' he said, quietly and forcefully, 'you all know me, and you know where I stand. I love this city. It is the best city in England, is York, the best city in the world, and I will work my fingers to the bone, I will give my last penny, if need be, to make it great again like it should be. I tell you, the railway is the future! It's no good shaking your heads and clutching your skirts like a lot of women scared of a mouse! Jumpin' on a chair won't keep the future away, but them as don't seize the chance will lose the benefit. We must have the railway, for if we don't have it, others will, and we'll be the losers! It means prosperity for all, does the railway. It means new opportunities, new trade, new jobs – in a word, brass, my friends, brass! Which one of you here couldn't do with a bit more of that, eh? Show me the man who despises brass, and I'll show you a liar.' There was uneasy laughter at that. 'The railway will make York thrive again: she will be at the heart of the country as she once was, instead of dying in obscurity.

'Now we've listened to a lot of talk from folks as have never been near a railway, never mind ridden on one! We've heard all the old wives' tales brought out, about aborting sheep and bolting horses and cows off their milk, and I don't know what else – and all from folk as have never so much as *seen* a steam locomotive! The Devil's horse they call it – superstitious nonsense! What are we, hysterical maids, or men of business? Now let's hear from a man as knows what he's talking about for a change. You all know Mr Stephenson. He's not called the Father of Railways for nowt: he has promoted schemes all over the north, schemes that are prospering at this very minute, bringing wealth and convenience to thousands and thousands of folk just like us, who had the vision to say yes to the future, instead of no or mebbe. He has come, despite his many pressing engagements, especially to speak to us about a scheme, a different scheme from them you've heard about so far – different and better by a mile! It's the right scheme for us, I promise you, but I'll let him tell it you. Now then, Mr Stephenson!'

Harry could only listen and admire, for though he was a plain man without much imagination, he could see how Hudson had manipulated the meeting, letting the opposition wear itself out on shouting down schemes he had no intention of backing, before bringing out something quite new, to which the exhausted gladiators could turn with a sense of relief, uniting them under the undoubted authority of Mr Stephenson. And the new scheme was one to appeal both to those with the greater vision of the line to London, and the more cautious who favoured a short, local line. Mr Stephenson spoke about his proposed North Midland and Midland Counties Railways, which were already under construction and which would join Leeds with Derby and Rugby. They had financial backing, he said, not only from Notts and Derby coal-owners, but from wealthy financiers in Liverpool and London, and could not fail of being profitable. Furthermore, there was no doubt that within a very short time Rugby would be joined by railway to London, and Leeds to Manchester and Liverpool. The new Midlands railways would thus be the central part of an extended net-work of lines joining all the great cities of the north with each other and with London.

'Now Mr Hudson has spoken to me of the various schemes before the York Railway Committee, and he has put up a further one, prompted in his mind by my own Midlands railways. Instead of building westwards to Leeds, says Mr Hudson, why not build southwards, and join up with my North Midland at Normanton? In that way, you will have your line to London without the expense of building it yourselves. You will also have a line to Leeds, and, in the fullness of time, across the Pennines to Manchester and Liverpool. Gentlemen, I must say that I have every confidence that this latter scheme will answer very well – so much so, that I have offered to Mr Hudson, if the York Committee decides on it, to do the initial survey myself.'

There was a buzz of approval and interest at that: Mr Stephenson's personal involvement was a strong recommendation. The great man sat down, and the meeting erupted into talk, as every man turned to his neighbour with comment or question. The talk was largely favourable, as Harry could tell by the tone of the buzz and the expressions on the faces. There were one or two still stony and unrelenting, some indifferent – and one in the centre scowling horribly. But by the time the meeting ended, the decision had been made to set up a new committee to survey the ground and raise the capital for a line from York to join the North Midland Railway at or about Normanton. The new committee was to be called the Provisional Committee for the York and North Midland Railway Company. Talk of an actual Company sent the meeting out into the open air seething with speculation, for a Company meant shares, and shares meant dividends – money in the pocket. It all made it seem more solid and probable, and less in the realms of fantasy.

Harry was detained in the hall, talking to a jubilant

Hudson, together with Stephenson and one or two others who were at the heart of the promotion.

'Well, lad, what d'ye think?' said Hudson, clapping him on the back so hard it almost knocked him down. 'We s'l have our railway now! You'll be attorney to the York and North Midland Railway before you can turn around!'

'I'm delighted, sir,' Harry said. 'The meeting went very well, I thought – on the whole.'

'Aye, and I haven't even told you the whole of it yet,' said Hudson, missing, in his excitement, that reservation. 'Time an' again I've begged Mr Stephenson to bring all t'railways to York, and now he's of my mind – aren't you, sir? Tell young Anstey the rest.'

Stephenson smiled. 'I have another scheme which is very dear to my heart: a great northern railway linking my home city of Newcastle with Edinburgh to the north, and London to the south. I had thought of routing it through Leeds—'

'Aye, that's right,' Hudson jumped in, unable to contain himself, 'but now we're going to link up at Normanton, I've persuaded him to take it through York instead. So, my lad, what d'ye think of that? York will be at the very heart of the country again – for once we have the Edinburgh to London line, they will have to come through us from Liverpool to Hull, so we'll be the pivot point! Ah, can't you see it: trade, traffic, people, pouring into our city! A hundred trains a day, and the name of York on every man's lips!'

It was hard to resist Hudson's enthusiasm, and Harry was kept talking for some time – or rather, kept listening, as the two railways visionaries designed their own future for England. At last he emerged, bemused and weary, to find the daylight going, and a mist coming up after the warmth of the day, which smelled a little of autumn, of dead leaves and woodsmoke and blackberries. He stepped out towards Gillygate, wanting to get home and tell Celia all about the meeting, but he had not gone more than a few yards before his arm was seized and he was spun round to find himself facing Nicholas Morland. He must have been waiting here for him, Harry realised; and felt for a moment an absurd shiver of fear.

'It's not over. I want you to know that,' was what Nicholas said. 'Indeed, your battles are just beginning.'

Harry tried to extricate his arm. 'Why you are so dead set against us?' he said.

'Us, is it?' Nicky sneered. 'What position have they given you in this ridiculous Neverland of theirs? Court jester to King Hudson, are you?'

'I am to be solicitor for the company,' Harry said reluctantly. 'That was decided long ago, before—'

'Ah yes, of course – you have long been Hudson's plaything. Well if I were you, I should get out now, while you still have your dignity. This railway will never be built. *I* will not allow it.'

'I don't see how you can stop it,' Harry said.

'I own the land,' Nicky said triumphantly. 'I will *never* allow you to cross my land; and I have enough influence to make sure you will not get a compulsory purchase order, so you may put that thought from your head, my fine friend.'

Harry shook his head. He almost hated to disillusion Nicky. 'Your permission won't be needed,' he said as gently as he could. 'The line to Normanton goes south, not west. It will not need to touch your land.'

Nicholas stared at him for a moment, his throat working, his face white with fury. For a moment Harry thought he might actually strike him; but then the bitter fingers released his arm, and Nicky turned away. 'You have not heard the last of this,' he said, and was gone into the gathering mist of dusk.

Aglaea woke from troubled dreams and thought it was morning. A moment later her mind and her vision cleared, and she realised that moonlight was shining in

266

her eyes: the bed-curtains had not been properly drawn. She felt oddly wide-awake, and on an impulse climbed out of bed. The room was flooded with a blue-silver light from the unshuttered west window, an unnatural light which carved the outlines of the furniture in black shadow, and gave a weird significance to everyday shapes – ewer, candlestand, her bedgown draped over the back of a convenient chair. It gave her an odd feeling, like being in a different world. When she had been a little girl, she had sometimes gone into her mother's bedroom, where there was a looking-glass on a stand. From a certain angle she could see in the glass the reflection through the door of the passage and the top of the stairs – a view so utterly familiar to her, and yet made strange by their reversal in the glass. She had sometimes stood there for half an hour together, staring at the looking-glass world and dreaming: she had imagined what it would be like if she could actually get into that other room, go out through that door and down those stairs. What would she find at the bottom? A whole different world, an enchanted place of extraordinary possibilities. She had yearned to pass into it, and though the logical part of her mind had told her there was no other place, the dreaming part had never doubted its existence.

She walked across to the window, hardly feeling the polished boards under her bare feet. Outside the high moon shone down from a clear sky, illuminating the scene – the glittering roofs of the outbuildings, and square bulk of the barbican tower, and beyond the open fields. There was a ground mist, which lay like thin milk over the grass; the trees rose out of it like willows growing in a river, and there was a line of dark knobs where the uprights of the stock fence poked up, marking the line of the track. Enchanted, she opened the casement and leaned out. The air was cold, but not unpleasantly so, and there was a smell of autumn on it, sad but enticing. She leaned out into the moonlight and the mist, and felt as light as a feather. She might lean on the air and float away, she thought: float on the river of silver into the other world she had never been able to reach . . .

A scream tore through the air, making her start so violently she hit the back of her head on the window-frame and almost lost her balance. Recovering herself she listened for reaction from the house, for a tumult of enquiring voices and pattering feet, but there was nothing. Inside and out all was quiet; not even a yard-dog stirred. Had she imagined it? She had been dreaming as she leaned out of the window – drifting in her mind? Perhaps she had actually fallen asleep as she stood there. But the scream had sounded so loud and so real.

She crossed the room and put on her bedgown and went to the door, opened it cautiously, looked out, listened. All was quiet in the house. And then she heard, not a scream this time, but a moan – such a pitiful moan that it made the hair rise on her scalp. Someone was having a nightmare. She thought first of all of Jemima: the poor little girl, locked up in the nursery, might well be plagued by the night fantasies of her disordered mind. But Miss Smith slept in the night nursery with her. If she had screamed, the governess would have woken and would be soothing her. Aglaea frowned. Would she have heard a scream from the nursery, in any case? It was in the opposite corner of the house, two long passageways distant. She stepped one pace forward, out of her room, listening. The silence of the house seemed to breathe, like a beast lying unseen in the dark. The passage along the upper part of the great hall was lit by moonlight, but to her right the passage to the chapel gallery was dark, the opening onto the chapel stair a blacker mouth in the blackness. Anything might be concealed in that blackness. Did she hear something move, rustle? But an old house was full of little sounds.

Then she heard the moan again – quieter, almost a murmur, but still distressed. Someone was troubled. She could not ignore it. She walked forward as though in a dream, her feet silent on the drugget, the walls bellying out of shape as her shadow crossed the moonlight. When she reached the railing she stopped and looked down into the great hall, black and white and dramatic; the massive lantern which hung down from the centre seemed to be swaying on its chain as though someone had set it swinging long ago, and its momentum was just running out. She shivered lightly and walked on.

The moan again, and a babble in a high voice, like a child's; but now she had no doubt. It came from Nicholas's room. It must do – he occupied the North Bedroom, and no-one else slept down that passage. It looked very dark, windowless and with its doors shut; she didn't much want to go into it. To her right the other passage opened out, and a draught came from the backstairs, touching her bare neck and making her shiver. There was darkness and menace everywhere, but no-one else had heard Nicholas cry out, no-one else had come. She could not leave him all alone in a nightmare. She stepped into the black passage, putting her hands out before her to feel for the end.

Something moved, touched her legs, and she gasped in terror and bit her tongue. For a moment her heart seemed filled with an iron pain, as though it might really burst in her chest; her throat was rigid and she could not draw a breath; she tasted blood in her mouth. And then something cold touched her hand, and immediately afterwards something warm and wet caressed it roughly, and her heart started beating again as she realised that it was Minna, who slept lying across Nicholas's door. She stooped, shakily, to find the smooth, warm head in the darkness, felt another long lick and the wriggle of a rump against her calf.

'Hush, Minna,' she whispered, but even a whisper seemed too loud in that listening silence. With one hand on Minna's neck and the other out before her, she inched forward until she encountered the door at the end of the passage; found the handle; hesitated, and then opened it. She had never been in Nicholas's room, had no idea how the furniture was disposed; but his room, too, was filled with moonlight, and she saw the fireplace, table and chairs before her, and the shape of the bed to her left, dark and tall, a ship with furled sails floating in a sea of invisible blue. He had left his bedcurtains completely open. As she walked nearer she saw him lying on his back, his arms flung out free of the covers. His eyes were closed, but as she neared him he muttered and thrashed, and then suddenly jerked upright, thrusting his hands out before him in defence, fingers splayed, and cried, 'No-o-o!'

She crossed the last remaining space in a flash. 'Nicky, Nicky, wake up,' she said. 'You're dreaming. Wake up.'

'Piepowder!' he cried out. His eyes were open now, two wide, black holes in his white face; his mouth another. 'Piepowder!' His voice was high and small and shrill like a child's.

'It's a dream,' she said, close to him now, urgently. 'Only a dream. Wake up, Nicky.'

She saw his body jolt violently, as though he had dropped to the end of a rope, and his face turned to her, stretched wide. 'Who is it?' he whispered, and she knew he was at the end of terror, hanging by a thread. She had never borne a child or cared for one, but nurture is in all creatures. Instinct directed her. She put out her arms, took hold of his shoulders, drew him to her, saying all the while, 'It's all right, Nicky, don't be afraid. It was only a dream, only a dream.' And, wonderfully, he came to her, yielded into her arms, put his around her, pressed himself into her, his face to her neck. She perched up on the bed the better to hold him, smelling the sharp, cold odour of his sweat, feeling his thin body vibrating like drum-skin. 'Mama?' he said tremulously. He could not yet be properly awake, she thought.

'You were dreaming. What was it?' she said softly.

270

'It was him, the Piepowder Man,' he said, still in that strange, high voice. 'He came for me.'

'It was just the moonlight on your face,' she said tenderly, 'that's all. You should pull your curtains at night.'

'I don't like the dark,' he said; his voice was coming down now. 'I don't like being shut in in the dark.' He pushed himself back a little to look at her. 'Aglaea?'

'Yes, Nicky, I'm here.' He seemed to want explanation, so she said, 'I heard you scream.'

'You came to me?'

'To see if you were all right,' she said.

He looked at her a long moment. 'How good you are,' he said, and sank back against her, nuzzling in like a puppy. 'How comfortable this is.'

She dared to stroke his head. His hair felt rough and sticky – she supposed he had sweated with fear. 'Tell me about your dream. It will help to make it go away.'

'It was—' He paused a long time, as though assembling his thoughts, and then began again. 'When we were children, I used to make up stories to tell Bendy. I made up a character called the Piepowder Man. I don't know why. I suppose I got the name out of some book or other. He had adventures – Bendy loved it. He was always pressing me for new episodes. But then I—' He stopped.

'Yes,' she prompted.

It was a long pause before he went on. 'I made him real. I brought him out of the stories. I used him to make Bendy do things – like a Bogeyman. The Piepowder Man would come and get him if he didn't – didn't—' He stopped again, and then went on in a subdued voice, as though ashamed. 'Once I made him burn his dog – his toy dog. It was an ugly old thing, made of cloth, not much like a dog really, but Bendy loved it. He took it to bed with him. So I told him the Piepowder Man wanted a sacrifice. I told him a sacrifice was always the thing you loved best. So he burned it. I made him do it.'

'Why would you do that?' she asked as gently as possible, so as not to disturb the mood. He had never told her anything about himself before. She was afraid if he noticed he was doing it now, he would stop.

'I was jealous of him,' Nicholas said after a moment's thought. 'I was always ill, and he was so healthy. Strong and healthy, and everyone loved him. The maids all cooed over him, and Mama petted him like a little dog, and my father – my father—'

'Yes?'

'I loved him so,' Nicholas said painfully, 'but he preferred Bendy. He taught him to ride, gave him presents, everything. Me he could hardly bear to look at. He was ashamed of me.'

'No, I'm sure not,' she protested.

'He never touched me,' Nicky cried out. 'He used to play rough and tumble with Bendy, throw him up in the air, wrestle with him – but he never touched me.'

'I expect he was afraid of hurting you, because you were delicate,' she suggested. He said nothing. She could feel him hitching and swallowing against her as he tried not to cry. Her heart ached for him. She wanted to cradle and soothe and protect him. The tenderness she felt for him was overwhelming, and she thought it must be love. I do love him, she thought wonderingly. Mary was right: I have come to love him.

She sat still for a long time, and there was no more talk, and gradually he relaxed in her embrace. She thought he was drifting off to sleep, and when she thought she had waited long enough not to disturb him, she tried to extricate herself, for her long immobility had made her stiff, and one of her legs had gone to sleep. But as soon as she moved he started and tightened his grip on her. 'No, don't go!'

'It's all right,' she said, 'I'll stay as long as you like.'

272

But she couldn't help shivering; she was beginning to feel cold.

'I suppose you wouldn't—' he began shyly. Nicholas, shy, of her? Her husband who might command her in anything. She was touched.

'I will do anything you want,' she said. 'You know that.'

'You will?' he said, and then, on a different intonation, as though discovering something, 'You will.' He eased himself back from her. 'Will you sleep in my bed tonight? I'm afraid of having another nightmare if I go to sleep alone.'

'Of course I will,' she said. He made room for her, pulled back the bedclothes; she climbed in. He took a moment or two disposing her as he wanted her, on her back, propped up on the pillows, and then crept into her arms, lying on his side with his legs drawn up, his head in the hollow of her shoulder and one arm lying across her to keep her still. In that position he soon fell asleep, and slept quietly without moving for the rest of the night. She could not sleep, her surroundings too strange, her emotions too disturbed. Holding him like a child, she dozed a little, waking with a nervous start every few minutes. She heard clocks strike quarters, halves and hours, heard sometimes Nicholas and sometimes Minna snoring, saw the moonlight cross the room and disappear, finally heard the first enquiring note of a blackbird and saw the grey chilly light of dawn creep in. Then she roused herself, thick-headed and prick-eyed with lack of sleep, thinking the servants must not find her here: Nicky had told her that people of their rank never slept together. She would not expose him to speculation or scandal. He was sleeping heavily now, and did not stir as she slid out from under him, except to snuggle into the pillow in place of her, as if he did not know the difference. Minna, who was lying on the foot of the bed, lifted her head, and then put it down again on her paws with a contented grunt.

273

Would he be surprised to find her there in the morning? she wondered.

The house was still quiet, and Aglaea padded undetected back to her own room and the unwelcome coldness of her own sheets. She thought as she lay shivering that she would not sleep, but once she had warmed the bed with her body's heat, she drifted down into a blissful oblivion from which it was agony to be roused when the housemaid came in with her water.

Nicky was already there when she came down to breakfast. He seemed remote, not meeting her eye as he poured her coffee and offered curtly to carve her some ham. Minna came to her chair and touched her hand and then went back to him, sitting beside him, looking up adoringly and completely unnoticed, for Nicholas was reading the newspaper. Aglaea ate her breakfast as though it was going on at a great distance, swallowing without tasting, her hands cutting, forking, lifting, all on their own, without help from her. She felt strange with lack of sleep, as though her mind were stiff and cold; she wondered now in this oddly flat and shadowless light of day if she had imagined the whole episode last night. There was nothing in her husband's manner to suggest he had spent the night any differently; and surely if he had really screamed, one of the servants would have heard it. No, she must have dreamed it.

He finished his breakfast, folded the newspaper, pushed back his chair, without looking at her. Moon came shuffling in at the same moment, with letters on a tray, and he sifted through them rapidly and put them back. 'I'll look at them later,' he said. 'I'm going up to Twelvetrees now. I shall walk up and go on to Colton from there, so have the curricle sent up to me there at noon.'

'Very good, sir,' said Moon.

274

He would not be back to take a nuncheon with her, then, she thought dully. He had not even told her where he was going – his remarks had been addressed to Moon. Nothing had changed. She had been foolish to suppose it might.

But then as he passed behind her chair on his way to the door, Minna at his heels, he laid a hand on her shoulder, and lingering just an instant, pressed it hard. She sat very still, long after he had gone, as if to move might cancel out the touch and all it meant. In the end Moon's voice brought her back to the present.

'Excuse me, madam, shall I clear?'

'Yes,' she said; and the butler was quite startled when she looked up and smiled at him.

The warm weather had brought out a few late roses, and she went into the rose garden to pick them for the house. She felt happy, and she hummed a tune as she walked amongst the bushes, feeling the misty sun warm on her back, smelling the faint, sad odour of autumn in the leaves and grass, hearing from somewhere nearby, piercingly sweet and melancholy, the song of a robin. She had given something back: that was the substance of her happiness. She had found a way to be useful. For the first time in her life she felt that it mattered to someone that she existed; that there was something only she could do.

She walked back beside the moat; a swan on the gilded water, his jet-bead eye glancing sidelong at the basket on her arm, tailed her casually, pretending he just happened to be going the same way. The low angle of the sun brought the grain of the bricks into sharp relief, and there seemed to her heightened senses something almost unbearably beautiful about them, something that went with the robin's song, tender and significant and sad. She paused at the end of the drawbridge and turned to look around, seeing the same unnatural clarity in everything, every blade of grass, every fallen leaf, every tree, as though

they had been outlined in light for her special consideration. Her soul seemed to be expanding inside her, its
damp, creased wings unfurling and stretching themselves
in this new sunlight. It's only because I haven't slept all
night, she told herself; but it didn't feel like that.

A horseman was riding along the track towards the
house. She screwed up her eyes against the hazy sun,
trying to distinguish the dark, jogging shape, wondering
was it Nicholas, coming back to see her, to tell her— ? But
no, in a moment she could see that it wasn't Checkmate,
but a darker chestnut; and that was a blue saddle-blanket,
not Nicholas's black sheepskin numnah. A moment more,
and she saw it was her brother Harry. Disappointment
and faint apprehension mingled. She stood her ground,
blocking the entrance to the drawbridge, feeling the eyes
of the house on her back.

He halted in front of her. In the warm, still air she could
smell the horse's sweat and the pungency of leather. The
chestnut stretched its neck and mouthed the bit, and the
bit-rings clinked with a small, clear sound. Everything
about the horse was clear in that same, rimmed-with-light
way, but oddly she couldn't see Harry at all: he seemed
to be obscured by a mist.

'Hullo, Aggie,' he said at last. The horse turned its
nose to her, and she put her hand out automatically;
it explored her fingers with its lips, and then turned
away, indifferent. It came to her that she had never
liked being called Aggie, but there seemed no purpose
in saying so now. Indeed, she had left it too long to
say anything in response to his greeting, and he spoke
again, anxiously, wondering at her silence. 'Are you
all right?'

'Of course I am,' she said. 'I've been picking roses.' It
made sense to her, but she could hear it sounded an odd
thing to say.

Plainly it worried Harry. He leaned forward in the
saddle with a creak of leather, his heels going down and

his calves stretching to counteract the shift of weight, and he spoke urgently and intimately, as though someone might be listening. 'I was worried about you. I haven't seen you for so long. No-one has seen you in York for weeks, and Nicky – Nicky's been—' He stopped, which was probably just as well, for there was nothing he could have said that would have been proper to a man's wife behind his back.

'I'm quite all right,' she said, looking at his boots; she wished she could see his face but it still seemed to be impossible. 'I don't go out much now, not into York.' He seemed to be waiting for her to go on, and there was a pause. She had nothing to say. Her mind lay quiet, dreaming in the sun. Behind her she could hear the swan smattering at the water with its beak, sifting weed, and far off, with that odd clarity of a still, misty day, a dog barking.

The silence seemed to break down his caution. The words burst from him. 'Aggie, does he treat you well? Are you happy?'

She roused herself. 'I can't invite you in,' she said. 'I am not to see any of you alone.'

'He said that?' Harry said, appalled.

'It's his wish. You must go away now, Harry. I should not be speaking to you.'

'But I'm your brother! He can't – I mean, surely you must—' He shook his head, helpless between outrage and propriety. It was wrong for any to try to come between a man and his wife – but the ties of family were strong, especially for an Anstey.

'His wishes are mine also,' Aglaea said dreamily. 'I will not go against them.' She looked up at his cloudy face. 'Tell Mary she was quite right. It is all one needs to know.'

'What? What is?' he asked, confused, unhappy.

'I am his wife now. I will always do what he wants,' she said. He did not know if that was an answer or not, but she

277

turned away in any case, walking across the drawbridge towards the house, and there was nothing more he could do or say.

CHAPTER THIRTEEN

The undulations of the land being what they were, a short cutting was usually followed at no great distance by a short embankment, so the soil taken from the one could be transported more or less on the level to create the other. It always gave Benedict a pleasantly logical and orderly feeling, to be evening up the landscape in that way. But the Tring cutting was different: forty feet deep and two and a half miles long, so there was no immediate use for the spoil. It had to be carried up to the top of the cutting and dumped at the sides, with considerable labour and no little danger to the navvies.

He was standing at the top of the bank, looking down and along the workings, the spring sunshine delightfully warm on his back. In six months the work had progressed very well, largely because the season had been dry. Wet weather was the very worst of ills: nothing could be relied on, embankments slipped, rails buckled, tips collapsed; the earth underfoot turned to mud fathoms deep that clung to everything and weighed like lead, so that every step was a colossal, heartbreaking effort; the horses suffered from galls, cracked heels, mud-fever, sprains and splints. Working in mud and living in shanties, the navvies never had the chance to get clean or dry. In wet weather the men grew dispirited, and the horses simply died; the work did not advance, and the contractors went broke.

But they had been remarkably lucky so far, and now a pleasant spring was following on the heels of a dry winter. Everything about the scene below him transmitted to Benedict's experienced eye a sense of satisfaction. The muddy gash in the earth, its sloping walls pocked with outcrops of chalk, was a hive of orderly activity. It must be warm down there now, for the men had taken off their shirts, and their bare backs and chests and arms gleamed in the sunlight as they bent and straightened at their work. The pickmen swung downwards, making a curious little grunt as the pick struck the earth, wiggled it softly to free it from the loosened soil, raised it up for the next stroke. The picks threw little hot sparks of light back from the sun as they made their arcs, one going down and one going up: from up here it was like a sparkle of musket-fire up and down the cutting. Behind the pickmen the shovellers followed with the barrows, swinging with a quicker, smoother rhythm, like a dance; a low flat curve of a swing, and the dirt flew up like a flock of starlings rising from a stubble field, a dark cloud that lifted into the air and landed with miraculous precision in the barrow.

In contrast to the torn and ugly rent in the earth, the men worked with a beautiful antlike orderliness; and in antlike silence, every man at his post, the gangers walking about amongst them seeing that all was well. Clay-coloured the navvies were: high-low boots, moleskin trousers, bare torso and felt hat all streaked and stained with clay. From up here they were marked out from the earth only by the little scrap of colour at the neck, the handkerchief knotted there, as much for decoration as use, like the markings of a male bird which made it different from a female. They were workers, these men: profoundly ignorant, rough, coarse, profane as they were – sometimes violent and often drunk – reckless, feckless, boastful, vainglorious, loyal, sentimental – above all, they were splendid, prodigious workers. Twenty tons of 'muck', as they called it, per man per day they could move. Up and down the country, by the sheer power of their muscles – almost with their bare hands – they were carving the naked earth into new shapes, cutting down hills, filling up valleys, erecting lofty, magnificent viaducts, boring vast stygian tunnels through the hearts of mountains. They performed feats and survived hardships that would have seen off a normal man in a matter of days. And even for navvies, the strenuous life was not without its toll. Forty was reckoned a good age for a navvy – if he was not killed in an accident long before that.

The soil here – chalk and mud mixed – was easy enough to work, though treacherous, easily loosened, and therefore given to slipping, especially after rain. Digging it was easy: the hard part was getting it up to the top of the cutting. Going up the barrow-runs – 'making the running', the men called it – called for prodigious strength, sure-footedness and nerve. The runs were simply planks laid up the sloping sides of the cutting, up which the loaded barrows of earth were wheeled. A rope was attached to the barrow, and passed through a pulley at the top, to which a horse was harnessed. The runner was similarly attached by a rope tied to his belt. When the barrow was loaded, the runner at the bottom gave a signal to the horse-boy at the top, the horse was led forward, and the barrow was drawn up, with the runner pushing and guiding it from behind. At the top the load was tipped and the man ran back down, the barrow resting against his back and the horse keeping the ropes taut. It was a spectacular feat, when all went right: Benedict could stand and watch it all day. But there was plenty of scope for things to go wrong. The planks became muddy and slippery, especially when the muck was wet, and a man could easily lose his footing or his balance. The horse-boy needed to know his business, too, for the horse had to pull steadily, without stumbling, faltering or slipping, to keep an even pull on the ropes; even more difficult, it had to be made to back steadily, to take the weight of man and barrow on the way down, and God had not made horses with smooth backward motion in mind.

If anything went wrong – and it often did – the runner's only chance of saving himself was to tip the loaded barrow over one side of the plank and himself over the other; if both went over the same side, he ran the risk of being crushed or smothered. The worst thing that could happen was for the barrow-rope to break. So far that had not happened, thank God, but when the cutting got down deeper, it would be more essential than ever to check the fastenings, and see that there was no fraying, or wear over the pulley-wheel. Last week one of the runners – Jackdaw – had suffered the opposite fate: on the way down the run, his leather belt had broken; his legs had gone from under him, and the empty barrow had run over him, breaking his collar-bone and two ribs, and tearing his scalp from front to back like a parting made with a bread-knife instead of a comb. But the cutting was still relatively shallow, and there had been no deaths so far, though there had been the usual crops of accidents. Navvies made a point of scorning danger, often to the length of courting it; they were given to issuing and accepting stupid 'dares' out of bravado, which ended in broken heads and broken limbs and sometimes even death.

It would have been easy enough to have designed a machine to take the muck to the top without a navvy having to go with it – indeed, Benedict had already sketched out something on the lines of a moving platform with a flanged wheel underneath to keep it from slipping from the run, which could be hauled up by horse-pulley or man-operated winch. He had even started to modify the design to incorporate a leverage system for easy tipping at the top, but when he had shown his drawings out of inter-est to Kibble, the contractor, the man had turned pale under his mahogany tan and begged Benedict to destroy them. 'The men hate machines,' Kibble said. 'They're convinced that every machine is designed simply to cut their wages. If they think you're working on something to cut out barrow-running, and that I agree with it, I shall have a riot on my hands.' And he told the story of how an American engineer had showed up on the Wigan workings with a design for a steam excavator which he said could do the work of thirty men, and had barely escaped with his life.

So Benedict stood at the top of the cutting and watched the men 'making the running', and felt the contentment of his new life wash over him. He was happy here. He had good lodgings at the New Inn, where Mr Knight, the landlord, kept good ale, Mrs Knight was an excellent cook, and Miss Knight was very agreeable to look at. Although he could have afforded to take a house for himself, he did not now see the point: he'd have needed at least two servants, plus a groom, who'd have had to be given daily instructions about when to expect him home. Lodgings were much cheaper – he was putting aside quite a lot of his salary – and more comfortable because he could come and go as he pleased without having to plan ahead. He had a friend who lodged there too: Philip Hastings, another engineer, someone to drink and jaw with in the evenings. He liked the life, the satisfaction of the job, the challenge of the terrain, the tough, capable men he led and directed. He was beginning to earn a reputation amongst his seniors, which pleased him; and the navvies liked him, which was a great compliment, for they quickly saw through anyone who was incompetent or who put on airs.

It was an exclusively masculine life, and that had its attractions too: it was easier and safer where no emotions were involved, and there were no obscure rules for pleasing people to be learned or guessed at. In any case, the work was hard, and there was little leisure in which to feel the want of female company. Once or twice he and Philip had dressed up in their best and gone off to Tring for their own muted version of a navvy 'randy'; but at the end of each long day a hot meal, a jug of good ale, and a comfortable bed was all he craved, and all were to be had at the New Inn. He slept like a log every night, and the morning always came too soon; with the physical effort involved in his job his appetite grew enormous, and his boyish body was filling out with a man's muscle.

Here was Walsh, one of the gangers, coming towards him with trouble in his eye. 'I think we found another of 'em, sir,' he said apologetically. 'Looks like a bad 'un. Will you come?'

In this chalk terrain, underground springs were only to be expected, and they could – and did – pop up anywhere. This one was worrying because it was near the bottom of the cutting's side. Benedict stood hands on hips staring at the water welling from the hole where a pick had recently loosened a large lump of chalk. The excavators stood round him at a respectful distance, resting on their tools, waiting for instructions; in the still warmth of the cutting he could smell their sweat like a sharp sauce over the flat, pudding smell of earth. The flow of water wasn't slackening.

'You'll have to put a drain in,' he said to Walsh. 'It'll soak away all right. The deuce of it is, where's it coming from?'

'There's a big damp patch up a-yonder, sir,' said one of the pickmen, gesturing higher up the cutting side. 'I think 'er were rising 'fore we bust 'er out.'

Benedict squinted upwards. Yes, he could see the different colour of the damper soil. 'You could be right,' he said. Natural pressure could force water quite a height through narrow fissures, until an easier path became available. Given the size of the present hole, and the volume of water, there must have been a considerable flow down here. He walked to the nearest barrow-run, and, laying hold of the slack rope – the barrow was at the bottom being filled – began to walk up the run, using the rope to steady himself. When he got opposite the damp patch, he let go the rope and climbed onto the rough cutting-face. There were plenty of foot- and hand-holds, and he scrambled across easily enough. Yes, it was definitely damp here. Draining out the water further down would dry that out, of course, but the danger was that without the pressure of water through them the fissures would collapse in on themselves and create a landslip. Only time would tell; in the meanwhile, it would probably be wise to improve the slope a little in this place. He would have to take some measurements to see what could be done . . .

Even as he was thinking that, he felt the ground under his feet shift very slightly. The information passed so rapidly through his brain that his hands and feet were already transporting him spiderwise back towards the barrow-run before he had properly registered it. Simultaneously he saw the fine fissure of a hairline fracture run past him, flickering zig-zag like an adder, but at great speed, across and upwards; and heard a clamour of warning shouts from below, where some of the halted gang were watching him. Reaching the planks, he grabbed the rope and raced upwards, feet slipping on the mud, feeling the hairy hemp scorch his hands, his brain blank to everything but effort, his every nerve and muscle dedicated to getting him to the top before the whole cutting-side slipped away. At every second he expected to hear the dreadful slow, rumbling thunder of a slip; only as he leaped over the edge towards the comfortingly solid timber supports of the pulley did he register that there had been no rumble and no further movement, and he had time for an instant's relief. His eye took in a mass of small detail: the nearest horse, standing with one hind foot cocked at rest, its tail swishing against early flies; the horse-boy holding the halter, staring at him in surprise, suspended in the middle of scratching his head, for which purpose he had pushed his cap forward and to the side; the link-man waiting at the edge of the cutting to pass on the signal, his hands jammed comfortably into his pockets. It had all happened so quickly they had not yet registered any alarm from his hurried scramble. Benedict drew a gasping breath to tell them to get back from the edge, and at that moment the black jagged snake of the fissure whipped out from under the planks across the flat surface of the cutting's top.

Then with a strange creaking sound, which was almost like the earth sighing with pain, a vast chunk of land detached itself from the lip of the cutting and slid downwards. It seemed to happen unnaturally slowly; only when the chunk began to break up and the rumbling sound started did things accelerate to normal speed.

Benedict's yell reached his own ears at the same time as the image of the link-man's fall reached his eyes: the man went feet first, his hands still in his pockets, his eyes bulging with surprise. Benedict had instinctively grabbed hold of one of the timber uprights; now as he locked his arms round it, he saw the ground underneath it collapse in its turn, right up to where the horse and boy were standing. It looked as though giant, invisible fingers had broken a piece off the edge of a cake; and like cake, it crumbled at the broken edge, lumps like currants rolling down the exposed face. He saw the horse's hind legs go over the edge, heard it whinny with alarm as it tried to keep its footing – but that was registered with one tiny part of his brain, for his own peril was immediate. With the ground slipping downwards the upright he was holding lost its support. It lurched frightfully, the gantry jerked and tilted over, his foothold went from under him, and he was swinging in space, clutching the timber to him, feeling its rough kiss against his face as the structure sagged and shuddered.

And then it held. The rumble of the fall was still in his ears, the clouds of chalk-dust were still rising round him, but the gantry stopped moving, canted over at a fantastic angle, but miraculously supporting itself on three legs; held in place by the various timbers connecting it to the tipping platform, and the bracing effect of the platform itself. It could all go at any moment: he had one instant of respite in which to save himself.

Jerking up his legs he wrapped them round the timber as well, clutching it with all four limbs like a monkey. Digging the edge of his heels into the roughness of the wood, he was able to exert just enough effort with his calves to hitch his body up, grip with his knees, and support himself long enough to free his hands to reach up for the cross-strut. He had to swing himself out, holding on for a terrifying moment with one hand only as he brought the other round the upright; then both hands were on the cross-strut, and he went along it hand over hand. The whole structure jerked and settled again, and his legs swung with a colossal, impeding weight like a pendulum, threatening to drag him loose. But he reached the end of the strut, and now he needed that pendulum, for when he let go with his hands, the swing had to carry him across the gap to the edge of the slip. Twice he swung his legs, to build up the momentum, and then he let go. His body arched heavily through empty space, his feet and then his body struck earth, and then he was scrabbling, scrambling, slipping in the loose spoil, over the edge and on hands and knees to safety.

There were people around him, hands clutching him, patting him. It had all taken seconds only: at the bottom of the cutting the slip was still rumbling and settling. Benedict sat gasping, his mouth full of dust and grit, his clothes white with it, and slowly became aware of the pain in his hands – cut and bruised and full of splinters – and in his arms – the muscles wrenched with his efforts. But he had made it! Someone was thumping him on the back and a foolish grin was on his face, which he made haste to wipe off as it came to him that he was still in charge, and if he was not hurt, someone else surely must be. He pushed his friendly assailants away and scrambled to his feet; at that moment the gantry creaked horribly and went over in a crashing of boards and a fresh rumbling of loosened soil.

'Jupiter,' he said, 'this is the devil of a mess.' His voice was dry with chalk, and he coughed and tried to find a clean bit of hand or arm to wipe his mouth with. Standing at the edge of the slip he could see the gantry lying almost at the foot of the slope, head downwards in a heap of soil and broken timber. A huge piece of the cutting-side had gone, and a mountain of muck would now have to be removed from the bottom of the cutting. That much was immediately visible: it took longer to find out about the casualties. The link-man had survived miraculously unhurt: having slid all the way down the slope feet first on his back, he was snatched to safety out of the path of the falling debris by a quick-thinking navvy at the bottom, for with his hands trapped in his pockets he could not have saved himself. The rest of the men at the bottom of the cutting had scrambled out of the way in time, and there was nothing more than a few cuts and bruises from flying rocks. The horse which Benedict had seen go over the side had managed to keep its feet and had slid and scrambled to the bottom, but it had a split hoof and was much cut about the legs, and was lame in the shoulder besides: it would be weeks before it was fit again, and its nerves were all to pieces.

It was the horse-boy who had suffered. He had not let go of the halter and been dragged over the side by the weight of the horse. When the horse had managed to scramble away sideways, the boy had tumbled straight down, and when the pulley-gantry fell, he was underneath it. He had been dragged all the way to the bottom by a combination of timbers and rubble. When Benedict wincingly inspected the poor battered body, he thought the boy's mother would not have known him. But of course it was because his mother – still less his father – had refused to know him in the first place that he had become a navvy-boy. Nobody even knew his rightful name. He had been called Nobby – a nickname given to a great many navvies, a sort of verbal shrug of indifference, like calling a person What's-his-name or Thingum-a-jig; and because there were so many Nobbies in the cutting, he had been further differentiated by the title Mack's Nobby, because he was in Macdonald's gang.

So it was as Mack's Nobby he would be buried; and as Benedict made his painful and weary way home that night, he comforted himself on Nobby's behalf that he would not go to his grave unmourned. Navvies were loyal to their own, and notoriously sentimental. Not only Macdonald's gang – the boy's 'family' – but the whole contract would walk behind his coffin on Sunday, wearing white favours. Kibble had spoken to the men. He would arrange the funeral – coffin, headstone and all; the navvies had agreed to pay for it out of their next week's wages.

There was no more work done that day, beyond the essentials of making the site safe for the night. Then the men by common consent knocked off out of respect for the dead, though they might have done several hours of over-time and earned themselves a bonus. But there was no question of it, and Kibble had not even bothered to press the matter, knowing his men as he did, even though the accident was going to put his contract behind. Benedict was glad enough to be getting off at a reasonable hour. He ached all over, and his hands were so painful he had difficulty holding the reins. Mrs Knight would dress them for him, he thought, and provide him with a hot bath – perhaps, if he laid the story on thick and rare enough, without charging extra for it. And then – supper!

He was sitting down at the host's table making a start on a tureen of excellent pea soup when Philip arrived, and sat down opposite him.

'Well, tell me all! I seem to have missed all the excitement – and you're the hero of the hour, by all accounts!'

'Victim, not hero,' Benedict said in mild surprise. 'I came off with sore hands and strained muscles, but I didn't do anything valorous, I promise you.'

Philip raised an eyebrow. 'You ran up the barrow-run to give the warning, instead of saving your own hide. That's what they are saying.'

'It was the only way I could go. Really, they must be hungry for heroes if they can make anything of that,' Benedict said with an uneasy laugh.

Philip grinned. 'I should let 'em, if I were you. After you with the soup, there! It's a hard job keeping on top of these tough customers: a little hero-worship will ease your passage mightily – and mine with it, with any luck. I shall get all the details from you tonight, and bathe in reflected glory tomorrow.' He took the ladle from Benedict and held his bowl in position, ladling the glorious stuff with a generous hand. There were chips of ham floating in it, and little balls of forcemeat. 'God, but Mrs Knight's a wonderful woman! Thank the Lord she's married, or I might be tempted to make a fool of myself.'

'It's all very well,' Benedict said, suddenly guilty, 'but someone was killed.'

'Yes, I know,' Philip said. 'Poor little devil! But life goes on, you know. I mean him no disrespect, but it would be a crime not to relish this soup. Eat up, old man! It wasn't *your* fault.'

'I know,' Benedict said, and sighed, and tasted his soup. 'It was the shock, that's all.' It was a shock when he had looked down at the torn and bloody body of poor little Nobby Nobody; what he could not tell Philip was that in that instant he had seen, first Dandy Dick lying there, and then his own son, grown up in obscurity to be just old enough to die without a name on the railway workings. He hardly ever thought of Liza and the child since he had come to Tring: life was too full and too satisfying. On the few occasions they had crossed his mind, it was with relief that he was rid of his burden, and a realisation that he had been a fool voluntarily to take them on at such an early age. When Philip wanted a woman, he had an arrangement with a nice, clean girl in the town who, in return for an agreed sum of money, not only gave him his pleasure but also accepted responsibility for her own welfare.

He had had one letter from Dandy, in January, telling him that they were all well, and that Fand was happy and not pining for him. Dandy's writing and phraseology had improved greatly, and Bendy was amused to note he was now acquiring an agricultural turn of phrase to replace his horse-boy's vocabulary. Liza was happy cooking and cleaning, and in her new status as widow had been able to make friends with some of the other estate wives. Little Thomas, going on two-and-a-half now, was showing a great affinity for animals: he liked to go with Dandy to the Home Farm, where he helped feed the pigs and calves; but his favourite trip was to the pheasant coops, where he demonstrated the remarkable ability in such an active child to sit quiet for hours together if there were birds to watch.

Just for a moment while reading the letter Benedict had felt a little left out. *After all he had done for them*, the thought began, to be hastily abandoned. They were doing very well without him, making a better life for themselves. He wondered, though, what would become of the boy, and whether he would ever see him again. And the shocks of this day's events had proved to him that one part of his mind at least had been brooding over his former family.

Philip had been eyeing him covertly, and when he finally shook himself out of his reverie, he said, 'You need taking out of yourself. What a pity we're so far from the town here – a little flirtation is just the thing to buck a man up when he's in the doldrums.'

Benedict was about to answer when, as though on cue, the landlord came in, bearing a magnificent beefsteak pudding, and his daughter followed behind him, carrying a vast tray on which the rest of the meal reposed.

'Gentlemen? Ah, Mr Morland! I've only just heard

about the accident. I was down in the cellar when you come in, sir, and I've been in the tap ever since, but now in comes one of your fellows with such a garbled story I can't make head nor tale of it, 'cept that some wretched boy has been killed. But my missus tells me you've been hurt too, sir, which I am heartily sorry for, and if I had known earlier, I'd have been along to say so in person.'

While he talked he had put down the pudding and quickly transferred the other dishes from the tray to the table – mashed potato and a dish of cabbage, the end of a cold mutton ham, a rabbit stew with onions, and a basket of bread.

'Now then,' he said. 'There's pudding afterwards, Mrs Knight's ginger duff, and a bite o' cheese if you're willing, so set to, gentlemen, and I'll fill up your jug. Now, by the Holy, if I hadn't gone and forgotten your hands, Mr Morland, which Mrs Knight says you'll find it hard work a-serving yourself. Let my 'Linda do it for you, while I go and see to the jug. 'Linda, put the tray down, child, and serve Mr Morland. Don't mind if she's shy, Mr Morland. A real hero don't come in her way very often!'

So Benedict had the double pleasure of being served by Belinda's own hands – of having her soft arms and tender bosom heartbreakingly close to him as she leaned across for the various dishes – and of telling her the story of his heroic day and seeing the light of admiration in her blue eyes. Across the table Philip egged him on, and gave him such meaningful looks that he had difficulty in keeping his countenance. But it all had the effect of driving away his momentary melancholy.

The food played its part, too: Bendy had a day-long hunger on him, and Mrs Knight's cooking was superb as always. Half the beefsteak pudding, all the ham and most of the rabbit stew disappeared inside two hearty young frames, to be followed by ginger duff with sweet sauce –

two helpings a man – and a large piece of sweet Leicester cheese with the last of the bread. When they were both sighing and stretching out their legs under the table, and Bendy's wounded hands had settled down into a distant and half-hearted grumble, Mr Knight came in from the coffee-room to check the level in their jug, and suddenly clapped his hand to his brow and said, 'Stuff my head with eels, if I haven't gone and forgotten all about the letter! 'Linda! B'linda! Bring in that letter for Mr Morland, on the kitchen chimney-piece. I beg your pardon, sir. I hope it wasn't something urgent.'

'No, no, I don't think so,' Benedict said, taking it from Miss Knight's fragrant fingers with a smile, and seeing George Findlay's fist scrawled across the front. 'It's only a note from a friend.'

'Here, you'd better let me open it for you,' Philip said. 'You'll never manage with those bandages. I must say, they look quite heart-rending. It's a pity you have to waste them on me. Oh, go ahead and read it, by all means,' as Bendy made a polite gesture and an enquiring sound.

Benedict received the opened and unfolded letter across the table gratefully, and settled down to read it. In his usual racy style, George imparted scraps of local news that he knew would interest Benedict, and in more detail the course of his own true love. It was the end part which made Benedict sit up with a start and read with closer attention.

'I don't know whether you will have heard from other sources, but the divine Miss Fleetham is soon to take another name. Her engagement is announced to a man called Partridge, who ought rather to have been called Gundog, by the way he has put the local females in a flutter. Supremely handsome (so Georgy assures me) and in air and manners just what is pleasing (again, *apud* Georgy) he had only to reveal his possession of a large income and a family seat in Derbyshire to have every woman in a twenty-mile circle swooning over him. The rest of us eligible bachelors could do nothing but fume until the bold Miss F snatched him away from under everyone's noses and won our eternal gratitude. *Some* young ladies – says Georgy – are saying unkind things about Miss F: that she threw herself at P's head, even that she is *fast* (horrors!) – but we need not pay any heed to that. Young ladies will say these things, in spite of every warning. I have seen Miss F in Selby, looking very pleased with herself and sporting a vast diamond ring. I fancy you had a *tendresse* for her once, so you will be glad to know she has disposed of herself to such advantage. Comfort yourself you could not have competed, even had you been here.'

Benedict put down the letter at last, and stared at nothing, his mind filled with memories of Miss Fleetham. It was true, he could not have competed; and it was a comfort to know she was to marry well. A small comfort, though. Miss Fleetham was to be Mrs Partridge, to lie in another man's arms and be lost to him for ever. One part of his mind had always told him that she was too good for him, that he had no chance of ever winning her, and when he had left York for Tring, that part of his mind had told him that he would never see her again. But there was another part which had insisted on keeping her image to the fore, had gone on hoping against hope, and believing – as one can believe, quite irrationally, in magic – that he would somehow make his fortune and go back to find her still waiting for him. The memory of her face when she had said, 'Do it quickly – and come back for me!' had seemed more vivid than anything his sensible half could produce in evidence. He had loved her at first sight, and surely that must count for something – some Divine plan, some inescapable destiny?

But now she was engaged to be married, and he would never see her again. He drew her image out of his memory and gazed, heartsick, at her beauty, her sweetness, which had been his in imagination. The lovely Miss Fleetham! And what sort of a name was Partridge, for God's sake?

'Something wrong, old man?' Philip enquired cautiously from behind the pipe he was trying to light. 'No-one ill, I hope?'

'No – no, it's not that,' Benedict roused himself from the torpor of disappointment which was overcoming him. 'It's just – well, a friend of mine tells me that a young lady I was – that I admired—'

'She's married someone else, eh?' Philip finished for him with unusual acuity. Benedict nodded. 'I guessed there was someone. At that ball at Christmas, I couldn't interest you in any of the females, though they were dashed pretty, some of 'em. And there's a *look* about you sometimes – I guessed you were carrying a torch for someone.'

'She's betrothed,' Bendy said, not without bitterness, 'to a very rich man called Partridge.'

'Damned rotten luck,' Philip said warmly. 'That's the penalty of our kind of life. Johnny-on-the-spot always has the advantage. But if he's very rich, you can't begrudge her. A girl has a duty to marry well, if she can.'

'I know,' Benedict sighed.

'It wouldn't show much sense if she turned him down for a penniless engineer who ain't even on hand to make love to her.'

'I know,' Benedict said again, rather more shortly.

Philip sucked his pipe thoughtfully, and then said, 'Look here, on Saturday night we'll go into Tring and have some fun. I'll get my girl Molly to find one for you – you need to let off steam a bit. What do you say?'

Benedict shook his head. 'Thanks, but I don't think it will help.'

'Lord, you have got it bad! Look here, if this Miss Whatsername was still free, you might have found yourself marrying her, and then – no more fun, just debts and babies; and the nice, pretty girl you fancied turning day by day into her ugly, bad-tempered old mother! Marriage is for fools. And you know it really – you were happy enough until today, weren't you?'

'I suppose so,' Benedict sighed. He wondered what sort of domestic happiness he could ever look forward to. Perhaps Philip was right, and he would do better to remain a bachelor, living in lodgings and relying on the Mollys of this world to warm his cold bed once in a while – ah, but not his heart! There was the rub. In a moment of insight he put his finger on the flaw. It was love that he wanted, not just female company. It was in his nature. What he wanted was a wife – in spite of everything Philip said – because he wanted to love and be loved in return, to spend his life with a woman he could trust, admire, cherish, a woman who would be a companion as well as a lover. Surely he would find such a woman some day? Surely he would not be condemned to the pointlessness of this lonely life for ever?

'We'll go into Tring on Saturday,' Philip asserted confidently, 'and you'll forget all your troubles. And on Sunday we'll go to church, and you can look at all the pretty girls as they come out, and realise that your Miss Whatsername wasn't the only one in the world.'

'It's the funeral on Sunday,' Benedict said.

'You don't have to go.'

'I think I must,' Bendy said, and was glad of the excuse. Poor Nobby – but he didn't want to be looking at pretty girls with Philip nudging him and blowing in his ear like an enthusiastic horse.

To the surprise and gratification of everyone on the contract, Nobby's funeral was honoured by the presence of Mr Robert Stephenson, who was paying one of his periodical visits of inspection. Bendy was glad for Nobby's sake, and Macdonald's gang plainly took it as a direct compliment, and filed out of the church past him in reverent solemnity, breaking into grins and chatter as soon as they were beyond the gate. When Bendy reached him he was given a hearty shake of the hand, and, most flatteringly, an invitation to dinner at his inn that evening.

They talked at first about the contract and the accident.

'How long to you think it will put you back?' Stephenson asked.

'I went down to have a look at it this morning,' Benedict said, 'and I think not more than a fortnight – if there are no more slips, and if the weather holds.' He almost shrugged as he added the last part. Such things were incalculable.

Stephenson nodded. 'That's the best we can ever say. I'm afraid most of our contractors are discovering that their estimates were no better than blind guesses. How could they be, indeed? We are undertaking tasks without any precedent in engineering: the expenses involved couldn't be foreseen by any experience. It was impossible to know beforehand how things would go.'

'Is the line going to come in much over budget?' Bendy asked.

'Enormously, I should think,' Stephenson said. 'We shall have to apply to the shareholders again, I don't doubt. That's why one must choose them carefully in the first place, to be sure they understand the unpredictable nature of the undertaking. Your friend Mr Hudson of York will find that out soon enough with his new line. He fixed his capital at £300,000, but he had better assume it will be twice that.'

'Have you news from York?' Bendy asked hopefully.

'I met Hudson in Town,' Stephenson explained. 'The York and North Midland company has got its Bill forward, and Hudson and some of his friends were in London trying to ease its way through Parliament.' He eyed Benedict curiously. 'You know, I suppose, that your brother has got together a group of landowners against the railway?'

Benedict nodded without embarrassment. 'He swore he'd stop it, but I don't see how he can.'

'He's persuaded the landowners not to invest in it, which is a setback. Hudson's trying to sell shares to his capitalist friends in the City. However he told me when I met him on Wednesday in Westminster that the shares are beginning to trade, which will encourage the investors – he mentioned a premium of £4 on a £50 share, though he may have been exaggerating. But if it's true, it may turn out that your brother has done his friends no service.'

'He didn't set out to benefit them, but to stop the railway,' Benedict said.

'If the Act is passed this session,' Stephenson said, 'they may be able to start work this autumn. My father has promised to peg out the line himself – or the first few miles, at any rate – as a gesture of support. That will look well in the reports.' He smiled a little. 'It's always important to have the backers in good heart at the beginning: their courage is bound to be tested when the delays and difficulties begin.'

Benedict was silent, thinking of York, Hudson, the railway, the position he had been promised as engineer – and Miss Fleetham. If the position were offered now, would there be any point in taking it? It would expose him to his brother's enmity again; and if *she* were married, he would as soon be far away from any chance of seeing her.

Stephenson watched him during this brief reverie, and his next question seemed almost to have read his thoughts. 'Are you happy here, on this contract?'

Benedict felt awkward, as though he had been caught out in some act of disloyalty. 'Oh, very happy,' he said hastily. 'And I like working for you, sir. I am very grateful for all you have done for me.'

Stephenson smiled. 'I'm glad to hear it. But does that mean you would not like to be moved? I was thinking of asking you to transfer to Crick.'

'To Crick? To the Kilsby Tunnel?'

'Just so,' Stephenson nodded. 'We're having a great deal of trouble there, as I suppose you must have heard. We knew there was sand under Kilsby Hill – we found it in our trial borings, as the canal companies did before us – but I had hoped that by taking the line further west towards Kilsby we might avoid the worst of it. But the working-shafts are running into water and sand in such volume that they're unusable, and when the contractors tried opening a parallel driftway to drain the site, that blocked with sand as well. And now – I suppose you heard that Nowell, the contractor, died?'

'I heard he was ill,' Bendy said.

'His sons don't want to carry on without him. There seems to be a curse on the Kilsby contractors – Chapman and Hughes are both bedridden now, as well,' Stephenson said. 'The directors were all in a gloom and panic, but I told them it *can* be done, and it *will* be done. My solution is to bring in a new workforce, and to oversee the works myself. Lean will be District Engineer under me – he's a good man – but I would like to have you there as well, Morland, if you will come. You have done satisfactory work here at Tring, but you are a good tunnel engineer and you were with me on the Glenfield Tunnel when we hit the sand there. If I have learned one thing in my life, it is that specific experience like that is precious.'

Benedict smiled inwardly, thinking that it was like Mr Robert to frame the move as a request: under the terms of his contract he was obliged to go anywhere he was sent. 'I'm flattered, sir,' he said, 'and I'll be happy to go anywhere you think I will be useful.' Tring or Kilsby, what did it matter if Miss Fleetham was out of reach?

'Good man! It's going to be a tough job – I fancy the hardest battle I ever fought – but we *will* do it.'

'Certainly we will,' Bendy said with a grin. 'No mere hill – even with quicksand underneath – can stand in the way of history.'

Stephenson's tired face lit with a smile. 'Hold on to

that spirit – you may need it! Kilsby isn't much of a place, I'm afraid, just a small village. You can base yourself comfortably at Crick, though – a nice little place, with a good inn. It's about two miles away, so you'll need a couple of good horses. And of course there'll be times you'll have to bed down in the village, which I don't disguise from you will be rough.'

'I didn't become an engineer for a life of comfort,' Benedict said.

'There'll be a rise in salary for you, too,' Stephenson went on. 'Another fifty pounds per annum—'

'I'm most grateful, sir.'

'—though the way things look, I doubt you'll have much opportunity to spend it.'

'All the better,' said Benedict. 'I can save up for my comfortable retirement.'

CHAPTER FOURTEEN

Miss Smith found Ferrars in the steward's room going over the books, as he did every Friday morning. He looked up quickly as she came in and immediately drew a sheet of paper over the figures he had been working on. Miss Smith noted the action with an inward smile.

'Where is your charge?' he said sharply.

She lifted a key out of her pocket. 'Don't worry, I've locked the door. But it's her I've come to talk to you about.'

His eyes narrowed. 'Well, what do you want?'

'I want to know what you plan to do with her. We can't go on as we are.'

'Are you telling me you can't control her?'

Miss Smith snorted. 'Oh, I can control her all right, if I'm given a free hand. But I doubt you'd be ready to countenance the measures that'd be necessary.' She wondered even as she said it whether indeed that was true. She was beginning to think Ferrars might be capable of anything. 'You know that she's fifteen now?'

'Is she indeed?' he said without interest.

'Her birthday's long past. And fifteen is almost a woman.'

He looked at her steadily for a moment, and then replaced the pen in the inkpot, signifying his full attention. 'Sit down,' he said. 'Now then, what exactly is the problem? Is she becoming difficult to handle?'

'Oh, she's quiet enough. Ever since that illness she

seems to've gone inside herself. Lost interest in every-thing. When we go out in the carriage, she just sits staring at nothing. Same in the evenings – she might have a book on her lap, but she hardly turns a page; never speaks unless spoken to.'

'Well, well, that all sounds excellent. What are you worried about?'

Miss Smith hesitated: unsure of his mind, she did not quite know what it was wise to tell him. 'You can't keep a young woman locked up forever. What'll it look like to anyone outside?'

'She has no family. Mr Morland is her legal guardian – and he has no family either. Who is there to wonder?'

'We don't live in a desert, Mr Ferrars. I've seen looks cast—'

'Looks? From whom?'

'Servants. Tenants. Estate workers,' Miss Smith said with a shrug. 'Things get about, you can't help it. And the Master might have no family, but Madam has. Now, I don't know what you've told people, or what you hope they think, but I tell you this, Mr Ferrars, unless you take me into your confidence, I can't help you. Like I said, we can't go on like this for ever. Apart from the gossip, it's an unnatural life for a girl, and it's bound to have its effect. She's quiet now, but who's to know what goes on inside her head? She might turn fury any time, attack me and escape.'

'If she turns fury, as you put it, she can be restrained.'

Oho, thought Miss Smith. Now we're coming at it. 'Put her in fetters, you mean?' Ferrars said nothing. 'See here, Mr Ferrars, you'd better tell me what you want of this girl, for we've reached a crossroads, and she might go one way or t'other. Do you want folk to think she's mad? Or do you want to drive her mad?' She smiled, a horrid sight. 'If that's your plan, I can help it along. There are ways.'

Ferrars felt a revulsion for the death's head opposite him, but he concealed it. His mind worked under his blank expression. She was right: it was a crossroads. Fifteen was no longer a child, and he would soon have to decide whether to keep Jemima in restraint for the rest of her life, or to find some other way of making it impossible for her to leave Morland Place. Complete restraint of an adult was a difficult thing to manage, unless one went the whole hog. Fetters? Yes – well . . .

Ferrars stared ahead of him, frowning, deep in thought. After a moment he roused himself to say, 'Thank you. You've been most helpful. I shall take what you've said into consideration, and let you know my decision in due course.'

She looked a little surprised, but after a moment's hesitation got up and left the room. Ferrars continued not to look at her, but when the door closed behind her he got up and began walking up and down the room. That was a dangerous woman, he thought. He had noticed that all through the interview Miss Smith had referred only to Ferrars' wishes and designs – she had made no pretence that the Master was really in charge. And she had hinted at complicity – offered to help him in his schemes. It was only one step from there to blackmail. No, he concluded, useful though she had been, Miss Smith must go. It would have to be done quick and sharp, before she had a chance to talk to anyone, or to tell Jemima anything she ought not to know.

But then, who would look after Jemima? Not Mrs Moon, not now the girl was fifteen – she would take too much watching. Fifteen? A thought came to him, and he turned it round in his mind, looking at it from all angles, letting it expand. Yes, that would be the way. That would have to be the way. It would solve a number of problems in one fell swoop; and given the natures of the protagonists, it ought to work.

'May I speak to you, Madam?' Ferrars said respectfully.

Aglaea startled. Though she had been facing towards

the door, she had not seen him come in; she had been too deep in her painting – so deep that she had no idea how much time had passed since she had taken up her brush. It was often like that when she painted. It was as if she went away into the picture, and lived there, in another time outside the world. The world was well escaped today: grey, overcast, dull, and damp, cold for August, a rainy day without rain. Ignoring the view from the window, she looked curiously at what she had done. The picture was three-quarters finished: a storm at sea, and a wrecked ship, broken masts and rigging trailing in the water. The ship was about to be overwhelmed by a great wave: she had put her bowsprit into the underside of it, and she would not recover. Aglaea felt mildly annoyed to have been disturbed, and she looked away from Ferrars (even obsequious, he was a horrible sight; no, especially obsequious) and towards the clock on the chimney-piece. Two hours. She had been painting two hours, and it felt like a few minutes.

'Yes, what is it?' she said.

'It's a delicate matter, Madam – concerning Miss Jemima.' He smiled a little, like an ingratiating dog. She wished he wouldn't. His teeth were like slimy tombstones, outward markers of hidden corruption. 'I suppose you know, Madam, that she is now fifteen?'

'What of it?' Aglaea said non-comittally. Was she indeed? Fifteen? She had been thinking of her as a child.

'Too old for a governess, really. It is a time of life when a girl begins to come out of the schoolroom and join the society of adults.'

'What concern is it of yours?' Aglaea said bravely. 'The Master looks after her interests, I am quite sure.'

'Everything that concerns the estate concerns me, Madam,' Ferrars said. 'My duty – and my pleasure – is to seek new ways of serving my master, making sure everything runs smoothly. The fact of the matter is, Madam, that Miss Smith must go away – for personal reasons, to do with her family – and it occurred to me that rather than engaging another governess for Miss Jemima, she might be allowed to come out of the schoolroom and act as your companion – if you were willing, of course, to take charge of her.'

With any other servant, and on any other subject, Aglaea might have made a sharp reply; but aside from her dislike and fear of Ferrars, her interest in Jemima had always been keen. 'Would that be wise?' she said slowly. 'I had understood that – that her mental constitution was delicate.'

Ferrars bowed. 'I understand you, Madam. I think I can assure you that Miss Smith has exaggerated matters – probably for her own purposes, to make herself more indispensable. From my own observations and from what the other servants say, I believe Miss is quite docile; not deranged at all, only a little slow and – shall we say, backward?'

'And you think that I could be useful to her?'

'I had thought rather in terms of her being useful to you, Madam: I have served amongst gentlefolk long enough to know the value of a female companion to a lady, especially one who lives rather retired. But without a doubt, it would be of the greatest possible benefit to Miss, to be around a lady of such refinement, whose conversation and example cannot but be improving.'

A companion, Aglaea thought, half eagerly, half doubtfully. Well, yes, she had sometimes felt isolated, since Nicholas had forbidden her visits to town, and a female companion, even if she were slow and backward, would introduce a welcome variety into the days. It would be good to feel herself useful, too – and Jemima might grow fond of her. It would be pleasant to have someone who looked up to her and depended on her.

'It may be as you say,' Aglaea said at last, 'but you know very well that decisions about Miss Jemima are not mine to make. You must speak to your master, not to me.'

Ferrars bowed again. 'Indeed, Madam, and so I shall. But I would not raise the subject with him without knowing first whether it would accord with your wishes.'

She hesitated. 'You may tell Mr Morland I am willing, if you think it is your place to raise the matter.'

'My wish is only to serve,' Ferrars said, and bowed himself out. Aglaea went back to her painting, but her concentration was broken, and she soon put it aside. Thinking over the conversation, as she did again and again in the hours that followed, it did seem to her odd that Ferrars had approached her before Nicholas. But then Nicholas had not been well lately, suffering from dreadful headaches, nausea and a deranged bowel, and his sleep had been troubled with nightmares night after night. Aglaea had been sitting up with him, and sometimes sleeping in his bed to try to keep them at bay. Presumably Ferrars knew how poorly Nicholas went on, so perhaps he was only trying to save his master trouble.

Nicholas sat in the fireside chair in his room, his elbows resting on the padded arms, his head in his hands. Despite the fire burning in the grate, he still felt shivery; his head was whirling unpleasantly, and he had not yet discovered whether it was worse when his eyes were shut or when they were open. When they were open, the room seemed to jerk and flicker about him like the skin of a dog with fleas; things moved at the corner of sight, the whole room turned away from him when he tried to follow it with his head. But when his eyes were closed he kept – passing out of the world, he supposed he might say. It was not like falling asleep, for the lapses lasted only moments, and he was conscious that they *were* lapses, though they were unpleasantly real. During them people spoke in loud, toneless voices, saying words which meant nothing; objects of huge significance rolled slowly past him, unidentifiable, just out of grasp, disappearing when he was on the brink of understanding what they meant. Worst of all, the patterns were repeated over and over again, like recollection gone mad.

He took his hands from his head and grasped the book in his lap and tried to concentrate on it, but the images there which ought to have stimulated him seemed dull and coarse to his sated senses. Yesterday – ah, yesterday had been a bad day, ending with what he thought of as a good night, which was why he felt so ill this morning. The surface of his body seemed to be shimmering, a feeling like the look of mother-of-pearl. Meat that was going off had that iridescence sometimes. No, he mustn't think about meat. He had been sick already this morning, and further vomiting would only make his stomach sore, for there was nothing more to bring up. Too great a variety of stimulants last night at the Golden Cage; and three girls! The expense! Two would have done. The third was sheer waste, extravagance brought on by his anger and disappointment during the day – his attempt to make up to himself for the bad news.

For as soon as he got to York yesterday, he had heard that the York and North Midland Railway Company had held its first formal meeting, registered the shares, and elected its board of directors. That was how well matters were going! The railway Bill had cantered easily through Parliament, thanks to whatever greasing of palms Hudson had been up to in London.

'He knows the way the game's played,' said Jack Cox, Nicholas's informant about the board meeting, tapping the side of his nose with a knowing wink. 'Remember how he got the Tories elected in 'thirty-four?'

Last year complaints had been made against Hudson and he had had to appear before a Commons committee to explain the vast sums of money he had spent during the election campaign. He had been accused of gross bribery, and the only reason he and the rest of his committee had

307

escaped prosecution was by the counter-accusation that the Whigs had been guilty of organised intimidation in the same campaign.

'Oh, he knows all about oiling the wheels, does our Mr Hudson!' Cox went on. 'Well, so long as he uses his own fortune, who cares? Our noble MP Mr Lowther will gather some support, and Hudson will buy the rest. The result is as sure as a gun.'

The Act had authorised a line from York to join the North Midland at Altofts, near Normanton, together with a branch from Whitwood to give access to Leeds, three short curves joining it to the Leeds and Selby at Milford, and an extension to the river in York for goods. It all looked as settled as could be.

'Who is on this damned Railway Company board?' Nicholas asked. 'I suppose Hudson has got himself made chairman?'

'Of course,' Cox said. 'And there's the Lord Mayor, of course, and the Town Clerk, and all the other Corporation toadies.' He gave Nicky a sidelong look of amused malice. 'Your brother-in-law is elected solicitor to the Company. He has his seat on the board and his place in history secured. You've allied yourself with the wrong side, Nicky, my boy! Always side with the winners.'

'They haven't won yet,' Nicholas snarled. 'The battle isn't over.'

'It looks tolerably over to me, old fellow,' said Cox, enjoying himself. 'I was chatting to George Baker this morning – he's secretary to the Board – and he says Stephenson means to start pegging out the line early in September. And of course, taking it across Micklegate Stray and Chaloner's Whin means they don't have to worry about landowners, for that's common land. All that's needed is the Corporation's permission, and the Corporation belongs to Hudson, heart, soul and pocket.' He grinned. 'You'll have the railway right on your doorstep, Nicky! You'll be able to stand at the edge of

Hob Moor and watch the locomotives chugging along on the other side!'

Nicholas had snarled helplessly; after that, things could only get worse. Needing comfort, he had taken an extensive and well-lubricated luncheon with Jack in the Maccabbees, and they had stayed on all afternoon playing billiards for large sums of money, and drinking brandy. But Jack's sense of humour had led him to bait Nicky continuously over the failure of his attempt to stop the railway. Finally he went too far, and commiserated with Nicholas that his brother Benedict had not been appointed Engineer to the York and North Midland, instead of Thomas Cabery.

'It must be such a blow to you,' he said sympathetically.

Nicky had lost his temper – 'And here's a blow to you!' – and there had been a most undignified scuffle in the billiard-room, which had led to a broken cue and an embarrassing confrontation with the proprietor: he could not quite ask two such free-spending members to leave, but he said enough to embarrass and shame Nicky, leaving him with no resort but an angry and scornful retreat. And as they were staggering out into Stonegate, Nicky had the further rotten luck to bump into Harry Anstey, walking by on his way home.

A sober man who has been working all day at his respectable profession and is returning to his virtuous wife and domestic hearth is not the best person to be met by his drunken brother-in-law, emerging from an establishment devoted to idle pleasure and high-stake gaming. He looked at Nicky steadily, gravely, but he could not prevent his lip from curling.

'Well, Nicky,' he said. 'You seem to have been enjoying yourself today.'

'What the hell business is it of yours, you infernal puppy?' Nicholas snarled, leaning against Jack Cox and making them both stagger.

Despite himself Harry smiled slightly. 'Puppy? We're the same age exactly – though I must say you look ten years older than me at the moment.'

'Puppy I said and puppy I meant! George Hudson's lapdog, that's what you are – and all the world knows it. He snaps his fingers and you come running, tail-awag. Oh yes, master! Oh no, master! Fawning on a draper's assistant with dirty fingernails. My God, you should be ashamed of yourself!'

Harry knew he ought not to respond – Nicky was plainly drunk – but the open hostility and the thought of Aglaea at Morland Place, forbidden to see her own family, were too much to bear. 'I have nothing to be ashamed of in working to bring about something that will be to everyone's good.'

'Ha!' Nicky interposed scornfully.

'The railway will bring prosperity to York.'

'You mean to line your own pockets, that's all. Why else would you tag along with a crook like Hudson?'

'How dare you criticise me? Anything I do must be better than sousing all day in a club as you do, addling your brains and wasting your fortune – while your wife stays home alone and neglected.'

'You leave my wife out of it,' Nicholas panted in fury. 'She's my sister!'

'Not any more. She repudiates you. Sent you away, didn't she?' Nicholas grinned in trumph as Harry could not deny it. 'Ha! You see? You're nothing, Harry Anstey – you're no-one! Youngest son of a tradesman's family! Who was your great-grandfather? You thought you could ally yourself to the great families by foisting your sister on me. Well, you were mistaken!'

Jack Cox tugged at his sleeve anxiously. 'Come away, Nicky. You'll only say something you regret.' He tugged again, glancing at Harry's furious face, and lowered his voice. 'Come away, old man. He might call you out.'

'Call me out?' Nicholas said in the loud, careless voice

of the very drunk. 'I wouldn't *go* out with a – a – *thing* like him! Hudson's poodle!' He became aware at last of the hand tugging at his sleeve. 'Oh let me alone!' he cried, pushing Cox so hard that he staggered and almost fell, and Nicky hiked off, half running, half stumbling down Little Stonegate and into the maze of low alleys and courts which seemed at that moment to offer him safety and tranquillity. He had wandered for a while, revolving angry and incoherent thoughts, until roused by an inept attempt by an urchin to pick his pocket. He had cuffed the child with all his strength, lifting the skinny thing off its feet, but it had picked itself up and run off before he could administer a beating. It was a natural few steps in his mind from there to the Golden Cage, where he had sought such restitution for the pains the world heaped on him that he had left himself feeling weak and shaken this morning.

The railway! he thought bitterly. It was all the fault of the railway! And he felt so very poorly – no-one understood. His constitution was not strong, and people abused his patience all the time in a way that would wear out a far stronger man. Oh, his poor head! He abandoned the book and sank his head in his hands again. That damned railway . . .

Ponderous, gigantic, a vast black engine of unimaginable purpose and no particular shape was bearing down on him, so slowly he ought easily to be able to avoid it, yet his feet would not move him, he could get no purchase on the ground, no matter how hard he tried. He jerked violently and opened his eyes, realising they had closed without his knowing it. Something *was* looming over him, the image persisting past dream into reality so terrifyingly that he screamed, and screamed again, the thin high sound fading in reverse, so that he heard it at last outside himself, just as he felt the hand shaking his shoulder and heard the voice telling him to wake up.

'Sir! Sir! You're dreaming.'

It was Ferrars. Nicholas slapped his hand away, panting for breath, feeling his heart pounding so fast it hurt. 'I'm awake,' he gasped. 'Leave me alone!'

Ferrars stood back, and Nicholas slowly came to himself. He was too warm now, bathed in sweat; his hand trembled violently as he reached into his pocket for a handkerchief to wipe his face. At his feet Minna crouched, tucked back out of the way, but still keeping her eyes on him hopefully, waiting for a word or caress. Idiot bitch, he thought. He wanted to kick her, but he had not the energy to move his foot.

'Drink,' he croaked. 'Get me a drink.'

Ferrars crossed the room to the bedside table and filled the glass from the decanter, brought it back and watched impassively as Nicholas sipped it, slowly turning from green to his more normal white.

As loathsome reality replaced loathsome fantasy, Nicholas felt very slightly stronger, and looked up at Ferrars, half in anger, half in fear. What was he doing here, in Nicholas's own room, without having been sent for?

'What are you about? You startled me. Why didn't you knock?'

'I did, sir, but you didn't hear me. I'm afraid you must have been asleep.'

'Well, what do you want?' Nicholas said uninvitingly.

'A moment of your time, sir, to speak to you on a particular subject.' Nicholas groaned, but he was listening. 'Perhaps I might be permitted to sit, sir,' Ferrars added, and without waiting for an answer, drew a chair up and sat. It was a hard chair, so he was still higher than Nicholas, but not so high that the effort of looking at him would make Nicholas sick. 'I have been considering the future of Miss Jemima,' he began.

Nicholas looked at him in slow amazement. 'The Devil you have! And what business is it of yours?'

'Everything which concerns your welfare is my business,' Ferrars said smoothly. 'I don't know if you are aware of it, but your ward is no longer a child.'

'The Devil!' Nicholas said again, though whether that was a comment on Jemima's age Ferrars could not tell. He decided for once on straightforwardness. He wasn't at all convinced Nicholas would understand anything very subtle in his present state.

'It will be impossible to keep her under the same sort of restraint much longer, unless you actually lock her up as insane. A child accepts things without question, but fifteen is almost grown-up, and the time will soon come when she will start to wonder if this is a normal way to live. Even with the limited contact she has with the outside world, there are risks involved. Stories are bound to get out sooner or later – unless, as I said, you actually put her permanently under lock and key.'

Nicholas stared at him owlishly. Jemima – his ward Jemima. Little Jemima, his mother's favourite grandchild. Fifteen already? She was a young lady. She would want to go to dances, wear pretty dresses – attract a husband. But he couldn't let her marry, could he? For a moment he didn't remember why not. Because she was mad, poor child. No, that was only what they pretended. Because he would lose her fortune if she married – and he so badly needed her fortune. He thought of the bills to come from the Maccabbees and the Golden Cage (oh, the Golden Cage! He knew exactly why they had chosen that adjective!) and his tailor and the wine-merchant, and the money he had lost to Jack Cox at billiards, and the little man who ran the books on the races. He wondered indeed whether there was any of Jemima's fortune left by now. No, she must not marry. If only he hadn't married Aglaea, he could have married her himself and made all safe. Incest didn't look so very horrible from his present vantage point, and he wondered why he had been so afraid of it before. But then, he was rather fond of Aglaea. He thought of the way she soothed him when he had had a nightmare, the way he put his head on her breast and had her stroke his hair, just as he had done with his mother. She was a good wife to him, he thought sentimentally. He would not want to part with Aglaea.

'So you think we – I should lock her up entirely?' he said at last.

'No, sir. I think that would be very difficult; it would require the co-operation of a number of people, and the fewer people who are involved the better. And besides, if she were to escape and managed to convince anyone she was not mad, it would be very difficult to explain. No, I have another plan.'

'Well?'

'Dispense with her governess, and let her out.' The shock of the words got Nicholas's attention. Ferrars nodded. 'She is a docile girl, according to Miss Smith, and since her illness, inclined almost to lethargy. No doubt the tedium of her life adds to the depression of her spirits. I think she would regard even a small increase in indulgence with such gratitude, she would be easily biddable.'

'But who is to take care of her?' Nicholas asked.

'Mrs Morland. She already accepts your command that she should not go beyond the grounds, and, as the most dutiful of wives, seems to have no thought in her mind but to obey your desires. In her company, Miss Jemima would not stray far. And to the outsider, nothing would be more natural than that Miss Jemima should be a companion to Mrs Morland: it is what the world would expect, if the world thought about it. Madam's attitude and behaviour will rub off on the girl. They will go about quietly together, sewing, picking flowers, taking walks and the like. The estate workers and servants and anyone passing casually will see the normality of the situation and the world will stop wondering. We – you will be safe.'

Nicholas considered the scene. 'All very well – until someone comes courting her. How do I keep her then?'

Ferrars smiled smoothly. 'We will cross that bridge, sir, when we come to it. I have other plans to cover all eventualities.'

'What plans?' Nicholas asked.

'I don't think you want to know, sir,' Ferrars said. 'Sufficient unto the day.' Something about his voice made Nicholas shiver with foreboding.

'Give me some more wine,' he demanded shortly.

Ferrars went and poured another glass and handed it to Nicholas, and the rim chattered against Nicky's teeth as he drank. Ferrars watched with satisfaction, and when the glass was empty, he said unemphatically, as though they had been discussing something as unimportant as having the chimneys swept, 'So then, shall I go ahead with the plan, sir? Shall we bring Miss out of the schoolroom?'

'Out of the schoolroom into the fire,' Nicholas muttered confusedly. What were they talking about? Oh yes – Jemima, Jemima, concentrate on that. The change suggested would be to Jemima's benefit, wouldn't it? It was the right thing, the good thing to do. She was his ward and he always had her best interests at heart, and how grateful she would be to him for his kindness in the present instance! That was a good thing to think about, little Jemima's gratitude.

And Aglaea would be grateful too: women always liked to have a female companion to chatter to. Aglaea and Jemima both grateful and happy, and it would all be his doing, his own thought entirely. 'How clever of you to think of it, Mr Morland!' – he could hear Aglaea saying it. 'With all the thousand cares you have to deal with every day, you found time to devise this scheme to make me and Jemima happy!' 'I always have your good at heart, my dear,' he would reply, and she would look at him in that way she had sometimes, which made him feel – almost – almost *happy*.

'Yes, it is a good plan,' he said aloud. His voice creaked. He cleared his throat and tried again. 'You may speak to Miss Smith, make whatever arrangements are necessary. I shall speak to Mrs Morland myself, and she can take the news to Miss Jemima.'

This last was a happy thought of his – Aglaea would put it in exactly the right light to Jemima, emphasising his thoughtfulness and beneficence. It could not safely be left to a servant. Servants were so coarse and crude, they might leave entirely the wrong impression.

'As you say, sir,' Ferrars said. The bow of acquiescence he gave concealed the expression on his face, which would hardly have recommended itself to Nicholas.

'I can't say more than it's your own fault,' Mrs Moon said, watching Miss Smith packing. 'Whatever did you want to go stirring things up for?' She had a pretty good idea what for, which accounted for her entire lack of sympathy for Miss Smith's predicament. She had wanted to take over the whole show, that was what. Ferrars had let slip enough hints to warn Mrs Moon that you couldn't trust anyone, not even an old friend you had got into the job in the first place. Well, it would rain monkeys the day Martha Moon was got the better of by such as May Smith. Wanted to rule the roast, did you? Now see where it has got you.

Miss Smith was not willing to give Martha the satisfaction. 'I don't care,' she said. 'I'm sick of this place anyway. Shut up here in the country with nothing to do. I've made my little bit out of it, and I'm off to somewhere brighter, where I can have a bit of fun.'

'Oh?' Mrs Moon was interested in spite of herself. 'And where might that be?'

'London, o' course. I've got plans! I'm going to make my fortune.' She straightened up and eyed Mrs Moon consideringly. 'Why don't you come with me? Shake the dust of this place off your feet, and come where there's real money to be made.'

Mrs Moon gave her a sad smile and a shake of the head. 'There's many have said that, and ended up in the gutter. London's no bed o' roses, as you'll find out.'

Miss Smith laughed. 'You talk as if I was some green girl with air in my head! No, I mean to set up a business which can't fail – and it's here I got the idea of it. You could be useful to me, too. Come with me, and we'll put our capital together and make a fine life for ourselves.'

'What business?' Mrs Moon asked, though she had an idea.

'A high-class brothel. Everything swanky, all red velvet and big looking-glasses, pretty girls, and high prices so only the richest can afford it. What do you say, Martha? You and me, eh? We've got all the experience we need in running girls and keeping 'em in order: a brothel'll be a damn sight easier than Women's Side on a Saturday night! We'll make a fortune! You can be housekeeper and I'll be madam – and we'll even find a place for that daft old man of yours. Put him in livery and stand him at the door – he'll add tone to the place. What do you say?'

For a moment it all swirled before Mrs Moon's eyes, glittering and inviting; and then she felt the twinge in her back, and remembered that May Smith had been conspiring with Ferrars against her. Better a big fish in her own pond, than risk the upheaval and the dangers of the hostile sea London might prove to be.

'Oh, I don't think so, thank you all the same. I like it here. I'm comfortable – and there's pickings still to come. I haven't finished with this place yet. Maybe I'll come and join you one day, I don't know. But it's like home to me now, this place – and Moon's happy here. He's not touched a drop in I don't know how long.'

'Suit yourself,' said Miss Smith with a shrug, and turned back to her packing. She wouldn't be sorry to be starting up alone. A partner was always a dangerous thing, never to be entirely trusted. And though Martha Moon was the best hand in the country at breaking up a girl-fight and making rations go round twice, she was as devious and underhand as a mountebank. Better to have a one-woman business, and keep all the profits herself. And one day when she'd made her fortune, she might come and pay a visit, all dressed in furs and diamonds, and show Mrs Moon what she'd turned down. That would be an agreeable prospect to contemplate.

CHAPTER FIFTEEN

Benedict was so tired that he dozed on and off in the long coach-journey from Kilsby to York. Since he had changed contracts, he had had little time off, and less sleep than he was used to: his comfortable lodgings at Crick had been so long unused he had transferred himself to Kilsby village itself, and slept in the hayloft above the stables of the inn, which had been transformed into temporary accommodation for him and two other assistant engineers.

The physical conditions at Kilsby were hard. The tunnel was to be almost one and a half miles long – a project the like of which had never been contemplated before. The doom-sayers had predicted that even if the tunnel could ever be dug, anyone foolhardy enough to travel through it would be suffocated in its black depths. To counter these prognostications, Mr Robert had sunk two vast ventilation shafts, sixty feet in diameter and more than a hundred feet deep; but the rumblings from the anti-railwayites still went on.

There was no way round. A great ridge of upland went right across the country from southwest to northeast, and anyone wanting to drive north must go over or through it at some point. Just north of the village of Watford was the Watford Gap – something of a misnomer, for it was not a break in the line of hills, but merely a place where the ridge narrowed. Here the canal builders had already tunnelled through, though it had taken them several attempts because of the same quicksand that Stephenson was now fighting. He had hoped by moving further west to avoid it, but there was evidently a great lake of water and sand under the whole of the Kilsby Ridge: of the first six working shafts sunk, three were drowned. There was nothing to be done but to drain the lake.

Month after month Benedict and the others had struggled with what seemed a hopeless task. Stephenson had brought in an army of 1,250 men and 200 horses. They had sunk a line of new shafts parallel with the line of the tunnel, and steam pumps had been set up at the heads to drain away the water from the working shafts so that they could be dug down to tunnel level. Week by week the water levels remained unchanged; then a steady fall would occur for several weeks, raising hopes – which were dashed when a new rush of water from somewhere brought the levels back up to what they had been in the beginning. More shafts were dug and more pumps set up; there were thirteen now, and still they seemed to be making little impression on the waters. Benedict dreamed of sand and water whenever he closed his eyes. He felt as though he had been engaged in this same struggle for ever.

There were other troubles at the workings: most of the navvies were living in a camp of turf huts all around the little village of Kilsby, and the inn and the green outside it had become the focus for their wild 'randies'. Here they danced, drank, fought, organised dog-fights and cock-fights, roasted oxen and pigs on huge bonfires, and sallied forth when roaring drunk to rat-hunt in the barns, fornicate in the fields, and terrorise the villagers in their houses. On one occasion the villagers retaliated, actually capturing and tying up two of the worst of the navvies; but the others had come to the rescue of their mates, and warfare had broken out. The troops had had to be called in to restore order, and fourteen men were arrested and marched off in shackles to Daventry gaol.

It was no wonder that most of the local landlords were

hostile to the workings; what was more surprising was that one, Sir John Leytham, was extremely friendly, and frequently invited the young engineers to dine and meet other local people. He was a cheerful, hospitable, vulgar man, who had made his fortune in soap and bought his knighthood with political donations. He had married into the gentry by taking the daughter of an impoverished peer, a languid woman who never allowed her personal lack of fortune, looks or intellect to interfere with her sense of superiority. But Sir John more than made up for her chilly hauteur. He liked nothing better than to gather a large party of handsome young people around him, and indulge them with fine food, good wine, vigorous dancing, and noisy games. His generosity was the more remarkable since he had four daughters of marriageable age at home, whom a careful father might have wanted to shield from the dangers of falling in love with a railway engineer. But to Benedict and the others it was like a glimpse of heaven, to leave behind the dirt and noise and toil of the battle with the quicksand, to render themselves as clean and decent as primitive facilities allowed, and hurry along to Leytham Hall. There they found bright lights and large fires, acres of food (Sir John was a shrewd judge of railway appetites), pleasant, foolish noise, and pretty girls to dance with. Some, indeed, may not have been so very pretty, and some – distant cousins of Sir John and daughters of his old associates – may not even have been genteel, but after ten days without a break on the tunnel shafts, they were as lovely and desirable as Houris to the weary young men.

Sir John's youngest daughter, fifteen and barely out of the schoolroom, had taken a particular fancy to Benedict. She was not yet 'out', but Sir John's indulgence thought it unfair to keep her from the 'fun and frolic' which her sisters enjoyed, and so she was always allowed down when the railway people came. 'It ain't as though I was entertaining Ministers and Dukes,' he often said to her, in Benedict's hearing. 'When I get the best plate out, Sib, you must stay above, but the young people ain't so particular about etiquette. The outs and not-outs are all nonsense in my book – but don't tell your Ma I said so!'

So Sibella joined in, and from the first meeting attached herself to Benedict with the frank lack of shyness that came from her youth and being her father's daughter. She claimed him as partner when there was dancing, made sure she got on his side when teams were picked for games, openly swapped chairs at the table to sit next to him. Sir John found it vastly funny, and teased her about her preference. Benedict enjoyed her as he might have enjoyed a younger sister or a playful puppy – indeed, there was something of both about her. Her conversation was lively, she laughed at his jokes, and told him frankly that he was the handsomest of all the engineers. 'When I come out, you will come to my ball, won't you?' she said once when they were dancing.

'If you learn to dance more like a lady and less like a Hottentot, I will,' Benedict replied. 'You've trodden on my feet so often I haven't any polish left on my boots.'

'Well,' she retorted, 'I don't call it very handsome of you to say so! If you was gallant, you'd say it was *your* fault. Which it is, for every time I go to put my foot down, yours is always underneath.'

'Oh, you want me to be gallant, do you?' Benedict laughed. 'You want me to play the courtier with you?'

'I don't suppose you'd know how,' she said kindly. 'Ma says you are the best of the bunch, but still a raw provincial.'

'I'll have you know,' he said, pretending a huff, 'that my mother was a countess in her own right.'

'Yes, but only a French one, Ma says, which don't count.'

'Not at all. Her title was granted by King George III, so you may put that in your pipe, Miss Minx. And that was my foot you trod on again.'

'Who else's foot would you like me to tread on?' she said smartly.

'No-one's. I like to dance with you. You don't giggle and flutter like the other girls.'

'Well, I suppose I ought to learn, if I'm to *take* when I come out,' she said judiciously.

'Don't you dare! You are perfect just as you are,' Benedict said quickly.

'There, you can say pretty things when you try,' she said. 'I tell you what,' she added generously, 'when I've come out, you could marry me. I shouldn't like to marry anyone else half as well. And I promise I'll never giggle or flutter, ever.'

He looked down into her face affectionately, noted the bright, wide-open grey eyes and the pinkish-gold hair that would break into fuzz whenever she exerted herself, no matter how long it had been brushed beforehand to make it smooth. The nose was indeterminately pudgy, the mouth wide but without distinction, the chin not sufficiently marked; it was a jolly face, passionate, full of the joy of life, but it was not beautiful. For an instant it was overlaid in his mind with the image of elegant, classical features, glossy, guinea-gold ringlets and blue eyes half hidden under rose-petal lids of dewy whiteness. Miss Fleetham was lost to him for ever, but she would always be his ideal of womanhood. 'I think your parents would have something to say about that scheme,' he said with an effort.

'Oh, they won't mind it. I'm only the youngest after all, and Pa likes railway men excessively, and Ma only cares about my brothers. I expect they'll be glad to get me off my hands by then . . .'

Benedict's head rolled and he jerked himself awake. He had been dreaming of chandeliers and music, whirling

323

round and round in the waltz, and it was a deep disappointment to discover the whirling was in his head, and that he was in a stuffy, crowded coach with seven other people, assailed by an assortment of smells, and with his sit-upon protesting bitterly about the inadequacies of the upholstery. He had decided to take the stage coach to Market Harborough and Stamford, and pick up the northbound mail on the Great North Road there. A chaise and pair all the way would have been more money than he felt he could justify, even for the sake of the speed. When the railway was finished, he thought, he'd be able to do the same journey in a matter of hours. In three or four years' time, people would laugh to think of the tiresomeness of this simple journey. Steam locomotive from Kilsby to Rugby, from Rugby to York, and back the same day – that was the future! And when his son was a man, the railways would stretch all across England—

Ah yes, his son. The letter had come as a complete surprise: Liza's words in Dick's handwriting, hopeful, anxious, grateful, doubtful.

'. . . He is a good man, as everyone agrees, and will be a good husband to me, and a good father for little Thomas. I hope you will see your way to allowing it to go ahead, for I want it very much, and feel sure it will be the best thing for all. I shall always be grateful to you, more than I can say, but our lives are so different. I'm not of your station, and I believe our ways lie apart. Please let me know as soon as convenient what you think. If you agree, we would like to marry in October, after the harvest, which is best for Joe. And if you will think of it, we would be honoured if you would come to the wedding . . .'

He had written back at once, of course, wishing them well, assuring them that his permission was not necessary and that he had only their welfare at heart. And on a second application, he had agreed, a little against his better judgement, to attend the wedding. He had had no difficulty in obtaining the time off from Mr Robert, for he had had no vacation in over a year; and he had arranged to meet George Findlay for dinner, to catch up on old friends and railway news, to round off the trip. The only difficulty was a wedding-gift, for it was not in his power to go shopping before the date of departure. In the end he had asked Sibella – with her father's permission – to buy something for him the next time she went with her mother and sisters into Northampton. Sibella had agreed enthusiastically to the commission, and had come back with a beautiful silver filagree cake-basket for the money he had given her. Bendy was doubtful about her choice – she had mistaken the degree of person she was buying for, he said, and described Liza's situation in more detail. There must have been many more useful things she could have bought. Sibella listened gravely and then pooh-poohed his doubts. Brides didn't want useful things, but glorious things, and to a humble estate-worker's wife, a silver filagree cake-basket would be a trophy to be cherished and displayed with pride. Even if she never had use for it, Sibella assured him, she would treasure it far more than anything practical and sensible he could have given her. Bendy could only hope that she was right, and that Liza did not take it for a piece of tactlessness on his part.

The wedding was over. Liza now had a surname to speak openly – she was Mrs Joe Thompson – and Thomas had a father who, Benedict could see at once, would be kind to him. Joe was a huge man, six feet high in his stockings and broad to match, red of face and barley-blonde of hair, with vast hands that would each have made two of Bendy's. He had few words, but his shy smile made up for the lack. He was a slow-moving, slow-talking man, with the long, quiet stare of the countryman. He evidently adored Liza, and hardly took his eyes from her through the whole ceremony, enduring it all for her sake, though he evidently felt ill-at-ease in the strange surroundings and the stranger clothes. And as for Thomas, Bendy only had to see Joe hunker down to twitch the boy's skirts straight after a tumble, or pick him up to ride against his shoulder, to know that he would make a tender father. He would whittle sticks for the boy, and show him how to snare rabbits, and Thomas would worship him and model himself on this silent, capable giant.

He had accepted Benedict's presence impassively, without demanding explanation. But Benedict had found Joe's eyes on him at one point, and though there was no expression on that broad, fair face, he had been convinced that Joe was not so slow that he had not worked out what the connection was between him and Liza and Thomas. The boy did nothing to betray his mother: he plainly did not remember Benedict, and though he allowed himself to be picked up and spoken to, he was much more interested in Joe's young pointer bitch, and soon wriggled to be put down. Fand did not give them away, for Fand had died back in the summer; a quiet, old-dog's death. Dandy had buried her behind the vegetable patch, and Benedict found time to go and stand a moment at the spot, saying goodbye. He would not replace her: an engineer's life was too hard for a dog; but it meant he now had no-one, no-one at all, to love him.

Liza had cried a little when, after the ceremony, Bendy had come up to congratulate her. She slipped her hand under her husband's arm, looking up at Bendy from under her white, ribbon-trimmed bonnet with a painful mixture of emotions. Then Benedict shook Joe's vast hand, and Joe took it gingerly, as if afraid he might damage it.

'Take care of her,' Bendy said.

'I will, sir,' Thompson replied, looking down into Benedict's face with a blandness that made him feel absurdly uneasy. 'Don't you worry, sir. And we thank you most hearty, the wife and me, for coming to t' weddin'. It were right kind of you.'

The wedding breakfast was at Joe's cottage, so he had the chance to see where Liza would live, and where Tommy would be brought up. It was more spacious than Dick's, and not more than a quarter of a mile away, so Tom would not lose touch with his uncle. It was simply but solidly furnished, and many of the items Joe had made himself, for he was a wood-worker of some note, and liked nothing better than a bit of carpentry in his spare time. It had a tiny best parlour – at present unfurnished – as well as 'the house', a large, stone-flagged room with a handsome fireplace; and upstairs three bedrooms, to house all the little Thompsons to come. Benedict didn't want to think about those. He remembered that Liza and her brother had been driven out of their childhood home by the brutality of a stepfather who preferred his own children to his wife's. No, it was absurd – Joe would never behave like that. But would Thomas grow up aware that there was a difference between him and his younger siblings? Would he feel less loved, less belonging? Would he feel like a stranger at his own hearth?

And if he did not – Benedict had to come to terms with an ungenerous feeling of his own, that if Thomas grew up to be entirely and completely Joe Thompson's son, it would be a sad waste. He did not want his son to grow up an ignorant clod, to follow his father into the labour of the soil; to wear heavy, common boots and a foolish smile, to marry an unlettered girl who would lose her teeth as she had her babies; to die in harness at fifty, and be remembered only as a good man who did not beat his wife.

Benedict had to cast away those thoughts. Thomas was Liza's son now, and he had no more rights over him. He had given those away with the responsibility, and it was not possible to have one without the other. As he left the merry-makers to make his way back to Selby and his dinner engagement with George Findlay, he knew that he would never see Thomas again; and that, while Liza would probably always retain a tender spot in her heart for him, the boy would equally probably never even know his name.

But Sibella had been right about the cake-basket, he reflected. Liza had been dazzled by it, and plainly more thrilled by its frivolity than by the utility of her other presents. Looking round the kitchen, Benedict couldn't quite see where she would put it, but Thompson soon cleared up that worry. 'When we do out the parlour, it'll look grand standing all on its own on a little table. I'll make 'e one, Lizzy, soon as I get a bit o' wood by – with them curly legs, if tha likes.'

And so that was that. It must have been hunger – he was ready by now for his dinner – that made him feel so hollow as he rode away on his hired horse; as if everything inside him had been emptied out.

Dinner at the Grey Horse was handsome, and George Findlay was satisfactorily full of gossip. Much of their conversation, naturally, was of railway matters.

'You've heard about the Great North of England Railway, I suppose?' Findlay asked through a mouthful of fat duck. 'They got their Act through at the same time as the York – the first part, anyway – a line from Gateshead to Darlington.'

'Yes, I heard that,' said Benedict. 'And Hudson used to talk about building a line from York to Darlington, to link London with Edinburgh through York. It looks as though he will get his way again.'

'Not so simple,' George said elliptically, sucking a wing-bone. 'The GNE want to take their line through Tadcaster, not York.'

'Tadcaster?'

'Say they've always planned it that way, and why should they change now? And of course, Tadcaster is all for it. They were pretty peeved that the York and North Midland missed them out.'

'But if York already has a line to the south, what's the point in duplication?'

'Profit, of course. They want people travelling on their line, not Hudson's.'

Bendy shook his head reprovingly. 'Hudson isn't taking it lying down, I hope?'

'Lord, no. He and the rest of the directors have gone haring off to Newcastle to talk to the GNE directors about it. And just in case they don't manage to persuade, Hudson's asked old Stephenson to survey a line from York to Darlington, so that he can oppose the Tadcaster scheme in Parliament if it ever comes to a Bill. But it won't. He'll persuade them, one way or the other, I've no doubt. When it comes to persistence, Hudson's got it with the gilt on.'

'And how are things going with the York and North Midland line?' Bendy asked after a pause during which he gave a vast pork cutlet the attention it deserved.

Findlay shook his head. 'Not at all. Something's happened, some snag or other, and the work's stopped. They staked out as far as Chaloner's Whin, and no further.'

Benedict frowned. 'I wonder what could be wrong? They got the Act through all right, that I do know.'

'I heard it was something to do with a landowner objecting,' Findlay said casually, 'but I don't know more than that.'

Nicholas, thought Bendy – it must be! But how could he still be causing delay, now that the Act was through? He saw now what a lucky thing it was that he had not been engaged as engineer to the York and North Midland – the embarrassment would have been intense. 'I thought of going into York tomorrow,' he said, 'before I go back to Kilsby. I could call in on Harry Anstey and get the story from him.'

'Good idea. And I dare say there are plenty of other people you want to catch up on.'

'Not really. I left it all behind when I went to Tring. And

329

now Miss Fleetham's married, there isn't a soul, really, that I care about back here – apart from you, that is.'

'Much obliged, old chap. Have some of this duck, and pass me the chops, there's a good fellow.' The exchange was effected, and Findlay went on indifferently as he held his cuff carefully out of the gravy and served himself, 'All is not going smoothly, however, for the divine Miss Fleetham. I fear she will never now be Mrs Partridge – or Mrs Anyone.'

'What? What do you say?' Benedict was startled. 'Has she jilted him?'

'Rather the other way around, I'm afraid.' George looked across the table at him. 'I'm sorry, am I treading on sore toes? Don't tell me you still have a *tendre* for her?'

'I'm – interested in her welfare, that's all.'

'That's what Georgy says,' Findlay grinned. 'I find it easy enough to believe in her case.'

'For God's sake, tell me what's happened to Miss Fleetham,' Bendy said stiffly.

'I was just about to. Keep the governor on, old man! Well, I got all the details from Georgy, of course, and it seems that everyone was quite taken in by the Partridge cove. He wasn't what he claimed to be – no fortune, no country seat, no noble connections. Once he'd run up debts in the neighbourhood too high for the tradesmen to ignore any more, he took to his heels and skipped – and now, no doubt, he's doing exactly the same thing in a different part of the country, with another set of gullible country maidens and their avaricious mamas.'

'But Miss Fleetham?' Benedict said in agony.

'Is much to be pitied – at least by us chaps. Even the diamond ring turned out to be fake. Unfortunately, she behaved so badly in cutting him out in the first place that the females she cheated of him are only too happy she's been shown up. And what's worse – well, she relied rather too much on her betrothal, I'm afraid, and behaved altogether too familiar with the Partridge.

She's compromised herself hopelessly, and now they say no-one will have her on a bet. Even Georgy, who has the world's kindest heart – and I should know – says that Miss Fleetham is fast, and a flirt, and not at all nice to know. Mrs Phillips won't have her in the house any more, and Ned Phillips told me he'd had a lucky escape – he was thinking of offering for her before this Partridge came along and flushed her out. He says he's grateful to the man for showing her up in her true colours.' He looked at Benedict's set face, and said, 'I'm sorry, old fellow. But you've had a lucky escape too, wouldn't you say? She was nearer taking you than she ever was Ned Phillips. But you know I always warned you she was a shocking flirt. That's all very well for fun, but it's not what a fellow would want in a wife, after all.'

'Please, don't say any more,' Benedict said grimly.

'Of course, of course, not another word. They say her father will have to take her to London now to get her off his hands. But even then, they say his fortune ain't what it was, and it's not as if she's in her first flush – she's been out five years if it's a day. I'd lay any money she ends up on the shelf.'

'George, old fellow, I love you like a brother,' Bendy said, 'but if you say one more word about Miss Fleetham I shall be obliged to shut you up by force.'

'Pax, old man, pax. The subject's closed. I'm sorry, I didn't realise you still had it so bad for the F— *Pax*, I say! We'll change the subject – truly. Now don't waste good grub— !'

He rode out first thing the next morning to Fleetham Manor, in order to present himself at the earliest reasonable hour for visiting. All the way there his heart was jumping erratically and his thoughts were whirling. He hadn't the slightest idea what he was going to say when he got there. Commiseration was out of the question – in fact, there was hardly an approach which would be tactful, for even saying nothing would look like pointedly avoiding the subject. The simple fact of his being there would prove to her he knew the whole story. He didn't really know what he was going for, except that he couldn't bear the thought of Miss Fleetham shunned by the polite world for something out of her control, for no other crime than being jilted, cozened and betrayed by a scheming rascal.

If all her former friends had abandoned her, she should know that he at least was faithful. She should know there was one soul who believed her still to be the most perfect woman in the world. Quite how to tell her that, other than simply by presenting himself at her door, he had no idea. He rode in a fever to lay his sword, metaphorically, at her feet. Indeed he would be happy to pound the Partridge to a paste for her should she desire it, and should anyone know the villain's direction.

As it happened – and probably fortunately – he was not required to explain his presence, for when he rode up to the house, he found it all shut up; and when he hitched his horse and rang the bell, the butler emerged to say that the Master and Miss were away, staying with friends in Leeds for a few days. He did not know exactly when they would be back. Would sir like to leave his card? Bendy thought yes and then no, and finally said, 'Yes,' out loud, and was instantly sorry, but was committed by the word, for the butler was poised and waiting for it. Bendy produced his card case and handed over his ticket, feeling that its presence when the Fleethams returned was as likely to be misinterpreted as anything he might have said had they been at home. Where sensibilities so refined and feelings of such delicacy were involved, it was hard to know what to do for the best.

He rode away from the house and out of the park, thinking how sad and autumnal everything looked, in sympathy with his feelings. The grass was not at its best in October, and the leaves had started to turn, but had not reached the peak of their colour, which made them look merely shabby. It was grey and overcast, and the low clouds caught like mist in the tops of the highest trees, and there was a depressing mizzle, enough to annoy and wet without actually being wholehearted rain one could respect. His horse wanted to turn homewards as they left the park gates, and when Bendy tried to send him the other way, he became quite insistent, set his jaw like iron and glued his hooves to the ground. A brief struggle ensued. After repeated drumming of his heels against the resounding flanks, Bendy persuaded the animal to move off sulkily in the other direction, but it trailed its feet in protest like a schoolboy, and showed a tendency to try to dash down every side turning they passed that led in the right direction.

York was only about twelve miles away by road, and once he got to Towton he knew the country, and could cut across the fields and save a bit. He ought to be in York by noon, and then perhaps he could entice Harry Anstey out of his office for a spot of something.

He left his horse at the Jolly Bacchus and walked on up Micklegate, but he had only got as far as St Martin's when he saw a familiar figure emerging from the narrow lane opposite, which led to Tanner Row. Muffled up in a greatcoat with a vast fur collar, tall hat clamped well down over the ears, it was still unmistakable by its bulk and rapid movements.

Hudson saw him at the same moment, and stopped dead, making an expansive gesture of welcome. Bendy glanced at the traffic, waited his moment, and dashed across.

'Well, well,' said Hudson, pursing his lips in a funny little smile. 'Well, well. If it isn't thee! I thowt tha was in Leicestershire diggin' tunnels.' His accent was always broadest when he was in whimsical mood.

'I thought you were in Newcastle, pleading causes,' Bendy countered.

'Oh, tha knaws about that, does tha?'

'I was speaking to my old friend George Findlay last night. He told me all about the great North Eastern, and how they meant to snub York.'

'Oh, that's over and done, never worry! They'll come our way in the end, I make no doubt. I've had other things to think on.' He gestured behind him. 'I've been inspecting the site for the station. George Stephenson reckons to terminate outside the city walls, with a snecky bit of a station, made o' wood wi' nothing about it. You engineers never think owt t'th' station – the lines is all you're interested in! But it won't do for me. York station must be *in* York, for my money. There's a passel o' land just inside the wall to the north o' Tanner Row that'll do grand – where the Women's Hospital and the House of Correction stand, and some folk's gardens. I put it in the Act, in spite of what Old George says. A great fine building is what we want, big as a church, that'll stand for a thousand years, and folk'll be proud to walk by. I have it all up here,' he tapped his brow. 'We s'll have it, I warrant thee – though it may take a while. But we s'll have it.'

Benedict smiled. 'I don't doubt it, sir. You have a way of getting what you want.'

The brows darkened. 'Aye, well, it's no thanks to thy brother, damn his hide! By God, he's a thorn in my side, I can tell thee! I had the man sewn up nicely, till he goes poking his nose in!'

'What has he done now?' Benedict asked, a little coolly, because of the immoderate language. 'What man?'

'Lord Howden, damn him – owns some o' the land to the south that the line goes over. He was against the railway at the beginning, but I sweetened him up, and the Bill went through nice as pie.'

'So I heard,' said Bendy.

'But your damnation brother has been pokin' at him like a wasps' nest, and now he's gone back on his agreement – claiming that I promised him five thousand pound not to vote against us in the House. Five thousand! Damn his eyes!'

'I'm sorry to hear it,' said Benedict, concealing a smile at Hudson's frantic rage. 'But did you promise it?'

'I may have promised him this or that, I don't rightly recollect. There were so many folk to see, and everyone wanting his back rubbed. I dare say I might have hinted that there was something in the purse for the man that showed himself our friend – but five thousand! Is it likely? And for a miserable bit o' land you couldn't raise turnips on!'

'If he has nothing in writing, it will be his word against yours,' Benedict suggested.

Hudson narrowed his eyes fiercely. 'True enough – and I'll beat him. I will! Five thousand! And makin' a liar of me! And your damned brother has the cheek to come round to me and ask how I'm getting on, and asks if I'd like his influence with his lordship, seeing they are *great friends*. Smirking and laughing up his sleeve at me like a damned ape! I don't doubt he'd come in for a share of the brass if we paid up. Well he won't get five thousand dried peas out o' me! I've told young Anstey he's not to settle on any account.' His steam ran out, and he sighed. 'But it all takes time. Four months on, and not a sod turned,' he concluded mournfully.

'There's no setting times when it comes to railways,' Benedict said soothingly.

'Aye, you've had your bellyful up at Kilsby, so I hear,' Hudson said, with a certain relish at someone else's problems. 'It'll be a long job, will that – and it'll cost a few lives, I don't doubt. Water's the devil! Have you got any men into the tunnel yet?'

'Oh yes, some of the shafts went down to tunnel level

without striking water. But it's slow work until we can get all the shafts cleared.'

Hudson nodded. 'And diggin' in those conditions – damp and foul air – they'll be droppin' like flies. There's nothing pulls a man down so fast as foul, damp air on his lungs. A man can go down in months and—' He stopped, apparently reminded of something by his own words. 'Where were you off to, when I called you over?' he asked in a different tone.

'I was going to call on Harry Anstey.'

'Ah, well, you're bahn the wrong road. If you turn to the right-about, you'll find him at the widow Makepeace's house.' He studied Benedict's face as he said it, and then added, 'You don't know, then? You haven't heard?'

'Heard what?'

'Eh, it's a terrible thing for a woman still in the prime o' life, and not a bad piece to look at, neither, when she was well – to say nothing of a good brain for business, which it's a crying shame to lose. She's sick, lad – at her prayers. A consumption. She went from owt to nowt in a few weeks. I walked down with Anstey half an hour since on his way to her. He's her man o' business – and if she's called him in, you can bet it's all holiday with her.' He eyed Benedict with sympathy. 'I'm sorry to be the one to tell thee, lad.'

Benedict didn't know what he said. He wasn't really aware of leaving Hudson, or of crossing the road again. Serena dying? He remembered the last time he saw her, at the races, and how healthy she had looked, and how he had wondered that he had ever loved her. He felt guilty, horribly guilty; he hardly knew what about, but he felt it all the same as his hurrying feet took him back down Micklegate towards Nunnery Lane.

Avis, the elderly butler, opened the door to him, red-eyed and trembling, and broke into tears as soon as he tried to speak.

'I didn't know, or I'd have come sooner,' Bendy said. 'Someone should have told me. How is she? Avis, it isn't – it isn't as serious as I've been told, is it?'

'Oh, Mr Morland, she's so young! I never thought I'd live to see—' He couldn't complete the sentence.

'Surely it isn't so bad?' Benedict said. He felt a coldness in the pit of his stomach. He hadn't really believed it until this moment.

Avis shook his head wordlessly, and fumbled with trembling hands for a handkerchief to wipe his face. 'Doctor says there's no hope,' he said.

'Which doctor is that?'

'Doctor Havergill. He was here a bit since, and he's coming back this evening. Mr Anstey's in with Madam at the moment. She's making her Will.' He dissolved again, and Benedict laid a comforting hand on the brittle forearm. He had to swallow a few times before he could speak.

'Do you think I might see her?'

But Avis was saved from having to answer, for the door to the drawing-room opened, and Harry Anstey put his head out. 'Avis, is that—' Then he saw Benedict. 'Bendy! Good God, what are you doing here?' He came out and shut the door behind him. 'I thought it was Havergill coming back.'

'Why didn't you tell me?' Benedict demanded in a trembling voice. 'I would have come before, but I didn't know. You ought to have told me!'

Harry came closer, lowering his voice as an indication that Benedict should do the same. 'My dear fellow, I didn't know myself until today. I would have written to you – I was intending to write this very evening – but until I was summoned here today I swear I had no idea she was ill. Havergill says it has come on very quickly, and that she wanted no-one told. In fact, it was only because he pressed her that she called me here today.'

'How bad is it?' Bendy asked. 'There must be hope? She's so strong – she's always been so well.'

Harry shook his head in pity, which was answer enough. 'Havergill says it's a matter of days now. She's very weak. I'm so sorry, Bendy.'

'How did it happen?'

Harry frowned. 'If I tell you, you must promise to keep it secret. I was bound to secrecy by Havergill – she doesn't want it known.' Benedict nodded. 'She has been doing good works amongst the poor. You know that there's a very poor area to the south of Nunnery Lane – on her very doorstep – and consumption is rife, because of the damp conditions and bad air generally. She – she had particular interest in the prostitutes who live in the worst of the tenements – some of them mere children. Havergill says that the infection is passed on through the air, and that being frequently with consumptive people and breathing their air is the most usual way of contracting it.'

'But she was always so strong and healthy!'

'That was part of the trouble, Havergill says. In a sickly person the symptoms would have shown earlier. With her, the disease had taken firm hold before there was any way of knowing.'

'Oh God,' Benedict said, putting his hand over his brow. The awful weight of guilt and regret sat like a stone on his chest.

'I must go back to her,' Harry said. 'She will wonder what I'm doing.'

'Can I see her?'

'I'm sure she will want to see you, but I will just ask her, in case it is a shock. Wait here a moment.'

'She's in the drawing-room?'

'For the last three days. Avis isn't strong enough to carry her upstairs, so she sleeps on the sofa. It's better not to move her.'

Benedict waited, head bent, staring at the familiar carpet, while Harry went into the room, closing the door

338

behind him again. In a little while he opened it again and beckoned.

'She wants to see you. Try not to agitate her, Bendy. Be calm and pleasant.'

There was a great fire burning, and the drawing-room was stiflingly hot, for though damp it was mild outside. Benedict's eyes leaped to the sofa by the window, but he did not recognise the woman lying there, propped up by pillows and covered from the waist down by a shawl. Only the hair was the same, glowing red-gold, hanging loose in a thick coil over her shoulder, as though it fed on her failing body. But within the frame of hair was a skeleton-face with a bony, prominent nose and bistred eye-sockets; and under the elaborate lace of the bed jacket there seemed only sticks which failed to fill out the shape of a woman. The lustrous flesh had melted away; the hands that rested limply in her lap were all joints and knuckles.

He could hear her breathing long before he reached her: the hoarse dragging sound seemed to fill the room. He went towards her, numb with pain and pity, but it was pity for a stranger – he could not see this person as Serena, whom he had loved.

'Bendy,' she said, and lifted her hand from her lap. He could see how much of an effort it was, and he hastened to take it. It was light and hot, like a small bird, but the fingers closed round his with surprising strength. 'I am so glad to see you,' she said.

'Why didn't you send for me?' he said. 'I would have come at once.' He sat down on the chair drawn up beside her; Harry went to the other side of the room to write at a table there.

'I didn't want you to know,' she said. She had to draw breath between each word or two, so speech was slow and laborious. 'I didn't want you to see me like this.'

'Oh, my darling!' The pity of it struck through the blankness; but more than that, it was because her eyes were the same. Looking into them and ignoring the rest, he saw Serena there still, like someone trapped in a wrecked ship, and sinking. 'As if that matters! But now I'm here you'll get better. We'll make you well again. We'll—'

The fingers tightened to stop him. She shook her head, just slightly – arguing was an effort which wasted strength. 'No time,' she said, and then went into a spasm of coughing which terrified him. Anstey hurried over, but there was nothing they could do but wait until it stopped, and then give her the water she reached for. At last she leaned back on the pillows, exhausted, and turned her eyes to Bendy's face again. 'Stay?' she said.

He took up her hand again. He wanted to say that he would stay until the end, but he couldn't frame the words, so he just nodded. It seemed to be enough. Harry leaned into her line of sight.

'I have the document finished now. Do you want to read it, or shall I read it to you?'

She shook her head. 'Sign,' she said.

'Then I shall need to call Avis, to fetch someone to witness the signature. There must be two witnesses, you understand, both present at the same time.'

'I will be a witness, if you like,' Bendy said to Harry. 'No need to put poor old Avis to such trouble.'

Harry shook his head. 'You won't do, I'm afraid. I'll get Avis.' And he hurried off, going out of the room rather than pulling the bell, guessing that Avis would be nearby. Bendy stayed where he was, holding Serena's hand. Her eyes were shut, but when he stirred slightly to ease his position, her fingers tightened as though she feared he would leave her. Her breathing, rough as an iron sled being dragged over cobbles, staggered on very slowly. Bendy tried to remember her as she was when they had been lovers, but he could not. In his mind, strangely, there was an image of railway lines, running away straight as arrows to that place on the horizon where all parallels

340

meet; shining silver lines, gleaming wetly under a damp grey October sky. It was a peaceful image. He let it have its way.

In a little while Harry came back in, with a shopkeeper Avis had fetched from nearby. The necessity of signing seemed to rouse Serena, and she sat up and took the pen with surprising vigour. Bendy helped to move the pillows and prop her more comfortably, and then withdrew to the other side of the room while Harry took her through the document, and he and the shopkeeper witnessed her signature. But when it was all done, the surge of vitality seemed to leave her, and she seemed almost visibly to sink like a guttering flame. She lay back exhausted on the pillows, and Bendy resumed his place and took her hand. After a while she had another coughing fit, which left her drowsy. Benedict suggested leaving her to sleep, but she said, 'Don't go. It is so comfortable to have you here,' and so he stayed, sitting quietly with her, unable to tell if she was awake or asleep. Harry stayed too, sitting nearby, looking thoughtfully at the fire. Neither of them spoke. There seemed nothing to say.

She died just before six that evening, quite simply, between one breath and the next, without speaking. Havergill arrived ten minutes later, and seemed not surprised. She could have gone at any time, he said. 'Are you the executor?' he asked Harry. 'Then you must give orders for the funeral.'

'Yes,' said Harry. 'Tomorrow. Bendy, you had better come home with me tonight.'

But Benedict shook his head. 'I can't. I can't just leave her. It wouldn't be right.' Someone ought to sit with her, through this first night, when her spirit would be hovering near, puzzled and uncertain. 'Someone must keep vigil.'

'Very well,' Harry nodded, accepting the necessity. 'But you must come and see me tomorrow, at my office. There is much to discuss.'

'Is there?' Bendy said vaguely.

Harry gave a grim half-smile. 'Don't you understand? The reason you could not be witness to the Will is that the witness cannot be a beneficiary.'

Bendy looked at him stupidly. The words passed through his brain, leaving no mark. 'What?'

'She left you everything.' He held up the folded document. 'Apart from one or two small bequests to servants and the like, she left everything she had to you.'

CHAPTER SIXTEEN

Benedict arrived at Harry's office early the next day in the state of bemused numbness that comes of sitting up all night. When the coffin-maker had arrived in the morning, he had gone upstairs to bathe and shave, and Avis had done what he could in brushing his coat and blacking his boots. But there was nothing he could do about a shirt, and Bendy felt distinctly frowsy in body as well as in mind.

Harry, seeing the state he was in, sat him down and sent for coffee, and engaged him while he drank it with some neutral talk about railways. Bendy revived enough after a few sips to ask, 'What's behind this business with Lord Howden? You had your Act through, I know, so how can he be holding you up?'

'He has introduced an amending Bill into Parliament, and of course the Select Committee is bound to consider it, which means we have to contest it. And if it goes to the Courts, it'll be a long business,' Harry said. He sat on the edge of his desk and folded his arms, frowning into the fire. 'I'm pretty sure it's Nicky who has put him up to it – they've been as thick as thieves all summer – Howden's even dined twice at Morland Place, and no-one ever dines there now.'

'No-one?' Bendy said, startled.

'They don't invite, or accept invitations. We never see Aglaea now.' He sighed. 'I wish I knew *why* Nicky's so dead set against the railway. I know there are people who think locomotives are the Devil's engines, but they're mostly ignorant people who know nothing about it. Nicky's not one of them. He knows as much as any layman about railways: when we had our trip to Northumberland as boys, he was as interested as we were.'

'What exactly does Lord Howden want?'

'He claims that Hudson made promises to him to get his agreement to cross his land, which Hudson hasn't fulfilled, and that therefore the Act was got through fraudulently.'

'And did Hudson in fact make the promises?'

Harry shook his head in exasperation. 'It's impossible to tell. *You* know what Hudson is, how he talks nineteen to the dozen without remembering half what he says. He'll promise anything in the heat of the moment; at the lowest estimate, he might well have mentioned sums of compensation in a general way in Howden's presence – you know the kind of thing: "We generally pay important landlords five thousand pounds" – thrown out loftily while gazing at the ceiling or out of the window. But it's beside the point. We'll fight it, of course, but Howden's better able to withstand the cost of the lawyers than we are, especially as we can't do anything until the matter's resolved. I've told Hudson we'd do better to try and settle, but he won't hear of it. I think Nicky's been baiting him, deliberately to make him fight, and now he's got the bit between his teeth. I'm afraid in the end it will come to a choice between paying Howden what he asks, and changing the line of the railway, and of the two, paying the bribe will come cheaper. But if we have to pay, I say the sooner the better. *I've* no wish to spend the next six months in London, standing before this committee and that, while my practice back here goes to rack.'

'Your practice is thriving, I hope?'

'Yes, thank you, I am doing very well. But Celia is increasing again—'

'Oh, congratulations! You must be very pleased.'

344

'We are. But we'll need a larger house when the new baby comes. It already seems intolerably small with young Arthur rushing about everywhere. I can't afford to let things slide. And I don't want to be away from home when the crucial time comes. Cely tends to be nervous, after we lost the last one.' He sighed. 'Which brings me to the business in hand. I lost a valued client last night.' He looked closely at Benedict. 'Are you all right?'

'I feel as if I'm in a dream. Everything happened so suddenly. I hadn't a thought of it when I arrived in York, and now, just a few hours later—' He shook his head. 'Perhaps I am dreaming. I thought last night you said that Serena had left me everything.'

'I did. She did.'

'The shop and everything? So now I'm to be a draper. I wonder what my mother would say?' It was not quite a joke.

'There's a great deal more to it than just the shop – though indeed that's a very profitable business. But old Makepeace invested well, and his widow – Mrs Makepeace, I should say, had a sound business head too. There are three small factories, some property, a good piece of agricultural land out past Shipton, a mass of shares, and a considerable amount of cash in various deposits. The whole is worth about three hundred thousand pounds.'

Benedict stared blankly. The figures sounded like nonsense to him. 'Did you say three hundred thousand?' Such a sum invested in the Funds would give him an income of fifteen thousand pounds a year. His present salary was five hundred. It was wealth beyond counting. It was preposterous.

'I think probably she didn't know the full extent of it,' Harry said sympathetically. 'There are other bequests, of course – a pension for Avis and the other servants, some gifts to friends and to charities. And one bequest in particular – it will make strange reading. There's a house

345

down by the river at the end of Clementhorpe: it used to be a warehouse, but it was converted into a lodging house in the days of old Mr Makepeace. Mrs Makepeace has been using it as a refuge for her fallen women for some time now, and in her Will she leaves instructions for it to be rebuilt to a design she has registered, and for a trust to be set up to administer it in perpetuity for destitute women and their children. The details will take some working out, but it can be done. I estimate that, together with the other legacies, it will remove about sixty or sixty-five thousand pounds from the estate. The rest is yours.'

It seemed Benedict had to say something. 'Did she say why? I don't understand why she left it to me.'

Harry shrugged. 'She had no-one else, no kin, just a few friends amongst tradesmen's wives – and her grateful prostitutes. I expect she just remembered you fondly, and thought you would find the money useful.' He saw his levity, mild as it was, was not going down well with Benedict, and he said more seriously, 'I remember a conversation we had some months ago, when she told me she believed your mother was on the verge of altering her Will in your favour when she died – or at least of restoring you to it in some way. Perhaps Mrs Makepeace blamed herself for not having spoken sooner.'

'It – it seems wrong. I don't think I want it,' Benedict said after a pause.

'Nonsense,' said Harry warmly. 'I shall think very little of either your sense or your chivalry if you refuse her last wishes. Besides, if it doesn't go to you, it goes to the Crown. Now I'm as fond of King Billy as the next man, but I don't see why he should have the Makepeace fortune, do you?'

'The Makepeace fortune. That's the trouble – most of it was accumulated by old Mr Makepeace. What would he think about it going to his wife's lover?'

'I don't see that you need to feel uncomfortable about

that. You did him no wrong. He was long dead when you met her, and she was free to take a lover or a new husband for that matter. There's no issue of conscience here, Bendy. It's simply a matter of whether you accept her generous gift gracefully, or snub her now that she is helpless to prevent you.'

Benedict smiled just a little. He felt desperately tired. 'Well, I suppose you're right. If it was what she wanted—' He stopped abruptly, and then added, 'I can't think that she's dead. It doesn't seem possible.'

'I know. I feel the same.'

'What do I do, then?' Bendy asked.

'Nothing, just at present. The Will will have to be proved, which will probably take a year or so – though I can advance money for the upkeep of the property and the payment of wages and so on. The house on Nunnery Lane is yours, of course, and you can move in straight away, if you like. And it is perfectly possible for me to arrange for you to draw on the profits of the shop, so that you can have an income while we wait for probate.' He smiled. 'As I am sole executor, you will have to get used to my knowing everything about your business. It's a good thing we are friends.'

'Yes,' said Bendy.

Harry cocked his head. 'You are on leave, I take it, from the railway? Will you have to go back to give your notice? I assume you will be leaving your career, illustrious as it has been?'

'I don't know. There's so much to think about.'

'Well, don't think about it now, that's my advice. Sleep on it. It's the very worst thing in the world to take decisions when you are in a state of shock, as I can see you are.'

'I suppose I am.'

'No suppose about it. You are welcome to come and stay with me and Cely; or you can use the house, as I said – though I don't imagine you'd want to stay there until after the funeral.'

'I think I have to go back to Kilsby. They are expecting me back tomorrow, and I would not like to let them down. But I suppose I'll come straight back. When will the funeral be?'

Harry considered. 'Tomorrow's Sunday – I can't do anything then. If I make the arrangements on Monday, we can hold it on Tuesday. Can you be back by then? I imagine you'd want to be present?'

'You don't think it would be— ?'

'There'll be very few other people there.'

'Then I'll come.'

'Very well. Now my advice to you is to go back to your hotel and sleep. You look all in. Is there anything you need for your immediate expenses?'

Bendy forced himself to think. He had enough for his reckoning and his fare to Kilsby; but he had kept the horse an extra day, and he would have to pay for its overnight keep at the Jolly Bacchus, and then pay his reckoning in Kilsby and Crick, and his fare back to York again. 'A few guineas wouldn't come amiss,' he said diffidently. Borrowing from a friend was not really the thing.

Harry seemed to understand his difficulty. 'It's your money, remember, not mine. No need to be embarrassed.'

He took the money from the safe, counted it out, handed it over, wrote the receipt for Benedict to sign, and then saw him to the door. 'Go home and sleep,' he said, giving his friend a farewell clap on the back.

It was advice that Benedict had every intention of following. He stopped first at the Jolly Bacchus for breakfast – the coffee had stimulated his appetite, and his stomach was now reminding him that he had not dined last night – and when he had got himself outside a vast, sizzling steak, a mound of spinach and three fried eggs, the blood started to circulate his numbed brain for the first time since he had left Hudson standing in Micklegate. He had money, he was rich, he could do anything he liked now, even come back to York in spite of Nicky. He could buy himself a house and estate, if not quite to rival Morland Place, at least to give him gentlemanly status in the city, and security for life. He could—

He could get married. He almost choked on the last mouthful of coffee as the thought came to him with such blinding clarity he could not understand why he had not thought of it before. Miss Fleetham! He could marry Miss Fleetham – if she'd have him. But surely, surely now that he was to be rich, there could be no difficulty. She had said that if he made his fortune and came back for her – she had said *come back quickly*, and he remembered the look in her eyes as she said it. His blood raced at the thought of it. Her beauty, her elegance, her sweetness – they could all be his now. Not Mrs Partridge, but Mrs Benedict Morland! It was the realisation of a dream, and it was all thanks to – yes, well, thanks to Serena. A moment's check in his exuberance. What would Serena think about his using her fortune to marry the lovely Miss Fleetham? But that was silly thinking! Serena, God rest her soul, was dead, and could hardly object to his marrying someone else – especially since he had begged her and begged her to marry him when they had been lovers, and she had consistently refused him. 'One day,' she had said, 'you will marry someone handsome, accomplished and rich, and if you think of me at all, it will be as a distant memory.' I will never forget you, Serena, he vowed; and if you had known Miss Fleetham, you'd have approved my choice, for she's everything lovely.

Having settled that last awkwardness in his mind, he could not bear to wait any longer. Perhaps Miss Fleetham and her father might have returned from Leeds already. He had a horse – it was only ten or twelve miles. Why wait any longer to secure his happiness? At this very minute she might be despairing of him and considering another offer. And if they were still from home, he would write a letter. He would ask the butler to allow him to write it there and then. *Carpe diem!* He was not going to lose her again if he could help it.

He pushed back his chair and yelled for the waiter, and a quarter of an hour later he was on his way, posting down towards Micklegate Bar with his mind in a fever of excitement and anticipation.

There was a post-chaise in front of the door when he rode up to Fleetham Manor; two footmen were unstrapping luggage from the back, and a figure he would have known anywhere, in any crowd, was halfway up the steps. Hearing hooves, she paused and turned her head, and then froze in that position, one foot up, one hand in her muff, the other lifting her skirts clear of the step. It was a picture at once etched on his mind, which he knew he would never forget. She was wearing a three-caped mantle of grey merino, piped with emerald, and a grey felt bonnet with three emerald-dyed ostrich plumes. Within its frame, beneath a front of delicate gold curls, her face was turned towards him: exquisite as eggshell porcelain but deathly pale, the mouth drooping with unhappiness, lavender shadows under her eyes. She looked worn, tired – older. He had taken her to be about eighteen at their first meeting, but now she looked more his own age. To the ferment of excitement in his breast was added an ache of pity, a longing to serve, to protect. He wanted to gather her to him, and make sure nothing ever distressed her, ever again.

He reached the foot of the steps and halted his horse.

'Mr Morland,' she said rather doubtfully, as though not knowing what degree of welcome would be appropriate. From the corner of his eye, he saw Mr Fleetham emerge from the carriage in his turn. 'What brings you here?'

'Miss Fleetham, forgive me, but I come with news.

Most important news.' He glanced at her father, steadily encroaching, and then back at her. Suddenly his pretensions seemed absurd. Mere money could not win this angel. If she did not love him, it would mean nothing – and he had no reason to believe that she loved him.

'News, Mr Morland?' She was not smiling at him yet. She seemed still doubtful; her father's face as he climbed the steps was grim.

'About my circumstances,' he stammered.

'Have you won your fortune and come to claim me?' she asked playfully, but the lightness did not touch her eyes – there seemed something almost sharp about them.

'Yes,' he said. 'At least, I have my fortune, and I – I—' How pathetic it all sounded. He felt sixteen again – a boastful boy.

But a miraculous change had come over her. The rose-petal lids had lowered over the glorious eyes, the sweet, shy smile he remembered so well touched her lips. She slipped her arm through her father's, and turned to face him. 'Papa, Mr Morland has ridden a long way, and must be tired. It would be shameful if we did not offer him refreshment.'

Her father jerked a little, almost as if he had been pinched or kicked – he must have been in a dream, and her words brought him back. 'Oh, very well – that is, yes indeed. Just as you please, puss.'

A radiant smile for him now, briefly bestowed before she turned her attention to the footmen. 'Harris, take Mr Morland's horse. What are you thinking about? Mr Morland, won't you please come in and rest awhile, and share a nuncheon with us? I have no idea what there may be,' she laughed ruefully, 'for we have been away some time and returned unexpectedly, but if you will take pot-luck, we should be honoured.'

'The honour, and the pleasure, are all mine,' Benedict said, dismounting.

★　　★　　★

The Fleethams went straight upstairs to take off their outer clothes, while Bendy waited below in the morning-room, where a housemaid hurriedly kindled a fire. The room had been partly warmed by the sunshine, but it had a stale, cold smell of unuse, and even his untrained eye could see the dust on the polished surfaces, and the tarnish on the silver. He turned to look out of the window instead. A terrace gave onto a rose-garden, which looked neglected too – he noted the straggling growth, brown, dead heads which should have been snipped, and here and there even a rose-hip flaunting itself. Beyond again was the park. It was a pleasant, misty, sunny autumn day, and a large horse-chestnut, the nearest tree to the house, was surrounded by a ring of yellow fallen leaves, like a pool of mislaid sunshine. Amongst the leaves a blackbird rooted, peered and stabbed. He could hear through the closed french doors a faint ghost of birdsong. The house behind him was very quiet – so quiet it made him feel faintly uneasy. In his state of excitement, over weariness from having lost a night's sleep, he could not quite pin down what was odd about the quiet. But when he turned from the window he saw that the clock on the chimney-piece had stopped, and put it down to that.

In any case, Miss Fleetham was re-entering the room, and there was no room for any thought but of her. Her travelling-gown of dull green cotton was bang up to the mark, with a pleated cross-over bodice worn over a delicate muslin tucker, and the sleeves much ruched and pleated, with a double flounce over the elbow, and then close-fitting down to the wrist. Below her small waist – was ever any waist so tiny? – the skirts were very full, with an exciting hint of bustle at the back. She wore her glorious golden hair in a knot behind, with long ringlets in bunches over each ear. Miraculously, every trace of tiredness seemed to have gone from her face. Her cheeks and lips were delicately pink, her eyes unshadowed – and he marvelled again at how dark a golden girl's eyelashes could be.

She smiled at him – one glance of flashing blue before she lowered her eyes modestly – and said, 'I am so sorry to have kept you waiting. And Barnes has not offered you sherry! How remiss of him. Papa, you really must speak to Barnes.'

Mr Fleetham, entering behind her, gave her a look Benedict could not fathom, but it did not seem particularly loving. 'Aye, as you say,' he said shortly. 'Well, Mr Morland, you look in fine fettle. Where have you ridden from today?'

'Only from York, sir. I am here on a few days' leave of absence.'

'Ah, here is Barnes now, with the nuncheon,' Miss Fleetham said quickly, as the butler entered with decanter and glasses, followed by a footman bearing a loaded tray. 'Shall we have the table set up by the window? The fire is rather sad still. Barnes, bring the round table into the window. Put the sherry down there, and I will serve our guest. Mr Morland, will you take sherry?'

She directed the conversation skilfully for the next hour, as they took their places round the table and applied themselves to eat and drink. It certainly was pot-luck – a cheese, a small piece of rather dry cold beef, some stale game pie, a bowl of apples, a dish of hard-boiled eggs and radishes, and a large, tasty but inelegant fruit-cake which had surely been destined for the kitchen table until promoted in the field to cope with the emergency. Miss Fleetham, after one desparing glance round the assembled forces, made no further reference by word or expression to their inadequacy, and Bendy was struck with silent admiration of her handling of the campaign. Mr Fleetham ate stolidly and in silence, as though indifferent to everything around him. Benedict thought he looked unwell: surely his face was more lined, his hair more grey, than when he had last seen him? No doubt he had been bitterly hurt by Partridge's treatment of his daughter. Benedict did what he could by following Miss Fleetham's lead and chattering lightly and unimportantly on the neutral subjects she introduced – the weather, the harvest, the King's health, the York races, the latest fashions, and so on.

When it was not possible to pretend any longer that the meal was not over, Miss Fleetham rose and went to pull the bell, and returning to her father's chair, hung very prettily about his neck and said, 'You look so very tired, Papa, I'm sure that horried carriage-drive has given you a migraine. Now do admit it! Yes, I thought so.' She looked up at Benedict. 'Carriages never did suit Papa's constitution – he is always quite done up by the shortest drive. I'm sure Mr Morland will understand if you go up to your room to rest. The only thing that helps, Mr Morland, is to lie down in a darkened room for an hour or two. Do go at once, Papa, don't mind us a bit. I will take my little walk about the grounds while you are resting – I must have my walk, and there was no opportunity this morning, for we were in the carriage by ten. I'm sure Mr Morland will be kind enough to give me his company. You will not mind if it is a little damp, Mr Morland?'

Benedict, who had been considering with despair the defection of Mr Fleetham – for it would not have been proper for him to remain alone with Miss Fleetham within doors – hastened to give his consent to all parts of the plan, and was struck again by what an able general she would have made, which was astonishing when one considered her youth and gentleness. In a little while Mr Fleetham had taken his departure, Miss Fleetham had sent upstairs for a fine, thick cashmere shawl, and they had walked out through the French doors onto the terrace, and were alone at last. Benedict walked beside her in silence at first, so completely unable to feel his feet he was sure he must be floating an inch or so above the ground. After three or four glasses of sherry – he had lost count – he had passed beyond tiredness into euphoria. He had never thought to see her again, and here he was walking alone with her, close enough to catch the familiar perfume that seemed to hang around her.

They passed from the end of the terrace down some steps and onto a sunken path that ran along the length of the lawn, every step taking them further away from the house and prying eyes. The hazy sun was pleasantly warm, the air smelled of grass and leaves, the birds were singing happily in every quarter. She walked in silence, her eyes fixed on the sights of nature around her, and he realised that it was up to him to open the subject.

'Miss Fleetham, I must say first of all that I heard of the terrible thing that happened to you. The appalling treatment of you by that wicked—'

'Oh, pray, do not say his name,' she said quickly. 'I cannot bear it.'

'He must be the blackest villain that ever lived,' Benedict said, 'and it would give me the greatest pleasure to be able to knock him down.'

'I should be glad to watch you do it,' she said, 'except that I am gladder still to think I shall never set eyes on him again. All I want to do now is to forget he ever lived. Unhappily,' she added, looking away from him slightly, 'there are those of my acquaintance – I cannot now call them *friends* – who seem to think I am in some way to blame for my misfortune.'

'I can only say that they are not worthy of your notice,' he said warmly. 'Anyone who could blame you for being taken in by a designing blackguard deserves to suffer the same fate themselves. That would show them!'

'I would not wish my misery on anyone,' she said in a low voice, 'no matter how cruelly they have spoken to me.'

'You are as generous as you are good,' Benedict said. He longed to strain her then and there against his heart. The word 'misery' from her lips filled him with an odd mixture of fury and despair. She should never be hurt, never! She should know nothing but perfect, endless happiness!

'You had something to tell me, Mr Morland?' she enquired gently after a moment, unaware of his internal struggle. 'You mentioned some news concerning your situation?'

'Yes,' he said. They were at the foot of the lawn now, and to the right the path led round a shrubbery, which would conceal them from the house. He turned that way, and a few steps along stopped and turned to face her. She lowered her head a little in automatic modesty, so that most of her face was hidden from him, and he addressed her smooth brow, her lowered eyelids, and the tip of her nose. 'Miss Fleetham, a long time ago I asked you if I might address you, and you told me that it would be out of your power to listen to me unless I was possessed of a fortune.'

A flicker in her face; she seemed about to say something, and then thought better of it. 'It was true – then.'

'I have come to tell you that by an extraordinary series of events, I now have my fortune.'

'You have?' She looked up at him now, with a mixture of hope and doubt.

'A very large fortune,' he said. 'Large enough to buy myself an estate and live comfortably for the rest of my life.'

'You're not going to be an engineer any more?' she asked. She sounded breathless.

'That depends.'

'On what?'

'On you,' he said. He saw her lips say, 'Oh,' but she made no sound. Her eyes were on his, and she looked pale under the pinkness of her cheeks, an anomaly his brain registered but could make nothing of at that moment. 'I have never stopped loving you. I was in despair when I heard you were engaged, and now by a miracle you are free again – I know it must not seem a miracle to you, and I'm sorry to use the word, but it is one to me. Your feelings must have been dreadfully hurt, and it will take time for you to get over it, but if you feel that one day you might be able to forget that villain and come to care for me, I will wait. I will give up the railways and become a landed gentleman, and wait for ever if need be, as long as there is hope for me. But if you feel you could never care for me, I will go back to my trade, and be an engineer. A man must have something to occupy him, and it will help me to get through my life without you.'

She did not reply at once. It was a long speech, and probably she was not sure it was over, he thought. And her feelings must be painfully confused. 'I do not expect an answer at once,' he assured her gently. 'You will need time to—'

'No, no,' she said breathlessly. She put out both hands to him, and with an excited rush of blood to his face he took them and held them. 'I do not need time, not at all! That man – that hateful man – I don't care about him! I never did! It was you I loved, always, always! I don't want to wait. I know my heart, I assure you. Pray – pray do not hesitate a moment.'

The words tumbled out almost in a stammer; she seemed to flutter in his hands like a startled bird. It was so unlike her usual composure that it delighted and terrified him. 'You love me? Is it possible? You love me?'

'Yes, yes, I love you. For God's sake, go on!'

He gripped the hands tighter, bemused and excited by her passion, and had to force himself to do the thing properly, as was her due. 'Miss Fleetham, I love you entirely – will you marry me?'

'Yes, yes, you know I will! Oh, Benedict!'

He did not know how it happened, but she was in his arms, and he was kissing her soft lips, his arms around her slender body, his own body feeling hot and hard and ready to burst with the sensations aroused by the physical contact with the woman he had adored so long. At the moment when he thought he would not be able to control himself any longer, she drew back from him, gasping a little for breath, put her hands up to her cheeks, looked at him tremulously, said – whispered – 'Now you know. I loved you from the first.'

'Oh, my darling! My Rosalind!'

'No, no, don't touch me again, not yet. It is too much!'

'You are right. And I must speak to your father.' A sudden doubt. 'But will he accept me for a son-in-law?'

'Oh, it is nothing to do with him. I am over twenty-one,' she said quickly.

He remembered what she had said about not being able to leave her father all forlorn. 'But you will still want his permission. And when you tell him that I will not take you far away—'

'Yes, that will weigh with him,' she said hastily. 'I am sure he will agree. He always liked you, Benedict, and it was only your lack of fortune – you are very rich now, are you?'

He laughed, not at her, but with pleasure. 'Very rich. It is an astonishing thing to contemplate, but I have come in for a legacy of two hundred and fifty thousand pounds.'

'Two hundred and fif—' Her eyes opened wide. She looked almost frightened. Then she swallowed and said, 'Oh, my dearest, let's be married right away, as soon as possible! I cannot bear to think I might lose you again. I was in despair when I was forced to accept that man's proposal, because it meant I would never see you again. And now you are here, it is like a dream. I'm so afraid I may wake up and find you gone!'

'I feel like that, too,' Bendy said. She allowed him to take her in his arms again, but gently this time; passion was under control, and tenderness for her was paramount. After being so cruelly jilted once, she would naturally be afraid it might happen a second time. He must do everything he could to reassure her. 'You mustn't be afraid. I long to make you my wife. We will have the wedding as soon as you like; and once you are mine I shall never leave you again, not for a minute. The world will marvel to see how completely one we are.'

'The world! Yes, I long to tell the whole world of our love,' she said eagerly. She extracted herself from his embrace, slipped her hand through his arm, and guided his steps back along the path. 'We had better go and see Papa at once.'

'But he is unwell – we ought not to disturb him,' Benedict said doubtfully. A man with a migraine might not be favourably inclined towards the proposal that dragged him from his bed of pain.

'Oh, he will be well enough now. A few minutes in a darkened room is all it takes – his headaches are never very bad. And you ought to speak to him as soon as possible, my darling. It would not be proper for me to rejoice in our love until he has given his consent. I would not for the world do anything the least undutiful.'

'You're right,' he said. 'If you think he will be able to see me, I will ask him for your hand at once. After all, if I don't see him now, it will be some days before I can come back, and the uncertainty—'

'What? Why? Are you going away?' she interrupted sharply.

'I must go back to Kilsby – to the railway workings.' Her fingers were biting into his arm, and he was filled with pity for her panic. How that man had hurt her! He would like to kill him. 'Don't worry, it is only to clear matters up there. I shall be back on Tuesday, for sure. There is some business I must attend to in York on Tuesday, and after that, my time is all yours, every moment of it, for ever. For the rest of our lives.' He lifted her hand, freeing its fingers from his arm, and kissed it. 'Don't those words sound good to you? For the rest of our lives.'

'Yes,' she said, a little absently; and then she smiled,

and looked up at him. 'Yes, very good. And our lives together can begin in three weeks – just time to call the bans. I don't want to wait a moment longer than that to be entirely yours.'

'Three weeks,' he said, kissing her hand again. 'We shall have to take a rented house then, to begin with, until the Will has been proved. I shall not have my fortune for about a year, I'm afraid.'

She seemed to turn pale. 'What – but – but it is certain? There is no doubt?'

'Not the least doubt in the world. But it is all very new news, you see.' Serena had died only yesterday. Was it possible? It seemed several years ago, at least, that he had sat beside her in the flickering firelight and heard her die. For a moment he felt bad, so bad it almost made him sick, that he had hurried from her bedside to Rosalind's arms, as though he cared nothing. It was disrespectful. It was almost indecent. But no, Serena would have understood. She was a woman, she would have known how important it was to rescue Rosalind from her *misery* without delay. 'I only heard about it this morning.'

Rosalind looked up at him with an expression he could not quite fathom. It was as if some profound revelation had come upon her, a realisation of something extraordinary and perhaps not quite comfortable. 'You mean – you mean that you came here as soon as you heard? It was the first thing you did?'

'The very instant. The very first thing,' he said, smiling down at her. 'Does that shock you? I was afraid of losing you, you see. If I'd arrived to find you'd accepted someone else five minutes earlier, I'd have had to shoot myself.'

'Don't joke,' she whispered. 'It frightens me. Do you really love me so much?'

'Can you still doubt it?' She shook her head, and looked away along the path. 'Darling, what is it?'

'Nothing,' she said. She drew a breath and smiled again. 'Only that I love you. Let's go and see Papa.'

They walked on up the path. She was light as a feather on his arm. The afternoon air was cooling and there were yellow leaves underfoot, blowing across the path on a little, fitful breeze. He was very, very tired now, and was beginning to feel it; by a trick of the light and his weary eyes, the house did not seem to get any closer, no matter how many steps they took towards it.

CHAPTER SEVENTEEN

Robert Stephenson was philosophical about letting Benedict go.

'I suppose I must congratulate you – you will be able to take your place in society. It's what every man dreams of, to come into a fortune. But I shall be sorry to lose you. You are a good tunnel man. I suppose you wouldn't care to come back after the funeral, just for a few months, until the legal business is sorted out?'

Benedict explained about Miss Fleetham.

'Ah, well, if there's a lady in the case, it's a different matter.' He offered his hand. 'I wish you good luck.'

'Thank you, sir. And I you, with the tunnel.'

'If you ever want another job,' Robert said with a faint smile, 'come to me. I can always use a good engineer.'

Benedict went outside and paused a moment to look around at the familiar scene: the steam pumps grinding and roaring, the horse-gins revolving silently like ballet, the men off-shift sitting about in patches of sunshine enjoying their pipes, the smell of coal and clay and manure and wood-fires. A world different from any other, which had become his and as familiar as his own heartbeat: but now he saw it as if rimmed with light, as something apart from him, a ghost-scene which he could not enter or touch. Or perhaps he was the ghost now, as any creature out of its world would be – a phantasm drifting from one reality towards another.

He shook the thoughts away and walked down to the

barn where he had left his horse. Before he reached it he heard the drumming of hooves behind him: Sibella Leytham was cantering towards him on her big, black horse. She was in her usual black habit and jacket, white stock, and a close-fitting low-crowned hat, but her hair had been fluffed by the damp air into a fuzzy mass like fine copper wires matted together. She was reining back as she passed him, but it was some paces before she could get the horse to turn. Benedict watched it come trotting back towards him, flashing its forelegs in a showy way and snatching at the bit, its neck arched and its ears almost crossed with excitement.

'He's too big for you,' Benedict said by way of greeting. 'I've said so all along. You can't hold him.'

'I can hold him perfectly well,' she retorted automatically, halting the black before him and making it back a step so that it was standing square. It was neatly done: she was a fine horsewoman. He admired the straightness of her back and the sureness with which her small hands managed the double reins. Sir John was proud of Sibella's prowess. He had bought her a horse he'd have been glad to ride himself, and had it specially broken to sidesaddle.

But Sibella didn't want to talk about her horse. The next words burst out of her. 'Is it true you're going away?'

'News travels fast. Who told you that?'

'I rode up here to see you, and I saw your horse tied up here instead of at the horse lines, so I guessed you weren't staying long. I've been all over the hill looking for you, and I asked Gallagher where you were and he told me. But is it true? That you're going away for ever?' Her face was a mask of tragedy.

'Yes,' he said, 'I'm afraid so.'

'But *why?*'

'Someone died and left me a lot of money, so I'm not going to be an engineer any more. I'm going home to be a gentleman.'

'Home?'

'To York. You know I come from York.'

She leaned forward urgently. 'If you're going to be rich, you can live anywhere you want. You could live near us.'

'I could,' he said, 'but I want to go home.'

'But you'll come back and visit?'

'Perhaps I may some day.'

She straightened up and looked at him with some sort of dawning realisation in her eyes. Her lip quivered, and she drew a terrible dignity over herself like a mantle. 'You were going away without even saying goodbye,' she said, and it was not a question. 'I think you're hateful!' And she gathered the reins and dug in her heel, turning the black sharply.

Benedict had to stand back from the whirlwind or he'd have been bounced out of the way like a ninepin, but he called 'Sibella, wait!' It was not easy to do; she managed it only by turning the black again on the spot. 'I'd have written,' he said. 'Of course I would. To thank your father for all his kindness.'

'To Father – not to me!' she said tragically. He saw there were angry tears on her cheeks – they caught the light as the horse revolved.

'I couldn't write to you, dear Sib!' Benedict said coaxingly. 'It wouldn't be proper. But I'd have sent you a message through your father.'

She got the horse to stand again, and looked down at him consideringly. 'I thought we were friends,' she said.

'I hope we are,' Benedict said.

'Then you'll come to my coming-out ball? You promised you would.'

'I will if I can.'

'You promised. People are supposed to keep promises.'

He looked up at her soberly. 'I think they generally try to. But sometimes things happen that they can't help.'

364

She gazed at him for a long moment with wide, rain-coloured eyes, and then she turned the black again and was off, cantering over the brow of the hill and out of sight. Benedict stood for a moment watching the space where she had been and feeling her heart-soreness as if it were his own. And then he shrugged and turned away. She'd have forgotten him in two weeks, and made a pet out of some other engineer – or puppy, or orphaned fox-cub. That was her nature.

The day of the funeral was appropriately grey. The paths of the churchyard were slippery with mats of black wet leaves, and a fine, penetrating mist of rain blew directly into the mourners' faces whichever way they stood. There weren't many of them: Harry and Benedict, the servants, employees from the shop and the factories, and a few women-friends, shopkeepers' wives. But in the background, keeping a modest distance, was a small group of the women she had helped; poor women with shawls over their heads and young children in their arms. They shrank back and avoided eyes when anyone looked their way, but when the coffin was lowered into the muddy gash in the ground, they wept. Benedict stood at the graveside, hat in hand, the rain soaking his hair, trying to feel something. This was Serena, this was the end of her, her wasted body in this coffin, going down into the yellow clay. But he could not shake off the dazed tiredness and bewilderment which had held him fast for the last few days.

Afterwards they went back to the house, where funeral meats had been provided, and Benedict was obliged, awkwardly, to play host. He could not help wondering what these decent folk were thinking about him. It must be awkward for them, too: they could hardly walk up and commiserate with him, as with a widower. It was Harry who saved the day – Harry and Celia, who had not been at the graveside because of her condition, but who now quietly made people comfortable and saw they had enough to eat and drink. She gave them a focus which they badly needed, for her presence was unambiguous, at least, as the wife of the deceased's man of business.

To Benedict's great surprise, some time after they got back to the house Hudson arrived, soberly dressed and sporting 'weepers'.

'I couldn't get away before,' he said, 'but I would pay my respects, though I can't stay but a minute.'

'I'm delighted to see you,' Benedict managed to say.

Hudson shook his head. 'Nay, lad, don't look so mazed! Us drapers mun stick together, tha knaws! Aye, aye, Anstey told me all about it. I'm right sorry the widow went off so sudden, poor woman, but there, it comes to us all, whenever and however. But I'm right glad tha's come in for a fortune. There's no man I'd sooner see well-lined than thee. But Anstey tells me it'll be a bit before all't papers are signed – as much as a year, mebbe?'

'So I understand.'

'Well, then, tha'll want summat to do. I can't offer thee the old job, for we've got a chief engineer, but there's a place for thee as assistant, if tha likes. There'll be a tricky bit o' work around South Milford where our line crosses the Leeds an' Selby, and that's the very land tha knaws best. What dost say? We could use thee, I don't deny it!'

Benedict almost laughed. 'I don't know what to say! I haven't a thought of working at the moment.'

'It'll be a while before we can start anyway, because of this trouble with Howden. But tha'll need summat to do while the lawyers weave their toils. And besides,' he cocked an eye at Bendy cannily, 'what if it all comes to nowt? It don't do to rely on fortunes until they're in the hand.'

Benedict shook his head, bemused. 'When the work begins, ask me again. I don't entirely relish the idea of giving up my profession, but I have other plans afoot which may not be compatible with it. You see, I mean to get married.'

'Oh, aye, to Miss Fleetham,' Hudson said with a nod.

'How do you know that?' Benedict asked in surprise.

'Stale buns,' Hudson shrugged. 'They talk o' nothing else in Selby. There were a few saying it were nowt but rumour, but where there's brass there's spite, 'specially amongst the females. Well, she's a tasty piece, so I don't blame thee. But tha'll likely find her expensive, and weddings don't come cheap. If tha wants to earn a few guineas, come to me.'

He plunged off to talk to the shopkeeping contingent, but he did not stay much longer. Soon after his departure Harry came to say he was taking Celia home. 'Come and see me tomorrow,' he said. 'There's a lot to discuss.'

'I can't tomorrow,' Benedict said. 'The day after?'

'Very well.'

Harry's departure seemed to be the general signal, and one by one the guests said goodbye and went out into the misty afternoon. In half an hour they were all gone, and Benedict was left feeling at a loss, not sure what to do next. He was staring about the drawing-room in an absent way when Avis coughed gently to attract his attention.

'If I might be so bold as to enquire about your immediate plans, sir? I have not yet made up a bed for you, but it can be done at once if you would indicate which room you prefer. I did not like to anticipate your choice. And will you be dining here tonight, sir?'

Benedict looked at him helplessly for a moment. This was his house now – as good as – but no, he didn't think he could sleep and eat here, not yet. She was too recently gone; she had died there, on that sofa which he could see out of the corner of his eye. The room was crowded with her things and with her presence. He had to get out.

'I shan't be eating here or sleeping here tonight. I – I have to go away for a couple of days.'

'Very good, sir,' Avis said imperturbably. 'Shall I have

367

one of the guest rooms made up for you, so that it will be ready whenever you wish to return?'

'Yes, thank you,' Benedict said gratefully; and in his gratitude realised that he was probably not the only one who felt unsure about the future. 'Perhaps you would like to tell the other servants that I do not anticipate making any changes. Anyone who wants to stay shall do so – and that includes you, of course, Avis.'

'Thank you, sir,' he said. 'You are very good. I'm sure everyone will want to stay.'

Bendy got to Selby before dark and secured himself a room at the Grey Horse for that night and the next, and since it was too late by then to go visiting, bespoke himself a dinner, and then went out for a walk about the town. The Abbey loomed pale in the darkness, a tiny seed of light showing in one of the windows where a candle was lit somewhere in the vast depths. At the bridge the smell of the river came up, a flat, grey-brown smell overlying the sharpness of horses; a seagull cruised past him in the dark, startling him for a moment. The wharves were empty of people, but along the far bank he could see the bulky shape of barges, and here and there a glimmer of light and a pale wraith of smoke showed where the crew on board were snugged down for the night. With a change of the light wind he could smell someone's bacon frying; and then the rain began again, light for a few seconds, then growing heavier, settling in. He felt suddenly lonely – and hungry and cold. He turned on his heel and hurried back towards the Grey Horse and his dinner.

'Benedict!' He turned from watching the cold rain falling to find her holding out her hands to him. In a gown of rose-pink muslin with a white embroidered tucker, with her shining gold ringlets and radiant smile, she seemed to fill the morning-room with sunshine. 'Oh, I thought you would never come!'

He caught her hands, flattered by her eagerness. 'It

can't be more than ten o'clock.' He glanced at the chimney-piece, but the clock was still stopped. 'It would hardly have been decent for me to arrive any earlier.'

'Have you seen the paper this morning?'

'Only yesterday's *Times*.'

'Oh, it will not be in the *Times* until tomorrow. I meant the *Chronicle*. Wait, wait, I will get it!' She flew out of the room and was back in an instant with the paper folded open at the announcements. 'There,' she said, pointing as she handed it to him.

The betrothal is announced of Benedict, second s. of the late James Morland of Morland Place, to Rosalind Maria, only d. of Joseph Fleetham of Fleetham Manor.

He looked up at her in some surprise.

'What is it? Is it not right?' she said quickly. 'I did not know if you had any second name; you never mentioned one.'

'No,' he said. 'No, I haven't. But you could have asked me if you had waited until I got back.'

She raised an eyebrow. 'I had not thought there was any need to wait.'

'No, not *need*, of course,' he said. He felt a little taken aback, but he could not put his finger on any reason for it. 'I just—'

'It is for the bride's family to issue the notices, you know. Or perhaps you have changed your mind since Saturday?'

'Of course I haven't,' he said. 'I was surprised the news spread so quickly, that's all. I met Mr Hudson in York yesterday, and he told me everyone knows about it.'

'Such happy tidings are hard to keep secret. I could not keep it from my maid – and I dare say Papa told his man, too. Once the servants know, there is no holding it back. You don't mind, I hope?'

'Of course not,' he said. He lifted her hand to his lips. 'How could I mind the whole world knowing that I am the luckiest man alive?'

Now she smiled. 'And I am the luckiest female. It's not every woman who is able to marry for love.'

His heart lurched in a most undignified way. 'Do you really love me? Is it possible?'

'Since the first moment I saw you, I have wanted no other man,' she said. He put away the paper and took her other hand too, drew them against his chest, and then, reading permission in her eyes, bent his head to kiss her soft mouth. After a moment she drew away. 'My darling, I wish we could stay here like this for ever, but there are tiresome things to be discussed with Papa – legal things, you know, about settlements and such. I hate the idea that business must intrude on our love, but if it must, the sooner it is done the better. Will you come and see Papa now?'

'It's rather early: will he be at liberty?'

'Oh, certainly. I told him – that is, he told me he would be in the book-room, waiting for you.' She put her arm through his and led him away. As they stepped out of the morning-room he noticed again that strange silence about the house; and on a little table in a dark corner of the passage there was a vase of dead flowers – dead so long they were only brown skeletons. It was odd, he thought, in a house full of servants that no-one took away dead flowers or wound the morning-room clock. At home, when his mother was alive, such things would have been noticed.

But it was only a passing thought. She opened the book-room door and led him in, saying, 'Papa, I have brought Mr Morland to you, as you asked.'

Fleetham was sitting at a desk with a newspaper open before him, and he looked up unsmilingly at the interruption.

'So you want to marry my girl?' he said at last.

'Yes, sir,' Benedict said uneasily. This was old ground. He had already asked for and received permission – or didn't Fleetham remember? And the notice was in the papers – surely he knew that? 'If you please,' he added at last, as the silence prolonged itself.

'Papa,' Rosalind prompted, warningly.

Fleetham sighed and made a gesture with his hand. 'Sit down, Mr Morland. And you, Miss, sit there and don't interrupt. Now then,' he said when they had settled themselves, looking across the desk forbiddingly at Benedict, 'how do I know you ain't just a fortune-hunter?'

'I love your daughter, sir, sincerely.'

'That's no answer.'

'I shall have a fortune of my own,' Benedict said. 'I'll settle on her whatever you wish.'

'But you don't have the money in your hand at this moment?'

'No, sir. The Will has yet to be proved.'

'And that takes for ever,' Fleetham said.

'The attorney says perhaps a year – at most.'

'Anything can happen in a year,' Fleetham said. 'The Will may be contested. You may come in for nothing at all. What do you say to that, hey?'

Benedict was puzzled. 'Only that it is very unlikely. There's nothing ambiguous about the Will and no-one to contest it. But if the worst came to the worst, I would always find the means to support your daughter, sir. I have a profession, and the offer of a job any time I want it.'

'Railway engineer! My daughter – Miss Fleetham of Fleetham Manor – to be living in a poor little engineer's house with hardly a servant but a maid-of-all-work, and I dare say no carriage of her own. A fine thing that would be!' Benedict saw Rosalind give her father an anxious look. She seemed to be trying to catch his attention, but Fleetham did not, or would not, look. 'It seems to me, Mr Morland,' he went on, 'that you had better wait until this fortune of yours comes in, before you ask me for my daughter's hand.'

'No, Pa!' Rosalind snapped. 'I told you— !' She stopped herself. Benedict looked at her, surprised by

371

the hardness of her voice. She smiled a little nervously. 'Now, Papa, it's no use going on like this. You've already given your consent, and you know that my heart is given to Mr Morland. I couldn't marry anyone else now,' she said with some emphasis. 'I don't care if he has a fortune or not, I just want to marry him as soon as possible. And that's what he wants too, isn't it, Mr Morland?'

'Yes,' said Benedict.

'So just be a good old Pa, and say we can be married in three weeks, as we've planned.'

Fleetham shot her a look which, had he not been her father, Benedict would have thought was almost one of malice. 'Very well, my dear,' he said, 'it shall be as you wish. But now you must leave the room while I discuss matters of finance with Mr Morland.'

'No, Papa, please,' she said nervously.

'Yes, my dear. Off you go now. This is men's business. Show Mr Morland how dutiful you can be. And close the door behind you.'

Benedict rose as she did, and she passed him with a look of great significance, though unfortunately he could not determine what she was trying to tell him. Fleetham watched until the door had closed with a faint click, and then he said, 'I suppose I should offer you a cigar at this point, but I haven't any.'

'I don't smoke, thank you, sir,' Benedict said.

Fleetham looked at him flatly. 'I didn't say I hadn't got any here, I said I hadn't got any.' Benedict didn't know how to reply. Fleetham went on, 'You will want to know about Rosalind's dowry. She is my only child, as I think you know. My estate is not entailed. Everything I have goes to her. Does that suit you?'

'I assure you, sir, that I have never given a thought to her dowry. I love her for herself alone. I would take her without a penny.'

'Is that the solemn truth?'

'I will swear it, if you wish,' Benedict said, on his dignity.

'Ha! Very well. I take your word. You love her for herself alone, eh?' He smiled sourly. 'That's just as well, because I'm all to pieces.'

Benedict could only stare.

'That's right,' Fleetham said, 'I haven't a feather to fly with. My investments have gone bad on me, and what with one thing and another – well, I won't trouble you with the details. You'll find out for yourself, when you're a man of property with a wife and brats to support, that there are more ways of losing money than you ever dreamed of as a bachelor. The duns are on my heels and I've sold everything I can sell. This place is mortgaged to the hilt, and mortgaged or not, it'll be the next thing to go if something doesn't turn up. That's her dowry, Morland. What do you say to that?'

The image in his mind was of brown, dead, ghost-flowers, neglected on a dusty table. The silence of the house was accounted for: they had dismissed most of the servants.

'I can only repeat what I've said before, sir – that I love your daughter and want to marry her. I don't care about a dowry.'

Fleetham's face relaxed and only then did Benedict appreciate the tension which had inhabited him until that moment. 'I believe you.' He put his hands over his face an instant, rubbing it wearily. 'You're a sound man, Morland,' he said when he emerged. 'A gentleman. And you're well known in these parts. Old family, the Morlands. You won't rub off like that damned rascal.'

He was trying to reassure himself, Benedict saw. He said simply, 'No, sir.'

'Nothing but a damned fortune-hunter, Partridge. That's why I tested you. She didn't want me to tell you – afraid you'd change your mind.'

'Sir, please set your mind at ease. Everything I have or will have is hers.'

'And what do you have, for the matter of that? If you wed in three weeks, how will you support her? Where will you live?'

'I have inherited a house in York, which the attorney says I can occupy at once. A large house, fully staffed. The business I have inherited will provide an income until the Will is proved. And if more is needed, I can work. The York and North Midland Railway will need an assistant engineer. I assure you your daughter won't want for anything – and the Will may be proved in much less than a year, after which she will be as rich as you could wish.'

Fleetham had been listening attentively. 'But Morland Place – that won't come to you?'

'No, sir. There is no likelihood of that.'

He nodded, and was silent, as though pursuing some line of thought. 'Well, well,' he said at last, 'we'd better get it all sewn up. I shall have my man of business go and see yours, to draw something up. I'll write a note to him today.' He nodded dismissal. 'You'd better go to her now, and tell her it's all right.'

He found her in the morning-room, walking up and down. She whirled as he entered, her face drawn with anxiety. He felt an enormous surge of pity that she should be so afraid of losing him: her experience of life had not been a happy one.

'My darling,' he said, 'how could you trust my love so little? I love you as you love me. Nothing changes that.'

She scanned his face urgently. 'He told you?'

'Your father told me he is ruined. It doesn't matter – I shall have enough for us both.'

'And you still want to marry me?'

'More than ever.'

She came up close to him, looking down at the ground, her fingers nervously playing with the end of her sash. 'You – you don't blame me for not telling you?'

'It wasn't your business to tell me – it was your father's. You have done nothing wrong.'

The eyes turned up to his – blue as sapphire, blue as the sky, shining with tears. 'And we can still marry at once?'

'Unless you want to wait until the Will is proved after all?'

'No,' she said quickly – a little gasp of anxiety.

'Then we shan't wait. I want to make you entirely mine as soon as possible.' He tried to make her smile. 'You forget, you put the announcement in the paper. There's no going back on that.'

'Oh, Benedict, you are so good to me!' She reached up and kissed him on the lips, a proceeding so novel it seemed to set him on fire. But before he could lose control, she moved away, and walked lightly across the room to the writing-desk in the corner. She pulled down the slope and extracted paper, ink and pen. 'Now, we ought to start planning the wedding at once. Three weeks is very little time, you know. The guest-list, to begin with – have you many people to invite? I suppose you will want to have lots of your railway friends?'

'No,' he said. 'It is too far for them to come. Besides, they were acquaintances, rather than close friends.'

She smiled. 'Oh good! Because you know I do think a lot of railway people would give the wrong sort of tone to the occasion. It is important to show the sort of society we expect to keep after we're married.'

'I must have George Findlay. I stipulate for him,' Benedict said, amused by her concern: it was so very feminine, and charmingly nonsensical.

'Oh, George Findlay! Well, I suppose if it is important to you. And I suppose he will want to see the Phillips girls there,' she said, writing.

'Surely you won't wish to invite them, when they

have behaved so shabbily towards you?' said Benedict in surprise.

'Oh, but I want them to see how I've – I mean, I want to show them I can be generous and forgiving,' she said modestly.

He lifted her free hand and kissed it. 'You are a paragon amongst women.'

'One tries to do what is right. Now, as to the rest – Sir Carlton goes at the top of the list: Papa's oldest friend, and he knows everyone, which is the best of it! I don't suppose your brother will come, but I'm sure you have lots of influential friends in York. After all, you are a Morland! Lord Anstey will come, won't he? And what about Lord Howick – didn't you say he was a family friend? Unless he goes to London for the winter – what a bore that would be! We'll have the wedding-breakfast here, of course, so there will be room for everyone. It will mean hiring extra servants at once to clean and polish – gardeners too – everything has been so neglected of late.'

'But, my love, what will your father think of that?' Benedict said, worrying about the expense. 'Wouldn't a quiet wedding be less trouble?'

'Oh, it won't be any trouble,' she said, flashing a brilliant smile at him. 'You forget, I have been mistress of this house ever since my mother died: I am quite used to ordering domestic matters. I am an old hand – you may safely leave everything to me, I assure you.'

'I wasn't worried on that score—' Benedict began, but she had run on.

'Now, as to bridesmaids – shall it be four or six, do you think?'

Benedict felt as though he were being carried away on a flood of bright, bubbling water. The volatility of her moods enchanted him – from deepest gloom to high elation in moments. It went along with her tiny waist and modest blushes, her elaborate gowns and the delicate fragrance that hung about her, in confirming her to him as the apogee of femininity, the very pattern of womanhood. He loved her more than ever, and he hadn't thought it was possible to love her more than he already did.

'Bendy, I've heard the oddest rumour concerning you,' Harry said anxiously. 'I can't think how it is getting about, but they're saying you are engaged to be married.'

'I am,' Benedict said. 'It's quite true.'

'But when I saw you last week—'

'I proposed to her on Saturday and was accepted. And of course I went straight to Kilsby on Sunday, and yesterday didn't seem to be the right occasion. I'm sorry you heard about it from someone else. I was going to tell you today, of course.'

'Of course,' Harry said dazedly. 'It's Miss Fleetham, I've heard. Of Fleetham Manor, near Micklefield.'

'That's right. Do you know Fleetham?'

Harry shook his head. 'I've heard of him, but we've never met. Jack is acquainted with him, just. But what brought it about? When did you become acquainted with Miss Fleetham?'

Bendy told him the whole story. Harry's face grew longer through the recital.

'I told you to do nothing without sleeping on it,' he said when Bendy stopped. 'I warned you you were in no fit state to make decisions.'

'A man in love is never in a fit state,' Bendy grinned. 'But there was no difficulty about that decision. I told you I've been in love with Miss Fleetham for ever. I'd have married her years ago if I'd had any money. I haven't done anything rash, Harry, I promise you.'

'I don't know so much,' Harry said slowly. 'Look here, old fellow, I don't want to pour cold water on your enthusiasm, but Hudson was here yesterday, and it seems he knows the Fleethams very well. He says Fleetham is under the hatches – put everything into a series of bad investments, and got rooked by a sharp, at the end of the last of his capital – forged share certificates or something of the sort. The upshot is that he is well and truly up the River Tick – his place is mortgaged and he's heavily in debt.'

'I know,' Benedict said lightly. 'They told me so themselves.'

'Before or after you proposed?' The words jumped out of him, and Harry cursed himself.

Bendy's smile grew taut. 'You are an old friend, but there are liberties even an old friend can't take.'

'I'm sorry, truly; but it's my professional duty to be cautious. And as your friend I have an even stronger interest in your welfare. In a case like this – you will be enormously rich, you know—'

'Look here, would you have married Celia if her father had been ruined?'

'Of course, but—'

'And if you had inherited a huge fortune, would you have wanted to change your choice?'

'No, never,' Harry said unhappily, 'but the cases are different. I had known Cely from childhood. I'd run tame about the house – I knew her brother – she knew my sisters. But what do you really know about Miss Fleetham?'

'I know I love her, and that's all I need to know,' said Bendy, with a mulish and dangerous glint in his eye. 'I don't know what you are suggesting, anyway. It was I who proposed to Miss Fleetham, not vice versa. I'm not a helpless female in danger from a fortune-hunter.'

'No, of course not,' Harry said. He could not repeat half of what Hudson had told him without alienating Benedict, and he did not want to lose his friend. The best he could hope to do was to tie up Benedict's fortune as far as possible so that she could not run through his money as she was supposed to have run through her father's. But any marriage was an expensive thing, and he would have difficulty in refusing to advance sufficient for an establishment.

'I'm very happy for you, and I hope you will be as happy as I have been with Celia,' he said, trying to inject some enthusiasm into his voice.

'Thank you,' Benedict said, with only slight reserve. 'You'll read the announcement in the *Times* tomorrow.'

'That was quick work!' Harry said. So, he thought, Bendy could not back out even if he wanted to. Publicly to jilt a girl would condemn him forever in the eyes of decent people. There was nothing to do but put a brave face on it. 'Do you have a date in mind?'

'The third of November. I hope you and Celia will come.'

'You are an eager lover.' The barest three weeks for the banns!

'So would you be if you saw Miss Fleetham!'

'And where will you live? Mrs Makepeace's house, I suppose? It's large and handsome enough, though the furniture is perhaps old-fashioned – but that can be changed bit by bit.'

'That's what I thought to begin with, but Miss Fleetham has a different idea. She suggested we ought to live at Fleetham Manor, and rent out the other house.'

'Oh?' Harry's suspicions were immediately aroused, but he kept the query neutral.

'Well, you see, it is her childhood home, and as I don't have a seat, I might as well have that one as buy another when my fortune arrives. It comes to her on her father's death, of course, but it's heavily mortgaged, and it won't do her any good if the banks foreclose on him and sell the house from under him.'

'But will you like to live with her father?' Harry said carefully.

Benedict shrugged. 'It's a big house. And if he loses it, he'll have to live with us anyway. Besides, Miss Fleetham is a very fond and dutiful daughter, and doesn't want to go away from him in his declining years. Her idea is that if we rent out Makepeace House, the rents can be applied to the mortgage, which will keep the banks from foreclosing until my fortune arrives, and then I can buy it outright and pay off the debt.'

Benedict smiled happily as he described the beneficent scheme, but Harry's legal blood ran colder even than legal blood runs normally. They had already got their hooks into him, then! 'Yes, I see the beauty of it,' he said, with a slight cough. 'If you will permit me, I think I ought to look into the exact state of the property and the amount and conditions of the mortgages. It may not be the best way to use your fortune – another house, unencumbered, might be a better bargain.'

'But I'm not interested in bargains. Miss Fleetham naturally wants to inherit her own home. It would upset her very much if it went to strangers, and she wouldn't like another seat half as much.'

Harry nodded, finding himself up against the blank wall of infatuation again. 'I'll look into it,' he said. 'But I do advise against running yourself in too deep before probate is completed.'

'You needn't worry,' Benedict said. 'I hate debt, and I've been used to live frugally. As Miss Fleetham points out, the beauty of this scheme is that it will save me the cost of forming an establishment: all that will be needed are a few alterations and additions to the existing house – a few extra servants, a little refurbishment and so on. No plate and linen – they have it all, which will be a great saving!'

'Yes,' said Harry.

Benedict cocked his head. 'You don't sound convinced. But I assure you she is fully aware of the need for economy. Her proposals for the house are very modest – and here's for you: she doesn't even mean to buy wedding clothes! She says she has all she needs, and can make over existing gowns to look like new.'

'That is very laudable,' Harry said, surprised. He well remembered the frenzy of warehouses and mantua-makers that preceded his marriage to Celia, and the vast collection of new gowns everyone had deemed necessary for the first month of her married life, to say nothing of the folderols. Going away on their honeymoon had been like an army manoeuvre. He had wondered if he ought to hire a separate hotel room just for her boxes and trunks.

Perhaps Hudson had exaggerated after all; or perhaps the leopardess had changed her spots. One brush with near disaster might have taught her the folly of counting unhatched chickens. Certainly her willingness to marry Bendy *before* he was secured of his fortune was a point in her favour. Harry hoped so: he could not be more eager to think well of Bendy's affianced.

CHAPTER EIGHTEEN

The days at Morland Place passed in an orderly and peaceful fashion. The routine hardly varied: Aglaea and Jemima walked about the gardens and grounds from ten until noon every day, and from noon until one o'clock, when a nuncheon was served them, they played the piano – half an hour's practice, and then half an hour playing duets. The rest of the day was occupied with working and reading. Together they had begun a new set of dining-chair seats in petit-point, which, since the pattern was elaborate and there were twenty-four chairs, would take them a good, long time. Aglaea drew and painted, often using Jemima as a model. Sometimes Jemima sketched too, and sometimes she read aloud to Aglaea while she painted. And in the evenings they read or worked, or sometimes had more music.

It had made an agreeable difference to Aglaea's life – she appreciated keenly the value of having a companion in her quiet daily rounds – but for Jemima it was like being let out of a dark dungeon into the sunlight again. She almost blinked in the comparative radiance of her new life. Instead of the four walls of the nursery rooms, varied only by the confines of the carriage, and the uncongenial presence of Miss Smith, she had the whole house and grounds to roam in, and Aglaea as her friend and mentor. Aglaea did not talk much, but when she did it was kind and pleasant, and even when silent she exuded companionability. In her relief and gratitude,

Jemima wanted only to please, and she fell in willingly with whatever Aglaea suggested.

Aglaea was happy these days because since September Nicholas's health had taken a turn for the better. His stomach upsets had gone away, and he was sleeping more soundly. The improvement seemed to coincide with his sudden friendship with Lord Howden, which had introduced almost an element of excitement into life, for they had dined together at Lord Howden's seat twice, and had him to dine at Morland Place, too. Nicholas was altogether more approachable when his health was not deranged, and he had dined at home several times lately, which always meant an improvement in the food. Mrs Moon seemed to think nursery fare was good enough for Aglaea and Jemima – boiled mutton and rice pudding every day.

Nicholas had been reserved with Jemima at first, and since Jemima seemed almost afraid of him, conversation at the table had lagged. But as September turned into October, the atmosphere round the dining-table eased to the point where Nicholas and Jemima talked to each other with something approaching normality. Aglaea still had to be on the look-out for subjects that would annoy him, and steer the conversation another way if necessary: he could change from warmth to chill with a rapidity that nipped like frost in May.

She had been glad so far not to find any symptoms of instability in Jemima. The girl was reserved and shy, which seemed natural to Aglaea, since she was so herself; the only thing unusual about her were the occasional periods of a subdued mood which was almost like mourning, when she would sit silent with her hands in her lap, staring out of the window at nothing.

They were returning from their walk one October day. As they walked up the steps and into the Great Hall, Aglaea said, 'We have been very lucky with the weather so far – only two days that I can remember when we could not take our walk. I don't know how much longer we can be safe however.'

'I do so like to be out,' Jemima said, pulling at the strings of her bonnet. 'Even if it rains, I hope we can still go out.'

'I don't mind a fine shower, but we can't walk in heavy rain. And what about snow? We must think what we can do by way of exercise when the bad weather comes. I wonder if I might teach you to dance? I was never very good at it, and it is poor sport without a partner, but the exercise is good for the figure and the circulation.'

'Oh, yes, ma'am, I should like that very much,' Jemima began eagerly, but then stopped abruptly, folding her lips tight and seeming to shrink into herself in a way that told Aglaea without having to look that Ferrars had come into the hall. Jemima disliked him even more than Aglaea did, and being so much younger, was less able to disguise the fact.

'Good morning, Mrs Morland,' he said. 'I hope you had an agreeable walk.'

'Yes, thank you,' Aglaea replied without looking at him. She turned instead to Moon, waiting to receive their outer garments, who may have been decrepit, but at least was not repulsive.

But Ferrars addressed her again. 'Mr Morland asked me to tell you that he would like to speak to you immediately. He is in the steward's room.'

'Very well.' She turned to Jemima. 'You run on up to the Long Saloon and begin your practice. I shall join you in a little while.'

Nicholas was standing by the window in the steward's room, looking out. His hands behind his back twiddled restlessly, but when he turned round Aglaea saw he was beaming, and the twiddling was jaunty rather than irritable.

'Ah, Mrs Morland! I've had the most interesting letter. The most interesting, amusing letter,' he said, indicating the item on the desk. 'Come and sit down,' he added expansively. He was really almost genial, she thought, taking the seat offered, and gently pushing Minna away as she came to greet her. Nicholas didn't like Minna to make a fuss of her when he was in the room.

'It's a letter from my brother, Mrs Morland,' Nicholas went on.

'Indeed, Mr Morland?' Aglaea was puzzled. Normally his brother was a subject which put him in the worst of moods. For an instant she wondered if Benedict were dead, but quickly dismissed it. He would surely not call his brother's death 'amusing', even if he rejoiced in it.

'Yes, indeed. He has written to tell me that he is getting married— "I thought that you, as head of the family, ought to know," he says, the impudent puppy! It is all coming about in a most unseemly hurry – the third of November is the date – just time to read the banns, you see, which might betoken an excess of ardour on his part, but in fact is something quite else.' He chuckled. 'I know the lady concerned, you see – or I know of her, at any rate, and in fact I've been hearing all about it this morning from quite another source. My brother would be amazed to know how many people are talking about him! To be married in three weeks – and the urgency is all on her side, you may be sure. She wants to secure him before he finds out what everybody but him knows. My brother, you see, Mrs Morland,' he put his fists on the table and leaned, pushing his beaming face at her, 'my simple-minded brother is marrying the most notorious girl in the three Ridings! She's a common, vulgar flirt who has behaved herself so badly no other man would offer for her if she had fifty thousand pounds – and the best of the joke is that she has nothing, nothing at all! Her father is all to pieces, her dowry is spent, and she was jilted not three months ago by a fraudster and left looking nohow!'

'Poor girl,' Aglaea murmured, but fortunately Nicholas didn't hear her.

'It's glorious! Quite glorious! She'll make him as miserable as he can be. She's so desperate to cover her shame that she's picked on my brother, probably in the hope that he may come in for something from Morland Place some day. He's the only man gullible enough to take her, and he's such a fool he fancies himself deep in love!'

'Does he mention her name?' Aglaea asked tentatively.

'It's Miss Fleetham, of course.'

'But I met her!' Aglaea discovered. 'One Sunday outside the Minster. I thought her very pretty.'

Nicholas didn't hear. He tapped the letter. 'He asks me particularly if I would come to the wedding – trying to show off his respectable connections, you see. In normal circumstances I would be delighted to crush such pretension, but the thing is, I simply can't resist seeing him leg-shackled to such a woman! What do you think, my dear? Should we snub him, or should we go?'

He actually seemed to want an answer, beaming at her across the desk with the letter in his hand. 'I should like to go very much,' she said cautiously, 'if it is what you wish.'

It seemed to have been the right answer. 'I like to give you pleasure whenever I can,' he said genially. 'If it will amuse you, that's enough to persuade me. Very well, I shall write an acceptance today. What a joke it will be! I can hardly wait to see that harpy drag him down the aisle!'

He was reading the letter again and chuckling. Aglaea's part in the interview seemed to be over. She excused herself, and was almost at the door when he said, 'You must have a new gown for the occasion.' She turned enquiringly. 'Oh yes, something bang up to the mark, from the best mantua-maker in York. I want to show the world the difference between my choice and his – between a real lady and the doxy he's been snabbled by! You shall wear jewels, too – we'll get them out of the vault and see what will suit you best. There's a sapphire set, as I remember, that my mother used to wear.'

Aglaea left in a state almost of euphoria. Going to a wedding – a new gown – and the family jewels, which he had never even shown her before! Things were decidedly looking up. Her life of tranquil content seemed about to erupt into positive excitement. She almost ran up the stairs to tell Jemima.

It snowed on the second of November, not heavily, but enough to cover the ground; and though it thawed overnight, the third dawned grey and cold, with a lead-coloured sky, pregnant with further snow. It was fortunate, Benedict thought, that they were not going far for their honeymoon – only to Leeds for a few days, a journey they could now do by railway. It would be Rosalind's first time on a railway train, and the thought of it almost reconciled her to the disappointment of not going to London, which she had been urgent for. But Benedict had baulked at the expense in their present, precarious state of finance, as well as the long coach journey at such a time of year. He had suggested Scarborough rather tentatively, but she had pointed out with perfect truth that there was nothing to do at the seaside in winter. She wanted shops, parades, balls, theatres – civilised amusements and smart people. If Leeds was the best they could do, so be it; at least she knew some people in Leeds. It would be deadly to go to some place where they knew no-one – an objection, he noted with amusement, that did not apply to London. He loved her inconsistencies.

He agreed to Leeds, and to the best rooms in the best hotel. That much he owed her. 'And I'll make it up to you,' he promised. 'When the Will is proved, I'll take you anywhere you choose. To London for the Season if you like. Or even to Paris.'

'Paris!' she breathed, her cheeks flushed, her lovely eyes like stars. Unconsciously she clasped her hands together, and for a moment in her rapture she looked like a little girl. It made him feel almost wistful. Perhaps one day they would *have* a little girl, who would look exactly as Rosalind looked at that moment. Perilously delightful thought!

The refurbishment of Fleetham Manor had gone on at enormous speed, and during his frequent visits there in the three weeks of their engagement he had sometimes wondered that Mr Fleetham could afford such an army of servants and workmen. The results were remarkable, however, and, Rosalind assured him, were achieved without great expense. There had been some repainting done, but the wallpaper and carpet in the drawing-room only looked new because they had been so skilfully cleaned; the pieces of furniture he thought were new had merely been cleaned and polished, or brought from other rooms.

'It is amazing how one's eye can be tricked,' she said. 'Only putting a thing in a different place makes it look quite different. The table there, for instance – it used to stand in that corner, don't you remember? You must have seen it a hundred times.'

'I really don't remember it at all,' Bendy confessed, and she laughed.

'There you are, then. My point is proved.'

The final guest-list had proved very long and very illustrious, and once again Bendy had wondered privately how Mr Fleetham could afford to provide a lavish wedding-breakfast for such a throng. Perhaps he had funds put aside for the occasion; perhaps he planned something that Rosalind could remember with pride, not a hole-and-corner affair that might remind her of her unhappy previous experience. For his part, Benedict wanted to claim her triumphantly before the whole world, and had this been a year hence, he would not have thought Westminster Abbey too much.

It was for that reason he spoke to her tentatively one

evening about her wedding-gown. 'Economy is important, and I think it is quite wonderful of you not to care about finery,' he said, 'but as to the wedding-gown itself, don't you think you might have something new? I know your skills with the needle, but I should hate anyone to look askance, or say anything that might upset you. If your papa can't manage it, perhaps you might feel able to accept something from me? I wouldn't hurt his feelings for the world, but I want everything to be as you would wish it.'

She looked at him rather oddly for a moment, as though not sure what to say; and then she smiled a little stiffly and said, 'But it *is* new. I thought you understood that. I mean, it is a gown that has never been worn. All my wedding clothes are new.'

Now he stared. 'I'm sorry, I don't know how it came about, but I could swear you told me that you did not need any new clothes, that you had enough already.'

She laughed gaily. 'Indeed I did! Don't look so struck, I know just how it happened! I said I had enough clothes already, and I have: they are what I bought before, when I was to marry That Person. I shan't shame you on the day, never fear! I shall look as fine as you could wish, and not a soul except my maid and the mantua-maker has ever seen any of the gowns.'

It cleared up the puzzle, but Benedict couldn't help feeling a little uncomfortable with the knowledge that his bride would be wearing a dress ordered for another man. It was foolishness on his part, he acknowledged; but he wished the wedding-gown, at least, had been bought with him in mind, and him alone.

On the evening of the second of November he had his bachelor party at the White Lion in Selby with George Findlay and a select group of friends. It turned out to be a drunken evening, and when the others had finally departed into the thawing night, George remained, and the two of them sat staring waveringly into the last of the fire. George was to be his groomsman, and the thought drifted across Benedict's mind that they ought perhaps to go to bed, if they were to be fit for anything in the morning. Then George passed the decanter again, and the thought drifted away.

'Fine institution, marriage,' George said at last. 'You should try it.'

'I'm going to,' Bendy reminded him. 'It's you that's the confirmed bachelor.'

'Marry Georgy like a shot if her people would let her.'

'If you came into a fortune they wouldn't say no.'

'Yes, but I'm fond of my guv'nor. Damned fond. I'd sooner not have the money and have him alive.' George goggled sadly at the flames. 'S'trouble with inheritance – someone's got to die.'

Bendy tried very hard to think about Serena, but simply couldn't. Oddly enough, the image his mind came up with was of Liza. But she hadn't died. She was as happy as a pig in a turnip field. With Joe Thompson. And little Tommy. Best not to think about little Tommy. 'Haven't you got a great-uncle you could spare? Like Hudson?'

But George had been following a train of thought of his own. 'Still time to call it off, you know,' he said.

'Call what off?'

'The wedding.' He turned his head with an effort to look at Benedict. 'I mean it, old man. Don't do it – that's my solemn warning. It's the money they're after.'

'I haven't got any money,' Bendy said, puzzled.

'But you will have.'

'Oh yes. I'd forgotten. But that's not it – you've got it wrong.'

George shook his head laboriously. 'Wouldn't say this 'f I was sober. Shouldn't say it now, really. Forget it in the morning, won't you?'

'Forget what?'

'What I'm saying. What I'm saying is, don't do it, old

fellow, for friendship's sake. She's a bad lot, and she'll make you very unhappy.'

Bendy knew with the last sensible bit of his brain that he ought to take offence at what George was saying, but he really didn't have the energy. And George was a good fellow – the very best. He reached out and patted George's forearm comfortingly. 'Don't take on so, old chap. I know what I'm doing. It will be all right, you'll see.' By the end of this speech he had already forgotten what he was comforting him for; he put his head down on George's shoulder and followed the words into oblivion, and didn't even wake when George and the night-porter carried him to his bed ten minutes later.

And now his wedding-day had dawned, chilly and dark with a low grey sky. Benedict woke feeling that death would be a pleasant alternative to getting up, but as the landlord considerately sent up a hair of the dog along with his hot water, and George insisted on a hearty breakfast to 'see him through the day', he set off at last for his appointment with fate feeling no worse than as if he had missed a night's sleep. As they drove up to the little church just outside the gates of Fleetham Manor, he felt a tremor – not quite nervousness, but a kind of solemn excitement, which seemed to him the right mood in which to approach his wedding. There were coaches drawn up along both sides of the lane for some distance, and a crowd of villagers had assembled at the gate despite the cold, drawn by the prospect of seeing so many important people at one go.

They cheered Benedict as he and George went in – a little feebly, since they did not know him. Inside the church was as dark as dusk, and the candles shone like pin-pricks of gold against the gloom. The pew-ends were decorated with evergreens – holly and myrtle and wreaths of ivy – which in his bemused state made him think it was Christmas. As he walked down to his place at the front, pale faces turned up to him on either side, amongst which he distinguished only that of Harry Anstey. There was a subdued humming of conversation and a smell of stale incense and dry rot on the chilly air. And then the wheezy little organ began to play, and George jabbed him almost violently in the ribs to get him to his feet.

There she was, glowing like a spectre in the gloom, spectrally shining white, the golden candle light reflecting in little sparks from her as she glided towards him on her father's arm. She looked magnificent, and he entirely forgot that the gown was intended for the Partridge wedding. It was of almost transparent floss-silk over white satin, very full-skirted, with a deep flounce at the hem and triple flounces above the bell of the sleeve. The bodice was draped and pinned at the centre with a sprig of flowers made of crystal and gold, and as she came closer he could see why she sparked in the candlelight: the over-dress was sewn all over with tiny spangles. She wore a white silk bonnet laden with white ribbons, flowers and crystals, and from the high, ruched poke a lace veil hung down concealing her face. She reached his side and stopped; he offered his arm and her satin-gloved hand rested on it, trembling lightly. He placed his other hand briefly over it and she turned her head towards him. Behind the veil her exquisite face, framed with golden ringlets and silk flowers, was seen as though through a mist. She looked very young, and very frightened: he saw her lips quiver, and her eyes were wide as he had hardly ever seen them. She looked at him like a bayed deer, and he told himself that marriage was a frightening thing for a delicately nurtured young woman. She could have only the vaguest notions of what was to happen to her, and the vagueness itself must be terrifying. He wanted to tell her not to be afraid, that he would never hurt her, that he would always take care of her and protect her, but it was not the moment to speak, for the vicar was already clearing his throat to begin. And then he thought, this whole ceremony is the way of my saying publicly just those things. He felt again that solemnity. I am dedicating myself to her, he thought; and he felt as though his whole body were shimmering like moving water in sunlight.

The service moved through its familiar cadences. When the vicar paused after asking if anyone knew any impediment, her hand tightened on his arm and she swayed a little, as though she might faint; and when it was time to speak the vows, her voice was almost inaudible. He spoke his vows loudly and firmly, so that no-one might have any doubt of his intentions; then George handed him the ring and he put it on her hand, and the vicar spoke the final words, and it was done. Cheers broke out all round the church, and applause, and she put up her hands and threw back her veil over her bonnet, and there was her face fully revealed at last, turned up for him to kiss. She was smiling, but there was strain in her eyes, as though she had survived an ordeal; and kissing her, he felt a wet touch on his cheek that might have been a tear.

When they went into the vestry to sign the register, she did in fact swoon, and had to be fanned vigorously, and brought a glass of wine to restore her. 'These tight corsets!' the vicar fulminated under his breath as he administered the impromptu sacrament. 'Young ladies damaging their health for the sake of an eighteen-inch waist! All nonsense and folly!'

But she soon revived enough to sign the register, 'Rosalind Maria Fleetham', and then turned to Benedict with a radiant smile. 'Now we are really one!' she said, and the note of triumph in her voice made his heart lurch. Not quite, not until tonight, he thought; but that thought made him feel unsteady, and he put it away resolutely for the moment. For the moment, there was feasting and rejoicing waiting for them at Fleetham Manor.

Sir Carlton Miniott was one of the first to come up to him and shake his hand heartily, covering it with both of his.

'My warmest congratulations, Morland,' he said. 'I am damned glad it was you that won her.' He seemed to scan Bendy's face for a moment for some information; and then abandoned the quest evidently unsatisfied. 'You're just the husband I would have chosen for her,' he went on in a slightly different tone. 'You know that I've been fond of her since she was a little girl – almost an uncle to her. You will permit me an uncle's privilege, I hope, and allow me to kiss the bride?' Bendy laughingly assented, and Miniott stepped in front of Rosalind and looked down for a moment into her face, with a smile that was both affectionate and amused. She did not smile, but looked at him steadily, almost gravely. Then he bent to kiss her, his head and the poke of her bonnet hiding the action from Benedict, and moved on to allow the next person room.

Benedict shook hands and smiled until he was bemused, hardly knowing who it was before him most of the time. Smartly dressed men and women smiled, congratulated, inspected him and Rosalind with various degrees of keenness, and then moved away towards the groaning buffets. Someone put a glass of champagne in his hand and he drank it thirstily, and it was instantly replaced. This was the kind of hospitality he liked, he thought – nothing paltry, nothing mean. Fleetham was giving his daughter a good send-off! Here was Harry Anstey, managing to smile and frown at the same time.

'Wonderful reception, Bendy. Nothing but the best, I see!'

Benedict grinned. 'Don't worry, you old skinflint, I shan't be applying to you to foot the bill.' He turned to Celia, blooming of face, her shape concealed with a loose mantle of Spanish-brown silk. 'You look wonderful,' he said. 'I am so glad you felt able to come.'

'I am very well, thank you, as long as I do not stand up for too long,' she said, and turned to Rosalind. 'Mrs Benedict Morland, I do hope we shall be friends! I hear you fainted in the vestry: I hope you are quite recovered now?'

'Thank you, yes,' Rosalind said coolly.

'I'm sure I felt faint all through my wedding,' Celia said, undeterred. 'It is a time of great emotion for a woman – no wonder we are so often overpowered. In fact,' she added smilingly, 'I should think a female unbecomingly bold who did not swoon at her wedding.'

Rosalind smiled at last, and said with some warmth, 'You understand so well! I am very pleased to make your acquaintance, Mrs Anstey. I hope we meet again soon.'

And now it was Nicholas approaching him, in an obviously new frock of mulberry-coloured broadcloth with velvet collar and cuffs, worn over a waistcoat of white velvet, at the neck of which the under-waistcoat of dark blue wool showed just the fashionable amount. A gold chain stretched from his fob, a diamond pin twinkled in his neckcloth, his cane had a silver head and silver inlay for three inches down the sides. Yet in spite of this finery, all Benedict saw was that he looked ill and shockingly old. His hair had gone grey at the temples and in streaks here and there; his cheeks were hollow, and deep grooves were etched from his nose to his mouth corners. He looked more like a man approaching fifty than thirty.

Yet he smiled with high-spirits as he approached Benedict, even if there was a touch of malice in it. 'Well, well, you have joined the ranks of married men! Now you will discover the delight of having a faithful and loving companion to support you in everything you do. Mrs Benedict, I salute you.' He bowed to Rosalind, who curtseyed slightly in reply, unsure what sort of salute it might be. 'I wish you both every joy which is possible.' His emphasis on the last word suggested he did not think that would be much.

'Thank you, Nicky,' Benedict said, hoping for the best, and turned to greet Aglaea. She was dressed with far more finery than usual – a new and obviously expensive gown, much trimmed, a bonnet rivalling Rosalind's in elaboration, a fur tippet with gold aiguillettes around her shoulders; a large diamond brooch on her bodice, several bracelets on each wrist, and a sapphire necklace and earrings he vaguely remembered his mother wearing. In spite of all this, she did not seem to have changed; her serene expression was just the same. He kissed her cheek and presented her to Rosalind.

'I hope this can be the start of a new understanding between us,' Benedict said cautiously to Nicholas.

'Well, perhaps it can, perhaps it can. What do you say, my dear?' He drew Aglaea's hand through his arm and patted it. 'I think we might invite Mr and Mrs Benedict Morland to dine with us some time, don't you? It might do them good to see how a happily married couple goes on. And it would be the greatest amusement to me, to witness the progress of their successful love.' Nicholas almost grinned; Aglaea smiled nervously. 'Oh, I see no reason why not.' And he gave a final, slight bow to Rosalind and moved on. Bendy watched them go, feeling that the couple presented the oddest spectacle in the room, though he could not quite decide why.

'Your brother seems a very agreeable person,' Rosalind said, 'though I must say I was surprised to see him look so unwell.'

'He did look ill,' Bendy agreed absently.

'And your sister-in-law shows no sign of increasing. Two years now, is it not?'

'Two years last June,' Bendy said. 'But that is nothing.'

'Nothing at all. There is still plenty of time,' she agreed, with such a kind smile that he was struck again with the womanly warmth of her sympathies.

The bride had gone up to change, and some of the ladies, Celia amongst them, had withdrawn. Harry saw Nicholas and Aglaea standing to one side of the room, a little withdrawn from the crowds, and took the opportunity to go over and speak to them. He was agreeably surprised at the openness of Nicky's greeting – he had half expected to be snubbed. The reason soon became apparent.

'Well, now that your railway plan is scotched,' he said when the first greetings were over, 'we can rejoice together that reason has triumphed. When the York Railway Company is discontinued, which will be very soon, I shall hold a celebration, and you shall come and dance on folly's grave with me.' He chuckled at the pleasant thought.

'Do you really think you will prevail?' Harry asked.

'Certainly. This scheme will get no further. Howden is firm, and we have friends in the Upper House.'

'But even if you manage to defeat this Bill, we will introduce another.'

'Ah, but you will have missed the final date for the next session. That means you could not have a Bill considered until January '38 at the earliest. Do you think your sponsors will wait that long? No, no, they will melt away like morning mist. There will be no railway at York, my friend, I promise you. Why not accept defeat with a good grace, and let us be friends again?'

'You're wrong, Nicky,' Harry said quietly, though he knew this was not the time or place to start an argument. 'The railways will come. Even if you stop this one, there will be another. The benefits are too great simply to be forgotten. Do you think once the wheel had been invented, anyone could have suppressed it? The railways are the future. You can't hold back the future, whatever you do.'

Aglaea's face tightened through this speech, and she looked at her brother with anxious urgency; but for a wonder Nicky was not annoyed.

'Dream your dreams,' he said. 'We shall see who is right. We will still be breeding our fleet and beautiful horses at Morland Place when your ugly locomotives are rusting in forgotten corners, with weeds tangling their wheels.' He held up his hand as though making a pledge. '*That* is the future.'

Harry swallowed the argument, and said instead, 'I am glad to see you looking so well, Aggie. I wish we saw more of you. Do you never come to York now?'

Nicky's hand went across and folded over hers where it rested on his arm.

'No, I never stir beyond the grounds, now,' she answered placidly. 'I have everything I need at Morland Place.'

'I wonder you don't get lonely sometimes – coming from a large family,' he added hastily, afraid it sounded like an accusation.

'Oh no, I'm never lonely,' she said. 'I am quite happy with my own thoughts. And now, of course, I have Jemima.'

'Jemima?'

'She is old enough to do without a governess now, and be a companion to me. We go on very comfortably, I assure you. But tell me, how is Celia? Is Doctor Bayliss happy with her progress?'

It was an obvious change of subject, but she had sounded quite sincere when she said she was content; and Nicky had seemed like a normal, affectionate husband today. There was nothing to worry about.

The carriage was at the door, loaded with luggage, and Rosalind came down in a new outfit, a travelling-dress of warm, coral-coloured wool trimmed with black silk cord and black velvet ribbon, and a mantle and bonnet both trimmed with fur to match the fur muff. There were little cries from the women in the company, and Benedict stepped forward to receive her with enormous pride. Before he reached her, Harry emerged from the crowd as he passed, grabbed his elbow and tugged at it urgently.

'When you come back,' he said in a quick, low voice,

'we must meet. There are important financial matters to discuss.'

'Very well,' Benedict said, but that did not seem enough for Harry.

'As soon as you get back,' he insisted. 'Don't fail.'

Benedict smiled and shook him off gently, and hurried forward to take his wife's hands. *His wife!* Extraordinary, precious words. He kissed her upturned face to a roar of acclaim from the company, and then they waved and hurried out of the door and ran down the steps. It had turned bitterly cold while they had been inside, and the sky was darker than ever; even now a single flake broke loose from the sky and wavered down past Benedict's nose. But they scrambled into the coach, the step was put up and the door closed, and they lurched forward, the horses going at once into a fast trot. Rosalind leaned to look through the window at the crowd which had spilled out of the door to wave goodbye; and then they rounded the laurels and were out of sight.

'So that's that,' she said with enormous satisfaction.

Even at the time it seemed an odd thing for her to say, but between champagne and anticipation Benedict was in no condition to be analytical.

The best suite in the Royal George was palatial enough even for Rosalind, and she walked from sitting-room to bedroom to dressing-room with little nods of approval, touching things here and there with admiration, while relays of hotel servants brought up the luggage. It had been a wretched journey through thickening flurries of snow, and Benedict was only glad that they had been travelling by railway, for they would not have got two miles behind horses. Even the locomotive was slowed by the snow, for the driver could hardly have seen ahead more than a few feet as it blew towards him like disintegrating darkness. By the time they reached their destination Leeds was white. The cab that was waiting for them might have been sugar-iced like a wedding-cake, and the horses were caked thickly over their backs and brows. They drove off over a thick blanket, making no sound and leaving deep tracks with crisp edges. The streets were almost empty, and the newly installed gas-lamps laid their buttery pools for no-one. With no wind the snow was falling vertically now, like slow white feathers drifting out of oblivion.

They were chilled and stiff with long sitting by the time they reached the hotel, and were glad to step into the hall and see a huge fire, an enormous lit chandelier, and a smiling host waiting to greet them. There were large fires in all of their rooms, and a multiplicity of wax candles – five shilling's worth in the sitting-room alone, Bendy thought wistfully, but they gave everything a cheerful brightness. 'A wretched day for travel,' the landlord sympathised. 'I hope you are not too chilled, Madam. May I bring up a hot toddy for you both, to warm you before your dinner? It is as well to take no chances in such weather as this.'

Rum and hot water and lemon-juice and a little sugar: by the time they had drunk it before the leaping fire, they were tingling with returning warmth. Betty, Rosalind's maid, collected up their outer clothes and went away, and then at last Benedict was able to gather Rosalind into his arms.

'Well, my wife?' he said, looking down at her tenderly. She looked tired, he thought; the strain of the day perhaps. He hoped not apprehension for the night. 'Did you enjoy your wedding? I hope so, for it's the only one you'll ever have.'

'Yes, dearest, very much,' she said. She watched his scanning eyes, and said nervously, 'I must look a perfect fright after that journey. My hair – and the smuts from the railway – I must go and change for dinner.'

'Not just yet. You look perfect to me,' he said. 'First I want a kiss from you. Do you realise we've been married nearly six hours?' He tightened his arms around her and bent his head to kiss her, but he could feel her heart was not in it, and her body did not relax. At last she made a little struggling movement, and he loosened his hold.

'I must tidy myself,' she said apologetically, and freed her arms to push herself away from him. He let her go, disappointed. She paused at the door and looked back at him. 'When you see how lovely I look in my evening-gown, you will be glad you married me.'

'I'm glad now,' he said, smiling. 'Do you think I married you for your gown, foolish? Come back and kiss me some more.'

'No, no, there isn't time. You must want your dinner. I mustn't keep you waiting.' And she whisked into the bedroom and shut the door.

She did, though. He did his washing and changing in the dressing-room, and then he waited in his evening-clothes in the sitting-room for an hour more before she appeared. A servant had been up twice on the pretext of tending the fire to see if they were ready for their dinner, and Benedict was feeling frail with hunger by the time the bedroom door opened, and she came out.

'Well,' she said. 'Was it worth the waiting?'

He stared in wonder. 'You look like something out of a dream; not real at all.' In white gauze over pale pink satin, and with her shining gold hair pinned with flowers and gauze bows, she looked like a Sèvres figurine, too delicate and dainty to be handled. 'My snow princess,' he said. And she smiled, and something of the tension went out of her eyes. How uncertain she was, he thought tenderly – still doubting his love. How that villain had scarred her trusting nature! She should learn to trust again. He would love her so much she would never fear anything again. 'I love you, Rosalind,' he said.

She did not answer, but she smiled, a closed and mysterious smile that made his blood rush about his body. And then there was a scratching on the door, and their dinner was announced.

*　　*　　*

401

They sat up a great deal later than he would have expected. Dinner was vast and went on and on, but they both had good appetites, and had sampled very little of the wedding-feast. But when it was cleared and the dessert laid on, Benedict had been prepared to hurry; Rosalind, on the other hand, seemed to want to linger. Her elbows comfortably on the table and her glass between her two hands, she chatted to him and drew him out, flirting with him as though they were not man and wife at all, weaving a delightful web of words and laughter about them both, in the toils of which he somehow managed to drink a great deal more than he had intended. At last, with his head whirling, he said firmly that it was time for bed. 'If I don't go soon, I shall be asleep in my seat.'

She rose at that point, her eyes modestly downcast. 'May I go first and prepare myself? I am not yet used to the idea of – of a man seeing me in my nightgown.'

'Of course,' he said gallantly, supporting himself with both hands on the table. 'Call out to me when you're in bed. I won't come in until you call.'

She kissed her fingers to him and glided away. Benedict went into the dressing room, took off his clothes, washed, cleaned his teeth, put on his nightshirt, and went back into the sitting-room. He sat down by the fire, but he soon found himself nodding, so he got up again and went to the window. It was very stuffy in the room, with the fire and all the candles together, and he pulled back the drapes and opened the shutters, which let in a dribble of icy air from the frames of the windows. Walking up and down, he managed to ward off sleepiness to such effect that he had got his second wind by the time Rosalind called him. She called so softly he only just heard her, and he thought tenderly that she was probably so nervous she might almost be hoping he would not hear!

He went into the bedroom. All was darkness apart from one candle at the near side of the bed. She was lying at

402

the far side, almost invisible, the covers pulled close up. Moving quietly, not to frighten her, he climbed in, and leaning on one elbow, drew the sheet down so that he could see her face. Gently he pushed a curl back from her brow. In the shadows he could not see her eyes, but he knew she was looking at him. 'Don't be afraid,' he said. 'I love you, and I will never hurt you. You know that, don't you?'

'Yes,' she said, after a pause. 'Could we— ?'

'Yes, my darling?'

'Could we have the light out, do you think?'

He turned away from her and snuffed the candle, and the darkness flowed in around them like black water. Yes, she was right, it was better like this – the first time, at least. He wanted to look at her, but if he had seen apprehensive eyes he might have lost his nerve. She was so delicate and fragile, his porcelain princess, not like the women he had known before; not like Liza or any of the other willing girls of that class; not even like Serena. His love surged up in him so fiercely that he had to swallow hard and struggle to control it before he took her in his arms: he loved her so much, he was terrified he might break her.

He thought it would be difficult; but he was astonished at how easy it was. It must be love, he thought confusedly as he drifted off to sleep. She was soft and warm in the crook of his arm, and, yes, he felt certain of it. It was love that had made it so remarkably easy.

BOOK THREE

The Terminus

I am the self-consumer of my woes;
They rise and vanish, an oblivious host,
Shadows of life, whose very soul is lost.
And yet I am – I live – though I am toss'd
Into the nothingness of scorn and noise,
Into the living sea of waking dream,
Where there is neither sense of life, nor joys,
But the huge shipwreck of my own esteem.

John Clare: *Written in Northampton County Asylum*

CHAPTER NINETEEN

The honeymoon passed in a whirl of shopping, taking meals, paying visits, and dancing or going to parties in the evenings. It amused him to see how proudly Rosalind paraded him before her old acquaintance and moved her hand so that her wedding-ring caught the light. It amused him also to see her eagerness for shops, and to discover how many things she managed to wheedle him into buying for her. It was useless to tell her that she had everything she needed – and her wardrobe of wedding clothes was vast – because she would simply remark, 'Oh, but look how pretty! One can't resist. Oh, dear Mr Morland, do say I can have it!'

And then the shop assistant would look at him coolly, as if wondering how he could be so parsimonious over a trifle, and Rosalind would put her head a little on one side like an eager bird, and he would give in. 'My little jackdaw,' he called her; and she laughed, showing her pretty teeth, and said, 'But I want to look my best for my lord, that's all. You will see how delightfully it becomes me.' And of course it always did. Her radiant beauty was his reward, and her high spirits – and at night in the darkness the tender love which at last overcame her shyness and modesty and responded to him with a passion he would not have expected in so young a woman. To make love where he truly loved was a completely different experience from anything he had known before, and it left him feeling weak inside. All day he could not take his eyes from her, fretted if she were out of his sight even for a moment, touched her whenever he could without shaming them both, and longed and longed for the night. He had thought before their wedding that he could not love her more, but by the time they returned to Fleetham Manor, he knew his previous feelings had been a mere candle to the sun.

He remembered Harry's urgent request to see him on his return, and reluctantly sent a note suggesting a date and time, only to receive a note by return that Harry had been obliged to go to London on railway business. He felt an obscure sense of reprieve, and settled down to enjoy his wife's company. The days flew by, and between making and receiving all the visits a bridal demanded, dining out and giving dinners, and, as Christmas approached, attending parties and balls, he began to feel that no price would be too much for a day alone with her. But Rosalind loved the company and activity, and he could not begrudge her.

The only time he could be alone with her was when they went out riding together. She had no horse of her own, but with a little experiment he discovered that the quieter of his road-horses would carry sidesaddle, and there was tack enough in the stables to suit. Both his animals were very well mannered, so he had no fear for her, though she mounted Star very reluctantly. But she soon discovered how quiet the gelding was, and they ambled about the park together, and began to explore the country round about.

'We must set up our stables as soon as we can afford it,' he said. 'I hate to see them empty and full of nothing but cobwebs and mice. Next winter we shall be hunting, I promise you – and if I can keep on good terms with my brother, you shall have a Morland horse to hunt.'

'So long as it is black,' she said, 'I don't mind what it is. But I must have a black horse. I can't bear any other colour.'

He smiled. 'Have you been taught some strange prejudice? A good horse is never a bad colour, you know.'

'Oh, but brown horses look so dull – like these two. Worthy animals, perhaps, but one does not like to be seen on them. A horse must be either a good, bright chestnut, or black, and since I am so fair, a black suits me best. A true black, mind you, none of your rusty sorts. And no white feet – that makes them look so clumsy.'

He laughed so loud that Tonnant turned back his ears and snorted in surprise. 'My darling girl, you are so delightfully nonsensical! Well, a black it shall be. I can refuse you nothing.'

'I know,' she said teasingly, looking at him sideways from under her eyelashes. She was wearing an absurd little tricorne hat with a long feather which curled round and brushed her cheek, and she looked adorable.

'I wish it were tonight,' he said huskily.

She turned her face away shyly, but she said, 'So do I.'

On Boxing Day they gave a ball, with a dinner for twenty beforehand. Nicky and Aglaea were amongst the dinner guests, and Nicky made himself agreeable all evening, for which Bendy was profoundly thankful. He even danced with Rosalind, and she handled him so well that they spend the entire dance chatting, and he even laughed once or twice. Benedict still found it difficult to talk to him, but he hoped that a mellowing must surely take place over time. After his dance with Rosalind, Nicky retired to the octagon room, where Mr Fleetham had got up several tables of whist, and Bendy breathed more easily. Aglaea sat and watched the dancing with interest, but when Benedict went and asked her if she would like to stand up with him, she smiled and said, 'Oh, no, thank you. I do not care to dance.' And when he pressed her, she said, 'I am very happy sitting and watching. I have been wondering, you see, whether I could paint such a scene as this, and I've been trying to fix the shapes and colours in my mind.'

'It would make a very attractive canvas,' he agreed, searching the whirling couples for his wife.

'I'm afraid it may be beyond my powers. But I shall try.' She looked up at Benedict. 'I should dearly love to take your wife's likeness,' she said wistfully. 'Mrs Benedict Morland is so very, very beautiful.'

'She is, isn't she?' he said, gratified. He loved to hear her complimented. 'I'm sure she would be very happy to sit for you some time. I have been looking for her, but I can't spot her. So many seem to be wearing pink tonight.'

'There she is,' Aglaea said at once, pointing discreetly. 'Dancing with the very tall gentleman.' Ah yes, there she was, revolving in the arms of Sir Carlton Miniott. 'The waltz is a pretty dance, and Mrs Benedict Morland does it so gracefully.'

'Yes,' said Benedict. It was his turn to be wistful. Rosalind and Sir Carlton certainly danced with practised ease, their movements blending as pleasantly as those of a good rider and his horse. What an absurd analogy, he thought, laughing at himself. But he wished it was he who was dancing with her. He would like her to dance with no-one but him, ever.

Harry had brought Celia – he had come back from London on Christmas Eve – and now they came up to say goodbye. Celia was looking uncomfortable. 'I must take Celia home – I hope you won't think us rude, but she tires easily, and the heat and noise have brought on the headache.'

'I'm very sorry. I do hope you're not unwell,' Benedict said.

'No, really, it is nothing,' Celia said. 'Just a little fatigue. I shall be quite well when I have rested. Please give my apologies to Mrs Benedict – we do not care to disturb her while she's dancing.'

410

'Of course. Just slip away – no-one will mind,' Benedict said.

Harry turned back to say, 'I must speak to you on business, Bendy. May I wait on you here, next week? On the seventh, perhaps – will that do?'

'Oh, don't trouble to come out here. I have lots of things to do in York, and I can just as easily call in on you while I'm there.'

'Thank you. The seventh, then.'

But a day or two later the news came that Celia had miscarried of her child that night. She was very ill for a long time, and Harry was sometimes in despair. The meeting on the seventh was postponed indefinitely. Benedict was surprised at how much the news affected Rosalind. She turned quite white, and then burst into tears, and ran away to the bedroom and cried for several hours.

The first shock came at the end of January, when a series of bills arrived for Benedict. He opened them at first with puzzlement, and then with increasing anger. The caterer, the wine-merchant, the draper, a furnishing warehouse in Leeds – the piano tuner – a man who had cleaned the silver and bronzes – candles and coals, an astronomical amount – hire of musicians – even a polite request from the vicar for payment for the organist and bell-ringers, to say nothing of his own fee. Benedict looked at them, and then looked at the direction at the top again, but his eyes had not deceived him. It was the reckoning for the wedding, winging its way home to him.

After a few moments of hard breathing, he gathered them together and went in search of Rosalind. Her father had gone away after Christmas to stay with friends in Harrogate while he took the waters, and Benedict wondered now if this was a deliberate retreat in the face of what he knew was coming.

Rosalind was in her dressing-room, changing out of her riding-habit. One glance at his face made her send

411

Betty out of the room. Benedict laid the bills down on her dressing-table, and said, 'What have you to say about this, Madam?'

Rosalind did not look at them, but put her hand up to her throat, falteringly. 'You are angry, I can see, but pray do not shout at me.'

'I wasn't shouting, but I feel like doing so. These bills – look at them! All addressed to me. The entire wedding – food, drink, everything! It's the bride's father who pays for the wedding, not the bridegroom!'

Rosalind sat down, looking up at him at her most appealing angle. 'Did he not, then? I thought he did. Oh, poor Papa, he must have forgotten.'

'No, he didn't forget. The bills are addressed to me. He ordered everything, and told the tradesmen to send the bills to me!'

'Oh dear,' said Rosalind.

'Is that all you've got to say, *oh dear*?'

'Well, I suppose he couldn't afford it,' she said reasonably. 'You know he is under the hatches – he told you so himself. He concealed nothing from you.'

Benedict bunched his fists in exasperation. 'But then why didn't he *tell* me? If he had come to me and said that you couldn't afford the wedding, I would have undertaken it – though it would not have been on such a lavish scale, I can tell you! Twelve dozen of champagne at seventy shillings the dozen! How was half so much drunk in just a few hours? And food enough to feed an army!'

'Perhaps you have answered your own question,' she said reproachfully. 'If he thought you would only give me a paltry, pauper's wedding, he might well not tell you.'

'It's unforgivable! It's – it's sharp practice.'

'Oh, how can you say such a thing? How can you insult my poor father to my face? I'm sure it was all a misunderstanding. He must have believed you meant to pay for it. After all, he knew that you knew about his situation.'

412

'But he should have spoken to me about it! Just to assume – oh, never mind,' Benedict broke off wearily. This was a pointless argument. 'I don't know how I am to pay for all this.'

She looked slightly alarmed. 'Why, it can be no difficulty, surely? Mr Anstey will advance it.'

'I can't keep applying to him for money. He is only supposed to advance it in an emergency. It places him in an embarrassing position if I keep asking him for sums for unessential things.'

'Unessential things? My wedding?' she cried indignantly. 'And what about embarrassing me? You don't seem to mind the thought of that! What would people have said if I'd been married in the hole-and-corner way you seem to favour? I'd have been shamed forever before the whole neighbourhood! If that was not an emergency, then there never will be one!' She gave a kind of angry sob, and drew out her handkerchief and applied it to her eye. 'If you begrudge me my wedding, I shall never forgive you.'

He softened. 'Oh, of course I don't begrudge it.' He sat down and reached for her free hand, but she snatched it away. 'It was my wedding too, don't forget,' he said coaxingly. 'I'm only angry that I wasn't consulted.'

'Well, poor Pa was probably mortified about the whole thing. You don't think of that. Imagine his feelings, having to apply to you to pay for my wedding.'

'I suppose so,' Benedict said grudgingly. He took up the sheaf of bills again. 'All the cleaning and refurbishing that was done before the wedding – it seems I am to pay for that, too. And you told me it was all being done without expense.'

'It was done as cheap as possible,' she said.

'But here's a bill from a warehouse in Leeds for a new carpet and wallpaper for the drawing-room. You told me they were *not* new. When I asked how your father could

413

afford them, you said they had only been cleaned very skilfully.'

'Well, so I thought they had been,' she said. 'Pa must have thought it wouldn't do after all. But I don't see the harm. All the work that was done would have had to be done sooner or later. The drawing-room was a disgrace, you must agree, and look how much use we have had out of it already. I'm sure Mr Anstey will see the necessity. We could not have had a splendid wedding with the house looking dirty and disagreeable. And now, do you think we could drop the subject? It is giving me the headache.'

He was instantly contrite. 'Oh, my darling, I am so sorry. What a brute I am, to come and take out my spleen on you. I should not have mentioned it to you at all.'

'Well, no, I think you should not have,' she said candidly. 'This was business between you and Papa, and it was not necessary to harrow my feelings with it.' And she applied her handkerchief to her eyes again.

'I beg your pardon – please forgive me, my dearest. Women don't understand matters of business, I know. I shan't trouble you with them again.'

She looked up and smiled – his reward. 'Thank you, Mr Morland. There are far better things for us to do together, I think, than discuss horrid old bills.' He took her hands and kissed them, and thought about the night to come. 'But it does bring forward another subject,' she went on, 'which I was waiting for an opportunity to mention to you. It's about Papa. Can I speak to you now without your getting angry?'

'I'm not angry any more,' Benedict assured her. 'You can say anything to me.'

'Well, then, Papa spoke to me before he went away, to say he was thinking of retiring permanently to Harrogate. He finds it too damp and cold here. The town is more convenient, and he has a large acquaintance there, all within easy reach – no fear of being trapped at home by fathoms of mud. And there is a large number of

414

physicians in Harrogate, which is always a consideration for an elderly man.'

Benedict was surprised, not having thought of Mr Fleetham as elderly or frail. 'He's not sickly, I hope? There's nothing in particular wrong?'

'Not that he has told me about,' Rosalind said, and added a sigh, 'but of course he may well want to spare me any worry on his behalf. However it is, he wants to go and live in Harrogate, and perhaps after this little misunderstanding, it might be better if he did.'

'It must be as he pleases. I could not be the one to drive him from his own home. But how could he afford it?'

'Ah, that is where it is very much as *you* please. His suggestion to me was that you should pay him a pension for as long as he lives, enough for him to live comfortably at Harrogate, and in return he will sign over to you the whole estate at once, everything that I would inherit when he dies.' She looked at him carefully. 'I know women do not understand business, but that seems very fair to me, does it not to you?'

Benedict remembered he had already thought he might have to buy Fleetham Manor when his fortune arrived, to keep it safe for Rosalind. This would be just the same thing, except that he would pay for it piecemeal.

'I can't see any objection,' he said. 'I had better speak to Harry Anstey and get him to draw up some documents.'

'Oh no, don't trouble him, poor man!' Rosalind said. 'Our man of business can do the job just as well – better even, for he knows the property, and Papa will be happier to deal with his own man. It's a delicate matter,' she added as Benedict was about to argue. 'He won't wish to have a stranger probe into his personal affairs at such a time.'

'Very well, I'll write to Mr Palliser,' said Benedict.

'Don't you trouble,' Rosalind said with a gay smile. '*I* shall do it all. I've know Palliser all my life, and I shall be glad to have the excuse to call, because Mrs Palliser hasn't been quite well, and I ought to pay my respects.

She was kind to me when I was a little girl. Let me speak to them, and you need not be bothered until it is all drawn up, ready to sign.'

'Very well,' Benedict said. As Rosalind said, it was better not to trouble Harry just now. Celia was still very ill, and Bayliss had said that she ought not to have another child, which must be distressing for them both. Palliser was perfectly competent – let him do the work.

The second shock came only a fortnight later. They were sitting at breakfast together in the morning-room, and Benedict was feeling content. Outside a spell of pleasantly warm weather was spilling sunshine onto the rather dreary scene of winter grass and bare trees. There were kippers for breakfast, and he was partial to kippers. Rosalind, sitting opposite him in a very pretty dress of forget-me-not blue, was looking ravishing, and had been making him smile with her chatter about various females of her acquaintance and their foibles. And he had just opened a very agreeable letter from George Findlay announcing that he had at last become engaged to Georgy Phillips. They were to marry on the same day that her elder sister Lizzie married an officer friend of her brother's.

The second letter he opened was in a hand he did not recognise. He broke the wafer and unfolded it and began to read; and as he read he felt a rush of blood to his head. It was from Madame Duclos, mantua-maker, of Stonegate, York – Bendy had heard of her, of course, for she was York's leading dressmaker to the wealthy and fashionable. It was a polite letter, but with an underlying hint of firmness. Mrs Morland's account had gone so long unpaid that it was quite out of her power to extend the credit any longer, and since her reminders to Mrs Morland had gone unanswered, Madame Duclos saw no alternative but to apply to Mr Morland for discharge of the debt, as she would be most reluctant to take legal proceedings which would be painful to all parties. She had pleasure in attaching an itemised copy of the account, and begged to remain Benedict's obedient servant, etc.

He turned back the page and looked at the account. He did not understand all the dressmaker's terms, of course, but some of the garments he could not fail to recognise. Item – wedding gown of ivory satin with over-dress of white floss-silk . . . Item – carriage-dress of dull coral barathea piped with corded black silk . . . Item – ball-gown of pink silk taffeta with over-dress of silver gauze festooned with silver rosebuds . . .

He went on down the list. All her wedding clothes, as far as he could tell; all the wedding clothes she had ordered for Partridge. They had not been paid for. And the total at the bottom – another surge of blood made his head pound. How could clothes cost so much? It was an abominable sum.

He was aware of a silence, and slowly, reluctantly, raised his eyes. Rosalind, discerning at last that he was not listening to her, had stopped chattering and was looking at him with enquiry. 'Is something wrong, dearest?' she asked. 'You look so strange and uncomfortable.'

He found he couldn't speak, so instead he passed the letter and bill across the table, and then turned his head to look out of the window. He felt he could not bear to see her face as she read it.

At last she said, 'Well?'

He turned to look at her. Her expression was guarded, as well it might be. 'Your wedding clothes. You ordered them for your wedding to Partridge, but you didn't pay for them. All this time, all this time, you've been deceiving me.'

Her cheeks coloured. 'How have I deceived you?'

'You told me you had bought them.'

'So I had.'

'Not so, Madam. They're not bought until they're paid for.'

417

'Well, how could I pay for them?' she said irritably. 'You know Pa was all to pieces. I don't see what business it is of yours, anyway.'

'It's my business now, now that she's applied to me for settlement. And what about all these other things that you've ordered since? Two more even since the wedding! How could you order more dresses when you knew you couldn't pay for the wedding-clothes?'

'I had to – it was the only way to keep her quiet,' Rosalind said, a hunted look coming into her eyes. 'She wouldn't press the bill as long as she thought I had plenty of money, for she'd be afraid to offend me, and the only way to convince her I had money was to keep ordering more clothes. You must see that! What else was I to do?'

Benedict spread his hands helplessly. 'But why didn't you tell me?'

'If you'd had your fortune already, I might have,' she said, 'but ever since you proposed to me you've been raving on and on about economy, and I didn't think you'd like to pay for my wedding clothes, when you knew they were ordered for another man. Men can be so odd about such things. Well, you must admit you didn't like it when I was forced to tell you.'

He looked at her despairingly. How could he make her understand that it was the lack of frankness which upset him most, not the money. While he sought for words, she added angrily, 'Anyway, I could have paid it off myself bit by bit if you hadn't kept me so abominably short of pin-money. My allowance is pitiful! Molly Coulsden – Creed that was – gets twice as much, more than twice as much. I'm ashamed to have to count pennies, after the way I have been brought up. You don't seem to realise I have a position to keep up!'

He strove for calm. 'Rosalind, my dear, I can't have my wife running up debts. We cannot order things we cannot pay for: it's dishonest.'

'Oh, you are too nice!' she cried impatiently. 'Everyone orders on credit! It's only dishonest if you know you can't ever pay, and mean to run away at the end. But when your fortune comes in, everything will be paid for all right, so what's wrong with that?'

'It's wrong to make honest tradesmen wait for payment. Why should they wait for their money, when we won't wait for their goods?'

'You are a simpleton,' she said scornfully. 'The tradesmen know how the game is paid – and they will be very happy, I assure you, to give you a year's credit, for the sake of keeping your custom. They think it will make you so grateful you will never order from anyone else.'

'Oh, Rosalind!' he cried, exasperated. 'You are so wrong! I tell you I can't, I won't have my wife order things I can't pay for. I hate a debt! And how am I to pay Madame Duclos? I haven't such a sum as this. What am I to do?'

'Pay her a bit on account, and tell her she'll have the rest when your fortune comes. She only wants reassuring.' She pulled out her handkerchief. 'I do think you are being unkind.'

'Unkind? I?'

'Asking *me* what *you* should do. A husband is supposed to take care of his wife, not scold her and upset her and bother her with business.' A tear glistened, and she put her face into her handkerchief. 'And at a time like this, of all times, when I shouldn't be upset,' she said, indistinctly.

'At a time like what?'

'I can't tell you when you scowl at me like that. You make me quite afraid of you.'

'Nonsense, you can't be afraid of me. Really, Rosalind—'

She lowered the handkerchief and looked at him with trembling lips. 'But I have something to tell you, something very special, if you will only be kind to me. It's supposed to be a happy time, and if you make me cry it will all be ruined.'

Something stirred in his mind, and he looked at her with dawning realisation, mixed with astonishment. 'A happy time? You don't mean— ? My dearest, tell me quick! I'm not angry any more, truly I'm not. Please don't cry. Look, I'm smiling!'

It was a very crooked effort, but it seemed enough for her. She said, 'Well, then I'll tell you – though perhaps you've guessed. Oh, it's so embarrassing!' The handkerchief again, and from behind it, 'I'm going to have a baby.'

He reached across the table slowly, took hold of her hands, peeled them away one by one. 'It is really true?'

She nodded cautiously, watching his face. 'Are you pleased?'

'Pleased?' It didn't seem like the right word. Bewildered, perhaps. 'I can't take it in. Oh, my darling! A baby! You're sure?'

'Of course I'm sure,' she smiled indulgently. 'What a foolish question.'

'Are *you* pleased?'

'Well,' she said, 'I think I would sooner have waited a bit, but one cannot order these things. You are too good a lover,' she added with a lowering of eyelids.

Thought was catching up with him now. 'But when? When will it be born?'

'Doctor Cornwell says the beginning of August.'

'You've seen the doctor? How long have you known, then?'

'I've suspected for a while, but I saw Cornwell on Monday, when you were over at the farm.'

'August? That means – the very first moment! Perhaps the very first night?'

'Perhaps.' She put her hand across the table and he took it and held it. A vast tenderness filled him. She was to be the mother of his child. Inside her this very moment his child was growing, sweetly cradled. His beautiful goddess, a mother! Perhaps the little girl he had dreamed of once for an idle instant.

'You must take care of yourself,' he said, as young husbands have been saying since time began. And she laughed, as young wives have done for just as long, and said, 'There's no need to worry. It will be a long while before I need to be careful.'

But he thought of Celia Anstey, and remembered how Rosalind had cried when she heard of the miscarriage.

'You should have told me sooner,' he said with gentle reproach.

'You'd only have worried the sooner, as you're worrying now. But you needn't. I will take care of myself. And there was another reason I didn't tell you. Can't you guess it?'

'No.'

'Doctor Cornwell says we must not – must not be lovers any more. Until after the baby is born. Now I've told you, I shall have to move into a separate bedroom. I was putting it off, you see.'

He was taken aback. 'A separate bedroom?'

'You don't want to harm the baby, do you?'

'No, of course not – but can't we still sleep together? Just for the company? I don't want to be apart from you.'

'Nor I from you, my beloved. But it is safer. Loving me as you do, you might be overcome one night. And loving you as I do, I might not resist.'

'But—'

'No, it must be. Do you think I could bear to be close to you every night and not be able to love you? I shall move into my mother's old room – that will be far enough away from you to avoid temptation. I'll tell Barnes immediately after breakfast to have my things moved.'

It was a blow. Benedict had assumed that once you were wed, you slept together for ever and ever; he was sure his

421

mother and father had. But as arbiter of what was the right and fashionable course of action, Rosalind reigned supreme, and he had already once or twice fallen foul of her lifted eyebrow. It made him feel like an apprentice engineer with grimy fingernails to have her shake her head at him. He loved her so much he was terrified of losing her love. It seemed so unexpected and inexplicable a benison, he was always afraid it might be correspondingly fragile, like a hot-house plant – unable to bear frost.

But it was a sad thing to see Betty hurrying along the bedroom corridor with a basketful of Rosalind's belongings, followed by a housemaid with her arms full of linen. And when he saw two of the footmen shifting a large brocade chair from one of the spare rooms, it seemed as though she meant to make a long stay. Rosalind found him standing near the door of her mother's room, looking in wistfully, and she laughed gaily as she danced by and tapped him affectionately on the cheek.

'You look like a puppy with your tail down! Cheer up, my love, it's only for a few months.'

Two days later Benedict was solicited for an interview by Rosalind's physician, Doctor Cornwell, who asked to see him in private and in confidence. Alarmed, he had Cornwell shown into the book-room. He wished he could like the doctor better: he was well thought of in the neighbourhood, and his fees were high enough to be reassuring, but there was something damp and furtive about him to Bendy's eyes.

But Rosalind swore by him, so he did his best to be cordial. 'You wanted to see me?' he said, covertly wiping the hand that had shaken Cornwell's on the back of his trousers.

'Indeed, indeed, sir, and it's most kind of you to allow me to take up your time. But it is a matter of the greatest urgency, I assure you, or I should not have troubled you,' Cornwell squirmed like an ingratiating dog; his voice was like a wet lick on the face. 'A matter also of the greatest delicacy, which I would hesitate to raise were it not—'

'Please speak frankly,' Benedict said, without much hope.

'It concerns Mrs Morland.'

'So I assumed. Her condition is satisfactory, I hope?'

'Yes indeed, Mr Morland! She is the very picture of health! That is – I fear her constitution is delicate, however. Not so delicate as positively to alarm, in the general way, for I must say she is so robust as to have needed very little of my attention in the years gone by. But, however, in the present circumstances it would be folly to be complacent, for I must say they present a consideration, which, while not absolutely alarming, may be said to be—'

'Spit it out, man,' Benedict said irritably. 'If there is something to worry about, I must know what it is.'

Cornwell hesitated, his eyes everywhere but on Benedict. He seemed torn between the desire to display Rosalind as the perfectly healthy result of his previous care, and the ailing dependent on his future care. 'Very well, sir,' he said at last, swallowing visibly. 'I must tell you that I have good reason to believe that Mrs Morland may have difficulty in carrying to term.'

Benedict's heart turned cold and leaden inside him. He thought of Celia Anstey, of the danger to her, and the misery she suffered. 'Why do you think that?' he managed at last.

The question seemed to take Cornwell by surprise. 'It is my professional opinion, sir,' he said at last, as if explaining the obvious to an idiot.

Benedict frowned. 'But you must have some reason, surely?'

'Ah – well – er – yes, of course. Naturally. It – er – it is my opinion that – that in her general constitution

423

Mrs Morland closely resembles her late lamented mama. I did not personally attend the late Mrs Fleetham, but I have been able to consult the notes kept by her physician, as far as they relate to the present case.' He was picking up speed and confidence now. 'The late Mrs Fleetham was brought to bed some weeks early. The event was happy, of course – the child flourished, as we know.' He bowed in compliment, and Benedict bowed back automatically. 'There is no reason to think the same happy outcome will not be true in the present case.'

'Then what are you telling me? Pray speak plainly.' Benedict caught the doctor's wandering eye and held it, though it seemed most unwilling to be held.

'The similarity in constitution between Mrs Morland and her late, respected mother bring me to believe that the child she is now carrying may be born prematurely,' Cornwell said unhappily.

'Prematurely?'

'But there is no need to anticipate that the result will necessarily be unhappy. Mrs Morland and her expected offspring may both be safe. And indeed, you should try not to display any doubts or fears before her.'

'You haven't told her this, then?'

Cornwell swallowed, and fingered the lapel of his coat. 'No, sir, no indeed. She knows nothing of it. I judged it best. Worry or alarm would be the worst thing for her. She must be kept in a state of tranquillity at all times.' He seemed to gather confidence at this point. 'Do not fret her, or cross her in anything. Do not drive her into a passion. Let her have her own way, for the sake of peace. Oh, and I strongly recommend that you do not sleep together until after the happy event.' He smiled with all the warmth of a gargoyle. 'Keep her happy and tranquil, and all may be well. And remember, sir, that I am at your command at any time of the day or night.'

424

It was the oddest performance he had ever seen by a doctor, and he would have given anything to be rid of him, and have someone else to attend Rosalind. How Cornwell ever won anyone's confidence was a mystery to Benedict. But of course if Rosalind was not to be fretted, the last thing he could do would be to change her doctor, or tell her he thought Cornwell was no good. He decided all the same that he would take a second opinion, and from someone who spoke straightforwardly, and who met your eyes while speaking to you.

Havergill listened quietly and intelligently, his eyes never leaving Benedict's face. He knew the Morland family well, had attended many of their aliments, and was besides a leading figure in the drive towards better public health. His knowledge was cyclopaedic, his intelligence formidable, and Benedict would have trusted him with his life – or, more to the point, with Rosalind's.

'I know nothing of the present case, of course,' he said at last, 'but it is perfectly true that a tendency to carry for less than the normal term can run in families, and that the outcome can be perfectly happy. And the advice you have been given is sound. No excitement, no alarm – a calm, peaceful, happy frame of mind is the best safeguard. And not too much exertion – the patient should avoid strenuous activity.'

'Like horse-riding?'

'Certainly no horse-riding,' Havergill said. He eyed Benedict sympathetically. 'Try not to worry. Child-bearing is, after all, what women are designed for; and most of them are a great deal more robust that we think. They have not the physical power that men are endowed with, but they endure, Benedict, they endure.'

He tried to smile. 'Thank you,' he said. 'I only wish I had more faith in her doctor.'

'Engage a good midwife,' was Havergill's practical advice. 'That will make up for any shortcomings.'

Rosalind accepted the ban on further horse-riding surprisingly meekly. 'Very well,' she said. 'I had expected it. I am only sorry I shall not be able to accompany you any more.'

'I shall give it up too,' he said on impulse, 'until after the baby is born.'

She laughed. 'You will do no such thing! How could I bear to see you moping about the house and know it was my fault? No, no, you shall ride every day as before, I insist upon it. Remember, Cornwell says I am not to be crossed!'

He remembered *that* very often, particularly as her tendency to spend the money they had not got showed no signs of abating. Now when bills arrived he could not remonstrate with her, except in the most gentle and ineffectual way. He hated building up debts, and wished he could take to heart her philosophy, that as long as they paid eventually it did not matter. Marriage had not so far proved the Elysium he had anticipated, and he wished fervently that she had not become pregnant so very soon.

His only comfort for the added worry and the loss of his wife's company at night was that Rosalind seemed completely happy and contented in the new state of affairs. She seemed always gay, was often singing or humming as she passed him in the corridor, and had the blooming appearance of a young woman in love. He wished she did not go out alone in the carriage so much, but as she pointed out, she could not stay in the house all day and every day, and since she could not ride and the weather was not pleasant enough for walking, carriage-visiting was her best amusement. Benedict was generous enough to be glad that at least it proved that she had a numerous acquaintance. Given what George

426

had told him, about her being 'cut' after the distressing business with Partridge, he was delighted that society had apparently rehabilitated her. As Mrs Benedict Morland she had been restored to respectability, and he was so much in love with her he was glad to have done her such a service.

CHAPTER TWENTY

Benedict took Rosalind to the meet at Ledston Park at her urgent request, though he was not hunting, having still only the two road-horses in his stable.

'You should have bought yourself some hunters,' she said as they drove there. 'Now the season is almost over, and you will have no hunting until next winter.'

'I couldn't afford them,' he said. 'Please don't let us have that argument again.'

'Oh very well,' she said. 'I was only thinking of you.'

'I hope it isn't for my sake that we are going to this meet?' he asked. The road to Ledston was not a good one, and he was afraid the lurching might harm Rosalind. Sir Carlton Miniott was not a careful landlord, it seemed.

'Oh dear, you do sound disagreeable!' Rosalind said teasingly. 'No, no, it is entirely for my sake – will that do? I thought it would be very good amusement. And besides, we must keep our place in good society, for once we let ourselves slip, we shall find no-one invites us.'

There was not a very good turn-out of followers, being late in the season, and the field was largely farmers on cobs, children out with grooms, and grooms taking out young horses for their masters who had already gone up to London. But the local gentry had come for the social gathering, and Sir Carlton, if he was an indifferent surveyor of roads, provided lavishly of warming drinks and hot patties.

He greeted them warmly. 'So glad you could come!'

He took Rosalind's hands and kissed her upturned cheek. 'How delightfully you look, Mrs Morland! The picture of health.'

'Thank you, Sir Carlton. Don't you think my new mantle suits me?' The mantle was one of a new wardrobe of clothes she had declared she needed to conceal her pregnancy, but she gave Miniott such a droll look, Benedict thought he must guess.

Miniott, however, merely studied her with grave attention. 'It is a handsome garment – but everything becomes the beautiful woman.' He turned to shake Benedict's hand. 'Have you heard the latest railway news, I wonder? Hudson has ordered the York and North Midland Company to pay Lord Howden the five thousand he demanded.'

'No, has he? I'm amazed.'

'So are we all – Howden as much as anyone, I fancy. But it was that or see the summer go without progress. I spoke to Hudson yesterday. He is furious, and disgusted about the whole business, but I told him I thought he'd done the right thing. At all events, the tenders for the first section to Copmanthorpe have been accepted, and the work should start in a month or six weeks.'

'I'm glad to hear it,' said Benedict. 'I wonder how my brother is taking the news? But perhaps he hasn't heard it.'

'He'll know soon enough, when the navvies arrive and the first sods are turned. He won't have far to go from Morland Place to see the work.'

'I do hope he won't try to make more trouble,' Benedict said awkwardly.

'No-one holds you at all to blame,' Miniott assured him. 'Indeed, your name was mentioned in the conversation yesterday.' He glanced at Rosalind, and said, 'I hope you don't object to a little railway talk, Mrs Morland?'

'If I did, would it stop you?' she said, laughing. 'Shall

I test your resolve? No, I will walk over and speak to a friend, rather than put you to the blush.'

Benedict thought he saw Miniott frown at her for a second, as though in warning or disapproval. But they had known each other so long, it was not surprising if they sometimes had exchanges he did not understand. Or perhaps Miniott thought she was too saucy with him, given how much older he was than her.

When she had gone, Sir Carlton continued. 'I think you know that Thomas Cabery has been appointed Chief Engineer?'

'Yes, so I heard,' said Benedict. 'I met Cabery when I was working on the Leicester and Swannington.'

'He has spoken highly of you to Hudson, and as a result I have been asked to propose to you that you consider taking on the southern section of the first half of the line, from Church Fenton to Milford, as district engineer. I know,' he held up his hand in anticipation of an objection, 'that you are a landed gentleman now, and with a fascinating young wife into the bargain, but you are peculiarly well qualified for the job; and I thought it was just possible,' he added with a sidelong look which Benedict could not quite interpret, 'that you might have a little time on your hands at present.' Benedict was silent. 'At all events, I hope you are not offended?'

He roused himself from thought. 'Not in the least. In fact, I've been used to work for my living, and I must confess the change to complete idleness has come as something of a shock. Four months ago I was working on the Kilsby Tunnel, the most difficult undertaking of our age! Yes, why not? I could relish an engineering problem or two to solve.'

'You'll take it on then?' Miniott smiled. 'I'm delighted. Would you like me to convey your willingness to Hudson, or will you speak to him yourself?'

'Oh, you needn't put yourself to the trouble. I have business in York tomorrow. I can call on him then.'

Miniott bowed, and at that moment his eye was caught by someone across the room. 'Ah, it's time to get mounted. I'm afraid I shall have to leave you. What a pity you do not hunt today. I'm assured we shall have a splitting run! If I'd known you had no horse, I could have lent you one. I've a promising youngster my groom is taking out today – I'd have been glad to hear your opinion of him.'

Miniott took his departure, and Benedict looked round for Rosalind but could not see her. The crowd was pressing towards the door to see the hunt move off, and he allowed himself to be carried along. Outside on the lawn the riders were mounting; it was a warm, misty, damp day, perfect for scent, and for a moment Benedict felt wistful. There was a toot on the horn, and hounds appeared with the whips from round the side of the house, just let out from kennels. They ran amongst the standing spectators, mouths smiling, sterns waving, eyes bright, looking for mischief and unconsumed patties. The horses began to fidget and snort at the sight of them; one whickered and set another going; a chestnut having its girth tightened lashed out in protest and sent people scattering from behind. The whips called the pack on, their strange high chirrups echoing from the damp sky, and the huntsman rode out to the front of the field, looking round to see if everyone was ready. Benedict looked around for Rosalind again, afraid she was going to miss all the fun. There was Sir Carlton coming down the steps at last, to where a groom had a big bay waiting for him. He mounted off the steps while the groom held down the other stirrup, and the bay flinched and fly-bucked as the cold saddle pressed its back. Ah, and there was Rosalind, just appearing in the doorway, looking flushed and happy. Benedict could not get to her through the crowd, and she did not see him. He watched her as she watched the hunt move off, and he thought she must be wishing she was going with them. Certainly she did not take her eyes off them until they had quite disappeared beyond the trees.

Aglaea and Jemima were playing a duet in the Long Saloon when they heard Nicholas arrive in the hall downstairs. There was a jarring crash as the door was banged shut behind him, and then he bellowed for Moon, simultaneously damning his eyes for having to be bellowed for. Fours hands faltered on the keys. Even at a distance, there was no mistaking the sound of anger. Jemima looked at Aglaea questioningly. 'Go on playing,' Aglaea said. 'Practise that difficult part at the top of the page.' She stood up and walked quietly out to the railing and looked down into the hall. The view from up here was partly obscured by the bulk of the lantern, but she could see Moon's back, and Minna, creeping to the fire with her tail between her legs. She couldn't hear what Nicholas was saying to Moon, but the sound of the voice was like a rumbling volcano. Then he appeared walking rapidly across towards the staircase hall. She stepped back hastily into the Long Saloon, and took her place beside Jemima again. She would know soon enough what had vexed him; she was sorry that the sunny mood of the past few months had been interrupted.

Moments later she heard his boots on the passage outside, looked up to see a glimpse of his coat passing; then the boots returned, and he was in the doorway, scowling horribly. His face was white with anger, except for a small red spot high on each cheek. 'You will kindly stop that infernal racket!' he snarled.

They stopped. Aglaea looked at him with dismay. 'I'm sorry,' she faltered.

'When I want music, I'll ask for it!' he snapped. 'Does no-one in this house consider my feelings? Good God, am I Master here, or kitchen boy?'

'I beg your pardon,' she said humbly. 'Do you have the headache?'

'If I had not before, I have now, thanks to you, Madam. Kindly find something quiet to occupy you, or else go out of doors.'

And with that he disappeared, tramping heavily towards his own room. Aglaea composed herself with an effort to smile faintly at Jemima, who was close to tears at this rebuke. 'He is very sensitive, and his health is delicate. We must not do anything to upset him,' Aglaea said. 'Perhaps it will be best if we take our work to the schoolroom. We will be out of the way there.'

Jemima agreed with alacrity, and they took up their sewing baskets and hurried away on tiptoe. What had happened to upset him? Aglaea wondered. She hoped it was nothing to do with her family; but most of all she hoped it would not affect his health. He had been so well and strong through the winter, and his temper had improved proportionately, so that he had been positively genial towards her. She had hoped the change was permanent; now she feared irritation might make him ill again.

He did not appear at dinner. When the other servants had left the room, she asked Moon where the Master was.

'Gone into York, Madam.' He gave her a sad look from his watery old eyes, and an infinitesimal shake of the head, and she knew the worst.

Nicholas did not come home until the following evening, late. Aglaea had retired to her bedroom, but was sitting up reading, and had left the door ajar so that she could hear if he did return. When she heard his dragging steps on the stairs, she got up quietly, took her candle and went to the door. He had reached the top of the stairs and stopped, and was looking towards her bedroom door, his own candle tilting so much in his hand that the wax was dripping onto his toecaps. She waited, cautiously, for him to speak first. His gaze wavered and goggled sadly, and then finally found hers, and his mouth twitched in an unsuccessful smile.

'Damn them all,' he said weakly. 'Damn them – damn them to Hell. All of them. Every one. Do you know what they've done?'

'No,' she said. 'Tell me.'

'They've destroyed me. That's what they've done.' He swayed, and she went to him, put a hand carefully under his forearm. 'Destroyed me.'

'Come in and sit down a while, and tell me,' she coaxed. His arm resisted a moment, and then allowed her to guide him into her room. She installed him in an armchair, removed his candle from his hand and put it down on the table nearby, and then knelt and took up the bellows to blow a little life into the fire.

After a long time he spoke. 'I've seen them,' he said. 'They've started. The railway men. Men? They're the denizens of Hell, ploughing the Devil's furrow. What can stop them now? They've won, and I am destroyed.'

'No, not that, surely not,' she said soothingly. 'A little setback, that's all. You'll come about again.'

'Not this time. Too late. I've seen them, I tell you – they're destroying my land, and I can't stop them.'

'Not your land, Mr Morland. It's common land. Your land is safe. They won't come here.'

'On my doorstep,' he said with the logic of the very drunk. 'Same thing.' He shook his head, boggling at the fire. 'Flames of Hell. Oh yes, I've seen them, picks and shovels, raw earth, black pits! Black men, glistening and black, with terrible white teeth – grinning. They're coming to get me – coming to my land next. Plough a furrow right up to my door. And then He'll come – riding up on a black horse with eyes – eyes of fire. Riding right up to my door.' He began to cry. 'Couldn't stop it. Tried, but I couldn't. All up with me now. Now He'll get me.'

She moved to his knee, still crouching, sought his hand.

434

'Who, Mr Morland? Who will? Don't be afraid. Tell me what it is you fear.'

His fingers eluded hers but gripped her arm savagely, and she winced. 'Can't say his name,' he said, tears running down his cheeks. It was a terrible sight, for it seemed to her that he wept without effort, like bleeding. His wounded mind was bleeding, she thought confusedly. 'Mama says if you speak his name you give him power.'

Pity overwhelmed her. 'My dear,' she said, 'there's nothing to be afraid of. These are fancies of yours, not real things. I promise you, no-one will harm you. You are tired and ill, and your nerves are irritated, but you will feel better when you've rested.'

He shook his head, his breath hitching a little in his chest, and pulled her closer, his fingers biting into her arm. 'Can't sleep,' he said confidentially. 'Daren't sleep. That's when he gets to you. He waits and waits and as soon as your eyes close he creeps up in the darkness – *no*!' He jerked back, looking round him wildly. 'Mustn't sleep. Mustn't sleep. I've been awake for two days now. But I can't – oh I can't—' The tears fell faster. She could see he was exhausted, at the end of his endurance.

'You can sleep,' she said tenderly. 'I will guard you. Come, come let me put you in my bed. He won't look for you there; and if he comes, I'll be there. I won't let anything harm you.' She put her arm round him, coaxed him to his feet, and he came reluctantly, swaying against her.

'Oh, I want to sleep,' he sobbed, 'but I daren't.'

'Yes you can,' she soothed. 'Don't be afraid. Sleep in my bed, and I will keep watch.'

He got as far as the bed's edge, and then stopped, shuddering, staring at the white sheets turned back. 'Mama?' he said in a small, terrified voice; it came out so high, it sounded like a child's. 'Mama?'

'No, not your mama, my dear, it's your wife. It's Aglaea. Get into bed, my dear, and sleep,' she said, and thinking it might reach him through the confusion, called him by his name. 'Sleep, Nicky, and I will watch over you.'

He turned and clutched her, his eyes burning in the bistred sockets. 'You get in with me, hold me, hold me tight. I'm so afraid.'

There seemed nothing else to do. She climbed into the bed with difficulty, for he would not let go of her even for that long, and he scrambled in beside her, pushing in close, wrapping arms and legs around her, pressing his head to her chest. 'Don't let him get me.'

'No, I won't,' she said. 'You're safe now.'

'Don't go away, Mama.'

'No, love, I won't. Sleep now.'

He slept; and woke, crying and raving; and slept again, and woke again. It was a long night, and dreadful to her, caught in the middle of his nightmare, so that her own reality became blurred and distorted, and she saw things in the shadows cast by the dying fire and guttering candle. The night was peopled with the terrors of his wounded mind, and time slowed to a nightmare's crawl. She watched the half-open door, longing for the first gleam of daylight, the first greying of the black, and hour after hour knew it would never come, and that this torture would go on for ever. And even when she was sure the dawn was coming, still his thin body twitched in her arms, and he half-woke, crying out 'Piepowder!' so she knew that daylight would not end it. She didn't understand, but she knew.

Harry Anstey had aged since Benedict had seen him last.

'How is Celia?' was the first thing Bendy asked, and Harry shook his head slightly, an instant reaction that told a great deal.

'She is mending slowly, and Bayliss says she will be well again in the summer; but she grieves that we cannot

436

have another child. I tell her one is enough for me, but women see these things differently.' He sighed. 'I hope Mrs Benedict is well?'

'Bonny and blooming, thank you,' Bendy said, and then thought perhaps he should not have sounded so cheerful.

But Harry smiled faintly, and said 'Good! That's as it should be.' The smiled faded and he went on, 'I've been so much in London I haven't had a chance to speak to you until now about your affairs.'

Benedict heard the note of disapproval like distant thunder. 'I've been spending too much,' he said. 'I know it. I'm afraid I've been running up debts.'

'You have,' said Harry. 'I don't like to see it, Bendy. It makes for awkwardness all round.'

He tried Rosalind's defence. 'But we will pay in the end. It's not as if we mean to default. The tradesmen know that.'

'You are borrowing against money you do not have. Suppose the Will is not proved in your favour – what then? You will have debts that the rest of your life will not serve to pay off.'

'Do you think that's likely?'

'No,' Harry admitted. 'Everything is going well. In fact, we may have a settlement by the early summer, with any luck. But that's not the point.'

'I know,' Benedict said. 'I'm sorry. We've been spending beyond my income – but my income will improve now. You know I'm to be district engineer to the railway at Milford? My fees will help keep us above water.'

'I hope so,' Harry said. 'But that's not what I wanted to talk to you about. I've received applications from two mortgagors for payment of principal loaned against Fleetham Manor – short term loans of three years and five years, expiring this month. Bendy, what have you been about?'

'I don't understand.'

'No, I'm afraid you don't. While I have been otherwise occupied, you have entered into an agreement with your father-in-law, haven't you?'

'Yes, but it's all above-board. I was going to tell you about it. Fleetham's man of business, Palliser, drew it up.'

'I've been speaking to Mr Palliser,' Harry said gravely. 'He says that you have undertaken to clear Mr Fleetham's debts and pay him a pension in addition.'

Bendy laughed. 'Not quite! I agreed to pay him a pension in return for his signing Fleetham Manor over to me, which Rosalind would have inherited on his death anyway, you know.'

Harry's face was unrelentingly grave. 'I think you have misunderstood. Did you think you were being given just the house and land? Fleetham has signed over to you his whole estate: that means all his debts and mortgages. He goes clear, with a pension, while you take responsibility towards his creditors. You have Fleetham Manor, certainly, but you have to pay off the loans he raised against it, as well as all his other personal debts.'

'But – but that wasn't the way it was meant to be.'

'Certainly it was. Palliser showed me a copy of the agreement, which you signed. He was quite clear about it. You've been rooked, my friend. Oh, Bendy, why didn't you consult me?'

'Because you use words like that,' Bendy said angrily. 'Rooked? How can you say that about my family? You've been against them from the start.'

Harry looked uncomfortable. 'That's not true. But it is my duty to be vigilant on your behalf, and great riches make strange bedfellows.'

'Well, if there is a fault, it must be Palliser's. He must have drawn it up wrong.'

'Palliser received his instructions from Mrs Morland, with confirmation from Mr Fleetham. They both knew the state of affairs.'

'Perhaps Fleetham may have – but Mrs Morland doesn't understand the first thing about money, I assure you. And I'm quite sure neither of them had the slightest desire to "rook" me, as you put it. It must simply have been a misunderstanding.'

Harry saw there was no point in arguing. 'It may all be as you say. However, there's nothing to be done about it now. But please, Bendy, don't sign any more agreements without consulting me – however simple and straightforward they seem.'

Now Benedict was uncomfortable. Harry looked weary, and Benedict thought of the upsets he had been through lately. 'Does it make trouble for you? What will happen now?'

'I must try to stall the creditors until the Will is proved, that's all. Yes, it makes trouble for me, but then I am paid for my trouble. It is you I worry about. You will have bought your country estate for three times what it is worth. I hope it repays you in pleasure what it has cost you in guineas.'

Benedict rode home slowly, deep in thought. Rosalind couldn't have known what the agreement meant, she *couldn't* have. It was she who had insisted on having Palliser draw it up, had told him not to bother Harry Anstey; but that was her tenderness for Harry's troubles. She was a tender-hearted creature – she had wept when she heard of Celia's miscarriage. No, Rosalind did not understand the import of the agreement, he was quite sure of that. She had been used by Palliser. Palliser had been the villain – working on Fleetham's behalf, without regard for the embarrassment it might cause poor Rosalind.

Well, he would make sure no harm came to her because of it. He would not even tell her about it. No doubt she still thought her father had acted magnanimously by them, and he was not going to be the one to disillusion her. Fleetham Manor should be hers, whole, free, unencumbered, and she should believe to the end of her days that that was how her father had intended it. But one thing he could do, and that was to take the estate business out of Palliser's hands. He would tell Rosalind that it was better for Harry to deal with everything. He would not upset her with that, either.

He came into the hall from the passage that led to the stableyard, just as Rosalind came hurrying in through the front door. She stopped abruptly at the sight of him, and seemed for an instant quite frightened.

'I'm sorry, did I startle you?' he said, coming forward out of the shadow of the stairs.

'I – I was not expecting to see you there, that's all,' she said, and forced a smile to her lips.

He crossed to her rapidly and caught her hand. 'My darling, I'm so sorry. You've gone quite pale.'

'It's nothing, nothing really.' The colour came slowly back to her cheeks. 'I thought you would not be back until much later.'

'Oh, I finished my business early. There was nothing to keep me in York, when I had you to hurry home to.' He tucked her hand under his arm and led her towards the stairs. 'Have you had an agreeable day? Where have you been?'

'Oh, nowhere interesting. Only carriage-visiting – leaving cards.'

'And you're only just back? My dearest, you must have tired yourself out, going from place to place – and nothing to eat or drink all day, I'll be bound.'

'Oh, no, you don't understand. I only left some cards I owed, and then went to see Molly Coulsden. She gave me luncheon, and I stayed to chat. You know she's in the same way as I am, only further on. So we had lots to say to each other which would not at all interest you, I'm afraid.'

'Everything about you interests me. But you must not do so much. You look worn out.' She was climbing the stairs, he thought, very heavily, and as she passed the window at the turn the light showed up the circles under her eyes. But as soon as he said it, she straightened her back, smiled more brightly and climbed more lightly.

'I am not tired in the least, I assure you. Nothing tires me but doing what I do not like.' She had been undoing her ribbons, and as she reached the top of the stairs and turned along the corridor she pulled off her bonnet.

'Oh, you've done your hair differently,' he said. When he had seen her at breakfast it had been done in her usual elaborate style, but now it was drawn back quite simply into a plain chignon.

He saw the whites of her eyes as she glanced sideways at him. 'Yes – I – I wanted to see how it would look done differently, so I had Betty do it again after you had gone. But I don't think it's a success.'

'I like it very much,' Benedict said. 'The simplicity sets off your beauty.'

She smiled at him. 'Foolish! My beauty, indeed! As if a woman in my condition can be called beautiful.'

'You seem more beautiful to me every day,' he said, and she turned at her bedroom door and put her arms round his neck, and kissed him softly. A great rush of desire surged through him at the touch of her soft lips, and trying to contain it made him feel almost faint. He sought for something to say to distract himself. 'Yes, I like this style. But it's not done as well as usual – it's coming down a little, look.'

He seemed to have annoyed her. She withdrew her arms. 'What do you expect, when I had to do it myself?' she snapped. 'I cannot see behind my own back.'

'I thought you said Betty did it?'

She thrust him away. 'No, I said Betty did it the first time,' she said exasperatedly. 'Really, Mr Morland, why must you question me so, like a criminal – and when I'm tired to death from paying tedious visits all day?'

'But, my darling—'

'I will see you at dinner, when I have rested,' she said, 'and when you have recovered your manners.' She turned away, but not before he had seen the glistening of a tear at her eye's corner. She really was tired, he thought. He must put an end to this gadding, even if he was obliged to be stern with her.

But he was not obliged to be stern. She came down to dinner looking ravishing in one of her new gowns, but very pale and tired. When he raised the subject tentatively, she said at once, 'You may save your breath. I have done with carriage-visiting now until after the baby is born.'

She sounded low and depressed, and he looked at her with concern.

'There's no need to give up your friends entirely,' he said. 'There are four months to go yet. I only wanted you to do a little less, not to tire yourself out. Visit one person in a day, instead of four or five.'

'No, I tell you I've done with it. There is no-one I care about, anyway. It is all form and surface. Besides, I cannot bear people to see me like this, blown up like a balloon. I know I look hideous.'

He couldn't let that pass; but though her appetite for compliments was usually keen, she listened to him indifferently on this occasion.

'Whatever you say, I shall hide myself away here like a hermit until it is all over. I shall sit in a darkened room and sew and read improving books. That is all an ugly woman is fit for.'

In spite of his sympathy, that made him laugh. Little by little he coaxed her out of her mood, so that by the time she went to bed she was quite cheerful again. But she was still determined to give up visiting; and she still went to her own bedroom alone, leaving Benedict to a restless night, disturbed by dreams he would not have cared to have to describe to anybody. He rose early in the morning and sponged his heated body with cold water, and told himself he needed some good, honest hard work to tire him out. At Kilsby he had not been troubled with dreams. The sooner he was back on the railway the better for his peace of mind!

On the twentieth of June that year – 1837 – the old King died at Windsor, and England had a Queen again, for the first time in a hundred years: a young girl of eighteen who had hardly been seen in public, and about whom nothing was known. The nation seethed with a mixture of hope and trepidation. George III, though he had been a good man, had lost America and ended his life hopelessly mad; George IV had been debauched and profligate, William IV a kindly old buffoon. A change could surely only be for the better? A young Queen – a new age – a fresh start – the phrases tripped easily off the tongue; but she was untried in public life, and very, very young. What if she fell prey to unscrupulous ministers? What if she turned out to be as mad as her grandpa?

The subject was canvassed in every quarter, outweighed in importance only in railway circles, by the news that the Great North of England Railway was certain to get its Act through this session, which meant that the section from York to Darlington could begin building in September. Hudson's representations had borne fruit: Tadcaster was no longer considered for the route. So York would have railways being built to the north and the south simultaneously. Hudson's vision of York being the hub of the whole railway network was on its way to being realised.

Benedict's personal contribution to the dream began in June, when he set out the works for one of the curves which would join the York and North Midland line to the Leeds and Selby at Milford. On the thirtieth of June he was walking the staked-out line in the company of Mr Carter, one of the contractors who meant to tender for the work.

'It's a pleasure to be alongside a gentleman like yourself, Mr Morland, sir,' Carter said, 'who knows his business so well. It's plain you know the land here like your own face! It makes my job so much easier.'

Benedict smiled at the blatant flattery, and had half a mind to say, 'I have no influence over who gets the tender, my good man!' Instead he said, 'I'd sooner have my job than yours any day of the year! How you can begin to guess what anything is to cost I can't imagine.'

'Oh, it's not so bad here – no marshes, no mountains, nothing much out of the way. And you're giving us good, gentle curves I see.'

'I was trained by Robert Stephenson,' Benedict said. 'He had a nice eye for a curve.'

'Excellent, sir, excellent. On the London and Birming-ham, were you?'

'Yes, at Tring cutting, and Kilsby tunnel.'

'Ah! Them's the sort of undertaking I'm glad not to have to estimate! Kilsby is badly behind, I understand.'

'Yes, they are still pumping out water. Lord knows what the final bill will be.'

'Ah, they'll be glad to—' He broke off. 'Does that man want you, sir?'

Benedict looked round, and saw a man trotting towards them, waving his hat and shouting. As he drew nearer, Bendy recognised the cob from Fleetham Manor that was used to go for the letters, and the man lurching in the saddle with the unease of one who could not ride was the footman, William. He seemed in scant control of the beast, which fortunately recognised Benedict (he usually gave it a titbit when he said goodnight to his own horses) and changed direction, skidding to a halt with its whiskery muzzle pressed affectionately against Benedict's chest. William fell off very slowly, mouthing like a fish as he tried to give his message without having any breath for it.

'What is it? Is it your mistress?' Benedict demanded. William gulped and paddled his hands. 'Get your breath, man – just nod or shake your head. Is it your mistress?'

444

William nodded. 'Time, sir,' he managed to gasp.

'Is the doctor there?'

'Sent for—'

'And the midwife?' A nod. 'Very well. Get your breath and follow me home. I'll leave the cob at the Black Bull for you – Carter here will kindly tell you where that is.' And with a curt nod to Carter, he mounted the cob, swung it round, and cantered off towards Milford and the inn where he had left his horse. He thanked God he had brought Tonnant with him, who was faster than Star and a better jumper: Fleetham Manor was only about three miles across the fields, and he had explored most of the country on his long solitary rides since Rosalind had withdrawn from the saddle.

After an infuriating delay at the Black Bull while they saddled Tonnant for him, took charge of the cob and failed several times to understand what they were to do with it, he was off again. So Cornwell was right, he thought. The twelfth of August had been the official expected date: she was six weeks early. Much as he hated to grant Cornwell anything, he had understood Rosalind's constitution well enough to predict this from the beginning. The appalling consequences which might follow from such a premature labour opened up in his mind like an abyss, and he drove Tonnant on, almost frantic to be home.

The house seemed to be in turmoil, with servants rushing about carrying things here and there, but Cornwell coming downstairs met Benedict with a damp and ingratiating smile. 'I have completed my preliminary examination, sir, and I can assure you everything is quite satisfactory, proceeding in every way normally.'

'Normally?' Benedict exploded. 'Six weeks early? How can you call that normal?'

The smile slithered away, and Cornwell seemed thrown flat aback. 'Ah – I – er – I mean normally for a case of this sort,' he said, and then seemed to recover himself.

'If you remember, Mr Morland,' he said superbly, 'I did warn you that this was likely to happen. With my acute diagnostic skill, I anticipated correctly, and so of course I was completely prepared for this eventuality. I assure you there is nothing to worry about. That is, I do not see any *particular* reason for alarm, although in these cases one must always remember—'

'Can I see her?' Benedict demanded, cutting through the self-congratulation.

'For a moment only, if she is willing. She may not wish you to see her as she is – women often do not, sir – in which case I must consider her wishes first. She is not to be troubled or crossed at this stage.'

Benedict followed him upstairs. 'Where were you going when I arrived? Why have you left Mrs Morland?'

'Oh, my dear young man, nothing will happen for a long time yet,' Cornwell said with a patronising smile. 'First confinements follow a regular pattern, you know, and the first stage is very protracted. The midwife is with her, and she will not need my services for some hours.'

'But this is not a normal first confinement,' Benedict said, shocked. 'How can you know what she will need, or when?'

Cornwell coughed, coloured, and said, 'I was not intending to leave the premises, of course. I merely meant to wait downstairs.' But he reversed his direction and followed Benedict upstairs again.

Benedict was a little reassured when Mrs Adale, the midwife Havergill had recommended, appeared at the bedroom door. She had a kind, motherly face and intelligent eyes, her apron and cap were spotless, and her hands looked strong and capable.

'Ah, you will be Mr Morland, I can see from your worried face,' she said, smiling. 'Now don't you worry – she's a strong, healthy girl, and she'll make nothing of it, though at present she's inclined to feel a little sorry for herself. But that's natural. You'll be wanting to see her, I dare say?'

'If I may,' said Benedict. 'If she's willing to see me.'

The midwife nodded, her eyes crinkling as she smiled. 'Of course she'll see you. I'll just go and tell her you're here, and make sure she's decent.' In a moment or two she came back and said, 'Come in, then, and don't you be alarmed at anything, or you'll upset her. Everything's going just as well as can be.'

The late Mrs Fleetham's room was very large and grand, but it was cluttered with Rosalind's things, and now also with extra tables covered with white cloths and bearing bowls, ewers, towels, linen and so on, from which Benedict resolutely turned away his eyes. Rosalind was lying propped up on pillows, her hair in its night plaits, one hand clutching a handkerchief and the other a smelling-bottle. There was a light sheen of sweat on her face, and her eyes were wide with apprehension.

'Oh, my darling,' Benedict said, taking up her hand. It dropped the handkerchief and locked round his with surprising strength. 'How is it with you?'

'It hurts,' she said, with a mixture of petulance and fear. 'I don't want to go through with it. I wish I'd never started it, now. Oh dear, what's going to happen to me?'

'Doctor Cornwell and Mrs Adale both agree that everything seems quite normal,' he began.

'What do they know about it?' she said crossly. 'I'm sure it isn't supposed to hurt as much as this. I keep telling them something's wrong, but they pay no attention. I hate them, I won't have them near me. Tell them to go away, Mr Morland!'

She was becoming hysterical, and he stroked her hand soothingly, and said, 'Don't be frightened, my darling. Everything is going to be all right. You can trust Mrs Adale. She understands just what's happening.'

'No she doesn't! Nobody does! You're all in league against me! Send them away! I won't have them, I tell you!' Her hand tightened convulsively and she screwed up her face in pain, arching her head back. Mrs Adale appeared at Benedict's side and detached Rosalind's hand from his, pushed him gently aside, and slipped her hand inside the bedclothes. Benedict watched, feeling helpless and guilty. After a minute the spasm seemed to pass, and the midwife beckoned the housemaid over to wipe Rosalind's brow, and ushered Benedict from the room.

'I'm afraid having you there only excites her, and worries you. Much better leave her to me now, sir. She'll do very well, don't you worry. The best thing you can do is to find something to occupy you downstairs, and wait until we send for you – don't you agree, Doctor Cornwell?'

'How long will it be?' Benedict asked, directing the question to her rather than to the doctor.

'There's no saying with first babies,' Mrs Adale smiled. 'They come in their own good time.'

'But this one is six weeks early. Doesn't that make a difference?'

The midwife shot a frowning glance at Cornwell which Benedict could not fathom; and it was Cornwell who answered. 'I can only repeat, Mr Morland, that I can see no occasion for anxiety at present. We will do everything necessary, I assure you. I concur with Mrs Adale's advice – you had much better go downstairs.'

He went, but there was no chance that he would be able to occupy his mind. For all the confidence of doctor and midwife, he had the awful example of Celia Anstey before him. He tried to read a book and found he had been staring at the same page for half an hour without taking in a word; he tried to play billiards and found he was walking round and round the table without seeing the balls. In the end he went out onto the terrace and walked up and down until his legs were weary. The June afternoon turned into evening, Barnes came out to enquire whether he would take dinner and was sent away with a shake of the head, and the midges began to bite. Then, as the bars of cloud over the setting sun were flaming at their edges like molten metal, Cornwell came out.

Benedict stopped, and so did his heart. Cornwell was looking distinctly weary, but he was smiling.

'A fine girl, Mr Morland. Mother and child both well.'

'Thank God,' Benedict said. It was all he could think of for the moment. 'Thank God.'

Rosalind was looking remarkably well, only flushed and sleepy as if she had been dancing all night at a ball. He bent to kiss her tenderly, and could find nothing to say except, 'Oh, my darling!'

Her hand found his and held it. 'A girl,' she said. 'I hope you don't mind.'

'As long as you're all right, it's all I care about,' he said, kissing her again; and then, thinking that was a little tactless after all her hard work, he said, 'I'm glad it's a girl. When we first wed, I dreamed of a little girl who would look just like you.'

She turned her face away, her mouth trembling, and he saw the glint of a tear before she closed her eyes. His heart was stricken. Had her suffering been so very terrible? It was impossible for a man to imagine. He turned helplessly to look for the midwife.

Mrs Adale came bustling up. 'She's tired, that's all. She needs a good sleep. When you come back in the morning, she'll be as lively as a cricket. Say goodnight, now, and then Milly will show you the baby.'

The baby was in a cot in the dressing-room, and Milly, the housemaid, lifted the bundle out with a moony expression and placed it in Benedict's arms. The last child he had handled was little Thomas, and he had forgotten how tiny a newborn baby was. Inside the white wool was the crumpled face, looking like no-one on earth, sleeping hard after the ordeal of the journey into the world. Little indeterminate nose, mouse-triangle of a pink mouth, two tiny hands with nacreous pink fingernails. His daughter!

'Dear God,' he said. The perilous rush of love left him feeling terrified and vulnerable, as if someone had stove a hole in him through which his soul might easily leak out.

Milly took the exclamation amiss. 'She'll be prettier by and by,' she said indignantly, taking the baby back from him with a determined and protective air. 'She's only just been borned.'

CHAPTER TWENTY-ONE

The Coronation of the new Queen was on Thursday, June the 28th, 1838, two days before Mary's first birthday. Irrational as it was, Benedict could never get it out of his mind that the joyful celebrations which erupted all over the country – the flags and bunting, the fireworks, the parties and balls, the people crowding the streets in their best dresses – were actually for Mary's birthday.

Because her birth occurred so soon after the new Queen's accession, she had been Christened Mary Victoria – Benedict's choice, for Rosalind seemed to have no thoughts on the matter. Indeed, though she seemed rosily healthy and full of energy within days of her confinement, she displayed no interest in the child at all, which Cornwell said was perfectly natural, due to a disordering of the nerves after a difficult confinement. It would take time for her to recover, he said, and Benedict should be patient; and also do everything in his power to see she did not become pregnant again too soon. This made depressing news to Benedict, who had so far found marriage to be rather deficient in the one thing he had thought it would guarantee.

The odd thing was that Mrs Adale did not think it had been a hard birth. 'Bless you, she came through it with no trouble; and so she should, a healthy young woman like that! Not twelve hours in all – and I've known first babies take thirty!'

'I thought, perhaps, with the baby being so early—' Benedict said tentatively.

'Hmmph!' Mrs Adale, eyeing him sideways. 'Well now, I know that's Doctor Cornwell's opinion, and to be sure, he ought to know, having attended Mrs Morland for years. But I must say that child does not look like a premature baby to me, sir. Why, she's as large and well formed as any it's been my privilege to deliver. Are you sure you did not have the dates wrong?'

Benedict smiled. 'There's no possibility of that. Mrs Morland and I were only married in November.'

Mrs Adale's brow cleared. 'Ah, well, then, that must be right. To be sure, the human frame is a strange thing, sir, and there's no accounting for its oddity.'

Rosalind was out of bed in a week and going out of the house again in a fortnight, seeming no worse for her experience, and Benedict was so relieved and grateful, he accepted his continued banishment from her bed with patience. A wet-nurse was found for the baby, and she thrived. Benedict could not have enough of gazing at her and holding her. It scandalised the wet-nurse, who took it for granted that gentry-folk, if they noticed their children at all, would notice them only for five minutes a day and at arm's length; she confided to Milly that she believed little Mary's papa would even have bathed her if he had been allowed.

Little Mary's papa became a rich man when she was just less than two months old. Rosalind was exultant, and the overflowing of her spirits when the news came showed Benedict how worried she must have been. He celebrated the accession of wealth by paying off all the tradesmen and clearing as many of the debts as Harry recommended should be tackled at once. Rosalind celebrated by an orgy of spending. Benedict stood back and watched her indulgently, glad to see her happy, only protesting now and then when some more outrageous than usual purchase was mooted. He had a flutter or two of anxiety that they would go right through the fortune and out the other side, but a little calculation calmed him – even at the present rate, she could not spend all of the income from the capital, leave aside the income from the shop, factories and other properties.

She bought clothes and clothes and more clothes; she ordered a new barouche to go visiting in; she bought new furniture and ordered carpets and drapes and had Fleetham Manor done over from top to bottom. She planned to landscape the park, and Benedict joined in the planning with enthusiasm, for that was a thing to interest him. He had plans to improve the home farm – the last attached to the manor – and to buy back some of the other land which her father had sold off. They went up to York and looked at Makepeace House together, and decided when the present let was up to take it back and modernise it for a town house for themselves. Rosalind looked about with interest but, in spite of Benedict's fears, asked nothing about the former owner. Whether she knew what Benedict's relationship had been with the draper's widow he did not know, for it was not a thing he could properly discuss with her, but he supposed she must at least guess at it.

It would be convenient to have a house in York, for now that the Will was proved and all was legally his, there was a great deal of business involved with his inheritance which meant frequent trips there. Apart from the shop, factories and other property requiring his attention, he discovered that a man with capital could hardly help being besieged by investment opportunities, and people who a few weeks before would hardly have known him now lifted their hats to him and invited him and dear Mrs Benedicit Morland to dine. Indeed, the whole county wanted to entertain them or be entertained by them, and it was not long before Rosalind had the happiness of more invitation cards than would fit on the morning-room chimney-piece, and of knowing that they had not an unengaged evening for two months ahead.

The demands on his time meant that Benedict had to give up his close involvement with the railway, but he made himself available to Hudson as a consultant engineer. Hudson, too, had withdrawn a space from the undertaking, now that it was actually under way; his other interest, politics, had come to the fore. The local elections in the autumn of 1837 brought the Tories a majority on the city's Council, and shortly afterwards Hudson was made Lord Mayor. Benedict found it amusing and almost endearing to see how violently proud Hudson was of his new status. He let down the side window of his carriage as he passed Benedict in the street one day and bellowed at him in his broadest accent, 'Ah'm bahn to 'ave ma likeness took – in ma robes! What doost think to that then?' and grinned and waved as the carriage bore him on under the fascinated eyes and pointing fingers of the populace. He looked likely to prove a popular mayor, at all events: by a combination of benevolent acts towards the suffering poor of the city and lavish banquets and balls for the rich, he secured the good will of most parties.

Benedict's one worry about becoming a rich man was how Nicholas would react. He wrote to him on the subject, hoping to soften the blow of his good luck by mentioning that he would no longer be working on the railway, but the letter was not answered. Enquiries proved Nicholas had not been seen about town for some time, but that was not unusual in summer; however, as the autumn advanced he still seemed to be keeping to Morland Place, except for occasional visits to the Maccabbees, when he would sit in his customary corner and drink alone, occasionally calling for the fire to be made up or the candles trimmed.

Benedict finally called at Morland Place one day in October, his mission to buy hunters for himself and

Rosalind. The house had a shut-up look, and his summons was answered by a strange manservant who told him – rather mechanically, Benedict thought – that the master and mistress were not at home. Further enquiries only elicited the response that the servant was 'not at liberty to say', and Benedict gave up at last and rode up to Twelvetrees. There he found a normal scene of activity. He asked for the head man, and after a few moments a familiar figure came out of a stable block and approached him with a warm smile.

'Cooper! I'm glad to see a friendly face at last.' Cooper had been rough-rider in his father's day. 'How are you?'

'Good day to you, Mr Benedict!' Cooper was a handsome, strong-jawed man with blue eyes and tousled fair hair; his legs, clad always in leather breeches and boots, bowed slightly from having spent almost every day of his life on horseback. 'I'm tolerable well, sir, thank you. I'm head man here now, sir – Mr Hastings has gone. Retired.'

'Well, he couldn't have got a better man to replace him. Everything looks very neat and prosperous. How are things going?'

'Oh, main well, sir. Business was a bit slow in the summer, but it's picking up now. We've got a very promising new stallion coming along – would you like to see him?'

'Very much!' Benedict said, dismounting.

'He's out of old Rocket, sir – d'you remember her? What a mare! Eighteen foals we out of her, and not a wrong 'un amongst 'em! We had to put her away last winter, sadly, but she were twenty-six and sprightly up to the end. This feller was her last foal, and we could tell from the beginning he were a good 'un. D'you remember, Mr Benedict, that time you helped me foal her one Christmas Day – 1820 or '21 it must have been? Lord, I'll never forget the look on your face! Your eyes was like saucers . . .'

Some considerable time and much reminiscing later, they came out of the stallion box, and Benedict said, 'How is my brother? Do you see much of him up here?'

Cooper's honest face pulled down a little. 'Not so much this year, we haven't, sir. Last year he were up every day, and taking an interest in everything, but since about April we've hardly seen him. O' course, there's not so much routine work in the summer, but he usually likes to get the hunters up himself. He's been – oh – half a dozen times to my knowledge, since September; and then he don't hardly seem to take no interest. It's yes an' no to anything I say, and then he has a horse saddled and off he goes for a solitary ride.' He shook his head. 'I don't think he's a well man, Mr Benedict, to tell the truth. Awful dowly he looks sometimes, and I hear tell there's some days he never leaves his room. O' course, we can do the work, we know well enough what to do, but sometimes there's decisions to be made.'

'Yes, I see it must be awkward,' Benedict said. 'Well, perhaps I've come on a wild goose-chase, then. I came to buy some hunters, but if—'

'Oh, Lord, sir, don't you worry about that. I've got full powers, if it comes to it.' He gave a shy smile. 'We heard about your good fortune, sir, and mighty pleased we all were about it. Couldn't happen to a nicer gentleman, that's what Frogmore said, and we all agreed.'

'That's very kind of you,' Benedict said. 'Well, what can you show me by way of a hunter?'

'For yourself, sir?' Cooper eyed him professionally. 'What do you ride these days, Mr Benedict? 'Leven stone?'

'I'm afraid so,' Benedict laughed, slapping his waist-line.

'You been on good grazing,' Cooper grinned. 'Well, sir, I got a very nice brown gelding, five year old, would just suit you down to the ground – a bold, clean mover, and jumps very nice off his hocks.'

'I'll have a look at him, then. And I want something for Mrs Morland, too – but it must be a chestnut or a black.' He met Cooper's look with an apologetic smile. 'Mrs Morland insists on a chestnut or a black.'

'Ladies has their fancies, sir. We must see what we can do,' Cooper said tactfully. 'I have got a nice little black mare, as sweet-tempered as you could wish, just fit to carry a lady; but she's not broke to side-saddle yet. I could break her for you, but she'd not be ready for the beginning of the season.'

'Oh, there's no hurry. I'm sure we can borrow a mount for Mrs Morland if need be. The important thing is to get the right horse. I'll have a look at her too.'

Benedict decided to make a little ceremony of giving Rosalind the mare, and said nothing about her at home. The mare proved such a willing learner that Cooper reported he could have her ready for mid-November, so Benedict decided to miss the first few meets himself so as to go out for the first time with Rosalind and her new mount.

The tenant of the home farm, Bowles, was happy to be in on the conspiracy. 'No trouble at all, Mr Morland,' he chuckled. 'I'd be right pleased to help. Just have the mare sent to me, and I'll keep and bring her up whenever you say.'

There was to be a meet at Ledston Park on the nineteenth, and Benedict decided to make the presentation to Rosalind on the eighteenth, so that she could have the day to get used to the mare's paces. He went down to breakfast on the morning of the eighteenth feeling absurdly excited. Rosalind appeared in a drift of muslin, looking more exquisite than ever. They ate, chatting lightly of this and that. William brought in the letters, and Sarah, the wet-nurse, brought in little Mary for her morning visit to her besotted Papa. Then, when the baby had been taken away again and Rosalind was getting up from the table, Benedict said,

'Don't go just yet, Mrs Morland. I have a surprise for you.'

She stopped, a smile beginning. 'What is it?'

'A present. Come, come with me.' He held out his hand and led her to the French doors onto the terrace and threw them open; Rosalind drew back a little, frowning, and said, 'It's much too cold to go out.'

'Only wait,' said Benedict, looking along the terrace and waving to the boy stationed there. The boy passed on the signal, and round the corner of the house came Bowles, leading the mare. She was groomed to a high gloss, her mane was plaited, her hooves oiled, and wearing only a headcollar she gleamed in splendid naked beauty, walking daintily with her neck arched as if she knew how beautiful she was. She was a true black, with no markings except a white star. She looked so perfect, Benedict thought, she might have been carved out of jet for an ornament: you could have worn her as a pendant.

There was silence from beside him: Rosalind was evidently breathless with rapture at the sight. He put off looking at her as a child saves the best morsel on the plate until last.

'For you, my love,' he said. 'Her name's Jewel, and she's broken to side-saddle. She's as fleet as a bird and sure-footed as a cat. We'll go to the meet at Ledston tomorrow, and you can try her out.'

Now he looked. Oh, but something had gone horribly wrong. His exultation slithered away into his boots. She was not starry-eyed with rapture at all, but was frowning and slightly puzzled. 'You mean, go hunting?'

'Why – yes. That's why I bought her for you. I know how much you love hunting—'

'Love hunting? Me? Nonsense! Rushing about on horseback getting muddy and blown to pieces? Whatever gave you that idea?'

He was dumbfounded. 'But – but – I was sure—' Yes, he remembered: 'When I first met you you said you were

458

never happier than out hunting, that you tire out your horses and never want to come home.'

She stared at him a moment, and then laughed. 'Oh, Mr Morland, how can you be so absurd! I never said anything of the sort! You are quite mistaken.'

Benedict could find nothing to say. Rosalind looked at the mare again, critically, and said, 'Well, it's kind of you to buy her for me. She's quite pretty. Thank you, my dear.'

'You – you won't come hunting tomorrow?'

'Oh, I should hate it of all things. But you go. I wouldn't want to stop you.'

Benedict was bitterly disappointed – first because he had wanted to give her pleasure and had failed dismally, and secondly because he had looked forward to a whole season of hunting side by side with her, and talking over the runs in the evenings by the fire. He couldn't understand how he could have made such a mistake about Rosalind's wishes.

However, when he came back to the house from business later that day he found Rosalind coming downstairs dressed in her riding habit. She smiled at him and held out her hand. 'I'm so glad you've come back. Perhaps you would like to come with me? I am going to try out your charming mare.'

He took her hand and pressed it. 'I'll come with great pleasure. But she's your mare, you know, not mine.'

'Yes, and a kind, kind husband you are to buy me such a fine present! Sir Carlton was here this morning while you were out, and went to look at her, and he says she is a little piece of perfection.'

Sir Carlton was a frequent visitor, being a close neighbour. 'I'm sorry I missed him. But I'm glad he endorsed my judgement.'

'He says you are the best judge of horse-flesh in the Riding,' Rosalind said, and Benedict smiled. 'And he has persuaded me to come out hunting tomorrow.'

Benedict's heart lifted, but he was too generous to have her do something against her wishes. 'You don't need to come just to please me, if it is something you dislike.'

'Oh, I don't dislike hunting. Quite the contrary. I really enjoy a good gallop, if I have a good horse – as long as the weather is not foul. And Sir Carlton assures me that it will not rain tomorrow, and that the ground is not too muddy. If I find that the mare is as good as you say she is, I shall be glad to come out with you every fine hunting day.'

Benedict blinked a little at the change of heart, but was too glad to question it, especially as she was smiling so warmly at him. He put it down as a piece of femininity; it only made her the more adorable in his eyes.

The following day she rode with him to the meet, and the mare behaved very well, only frisked a little when hounds appeared and fly-bucked once or twice; but she settled down as soon as they were moving. They found at the first covert and had a short gallop, but checked at a large wood before running again. After that first check Benedict lost sight of Rosalind, and did not see her again all day. When he got home he found her there before him: she said she had taken her own line on the second run and gone the wrong way, lost hounds, and had no alternative but to give up.

'What a pity,' he said. 'You missed the kill. We had a fine day's sport.'

'Never mind. There will be others. And I had a nice ride, after all. The mare goes delightfully.' She laughed. 'I had always sooner go my own way, even if it takes me off the beaten track.'

'You weren't the only one to go missing. There was a big bullfinch that defeated half the field, and a twelve-mile point sorted out the rest. Hardly anyone was in at the kill – not even Sir Carlton. I don't know where he foundered, but he was not there at the end.'

She went out with him, as she promised, whenever the weather was good, and the meet was not too far away.

460

She could not be said to have had a lucky season: it was remarkable how many times she missed the kill, by taking the wrong line, or losing her way, or the mare casting a shoe or refusing a jump. Benedict began to suspect she did it on purpose, because she was too soft-hearted to bear to see the fox brought down. But she insisted she enjoyed herself all the same, and he was content. The exercise was obviously good for her: she always came home smiling and rosy on hunting days.

When the hunting ended, there were their plans for landscaping the park to keep them out of doors; and little Mary, growing fast, began to take up more of Benedict's time. By the beginning of April she had abandoned crawling for a slower but more dignified progression on two legs, and taking a walk with her father, her fist folded round one of his fingers, soon became a daily pleasure for them both. By the end of May she was running everywhere and chattering non-stop, though largely incoherently; by the end of June she had mastered enough language to be able to converse. Benedict was firmly convinced that she was the most remarkable child who ever lived, an opinion which every servant in the house endorsed; and now that she was no longer just a howling bundle, Rosalind's interest in her child had kindled too, and she regarded her with affectionate amusement and no little pride.

'Now she has her teeth, she is really very pretty,' Rosalind said one day as she and Benedict watched Mary chasing butterflies up and down the terrace.

'She's not just pretty, she's beautiful,' Benedict said indignantly.

'Well, she's certainly a pleasure to look at now,' Rosalind agreed calmly. 'Not like the first few months.'

Mary ran past laughing, simply enjoying her own mobility. Her hair was so fair it was almost silver, her skin was like cream and roses, her eyes clear blue – not the pale blue of the flax-flower, but a remarkable dark blue, almost *bleu de Nîmes*. There was nothing of Benedict's

461

dark colouring about her: she was all her mother. He was content that she should look like Rosalind. It was what he had dreamed of.

The Coronation was on Thursday, and there was to be a huge civic procession and banquet in York, organised by Lord Mayor Hudson, to which Benedict and Rosalind had been invited and felt obliged to go; so it made sense for them to have their own party on the Saturday and combine it with Mary's birthday celebration. The grounds were to be thrown open at noon to tenants and villagers, and there were to be side-shows, puppets, a luncheon-party in the open air, and a grand fancy-dress parade for the children. Then in the evening there would be a dinner for forty, and afterwards a ball and fireworks for the county. Benedict had determined – secretly, for he was sure it would not be approved – to get Mary up for the fireworks. As far as he was concerned, it was her day, and the Coronation came considerably second.

For her birthday present he had ordered from Obadiah's in York a miniature barouche, just six feet long, perfect in every detail from box to foot-plate. The coach-work was gleaming black, with gold scrolling and a flourishing gold 'M' on the panels, and the upholstery was crimson velvet. To draw this little masterpiece he had had to scour the country, following false trails and visiting scores of stables and studs, until he finally tracked down a pair of cream ponies of just the right size and temperament. The harness was of soft, crimson leather. He had had it made specially by Benjamin's, the saddler in York: he was glad to give York companies the work, to help reassure them that the railway was not going to mean the end of the world for them. Each of the collars had two little silver bells on it, individually made and tuned so that they would ring in harmony.

Rosalind was intrigued from the first about the barouche, and was glad to think that her child would have something no other child in the Riding could boast. It was her idea to have the children's fancy-dress parade, and for her birthday present she had her mantua-maker make up a habit for Mary in the style of Charles I's reign, in dark blue velvet, with a lace jabot and cuffs and a broad, feathered hat. Thus dressed, and sitting in her barouche, Mary would lead the parade, draw every eye and capture every heart.

'No-one will even notice any other child,' she exulted.

'How cruel you are,' Benedict laughed. 'Their mothers will no doubt slave over their costumes for weeks beforehand.'

'Let them.' Rosalind said with relish. 'It will be effort wasted. My child will be first in attention as she is in consequence.'

'You'll spoil her,' Benedict said, though he didn't believe it. 'You'll give her too high an idea of herself.'

'How could it be too high? Besides, she is so sweet-tempered she can't be spoiled. Look how you fuss over her, and it makes no difference.'

'It's true,' Benedict said. She came running over now, tired for the moment, to push her way in between his knees, where she liked to stand, and gaze up at him adoringly. 'Well, my sweetheart? Would you like to come riding with me this afternoon?'

'Yes please!'

'No, Mr Morland, it's dangerous,' Rosalind protested, but half-heartedly. Since Mary began to walk, Benedict had been taking her up on his saddle before him, and she showed not the slightest fear of horses or heights, and had now even begun to ask to hold the reins.

'I'll be careful. And if I teach her to handle the reins, she can learn to drive herself in the barouche,' he said to Rosalind over Mary's head.

'What's a barouche, Daddy?' Mary asked with interest.

'It's a secret. You'll find out very soon.' He looked at Rosalind again. 'It won't be long now before she's old enough to learn to ride.'

Rosalind laughed. 'You are ambitious, sir!'

'I want her to be like her mother in every way. I want her to ride just like her mother,' he said lovingly. Rosalind's smile seemed to falter. 'What is it?' he said at once.

'I hope she will be a better woman than her mother,' Rosalind said.

'That would be impossible,' Benedict said.

After a moment, Rosalind's smile reappeared. 'There's no arguing against such partiality.' She stood up. 'I must go and change. And you should be on your way to York by now, should you not, Mr Morland? You will be late.' He looked at his watch and exclaimed. 'I'll take Mary back to Nurse. Come, Mary.' She held out her hand and Mary went to her. Benedict hurriedly kissed them both and strode away, but still found himself compelled to turn at the end of the terrace to watch them going in at the French doors hand in hand, dressed alike in white muslin, one tall and slender and golden-haired, one little and chubby and silver-haired. They were everything in his life he loved, his two exquisite jewels. It was a moment of perfect happiness.

The Coronation ball was well under way. The ballroom at Fleetham Manor had been added by an indulgent Papa for Rosalind's come-out when she was seventeen, in anticipation of her making a brilliant marriage. That was before Mr Fleetham had started to speculate, when Rosalind had been a substantial heiress. It was a matter of great pride to Benedict that he was able to restore her to her proper place in society, and to gather around her at this ball the kind of people she wished to count as her acquaintance. It was a nice mixture of county and city, the local landowners, the substantial people of York, civic dignitaries, bankers and lawyers, church and army, and numbered amongst the throng four lords, two baronets and three knights.

Mr Fleetham was not there. Benedict had invited him

to come and stay, feeling that as Mary's only living grandparent he ought to be there for her birthday, but he had refused, claiming that his health was indifferent and prevented his travelling so far. He sent by separate cover a very pretty gold and turquoise bracelet for Mary, which Benedict thought an unsuitable gift for a child so young. Rosalind said it was a handsome present, and Benedict had to repress the unworthy thought that as Mr Fleetham was spending Benedict's money, he could afford to be handsome. He did feel, however, that Mary ought to have the chance to become acquainted with her grandpapa, and asked Rosalind if there were anything he could do to make the journey acceptable to her father. She replied rather shortly that it was not his health that kept him away, but disinclination.

'The fact of the matter is that he has got in with a set he likes and would sooner stay put. And there's a woman in the case.'

'A woman?' Benedict said, startled.

'Sir Carlton has a friend in Harrogate, who wrote to him some weeks ago that Papa has taken up with a rich widow. Your spa towns are full of them, you know, hanging out for husbands.'

Benedict wondered that Rosalind could take it so calmly. 'So he is meaning to present you with a step-mama, is he? Shall you mind it, love?'

'He won't present anything to *me*,' she said. 'Sir Carlton's friend says she's as vulgar as she can hold, well over fifty, and brassy. Her first husband made his fortune selling fish. I dare say Pa told her he had a country seat, and she's hoping to buy respectability by marrying him. Well, she'll catch cold at that, for even if he marries her, which I doubt, *I* shan't receive her.'

'Good God!' Benedict was shocked as much at her attitude as at the idea of Mr Fleetham's dishonesty.

She glanced at him, not understanding his concern. 'You should be happy. She's as rich as an abbess, so

Carlton's friend says. If he does marry her, you'll be able to stop his allowance.'

After that conversation, Benedict was glad that Mr Fleetham was not coming to stay. He was sorry, though, that Nicholas had refused the invitation. He had not seen him for over a year now, and had rather hoped the temptation of such a splendid ball would have moved him; but Nicky sent a civil excuse, though it was not in his hand. Benedict was afraid for his health, and resolved to call again soon and insist on seeing him, or at least Aglaea.

But these things could not dim the happiness of the occasion, or the splendour of the ball. The ballroom was decked with flowers and hung with ribbons and favours in red, white and blue, and there was a supper laid on of such magnificence that even the Lord Mayor, who by now knew a thing or two about banquets, caught his arm by the door of the supper-room and said, 'By God, Mr Morland, I've not seen a spread to equal this in all my born days! Tha's done us handsome, and no mistake!'

'Thank you, Mr Hudson,' Benedict said genially. 'But I'm sure when the opening day of the York and North Midland Railway comes, you will show us all a thing or two.'

'Aye, I will an' all,' Hudson said without unnecessary modesty. 'I'll knock everyone's eye out. But for a spread in a private house, this beats all, does this.'

'And when will that blessed day be, do you suppose? I've heard that things are not going too well on the workings.'

'You must come down and see for yourself. The survey was done too hasty, that's what it is, and there's unforeseen problems arising. But I will say,' he added handsomely, 'that the curves you laid out yourself have given us no trouble at all.'

'I'm glad to hear it.'

'And we still hope to be opening next summer. George

Stephenson reckons to have his line open to Derby then, so we can take a train right through, and show the world what I've been talking about these eight years past. If young Mr Robert gets yon tunnel of his fixed up, we can have a train to London by the end of next year! What doost think to that, then?'

'I think that the world will thank you one day – you and the Stephensons. Or at least, the good people of York will thank you, which will probably do just as well.'

Hudson laughed, throwing back his head, and then clapped Benedict on the shoulder. 'Aye, well, you could be right. And you s'd have your share o' the praise, for you've always believed in my vision, haven't you.'

'Enough to buy shares in the railway, now I've money to invest.'

Hudson nodded. 'A fortune couldn't have come to a better man,' he said. 'It's a damned shame you didn't inherit Morland Place instead of your brother. You're wasted down here – and it's wasted on him!'

And with that he walked off, saving Benedict from the necessity of thinking of a reply. Everyone was pressing into the supper room, and he removed himself from the doorway, where he was rather too easy a target for the people who wanted to shake his hand and be civil. Not that he objected to civilities, but he wanted to find Rosalind and make sure of having at least one dance with his own wife. She had danced every dance, from leading off with Lord Lowther, to the last before supper with the young Lord Lambert of Baldersby. Wherever she was in the ballroom, his eye had found her instantly, the most beautiful woman in the room, and the most vivacious. He had seen more than one group of onlookers watching her, many a group of chaperones discussing her behind their fans as she circled the room with one partner after another. She seemed to glow in her ball-gown of deep cream silk with the draped bodice and pleated puff sleeves, her lovely neck and bosom bare, her ringlets caught up with cream rosebuds, a necklace of gold filagree set with moonstones and pearls at her throat. That had been his present to her on Mary's birthday – given that morning over the breakfast table with a tender kiss, telling her that she had as much reason to celebrate that day as Mary. And Rosalind had looked up at him with a smiling promise in her eyes, and had said, 'I shall wear it to the ball tonight; and you shall take it off for me afterwards.'

His blood had rushed madly about his body at the words and the thought, and for the rest of the day he had felt as though he was flying. Little Mary's awestruck wonder at the sight of the barouche and ponies had not moved him more, nor the sight of her sitting in it and leading the children's parade, so proud and excited she hardly knew how to bear herself. He had gone through the day with his feet not quite making contact with the ground; and now he wanted to make the perfect day more perfect still by dancing with his beloved just once in front of the whole county. The first after supper, he thought, was the proper one. He determined that whoever she was engaged to, he would ask them – require them – to yield to him. The assembly should see him leading off the second half of the evening with the woman he had chosen out of all the world. And it should be a waltz. He would speak to the orchestra as soon as he had spoken to Rosalind.

The difficulty was finding her in that throng. She was not in the supper-room. He forced his way down the corridor to the ballroom, and could not see her there either. But some ladies had gone upstairs to repair their toilettes after the exertions of the first half, and perhaps, as hostess, she had gone with them. He stationed himself at the foot of the stairs to catch her coming back down; and then remembered that he had promised Mary to go up and see her at supper-time. Probably she would be sound asleep – as she should be at that hour – but he must not fail her, if by any chance she was awake. He turned away and headed for the staircase at the other end of the corridor, which the guests would not be using.

As he went up, he met one of the new housemaids coming down – a nice, pretty girl, she was, by name Anna, he thought. All the new maids Rosalind had hired recently had been exceptionally pretty, but he could hardly tell one from another, having no eyes for any woman but one. This one smiled sweetly at him, and said, 'Good evening, sir', and he said on impulse, 'Have you seen Mrs Morland, by any chance? I think she went upstairs.'

'I saw her go into her room a bit since, sir,' the maid said. 'I don't know if she's still there.'

'Thank you.' Benedict ran on up the stairs. Probably something had come unpinned and she'd gone to her room to repair it. She might still be there. He hurried along the empty corridor – the bedrooms set aside for the lady guests were at the other end of the house near the main staircase – and came to Rosalind's room, tapped softly on the door, and, hearing no reply, opened it.

It was a heavy, solid door which would keep sound in or out; as it opened, he heard a noise from within. Someone was moaning with pain. He went cold all over. Rosalind was hurt, was ill! He flung the door back and stepped in, his heart thumping with fear; saw her first in the long cheval mirror, a pale wraith indistinctly lit by a candle in the corner of the room; then turned to look at her.

There was a perceptible moment during which his brain could not make sense of the information his eyes were offering. Rosalind was standing near the bed, her head thrown back, her eyes closed, her hands stretched down and out a little from her sides, moaning. So much he understood. It was the rest that was difficult. In front of her, blocking most of her from his view, was Sir Carlton Miniott, in his shirt-sleeves. Sir Carlton's coat was on the floor near their feet. And the bodice of Rosalind's cream silk gown had been pulled right down, exposing her left breast to Benedict's stunned gaze. Her right breast he could not see: Sir Carlton's head was in the way.

CHAPTER TWENTY-TWO

Ferrars watched the deterioration in Nicholas's health and intellect with all the vital interest of a mother, if without the essential tenderness. When he had encouraged Nicholas in his vices, he had looked to reduce him to a helpless dependent, possibly bedridden, and in the long run to have him die. The taking of a wife had complicated matters, though much less than he might have feared, since there were obviously to be no children – and Ferrars congratulated himself for that – but it would be disastrous if Nicholas died too soon. Ferrars had not yet completed the transfer of the Morland assets into his own control – not by a long way – and there was still the question of Jemima. If Nicholas died while she was still a minor and unwed, her care would be transferred to another guardian, and her fortune would be snatched away out of Ferrars' reach. Considering the six years of hard work he had put in, supervising the Skelwith business and taking care of the estate, it would be deeply unfair in his view for someone else to reap the benefit.

As the summer went on, Nicholas sank further and further into his listlessness, and even a trip to the Golden Cage did little to alter his mood. He spent a great deal of his time sitting in his bedchamber with a bottle of brandy beside him, poring over his collection of curious books, or simply staring into the fire. He felt the cold a great deal, and a fire was kept burning in his room even through the hottest part of summer. Ferrars had always encouraged him in his opium habit, but, for fear of his mental state, now did what he could to discourage it. Nicholas's grasp on reality was fragile at the best of times, and the opium brought such dreams and confusion that Ferrars was afraid that one day he would simply not come back.

Besides, smoking stopped him eating, and he was already dangerously thin. In July he caught a cold which lingered and then went to his chest, hinting at the route by which he might most probably eventually leave the world. Aglaea nursed him tenderly, sitting up with him night after night when he was delirious; and Jemima, though she still felt an instinctive revulsion for Nicky's person, took her turns at the bedside to allow Aglaea to sleep. Mrs Moon, fearful for her position, was urgent for the doctor to be called in, and Ferrars, weighing the fear of what the doctor might discover against the fear of losing Nicholas untimely, endorsed the recommendation. But Nicholas reacted violently against the idea, and grew almost hysterical when Ferrars pressed him. He would not have Bayliss in the house; Havergill was even more unthinkable. He appealed to Aglaea for protection and, deeply touched, she promised him he should not be bothered by anyone, if she had to hold the door herself against all comers.

He recovered from that illness, but the fright had been enough to convince Ferrars it was not safe to leave the question of Jemima unresolved any longer. In the May of 1838 she was seventeen; quiet, gentle and womanly. Those scandalous times when she had danced round the table at Nicholas's bachelor parties and drunk wine and sung lewd songs were far behind her, and might not now be enough to keep off suitors, even if they were believed.

Ferrars tried to make friends with Jemima, but when he encountered her alone and tried to engage her in conversation, she drew back from him as from something horrid discovered under a stone, and fled to Aglaea's protection. Her unconcealed distaste blew on the dull spark of anger that glowed permanently in him. It was not his fault that he was small and ill-favoured, nor his fault he had been born to a servant's estate. With his intelligence, he told himself, he could have risen as high as anyone in the land, if he had been the son of a gentleman, or if he had been tall and handsome. All through his life, every insult he had ever received, every contemptuous look, every aversion of the eyes fed his resentment; and he tended his hatreds carefully, feeding and watering them, brooding over them like a gardener over some prize bloom. He would pay them out, all those who had despised him! And now Jemima was added to the pay-roll. She had drawn back her skirts from him: she should be forced to accept him – and accept him completely.

So he sought an interview with Nicholas, choosing his time carefully. One bright day the Master had Checkmate saddled and went out for a ride. He no longer went up to Twelvetrees to work on the young horses – indeed, Ferrars had to give the orders up there, another burden added to his already heavy load – but he still sometimes liked an amble along familiar paths, as long as they took him away from the railway line. He never rode across Hob Moor now, where the raw scar of the workings reminded him of the battle he had lost, but an amble out to Ten Thorn Gap and a canter across the North Field gave him a little fresh air and spiritual pleasure, and he came back from these infrequent outings tired but in a happier and – more importantly from Ferrars' point of view – rational frame of mind.

It was a mild, hazy August day, with a milky sky like gauze drawn over the sun. Ferrars went out into the yard to meet him, and stood in the sunshine watching him dismount while the groom held Checkmate's head. There was only one groom and a boy up at the house now, for apart from Checkmate, the only occupants of the stables were a pair of carriage horses and the cob that was used to go for the post. Just for a moment, Ferrars saw the yard in memory as it had been when he first came to Morland Place as Nicholas's groom, when James Morland was alive: seething with comings and goings all day long, rich with the smell and sound of a score of horses and all the activities involved in their care and use. It was a live place, and now it was half dead. A window was cracked over there; a tile had slipped on the stable roof and was balanced perilously in the gutter; the gutter leaked in that corner and a green stain was growing on the wall below it; a ragwort had secretly planted itself behind the rainpipe on the gatehouse. None of those things would have been tolerated in the old days. There was an air of neglect to the yard, an air of something ending, and there was a melancholy about it, like the feeling of shadows coming up at the close of a long summer day. The shadows were closing over Morland Place; and just for the fraction of an instant, Ferrars felt sorry. If it had been in him to love any place, he would have loved Morland Place as it had been when he first arrived. But it was only a momentary sadness. He remembered that James Morland had not wanted him, had opposed Nicky in his choice, and that the old mistress had treated him as a servant. They had paid the price, as all did who crossed Ferrars. And Morland Place, which they had loved, had been brought low.

He shook these thoughts away: Nicholas was coming up the steps towards him. With the sun behind him, he looked almost transparent, and a thrill of fear made Ferrars shiver: he had left it almost too late.

'May I speak to you, sir?' he asked, fixing the customary deferential look on his face.

'Yes, I suppose so,' Nicholas said. He sounded tired. 'What do you want.'

'In private, sir, if I may,' Ferrars said, giving a glance around to indicate that walls had ears, and therefore tongues as well. 'In the steward's room.' He took Nicholas's hat, gloves and whip and laid them on the side table in the hall, and then bowed him towards the passage to the steward's room. The door to the chapel was ajar, he noticed – probably one of the servants had gone in to refill the sanctuary lamp. Though Nicholas never went in there, he had given strict orders that the lamp was not to be allowed to go out. Nicky shivered as he passed the door, and Ferrars paused to close it as he followed Nicky into the steward's room. The cold smell of stale incense came through that open door like foul breath to him, even though there had been no priest to celebrate mass these six years. Ferrars could not help feeling that these old chapels had a life of their own, and he did not blame Nicholas for his aversion.

Nicholas was standing by the fireplace waiting for him. The fire was laid but not lit, and he rubbed his hands together and said, 'Be quick, it's cold in here. What did you want to say to me?'

'I must talk to you about Miss Jemima,' Ferrars said. 'She is seventeen now, of good age to be married. And you know that if she marries, we lose her fortune.'

Nicholas frowned at the 'we', and answered shortly. 'She can't marry without my consent. There's nothing to worry about.'

'At twenty-one she can marry without your consent; even before that she might give trouble, if she fancied herself in love. She might even elope.'

'Get to the point,' Nicholas said impatiently, to mask his nervousness.

'You may remember some time ago I told you that I had other plans to cover future difficulties. I have decided that to protect your interests I must marry her myself.'

Nicholas's eyes bulged in his grey, misshapen face, and his lips rehearsed in shocked silence before he managed to gasp, 'Out of the question!'

Ferrars shrugged. 'I have no desire for a wife. But I am willing to make this sacrifice, because I see no alternative. It is the only way to make her fortune safe for ever.'

'Safe for you!' Nicholas said explosively.

'I would take command of her fortune only for your sake. Naturally I would expect a reasonable remuneration for myself. But think, if she marries anyone else, you will lose it all. Much better let me have her now, and make sure.'

'I'd sooner see her dead,' Nicholas cried. He was afraid of Ferrars, but he hated him almost more than he feared him. 'I'd sooner see *you* dead.'

The red spark glowed brighter. Ferrars shifted his grip on his temper. 'You are not being sensible. I'm talking of a marriage of convenience – and the convenience would be yours.'

'No,' said Nicholas, setting his jaw. 'It's outrageous! Never!'

'You will agree to this,' Ferrars said slowly, 'because I can force you to. Do you want me to remind you of the services I have done you in the past?'

'You've been paid for your services,' Nicholas said; but there was fear in his eyes. He made a move towards the door, but Ferrars moved easily to block his exit.

'You're forgetting the secrets I've kept for you.' Ferrars smiled, and pressed the nerve a little harder. 'Shall I remind you of the girl – what was her name? Annie, was it? An unfortunate end, she came to – but fortunate for you that she died before she could tell anyone about the little games you and she got up to.'

'Let me go,' Nicholas whispered. He must not remember these things – dared not. 'Get out of my way!'

'So many things happened conveniently for you. How lucky that you had me to help you, or there might have been awkward questions asked. You might never have got to be Master of Morland Place.'

Nicholas was staring at him wide-eyed now, and trembling. A little more and he would go over the edge. Ferrars took his finger from the nerve.

'Think about it, sir. Master of Morland Place, and in control of the whole Skelwith fortune. But you must make sure you keep hold of that fortune. I can help you do that. You had better let me help you.'

He stood aside and opened the door, and Nicholas came to life like a wooden puppet and walked jerkily through. There was, Ferrars perceived, a danger in pressing him too hard. If his mind went completely, the marriage would not come about, and another guardian would be brought in. And another guardian would undoubtedly want to know what had become of the profits from the Skelwith estate.

On the 17th of September 1838 the Kilsby Tunnel officially opened. The last brick had been laid on June the 21st, and one train in each direction had been running through each Sunday since then; but only one rail had been laid and while work continued on the other all other services had terminated at Denbigh Hall or Rugby, at either end of the tunnel. For the official opening, a special train was to carry the London directors of the railway company to Birmingham, to dine at Dee's Royal Hotel with the other directors and invited guests, of whom Benedict was one.

It was a gentlemen-only dinner, and when the invitation arrived Benedict hesitated to accept it. 'I should have to be away for three days at least,' he said to Rosalind.

'I think you should go,' she said. 'You will like to see your old friends again; and think what a shocking snub to Mr Robert Stephenson if you refused.'

Still Benedict hesitated, and she looked hurt. 'You don't trust me. That's what it is, isn't it? You think that while you're away I shall—' She broke off, and put her hands over her face with a choking sob. 'Oh, must I pay forever for that one mistake? I am so miserable!'

Benedict looked at her helplessly for a moment. 'It isn't that,' he said.

She continued to sob. 'I don't blame you! What I did was terrible – unforgivable! And now you will never trust me again!'

He could not bear her weeping. 'I *have* forgiven you,' he said. And then, 'I do trust you, of course I do. It wasn't that at all. Please don't cry. I was only thinking that I shouldn't leave you alone for three or fours days because you would be lonely and feel neglected.'

She looked up, her blue eyes swimming. 'Truly? Is that really why?'

'Yes, truly.'

The sun came out, and she was smiling again as though there had never been rain. 'Oh, my darling, thank you, thank you! Then you do still love me?'

'Of course I do.' He laid his hand over hers.

'And I love you,' she said. 'Only you. Always, since I first set eyes on you.'

He lifted her hand to his lips, and then the servant came in and they had to resume their normal aspects.

'Well, then, I think you should go, Mr Morland,' she said brightly. 'It will be a grand occasion. And I shall be quite all right. I have plenty of friends to call on, and little Mary to occupy my days.'

So it was that on the 16th of September Benedict found himself in a carriage once more following the road to Stamford and Market Harborough. This time it was a post-chaise, however; and he paid for the extra comfort and privacy by having altogether too much time to think, and brood over past events.

It had been the worst moment of his life when he had walked in on Rosalind and Sir Carlton Miniott that night at the Coronation Ball. What he had seen was burned deep into his brain: he knew he would never forget it.

But even worse was the recollection of the sound she had made before she knew he was there. He had heard her moan like that; that was the frightful thing, that she had made the same sound with Sir Carlton as she had made with him in the sanctity of the marriage bed.

The instant later they had both become aware of him, and sprang apart. Rosalind gave a little stifled gasp, and pulled her dress up with both hands to cover her bare breast. She looked at Benedict not angrily, but wide-eyed and terrified. It was that, more than anything, which had ultimately brought him to forgive her – the memory of that cornered misery.

Sir Carlton had stood straight like a soldier under discipline, his face inscrutable. He had acquitted himself as well as a man in that situation could, blaming himself entirely, exonerating Rosalind, saying that he had pressed his attentions on her against her will. He apologised profoundly, and offered any reparation it was in his power to give.

It occurred to Benedict afterwards that this was probably not a new situation to him, and that he had had practice in how to face down an outraged husband. At the time, though, this self-possession had had the effect of taking the edge off Benedict's desire to hit out. It seemed to require of him an equal control. 'Please leave my house at once,' he had said with as much dignity as he could muster; and without another word, and with no glance at Rosalind, Miniott had walked out.

Left alone with Rosalind, Benedict had not known what to do. Hitting Miniott – even being hit by him – would have been a relief. Baulked of his anger, he had no defence against the pain. It felt like death inside him, a black bitter emptiness that there was no dealing with; an absolute nothing from which nothing could flow. In that moment he wanted to die, rather than face what had happened. But then she cried, 'Oh, Benedict, I'm so sorry!' and at the sound of his name he came to life again, and felt.

How could such pain be endured?

'How could you?' was what he said. 'How could you, with that old man?'

'I didn't mean to! It just happened! I came up to put on some more powder, and he must have followed me, he came in and started to kiss me. It wasn't my fault. I didn't mean to do it. It was the wine – the heat – the excitement. I was thinking of you a moment before. I don't know what came over me.'

The words babbled forth like a brook, and he heard them without hearing. After a time he recollected the guests downstairs, the ball, the necessity of keeping face. 'We can't talk about it now,' he said. 'We must go downstairs. People will wonder what's become of us.'

'But you do believe me, don't you? Oh, say you forgive me! I didn't mean to do it.'

'Not now,' he said, with an instinctively escaping movement of his head. 'I can't talk of it now. Straighten your dress and come downstairs.' He began to leave, and then remembered. 'I was looking for you to ask you to dance with me after supper. We had better dance the first two together. It will give the right impression.'

That dance had been agony. To waltz round the room with his hand at Rosalind's tiny waist, her hand in his, her smiling, lovely face tilted back to him, would have been exquisite pleasure in other circumstances; as it was, he had to smile and pretend all was well, when his insides felt as though they had been scored with sharp nails. The ball went on until four in the morning. He danced every dance, and would not let Rosalind leave, though she claimed a headache, and looked pale enough for it to have been true. But at last it was over, and he retired to toss and turn in his bed for four hours without sleeping, before rising so as to be at breakfast as normal when Mary was brought down.

Mary ran to him, full of questions and kisses, and seating her on his lap and talking to her, he had felt as though he were in a dream, with the strangeness that follows great shock and lack of sleep. But she concentrated his mind wonderfully, for she showed him what really mattered. How could Rosalind's error compare in importance to Mary's existence, to the wonder of her? What was more important than her happiness? What counted more than the love she bore for her papa?

Holding Mary, smiling absently at her chatter, he tried to reshape the events in his mind. Sir Carlton was a charming and sophisticated man, he told himself, and Rosalind had been drinking champagne all evening. She was thoroughly excited in body and mind, and if at that point Sir Carlton had seized her and started kissing her passionately, it was natural, wasn't it, for her to be swept away?

It was at that point that he had difficulty. Sir Carlton was a friend of her father's, and she had known him since childhood. Would she not be shocked into sobriety by his advances, would she not scream and try to fight him off?

Well, well, it hadn't happened that way. The point was, what was he to do about it?

When Mary had been taken away, he had gone out onto the terrace to walk – and walk, and walk. Rosalind had not appeared until the middle of the afternoon, and by then he had walked himself into loneliness for her. He wanted her desperately, and far from being angry enough to send her away, he had begun to fear that she might leave him.

She appeared before him at last beautiful, delicate-looking, penitent; had not spoken, but had held out her hands to him in supplication, with such a pleading look that his defences had crumbled. He had taken her hands and kissed them, and then clasped her in his arms, feeling her tears on his neck.

'I love you, only you,' she had whispered. 'I will never do such a thing again, oh never!' And, care-less of the servants who were undoubtedly watching from the windows, he kissed her, long and tenderly.

Sitting in the jolting coach on that interminable journey, Benedict restlessly crossed and recrossed his legs. Rosalind, the beautiful, the vivacious, the passionate, the tender. He loved her, more than ever. After that reconciliation their married life had resumed, and she had been warm and generous to him, and he had scaled heights of ecstasy he had never before imagined. It had been like the days of their honeymoon all over again – except that it wasn't, quite. There was a difference. As long as he didn't think about it, as long as he kept busy and gave himself no leisure to brood, he could believe that everything was as it had been before. He was happy, perhaps happier than he had been before it happened, but now he was aware of how thin the ice was underneath him, how fragile his tenure of that happiness. It was a kind of growing up, he thought: he had believed her perfect, and now he knew her frailty.

They had not seen Sir Carlton since the ball, and it left a gap in their lives, for he had been in the habit of 'dropping in' on terms of easy familiarity. Benedict felt that he had not acquitted himself as well as he ought; that probably he ought to have thrashed Sir Carlton, or called him out, or something. But he could not have thrashed a man twenty years and more his senior, after all; and the idea of calling him out seemed faintly ludicrous in these modern times. All the same, if the story ever got about, he might be generally despised as a poltroon for not having done something. If the story ever got about: there was an idea to bathe him in cold sweat! There was no end to the torment he could extract for himself, once he had the leisure really to think about the situation.

He had played his part in the opening of the great London and Birmingham Railway. He had joined the special train at Denbigh Hall, and with a glass of champagne in his hand, had stared out of the window in excitement and awe as they steamed slowly into the vast maw of the Kilsby Tunnel. It was an experience to raise the hair on the back of one's neck, to be plunging into the darkness, to be rushing through the very core of a massive hill as fast as a horse could canter, to hear the muffled, grinding roar of their passage, to smell the bitter smoke blowing back. The men with whom he was sharing a carriage began in talk and laughter, and ended in silence; and even he, who had worked in these depths, and who knew a tunnel for what it was, felt a superstitious rush of relief and joy when they burst out into the sunshine again, to normal noises and green banks and a glimpse of mazy sky up above.

Just over four years had passed since the first sod had been cut at Chalk Farm near London to mark the beginning of the works. The terrible battle with the quicksand had been won, and the tunnel driven, by dint of incredible labour on the part of the navvies, working in shifts night and day, toiling in conditions the ordinary man had never experienced and could not imagine. Many had died in the process. The heart had been carved out of a primordial hill by the labour of men's hands alone; and the result was this smooth and easy passage, a few minutes of roar and blackness and then back into the sunlight again. Benedict thought of the thousands upon thousands who would travel along this line in the years to come: they would notice the tunnel only as a few inconvenient moments of darkness, instantly forgotten, in their journey from London to Birmingham; and the journey itself would soon become an instantly forgettable element of their day's business or pleasure. None, not one, would ever think of the rough, foul-mouthed, violent-tempered, courageous men who had gouged their way through the hill in darkness and heat and peril and heartbreaking toil. Benedict raised his glass to their memory; and the locomotive steamed triumphantly into Birmingham, with Robert Stephenson himself riding on the footplate, to the reception of a brass band, bunting, and an admiring crowd.

That had been yesterday. Now, today, he had taken to horse-power again, for a long-promised visit to Leytham Hall. Sir John greeted him with simple warmth and a handshake that was like the embrace of a friendly bear.

'I want to hear all about your junketings yesterday,' he said before Benedict had even got in at the door. 'When I think of you hurtling through that tunnel— !'

'Hardly hurtling,' Benedict corrected him, grinning. 'The drivers are ordered to keep down to fifteen miles an hour for some time yet, until Mr Stephenson is sure it isn't all going to come down on their heads.'

'Teach your grandmother to suck eggs,' Sir John invited genially. 'I know the works all have to be consolidated before the locomotives can get up full speed; but stand there and tell me fifteen miles an hour ain't hurtling when there's a tunnel wall six inches from your nose!'

'It was very exciting,' Benedict agreed. 'You must try it yourself.'

'I mean to, the first chance. But come in, come in, don't let me keep you on the doorstep. Her ladyship has been in a froth all morning waiting for you to arrive, and the children are beside themselves.' The idea of Lady Mary doing anything so immoderate as frothing made Bendy grin.

'By God, it's been a long time!' Sir John exclaimed. 'And here you are a gentleman of means after all. You're looking mighty well on it – been living as high as a coach-horse, I'll be bound! You're getting a bit of meat to your bones at last, young Morland! Oh, I beg your pardon—' His face collapsed into comical dismay at the realisation that he had been over-familiar with a gentleman of means.

Benedict grinned. 'Don't pull your punches, Sir John! You were uncommon kind to me when I was nothing but a scrub: I ain't about to come the frosty with you, now I've come into a few guineas!'

Sir John smiled with relief, but said, 'More than a few guineas, by what I heard! But never mind all that – come in and try my new sherry, and meet the brats. It's a wonder Sib ain't come galloping down to meet you. She's spoke of nothing but your visit ever since we got your letter – ah, here she is at last!'

Ever since he arrived, Benedict had subconsciously been expecting Sibella to come rushing into the hall to fling herself at him as she used to do, plaits flying, front hair all awry, and as like as not a button missing from her habit – she was always dressed in riding habit unless positively forced into something else for a special occasion. But turning to follow Sir John's glance, he saw coming down the stairs the vision of a young lady, tall and slender, dressed in a muslin day-dress which, though plainer than Rosalind was wont to wear, was well-cut and elegant and outlined a figure fully formed and womanly. She didn't gallop, but glided; but the beautifully straight back was Sibella's, and the carriage of her head. She stopped in front of Benedict and looked up (not so far up as it had used to be) with such a combination of hope and doubt, desire to be approved and fear of not being remembered, that it touched him to the heart.

'Why, Sib,' he said, 'you've grown up since I went away.'

Sir John chuckled. 'Seventeen now, the hussy! And every Jack in the county a-begging to be her servant; but she switches her skirt at 'em all! I tell you, it'll be a long time before this 'un is broke to harness!'

'Oh, Papa,' she said reproachfully, colouring a little, and throwing him the only fraction of a glance she could spare from Benedict.

'Not sure if she ain't the pick of the bunch after all,' Sir John said proudly. 'Practice made perfect, hey?'

'I like the way you're wearing your hair now,' Benedict said to her. Her hair was drawn up into a knot behind, the side-hair plaited and drawn back to wind about the knot; and all the reprehensible fuzz that had framed her face was now become little copper-gold curls like duckling-feathers. Her features had fined down, her freckles retreated to a golden dusting like those on the throat of a lily; and lily-like her open face was lifted up to his, the rain-coloured eyes searching his face. There was something heartbreaking about this tender young beauty; he had an image in his mind of a yearling filly, full of its own grace and power, yet with melting eyes and a mouth soft as a glove.

'You've been gone such a long time,' she said. 'I thought you were never coming back.'

'Well, I'm here now,' was all he could think of to say to that.

'And still standing in the hall. Come in, come in,' said Sir John. 'The others are in the morning-room. We shall have a bit of something to eat by and by, and you shall tell us your adventures.'

There was something more wanting. Benedict understood what it was. He offered his forearm to Sibella. 'Miss Sibella, will you do me the honour to take my arm?'

She laid her hand on it with a gesture that somehow expressed gladness. 'You don't need to call me miss, really,' she said candidly. 'You can still call me Sibella.'

'I don't think I'd dare,' said Benedict, and it was truer than she thought.

After a luncheon, Sibella suggested with all the lightness of desperate urgency that he might like to take a ride about the estate and see the improvements Sir John had been bringing about.

'Aye, do go, let Sib show you,' Sir John said promptly. 'I'd welcome your opinion, after what you told us about Fleetham Manor. Take Thunderer – he's a youngster of mine – I'd like your opinion on him too. He'll give you an interesting ride. And, Sib, be sure and show him the new cow-house! A model dairy, to my own design. It'll make your eyes stretch, I promise you!'

So now they were out in the fresh air, the afternoon cool enough for riding to be a pleasure. Sibella had changed into habit and boots, and was looking more like her old self, except that it was a smart, well-cut habit, and she wore a tall hat with a veil. She was still riding Rocket, the big black gelding, but she had grown into him now – he didn't look so very big for her, though he was still a powerful horse for a slim young woman. Indeed, Sir John's Thunderer was not much bigger, though heavier built. They rode out onto the hills, and had a gallop to get the tickle out of the horses' feet, and then pulled them up to breathe them on the slope above Kilsby. The navvies had gone, the village was silent again, and only the abandoned turf huts, the fire scars and the debris told of the invasion which had turned the villagers' lives upside down for two years.

They walked on, letting the horses pick their own way, while they talked – about the railway at first, and about the York and North Midland.

'I was thinking, you know, what a pity it is that my brother opposes the railways so much. If I owned Morland Place, I'd be making friends with Mr Hudson and securing myself a contract for railway horses. But Nicky can't think like that. His mind is set in the old ways.'

'Well, you have an estate of your own now,' Sibella said. 'You can breed horses on it on your own account, can't you?'

Benedict laughed. 'I don't think Mrs Morland would care to have me become a horse-dealer. She wants me to be a gentleman and nothing else.'

'How silly,' Sibella said, but without heat. 'What could be nicer than a horse-dealer? Gentlemen are two-a-penny.'

'I'm glad you have found that to be so. I don't know

487

too many myself,' Benedict said. It sounded grimmer than he meant it to, and she glanced at him curiously for a moment.

'Does Mrs Morland like horses?' she asked next.

'Yes, very much. That is to say, quite. I bought her a lovely black hunter mare—' He stopped, a flood of memories overcoming him; and he realised there was very little he could say to Sibella about Rosalind and horses without sounding, or being, disloyal.

Sibella did not seem to notice the truncated sentence. She was following some train of thought of her own. 'Is she pretty?' she asked next.

'Very, very pretty. In fact, I think she's the most beautiful woman I've ever seen.'

He heard Sibella sigh. 'Yes,' she said, as though to herself, 'I suppose it would take that.' He did not understand, and waited for more, looking at her enquiringly. 'I'm not pretty or beautiful,' she said at last. 'I do have a dowry, but it isn't much. Only younger sons dangle after me, whatever Papa says.'

'You're very young still,' Benedict said. 'The right man will come along in time, and then—'

'Oh, he already has,' she said in her abrupt way.

Benedict felt a pang he could not quite identify. 'Is he in love with you?'

'I'm not sure,' she said judiciously. 'But in any case, it's no use.'

'Why? Is he unsuitable?'

'In a way,' she said. She vouchsafed no more about it, and he rode in silence beside her for a while, not liking to intrude, but rather wishing he could have five minutes alone with the brute who had made little Sib unhappy.

At last she turned and looked at him. 'I shall be having my come-out next Season. Papa is taking a London house for me.' She gave a small, tight smile. 'He has faith in me, you see – you heard his nonsense about me being the pick of the bunch. He thinks if

I am put up at a bigger market, I'll attract a better buyer.'

'Oh, Sibella, don't talk like that! I'm sure he doesn't think in those horrible terms at all.'

'Perhaps not, but that's what it comes down to. A London Season costs an awful lot of money, so he must be hoping I'll recoup it for him one way or another.'

'I'm sure he only wants you to be happy.'

'I'm sure of that too. It's just that he thinks the richer and more important my husband is, the happier I'll be.' She shrugged. 'I expect he's right. If I can't marry the man of my choice, I don't much mind who I marry.'

Benedict was silent, feeling uncomfortable at this kind of talk. After a moment she said, 'At any rate, I shall be launched next Season, and my ball will be in May – it must be either the first or the last of the Season, Mama says. Anything else would be insipid. So what I wanted to ask was, will you come to it? You did promise, after all – and now that you're rich, the expense can't be an object, can it?'

'I will come if I possibly can,' Benedict said. He felt obscurely bad about this, as bad as could be, but he didn't know why. 'That's what I promised – that I would if I could.'

She nodded briskly. 'I dare say Mrs Morland would like to spend the Season in London.'

'I dare say she would,' Benedict said, laughing, the clouds clearing as he thought of Rosalind let loose to spend money in London. The wonder of it was that she had not asked to go before.

'That's settled then,' she said with a little nod, and collected Rocket. 'Shall we canter? There's a good path along here.'

Rocket knew it, and began to fret at the bit and dance a little, and Thunderer caught the excitement and stuck his head up in the air, in a way that suggested Sir John had been heavy-handed with him. Benedict turned him in a circle to get him back on the bit, and said, 'Just a minute.' Sibella looked enquiringly. 'This damned animal needs a martingale! I wanted to ask you, Sibella – this man you're in love with—'

'He doesn't know. Oh, don't worry about it! I've got used to the idea by now. And anyway, I'm much too sensible to go into a decline or anything. There's always horses. One can forget almost any disappointment when one's galloping a good horse over good country.'

He felt a surge of relief at knowing she was not pining, and laughed at her panacea. 'He probably wouldn't be flattered to hear you say that.'

'I dare say he feels the same way himself,' Sibella said. 'Except that he's probably never had to think about it.'

And ascertaining by a glance that he was in sufficient control of Thunderer's gyrations, she let Rocket bound forward, and went streaming away in front of him across the hill-top, passing out from the shadow into the sunlight, which was low enough now to flush the grass with gold. Black on black she was, with just a touch of fire which was her hair below her hat catching the setting rays. Benedict closed his legs and sent Thunderer after them, and concentrated on keeping his nose out of the way of that tossing head.

CHAPTER TWENTY-THREE

Nicholas sat alone in the steward's room, in the old red-plush chair beside the fire where his father had used to sit sometimes when he had a problem to think out. He sat hunched forwards towards the fire, though it had died down to embers, and there was very little heat in it. He rubbed his hands together over and over as a man rubs them to warm them; he had been doing it for hours without noticing, and the movement had slowed until it now rather resembled an endless washing.

It was late; he had no idea how late, but the servants had long gone to bed, and the house was quiet – or as quiet as an old house ever is. When the human sounds drained away into night silence, the fabric of the house seemed to come to life: little whispering, pattering sounds, creaks, a murmur of wind in a chimney; and every now and then a long sigh, almost below the level of hearing, the sort of sigh someone on the point of sleep gives as they turn over one last time. The sounds made Nicky nervous. He felt as though he were being watched; the murmurs and whispers were critical discussions of him; the sighs were expressions of disappointment. Sometimes he thought he saw a flicker of movement out of the corner of his eye, or a surging of the darkness in an unlit corner as though the shadows were gathering up into some solid form. Since Minna had died a fortnight ago, he had seen her every day on the fringe of vision, had thought a hundred times he heard the clicking of her nails on the floor behind him.

He should have got another dog straight away, but he had not had the heart for it, nor the energy to contemplate training a new puppy. He thought perhaps her ghost was trying to fill the empty place at his heels. She had always been a good dog. Sometimes when he was dozing in his chair in his room, he was wakened by the touch of a cold nose on his dangling hand.

He wished she was here now to comfort him. He knew the house was watching him. Generations of Morlands, whose essence had seeped into the ancient walls, were hanging on his decision. He could feel their impatience, impotent as they were, having no physical presence, dependent on him to do what was needed to protect the Morland Inheritance. In a gesture of anguish he lifted his hands to his head, pressing the heels of them against his temples. Why had he ever wanted to be Master? He had not realised the silent weight that would lean against him, the responsibility to his ancestors which he had taken so lightly. Their expectations wore at his brain, constant and tireless as water, drip dripping until he felt his head must burst.

What do you want? he screamed inwardly. But he knew what they wanted. *I can't!* he wailed. But the stern imperative was there in the silence. You must. You brought the Serpent into the Garden – you! *I didn't know*, he whispered. What have you done? said the sigh of the house reproachfully, and the creak of the old wood was like a groan of pain. He couldn't bear it, he couldn't bear it, and he got up from his chair and paced up and down, washing his hands together endlessly. Ferrars – Ferrars was the Serpent. He had to do something about Ferrars.

He thought about the interview he had had earlier that evening with his manservant. (Manservant? questioned one part of his brain. Who was Master and who was Man now?) It was a simple proposition: Ferrars wanted to marry Jemima so as to take control of her fortune. The properties of a married woman became her husband's, irrevocably. Even if she left him and ran away, her property stayed behind. If she died – no, Nicholas did not want to think about that.

'For your sake, sir, only for you,' said Ferrars every time; and he was growing more urgent day by day. Jemima might defy him and marry without his consent. Such a marriage, while she was a minor, would not be legal, but in practice would be hard to overturn. And then her fortune would be lost to Nicholas. The consideration weighed less heavily on him of late. He could almost say he did not care about her fortune. He had no idea any more what money he had, what the estate was worth. It was long since he had looked into the books. Ferrars did all that. He had a suspicion that he was much poorer than he had been five years ago, but he did not feel inclined to test the theory, not if it meant asking Ferrars. If his fortune had dripped away in the intervening years, how could he ever discover where it had gone? It was something he emphatically did not want to ask. And what did it matter anyway? It would last him out, and he had no son. *Après moi le déluge.*

The house moaned, his ancestors moaned. It was not for this we fought and died, suffered persecution, took up arms, married and progenerated, built and repaired and tended. They had been laid to rest in the crypt, under the chapel, under the house; the house was built on their bones, and the mute bones cried out in silent protest, a deafening, accusatory silence. Here we lie, here we lie for ever, watching you, judging you. You cannot escape us.

Ferrars wanted Jemima. Why? For Nicholas's sake, he said, but somehow or other, Nicholas didn't believe that. The money, her fortune, the Skelwith estate, would all belong to Ferrars, and would he then meekly pass it over to Nicholas? He doubted it. In any case, whether he did or not, Nicholas would never know, since he did not see the accounts. And when Ferrars had the girl and the money, what then? Nicholas was afraid Jemima might not make old bones. (No, not bones, don't think about bones!)

He could not give Jemima to Ferrars. It was impossible to be party to handing her over, fresh young innocence, to that poisonous toad. The thought of Ferrars touching her, slobbering over her, fondling her white child's body, doing to her what men do, sickened him. He felt a cold weight in his stomach like poisoned meat. He could not give Jemima to Ferrars.

But Ferrars wanted her, and he had the means to force Nicholas. He knew Nicholas's secrets. He would tell. They rose up in Nicky's mind like a boulder thrusting up out of the earth, and he whimpered and tried to thrust them down again. He could not think about them, or he would go mad; and he must not go mad, because there was Jemima to think about.

Ferrars was smooth, always deferential, always smiling, but he had threatened. I will *tell*, he said. And then he said the other thing, the thing which had brought it all to a head, which meant that Nicholas could not sleep or rest or slide into blessed drugged oblivion, because the decision had to be made *now*, tonight.

'The other way for me to make sure of her, of course, is to have carnal knowledge of her. If I have her, she will be spoiled goods. You will have no choice but to let me marry her, because no-one else will have her. But I should not like to force your hand in that way. I would much sooner have her with your blessing than without. I will let you sleep on it, sir, and come back for your decision tomorrow.'

If he said no, Ferrars would defile her. He could do it – who in the house could stop him? And he would do it brutally. Nicholas could imagine her struggling and screaming – he clapped his hands over his ears even at the memory of the thought. And once it was done, it was done. Nothing could change it. Even if Nicholas

494

sent for the constable and had Ferrars arrested, nothing would undo what had been done to the child – his ward, his responsibility.

Ferrars knew that. That was why he had made the threat. Not because Jemima defiled would automatically be given to him as his bride, but because he knew that Nicholas could not allow it to happen. Better she be wed than raped. He could not let it happen. But to marry her to that man— !

Agony of mind drove him to pace again, like an animal in a cage. The ancestors watched him – on an impulse he opened the steward's room door and looked out. The passage was silent and dark, and the chapel door stood ajar. The hair rose up on his scalp at the sight. It had been closed when he came in here, he was sure of it. Just lately, the chapel door seemed always ajar, as if it were opening of its own accord, and from it he caught the smell of old incense and dust and decay, the corpse-breath of the untenanted place. He shivered with fright like a horse that smells death. *Who opened the door?* But he knew who. They were calling him to account. He found he had stepped forward, and looked down in amazement at his feet, as if they had done it alone. They stepped again, and again; he walked into the chapel.

It was not quite dark. The sanctuary lamp cast a dim glow which, in comparison with the unalleviated darkness outside, gave sufficient light to distinguish the contours. He walked forward, listening, every nerve on the stretch. And then he stopped. No use going further. They were here, all around him, underneath him. The bones under his feet groaned, the spirits in the air sighed. *Leave me alone*, he cried inside; but they answered, Decide! You let the Serpent in. You bear the blame. You must make reparation.

His mother's bones and his father's lay under his feet – no, no, don't think about them! His sister's, and the son she died giving birth to, who would have been the heir;

his elder brother, who would have been the heir. They stared up at him in the darkness, their reproachful eyes burning like coals, like the coals of Hell which awaited the sinner. He must act. The outraging of Jemima would be the outraging of the house. He could not let it happen.

And then he knew what he must do. In an instant he was calm and cold as ice. He turned and walked back into the steward's room, felt in his fob and drew out the key chain on which rested the only two keys he still retained – the key to the strong-room, and the key to the gun-cupboard. He selected the latter and went to the cupboard in the corner, and opened it. Amongst the weapons there was a pair of pistols. He took one out, tested the action, and then, with hands that barely shook, carefully loaded and primed it. He laid it aside and did the same with the other – one misfire in two was not unusual with pistols. Then he pushed them down carefully into the waistband of his trousers, let his coat drop over them, and walked out.

The great door of the hall was closed and bolted, of course, and the effort of undoing it was too great for him in his state of nervous exhaustion. He went down the passage into the kitchen, and out through the buttery door – both buttery doors were locked, but the keys were in them. They were intended to stop ingress, not egress. Outside in the yard the night was cold but not bitter, and there was a luminosity in the clouds behind the stable roof where the moon was rising. There was just enough light for the skyline to be visible. Ahead was the bulk of the barbican, and the gatehouse where Ferrars lived. Nicholas walked forward, carefully across the uneven cobbles, and suddenly the moon tugged clear of the clouds – a gibbous moon, pale-lemon-coloured – and its light swept wanly across the yard. Light and shadow – the face of the gatehouse thrown into rough contour, its windows dark in the shadow of the embrasures like blind eyes. And under the barbican absolute dark, like the mouth of a tunnel – like the mouth of the Abyss.

He walked forward carefully but without faltering, feeling the house behind him, his support now, not his inquisitor. Under the barbican he put his hands out in front of him like a blind man and found the door to the gatehouse by feel. He turned the ring of the latch and it lifted easily; inside the stairs began immediately, stone stairs worn a little in the middle with generations of tired feet. He walked up them, his hand touching the rough wall for guidance, the pistols heavy at his waist, but warm. At the top another door. He had to feel about for the ring, and missed it several times before a fourth sweep encountered it. It creaked as he turned it, and the latch slipped up with a loud snick, but his nerves were steady. He was in the grip of a greater power than himself, and he knew he was safe.

Inside, the living-room was moonlit, enough to see the shapes of the furniture, table and chairs, the seeds of a fire in the stove under the chimney, gleam of plates on a dresser, clothes hanging up on the back of the further door like a headless horror. No horror to me, he thought: it is you who must be afraid now, Ferrars. Through the farther door was where he lay. Serpent! Nicholas started towards it, eager now to close with him.

He was halfway across the room when the door opened, and he stopped dead with a sudden return of fear. Ferrars came out, gleaming pale in a nightshirt, something in his hand down by his side, something dark – the bedroom poker. Ferrars disconcertingly awake, frighteningly real and solid and dangerous. Not the Serpent, but human Ferrars. Serpents crawled and stung, but Ferrars might do anything.

'Ah, I thought I heard something,' he said. His voice was as steady as always. Was he never afraid? 'Did you want something?'

'I came to tell you,' Nicholas began, and his voice caught on his dry throat with a click, and he had to swallow and start again. 'I came to tell you my decision.'

'About Jemima?' Ferrars asked complacently. The assurance in his voice roused Nicholas to anger at last.

'Miss Jemima to you! You have made free with her name for the last time. I have come to tell you that you will not have her. I will not give her to you. You have overreached yourself.'

'Oh, I think not,' Ferrars said smoothly. 'If you think I will not carry out my threats, you are very wrong. You will give her to me, or I will take her, and expose you into the bargain. I will tell the world, about how you killed your father—'

'No!' Nicholas cried.

'And your m—'

'No! Don't say it!'

Ferrars smiled. In the moonlight Nicholas could tell by the writhing of the shadows on his face that he smiled. 'You see? You have no choice. I will do as I threaten. Make no mistake about it. You cannot beat me.'

With a vast effort of will, Nicholas took hold of himself, crushed down his terror. 'I know,' he said. He dragged out the right-hand pistol, raising it between both hands. 'That's why I have to kill you.'

For a fraction of a second – one lovely instant – Ferrars looked disconcerted, his smile faltered. But the moment passed, and his smile regained its normal confidence. 'Oh, I don't think so,' he said. He began to move forward again, very cautiously, his eyes on Nicky's face, his hand lifting the poker stealthily.

'Stay back!' Nicholas cried, his finger curling round the trigger.

'I don't think you will really pull the trigger,' Ferrars said. 'I don't think you have the bottom.'

There was a crash, and Ferrars stopped dead, his eyes opening wide, his jaw dropping as if in enormous surprise. The poker clattered on the floor. Ferrars' two hands came up, fumbling at his chest like a blind man feeling for his waistcoat buttons. And then he fell, shockingly, forwards out of the moonlight and into the shadow, his body thumping softly and his feet scuffling a moment against the bare boards as though he were trying for a toehold. And then there was silence.

The next sound Nicholas heard was a whimper, but it came from himself. He stood where he was, too frightened to move, staring until his eyes ached at the darkness on the floor where Ferrars had disappeared, waiting for him to get up. He would get up and come for him, he knew. He thought every instant he heard the rustling of movement, expected every moment to feel cold fingers grasp his ankles; but as the moments passed and the silence endured, he began to believe it would not happen.

He had done it. He had killed him. He had no recollection of having pulled the trigger. It must have been increasing and unconscious pressure on the trigger which had finally tripped it. He rested his eyes and listened. There was no sound of breathing. He must be dead, he must be! He knew he ought to kneel down and examine the body, but he had a helpless dread that if he did the fingers would flash out and fasten round his throat – dead or alive, it made no difference, Ferrars would get him if he went too close. The only thing to do was to run; but it took him some minutes more to get control of his legs and to bring himself to turn his back even for the length of time it took to get to the door and through it. Then he slammed it shut, and ran down the stairs, expecting to hear the door open again behind him. Out through the bottom door, and slam that shut. In the cold night air he stood panting, not with exertion but with fear.

The night was silent; no-one had stirred. The walls of the barbican were thick, and the sound of the shot had not escaped them, or not enough, at least, to wake anyone. He was safe. Ferrars was dead – probably; but how to stop him rising up and coming after him? The door at the bottom of the gatehouse did not lock; it would be no barrier. Nicholas looked round wildly. He must have help, but he had no way of summoning it; he could not leave the yard or turn his back on the gatehouse door, in case Ferrars got out during that instant. Then his eye fell on the window of the flat above the stable. He reached down and felt about for a stone to throw. At the third clatter, a face appeared at the dusty glass, and Nicholas waved and beckoned frantically. A few minutes later the boy came tumbling out, still pulling on his breeches, his nightshirt flapping behind.

Nicholas felt like giggling at the sight, but controlled himself sternly. The boy came up to him, half asleep still, wondering.

'Go down to the carpenter's cottage – do you know where Mr Johns lives?'

'Yessir.'

'Good boy. Go down there as fast as you can and get Mr Johns up, and tell him to come up here to me. Wait! Tell him I want the gatehouse door boarded up good and tight, so that no-one can get in, so tell him to bring boards and nails and whatever else he needs. Wait with him and help him carry. Run as fast as you can, and tell him to come as fast as he can. Do you understand?'

'Yessir,' the boy said, and was sufficiently in awe of the Master, who had never spoken to him directly before, to obey without hesitation or question.

'Sharp now!' Nicholas added, and the boy turned and ran. There followed an agonising period of waiting, standing under the shadow of the barbican with his back against the wall, watching the door opposite. His aching eyes played tricks on him, and again and again he saw the latch-ring move, the door begin to open; but he dared not close them to rest them. The moon passed slowly round the yard, altering the shadows and the shapes of things, and hours passed, days, aeons, he grew old and died, the world turned to coal; pain invested every corner of his consciousness; he suffered the torments of Hell through a thousand ages; and at last the boy came back with the carpenter and a bag of tools and lengths of wood carried between them.

The carpenter looked puzzled and annoyed in almost equal measure, and addressed his master doubtfully, sure the boy had got it wrong.

'You want the gatehouse door nailed up, Maister?'

'That's right.' Nicholas saw that for the older man, some explanation was necessary, if only to stop him speculating abroad. 'Mr Ferrars has gone. I – dismissed him. He's packed up and gone, and I want to stop him getting back in, if he should decide to come back.'

'Mr Ferrars gone, sir?'

'That's right.'

'Well, God sa' me,' Johns said in mild astonishment. 'I can't say I'm sorry. He wasn't well liked, wasn't Mr Ferrars.'

'Quite so. But get to work, will you. And hurry. I want it done as quickly as possible. And tight, mind! I want it so that no-one could get in there, however hard they tried.'

It was inevitable that the sawing and hammering should wake someone, and eventually old Moon arrived, a dressing-gown over his nightshirt, a stout billet of wood in his chalky old fist, an expression of bewilderment replacing that of tremulous belligerence when he saw Nicholas supervising the work. Nicholas gave him the same explanation and drove him away, telling him to keep the other servants away and send them back to bed if they were roused.

'Very good, sir. But won't you come in? You're shivering with cold. Mr Johns can finish the job alone.'

'I want to see it done. Leave me alone, I'm all right. Go away, will you, before I get angry.'

It was done at last. With Johns standing back, Nicholas felt over and tested the rigidity, and was satisfied. 'Good,' he said. 'Now listen to me, Johns: this door is not to be reopened, no matter who asks you, do you understand? Not for any reason, not on any account.'

'Very good, sir.'

'You may go, then. And thanks,' Nicholas said. Johns touched his forehead, picked up his bag and went away; the stable boy, gaping wonderingly at the boards, was driven away with one stern look. And Nicholas trudged slowly back to the house, aware of faces at windows being hastily withdrawn as he approached. He went through the buttery, locking it behind him, and found Moon in the kitchen, hovering anxiously. 'I thought I told you to go back to bed,' Nicholas said wearily.

Moon gazed at him earnestly, his hands quivering with the desire to pat his master's shoulder. He had never seen him look so exhausted; and he had got rid of Ferrars! 'I wanted to see you was all right, sir. Can I get you anything? A drop o' brandy? Or something hot? I can blow up the kitchen fire in two twos and boil a kettle.'

'I want nothing. Go to bed.' He met Moon's eyes, and read a number of things there. He softened a little. 'I'm all right. I just want everyone to go back to bed.'

'Very good, sir,' Moon said unhappily; but Nicholas stood there implacably until he went away towards the backstairs.

And then Nicky could be alone with his thoughts, and with reaction. He had done it. He had rid the Garden of the Serpent. Jemima was safe. Morland Place was safe. He could sleep. But no, there was one thing left to do. He walked back down the passage, across the hall, across the staircase hall. The steward's room passage was dark, the chapel door was closed, but he went forward with confidence, opened the chapel door, stepped into the chilly stillness.

The Sanctuary lamp glowed still: a lightless light, just as the silence was filled with sound. All things here were contradictory, here in the living heart of the house which contained all its death. He hated and feared and

502

reverenced this place; but now he had an offering to make, now he had come with what was acceptable. The Lady Chapel – that was where he must go. He knew without understanding that that was what was waiting for him. The dim glow from the lamp gave just enough illumination for him to make his way to it without stumbling. He could see the altar, a glint of light from the silver candlesticks, and the shape of the statue of the Lady, the edge of one outstretched hand, but not her face – that was in shadow.

'I have come,' he said, and the sound of his own voice was shocking in the silence. He spoke after that inside his head. *I have done it*, he said. *I have done what you wanted. I have avenged you.*

There was no reply. The whispering silence did not notice him.

I have killed the Serpent! he cried. *I have killed Ferrars.*

And now the eyes turned to him. He felt them in the darkness. The reply came: But that was not what we meant, not what we meant at all.

The eyes were everywhere. The watchers were there. He felt the shapes rise up before him, rising up like smoke, like shadow, up from the crypt below, up through the floor, black and forbidding. Whose bones were down there? His father's. His mother's. And how did they die?

Don't ask me, he whimpered.

Who killed your father?

Don't ask me. Don't ask me that.

WHO KILLED YOUR MOTHER?

'No-o-o!' cried Nicholas aloud. 'It wasn't me! It wasn't me!' There was light on the Lady's face now (how could there be?) and he could see her looking at him, stern, implacable, and grieving, bearing all the grief of his sin, even as she condemned him to eternal darkness. There were tears on her face, slow tears glittering in the faint, wavering light. It was the Mother's face; it was his mother's face! He turned to run away, stumbled a desperate

503

few steps, and then stopped in rippling fright, because a white shape barred his way, a white shape shimmering in unearthly light – the White Lady, the ghost that walked the house. His throat tightened with an unuttered scream; but she was not the worst thing to fear. She was only Hell's messenger. It was what came behind her that made his heart bolt, his eyes bulge with terror: behind her came nemesis, came Hell itself in almost human form, carrying a pall of darkness to wrap Nicky's soul in and take it away. He knew who it was, and as he stared into its face, he felt his reason stretch to bursting point.

'NO-O-O!' he screamed, his hands clawing for escape; and he felt the bubble of darkness in his head bulge and burst, and he fell down into the blackness, fell and fell for ever, like a star.

'Nicky!' Aglaea, wrapper over her nightgown, candlestick in her hand, ran forward the few steps that separated her and knelt down over the fallen bundle of her husband. 'Oh, Nicky, Nicky!'

And behind her Moon hurried forward, tremulous with anxiety. 'He's fainted, poor gentleman. Here you are, missus, put this over him.' And between them they covered him tenderly with the blanket Moon had snatched up when he had roused the mistress, for fear of the Master's health, the chapel being a chilly place and him being so susceptible to cold.

'It was just a faint, Martha,' Moon protested feebly. 'The missus coming up behind him like that frightened him. He thought she was a ghost.'

'Ghost, my eye! And since when did the Master visit the chapel in the middle o' the night – or any other time, for the matter of that? Hates the chapel like a cook hates mice, does the Master. No, there was something queer going on, and I don't like it.'

Moon shook his head – not in denial of the queerness,

but in puzzlement. 'Mr Ferrars going off like that, so sudden—'

'Aye, that's the other thing. Master must have found something out, and it must have been mortal bad for Ferrars to rub off, and not face him down.' She looked up at her husband with deep trouble. 'You know what, Moon – it won't be long before Master comes sniffing round us. It's time we were off as well.'

'But – but what could he find out about us?'

'Damn near everything,' Martha said briskly. 'Don't be more of a fool than you can help.'

'Oh, Martha, you haven't been up to your old tricks— ?'

'Godamighty, you are a snivelling old tosspot! Did you think I took this job for the pleasure o' being a housekeeper? I admit I'd begun to think it might see us out nicely, but after this— ! Well, thank God I've been salting it away. What did you think I was doing, going into Leeds every month on my day off? I've a nice fat account at a bank there – and a new name into the bargain. They think I'm running a respectable boarding house. Lord, you should see them touch their forelocks and open doors for me! Did me a power o' good after all the bowing and scraping I've had to do here.' She snorted, and if Moon reflected that he had never seen her bow or scrape to anyone in this house, he wisely kept the thought to himself. Martha was still thinking. 'We'll have to stay in Leeds for a while – a couple o' months, until I can get the money out. It'll rouse suspicions if I take it all out at once. But then we can be off, anywhere we want. I've a mind to try London—'

'You don't mean – leave Morland Place?' Moon interrupted in dismay.

'God bless us, the old fool has worked it out! Yes, donkey, leave Morland Place – and tonight, while we can. We're not safe here any more. If Master's twigged Ferrars, he'll be on to us next. And if Ferrars is caught, he'll squeak like a fieldmouse. We've got to get right away and leave no tracks, make ourselves invisible.' She struggled to her feet. 'Get on and pack our things while I have one last look round to see if there's anything worth taking. You've got the key to the silver cupboard, haven't you?'

'Now, Martha— !'

'No, no, you're right. They'd be sure to chase after us if we took anything they'd notice. But I want my little clock from the housekeeper's room, and the trinket box and the candlesticks as well. They won't miss them if they haven't already. Go down and get 'em – quiet! – while I start packing. We must start while it's still dark. It'll mean some walking, and God help my poor feet, but it can't be helped. Once we're clear we might find someone to give us a lift. Well, go on, then, hustle about! What're you standing there for?'

Moon stared at her a moment longer, thinking of the poor master, and how white and thin he had looked, thinking of the mistress with her sweet, anxious face – and Miss Jemima, too, who had helped her nurse when the Master was ill. And he thought of the house he had come to love, the comfort and permanence of it, the light in the various rooms and the views from the windows, the portraits of long-ago Morlands who looked down on him kindly, he thought, as he passed back and forth tending their inheritance. He had thought he might end his days here, and it had been a good thought, a restful thought, as though he had come home. He did not want to leave, to go on the road again, staying in cheap lodgings under false names, never feeling he belonged anywhere. For a moment he felt he might defy Martha, tell her he just was not going to go; but she stared him down, and after a moment his gaze wavered and dropped, and he turned and shuffled off. He had always done as she bid, and it was hard to resist her. Besides, she had looked after him, all those years before Morland Place, when his only refuge from his hideous guilty thoughts had been the oblivion of drunkenness. Without her he would have perished, and he was grateful to her – too grateful to separate himself from her now.

Nicholas lay propped against his pillows, white and ghastly, his lips blue and his eyes staring as he gasped for breath. His old trouble had come upon him again, and Aglaea did not know what to do for him, beyond putting hot flannel on his chest, and burning herbs on the bedroom fire. She had begged him to allow her to send for the doctor, but he had forbidden it, and grew so agitated at the very thought that she feared for his life if she pressed the matter.

She had tried, very gently, to extract from him some account of last night's events, but between his gasping breaths, only disjointed fragments came out which she could barely piece together. Ferrars had gone – thank God! – and Nicholas had ordered his apartments boarded up to stop him returning; an odd and unnecessary proceeding which made her wonder what had passed between them to provoke Ferrars to leave. And then Nicholas had fainted in the chapel out of fear.

'Thought – you were – White Lady.'

Aglaea had heard all the Morland Place ghost stories in her childhood, and those few words were enough explanation. The White Lady was the ghost of some poor mad Morland lady from mediaeval times who had drowned in the moat and was said to walk on moonlit nights, still dressed in her nightgown and streaming water. 'But what were you doing in the chapel?' she asked.

Nicholas only shook his head slowly from side to side, his eyes bulging; and she stroked his brow and brought up to his nose the dish of crushed camphor leaves, but he pushed them aside feebly. 'Mother,' he gasped. Which mother? she wondered. He was in the Lady Chapel – did he mean Mother with a capital letter?

'No matter,' she said soothingly. 'That horrid man is gone, and we shall be more comfortable without him. You

507

must rest and get well, Mr Morland. Don't be afraid, I will keep everyone away from you until you feel better.'

She was about to rise, when he raised his head from the pillow and grasped her hand and pulled her back with a grip so strong she winced a little. 'Statue – wept,' he said, and then fell back, exhausted, and closed his eyes. Aglaea released herself gently and took the camphor-dish away, moved softly about the room tidying things with the calm, unruffled movements of the good nurse. But she was weighted with a sense of dread. Like the ghost stories, she knew the legends. The statue of the Lady was old, older than the house by far, its origins lost in obscurity, and it had survived many an attempt to destroy the chapel. It had about it a strange aura of power, and the legend in the house was that when some particular disaster was about to befall the Morland inheritance, the Lady wept.

Ferrars was gone. She had long believed him to be a kind of evil genius, and his departure ought to have lifted a dark cloud from Morland Place. Why, then, had the Lady wept? Could it be that there was more evil in his going than in his staying? That he could continue to harm them from wherever it was he had gone? Or that the evil had not been in Ferrars in the first place? And if not there, where?

She thrust the thoughts away from her. First she must get Nicholas well again. She rang the bell for hot water to wash him, but it was a very long time before it was answered, and then the servant tapped on the door instead of coming in. When she went to open it, the kitchen maid, Feeb, was standing there, twisting her hands in her apron, her face agitated. She opened her mouth to pour out her alarms, and Aglaea shook her head forbiddingly, thrust her back and stepped out into the passage, closing the door behind her.

'We must not alarm the Master,' she whispered. 'What is the matter, Feeb? Speak quietly!'

'Oh, ma'am,' the girl whispered, her eyes darting here and there as if to escape the situation. She had never spoken directly to the mistress before, and now it was with bad news to tell. 'Mrs Moon has rubbed off, and Mr Moon as well.'

'Rubbed off?'

'Gone, ma'am, packed an' clean gone before anyone was oop, and what wi' Mr Ferrars gone an' all and the Maister ill, Thomas said as how there was summat queer goin' on, and how he didn't want to have no part of it, and him and Ned is gone 'ome and not coming back namore. And the maids is in the servants' hall talkin' what to do, and when the bell rung there was only me and Mrs Codling and Bella in the kitchen, and so Mrs Codling said as how it had to be me, because she had to mind the fire. And oh, ma'am, whatever is to do?'

All Aglaea's housewifely powers rose up at the challenge. 'Calm down, child, and stop looking so worried. Do as you're told, and no harm will come to you.'

'Yes, ma'am,' Feeb said, still with some doubt, but evidently relieved at the access of authority.

'Now just run down and ask Mrs Codling for some hot water for Master's room, and bring it up yourself, quietly. And tell Mrs Codling that there's nothing to worry about, the Master is a little unwell with his old trouble, that's all. There's nothing at all strange going on, and I shall come down by and by when I've made the Master comfortable and speak to all the servants in the servants' hall. Can you remember all that.'

'Yes, ma'am.'

'Good girl. Run along, then.'

She went back into the bedroom, and crossed to the bed. Nicholas seemed to be asleep, and his breathing was quieter, but as she approached he opened his eyes.

'Better?' she asked softly.

He nodded his head, just once, economically. 'What was that about?' he asked. He had improved to the point where, if he whispered, he could speak without gasping.

Aglaea hesitated, wondering whether to tell him, but concluded that he would know she was holding something back and might worry more. 'It seems Moon and Mrs Moon have packed their bags and gone. I'm not very surprised,' she went on, speaking lightly as if it didn't matter. 'I always had the feeling that they were in league with Ferrars. We will be able to replace them easily enough, I'm sure.'

'No,' Nicholas said.

She looked at him enquiringly. 'There are plenty of servants about, and everyone always wants to work at Morland Place,' she said mildly.

'Don't replace them,' Nicholas whispered. 'I don't want more servants. *You* keep house. Said you could. Said you wanted to, in the beginning.'

'Yes, that's true,' Aglaea said, suppressing her surprise. 'I could take over the direction of household affairs, if you wanted me to.'

He nodded. 'Do. Get Jemima to help you. Close some of the rooms if need be. But don't get more servants. No more strangers coming in. That's my order. D'you hear?'

'Yes, of course,' she said hastily as he began to get agitated again. 'Be easy. It shall be just as you wish, Mr Morland. I can manage very well, very well indeed.'

Even if most of the servants left she could manage, as long as she had a cook and a couple of housemaids, and the laundry-woman and the scrub-woman who came in from outside. The idea of rising to the challenge, of coping with the domestic siege, stimulated her: she had always wanted to be useful to him, directly useful, and now at last she would be given the chance. And what good training it would be for Jemima! With one part of her mind she wished she knew what had passed between Nicholas and Ferrars; but another part told her she had probably better not know. A discreet tap at the door told her the hot water had arrived, and she got up to go and fetch it. Now all she had to do, she reflected, was to think of something to tell the servants.

CHAPTER TWENTY-FOUR

During the late months of 1838 and the beginning of 1839 the work on the York and North Midland at last began to pick up speed, and at a meeting of the shareholders in February an opening date in May for the first section – York to Milford – was talked of. Benedict was there in two capacities, as consultant engineer, with special reference to the Milford curves, and as a shareholder. As an act of faith he had taken twenty thousand pounds' worth of shares in the Company, and through the winter had frequently been embarrassed by Hudson's repetition of the fact whenever shareholders grew nervous about progress. Benedict's name came second only to George Stephenson's as a panacea for restlessness and guarantee of eventual success: he was not only a York gentleman born, and a wealthy local landlord, but he was a personal friend of Stephenson père and had actually worked with both Stephensons, and could therefore be assumed to know what he was doing. Benedict grew tired of bowing politely every time his name was mentioned at a meeting and all eyes turned to scan him for signs of wavering.

But things were definitely moving forward now. The decision had been made to purchase the parcel of land inside the walls, and agreement had been reached with the Great North Eastern Company to share a station for the convenience of passengers travelling right through. Negotiations for the purchase were so slow, however, that it was decided to build a temporary, wooden station outside the walls for the opening of the first section, and extend the lines inside the walls when the work was done. Tenders were considered at the meeting in February for making the opening in the walls, a seventy-foot-wide arch, for which permission had been granted by the Corporation, provided the promenade along the top was restored when the work was finished.

After the meeting Hudson came across to Benedict to clap his shoulder and say, 'By, things are goin' like thunder now, eh, lad? I had word from Old George that our first locomotive is nigh on ready. We s'l have her by April, in time to give her a trial run. You'll be there, won't you?'

'Try keeping me away,' Bendy grinned. 'But I shall insist on riding on the footplate. Now promise me!'

'Aye, aye, if tha likes. Tha's been in on it from't beginning, after all.' His eyes narrowed. 'But what's this I hear about your brother?'

Benedict looked wary. 'I don't know. What have you heard? I am the last person to ask, you know.'

'Oh, they say he's—' Hudson hesitated, a piece of delicacy so unusual in him that it made Bendy nervous. 'They say he's behaving queer,' Hudson said at last. 'Sent away all the servants and shut himself up in the house with only his wife and that lass to take care of him. I don't know what truth there is in it.' He hesitated again. 'There's other rumours flying about too, but I don't put any faith in 'em.'

'Of course, my brother always has behaved oddly – as you know, Hudson, as well as any man,' Benedict said. 'I haven't heard anything; but I have been very much occupied these last weeks.'

'Oh yes, and how is Mrs Benedict Morland?'

'Oh, tol-lol, you know. Her health is good, but her nerves are all to pieces. The last little one came early, and the doctor thinks this one might too, which makes us all anxious.'

'Aye, it's a worrying time for man and woman alike,' Hudson said with sympathy. 'Whenever my 'Lizbeth was carrying I was like a cat on a griddle. Which doctor does she see?'

'Cornwell. He has known Mrs Morland since childhood.'

'Ah, that's a comfort to you, then. I suppose you'd like a boy this time out?'

Benedict smiled. 'Everyone supposes the same. But my little Mary is such a piece of perfection, I'd be happy with another girl, if she turned out to be like her.'

Benedict had engaged the same midwife, Mrs Adale, for the confinement at the beginning of April; but in the event Rosalind went into labour a month early, and an urgent message to Mrs Adale found her still in attendance on her previous patient and unable to leave. A substitute had to be found from the village, and although Cornwell said that he had used her before, Benedict felt no confidence in her, perhaps simply because she was a substitute. Mrs Garden was a scrawny, underfed-looking woman with a sunken face and gums innocent of teeth except for two lone survivors, one up and one down, like hitching-posts. However it was, the second labour went much harder with Rosalind than the first, Cornwell shook his head a great deal, and Rosalind sent for Benedict halfway through the first stage to clasp his hand and bid him farewell.

'I know I am going to die,' she said, staring up at him with enormous eyes. 'I wanted to ask your forgiveness, and to beg you to be kind to my poor child – children, if this one should survive.'

Benedict struggled against tears, for her sake, exclaimed against such terrific ideas, kissed her tenderly upon her salty lips, and was soon driven from the room by the resumption of the pains. It was nearly midnight on the 3rd of March before Cornwell came downstairs, looking grey and tired, to say that the child was born, alive, and that Rosalind looked like remaining amongst the living for the time being.

'It has gone very hard with her, however, and I don't doubt but that her nerves will be very much disordered for some time. In any case, ladies generally have a stronger reaction after the second birth than after the first, and it will not be surprising if she feels very low in spirits for some weeks, if not months. You must do everything you can to cheer and comfort her, make light of any difficulties, and do not cross her in anything. Whatever she wants, let her have it. It would be the worst thing in the world for her to be fretted.'

Benedict could hardly have been more eager to comply with these instructions. 'Are you sure she is out of danger?' he asked anxiously.

'As sure as one can ever be in these cases,' Cornwell said lugubriously. 'Motherhood is a great trial; it can never be taken lightly.'

It was only as Benedict was going upstairs to see Rosalind at last that he remembered that in his concern for the mother he had asked nothing about the baby. Mrs Garden met him at the door of the chamber with a wide, untenanted smile and said, 'Now then, Maister, coom to see your wife and daughter, eh?'

'It's another girl, then?' Benedict said, wondering for an instant whether he felt glad or disappointed, and decided in the end that he was glad.

'Aye, didn't you know?' She snorted at the idea. 'As big a babby as I've ever seen in twenty years o' mid'ifing. It's no wonder her ladyship had a struggle! As big and fat as a baby seal! Nigh on ten pun', if I don't miss my guess!'

'But is my wife really all right?' Benedict asked, eager for a second opinion – or rather a second reassurance.

'Well, Maister, how'ud *you* feel?' Mrs Garden said with a ribald cackle.

Benedict did not want to think about that; he wished more fervently than ever that Mrs Adale had been free.

He went across to the bed, round which a screen had been placed to keep the light and the draught out. Rosalind was lying back against the pillows looking flattened and very tired. There were marks of strain about her eyes and mouth, and she looked suddenly ten years older.

'My darling,' he said, and ran out of words.

'Well, that's over,' she said, and closed her eyes wearily. 'Never again,' she muttered. 'I swear, never again.'

Benedict took her hand and lifted it to his lips. 'Whatever you wish,' he said humbly.

A tear seeped out from under her eyelid. 'You don't know what I've suffered,' she said pathetically.

'I wish I could have borne it for you,' he said, and her eyes snapped open.

'Oh, don't be ridiculous! And have a little pity for my nerves! Don't hang over me like that, it oppresses me. Have you seen the baby?'

'Not yet.'

'Another girl. I hoped for a boy this time.'

'I don't mind, darling. Another little girl like our own darling Mary – another little girl to grow up just like you.'

Rosalind pulled her hand free and turned away her head. 'Oh, go away,' she said. 'Please – just leave me alone. Let me rest.'

He left her, unwillingly, to the care of Mrs Garden, and outside found the nursery-maid, Hannah, holding Mary by the hand, coming towards him along the corridor.

'Papa, we are going to see the new baby,' Mary said importantly as soon as she saw him. They halted in front of him, and she looked up from under her silken fringe of curls. 'Hannah says it will be my sister all the time, until I am old and die and be an angel.'

'That's right,' Benedict said. 'A little sister for you, and a second daughter for me.'

'But *I* are your daughter,' Mary said anxiously.

'Yes, of course you are. You are my eldest daughter.'

'Your best one,' Mary insisted.

Benedict laughed. 'I suspect so. But we won't tell the new baby that. It wouldn't be kind.'

Mary nodded agreeably, happy now that the important point had been settled. She slipped her hand out of Hannah's and gave it to Benedict like one bestowing a great honour and said, 'You can come and see it too.' Hand in hand they walked along the corridor, Hannah following behind, to the dressing-room where the new baby had been installed. There, as it lay in the white muslin-covered crib which once Mary had occupied, they inspected it gravely for some time in silence. Then Mary said, 'It isn't very little. Not like a puppy.'

'No,' Benedict agreed. Indeed, the baby was very fat, bundled up like a bolster, with wide red cheeks, and rolls of flesh about its wrists like bracelets. 'You mustn't call her "it", though: she's a "she". Do you like her?'

Mary looked for a moment judiciously, and then said, 'Can I have a puppy instead?' She had been wanting a puppy for some time, but Rosalind had vetoed the idea.

'No, I think we had better keep the baby, now she's here,' Benedict said, controlling his smile.

'A' right,' said Mary equably. 'What shall we call her?'

'I don't know. What do you think?'

'Shall we call her Raditch, 'cos she's very red?'

'Radish isn't a very nice name for a little girl,' Benedict said, hearing Hannah stifling giggles behind her.

'I think it is nice.'

'What about Rose? Roses are red too,' Benedict suggested.

'Iss,' Mary said, nodding vigorously with agreement.

'Rose it is, then,' he said, thinking privately that at present, Radish really was the more appropriate name. Afterwards, when Mary had been taken back to the nursery, he realised that she had not asked a single question about her mother. How wonderful to have such a narrow field of vision, he thought; to be able to concentrate on one thing to the exclusion of all worries.

Later that day he met Mary again, when it was time for her riding lesson. Though she was not yet two, she was well-grown and strong for her age, and Benedict believed you could not start riding too early, if you were to excel at it. The difficulty with very small children was always to find a small mount that was narrow enough, for most ponies tended to be too broad for short baby legs. He had scoured the country again, and a dealer had advised him at last that the wild ponies of Dartmoor tended to be narrower than others, and when broken had tractable tempers. He had advertised, and the result was a black mare called Clover, eleven hands high, with a fine-boned face and elegant tail-carriage. Mary adored her from first sight. She had been riding for two months now, on a felt saddle, and with a special bridle whose reins were narrower and made of softer leather to suit her little hands. Benedict thought she was showing great promise. So far Rosalind had not been out to watch a lesson, for in the last two months she had been fretful and unhappy in her pregnancy, and spent most of the time lying on a sofa bewailing her loss of freedom and looks. Benedict was half glad she had not come out yet. He was afraid she might object to the sight of her daughter riding astride – but really, so young a child could not be taught any other way.

He told the groom to lead her round while he stood back to watch her from a distance, the better to judge her progress; and as he watched, he suddenly thought of Thomas, his son. He must be eight now. Was he riding yet? Probably he had been scrambling on and off farm horses for years, but would he learn to ride like a gentleman? Would he ever have a horse of his own? It was an odd thing, Benedict thought, that he was so close to them here, but it had never once crossed his mind to go and visit. Well, it would probably only unsettle them all.

They had a life without him now, and Thomas would have forgotten him. Probably he had younger brothers and sisters, as well. Better not to think about him. Benedict had his own life, too – and two children, two daughters.

'Daddee, I can go round on my own!' Mary shouted, half boasting, half imploring. The groom looked at him enquiringly. Benedict considered. Clover was quiet, and the ground was soft. If she fell off, it would be a valuable lesson: as the old saying went, it takes seven falls to make a horseman.

'All right,' he said to the groom, with a significant nod, meaning, 'Stay close.' The groom let go of the bridle and took his steadying hand from Mary's leg. Clover walked on a few paces, decided that work must be over, and put her head down to graze, and Mary fell off over her shoulder, very slowly, as though in stages. Benedict started towards her, Mary looked around her in astonishment, and deciding that she had been affronted, she let out a bellow, which made Clover breenge and jump away. The groom hurried to catch the mare while Benedict reached Mary and scooped her up.

'Are you hurt, chicken?' he asked through her yelling.

'No-o,' Mary said, unwilling to forgo the distinction.

'Then what are you crying for, silly little woman?' he said tenderly. 'Look, you frightened poor Clover. If you're going to be a horsewoman, you must remember never to make loud noises near them.'

'But if I are hurt?'

'We'll cross that bridge when we come to it. Never cry when you aren't hurt, my love. Do you know the story of the boy who cried "Wolf!"'

'What wolf?' Mary asked, intrigued.

'I'll tell it to you later, when you have your milk. Now, here's poor Clover come back. You had better get on again, to show her you still love her.'

He put Mary back in the saddle, pleased with himself for distracting her so that she had forgotten the fall, and would not now be nervous of falling again. But when he had settled her and put the reins into her hands, she said suddenly, 'Mama does.'

'Mama does what?'

'Mama does cry when she aren't hurt.'

'When does she?' Benedict asked, puzzled. 'When does Mama cry?'

'When she comes back when she rides.'

'But Mama doesn't go riding – well, not for a long time,' Benedict said. She had given up riding last September, when she had been sure she was pregnant again. He could make no sense of this, and Mary could not explain further. Indeed, her attention had passed on to something else now, and Benedict let it go, as something unimportant.

Rosalind did not spring back so readily as she did after giving birth to Mary. She remained in bed for a long time, and did not leave her room until April began; and even then came downstairs only to lie upon a sofa. She seemed depressed, and did not want to do anything to amuse herself, not walk, or sew, or read, or even converse much. She lay staring blankly out of the window for hours at a time, though when Benedict asked her if she felt well, she would say indifferently, 'Well enough,' and when he asked her if there was anything she wanted, she would sigh and say, 'Nothing, nothing at all.'

But as April passed towards May, the wet, cold weather improved a little, and she began to sit up more on the sofa and looked bored rather than listless, which he counted an improvement. 'Wouldn't you like to go visiting?' he asked. 'You haven't seen any of your friends for such a long time.'

'I can't bear to see anyone,' she said at first. 'I look such a fright.' But after a while her protestations became weaker, and she began to say she might think of paying a visit – but not yet.

Benedict had not forgotten his promise to Sibella to attend her ball if possible, and thinking that a trip to London might shake Rosalind out of her gloom, he suggested tentatively, without mentioning Sibella, that she might like to spend the few last weeks of the Season in the great metropolis.

'Oh no! I couldn't possibly. The journey would kill me. I could not go half so far,' was her immediate reaction. And, 'What pleasure would London be to me? I am past my gadding. I am an old married woman with two children. There can be no more jollity for the likes of me.'

But it was the very next day that he came into the saloon, where she usually sat in the mornings, and found her sitting up instead of reclining, and with much more colour in her cheeks. As he came in she was just stuffing something down the side of the sofa-cushion.

'What's that?' he asked mildly.

'Oh, nothing. Just my handkerchief. Mr Morland, I've been thinking that I would like to make a trip, but not to London.'

'Where then, my love? I'll take you anywhere you like.' He sat down opposite her and clasped his hands between his knees, gazing at her and thinking how very lovely she looked when her cheeks were flushed and her eyes bright. 'You're feeling better, aren't you?'

'Just a little.'

'And ready for some merry-making. I told you it was not all over, foolish one!'

'Ah, but the trip I want to make is not for pleasure, but for duty. That is, it will be a pleasure to me, of course, but – well, to make a long story short, I want to go and visit my father in Harrogate.'

'Oh.'

'Oh dear, please don't look like that! I know you don't like Papa, but you must own that I owe a duty to him.'

'Of course, my darling, I understand your wishes entirely.'

'And I haven't seen him since Mary was born, and now he is a grandfather of two, his own daughter ought to spare a few days to visit him.'

'I have no argument with you, my love. When do you wish us to go?'

'Good God, not "us"! I mean to go on my own,' she said with a laugh. 'Not for the world would I drag you all the way to Harrogate to wait on a man you despise.'

'Nonsense,' said Benedict. 'Of course I will go with you. In such a case as this, where your duty is clearly to pay your respects to your father, my private feelings are not important. I know what is right.'

She looked down at her hands and then up again, from under her eyelashes. 'Dearest, I would sooner go alone. It would make me uncomfortable if you were there, knowing how you feel. And Papa would be able to speak to me more frankly if he had me to himself. Please, Mr Morland, grant me this one thing. I want to have one last small time alone with him. I fear – I fear from his letters he may not have long left in this world.'

He was uneasy on her behalf, but could not deny her request, and her gratitude when he consented was enough to repay him for his fears. 'How long will you be gone?' he asked.

'A few days, only. I will go on Tuesday, if I may – and then I can come back on Saturday. You will hardly have time to miss me,' she added with a playful smile. 'Especially since you spend most of your day playing with the children. There now, that must be the final argument: you could not come with me and leave the children behind!'

He smiled obediently in response to her pleasantry. It was true that he spent a great deal of time with the children, and the servants were growing quite used to his unfatherlike behaviour. The baby was not as lively as

Mary had been, though that was perhaps understandable, given the harder time she had had of it, but still he liked to hold and rock her, and look into her face, and try to make her smile. Rosalind had agreed indifferently to the name Rose – though occasionally Benedict found himself on the verge of calling her Radish. One of the most pleasant things he did with the children was to sit on the floor playing games with Mary, while the baby lay on a rug in a patch of sunshine nearby, kicking slowly and blowing bubbles. If only Rosalind had been one of the group, everything would have been perfect.

But perhaps if she had been worrying about her father, the visit would settle her mind, and she would come back in a happier frame, and enjoy their company more. He saw her off on Tuesday feeling sorry and hopeful, and a little comforted by the fact that she was in her own carriage with her own coachman and their own horses: travelling easily, they would not need a change, for it was only twenty miles to Harrogate.

Even though she had not been much of a companion for several months past, the house seemed empty without her, and each room he entered reminded him of a hearth with no fire lit. It made him realise, with some dismay, what it would have been like had he lost her in childbed; he resolved when she came back to make doubly sure she knew how much he loved her, and to make even more strenuous efforts to see that she was contented and had everything she could want.

Afterwards, long afterwards, there were many things he remembered, tiny insignificant details about the sequence of events, which stuck in his mind like tiny slivers of broken glass catching the light, after you think they have all been swept up. He remembered, for instance, that he had stopped halfway across the back hall to fasten his boot-strap, which had come undone, when Barnes found him to give him the letter.

'This came by special messenger, sir, from Harrogate,' the butler said; and Benedict stood up hastily and reached out for the letter in dread, until he saw Rosalind's round, unformed hand on the cover. If she had been taken ill she would hardly have written herself to tell him of it. She must be writing to advise him what hour to expect her tomorrow. He opened the letter, flattened it out, and read it, dread changing to disappointment. It was addressed from the hotel where her father lived. She was well, was enjoying her father's company, but had a great many things to talk to him about, and would therefore not be coming home tomorrow. She would stay at least until Tuesday, perhaps a little longer if circumstances seemed to warrant it; knew her dear husband would understand and approve of this filial duty towards her only parent.

'Is the messenger still here?' he asked Barnes.

'No, sir. He said there was no answer and went away.'

Benedict stood irresolute for a moment; and then he thought, Harrogate is only twenty miles. No sense in sending a messenger. I will go myself and surprise her. The sun from the staircase window was throwing the pattern of the banisters across the hall floor, dark bars on black-and-white squares. He remembered that too, afterwards.

'Have Tonnant saddled, will you,' he said to the butler. 'And have some necessaries packed for me in a cloak bag. I am going to Harrogate for a few days. Perkins had better come with me in case I want to send the horses back: I might travel back with the mistress.'

'Very good, sir.'

'See to it, then, Barnes. I shall want to leave in half an hour. I shall go and say goodbye to Miss Mary first.'

Mary seemed unmoved by the news of his impending journey. Benedict thought she probably did not understand how long he would be away. 'Are you going to fetch Mama back?'

'Yes, poppet.' He scooped her up and kissed her, and she settled herself in his arms and reached out to test one of his coarse dark curls.

'When I'm growed up, Daddy, I will marry you,' she said magnanimously.

'You sound like Sibella,' Benedict laughed.

'What's Sibella?'

'Never mind. But I can't marry you, chicken, because I'm already married to Mama.'

'Praps you won't be when I'm growed,' she said, rolling the curl round her finger with intense concentration. 'What will you bring me back?' she asked, reverting to more important matters.

'From Harrogate? What would you like?'

'A puppy,' she said promptly.

At Fremlin's Hotel in Harrogate, Benedict left Perkins with the horses while he went inside. The proprietor came hurrying to meet him, seeing the quality of his clothes under the dust of the journey.

'My wife and father-in-law are staying here, and I wonder if you have room for me as well. My name is Morland. Mr Fleetham is my father-in-law.'

'Oh, yes sir, Mr Fleetham is one of our most valued guests. But your wife? I'm afraid Mrs Morland is not staying with us.'

'Oh? Well, perhaps you know where she *is* staying?'

'I'm afraid I don't, sir. I have not had the pleasure of speaking with Mrs Morland. Shall I send a message up to Mr Fleetham? He is in his room at this moment.'

'No need to trouble yourself,' Benedict said. 'I will just step up and speak to him myself, if you will kindly direct me to his room.'

A boy took Benedict up the stairs to Fleetham's room. When Benedict entered, he found Fleetham in his shirt sleeves standing in front of the fire drinking a glass of sherry. He had changed a little in the years since Benedict had last seen him. He seemed to have grown shorter, and his bulk harder, as though he were consolidating with age. His face was much redder, tending to purple on the nose, and his hair was both scanty and grey. At the sight of Benedict his face contracted to a fearful scowl, and the colour deepened on his slab-like cheeks.

'Good God, sir, what are you doing here? Come to make the reckoning? Come to demand satisfaction of me, have you? As if being condemned to live in this place ain't punishment enough. God damn it, sir, what do you want?'

'Be easy, sir,' Benedict said, taken aback, 'I shall not disturb you long. I should not have troubled you at all, if Fremlin had known where Mrs Morland is staying. If you will but give me her direction, I shall trouble you no further. Unless – that is, perhaps you have made arrangements to see her this evening?'

Fleetham stared at him in angry puzzlement. 'See her? What the deuce are you talking about? How the devil should I know where she is staying? Are you bosky?'

Benedict stiffened a little at the language. 'Since she came to Harrogate to visit you, I think my questions are not unreasonable. Or have you so little curiosity as not to want to know which hotel your daughter is staying at?'

'Came to see me? She did no such thing! After the way the ungrateful minx treated me, I've no wish to clap eyes on her ever again.'

Now Benedict was bewildered. 'Wait, please, let me understand you – are you saying that Rosalind has not been here, that you have not seen her?'

'Got it at last! No, she hasn't been here. Why should you think she had?'

'But – but – where is she, then?'

'How should I know?' Fleetham snapped with unpleasant relish. 'If you have mislaid your own wife, don't come bleating to me.'

Benedict was reduced to silence, his brain whirling.

Had she met with an accident on the way? But no, she had written from this direction, saying that she had much to talk to her father about. But he said he had not seen her. Was he lying, and if so, why? What was going on? Where was she?

Fleetham watched his bewildered face with contempt. 'I never liked you, Morland. You were an upstart. But she would have you – and your fortune came in, in the end. She was right about that. But giving up my home and living the rest of my life in Harrogate is too high a price. I'd have done better to go bankrupt. It would have been less of a dishonour than this.'

'But she said you wanted to live here,' Benedict said, struggling to cope with this fresh mystery as well.

'She said, she said,' Fleetham sneered. 'You'd have done well to pay more attention to what she did than what she said. Oh, go away, I've no patience with you! You'd better go and look for her. You won't find her here.'

Outside in the street Perkins was walking the horses up and down to keep them from getting chilled. He looked at his master's face as he emerged, and hastily schooled his own into complete immobility. When a master's face was set like that, it boded ill for the servant who caught his attention.

He found them quite by accident. He had sent Perkins off with the horses to find lodgings, and appointed a *rendez-vous* with him later; and then set off to make enquiries at all the principal hotels. Since Harrogate was a spa town, hotels were as plentiful as blackberries, and he had set himself no light task; but as he was waiting to cross the main street, he suddenly saw them, through the traffic, on the pavement opposite. It was growing dark, and there was a hint of rain on the light breeze, and they were walking along quickly as though anxious to be home.

The sight of them was a like a blow falling on a place

already bruised: there was no pain, only a sickening sense of damage. They were not behaving furtively, nor laughing together, not exhibiting either shame or great delight. Rosalind's hand was through Sir Carlton's arm and they leaned together and a little forward as they thrust against the damp wind; they looked tired. The worst thing of all, to Benedict, was that they looked so much like an accustomed couple, united in silent purpose without the need for smiles or conversation, as though they had been long married.

With the thought came anger at last, and anger released him. He hurried across the road, dodging the traffic, and followed them. They went a little way along the main street and then turned down a side road; he lingered cautiously at the corner, but looking back was not in their minds. They walked on a dozen yards and then turned up the steps of a quiet, decent-looking hotel. Now they were quarried, Benedict hurried forward, moving so rapidly that they were still standing in the vestibule, and Sir Carlton was shaking the rain drops from Rosalind's mantle while she inspected her skirt for damage. They both looked round as he came through the door, and froze in the positions they had just assumed. That was where similarity ended. Sir Carlton, on seeing who it was, looked weary to death, a little sick; Rosalind looked furious.

Sir Carlton moved first. He took two steps towards Benedict and said, low and urgent, 'Not here, I beg you. Come upstairs to my apartment.' It was well that he said 'my' apartment: had he said 'our', Benedict would probably have struck him. As it was, he was able, just, to realise the folly and indignity of attacking there and then in a public place, and after a moment nodded curtly. Miniott turned back to Rosalind; Benedict saw her look into his face and open her mouth to speak, and then saw her expression change. What Miniott's look was he could not tell, but the realisation that Sir Carlton could control her with a look devastated him. It was the beginning of his defeat. He followed them up the stairs with his anger draining away, leaving him each moment more helpless.

He was led into the sitting-room of a large apartment on the first floor. A fire was burning, a tray of decanters was set out, everything was homelike and comfortable. A door in the corner called his eye insistently, but he refused to look at it, knowing where it must lead. But as Miniott closed the door behind them, it was Rosalind who spoke first, rounding on Benedict in fury, her face contorted with rage.

'What are you doing here? Oh, why must you come following and spying on me every minute? You have ruined everything with your horrid spying!'

Sir Carlton stepped between them. 'Go into the other room,' he said quietly, but with absolute authority. 'I must speak to Morland alone.'

'If you are going to talk about me I have the right to hear,' she said indignantly; but Sir Carlton was unmoved.

'Do as I say,' he said, still quietly, steadily. 'Go in to the other room. I will call you when it is your turn to speak.'

There was even humour in the last words, but none in his face; Rosalind gave him a baffled look, and turned and went out with a toss of her head. Benedict watched her go as he might have watched a loved one led away to the condemned cell; part of him knew then that he would never see her again.

When the door had closed, Sir Carlton turned to him. His face was grave, and he looked old and very tired.

'What can I say, except that I wish this had not happened? No, there is nothing I can say which is equal to the injury I have done you. Say what you will to me, and I will listen patiently.'

Benedict heard his words first with astonishment, and then with utter dismay. The last of his anger seeped away in the face of this meek acknowledgement of error. Had

Miniott blustered, Benedict might have raged, might even have been able to knock him down, in which there would have been some satisfaction; instead he felt a growing dread inside him, something cold and insistent which, like a malignant tumour, he feared would destroy him. He looked unwillingly into the older man's eyes, and read there his own knowledge, which he had assiduously denied to himself. This was no casual affair; this was love – and not a new love.

'What have you done?' he said in the low tone of horror.

'I can't excuse myself,' Miniott said. 'I can only say that I have loved her since she was a little girl – since she was ten years old, and looked me saucily in the eye and called me by my surname to see if it would annoy me. She was so fresh, and full of innocent high spirits. I watched her grow up, loving her more every year. You did not know her at fifteen, at seventeen. I would have married her if I could, but I could never have afforded her. My affairs are badly involved, and her father—' He shook his head hopelessly. 'When you came on the scene, I wished you well, because I knew you could never succeed any more than I could. Fleetham wanted a fortune for his treasure, and who could blame him?'

'Don't,' said Benedict – feebly, like a helpless victim trying to ward off another blow.

'Then Fleetham lost all his money – was more in debt than I was. Now I was not so mean a suitor. I would have kept her from starving at least. I made my offer; but she laughed, and said she would not marry me. Would not—' He closed his eyes and passed his hand across them. 'Would not marry me. Oh God!'

Benedict stared, unable to speak. The dread was consuming him, cell by cell, spreading towards his heart. Miniott removed his hand from his face, leaving behind a trace of moisture. 'I thought she would relent at last, but then you came back with your promise of wealth. What could I do? I couldn't tell you. I hoped all would be well.' He stopped, swallowing hard, and then went on rapidly, as though there were things he must say before time or his courage failed him. 'You must blame me entirely. It is all my fault, everything. Whatever has happened, I could have prevented if I had been stronger. There's no excuse for me. I should have resisted, but I was weak – utterly culpable! I am the only guilty one. You must not blame Rosalind.'

Benedict stirred. 'Don't,' he said through clenched teeth, 'don't you dare to speak her name to me.' And then he moaned with pain as the memories came back to him, clues he could have followed, hints he should have been able to piece together. 'I have been such a fool,' he said aloud. 'Such a blind, self-satisfied block. How long, Miniott? How long? All the time we have been married?' Sir Carlton made no answer, standing straight and looking at him, not in defiance or shame or even sorrow, now, but with the patience of death.

But now there was a distraction: Rosalind, unable to bear her banishment from the scene, burst in again. She had taken off her bonnet and her lovely hair was tumbled and a little damp at the ends, and there were the marks of tears on her cheeks. She rushed at Benedict in a passion, and before he could steady himself had struck him such a blow that it rocked him off his balance.

'You've spoiled everything! Oh, you selfish, selfish brute!' She struck him a perfect flurry of blows, and he caught her by the arms in the middle of it and diverted them harmlessly to his chest.

'Rosalind, don't! What are you doing?'

'Everything would have been all right,' she went on crying, 'if you had just done what I told you to. Why couldn't you stay at home out of the way? Why did you have to come following me and spying on me and spoiling everything?' And she made an inarticulate sound of rage, and dealt him one last strengthless blow on the chest.

He looked at her with pain and astonishment, seeing in her face thwarted fury and tearful self-pity, but not the least acknowledgement of error. She did not know or understand the enormity of what she had done. She had been thwarted in her pleasures, that was all. He had been right to say goodbye to her in his heart when she left the room that last time. The Rosalind he had loved had disappeared then. This was the real woman, and he had never seen her before.

Miniott had stepped forward, and was hesitating, wanting to help Benedict, but afraid that touching her in his presence might be even more of an affront. At last he said, 'Mrs Morland, control yourself. Be still!'

Rosalind was sobbing now, more in anger than grief. 'You never loved me!' she raged through her tears; one last outburst before she obeyed.

And then, looking from her to Miniott, Benedict somehow arrived at the final knowledge. A breaking wave of pain engulfed him. It was Miniott he looked to, not the weeping woman he still held by the elbows.

'Since before we were married, then?' he said. His pain was mirrored in the other man's face; there was no triumph in Miniott. He wished the past undone as desperately as Benedict could; he wished the next words unsayable.

'Mary – Mary is not mine.' Benedict looked down at the woman, and hardly knew who she was. Dazed, he set her away from him, carefully, courteously, removing his hands only when he knew she had her balance, and then turned away from them both towards the door.

'Benedict, where are you going?' Rosalind cried; and Miniott hastened towards him.

'Morland, for God's sake—' he began urgently; but Benedict shook his head.

'I can't,' he mumbled, like a fighter who had been struck too often. 'I can't now. Let me be.'

And Miniott fell back and let him go, and he fumbled

with the door-knob and made his escape, hearing the woman still calling to him in rising anger; but the cries were like the shrieks of a seabird, and carried no meaning to him. They were just sounds.

CHAPTER TWENTY-FIVE

Perkins found Benedict at last sitting on a bench in the gardens. He had not been at the *rendez-vous*, and the man had searched with increasing alarm; he had been on the brink of seeking out the constable when he saw the hunched shape through the darkness and hurried over.

'Sir, you're wet through,' he discovered. Benedict looked up unseeingly, and, shocked, Perkins said, 'Are you all right, sir? Has something happened? Have you been robbed?'

He received no answers, and seeing the state of exhaustion his master was in, took the liberty of ascertaining quickly that there were no obvious injuries, and then helped him to his feet. 'I've got rooms at the George, sir. Let me help you back there.'

Benedict went with him unresistingly, like a tired child. Once in the hotel chamber Perkins looked after him as he would one of his horses after a long day in the field, stripped off his clothes, bathed him, fed him some hot wine and a little cold meat, and put him to bed with a hot brick at his feet. Then he tended the fire, wrapped himself in his cloak, and settled himself in an armchair, in case he should be wanted. He was woken once in the night by the sound of Benedict weeping quietly, but after a moment's consideration decided it was kindest to pretend he had not heard, and went to sleep again.

In the morning Benedict woke early, to the vague sense of impending doom which briefly preceded the remembering of yesterday. A sickening grief overwhelmed him, and he closed his eyes and wished for sleep again, but sleep was gone. Instead he found himself unable to stop going over and over all the hurtful, shameful things: how she had not wanted to go hunting, for instance, until Miniott persuaded her, and how they had gone missing after the first draw. All those mornings she had gone carriage-visiting – who was it she had visited? And her morning rides alone – where had she ridden to? He would never know when and how often he had been deceived, or whether any of the things she had said to him were true. Her loving words, her loving actions in the precious hours of darkness – had they, too, been lies? Did she say the same things to *him*, do the same things – ah no, he couldn't think about that! If he thought of her in Sir Carlton's embrace, there would be murder in his heart.

He remembered suddenly little Mary saying that Mama cried when she came back from riding; the thought was agony. Did she, then, care for Miniott so much? Or were they the fretful tears of the spoiled child at her pleasure's curtailment? But he must not think about children either – and yet he could not help it. Mary, born six weeks prematurely – he remembered Cornwell's warning words, and the unsteadiness of the doctor's eyes as he spoke them. She had been with child already when they married – that, of course, was why she had wanted to marry so quickly. Probably Fleetham knew, and that was what changed his mind. Indeed, everyone in the world probably knew, he thought in a passion of shame, and laughed at him.

And Rose – Rose was born a month early. In June, then, before the Coronation Ball? She had taken him back into her bed as soon as she knew, to cover her sin. Oh God, he had been the easiest, most complacent cuckold in the world! He swaggered in his horns, while the world laughed behind his back!

He thought of Rosalind, of her beauty and high spirits.

Like the epitome of shallowness himself, he had fallen in love with golden curls and long eyelashes and a tiny waist, with the impression of childlike innocence such beauty created. He had behaved like an idiot, like a man without intellect or reason or judgement. He made her up in his mind to be what she was not: a goddess, a creature of infinite wisdom – the perfect woman. Looking back on his own behaviour these six years past, he was ashamed of how little he had tried to know the object of his adoration. Well might Rosalind cry 'You never loved me!' Miniott, knowing her as an innocent, high-spirited child, had gone on loving her, wistfully, when her adult appetites had outstripped her childish comprehension. Rosalind was not a woman, but a child grown old.

But what to do? The hurt and angry part of him wanted to strike out wildly, to banish her, to say to Miniott, 'You keep her, then, since you wanted her so much! I want nothing more to do with her!' Ah, but there was more to it than that. If she were to leave him and go to Ledsham, everyone would know how he had been served. Everyone would *know*, rather than just suspect. The shame, the humiliation – the pitying eyes, the secret laughter! He could never hold up his head again. And Rosalind – she would be expelled from society, and society was the sole thing she craved. Even if he were to divorce her (and the expense! the public ritual of shame!) and Miniott to marry her, they would still, all three, be involved in the most hideous and disgusting of scandals.

And, much, much more to the point, so would the children. Rose was still too young to remember her mother if she went away now, but Mary would miss her and grieve. Though Rosalind had not had so much to do with Mary as Benedict had, she was fond of her, and Mary idolised her beautiful mother. How could he deprive them of each other? And how could he condemn Mary to growing up motherless, and to all the shame and pain of eventually discovering, as one day she must, her mother's frailty.

No, it was unthinkable. Separation or divorce were both unthinkable. The only alternative was concealment. He had married Rosalind by his own choice, without finding out what manner of woman she was, and the blame was to him as much as to her; she was his wife, and he must somehow find the way to keep her respectable. He sat up in bed, his mind busy now, planning. He would have to interview them today and discuss what was to be done. It was a horrid thought, and he shrank from it, but it must be done – and therefore, the sooner the better. In the chair nearby Perkins was asleep, snoring softly as his head had fallen back at an awkward angle. He smiled a little. That was a good man, worthy of advancement; and his sad heart was warmed a little at the realisation that while mere duty might have brought him home and put him to bed, only affection would have sat up beside him, when there was a perfectly good bed waiting on the next floor.

He interviewed Rosalind alone. Rosalind, subdued now, her face drawn with the effect of tears and a sleepless night, seemed to have come to come realisation of her crimes. She sat with her hands in her lap and looked at Benedict, if not meekly, at least cautiously.

'Why did you do it?' he said – uselessly, stupidly, but still he felt driven to, wanting to know what he could never understand.

'How can you ask?' said she, as if it were a simple surprise. 'He is so charming, so sophisticated – such a man of the world.' She looked at him with something approaching pity. 'You were just a boy. I could see you adored me, but you were like all the other young men. Except—' She paused, frowning.

'Except what?'

She shook her head, unable to define it. 'There was one time – at the races – when you asked me to marry you. I thought then that you seemed different. If only we could

537

have married then, I think we would have been happy. Oh, I don't know.' She shrugged away the intangible. 'I didn't mean to make you unhappy, you know; but I couldn't help it. I meant to be a good wife to you, but I'd always been mad for Sir Carlton – all the girls were – and he was there, and—' She shrugged, as though it were a matter that needed no further explanation. 'I'm sorry,' she added.

Benedict looked at her tiredly. 'Yes, I think perhaps you are, just a little. Well, Mrs Morland, what are we to do? You are still my wife, after all.'

'Do you mean to cast me off?' she asked in a small voice.

He shook his head. 'I have spoken to Miniott, and he has agreed to sever the relationship.'

'Yes, he told me,' she said, her voice yet smaller. Did she find it humiliating that her lover had agreed to abandon her?

'It must be hushed up, for everyone's sake. We must appear a loving couple. No-one must know what has happened.' He eyed her closely. 'Does anyone else know?'

'Only Betty,' she said, and then added, 'and Paterson, of course. He drove me, and held the horses when I rode.'

Benedict closed his eyes a moment. 'Well, I suppose they must know how to hold their tongues, if they've done it so so far.' They would have to be sent away – he could not live with their knowledge – but they must be treated generously, so as not to provoke them to spiteful gossiping. He must pay for his wife's reputation – he must wear his horns with generosity. 'You have not spoken of it to any of your friends? Mrs Coulsdon, for instance, or Miss Phillips?'

'No,' she said. 'Of course not. Anyway, I've hardly seen any of them for months now.'

An unfortunate reminder – she had been seeing him, of course, when she had said she was visiting them. He looked at her in pity for her frailty, as he might have looked at a hunchback or a lame person; and it was this that made him realise that he still loved her. My God, it was true! It was not the same love – how could it be? – but it was perhaps a better love, based on reality and not on conceit. He wanted to keep and protect her, and to make her better, and those were not the impulses of indifference.

He would have to detach her from her old associates, and find a way of keeping her innocently occupied. It was too much to hope that she would occupy herself with her children: she must have society; he must involve her in a new circle of friendship. 'This is what we shall do,' he said. 'We shall go at once to London for the last few weeks of the Season.' That should give her enough immediate diversion to take her mind off her separation from Sir Carlton. 'And when we come back, we shall shut up Fleetham Manor and move into Makepeace House. There is always plenty to do in York. It will keep you busy.'

She looked a little strained. 'But – will we never live at Fleetham again?'

'I don't know,' Benedict said. 'Frankly, at the moment I would like to sell it and never see the place again; but I will do nothing in haste. We will need a country place for the summer, for the children's sake. We can rent somewhere until we decide where to settle.'

She was silent. He was being generous, she knew – more generous than she had any right to expect. That 'we decide' for instance – how many men would have said that, instead of 'I'? And yet – and yet – she could not help wishing he was more of a man and less of a boy. His generosity she saw as weakness. If he had been a real man, he would have called Sir Carlton out and killed him, burned down Fleetham Manor, locked her up in her room, perhaps beaten her. How could she respect a man so gentle – almost feminine in his ways? And if she did not respect him, how could she help deceiving him?

But he was a good man, and she wanted to be good to him. She must try. 'Very well,' she sighed. 'Just as you wish.'

He fixed her with a serious look. 'And you will not see Sir Carlton again.'

But there was just the hint of a question mark in the statement. She lowered her eyes demurely, her eyelashes making soft, dark fans on her cheeks. 'Of course not,' she said.

The visit to London seemed to Benedict afterwards to have been a dream, and not always a delightful one. The hotel, the streets, the shops, the crowds – and the Season was a full one – the sights of London did not fit comfortably into the spaces of his mind; everything seemed to have an odd, praeternatural brightness, like things seen in the strange light just before the breaking of a storm. Rosalind moved in this odd illumination too, rimmed with a doomed brightness. He saw her as though through glass, swimming slowly in an air he could not breathe; sometimes when she turned and looked at him, and smiled or spoke, he could not hear her words. He felt that he was divided from her, could not reach her, and yet wanted to snatch her back from the nemesis which was hurrying down on her, which she had not perceived.

They walked, shopped, went to the theatre, visited the exhibitions, showed themselves in all the fashionable lounges, drove in the Park at the hour of promenade. She seemed happy, and he gave her credit for concealing the recent unhappy events and behaving towards him in public as naturally and affectionately as if nothing had happened. She was even affectionate to him in private, and he tried to respond to her and play the part of fond husband, but he felt he had little success in it. Their hotel room had but the one bed, and lying as far from her as

540

possible each night was a sore trial to him; but one night she moved close to him in the darkness, put her arms round his neck, kissed him. He struggled against his feelings, reminding himself of what she was and what she had done, but his body and his mind were not of one opinion. Afterwards he felt bad, very bad about it. He wondered what had been her motive, whether affection or pique or merely the idea that it would make things easier between them; but he could not ask her. In the daylight he could not speak to her of such things, and she seemed oblivious of what had passed in the night; in the darkness, his traitor body responded to what it had loved, and his mind stood apart, bleeding and panting like a torn hart.

And so the day came for Sibella's ball – the last day, also of their stay. The house that Sir John had hired was a good one, in Mount Street, and the throng was phenomenal. When their carriage drew up, they were twenty carriages at least from the awning, and it was an hour before they were walking up the staircase and hearing their names announced.

'Mr and Mrs Benedict Morland.'

Sir John clasped his hand ecstatically – large, red-faced, beaming with accomplished pride, a gigantic diamond pin in his neckcloth glittering fit to dazzle. 'So glad you could come! Wouldn't have had you miss this for the world. And this is your lady? By God, young Morland, you've picked a winner! How d'ye do, my dear? You won't mind if a bluff old fellow tells you you're the prettiest thing he's seen in a Season, I hope? No harm meant – not the least! Delighted to make your acquaintance at last!'

Rosalind smiled her willingness to be complimented, while Lady Mary looked pained and greeted them with the most severe propriety. Benedict, glancing at his wife with Sir John's eyes, had to agree she was as beautiful as ever, golden curls, blue eyes, delicately flushed cheeks, white shoulders and bosom, tiny waist – as beautiful as a porcelain figurine – as beautiful as an expensive doll.

She was every little girl's dream of beauty, he thought wistfully. Perhaps she had been her own.

And now she was greeted by Sibella, and Sibella was turning eagerly towards him. How extraordinary! Sibella had stepped out of the storm-edged, strangely lit bubble that enclosed the rest of the world, and she alone was real, and there, and solid. She was holding out her hand in her usual frank way, but looking into his face with an enquiring anxiousness. She was a piece of normality so fresh and immediate it was painful to touch her and speak to her, as though his soul was newly shelled and tender.

'I'm so glad you came!' she said. 'But you have been ill! What is it?'

'No, no, not ill,' he said quickly. He saw he must tell her something, for she continued to look at him in that disturbed, disturbing way, as if she could read the words written on his heart. 'There have been troubles – private things. All over now.'

She allowed herself to be appeased, though her brow was still faintly troubled. She said, 'Mrs Morland is as beautiful as you said.' She turned her frank smile on Rosalind. 'He spoke so warmly of you, ma'am, but I see he did not say half enough! Thank you for coming to my ball. It is most good in you.'

Rosalind said something – Benedict was surprised at the coolness of her tone, and tore his eyes from Sibella's face to look at her, but she was already turning away, moving off to make room for the next comers. Benedict felt the silent pressure behind him and paused only to clasp Sibella's hand again (it was still as hard and strong as a boy's, he noted with an inward smile) and say, 'May I hope for the honour of a dance with you? Or am I out of the running, now I am an old married man?'

'I will dance with you with pleasure. The fourth or fifth – I'm not sure. I will give you a sign when to come for me,' she said in a businesslike way, and then released his hand as firmly as she had taken it, signifying his time was at an end. He walked on, a little ruefully, to rejoin his wife. Little Sib was growing up, and looked likely to prove as formidable as her father in her own way.

Their dance came. Rosalind had a partner and so was taken care of, and he went and claimed Sibella's hand with an easy conscience. She seemed a little preoccupied, and they stood in the set in silence for a time. Then he felt he ought to make conversation, and said, 'I suppose you will be tired of hearing this by now, but I must tell you how beautiful you look tonight.'

She looked up sharply out of her thoughts. 'Oh, don't,' she said.

'Don't what?'

'Don't flummery. I'm tired of being told I'm beautiful. I never was before, and it being my ball doesn't make any difference. I'm just plain little Sib, as I always was. Don't *you* spout polite lies. I expect better than that of you, Benedict.'

Benedict was surprised by a number of things in that speech, and had to assemble his thoughts. 'It wasn't flummery,' he began, but she wouldn't let him off.

'Your wife is beautiful, and if you know that, you can't be blind to the difference between us.'

'I am aware of the differences between you – no-one could be more so,' he said. She glanced at him in surprise, and he realised the tone of his voice had been inappropriate. 'Nevertheless, I can say you are beautiful with absolute truth. There is more than one kind of beauty. A horse and a rose can both be lovely, though they don't look anything alike.'

She seemed amused. 'Well, now, I know which of us is which. And to say truth, I don't much mind being called a horse. To my mind, the horse is the most beautiful part of creation.'

Bendy grinned. 'I didn't mean that, as you well know,

Miss Minx, but now you come mention it, I do think you are beautiful in much the way a horse is: gleaming and bright-eyed and graceful and strong – and lovely inside, too, the way a horse is. The soul is as important as the hide, wouldn't you say? God made horses good, and that's why we love them.'

'Gleaming and bright-eyed and – what was the rest of it? Now that's a compliment I can treasure,' she said, smiling up at him. 'I shall write it down in my journal.' Looking down into her near, warm, living face, he felt a mixture of tears and warmth, as though he wanted to smother her with kisses and pick her up in his arms the way he did Mary, both at the same time.

'Oh, Sibella,' he said, and couldn't go on.

'Yes,' she said, and it was somehow an answer to the things he hadn't said, whatever they might have been. She looked away, searching for someone or something in the crowd; and then back at him. 'She is certainly beautiful *outside*,' she said, with faint emphasis. 'Was that the trouble you talked of?' He stared almost in panic – how could she know? What had she heard? 'Oh, don't worry,' she said candidly, 'I don't know anything. But you were rather wearing your face on the outside when you first came in.'

'Sibella,' he said desperately, 'I can't talk to you like this. It isn't right. It isn't – *possible*.'

She grinned an urchin grin. 'But it's me talking to you, not vice versa. And we'll stop now if it makes you uncomfortable. Just so long as you remember that I am your friend. And you are mine. You came to my ball – you kept your promise. I shan't forget that. Now do stop looking like a poll-axed bullock, and smile at me as people smile at balls. Shall we meet again tomorrow? I ride in the Park every morning – do you? It's poor sport, but the best we can manage in Town. They say one can gallop in Richmond Park, but it's too far to go for just an hour, and I never seem to have much more than that to spare. There are so many invitations, and one can't refuse them all.'

'Dear Sib, how grand you sound!' he said, coming to life again.

'Do I? Oh, but I long to be home again! I have enjoyed my Season *very* much, but I miss the countryside. And I can't believe my brother is exercising Rocket properly. I told the grooms they mustn't ride him, because they'll ruin his mouth.' She grinned mischievously. 'Mama says that if I talk about horses in the ballroom I shall never get a husband.'

'Haven't you had any offers? I hope your father hasn't wasted his money.'

'Oh, I've had dozens of offers,' she said easily, 'but none that I'd accept. Fortunately, none of them was what Mama thinks of as suitable, so we shan't quarrel about it. But she is disappointed. Papa doesn't mind, because he'd like to keep me at home, but Mama thinks I haven't tried hard enough, and there are only five balls left: unfortunately, says Mama, and thank God, say I!'

They reached the top of the set and he took her in his arms to dance down. There was a wicked gleam in her eyes as he looked down into her face, and he felt himself smiling, and could not resist saying, 'I'm glad you haven't accepted any offers. You wouldn't talk to me in this comfortable way if you were an engaged miss – you'd do nothing but talk about the glories of your fiancé.'

'Ha!' she said triumphantly, and he was left to determine for himself what she meant by that.

In bed that night, as they lay without touching in the darkness, waiting for sleep, Rosalind said out of nothing, 'Is that the Miss Leytham you spoke of before? Or are there others?'

'There are others, but Sibella was my special friend.'

'But she must have been quite a child.'

'Yes; in pigtails.'

'She's very young for her age even now,' Rosalind said,

and it sounded disapproving. There was a long silence, and then she said judiciously, 'Her eyes are fine, but she hasn't another good feature in her face. They will never get her off their hands.'

Benedict preferred not to answer that. He made his breathing regular and heavy, hoping she would think he was asleep; he did not want her to turn towards him tonight, not tonight. And lying very still and breathing regularly, he very soon was asleep, and knew nothing more until the next morning.

Coming home there was Mary's delight to warm him, and the news of Rose's fresh progress, and Fleetham House did not seem quite so oppressive as he had expected; but still it roused painful memories in him, and he did not want to stay here, not yet. The next thing in the calendar was the opening of the York and North Midland Railway on the 29th of May – only two days away – and then in June there was Mary's birthday – they should stay here for that, he thought. And after that – well, it would be absurd to be taking the family to live in York at this time of the year, just when everyone else was moving outwards. Perhaps they might all go away somewhere for the summer, to Scarborough, perhaps, or Brighton – somewhere with sea-bathing for the children and a sufficiency of society to entertain Rosalind: no use thinking of a quiet country house. Then in September they could come back to York and move into Makepeace House, and he could decide what to do in the long term.

He had thought he would have painful feelings about Mary and Rose – particularly about Mary – and so he did. But as soon as he saw Mary in the flesh again, and she ran to him with her arms out and her imploring cry of 'Daddeee!', he knew that the painful knowledge made no difference to their relationship. She was his Mary just as before, herself and nothing more or less, and he could not love her any differently, or even feel with any essential part of himself that he was not her father. He might have deluded himself to ease the pain – told himself that Cornwell had spoken no more than the truth, that Mary was born six weeks before time and that was that – but the cold and intellectual part of his mind knew the truth. Yet the truth did not touch that little dragonfly-darting, bright and laughing creature. She was who she was, and fatherhood was more than being a progenitor. He was her father in everything that mattered; and when he had a spare fraction of his brain to think it, he hoped that Joe Thompson felt the same way about little Thomas.

The great day arrived, and dawned fair, one of those perfect, clear summer days that occur once in a while to gladden men's hearts: a sky of deep blue, the colour of chicory-flower and polished like crystal; a fresh, transparent warmth from the sun, and a little gentle breeze from the north east for invigoration. The whole of York was *en fête*, with bunting and flags in all the main streets, the Minster bells ringing, and everyone out and about in their holiday clothes. York's vast collection of inns did a brisk trade from early in the morning, and in the street pie-sellers and hot-chestnut merchants did their best to soak up the liquid exuberance.

The particular events of the day began with a massive breakfast at the Mansion House for the Directors of the York and North Midland, the shareholders, and the most distinguished of the guests. Benedict had his shoulder clapped so often on his way up the steps he began to feel bruised; at the top of the steps he met Harry Anstey, with Celia on his arm, held up by the bottleneck of the door and the receiving line.

'Bendy! There you are!' Harry cried in great good-humour. Celia smiled at him, but did not speak. She seemed to Benedict diminished, her sweet beauty dimmed. A third miscarriage last summer had led the doctor to decree that there should not be another attempt. Her son, Arthur, was five years old and sturdy: what need had they, Harry had declared, for any more? But either the physical strain or the spiritual sorrow seemed to have drawn her youthful spirits out of her: she had dwindled into a middle-aged wife.

'What a great day this is!' Harry went on. 'Did you ever believe it would come? When we were little boys, just back from visiting the coalfield tramways in Northumberland—'

'It all seemed an impossible dream then,' Benedict agreed. 'But here we are – and you never wavered for an instant, did you, old fellow?'

'Nor you – nor our illustrious Lord Mayor. Listen to him!'

From inside they could hear Hudson's harsh, booming voice, greeting, laughing, exclaiming – growing more consciously broad as he expanded into this supreme moment of his triumph. 'This time next year, Ah tell thee! No, no, Ah woan't listen to doom-sayers like thee, Arnold Catchpole! Ah was reet all along, and Ah'll be reet about this an' all! This time next year, there'll be four trains a day from York to London Town, Ah swear by this head! Two hundred and seventeen mile o' permanent way, uninterrupted. And Ah tell thee what else, an' all – it'll be a dom sight quicker than 'at twenty-hour journey we've been talkin' of an' promising folks!' An inaudible comment from someone and a burst of roaring laughter. 'Aye, aye, y' can laff all y' like, but the locomotives'll be doin' forty mile an hour next year. You'll see who's reet!'

'He's in high form,' Benedict said, smiling, as they shuffled forward. 'And of course he's right. When something quite new is brought out, like the railway, it gathers momentum far more rapidly than anyone expects. We believe the trains may soon run at twenty-five miles an hour, because we know they can go at twenty now; Hudson imagines that by next year it may be forty; but the reality will probably be nearer sixty – maybe more.'

548

'And it won't just be trains to London, but to Edinburgh as well,' Harry agreed. 'London the foot and Edinburgh the head, with York as the heart in the middle!'

They were through into the vestibule now, and Benedict fell silent as he looked around at the splendid surroundings, the vast chandelier above, the crimson carpet, the smartly dressed people all wreathed in smiles as they edged forward to be received by Hudson, vast and beaming and gleaming in his mayoral gold chain, teetering back and forth on his toes in his tight shiny patent-leather boots. Through the great doors, out of sight, a band was playing, and he could just see the end of a table, spread with a white cloth and a glittering freight of silver and china, flowers and fruit. In a little while they would all be at their places, eating, drinking, laughing, toasting – ham and beef and pickled tongue, kedgeree and game pie and sausages, porter and claret and burgundy and champagne – a throng of prosperous men and women rejoicing at the biggest and most important Christening of their lives.

But there was another scene in his mind, of a raw gash in the earth, the subcutaneous layers of chalk and clay and sandstone shockingly exposed to the air like the inside of a body at a post-mortem. He saw the barrow-runs, slippery with yellow mud, and the earth-coloured men cursing their way up them with cracking muscles and sweat-slicked faces; weary horses leaning to their harness, floundering for a foothold, their tails like many-stranded mud-soaked cords. He heard the gigantic, thought-flattening boom of blasting, the bitter smell of gunpowder-smoke, the rattle and rush and roar of cascading rocks and stones and soil. He saw men white-faced under their tan and silent under the pain of torn muscles, broken limbs, bleeding faces, missing fingers, crushed feet; he saw men dead and buried in a grudging churchyard far from their homes, their broken bodies laid out as the price of those gleaming rails running like inevitable fate to the horizon.

He came back from his reverie as Harry asked him a question, and had to ask for it to be repeated.

'I hope Mrs Morland is well? I had thought to see her here, but perhaps it is too soon after her confinement.'

'She's very well, thank you, and quite recovered from the birth. But she is not much interested in railway trains,' Benedict said, keeping his voice carefully neutral. It had been the cause of a quarrel between them that still hurt him in memory: he had tried to press her to come with him to the opening ceremonies, and she had accused him of not trusting her out of his sight.

'I gave you my promise, but you mean to keep me under your eye every minute, as though I were a criminal!' she had cried hotly. 'You can't think how it pains me to have my word doubted. Well, if you do not trust me, I shall act accordingly. If I am to be treated like a criminal, I may as well act like one.'

It had taken a long time to calm her down, and assure her that he had wanted her to come only because he thought she would enjoy it. At last it had been settled between them that she would spend the day in her own way, but come to the ball that evening at the Mansion House. He had left her all compliance and smiles, but the quarrel had hurt him, and the soreness lingered. Worse was to come, however: all through the breakfast, and afterwards when the guests streamed out to the waiting throng of carriages to be carried to the railway station for the inaugural journey, he kept scanning the company in vain for Sir Carlton Miniott. Sir Carlton was a shareholder and a close friend of Hudson, an early convert to the York and North Midland faith and a fervent adherent. He ought to have been on the top table, but Benedict could not see him anywhere. There was an infinity of possible reasons for his absence, including the chance that he had not come because he knew Benedict would be there. It hurt Benedict deeply that he should suspect even for a second that Miniott's absence had anything to

550

do with Rosalind's; but the suspicion did cross his mind, even though he dismissed it at once. He would not be the suspicious, unforgiving brute of Rosalind's morning tirade; but he realised, miserably, that this was the way his life would be from now on. Whether Rosalind was innocent or not, he was never going to be able to feel easy when he was away from her.

Aglaea sat beside the bed watching Nicholas sleeping. She was very tired, but she knew that if she got up and left him to go to her own room, even if she moved away to stretch her legs, he would wake and cry out for her. Jemima was asleep on the truckle bed on the other side of the room, as far from the fire as possible, for the room was stifling hot; despite the warmth of the day outside, Nicholas was taken with violent fits of shivering if the fire sank down. Jemima, good girl that she was, would willingly have taken over the vigil from Aglaea, if Nicholas would permit it; as it was, she was there to support Aglaea, and run errands.

At least he was quiet now; he had been raving earlier, and only a terrifying fit of choking had quieted him. When he slept, she could at least doze and drift, which restored her a little. She had lost track of how many days it had been since she last slept properly in her own bed. She had gone beyond sleepiness into a realm of tiredness which had its own laws; where it seemed life could sustain itself at this diminished level for ever.

He stirred and muttered, and her attention sharpened for a moment, but he did not wake. He was so thin he looked almost transparent against the pillows, white and delicate like some underwater thing; blue-shadowed about the eyes, and across the forehead where the great veins lay. His hands, too, lying on the outside of the sheet, were thin and blue-white and brittle, like the ghosts of starfish she had seen washed up on the beach at Scarborough – a thousand years ago, in another life. Sometimes lately she felt as though she were under water, drawn back and forth by the tide of his waking and sleeping; the medium in which she lived seemed denser than air, full of the drifting motes of his thoughts, and the looming, shapeless sea-monsters of his fears, half perceived in the dimness at the limit of vision.

She had watched him worsen through the winter, and gradually a foolish but beguiling notion had come to her: that he was stronger, more reasonable, more attached to the world when things were going badly on the railway; weaker in body and reason when things surged ahead. It was a mad idea, but in this house madness seemed to have become the norm, and it was hard to judge by any other standards. Certainly his interest in the railway was intense to the point of insanity, and every detail of every day's progress and every mishap or setback was seized on by him and pored over, mourned or celebrated. She had tried to turn his thoughts in other directions: 'Do not ask about the railway, Mr Morland; it only upsets you.' But he brushed away her words and her concern as though she were a bothersome fly, no more important than that.

His other obsession was with the long departed Ferrars. Every day – until he had become too weak to go out – he would go not once but several times to check that the gatehouse was still boarded up and had not been disturbed; and now he was bedridden, he asked about it constantly, needing to be reassured every time he woke. Aglaea had been infected by his fears at first, had half expected Ferrars to return – dreaded it – but nothing more had been heard of him. It was the one light patch in the otherwise lowering sky, that Ferrars had gone out of their lives. But through the winter things had begun to fall apart. More servants had left, all those who could get other places, and since Nicholas had taken to his bed Aglaea had had no time to oversee the remnant. Nothing got done now; the house was dirty, clothes were unwashed, meals were erratic. Mrs Codling had remained in the kitchen, but there was never any knowing what food she would have available to cook.

Cooper from Twelvetrees had come up to the house one day asking to speak to the master: fodder bills were outstanding, he said, and he had had no orders about what to do with the horses. It had been one of Nicholas's bad days: Aglaea had had to send a message down to him that the Master was too ill to see him, and begged him to manage as best he could for the time being. He had gone quietly away; and word had since come back through the remaining stable-boy that Mr Cooper had taken over all the estate matters and was running everything just like Mr Ferrars used to, only better, because everyone liked Mr Cooper and trusted him. It was one thing less to worry about, and Aglaea blessed him privately when she had a moment to think about it.

But that had been weeks ago. Things had gone on getting worse, and if she had not been so tired, she might even by now have begun to think they could not go on like this much longer. Yesterday – she thought it was yesterday – Jemima had said again that they ought to call in the doctor, but like every other time it had been mooted, Nicholas grew so hysterical at the idea of it that she could not insist. However weak he was, he was still Master of Morland Place, the ultimate authority between these walls; and more than that, he was her husband, whom she had vowed to obey in every particular. It was her duty not only before the world, but before God. So she kept vigil, and waited for deliverance.

His eyes were open; she had been drifting in her thoughts, and had not noticed him wake. He moved his hand on the counterpane, and she reached across and took it in hers. It was cold and damp and salty, like a stone recently washed by a grey receding wave.

'What day is it?' he asked, his voice hardly more than a whisper.

Aglaea was at a loss. She could not remember how

long this latest vigil had lasted. 'I don't know,' she said. 'Tuesday I think. Or Wednesday.'

'The date,' he insisted. His eyes were wide, fixed on the air behind her. 'I know. I know. It's the twenty-ninth of May, isn't it?'

'Is it? It may be,' she said vaguely. The date meant nothing to her.

'It is,' he said. 'I know it is.' It was what he had been dreading for six years, and through all his confusion, his fear had kept count of the days passing. His staring eyes strained at nothing, and his voice rose in panic. 'The Devil is come to York!' He began to struggle wildly, shouting, and choking as his breath shortened with panic. Jemima woke and jumped up from the truckle bed, and ran to help as Aglaea tried to soothe and calm him, and stop him injuring himself.

CHAPTER TWENTY-SIX

He was quiet at last, and the women managed to sit him up and give him watered wine to drink. He was shivering violently, and Aglaea wrapped her shawl around his shoulders while Jemima put more coal on the fire, and some wood on top of that to make a good blaze: he took more comfort if he could actually see the flames. Sweat was beading his face, though his hands were as cold as death. When Aglaea put the wine-cup aside, he reached for her hand and held it so tightly that her fingers went white under the pressure. But she endured it. If she tried to pull away, he only gripped harder.

The day broadened. He lay staring tautly, as though waiting, listening for something. Then at a little before one o'clock there came a distant, heavy sound, a sullen booming, very far off, but brought on the breeze and just discernible: the sound of cannon. Aglaea looked in surprise at Jemima, who shrugged minutely; but Nicholas's eyes had widened, his nostrils flared, his free hand clenched on the counterpane. He knew what it was.

'It's starting,' he said.

'What? What is starting?'

'The cannon were to be the signal – down by the river – an eighteen-gun salute. It has begun. Oh God, oh God, I have failed!' He lifted his fist and pounded himself on the chest with it. 'It's come. I've failed!'

'It's not your fault,' Aglaea said, only half understanding him. 'There was nothing you could have done.'

He fixed his wild eyes on her. 'She didn't want it. She said from the beginning it was wrong and evil, and I swore to keep it out. But I couldn't. Oh, don't be angry with me, Mama!' He tugged at Aglaea's hand, as though it were she he was talking to. She did not know whether he knew her or not; but the important thing was to calm him. His breath tore raggedly at his chest, worse the more excited he became. The ominous blue-grey shadows were growing around his lips.

'It's not your fault,' she said again. 'Not your fault, Nicky.'

He moaned. 'Oh Nicky's been bad, Mama! Oh forgive me! Say you love me! Say you love me best! Say it, say it!'

'I love you best. Only you, Nicky.' She reached out to soothe his brow, but he jerked his head away from her.

'You can't love *him*. He's been so wicked. Ran away from home because he'd been so wicked. Never loved you like I did. *I* was the one who stayed and took care of everything. I was always your good son, wasn't I?'

'Always, my poor Nicky!'

He closed his eyes, moaning. 'Oh, but there were so many sins! So many! If you knew about him, it would break your heart. Must keep it from Mama. Oh, the wickedness! He killed that girl, you know.' His eyes flew open, staring at Aglaea, not focused on her. 'He killed her and then pretended she'd hung herself. Oh, she looked so awful!' he moaned, rolling his head back and forth on the pillow. 'All black and blue, and the tongue sticking out – awful! All blue and horrible, and he hung her up and ran away!' He closed his eyes again. 'But Ferrars knew.' His voice dropped to a whisper. 'Ferrars saw. He was going to tell. He mustn't tell – mustn't— !' He choked, and went into a paroxysm of coughing, which left him wheezing and gasping for breath. Aglaea threw an urgent glance at Jemima and she came running, her eyes wide with what she had already seen and heard, and together they sat him up and leaned him forward. Jemima laid a cold towel over his forehead, and together they held him as his body jerked between their hands.

At last it was over, and they were able to lie him back and bathe his face while his tearing breaths grew slower. Aglaea and Jemima exchanged a look. Jemima was pale and Aglaea thought she should not hear any more of these ravings, meaningless though they were. In a low voice, she bid her go down to the kitchen for some aromatic balsam in hot water for Nicholas to inhale.

When his breathing had slowed to near normal, he opened his eyes and sought Aglaea's. He seemed rational, and pressed her hand with a more gentle urgency. 'I must tell,' he said. 'I want to tell you.'

'For God's sake, no more,' she muttered in spite of herself.

He lifted his head off the pillow with enormous effort. 'I must tell you,' he said desperately. 'Will you hear me?'

She pressed him back gently. 'Yes, yes, I will hear you,' she said remorsefully. 'Whatever you wish to say, if it will give you ease.'

He sighed and nodded. 'I must be free of it. I've carried it all so long. She was not the first, you know. She – the girl – just a trollop, nobody really. He used her – oh, the vileness!' He shuddered, and she thought he was growing too excited again, and pressed her hand on his shoulder. 'When he killed her, it was a merciful release – her life had become intolerable. But she was not the first. The first – oh my God! – the first was my father!'

'No,' Aglaea said, feeling herself pale. 'Don't say it! It's not possible. Your father died in a riding accident.'

'No accident,' he said sorrowfully. 'He had fallen, broken his ankle, that's all. We were all out looking for him. He heard him calling, went to him – they were alone – there was no-one to see or hear. It was done in a moment, almost before he knew. He killed him – broke his neck. It was so easy – so easy.' He sounded

557

wondering. 'Life is such a brittle thread, so easily snapped. And his father never loved him. It was easy for him to do, because his father never loved him. But afterwards – oh, the horrors! You can't imagine the horrors.'

'I don't believe you. It's not true,' she said. 'Don't tell me any more.'

'But I must, I must. I have to be free of it, or it will choke me! You must hear me! I say you must!' He dragged himself up by her hand which he held, and the effort made the veins stand out in his head and neck. His breathing began to rasp again, and the blue marks round his eyes darkened.

'Well, I will hear you,' she cried, 'but for God's sake hurry! I can't bear it!'

'Yes, I must hurry. There isn't much time left,' he muttered. 'Oh, but it hurts to tell. The first is easy, and then it's hard, and then it's easy again. It grows over, like knocking a nail into a tree, and the bark grows and covers it, till you can't remember exactly where the nail was. But inside it eats at you – the secret. Have you ever had a secret?'

'No,' she said. 'I've never had anything.' It was true, she thought. She had been a child at home, and then she had been married, but in neither life had she had anything that was hers and no-one else's. She had been a part of other people's lives, never her own. 'Only my painting,' she added, but she said the words too quietly for him to hear.

He was following his thoughts. 'A secret is like poison, slowly killing everything inside you. It's like the rotten apple in the box that rots all the others if you don't take it out. The secret ate at him, and ate at him, and poisoned everything he did, everything he thought, so that he couldn't think like himself any more. He killed his father, and that was one secret. And then at the end – oh!' He cried out in anguish, and tried to stuff his fist into his mouth, like a heart-broken child wanting to weep silently, so as not to attract more punishment.

'Nicky, don't,' she said hopelessly. She had a feeling of foreboding. Something bad was coming, the worst thing of all. She did not know what it was, but she was afraid she would not be able to witness it and live. She could not believe these things about Benedict, and yet Nicholas spoke of them with such conviction it was impossible to doubt. And the worst thing was yet to come. 'Don't,' she said.

'I must tell,' he said. 'I've seen her in the chapel – the Lady – weeping! Do you know what that means? Death to the house. Not death *in* the house, but something worse. Betrayal. That's why the White Lady walked again. The Devil has been let loose.'

'No, Nicky, there's no devil. You mustn't think it!'

'Listen to me,' he said in a low, dreadful voice. 'She's angry with me because I failed her. I knew what he planned, and I didn't stop it. I tried at the end, at the *very* end, but it was too late, because he'd already killed her. He killed my mother – do you hear me? He killed my mother!'

'No, Nicky!'

'It wasn't the cholera. It was poison. He bought it from a man in Well Lane, down by the Staith. He put it in her food. She trusted him – why shouldn't she? It was easy. And when she got ill, the doctor brought her medicine, and he put it in that too. She died so quickly, and everyone thought it was cholera. Are you listening to me?' He tugged her hand impatiently. 'This is the truth! He killed her – my mother.' Tears rolled from his wide-open eyes, and he did not seem to notice them. He cried as a man bleeds to death, too mortally hurt to feel the pain.

Aglaea stared, understanding coming in great rushes, understanding she wanted to resist but could not, drowning out her resistance, leaving her gasping and exposed on a bare rock of knowledge. Not Benedict. Not Benedict. Benedict had been long gone when his mother died. Benedict had been far away, in Leicestershire, had not even known about it until months afterwards – she knew that from Harry. It was not Benedict who had killed his mother. It was not Benedict Nicholas had been talking about, but himself. *Nicky's been bad.* So he had said at the beginning. And the worst thing, the terrible, sickening, death-dealing thing was that *now* she believed. She could not believe Benedict had done those things, but Nicholas – her husband – yes, she knew it. Oh the wickedness, the wickedness! She *knew*.

'Now do you see?' he said to her, watching her expression, watching understanding come to her. 'Now do you see why I could never let him come here? She wanted me to keep him away, him and his Devil's works, and I tried, I really tried, Mama. Don't be angry with me! But he was too strong for me. The Devil always is. I couldn't stop him. He's killing the House. He is the Devil. Bendy is the Devil!'

'No, Nicky,' she said, gently, out of a terrible pity. 'Not Bendy, you. It wasn't Bendy, it was you.'

She saw the realisation fill his face, like the dawn of the Last Day, a terrible, dreary storm light illuminating without shadow. He fell back on the pillows, panting, his eyes flickering as if even at this last moment he sought to escape what was coming. And then he gave a terrible cry, like a spent and cornered fox, as his eyes fixed, bulging, on something Aglaea could not see.

'*Aiee!*'

She started to her feet, and even as she did, she saw his body jerk as though it had been thumped by some gigantic, invisible fist. His hands went up and clawed feebly at his throat, his face blackened, he made a gobbling sound; and then he fell back unconscious.

There was a crash from the door, and Jemima's voice. 'Oh God, what is it?' She had dropped the tray on which she had been carrying the bowl of hot water and the bottle of balsam, and now the powerful smell of eucalypt cut through the sour heat of the room.

'It's a stroke.' Aglaea turned to her, her face stern and sad, her voice calm. 'Run downstairs, Jemima, and tell the boy to run for the doctor – Doctor White from the village will be the nearest – as fast as he can go. You saddle up the cob—'

'But you'll need me here!'

'Mrs Codling will help me. There's something more important for you to do. You must find Benedict Morland and bring him here.'

'Where— ?'

'I don't know. Somewhere on the railway. That's why I must send you. Don't come back until you find him. Now run!'

Jemima ran. Aglaea turned back to the strange Nicky-puppet in the bed, black-faced and hoarsely breathing through twisted lips. There was nothing to be done here; the doctor must be sent for, but it was for form's sake only. That was why she had told Jemima to take the horse. Nicky's part in this play was finished, and the important thing now was the House. She felt them watching her, the ancestors, as he had told her so often he felt them; but she had no fear of them. She knew what had to be done, and after that, there was only the waiting. She did what she could to make him more comfortable, and then sat down to resume her vigil, folding her arms tightly around herself and rocking a little.

Benedict had travelled on trains often before, but there was still something about this journey that was different – more personal, more exciting. The lead locomotive – from Mr Stephenson's Newcastle works – was called the Lowther after Hudson's friend and leading patron of the York and North Midland, and it was driven by a man named Nelson, which seemed appropriate for this brave

561

day. The locomotive drew a train of nineteen carriages, with a second engine at the rear for safety's sake. Every inch of the line had been swept and inspected to make sure that there could be no mishaps, and railway staff were stationed at regular points along the line to keep the spectators back. The company mounted the carriages to the deafening noise of two brass bands, which had begun on the same tune, but were playing it with competing degrees of enthusiasm, so that they were now a bar and a half apart. Many, perhaps most of the company had never ridden in a railway train before, and the noise of exclamation was like the jabber of a roost of starlings.

Uniformed railway staff ran back and forth closing carriage doors, only to have them opened again as this luminary decided he wanted to be in the next carriage with his good friend, or that luminary's lady suddenly collected that she had dropped her gloves somewhere on the platform. Still, at last they were all pent up, the station bell rang, the engine whistle blew, the spectators set up a cheer, and the lead locomotive let out a great snort and grunt and jerked forward. The bands crashed into one-and-a-half last triumphant choruses, and the train crept out like a long, glittering snake under the arch of the Holgate Lane Bridge, which was lined with cheering, waving onlookers, like a row of spring flowers all bobbing in the breeze.

They passed out from the shadow of the walls and over Micklegate Stray, across land familiar to Benedict from childhood, land he had walked and ridden over almost every day of his life until his banishment. He thought of his childhood, and of his father and of his mother. Papa would have been with him today, riding the railway train with wonder, if he had lived. He would have approved of the railway. And Mama? Well, Papa would have persuaded her. He hoped she did not mind too much, that she looked down with better understanding, now, of the good that would follow. We did not despoil your land,

562

Maman, he whispered in his heart; and you always loved beauty and ingenuity, and this railway is a beautiful and ingenious thing.

They reached Chaloner's Whin and swung across the road, and still the crowds lined both sides of the track, waving and exclaiming, some of them holding up small children to stare in open-mouthed astonishment as the iron horse galloped by. Well, to be truthful, she was only trotting as yet. Once past Copmanthorpe she broke into a canter, her clouded breath streaming back, with the whiff of sulphur in it from her fiery lungs; over the flat, and over the flattened land she ran, cutting, embankment, cutting, embankment, scattering a herd of cows at Colton Breck, past Bolton Percy where there were more crowds waiting, over the River Wharfe. Then across the marshes, where they put up a skein of duck: an empty stretch populated by windmills, and one lone, gaitered farmhand who had evidently never seen a railway train before. When the carriages clattered by with no earthly horse pulling them, he fell on his knees at the trackside in such evident supplication to the Almighty to spare him that the whole carriage exploded with laughter.

They left the Mires and slowed to trot through Church Fenton, and now Benedict looked out of the window with keener attention than ever, for this was the section of line he had overseen, and this was the country he had newly learned, within riding distance of Fleetham Manor. Between Church Fenton and Sherburn there were a number of horsemen standing watching, or playfully racing the train across the fields, and he stared achingly, wondering, hoping that Rosalind might be amongst them, might have cared enough about his passion to have come out to witness the train passing. But he did not see her. And then they were slowing again, approaching Milford and the end of the line – for today at least.

Yes, there was the first of the curves he had designed for joining the line to the Leeds and Selby; he looked at it critically, and decided it was as perfect a curve as the eye could determine. The train slowed to a stop, and stood sighing and panting, ready for food and water after the run. The carriage doors were opening all along the train, and the gentlefolk were bursting out and jumping down like excited children let out of school, everyone wanting to tell his own impression of the journey, and no-one wanting to listen.

'I declare I felt quite faint—'

'I thought my heart would stop—'

'Oh, I wasn't frightened a bit—'

'I was thrilled when we went through that great chasm—'

Benedict passed through them, listening, smiling. He remembered how, before the Liverpool and Manchester had first carried passengers, learned papers had been written about the effects of being carried along at unnaturally high speeds. All the blood would inevitably be drawn up to the head, the learned men had pronounced, and the head would infallibly explode. How they had made their readers tremble! But it seemed they were not far wrong – these folk had evidently had their blood drawn upwards, and they were certainly exploding in conversation.

On the journey back, Benedict managed to get himself a ride on the footplate. Nelson was reluctant to allow a mere gentleman into his sanctum, but Benedict won him over when he revealed he had been an engineer and worked for both Stephensons. Old George was Nelson's especial hero. Under the influence of comfortable engineering chat, Nelson grew expansive, opened up the throttle, and let the Lowther have her head, and they galloped back to York at a heady twenty-two miles an hour.

At York station the company was to pile into carriages again to be taken to the Guildhall for a vast banquet, after which the ball would begin at the Mansion House, and Benedict would see Rosalind again. The thought of consuming more food and drink, when he had hardly digested the breakfast yet, dismayed him a little, though he was a good trencherman; but he need not have worried. As he stepped down from the engine, shaking Nelson's hand and contriving to introduce a five-shilling piece into the salute, he heard his name called urgently. It was one of the station staff, smart in a bottle green uniform winking with brass buttons, hurrying towards him, waving his arms to increase his chances of being noticed.

'Mr Morland! Mr Morland, sir!'

'Yes, here I am. What is it?' His stomach tightened with sudden apprehension. A message from Fleetham? A message from Ledsham? No, not that, never that!

'There's a young lady been waiting here with a message for you, sir – fair fit to take the rest, she is! From Morland Place, sir.'

'Morland Place?' The man was leading him away, shoving through the crowds and breaking Benedict's path for him. 'Is something amiss?'

'The Master, sir – your brother, Mr Morland – taken ill,' the man said. For many in this part of the country, even if they had not been directly employed by the estate, the Master of Morland Place was simply The Master.

They broke through the crowds with some difficulty, passed out of the station, and there out in the road, standing at the head of a sleepy cob, was Jemima – a Jemima grown up almost out of recognition since he had last seen her, grown tall and thin and – alas – plain, with an oldness in her face that had nothing to do with growing up. A wonder passed briefly through his mind, as to what her life must have been like at Morland Place these past years since his mother had died; but there was no time for more.

'My brother – ill? How seriously?'

Jemima looked at him out of a naked emotion, eyes flat, bare and undefended. 'It's very bad. I think he's dying. Will you come?'

He nodded, looking at the cob. His own horse was at

the York Tavern where he had left it before the breakfast; but this was a sturdy beast. 'I don't suppose you weigh more than a feather,' he said. 'The cob will take us both, if you'll ride with me.'

He took the reins and mounted, and put down a hand, and she put her foot on his boot-toe and came up lightly, like a bird. Without apology, he put his arm round her waist and held her against him (hollow bones, like a bird) and clicked to the cob. It woke itself only reluctantly, but once realising its head was pointing homewards, it pricked its ears and put down its feet with a will, making nothing of the double burden.

The doctor from the village came, in a violent hurry, as he always was, with too much to do and too little time to do it in. He was a good physician, but was inclined to good works, and frequently visited the poor for little or no reward, which prejudiced the great folk against him. His practice was amongst the prosperous farmers and middling sort; he had never been called to Morland Place, but he had known the old mistress, had often met her across the bed of an ailing villager or old pensioner, and came as much for her sake as for the potential fee.

There was nothing he could do, however. He confirmed Aglaea's suspicion, that it was a stroke, questioned her closely to see if she was likely to be able to cope, gave her some advice on nursing, and went away, promising to return later. Aglaea was almost glad when he had gone. Her tiredness was so great now that it was an agony to be roused to speech or response. She could sit with Nicholas for ever if she had to, holding his inert hand and listening to his ragged breaths, but to feel anything would be an effort beyond her powers.

The dark colour of his face had drained a little, but he still looked suffused and swollen, and there was a little streak of blood at his mouth corner where he must have bitten his tongue in the paroxysm. It had dried to rusty brown, and increased the lopsided look of his face, as though he were smiling on one side of his face and snarling on the other – a landscape divided into sunshine and shadow by a passing cloud. What was he, she wondered, almost idly in her exhaustion. Devil or man? The devil let loose in the house. No, that was not possible. He was her husband; he was the Nicky Morland that her brother Harry had schooled with and played with; he was one of the family she had known since babyhood, one of the pairs of feet amongst which she had first learned to crawl twenty-nine years ago. Devil or man? Had he really done those things he had said? It could not be. No man could be so depraved and not show it.

She slid away from the rock of knowing and into the green waters, letting tiredness and confusion carry her more comfortably. He must only have imagined those things, in the delirium of his fever. Perhaps she had only imagined he had said them. Motes drifting in the green water – oh carry me away, far away from here, never to return.

And then she remembered, like the shape of the Leviathan lurking at the limit of vision, the one element she had forgotten. Ferrars! Yes, that made sense of everything! Not Benedict, not Nicholas – but Ferrars! He was the monster, the evil one, the devil Nicky had referred to. He had only said 'he' – and Ferrars had been there all the time, when all those things happened. When Nicky realised the full enormity of it, he had confronted the man and sent him away. No wonder he had boarded up the gatehouse! No wonder he was afraid of him coming back!

Yes, but why did he send him away? Why not give him in charge?

She shook off the doubting voice. Because the deeds were so awful, he could not bear to have them spoken of, let alone dragged out into the glaring light of publicity. He had done the best thing, sent the man away to face

God's judgement in God's good time. But the shock of it all had been too much for his frailty. Yes, she thought, that was the right interpretation. She felt relieved and satisfied. He had turned his head a little on the pillow, and the sunlit side was uppermost, so that he looked two-thirds man and only one-third devil now. She rocked, waiting for deliverance.

He grew restless, began to move his head and mutter, frowning as though carrying on a conversation only he could hear. She leaned over and wiped his face with the damp cloth, and he moved with it as though following it in pleasure. His breaths dragged in and out like snores, hitching sometimes as though he was swallowing, and between them the muttering grew louder and more troubled. The conversation was an argument now, and he shouted with the tonelessness of sleep-talk. She watched him anxiously. His face seemed to struggle, as though the muscles of it were fighting with each other for supremacy; she could see the blood pulsing through the veins in his forehead. A crisis was coming. She felt afraid, and horribly alone. She began to pray under her breath, the words choosing themselves almost at random.

'Almighty God, Father of our Lord Jesus Christ, Maker of all things, Judge of all men—' It was the *Confiteor*. Every day of her life until her mother had died they had said it at family prayers; thereafter once a week at church. 'We acknowledge and bewail our manifold sins and wickedness which we from time to time have most grievously committed—' She rocked with the rhythm of the words.

His eyes flew open. The pupils were so dilated that there was no iris to be seen, and they looked like two holes into black nothingness. No humanity in that blackness, no man's soul or man's feeling, only eternal emptiness. It chilled her, so that she shivered in spite of the heat of the fire. She whispered more rapidly.

568

'By thought, word and deed against thy Divine Majesty—'

His head rolled over completely, so that the black holes were pointing at her; his face writhed as though she were witnessing some hideous transformation of the very flesh. His lips moved stiffly, a thing not used to human speech, a sound emerged, blurred, incomprehensible – not human.

'We do earnestly repent and are heartily sorry for these our misdoings—'

The sound became a gurgle, and the gurgle became words. 'He's coming!'

She caught her breath and stopped, and in the silence behind his breathing she thought she heard footsteps. She went on, the words tumbling out in panic. 'The remembrance of them is grievous unto us, the burden of them is intolerable.'

'He's coming!' It was strong now, not Nicholas's voice, but issuing from his lips, and charged with terror.

'Intolerable.' She could not remember the next words. 'Intol—'

'*God!*' The unearthly cry as the door opened behind her, she felt the cold air on her neck, felt her heart bursting with his terror, fell off the chair onto her knees beside the bed as his body jerked like a marionette plucked up and flung down again, rolled onto his back, twitched once, twice, and was still.

It was a man there beside her, a man smelling of bitter, sulphurous smoke and warm, earthly horses, a man crying, 'Nicky, Nicky!' in a human voice, not a devil's. Jemima there, too, Jemima's hands on her shoulders, her hands reaching up and clasping Jemima's as if that might stop her sliding down into the chasm where Nicholas had disappeared. Benedict was bending over the puppet in the bed, and through the blurring of sweat and tears she could see his familiar face, a little worn with care and exposed now in sorrow and love. She remembered the next words

569

at last, and went on whispering, not knowing what else to do. 'Have mercy on us, have mercy on us most merciful Father, for thy Son our Lord Jesus Christ's sake—'

Jemima knelt beside her, whispering with her, her young, less wearied voice hurrying along a little, carrying her with it. 'Forgive us all that is past, and grant that we may ever hereafter serve and please thee in newness of life—'

'He's gone,' Benedict said. He leaned in agony over that frail, spent body, looking down into that vacant face, where death was already smoothing out the lines of pain. He's dead; I'm too late. Too late – the saddest, most leaden words of all. He had wanted to be reconciled, to ask and give pardon. My brother, my only brother.

The gun-barrel eyes were open, staring sightlessly upwards in death, and Benedict leaned over, his chest hitching and tugging with tears as though he were four years old, to place his hand on the brow and draw down the eyelids over those pitiful mockeries of eyes. But as he touched the cold brow, the blue lips moved.

'Nicky?' He drew a sobbing breath. Was he mocked, or was it not yet, quite, too late? 'Nicky, it's me, it's Bendy.'

The lips moved, and he leaned down to try to catch the words. Suddenly he had a sensation of Nicholas being near, an extraordinary, clear thing, like the hot breath from an opened oven door, unseen and yet indisputably palpable.

In his offered ear, a whisper: there was no voice to it, only the breath. '*Piepowder.*' He drew back to look, and it seemed that Nicky was smiling, the corners of his lips drawing back to smile in the old and childlike glee. Then a long, slow sigh escaped him, that seemed to go on and on for ever, a last and absolute exhalation. And then no more movement. The drawn-back lips relaxed, the smile faded like dusk light, and the sense of him was gone.

Benedict knelt too, like the women, and tried to pray, but he could think of no words; only that last teasing whisper, and the gleeful smile, which in his mind streamed out past him and on into the aether, like the echo in memory of an unforgiven word.

'Young' Mr Pobgee looked gravely across his desk at Benedict, the June sunshine glinting on the bald front of his head. Benedict had long suspected that he deliberately cultivated that bald front, as giving him a safe and dependable look; he imagined him polishing it with wax at night to keep the shine deep.

'I'm sorry,' Benedict said, catching himself back; he was very tired and his mind tended to wander at the slightest opportunity. 'What did you say?'

'I said that I was glad to have the opportunity to speak to you alone. There are matters which it might be better for you to explain to the ladies.'

'Oh dear, more shocks?'

'I'm afraid,' said Pobgee severely, as though it were Benedict's fault, 'that the affairs of the Morland Estate are somewhat involved.'

'Involved?' Ah, yes, that was a legal euphemism he had heard before, applied to the estate of his father-in-law, for instance: it meant in financial trouble.

'You will understand that I have not yet been able to examine all the books in detail, but it is quite clear that matters had passed out of your late brother's hands and into those of unscrupulous individuals. The account books are quite shockingly revealing. Quite shockingly,' Pobgee repeated, shaking his head.

'Do you care to name names?' Benedict asked. He was too tired for circumlocutions. He wished Pobgee were not so ineluctably discreet.

'The steward – or I should say, former steward – of Morland Place, the man Ferrars, seems to have been transferring the assets of the estate into some place we have not yet located. Presumably for his own benefit.' A sigh. 'If we could get hold of Ferrars – but I suppose he is long gone, living under a false name somewhere, in luxury; perhaps even gone abroad. We will make enquiries, however. I do not counsel despair, Mr Morland. Never that. And if we don't find him, we may still find the money.'

Benedict nodded. 'What else?'

'Considerable assets are missing from the Skelwith estate – for which your late brother, as Miss Skelwith's trustee, was responsible. I can only assume they have gone the same way. I cannot believe the late Mr Nicholas Morland would so forget his duty—'

'Quite.'

'And apart from the deliberate depredations—' Pobgee paused a heartbeat, as though to savour the happy conjunction of words – 'the management of the estate has been let slip to the point where the income does not match the outgoings. I'm afraid that the inheritance is sadly depleted. A considerable sum of money will be needed to discharge the debts, if the family heirlooms and perhaps even the house and demesne are not to be sold. There is considerable livestock and deadstock, of course, which would naturally be sold off first, but—' He shrugged.

'So,' said Benedict. 'I can see why you would prefer me to break the news to Mrs Morland.'

'And to Miss Skelwith. It will not be a pleasant thing for either of them, to realise how their trust has been betrayed.'

Benedict nodded. 'And to the purpose, Pobgee, who does the estate pass to now? To Mrs Morland? I imagine my brother made a Will excluding me, and I can't think who else he might leave it to.'

Pobgee put both his arms on the desk and leaned on them, in the manner of a man about to be confidential. 'That is the odd thing. Such a Will was drawn up, dating from the time of Mr Morland's marriage: it specifically excluded you from inheriting any part of the estate, but after provision of a widow's portion, the residuum was left to the man Ferrars.'

'What!'

'I'm afraid it's true. "In recognition of his long and faithful service to me over many years, going beyond the natural calls of duty".' He looked closely at Benedict, and coughed a lawyer's cough. 'I have the gravest doubts whether it was drawn up by a professional man. I certainly had no hand in it: it was deposited with me with instructions that it was not to be read by anyone until after his death.'

'Deposited by whom?' Benedict asked suspiciously.

'By Ferrars,' Pobgee admitted. 'But the covering letter was in your brother's hand. I had no doubts of that – I knew his hand very well. I am fairly sure that his signature on the Will is genuine too – though of course it may have been written under duress, or even under the influence of alcohol. It has rather an erratic line and flourish to it.'

'But – God damnit, man— !'

Pobgee lifted a hand. 'Do not be alarmed. I am glad to say that if Ferrars was the sole author of the Will, his lack of legal expertise was his undoing. The two witnesses to the Will were Ebeneezer Moon, Butler – and John Edmund Ferrars, Steward. Under the law of this land, a beneficiary under a Will cannot also be a witness to it – for the obvious reason that coercion would thus be made all too simple.'

'So you mean that the Will is not valid?'

Pobgee bowed. 'To all intents and purposes, your brother died intestate. And in that case, the second clause in your late mother's Will comes into force. The estate was left to him with the provision that if he died intestate and without issue it was to pass to you.'

Benedict stared blankly past Pobgee's left shoulder. 'Did Nicholas know that?' he asked at last.

'Certainly. Your late mother's Will was, of course, explained to him in detail. The clause was put in as the merest precaution against your brother dying by accident soon after your mother, before he was able to make testatory provision; but as it happens, it was wisely added.'

Did Nicky remember it? Benedict wondered. Did he, on some level, acknowledge a natural justice; almost without knowing it himself, ensure that the estate went where it was supposed to go? Was that what that last, strange little smile meant? The last throw pays for all: all debts cancelled, all sins forgiven. All the spiteful tricks of childhood and the furious, suspicious hatred of adulthood cancelled out at last, the books balanced, the account closed; and Nicky went away on a long sigh of relief, having put things right at the very last.

'So, Morland Place will be mine?' he said, not meaning it as a question, more as a musing; but Pobgee took it literally.

'The house, the demesne, the estate real and personal, the livestock and deadstock – and the debts.' He permitted himself a small smile. 'If I may say so, it is well that you are an independently wealthy man. Apart from the debts to creditors, there is the question of the Skelwith estate: there is some evidence that income from that was used to discharge debts incurred by the Morland estate – a most improper proceeding. As I said, the affairs of both estates are exceedingly involved.'

'There's another thing,' Benedict was reminded. 'What happens to Miss Skelwith? She's still under age.'

'She will become a Ward of Court, and the Lord Chancellor will decide who is to be her trustee for the rest of her minority.' He looked at Benedict consideringly. 'I am quite sure that, if you were willing to undertake the responsibility, it would be awarded to you. Considering that Morland Place has been her home—'

'Yes,' said Benedict. 'I'm sure it's what my mother

would have wanted. But it must be as Miss Skelwith wishes.'

There was a great deal more to be discussed, and it was a long time before Benedict stepped out into the sunlit street, feeling bemused, and exhausted with emotion. He hesitated, and then turned his steps towards the buff pillars of the Black Swan in Coney Street, feeling the need of some comfort. The Black Swan was one of the great coaching inns of the city, where the Leeds Highflyer and the Harrogate Tallyho had their terminus, and where the Edinburgh Mail pulled in on her way from the Bull and Mouth in London, having done that leg of the trip in an incredible twenty hours. The Flying Machine, men called her. How much longer? Benedict wondered. The days of the Edinburgh Mail must surely be numbered, and there was sadness in the thought, as well as pride. In a decade – less perhaps – the railway would reach out from York to every part of the Kingdom, and there would be no more shining, rocking coaches swinging into the Black Swan yard, no great glossy horses steaming and snorting as the ostlers ran to unbuckle them, no thrilling toot of the yard-long coach-horn as the new team plunged against their collars ready to depart. A new music, the train's whistle and the station bell, would thrill men's wandering spirits, and the steaming, sighing, snorting horses would be made of iron, with real fire in their bellies.

And he, Benedict Morland, would have played his part in the change. He crept into the Black Swan almost guiltily, found a quiet corner and ordered a quart of their best ale. He, Benedict Morland, was to be Master of Morland Place after all. How would Rosalind like that? he wondered. It was what, he remembered, she had been hoping for all along, though he had been too simple to understand her hints. Rosalind mistress of his mother's domain? Well, she would be a beautiful ornament to it, at least; and perhaps it would be enough for her, and she would steady under the pride and the responsibility.

And the children – little Mary and Rose – how pleased he would be to have them growing up in the Morland nurseries, with the gardens to wander in and the swans to feed and the whole estate to ride over, just as he had done when he was their age. The House would be glad too, to have the sound of children's footsteps and children's voices echoing in it again. Mary and Rose – and perhaps, perhaps another, a son to carry on the Morland name? With the weight of the estate to steady her, Rosalind might be glad to give him a son – or if not glad, at least willing. No, he would settle for glad. He could not conceive of anyone's being unhappy at Morland Place.

That brought him to Aglaea. He must provide for her: duty as well as affection required it. She might stay at Morland Place if she wished – there was room enough for a relict. But perhaps she might feel uncomfortable in the same house with a new mistress. If she wanted to be on her own, he could offer her Makepeace House, perhaps. Poor Aglaea! But she was young enough still: she might marry again.

And Jemima – he would have a great deal of making up to do to Jemima for the wrongs she had been done. He hoped he would be given trusteeship for that very reason; he hoped, too, that Rosalind would be kind to her. But she was not pretty, and Rosalind had always been fonder of plain girls than pretty ones. The best thing he could do for Jemima, he decided, would be to find her a good husband.

He finished his ale, collected his horse, and rode back to Morland Place, for he had a great deal to explain to Aglaea and Jemima before he rode home to tell Rosalind the news. He had a passing thought that it would be much harder for her to stray when she was living at Morland Place, surrounded by servants and estate workers all loyal to the name – but he put the thought aside as unworthy.

She would be happy at Morland Place, and being happy would make her good.

As he rode in under the barbican, he had another passing thought, that they must take those unsightly boards down from the gatehouse door and clear the place out. They might even find some clue in there as to where the villain Ferrars had gone: Pobgee would dearly love to track him down and ask for the Morland and Skelwith money back – though it was all Lombard Street to an addled egg that he had spent it long before now.

Now he was in the yard, and Tonnant snorted and tossed his head as the boy came running out to hold him. Benedict paused a moment before dismounting and looked up at the familiar face of the house, the top storey glowing in the friendly sunshine and the lower part bathed mysteriously in cool shadow. And then all other thoughts were wiped out of his mind by the simple realisation that he was *home*.

DYNASTY 1:
THE FOUNDING

Cynthia Harrod-Eagles

Power and prestige are the burning ambitions of
domineering, dour Edward Morland, rich sheep farmer
and landowner.

He arranges a marriage, the first giant step in the
founding of the Morland Dynasty.

Robert, his son, more poet than soldier, idolises his proud
young bride, Eleanor, ward of the powerful Beaufort
family. But she is outraged. Eleanor's consuming secret
passion is for Richard, Duke of York, but duty is held
supreme and she must obey.

Against the turbulent years of the Wars of the Roses,
the epic unfolds, a passionate sage of hatred, war and
fierce desires.

978-0-7515-0382-1

DYNASTY 2: THE DARK ROSE

Cynthia Harrod-Eagles

The marriage of Eleanor Courtenay and Robert Morland
heralded the founding of the great Morland Dynasty.
Now, Paul, their great grandson, is caught up in the
conflict of Kings and sees, within his family, a bitter
struggle bearing seeds of death and destruction.

And Nanette, his beloved niece, maid-in-waiting to the
tragic Anne Boleyn, is swept into the flamboyant intrigues
of life at court until, leaving heartbreak behind, she is
claimed by a passionate love.

A magnificent saga of revenge, glory and intrigue in the
turbulent years of the early Tudors as the Morlands crest
the waves of power.

978-0-7515-0383-8

The complete Dynasty Series by Cynthia Harrod-Eagles

1. The Founding	£6.99	15. The Reckoning	£5.99
2. The Dark Rose	£7.99	16. The Devil's Horse	£6.99
3. The Princeling	£7.99	17. The Poison Tree	£6.99
4. The Oak Apple	£7.99	18. The Abyss	£6.99
5. The Black Pearl	£6.99	19. The Hidden Shore	£7.99
6. The Long Shadow	£7.99	20. The Winter Journey	£7.99
7. The Chevalier	£6.99	21. The Outcast	£7.99
8. The Maiden	£7.99	22. The Mirage	£7.99
9. The Flood-Tide	£6.99	23. The Cause	£7.99
10. The Tangled Thread	£6.99	24. The Homecoming	£7.99
11. The Emperor	£6.99	25. The Question	£7.99
12. The Victory	£6.99	26. The Dream Kingdom	£6.99
13. The Regency	£6.99	27. The Restless Sea	£6.99
14. The Campaigners	£6.99	28. The White Road	£18.99

The prices shown above are correct at time of going to press. However, the publishers reserve the right to increase prices on covers from those previously advertised without further notice.

TIME WARNER
BOOKS

TIME WARNER BOOKS
PO Box 121, Kettering, Northants NN14 4ZQ
Tel: 01832 737525, Fax: 01832 733076
Email: aspenhouse@FSBDial.co.uk

POST AND PACKING:
Payments can be made as follows: cheque, postal order (payable to Time Warner Books), credit card or Switch Card. Do not send cash or currency.

All UK Orders	**FREE OF CHARGE**
EC & Overseas	25% of order value

Name (BLOCK LETTERS) . . . .

Address . . . .

. . . .

Post/zip code: . . . .

☐ Please keep me in touch with future Time Warner publications

☐ I enclose my remittance £ . . . .

☐ I wish to pay by Visa/Access/Mastercard/Eurocard/Switch Card

Card Expiry Date ☐☐☐☐   Switch Issue No. ☐☐